THE LEGEND OF AERROW FIONN

SERAPHINA

Mychaila A. Rose

The book is dedicated to my Gram Gram!

Thank you for your support!

Love you
THIIIIIIIIIIIIIIIIIIIIIIIIIIIIIIIIIIIIIIIIIIIIIIIIIIIIIIIIIIIIIIIIIIIIIIIIIIIIIIIIIIIIIIIIIIIIIIIIIIIIIIIS

Much.

Table of Contents

Chapter One: No Rest

I kept my face neutral, but it was hard to do as I held back the turmoil going through my head. Orpheal took a breather in the midst of his longwinded explanation of what the mission details were, moving his lengthened dark blue bangs that had got displaced. A slight view of a ponytail that he didn't have three months ago appeared as he looked over his tablet to make sure he covered everything.

It was dinner time when he had called, but that was fine. I wasn't exactly hungry anymore.

I played with my sleeve, something I knew he wouldn't be able to see as my anxiety appeared physically, but out of my words. "This is the only way to get that machine working then?"

"Unfortunately," Orpheal answered, regretfully. "I would have waited but-"

"You're going to be overrun if this is delayed any further," I agreed with him before looking down at Azarias. He was also in the room with me, seated at the computers below. The communications room in Asylotum wasn't so different from the one in Siofra Castle; it was almost identical except the command chair was white instead of red. "Azarias, how many people in our records are capable of fulfilling a minimum of forty-five percent dragon?"

"Not many…" Azarias started, hesitantly. "There are only four people, two of them being royal."

Part of that I knew. My heart skipped a beat at my anxiety-fuelled worries for being so precise. "Who are the other two?"

"A set of twins. They were born two days ago, still in the hospital for obvious reasons."

A small tsk came out. I couldn't send them across the continent, let alone let them leave that hospital. Forty-five percent was dangerous on its own, but also being a set of twins… That left…

Dammit. It was too soon.

It had only been three months since the fall and Outland Monsters were forcing my hand. Outland Monsters and Outland Dragons probably pulled by strings held by Ciar. Things were steady, yes. But being king for only three months, for a trip that could take a third of that time if there weren't complications, which there would be, was not what I considered ideal. Atlamillia couldn't go, leaving…

A bitter taste of bile brushed my tongue as I addressed the Lord Director of Seraphina. "Lord Orpheal, I hate to ask, but… is there no other way?"

"My partner, Doctor Naftali Belenos, has been at this from the start and says there is no other way." Orpheal set his tablet down someplace off screen in front of him. "He's been dealing with that side of the project and has tried to use volunteers to possibly add to the total needed, but it's all been unsuccessful for it to work accordingly. Dragon blood is the only way the monsters will respond along with Outland Dragons. It's the closest link we have since Light Dragons came around the same time Outland ones had."

Didn't I know it… I held back my feelings somehow as the words that came from my tongue felt like acid. "Since I can't let Atlamillia go, I'll be the one coming to assist with this and hopefully, we can both have peace of mind once completed. I'll have to prepare for the trip and will need a couple of days. I'll call the day I'm leaving. It should take us about five days to get there if the winds and monsters are not in our favour."

"Thank you, King Aerrow. This is more than what I had expected," he answered with a curt bow. "I only wish that it didn't have to be so soon with the only two available for this mission being Princess Atlamillia and yourself, Sire. I know you're still adjusting."

"If there is nothing else that can be done, then there is nothing else that can be done. The rewards will exceed the effort and while it's a bit inconvenient due to circumstances, the machine will greatly benefit Absalom as well as the other kingdoms. Maybe get ahead of Ciar's game, whatever he's planning."

"Again, I cannot stress enough how grateful I am and how grateful Seraphina is for your time. I'm sure it's a little more than inconvenient."

"I've always been adaptable, this is no exception, Lord Director… Was that everything?"

"Yes, apologies once again."

"I'll start preparing for the journey now. It'll be a pleasure to meet you in person and actually remember it, Lord Orpheal."

"It'd be good see you too, Sire. Good luck."

The call ended and I gripped the railing in front of me, leaning on it. Being social with the other leaders, even if they were kind, was still hard to do.

And to add to it, the new mission just made me sick. Not that I had really adjusted to Asylotum fully yet, so that didn't help matters. It was better then three months ago, sure, but it still made me queasy at times and I found stress did not do me any favours. But leaving for the more stable world…

My stomach twisted. I didn't want to go out there.

Not with him.

"Fuck."

Deigh came to my attention, not surprised by the word that came out of my mouth. "*I know how you feel, but it'll be different from last time.*"

I didn't reply to her as optimism had long left my thoughts. If it wasn't going to be like last time, there was going to be only two other verdicts. The one where we won without casualties was a little less than slim. The second ending was death.

Azarias looked up at me with concern streaked across his violet irises, the silence from surprise left behind. "Are you sure you want to go?"

"I'm sure that if I don't, we'll be one kingdom less and refugees will be needing our help, so regardless… something must be done."

"But are you going to be-"

"I'm adaptable," I cut him off before getting off the railing. "I need to get the house leaders together. Get Cyrus to help you prepare for our trip, other servants around the castle, whoever is available. I'll join you afterwards."

"How many knights do you want to come along?"

"None. We don't have that luxury. Just Cyrus, you… maybe Owen… I need to speak with him."

He didn't look so happy about my decision, but nodded, and got up from his seat. "Did you want me to send out the word to the houses?"

"No, I'll do it."

"Before or after you eat?"

"I'm not hungry." I left the room and started down the hall, to where, I wasn't quite sure. Azarias came out not too long afterwards from the noise and I stopped walking as he stepped in front of me. "Really?"

"It's kind of my job to make sure you're eating and whatever. I let it go all day 'cause frankly, you looked like shit earlier-"

"Thanks."

He ignored my sarcasm like I hadn't said anything at all. "But you have to eat at least something now."

"I'll think about it later," I growled before stepping past him. "I appreciate the concern, but… I need to have some time."

A sigh of disgust came from him, but he didn't stop me. "I'll tell Ramsey to set a plate aside…"

"Thanks."

"Did you want us to be there for the house meeting?"

"I'll hopefully have it for eight if you want to come, but it's not necessary."

"Owen should be in the training grounds," the brunet called then I heard his boots hit the floor, heading elsewhere in the castle, the opposite direction of where I was heading.

Another sigh came out as I got back to current issues.

There was about two and a half hours to send a message to the other houses, but I did want to speak with Owen before hand.

The walk to the training grounds was quiet. The kids were eating along with my sister and Deigh, and it was relieving but at the same time mortifying. It left me to think, something I didn't want to do. I hadn't had much time to do that, thinking about the horrors that ran through my skull all this time. There was always something else that needed to be done, something else to be thought of. Someone talking to me, giving feedback of some sort from months worth of work. But now… I was alone with only the trip on my mind. The inevitable that I knew was coming but hoped it never would.

I ran a hand through my hair, trying to settle my nerves. They didn't settle, however. Instead, the halls changed slightly to the corridors of Siofra Castle, covered in bodies and blood from the attack. My breath caught in my throat. The last words of the king echoed the halls. The sounds of rain-

"Sire?" Jakob's voice came from behind me, and I jumped about a foot in the air before turning to him, not realizing that I had stopped my walk. Ice-blue eyes looked me over as the hall went back to normal. "Everything alright?"

I cleared my throat. "Y-yeah… yeah… Something the matter?"

He eyed me a little longer, concern staying on his face before he shared. "Sir Azarias had told me you wanted to see me about a meeting?"

"Did he?" I looked past the loyal butler and down the hall where Azarias was long gone. Deigh made a small comment on how perceptive the knight was, but I wasn't as pleased that he ignored me. Not that I wasn't in need for a distraction. "What a piece of work…"

"He wants to make your life as simple as possible," Jakob stated. "He's concerned for you like the rest of us."

"I know, but I'm fine. Really."

"I'm sure… but you haven't eaten today and barely ate last night."

"That's because I was nauseated, and then I threw it up."

"There goes your streak, you were doing so well…" he sighed. "If you forget to get food after whatever you're planning, I'll make sure your meal is delivered nice and hot."

"That isn't necessary-"

"As your family butler, it is my duty to make sure you're getting your necessities. Food is necessary and I'll make sure you're getting it even if I have to shove it down your throat."

I stood my ground though in reality, the thought of being force fed food was horrifying. "I ate food yesterday-"

"You're supposed to be eating three meals a day." He changed his tone to a softer one. "Please, Sire. I know that it's been difficult for you with all that has happened, but you're going to hurt yourself with all the training you've been doing without supplying the needed calories. I've been doing my best these last few months to accommodate, but you worry me."

"I'll… try to eat more if you're that concerned, Jakob."

"Thank you, Sire. Did you wish for me to set up a meeting for you?"

"I suppose it wouldn't hurt to have some help. I need each of the house leaders in the war room for eight. It's not negotiable."

He bowed. "It'll be done."

"Thank you, Jakob." I started to leave for the training grounds but was stopped as he wasn't done.

"One other thing, Sire," he started. "If you want someone to talk to, I am available at your beck and call."

I gave him a grateful glance before shaking my head. "I'm fine, really. Thank you for the consideration though."

He gave another bow, and we went our separate ways. Jakob's slender, ice-blue dragon, Kisa, came in from the window, her slight stripes of glowing white were basically a blur from her quick trot down the hall to her partner, blue eyes looking me over just as he had. I gave out a slight sigh once more. I hadn't meant to be such a pain to them… but there wasn't much I could do about it.

I turned the corner and saw the training ground doors just ahead. At least I wasn't left to my thoughts for long.

I came to the doors and opened them to find Owen and, surprisingly, Dani, sparring in the sandy clearing. I kept as silent as possible as I closed the door behind me and snuck along the wall. Eclipse clashed against Dani's double ended axes, Retribution and Regret, creating a loud ring across the outside space. I couldn't help but watch the axes move. They were a marvel to behold, custom-made upon her request. They were black, pointed, and cruel looking with jagged edges. Bits of red dragon stone glowed with power and matched the Seraphinean technology weaved into black armour that she wore against the equally armoured general.

I got to the balcony of the training grounds without being noticed and found that the major reason for it was because their fight had a lot more going on than what I first thought. It was more serious than I had seen in the grounds since we got there; each attack was meticulous and the movements from Owen were not simple off-hand practice. Looking over the battleground more, I saw a similarly designed compound bow that was on Dani's person at one point. It's bone-like design with the sharp edges at the riser, protecting the grip and sight, stood out like a sore thumb on the ground. How it got there was a mystery on its own.

Eclipse went black as Owen charged the golden blade with magic and struck, discharging as it hit the axes. Dani parried, sending a gust of air to blow up sand and to force the general off a second attack. She twisted the centre shaft and the axes split into two. A dark field formed under the sand that tried to grip at the girl, but the tendrils were sliced away. Owen charged the opening she made only to change his attack stance to a defensive one as a stream of fire came from Dani's second axe, slipping past his head.

A slight grin appeared on his face, apparently happy at the surprise. "You're getting better with your magic."

"It's a start," Dani answered, not sounding as pleased.

I frowned. From what I could tell, she was learning incredibly quickly, easily picking up from where she left off when she lived with the rest of the Raghnalls a couple of years ago. What was her goal if the progress wasn't enough?

The answer became very obvious as the sand twisted slightly behind the general. The two axes and blade clashed, bursts of fire sprung from the axe heads and the twisting breeze. The act didn't go unnoticed by Owen and caused her to lose concentration on the little twister she had by disarming both of her axes with a single motion. The blade sat on Dani's gorget and her shoulders dropped in defeat.

"Dammit..." she growled, frustration barely contained, and Owen put Eclipse away. Dark tendrils brought Dani her lost weapons.

"It was a good try, but maybe our king can tell you where you foiled yourself," he stated, looking up at me.

Dani looked just as surprised as I was and looked away in embarrassment. "How long were you watching us?"

"Only a few minutes," I answered honestly. "It was more passionate than what I was expecting."

"We were practicing," she huffed, flicking her medium, black ponytail over her shoulder. "So, what did I do wrong this time?"

Straight to the point... she wasn't in a great mood. But I didn't blame her. She had been working hard and purposely making sure that her practices weren't in my sight – timing them to conflict with my schedule. I came down from the balcony, the short way instead of the stairs, dropping down from the banister that was just over thirteen metres off the ground. Owen rolled his eyes at my laziness and I shrugged, walking over to them. "Your axes gave you away. You were using them as a conduit, but you didn't conceal that fact. This allowed Owen to know exactly how much magic was being used and what you could do with it."

"I see..." Her pale blue gaze looked away from me, turning to a glare at her axes that were whole once more.

"Your skill lies in element merging, this makes your ability incredibly invaluable, but it can be difficult to hide that extra surge of energy."

"Doesn't explain why Cyrus can do it just fine."

"Cyrus has been training a really long time with merging elements; his unique skill comes from magic concealment," Owen told her as he looked over at me. "Even the most powerful magic abilities barely show up to the most sensitive of people."

I gave a nod. "It's true."

She frowned slightly. "I'll have to focus on that then some more… But if you don't mind me asking, Aerrow… weren't you supposed to be eating, not out here watching us?"

"About that…" I felt my stomach twist again. "Orpheal called, he needs someone with a dragon blood percentage of forty-five or more to get his machine to work. They're being overrun and running out of time."

Her eyes went wide, and Owen's lighthearted smile turned to a slight grimace. The general asked his question, "You're the only one who is capable of that… aren't you?"

"Atlamillia is as well but, from the records that were just brought up, the only other people available are two-day-old, newborn twins in a hospital."

"And you don't want Atlamillia going anywhere near Ciar."

"I can't lose anyone else to him," I stated harshly before sighing, reeling my emotions back in. "I'm going to be holding a meeting with the other house leaders in a couple of hours to make sure that they are aware of my decision to leave and actions can be taken accordingly. I came out here to ask where you stand."

"You mean whether or not I'm going with you or staying here as Atlamillia's General."

I gave a nod, but he didn't think too long on the answer.

"I'm going and I have the perfect one for my acting position that will secure your decision with at least one of the houses. He gets along well enough with Atlamillia."

"You mean Ronial, he's the younger brother of Corraidhín Jósteinn, the head of his house, right?"

"Yes." He turned to Dani. "And I'm sure your presence here will help with the Raghnalls cooperation."

"I… can't do that," she disagreed. "I haven't talked to my parents since we arrived and… they have no idea that I've spent a good portion of my time here, being friends with the king and princess…"

He raised brow in question. "Why ever not? They'd be-"

"Smothering me to get favour and swindling courtship with you, Aerrow," she interrupted, turning to me. "I cannot be their puppet again. I'm sorry."

"It's alright," I told her, not wanting to bring up a sensitive topic that I only heard parts of from Atlamillia. "I won't even mention that you've been here."

She looked up at me with a grateful look. "Thank you…"

"But that doesn't mean someone else won't. If it comes up, I'll avoid the subject the best I can, but don't be surprised if you get a missive from them."

"Right… guess we both get to deal with things we don't want to, huh?"

"Everyone has their demon…" I muttered. "I'm going to deal with arrangements… you're both welcomed to join me. I would love both of your inputs on things…"

"I'll gladly help, even go to Seraphina with you," Dani suggested, and I shook my head.

"Atlamillia is going to need you here and the same thing applies; I don't want to lose anyone else."

"Then I'll be here for Atla, but I can still help prepare." Her smile stayed warm in understanding before turning to Owen. "If it's okay we cut our training short."

"This new development has a much higher priority…" He looked me over again. "After our meeting, I'm going to head to the armoury to get some gear to help our predicament. I have a feeling that you're going to like it if we face Ciar."

I swallowed with a small nod. He was trying to make me feel better, but all it did was make things seem worse in my head.

00000

The room was a little more than loud as the house leaders sat around the war table – thirty-six of them in total. One provincial leader for each of the six provinces, three major houses, two minor houses, and now that I was in the room, it brought the total to thirty-seven. Some of them were more difficult than others to make acquaintances with as I did rounds to get to know the leaders that helped lead Absalom. Bonita Munro, the granddaughter of Friea and Fern Sharrow, Oliver's daughter, were among them. Their houses were still major houses after many investigations into the treason, but while they had shunned their relatives, having the stigma of their former leaders imprisoned along with other criminals was there. Plus, I wasn't dumb enough to think I could trust the Munro or Sharrow families just because nothing came up.

The room went quiet upon entering with my two knights, Owen, and Ronial. The other leaders stood up from their seats in respect. Some were visibly confused like Corraidhín seeing his brother amongst my entourage, some were pleased to be called, and others weren't overly happy about being asked to the castle so late. We took our seats, the leaders followed, and I got straight to the point, not wanting to keep them any longer than necessary.

"All of you are aware of what happened three months ago, yes?" There was a collective nod and quiet agreements and I continued, "Then you're also aware that Seraphina was going to call for aid. Monsters and dragons are attacking their borders this very moment and like the monsters here, they have been boosted with foreign powers."

"We don't 'ave tat kind of power ta send when our own borders 'ave yet ta be secured," Óðinn Áed stated. He was Clovier's son and the new provincial leader of Maritemps. I nodded in agreement. "Yer plannin' on a smaller team ten ta assist."

"The plan to secure the borders is still my priority, the phases for that are already in motion and with this trip, it'll help us make sure we keep them no matter what Ciar throws at us."

His sea green eyes lit up in amusement as they always did when he was intrigued. A cocky grin placed itself on his face. It was one that when I first saw it, made me want to wipe it off, but after speaking with the twenty-year-old, he was just as mischievous as I was. He was on board with this plan. "Tis 'as ta do wit tat machine te Seraphs were askin' for 'elp awhile back, eh? Ya need someone ta take te mission?"

"The details of who's going have already been determined. What I called everyone here for was to prepare for that."

His grin wavered as he processed the information before it came back barely a moment later. He put his head on a propped arm, his short-medium black hair shifted slightly. "Yer a bold one, eh?"

I brought the conversation to the rest of the table. "The machine Orpheal has been working on needs a dragon blood percentage of forty-five percent or higher. Straight dragon blood is too much, and their experiment attempts for anything lower have been unsuccessful. Being that there are so few that fit the needs, I'll be heading to Seraphina three days from now in order to assist."

"Yer leavin' the kingdom so soon?" Fern asked, not rudely so. "Te kingdom needs ya 'ere."

"I know it does… unfortunately, the risk of staying is much greater than going. I'm not planning on staying long and will make sure I have full contact with Absalom as soon as I get there with the help of a CT. The machine will help put this kingdom back to where it stood and more so. We won't have to worry about Outland Monsters like we used to with it. But it needs to be built first and it's going to need either Princess Atlamillia or myself."

"And the princess is not an option," Owen added before someone could bring it up. "She's inexperienced and just as Óðinn kindly put it, we don't have the resources to send for her."

Fern seemed content with the reply. "So, you've gatered us for approval?"

"I have," I told her honestly. "I wanted to make sure that this decision is well received and if any other options could be presented that might not have been thought of. I respect the opinion of everyone at this table and elsewhere and wanted to have a reasonable window of leave that is appropriate for everyone here."

"A reasonable amount is not at all," Kaeden Lachesis, the provincial leader of Aesear, said in a deeper voice than his appearance would seem to have. His hazel gaze was not unaware of the horrors that Siofra had gone through as his property wasn't far from the city's southern border. "This is a fragile time for the kingdom, and it makes it sound like you're running away to stable borders."

My gaze narrowed just shy of a glare. "I'd never do such a thing."

"We're aware, but words and actions are very different things."

"Who are ye goin' wit?" Áskétill, leader of the Major House Curtis in the Drixula Province asked neutrally. His medium length, dark brown hair tied back in a ponytail moved slightly as he looked up from his tablet. "If it's a small group, are ya goin' wit just yer two knights? Tat's incredibly risky if Ciar is out tere."

"General Owen will also be joining me and while he's away, Ronial will be taking his place as Atlamillia's general from here on." A look of surprise came from Ronial and Corraidhín. "I don't want to leave this kingdom weakened. With this setup, Owen can portal my team back using waypoints that will be scouted over the next few days so that if there is an emergency, no matter where it is, we can respond and get there as soon as possible. The north, east, and west territories are being scouted come morning, taking extensive photographs, and we'll be observing locations as we head south. All that's left is your approval on how long is reasonable for me to be gone."

Salicia Harlan, the youngest house leader at the table, a year younger than Atlamillia, answered first with a strong voice, well versed in political trips. For a minor house of Aesear, she placed her worth on the table and then some which was a surprise since her uncle was the house leader before he was killed in the Siofra assault. "A typical political trip to Seraphina is up to two months of leisure, but in terms of missions, it can be up to six months. Due to the circumstances of the kingdom, I believe half of a mission's time would be appropriate. Lord Director Orpheal has stated that most of his machine is built, it shouldn't take longer than that to complete."

"I wouldn't want to be staying that long even if it wasn't done completely, the mission is just for me to provide it with the necessary requirements and hopefully return with a machine of our own," I told her, and she gave a small nod. "Is three months good for everyone else?"

There were a few mutters of agreement before a familiar, strong opinionated voice broke through it. "Half of that."

The room went quiet as we turned to Eudoxia, Dani's mother. Owen frowned. "Half?"

"You don't have an heir," she reinforced her objection. "No matter the purpose of that machine, an heir is more important to any of that and there are many suitors who require your attention."

"Lady Eudoxia-" I tried to reason but she wasn't done.

"Any time lost is lost time for you to find a consort and have an heir as soon as possible. Even above the kingdom's venture back out into Orithin and our allies. A month and a half, once you get to Seraphina, of course, but that is what I think is appropriate. Then, many suitors, like my daughter, Dani, would be quite content about having your full attention."

"I don't think finding someone in times like this is appropriate."

She put her black hair behind her ear, green eyes piercing me for the truth. "Are you saying that my daughter roaming the halls of this place is coincidence?"

I figured she would have got some word but who the hell told her that?! I kept myself as I had been before. "I've been a busy person these last few months. If I've seen your daughter, she's been here for other business and I haven't spoken with her."

"Is that so?"

"Yes… I am quite honoured that you believe your daughter is a perfect candidate, but this matter is something I wish to address only after I know that our home is secure. There is no point to having an heir if they are killed before they can speak, let alone be born."

"Yes… so tis trip needs ta be completed successfully as soon as possible," Scot Hildebrand, the minor house leader of Drixula agreed to both of us. He was older than both of us combined and times by three. While rough around the edges, he seemed to have a good heart. He, like a lot of the other citizens of Absalom, were adopting the heavier Absalom accent that dominated the capital before it turned into a multicultural hot zone. And being that the capital was sacked, there wasn't much of a fight against the lighter accent that the less malleable still had. "A mont and a 'alf upon arrivin' in Seraphina I believe is appropriate. Gets tose Seraphs motivated, keeps ya out of relative danger, and not in one spot for long if tose zealot pricks are out and about. Ten, you can come back and search for a wife wit no concern."

If only it was as simple as that…

Others around the table agreed with mixed replies of yeses and mentions that the Seraphineans would take their time if they didn't get a deadline. It wasn't much time… but it should have been enough. Then, I could be a part of a horrible experience of being forced to meet with so many suitors that… I didn't want to participate with. "If that's the final verdict, then a month and a half upon reaching Seraphina's island it will be. If it's not completed, I'll make my way back. In the meantime, however, I've already started on a list of things that are to be taken care of, so nothing slacks off. Most of it will be done by the council, but if anything has to do with your houses, you'll be given a detailed description of what that is before I leave in case you have questions… You're dismissed."

Chapter Two: Final Details

I came out of my room, notebook in hand as I wrote things out. It was almost done, but not quite. It felt like I wasn't doing enough, like I was forgetting something. I was leaving tomorrow, and it just felt like everything could fall apart at the seams. I knew that wasn't the case, but it didn't matter to me. Every part of me was telling me that leaving was the last thing that I should be doing. That it was a mistake.

It was unnerving.

Giggling came to my ears down the hall and before I could even look up from my book, someone dropped from above and onto my back, making me stumble forward. I caught myself with a small gasp, somehow not losing the book and pen as whoever fell from the sky struggled to keep themselves on, scrambling up as they slid down. A familiar grunt came from the culprit and I adjusted him into a piggyback before he could accidently choke me.

"Morning, Gasper…"

"How'd you know it was me?!" The boy asked and I lifted his leg slightly, showing off his footwear. I didn't want to point out that I had heard him first.

"How many kids do I know that wear adventuring boots?"

"Darn it… There is always something!"

"How'd you drop down on me anyway?"

"Look up!" He exclaimed and I did so, finding a little blue, red, and silver dragon overhead. "We've been practicing!"

The little whelp nodded and then his eyes went wide as he went too far to the right. He dropped down. My book and pen fell out of my hands as I sprinted a few steps. The bundle of scales dropped into my arms. "Careful, Zekrem… you're getting a lot bigger and I'm not going to be able to catch you soon."

A huff escaped, his pride a bit wounded. The voice that came from him was about the same treble tone as his partner's, "Sorry…"

I put him on the ground and Gasper got off my back, dancing around to stand in front of me. "You two have been working pretty hard over the last few months if you're already able to fly as a team."

"We've been working really, really hard! This was our first time actually flying though," the small dragon answered happily, his tail wagging swiftly back and forth. "Gasper wanted to catch you off-guard."

"You almost did," I told him. "Maybe next time."

"What'd I say," Claudius started, coming from down the hall from where the giggles could still be heard with Kalibora next to him. Like Zekrem, Kalibora had also grown significantly, her head at the same height as her partner's. "You're not going to catch him off-guard, not after what that Olin guy did at least."

"Big jerk," Kalibora huffed. "Abusing his position to try and continue that plan those councilmen started."

I gave a look of surprise. Admittedly, that wasn't someone who I had thought of in a while due to other issues. Olin was interrogated and determined to be an associate of Oliver's about two months ago. Fortunately, nothing more came from the incident and the former knight was stripped of his title and thrown in prison. The former councilman was then put on higher watch. Even after that though, no one had seemed to figure out what his and Friea's end goal for power was. But because of Olin, it was a wake-up call that it may not have been over.

I crossed my arms, taking myself out of my head before the kids could call me on it. "How did you two get a hold of that information?"

"Asked around," the black and blue dragon said, and I shook my head. She was a lot cuter when she didn't talk… Now she was just as smart and sassy as her partner and she could voice it. "To be fair on his side of things, you weren't in much of a position to fight back."

"Yeah…" Gasper looked away from the two of them to me. "You're still not, right? I heard you threw up again yesterday."

"That wasn't so much as me being ill but rather…" I didn't want to get into it being caused by stress. "I'm alright now."

"Was it true that if Uncle Cyrus didn't show up, Olin could have kidnapped you?"

"Or kill me… It wasn't exactly clear what he was doing there, but yeah, Cyrus rescued me." Olin had been just as silent as the two councilmen on any details further than what we knew which was, unfortunately, smart on their end if they had a bigger goal.

"I should have been there! I would've been able to protect you!"

"I'm glad you weren't," I told him with full honesty. "I don't know what Olin would've done to you if you were."

He pouted and went to argue when another familiar voice came from down the hall. I looked up to see the light brunette saint that was Larissa walking towards us. Her large, bright, violet eyes were lively as ever with Kris in her arms. "There you are, it's lunch time kids." She looked up at me. "Jakob told me you missed breakfast again."

"Did I?" I frowned. I hadn't realized the time. It was moving faster than I wanted it to. "I suppose I should eat something…"

"Uncle Aerrow is gonna eat with us!" Kris cheered loudly, looking at his mother. "I told you he would!"

She nodded briefly before looking down the hall with a small glare. "Juno, leave your sister alone."

A small whine came from the direction as Lyric came running from out of the room, through the horde in front of me, and directly into my legs. Her eyes slightly teary. "Aerrow, Juno wants to put a helmet on me… I don't want to be the Dragon Knight."

I turned to Larissa. "How do you keep doing that?"

"Do what?"

"Know when someone is getting into trouble."

"Oh…" She shrugged. "Just do, I guess."

I looked to Lyric and picked her up, wiping her tears away. "You don't have to be a Dragon Knight if you don't want to, okay?

"But someone has to be, or the game is ruined." Lyric sighed, "But it's scary…"

"It is… but you know what's not scary?"

She shook her head. "What?"

"Lunch. Are you hungry?" She didn't get to answer as her stomach growled. Her eyes went wide, and I gave a small chuckle. "Let's get your sister and the others so we can all have food together, and then afterwards, maybe I can be the Dragon Knight in your game. How's that?"

"That sounds great!" She cheered before frowning, looking past my façade. "Wait… is there something going on? You haven't been able to play with us a lot since being king and there's been a lot of-"

"We'll talk about it after food," I interrupted, looking at the two boys and their dragons in front of me. "Don't want lunch to get cold, right?"

Claudius wasn't buying my attempt to go around the subject and picked up my book and pen, looking at one of the many pages that had writing in it. "You do realize how tedious this is, right?"

"I don't know what you're talking about."

He and Kalibora rolled their eyes as he passed her the notebook. "The instructions in here are so simplistic that even Gasper could run the kingdom."

"Hey!" The red head shouted in anger.

"I'm just making the comment since Kris can't read half these words yet."

He was left a bit confused. "I can't tell if you just called me smart or stupid…"

"Yes." Claudius turned to me, ignoring his friend's struggle to be mad or not. "And if you want this book back, you're going to tell us why you're making instructions about what needs to be done while you're away or if the kingdom starts to fall apart."

"Claudius, I need that book…" I growled slightly, unable to hold back the frustration of it being held hostage for information.

The white-hair child raised a brow slightly, seemingly impressed by the reaction. "Kalibora will give it back after lunch when you tell us what is going on and actually eat a meal."

"Claudius, that's not appropriate behaviour," Larissa tried to intervene but Kalibora left swiftly out a window before any of us could react. "Claudius and Kalibora!"

"We know, we know… but honestly, sometimes you got to steal the candy in order to get the baby to cry."

I sighed, annoyed, but not angry. He certainly knew how to get what he wanted from me… and if I hadn't been working on that book all night, it wouldn't have mattered. But I had, and I didn't have the time to redo it all. "Just… make sure that book doesn't get damaged… okay?"

"Well lucky for you, Kalibora is a storm dragon. So, lunch?"

00000

The food was mostly eaten, more than what I had expected of me. The kids were unnaturally silent as I played with my food, all done explaining about the commotion happening around the castle. They had heard a lot of rumours flying about and they were mostly true. I didn't blame them for being quiet, it was more than obvious that they were scared.

It was Karros who managed to find his tongue first, beating out Claudius who wasn't as bold now that he knew. His question though, as always, was meticulously thought out and caused my heart to skip a beat. "What happens if you're killed?"

"If…" I didn't know how to answer that. I knew of what would happen theoretically, but not of what would really happen. I went with a more reassuring answer. "The trip isn't to fight anyone. It's to get a device working-"

"I don't want to know what the plan is… I… we want to know what happens if it doesn't work."

"Then I'm killed…" This was a much deeper conversation than what I wanted. Larissa didn't seem very happy about the direction it took. "Atlamillia becomes the queen and takes the throne. There are things in motion where it won't matter if I'm alive or not to make sure that the kingdom, and you guys, are able to return back to Orithin and Siofra."

"I see…"

"But I'm not planning on dying on this trip. Not from monsters and not from Ciar… okay?"

He gave a nod and Holly asked her question. "What if Ciar is waiting for you?"

"Then he's going to have an interesting time trying to get to me."

"Are you going to run away?"

"If I have to, yes." She gave a small frown. "Didn't like hearing that, eh?"

"No. I want you to beat him. But…" She gave out a sigh. "He's really scary from what everyone has said. You'll beat him eventually, right?"

"Maybe. But he's really powerful-"

"So are you!"

"And he's had time to plan. More time than I have."

She crossed her arms, puffing out her cheeks. "But you've been practicing almost every day... It's not fair."

A small laugh came out. "No, it's not... But if he shows up and things are in my favour, maybe I will beat him."

She brightened at the thought. "Stab his face in if you can!"

"Holly..."

"What? He's hard to kill, just hit him there a few times. That's what Daddy told me about fighting monsters."

Fair enough.

I looked over the table again. "There are a few things I have to do yet, but when I'm done, did you guys want to play something? I heard you needed a Dragon Knight and I happened to qualify for the job."

There was a collection of nods.

"Okay. You guys make sure you aren't changing the rules on me and that is the game you want to play, and don't give Larissa a hard time, alright? And Claudius... give me back my book."

00000

The war room was where the council meeting had concluded. I needed the high-tech table to go over the phases of getting the kingdom back in Absalom and to finalize details on the mission. The table itself was a marvel and insulated from pesky people who broke it such as myself and my sister. I got out of the view of the south wall that was broken but still had a live feed going back to the full map of the kingdom. Seeing it without anyone really living in it broke my heart, but if everything went well... everyone would be back before the end of the year.

I turned to my council, my sister, and Ronial. "I believe I've covered everything."

Archbishop Ailín Sowards, the councilman of housing and labour which wasn't too different from his job at Orithina's Temple, gave a nod as his old fingers flipped a page in my notebook. His voice was youthful and strong, quite the opposite to his fragile frame. "I have to admit when you said you wrote a detailed outline... I wasn't expecting a book."

"Anything missing from it?"

"Not from what I can tell, Sire."

"Let me see!" Priestess Hazel Nova, the new councillor of commerce, demanded, stealing the notebook from underneath her friend. "You've been hogging the damn thing for the past hour!"

A chuckle came from the elder priest. "Apologies."

She didn't spend long looking at it, moving her long, brown hair over her shoulder. "How do you have perfect grammar? What the fu-"

"May I?" Zephaniah asked, interrupting the priestess who looked up to the middle-aged man with a raised eyebrow. "You can explore its pages afterwards. Víðarr and I just want to do a quick look over of it's contents."

"Alright…" She gave a pout, passing along the book. "Might as well pass it to Owen and Ronial, Zeph… I'm going to be looking it over a lot longer than all of you combined."

"The book really isn't that interesting," I sighed as the brunet councilman of Health and Education took the book for him and Víðarr.

The slightly older blond, Víðarr, looked it over briefly before shrugging. His accent was still thick and unwavering from the rest of us who lived in or around the capital and one of the main sources that admittedly, I was starting to pick up on slowly, but not enough for anyone but Owen and Atlamillia to notice. "I'll look it over later… I'm sure it's covered more tan necessary. Tough I 'ave ta ask if tere is anytin' tat Zeph and I should report ta House Delany and House Annadh? My fater 'as been pesterin' me since ya called te 'ouse meetin'."

"No, not until we're ready to ask for Annadh's personal guard. The same for your houses, Zeph and Ronial."

"That'll please my brother." Ronial chimed in as Víðarr went to pass the book over to Owen who shook his head. "Not goin' ta look it over, General?"

"No. I'm more than certain a child can figure out what to do with the instructions inside, but you should look it over with great detail, Ronial. As the acting general for Atlamillia, you need to know everything that could possibly go wrong and I can guarantee you, that list is in it."

He gave a simple nod, not giving away on how he felt about reading the whole thing other than slight determination. "I'll look it over then once Councilwoman Hazel is finished with it."

The woman gave a giggle. "The name still hasn't set in yet, it's so professional sounding."

"Nothing like you," Ailín said, destroying any sense of pride she had.

"Grouchy, much?"

"No." A cheeky grin formed on the man. "You just make it incredibly easy to tease. Always have."

"Alright, time's up!" The woman in the cardigan growled, stealing the book from Zeph and caused the bearded man to scowl.

"I wasn't done with that…"

"Catch me if you can."

He rolled his green eyes as the councilwoman left swiftly, the door closing behind her. He turned back to the table. "Which one of you gave her an energy drink this time?'"

No one answered, either not knowing who had done the forbidden act or didn't say anything, too afraid to admit blame. I was part of the former.

A small smile formed on my face. It was nice having a council that was able to enjoy each other's company freely.

"Your Majesty, in the off-chance that I don't see you before your departure, good luck on your quest. You have the council's full support on this endeavour, and we'll do our best to quell house issues if they arise."

"That would be greatly appreciated." I turned to Atlamillia. "Anything else you think needs to be brought up? You're going to be regent while I'm away, so if you have anything…"

She shook her head slightly. "No, brother, I don't."

Thank the gods that there wasn't anything else. I dismissed the council meeting and I looked about the table further. Soon, there would be lights decorating the vast kingdom. I tapped on the layer button and picked the tunnels. The map changed from a coloured version to that of black and white lines of tunnels like spider webs covered across the map with small names of settlements near most of them. Delram and several other brigadier-commanders and generals were out, scouting out the tunnels across the kingdom in teams.

They were putting up cameras within the tunnels that were accessible and would eventually feed to the very table I was looking at once they got back. It was a plan in hopes to lessen the need of guards or knights to constantly patrol them for monsters or instability and simply act on problems as they arose on the sensors and cameras.

Suddenly, the table turned off and I raised my hands in a panic, looking it over. "I didn't touch-"

A giggle came from the other end and I realized I wasn't alone. Atlamillia had a mischievous grin across her face as Dani and Aoife stood next to her, both girls had a look of shock.

Aoife's expression changed to that of hilarity. "That was the funniest thing I've seen all week! Haha!"

"Aoife don't encourage this kind of behaviour..." Dani tried to say seriously but fits of laughter were coming out. "Atla, you're so mean."

"I never got back at him for putting crickets in my room before he left the first time to Seraphina," my sister said, pushing the button on the side of the metal table. The screen of the war table turned on again, exactly where I left off. "Staring at the table isn't going to make things go faster, so come with us."

My head tilted in confusion. "Go where though?"

"Well, there is someplace that might be interesting."

"There are knights already out looking for that place you've been sensing since we got here," I growled. "Let them find-"

"This is a different mini adventure," she cut me off with a sigh, annoyed. "Maybe help boost your mood a bit."

My head tilted. "How exactly?"

"It's a surprise. It'll be a good walk in the outdoors too, your favourite thing way back before you became a workaholic."

I rolled my eyes and sighed, letting her take me wherever she wanted me to go.

We started our journey through the castle, Aoife and Dani following us and somewhere along the way, Cyrus joined. I wasn't quite sure where or when as I was listening quite intently on the progress of the girls' training session they had. The disappointment from the brunette's loss over Dani was evident.

Cyrus offered a few tips on how to fight against an air elemental user and Aoife started brainstorming incredibly one-sidedly. She got some ideas; someone added their suggestion, and she grabbed it as well, combining it with something else.

She reminded me a bit of myself when I was a lot younger, just as creative and forthcoming, but the difference was she had control while, when I was like that, most certainly did not. I went too far while she knew just how close the edge was.

It was admirable.

We rounded a corner of the street that was bustling with people, some giving regards to us, but like in Siofra, no one really cared about the royal precession and a hospital sat at the end of the street.

I looked over at Atlamillia in confusion. "Why are you dragging me to a hospital?"

"It's a surprise," she answered but didn't explain further.

I looked to Cyrus who just shrugged, also unsure of what the girls had planned.

It didn't take us long to walk to the large building that, as expected, was a bit busy with people and dragons coming and going for a numerous of reasons. Inside, it was pretty with bright colours and dragon stone decorating the ceiling. Paintings from professional to children's works were on the walls dividing the wings into different parts of the hospital. The names of the wings that hung on the pillars, ceiling, and walls were proper nouns and not of what they held.

A code yellow went across the hospital for one of the wings, but no one really reacted to it except for a few nurses. The main foyer wasn't as busy as people went to and fro, making the outside a lot more cluttered than inside.

Atlamillia didn't head to the front desk but instead headed down one of the many great halls, following about half of the different wings labelled. A prominent sign of restrooms and elevators hung from the ceiling, and we continued towards the elevator.

"Can we take the stairs?" I asked and while Dani started to say yes, Atlamillia overruled her with a no. "Why not?"

"Because I don't feel like walking up the stairs and since you don't know where you're going, you're following me."

I gave out an aggressive sigh, throwing my hands in my pocket. "As you wish, oh great and powerful leader of the kingdom."

"Don't get snarky."

"I'll get as snarky as I damn well please. I don't like elevators and you know it."

"You know what Seraphina has lots of?"

"What?"

"Elevators. They have a massive one that leads from the mainland up to their kingdom so anyone can get to it without flying and that's not including the buildings there. They like to build tall."

A groan escaped as she pushed the button on the elevator.

"So, you better get over it, *Sire*. You're representing the whole damn kingdom when you get there."

If I got there...

"*You'll get there, because I'm going to make sure that you do,*" Deigh told me, reassuringly and I held back a sigh.

"*I know you would if it was just normal monsters.*"

"*If he can catch me... I'll set him on fire. We'll all make it to Seraphina and then we're going to come back. It'd be a shame if you couldn't enjoy a long reign like your predecessors.*"

That really wasn't what I was thinking of, but I appreciated the simple idea. It was easier to envision even if it was incredibly unlikely. All I had to do was not die until I was old. And to do that...

Gods, I was not going to make it.

"*All we can do is try. You've got a lot better with your clumsiness while scattered-brained.*"

"*Heh, thanks Deigh.*"

The doors to the elevator opened and we went in. I went to the back wall, mostly in the corner where I could happily brace myself against the horrible box of death.

"What floor was it again, Atla?" Aoife asked and my sister answered.

"Fifth."

"Right, oooh this is so exciting!"

"What's exciting?" I questioned, hoping to abuse her hyperactive nature but she wasn't gullible, something I already knew, but hoped anyway.

"Nice try."

"What if I ordered you to tell me?"

"Death before dishonour!"

I gave a sigh of defeat as Dani moved closer to me. "You'll be okay. Between Cyrus and I, I'm sure we could keep this elevator from falling in the off-chance it completely breaks."

"I know…" I gave a small smile. "I appreciate the reassurance."

She smiled back as the elevator started moving upwards, causing me to tense a bit. A giggle came out of her. "I forgot how you reacted to the elevator in Dragonstone."

"Is it better or worse from then?"

"The exact same."

Well, I tried.

The doors opened and I held back the urge to run out, following Atlamillia through the facility. The halls were much quieter than the hall below, the occasional baby crying which made me curious to know where she was taking me. Every so often she looked at the room numbers and I peeked in on the open doors slightly to find nothing out of the ordinary. Just family or women chatting within the room or no one at all. She stopped walking as we came across a door and let herself in. Aoife and Dani followed her while I hesitated a bit before going in, Cyrus not far behind me.

Inside was relatively dark and empty of anything but a lit window ahead and off to the right. Atlamillia looked at me, expectedly. I eyed her a bit as moved next to her. On the other side of the window was a family, two small whelps in little beds that had to be only a few days old, parents holding two, small newborns with a doctor and a few nurses standing by. The babies looked healthy enough, but the little encased cribs with medical equipment attached told me otherwise. They were stable enough to be held by their parents, but at any moment, they could require medical assistance.

"Who is this family?" I asked, finally finding my voice and Aoife answered.

"This is the family Azzy mentioned to us. Apparently, they're the first kids to be born of Siofra and the first to have such a high-level percentage in a long while."

I looked away from the family on the other side and Atlamillia continued.

"They're healthy, but they need to get back to Orithin as soon as possible. Like you and Owen, they aren't suited for Asylotum. She looked back to the window. "You helped them when you held the shield longer than you should have, I doubt that they were born just to never go head to the home you allowed them the chance to see."

"I thought this was supposed to be an uplifting experience…" I muttered, feeling the existential burden of failure. The failure of not bringing the machine back to secure the borders and have it safe enough for my people.

"It is. I'm telling you that you'll be fine, and it will turn out alright."

"Is this some sort of faith in destiny that you're trying to sell me?"

She nodded. "I believe, wholeheartedly, that those kids are going to see their true home with their parents, and it will be because of you once more… So, as long as you stay safe, play smart – stay out of Ciar's radar… you'll be just fine. I know you can do two of those things without issues."

"And Ciar?" Dani asked. I turned to her; a visible worried expression was on her face as she looked between the four of us. "What about him?"

I looked to the window and saw the little twins being played with by their parents. "I don't know… Run until a real weakness can be found."

"Ciar won't get anywhere near you, Aerrow," Cyrus assured behind me in his usual monotone. "And if he does… he'll be facing the wrath of nature itself."

I just gave a nod to the crimson knight, the weight not lifting nor the pit of my stomach filling. I knew the so-called god probably couldn't get through this wrath of nature that Cyrus and Tempest would create, but it didn't make me feel better. The monster thought I was some Godling and was determined to kill me, waiting years on end just to do it. Leaving the kingdom, the sacred realm of Asylotum, and heading to where Ciar was most likely from, was a sure way of falling right into his trap.

I felt my nerves get the better of me and I shoved my hands in my pockets to at least hide them. Just the thought of him made them shake and I didn't want anyone to see how scared and pitiful that their leader was.

Their sturdy pillar, shaken to the core.

Chapter Three: See You Again

A slight breeze swept through the field we stood in, shifting my bangs as I fidgeted with my armour. The gateway arch was active, as usual, and connected to Orithin wasn't sitting far. Azarias was casually joking around with Bretheena, who looked ready to punch him, and Elias. Cyrus and Mazaeh were going over last-minute checks to make sure everyone was geared up and had everything they needed. Owen was speaking with Atlamillia and a silent sigh came out.

It would have been a much louder goodbye if the kids had come, but I knew better than to trust them. They would have wanted to go on an adventure, one that wasn't safe for a group of knights, let alone a group of children.

The thought of them, living with them in the castle for the last three months was an experience, one I wouldn't trade for the world... but for the sanity of Larissa and myself... I wasn't letting them say goodbye at the arch.

I wished they could have come though.

I looked back at the arch trying to find a distraction, but it didn't work as my gauntlet felt like it wasn't sitting right which wasn't true. I was just nervous, though it did give me something to do while the others were busy. The gauntlets were a perfect fit as they were a gift from Owen, the armoury piece that he thought I would like if I had to face Ciar again. And he was right to a degree.

I didn't like them, I loved them.

They were awesome in both design and function, similar to my sister's gauntlets but for me. They were a carbon-steel alloy, based around the carbon material of primordium – the metal that Winterthorn was made of, but significantly less expensive and much easier to repair and make. The silver material went past the glove to make the fingers look like claws with red dragon stone tips, abusing the glass-like nature of the stone to it's full potential. They were sharp enough to cut glass and other hard to slice materials shown in demonstration that morning and my own clumsiness when I accidently dropped it. Saved it by catching the blades on the claws like an idiot.

Hands bleed when sliced up. A lot. Who knew?!

But, like the accident, it showed the potential they had. The options when things got less desirable. The ability to still do a considerable amount of damage with their tough structure to withstand any blows I could do or have to block in case I lost my sword again.

Along with the gauntlets, I took Atlamillia's example and brought a couple of daggers, attaching them to my belt and on my boots. There was a ranseur and a crossbow up on Deigh's saddlebag with multiple types of bolts, including Outland ones…

Everyone in the party had more than enough of the antidote in case I accidently hurt myself.

Atlamillia's orders.

Then there were a few miscellaneous objects… one of them being the plush dragon. Was it stupid for bringing it? Yes, but I wasn't going to abandon it. It was a hell of a lot safer with me in a waterproof, practically invincible bag than left alone. But luck wasn't the only reason why I brought it on this adventure, was it?

I withheld another sigh, trying to see past the white light of the gateway. Nothing showed on the other side. I knew it would be fine. The kingdom was safe in Asylotum from any monster. Atlamillia was safe from anyone inside the kingdom with Bretheena, Ronial, Jakob, Elias, and Mazaeh watching her – the latter two poking their noses into everything.

It should have been enough. All the hours of working, either in the council room, my study, or my room in perpetual darkness when I couldn't handle being in the light from the migraines and instability. Dinner parties with so many houses, education plans, law enforcement. The excessive training…

It had to be enough.

I turned back to the group. There were plans in case something happened, the roll of a twenty-sided die – each number with a different cataclysmic problem and solutions to those problems. The book left behind was more than tedious, but even with it, I was still uneasy about leaving. A dreaded thought of something awful happening if I left.

A lot of somethings.

Paranoia or gut feelings though, I wasn't sure.

Unfortunately, Seraphina needed their machine working or they were going to lose. I was their solution, so my feelings, even if instinctual, didn't matter. I had to go no matter the consequences if it saved as many lives as possible from monsters and Ciar. Hopefully, it didn't risk anyone else in the process.

I switched from playing with my gauntlet to my armguard, running through everything that needed to be done. The thoughts started forming out loud, "The people of Baiwyn had sent a request-"

"Yes, my dear brother," Atlamillia replied, interrupting me. I turned to her; the conversation she was having with Owen was apparently done. "They want some of their fishing supplies."

The list started to come out, involuntarily, the paranoia of missing something, evident. "Then there are some guards that want-"

"To explore more of Asylotum where the knights haven't yet, I know."

"Don't forget-"

"Aerrow, for the love of any god, chill." A sigh came out of her like she was dealing with a child and I stopped. "You wrote a book on what needs to be done and your council knows just as much as I do. These things are nothing new. We'll be fine."

"Yes, but-"

"No. You need to leave. The kingdom will be fine. You've done everything you could possibly do and the things that need to get done, are not going to cause this kingdom to collapse."

I took the hint. "Alright… I'm just worried."

"You're not abandoning the kingdom. You're aiding another so we can work together, better. With it, maybe someone can kill that bastard or, if he's lucky, to face you and be detained."

Both of those were easier said than done for a multitude of reasons. "What if this is an irresponsible decision-"

"*Your* council believes this to be the correct choice of action, even if it is dangerous. You have Owen and he's placed someone he greatly trusts to act for him while you're gone. This decision is better for the long run so you can come back in one piece, find a pretty wife, and make little babies. You're doing just fine and as king, there are going to be some decisions that are going to be difficult to make. Like, leaving your safe kingdom to aid another even with a psychotic monster waiting and wanting to kill you, and definitely using our friends to the south as bait."

I knew all that. "But it's only been a few months…"

"And you've been working constantly. You've recovered and that means so has Ciar. He's going to attack someone, if not a whole kingdom, if you don't go and help the Seraphs and take them Helena's samples and work so far."

More fair points. A sigh came out. "Once I get to Seraphina, I'm going to get a CT, something I can't break…"

"And then you can check in whenever you want to see if the grass is still growing." She rolled her eyes. "Remember when you weren't a control freak? I do. It was nice and honestly, I miss him."

I wasn't sure how to answer that and she filled the silence again.

"It's not a bad trait to gain for a king, but good gods."

I went to argue further only for more evidence to present itself against my favour when my mind turned to see if I could check in at the outposts. Another sigh escaped.

Deigh purred in amusement, the only one who knew what had happened. Suddenly, she picked me up and placed me on her back. "This is where you belong for the time being. So, enjoy the peace of the moment."

"You make it difficult to have any sort of dignity," I grumbled, and she nudged me with her nose.

"Who's my sweetest little king ever? You are!"

"Stop that…" I growled out and turned to Atlamillia. She had her retainers collected nearby and my party mounted, ready for this grand adventure that I would have wanted thirteen years ago. The grin on her face and the stifled laughs from them only made the embarrassment worse. I shook my head. "Don't do anything stupid while I'm gone, okay?"

"It's impossible when you're leaving."

Just had to get one final insult in there, didn't she? I waved. "Good luck."

She rolled her eyes and waved back slightly.

We were still terrible with goodbyes.

I gave Deigh a silent go ahead that I was ready, despite not knowing if we were ever going to come back. She strode to the arch. The bright world of Asylotum was left behind after an even brighter light and then it became dim. Two knights stood in a large space, dragon stone decorated the gate's domain in pictures above and on the walls. The space, now that we weren't being chased by monsters and I wasn't dying, was incredibly beautiful. It was like the other world, archaic, fascinating, and welcoming. But unlike the other side, this place felt right. The uneasy, sickly feeling I had grown used to back in Asylotum left immediately. My body felt alive and light, even with hundreds of metres of dirt overhead. I felt like I could breathe like I never breathed before. I looked back at the light of Asylotum.

How had Atlamillia found the space so comforting, I didn't know. It was weird to think that we were opposites, despite our same heritage. It wasn't something I was willing to investigate further, but it did have my curiosity. The world was missing something Orithin had, and while at first, I thought maybe it wasn't detrimental… but waiting for the rest of my party to go through the gate – the thought changed. It felt almost life threatening, whatever it was.

No… not almost.

It was.

The same level of requirement as oxygen.

A chill went up my spine at the prospects of what would have happened in the long run to the very few people that were affected by it like Gasper and the newborn twins.

The pit of failure came back, and I shook the thought away. Those kids needed to get back to Orithin as soon as possible. They weren't like most of my people that were healthier in that realm. They were missing the same thing Owen, Deigh, and I were.

Owen asked a silent question as Missiletainn came up beside Deigh and I, wondering if I was ready and I gave a nod. He led the way back down the tunnel I vaguely remembered. It was the same one that we went through before and while impossible to get lost, I didn't remember most of the trip the first time. We flew and in a much shorter time than before, and about two dozen knights later, we made it to the surface. The sun glared down, and I welcomed its harsh, warm touch of late Kalokairtas.

The last time I had seen the sun, the actual sun, had been… a long time ago. Sitting on Deigh's rock in the courtyard with…

I tossed the memory that returned aside.

It would have been a lie if I said I was over her… but I felt like I was doing better. Only certain things brought her to mind, and it was probably due to the work I threw myself into that didn't allow me the time to think. The harsh glow of the orb in the sky brought back another memory. One where the land

Deigh stood on was in twilight. I missed it a bit, but it did tell me of what I should do before leaving.

I turned to Owen. "Do we have time for a minor detour?"

"Depends on what that is," he started, passing me a confused look. "Where did you want to go?"

"I... I-I need to make a stop at the temple." The words were dry on my tongue.

"The temple? That's well past- oh... yes. We have time for that. They have to get the train prepared anyway."

"Alright..."

Azarias looked ready to ask why I wanted to go by our destination, but thankfully didn't, and we took off towards Mount Orithina.

It might have been a blessing that many of the tunnels had become too dangerous to use. It made the trip to the temple more reasonable. Then, it would be a short trip to the train station outside of Siofra. The progress of reclaiming territory from monsters that got through the unprotected and broken walls had been going relatively well, starting from the Absalomian Gate in the east. It was by Drakcovíssus, a port city that was built long, long ago for access to Akirayuu Ocean for the kingdom and was still incredibly active despite the assault and had to be protected. People used it to go on pilgrimages to the temple from around the world and it was my job to make sure that their time within the borders was protected.

It was still my kingdom and eventually, it was going to be sound everywhere within it. It was just going to take time to do it stealthily. If it were just Outland Monsters, it wouldn't even be a question of securing territory, rebuilding the walls, and use the barrier to do it all.

But Ciar wasn't an Outland Monster.

He was something else entirely.

I wasn't going to risk lives just to get it all back and have him do it all over again, for me to prove some point, whatever that point could be.

Strength?

Maybe. I had been meticulously training and studying whenever I wasn't completing duties, even oversleeping.

Petty pride?

Wouldn't be much of a leader if I went and did it for that reason.

Not being afraid?

Definitely not that. I wasn't an idiot. The creature was terrifying.

There was no point to prove. The next time I met with the creature… that man… I wanted him dead or captured. Maybe captivity was too risky. It probably would have been safer if he were dead. And if I was honest, I didn't care about who did it.

I wanted to complete the deed, but the minutes before passing out every night gave me time to think about it. If I were the one to kill him, I wasn't sure if I could do it for justice. I would be struggling against revenge for everything he took from Atlamillia and I. From my people. But if I did that… it went against everything I believed in.

But it'd be just a pity if he didn't force my hand.

A growl came out as I shook my head, trying to clear the horrible thoughts. It didn't work, but the action was satisfying in some way.

"Everything alright?" Cyrus asked and I found him on Tempest next to us.

I nodded. "Yeah. Just being left without something to do has given me more than a desirable amount of time to think."

The red and gold knight nodded, leaving it as it was, noting that I didn't want to talk about it.

Unfortunately, Azarias didn't care if I wanted to talk about it or not. "What were you thinking about?"

"Nothing overly important…"

"Seems important. Was it maybe about Ciar?"

"Perhaps…" What was the point of asking if he already knew?

"Thinking about if you want to dice him before you cook him? Or perhaps you want to straight up throw him on the grill."

My feelings escaped. "I want to. I really, really want to kill him, painfully-"

"Huh, you are capable of pent-up rage."

"But I don't." I finished after his sassy remark. I sighed. "You see the problem?"

"You could kill him not painfully. A mercy kill-"

"That's not what he means," Owen interrupted, joining in on the discussion. "Honestly, sometimes I wonder-"

"Oh, you meant you literally don't want to kill him," the brunet said, ignoring the general entirely. Azarias did know, he just set it aside for the more violent option. I wished he wouldn't do that… it fuelled a less than moral part of me. "That's a conundrum. But whatever you decide, I'll stand by you. The gods know I'm not a saint."

Well, wasn't that just so helpful.

I sighed again as the temple's gold tiled roof came into view, threatening to blind me if Deigh changed her altitude. I sensed her temptation to do so grow and I glared down at her. *"Don't."*

"But it'd be funny," she laughed, trying to lighten the mood, but it wasn't helping.

"You know what else would be funny?"

"Blinding you and then dropping from the sky?"

"Overcooking your next meal just before you take a bite of its juicy flesh."

"That's not funny…"

"Neither is blinding me."

"Fine."

She landed on the white stone of the mountain and kept walking towards the temple doors, not allowing me to disembark. The doors opened as we arrived with a priest behind them to greet us. He looked up in surprise to see me but kept on doing his duty.

"Can I help you with anything today, Sire?" He asked and I shook my head.

"No but thank you."

He bowed and we continued our way.

The entrance to the tomb came into view quicker than I had anticipated. It didn't allow me the time I needed to ready myself to go down. This would have been the fourth time I had been inside, but it felt just as hard as the second if not more so.

I didn't want to say I didn't belong, it was a tomb after all, so the living didn't belong, but…

"*You still feel guilty,*" Deigh simplified my feelings as we descended, leaving the three knights in the hall above. "*Hopefully, in time-*"

"*You already know that's not going to happen,*" I growled. "*Even if it was out of my control.*"

"*I know. But I hope anyway.*"

There was silence between us as she made it to the bottom of the stairway. The room was just as beautiful as I remembered. The battle scars from the Arachrom battle still remained as the repairs had to be done in small burst to hide the tomb from anyone looking, but the reconstruction was coming along nicely. Dragon stone created the soft purple light as it danced through the room. The soft sounds of water flowing came from the sides, and newly planted water lilies grew happily within the waterways.

I hated this place.

Deigh flew to the top of the raised platform and I got off. Two sarcophagi laid empty next to Father's and Mother's filled red and white quartz ones and I did my best to ignore the void that called from them. The beckoning of me to have my final rest.

I turned to the stone slabs that I had come originally to see. But…

I didn't entirely think through why I had come. Just that I should have…

What was I supposed to do now?

Half a million thoughts and emotions fought to try and give me an answer, but none of them succeeded in being prominent, leaving me numb.

I could just continue to do what needed to be done, but that wasn't a goal. Not an end goal, at least. It was something that was constantly changing. Easily muddled and eventually, there wouldn't be anything to be done.

What was I supposed to do then?

Silence answered my question. Silence and the quartz.

Of course, the dead couldn't speak. It was silly of me to think that coming here would give me answers.

I missed them.

They always knew what to do. The answers that no book could give. Even my memories from so long ago knew that I could turn to them with the wildest of questions, not even close to the kind I had now.

Was it enough with what I was doing?

Was I even doing it right at all?

What if leaving, left my kingdom vulnerable?

Why was it like this?

Would it get easier in time?

…

No answers. None at all…

A tsk came out in frustration. Coming here was a mistake and it wasted time to lend aid. Just another mistake.

I turned to leave and suddenly found a woman standing behind me, slightly taller than my shoulder. I took a step back in surprise as Deigh hadn't warned me that someone else had arrived. Not that there should have been anyone else. No one was supposed to be…

Familiar, large green eyes stared up at me with love and grief. Red-brown hair, done up like Atlamillia's half ponytail had the same dragon hair piece in it. A red, white, and silver gown…

I recognized her.

I took another step back, unable to breathe in a panic only to find that a sarcophagus was in the way, tripping me slightly. I drew my sword as Deigh growled, turning away from the entrance way to what stood in front of me. Suddenly, a second figure appeared, more familiar than the first, raising a hand which silenced her.

A reactive reaction to times before.

I looked between the two people before turning to the slabs of stone behind me for a second then looked back, terrified.

What the hell was the meaning of this?

"You're…" I couldn't finish my sentence as the woman took a step forward.

A voice I hadn't heard in thirteen years came from her lips, "Aerrow-"

"Don't…" The name stung as I raised my sword in defence, stopping her advance. "You're… you're dead! How… Why are you here?! Who are you?!"

"You already know who we are," the woman said softly, taking a glance over at Deigh before walking towards me.

I braced, but I couldn't move. I was unable to use the sword that had belonged to the man behind her. She moved around the blade gracefully, just as she always had been, and adjusted it out of the way slightly. She raised a hand and hesitated before placing it on my cheek. My heart stopped for a moment at the familiar touch. A hand smaller than what I remembered, but it was the same. The same, warm touch.

Tears started to form in the beautiful woman's eyes as she smiled a smile I had solely missed. "You're all grown up."

"Mother…" Winterthorn dropped out of my hand, clattering loudly on the floor.

Was this…

I couldn't stop myself as I wrapped my arms around her.

This was her…

Tears slipped out as I failed to keep composure. She was so small compared to me. But I didn't care… This was her. This was the woman I had been missing for so long. "I missed you so much."

A hushed voice came from her, "I missed you, too. My Little Dragon, I'm so sorry."

I had no words for the nickname that was worthy of only her. I held on tightly, but not so much that I could crush her. Before it used to be as such, squeezing her to show how big I was getting. But now… I didn't want to lose her again.

I couldn't lose her.

A hand dropped down on my shoulder and I looked up from my mother to see my father, a tiny bit shorter than I.

When did that happen…?

In my split concentration, the woman I had missed so much, slipped through my arms, but kept me within hands reach, holding onto my hands like she was afraid that I was the one who was going to disappear. A sad smile formed on both of their faces.

A dawning realization came over me. That this… this wasn't forever.

They were…

"I'm so sorry…" Mother repeated once more as Father moved from my side to hers. My heart skipped another beat at his presence leaving.

"Please, don't-"

"You know we can't," Father said. "We're not-"

"I don't care! You're here right now, right?! You're…" My voice caught. "What am I supposed to do?"

"Do what you think is right. Just as you always have."

"Do what I think is right? My actions got you both killed! How could anyone, let alone you, put that much faith into-"

"You did not get us killed," Mother stated with a firm tone that even after all this time shut me up. She squeezed my hands tightly. "While reckless, you've done nothing wrong. You've done everything you could and will continue to do so. Because you're my boy, Little Dragon… You always make the right choices no matter how difficult. Right?"

"What if it's not enough? Ciar is far beyond anything Deigh and I can compete against, especially after all this time…" I swallowed. "What can I do that you two couldn't? This world would be in better hands if I-"

"Don't say such things!" She knew what I was going to say. "I wanted to save you that night from that monster and in a blind rage, I was the one who made the mistake and paid for it. Ciar was the one who committed the act. Not you. And even if you didn't leave, he would have come. He would have killed you and your sister before either of us knew he was there. You left, yes… but it saved the both of you."

"But not you."

"No… it did not save me. But I would do it again and again."

"I didn't want that. I don't want that even now." Tears fell as my words caught in my throat. "I wanted to be with the both of you. See the world together. The sunrises and sunsets, oceans, and mountains that I've never seen. All of us having stupid picnics instead of being in the castle walls… looking up at the sky and wondering how I could have done something to change everything…"

"Someone was dying that night, Aerrow. It was fated."

"And it couldn't have been him?! Fated… who has the right to determine who lives and who dies? What purpose does it serve? Ciar wouldn't have become a problem if you two were there together. He wouldn't have stood a chance. What idiot decided that killing their best champions to deal with Ciar was a good idea?!"

She came close again, wiping away the tears of grief and anger. "It's not so simple. You're the best hope this world needs. Not us."

"You know how many people are dead because of me? For one reason or another? How can that-"

"Enough," Father growled, drawing my attention to him. "People will continue to die, whether or not you make a move. You've seen the actions of that. Pyrrha died when you could not and Ciar came back when you had to use magic in Baiwyn and in the north. But it also saved more lives than they claimed. Each action was caused by the need to save someone and you must continue to keep as many safe as possible from people and creatures that wish to harm the innocent and you. You do not have the luxury to sit in the past. We're dead and there isn't anything that can be done about it."

I looked away in disgust.

"You cannot change the past or punish yourself for the actions of others. What you can do however, is continue to protect this kingdom, this world, and maybe more from Ciar. You need to protect your sister." A sigh came out over the urgency of his words. "You deserve so much better. Better than a sword and a burden on your shoulders… but this is what we pass to you."

"I deserve nothing. You two deserved a better son. Someone who was more like you. Neither of you needed to die, never needed to leave Atla alone… She doesn't show it. Doesn't talk about it. But at night, she cries in her sleep, asking for help from you, from Orithina, and I can't do anything to ease whatever suffering she has. Why did it have to be up to fate? It's ridiculous to think we are all just pawns. Pawns that were you two. You were here with us… and then, suddenly, you weren't. I heard a woman tell me that you said not to grieve, but that's all I can do. And now, you're going to leave, and I'll never see you again." I pulled them into a hug that I wanted to last for eternity. "Please don't leave."

"We want to stay, Little Dragon," Mother said, returning the hug with the strength and love of someone alive and well, a voice that was breaking in undertone. It broke my heart even further. "You have no idea how much we wish to be with you. But we aren't a part of this realm anymore."

"Neither is Ciar and yet-"

"Yet he still remains… Please, my little Aerrow, do what we cannot. Protect this realm. Protect your sister. You are all you have left…"

"And keep denying fate her opportunity to have you," Father added, and parts of my puzzle clicked into place.

"Is this Orithina's fault? The one who keeps sending Atlamillia nightmares of my demise? Of your demise… or is she just the messenger?"

"She does what she wants. Atlamillia is just one of those who can see her intentions… whether or not it is for the right choices or herself. We don't know."

Her intentions? Was she trying to kill…? "Why would she want to see me dead if you said I'm supposed to do what you cannot? How am I supposed to avoid-?"

"You've stopped fate before, just as we had changed ours to keep you safe. Do not see this as her fault alone. Many will wish to end you and your sister just as many have tried before," Mother answered softly, taming my anger as she looked up with sadness. "You must deny them of that. Don't throw away the life we want for you… and always know that we love you. But please, please don't make me see you in the next realm so soon."

So… Orithina did have something planned, I just didn't know what the intentions were behind it.

Damn it all! I was just a mortal idiot against… what?

"How am I supposed to do this? If the teachings of even faith aren't going to help, the same teachings that you two brought me up on, what do I do?"

"You make your own path with the things you want to live for."

The things I wanted to live for was going to be my path… how vague was that? Everything I wanted was right here in my arms, Atlamillia in the sanctuary, my uncle and knights upstairs… This was all I wanted to live for and two of them were dead.

"Be strong. We'll be watching over you, okay?"

I didn't get to answer as I felt the figures I held, start to disappear. Suddenly, I was falling through them, and I quickly turned around to see them barely visible. "Wait-"

"We're sorry… but please, protect where we couldn't…"

I reached out for them, but they were gone, leaving Deigh and I alone. My knees hit the floor, disbelief as the anguish of them leaving again clouded my vision. Their resting places were all that stood in front of me.

It wasn't fair…

Would I ever see them again?

"Depends on if you die," the woman from the hall months ago whispered in my ear with her mezzo-soprano toned voice, making me very aware of her presence. Arms wrapped around my shoulders; a head rested on the right one as the left had a pauldron in the way. A comforting gesture, but not one I could see. "But your parents have told you to stay, haven't they? To move onwards, to protect… Whatever shall you do?"

"Who are you?" Silenced answered and the feeling of the woman was gone. I turned to Deigh who was looking at me in confusion. "Please tell me you heard her."

"I heard your mother, unless that's not who you're-"

"You didn't hear another woman? See another one?"

"No? Should've I?"

"She was… never mind…" I got up, picking up Winterthorn and sheathed it. It was possible I was hearing things, some adverse effect of the venom perhaps. As far as I was aware, I was the only one who lived after one dose, who knew what it did to the mind after two. I was going to have to keep it to myself if that was the case… The voice wasn't hurting anyone. "We should get going… We spent enough time here. Seraphina-"

"Are you going to be okay?" Deigh cut me off and I stopped my trek to her, turning to the two slabs of white and red quartz.

"Maybe… but if nothing else, they've given me a direction. A final task that I refuse to fail. Father was right, I cannot stay in the past or my inability to act will take more lives. I don't know if making moves will prevent more or less death… but it's worth trying, right?"

She nodded. "It's always worth trying."

My depression lessened on the grief of losing them again as acceptance started to flow. They were gone… but I was given something I doubted many got; a second time to see them, the ones that had passed. To have some of my questions answered. I only hoped that they would see Atlamillia just as they saw me. She was the one who deserved the honour the most.

A proper goodbye from the parents who loved her so very much.

Chapter Four: Ashes of Memory

Deigh and I left the tomb and met up with the others who were waiting patiently.

"You were down there a while," Owen started casually, but there seemed to be something more underneath. Unfortunately, his face was neutral, and I was too preoccupied to ask. "Did something happen?"

I looked back down the stairwell that was dark and unending from the entrance. I couldn't tell them that ghosts showed up, let alone the former king and queen. And not even incorporeal, but physically there for a time. "No, I just lost track of time. Sorry."

He didn't press the subject further, seeing that I didn't want to talk and accepted my answer as it was. In time, I might tell them, but now wasn't it. There was still the question of whether or not Deigh and I were crazy. And if we weren't, why had they come with their mission?

"*I don't think we were both imagining what happened...*" Deigh said as we started to leave the temple. "*But we do have to be careful and analyze their words thoroughly.*"

"*Because they basically said that Ciar is going to do something on a global scale, or because they said that Orithina wants me dead?*"

"*They did mention her... but they also mentioned that there are others that we don't know of. We have to prepare for whoever that could be.*"

I forgot about that aspect... maybe because having a god and a monster wanting to kill me was higher than some mortal being doing the same. But I guess it didn't entirely matter if I was killed, I wasn't invincible.

"*That means telling Owen. He needs to know, or he'll be risking his life unprepared and he's going to be very angry when he finds out that you knew. And when he does, I'm not going to listen to it. I'll fly away and shut off the link.*"

"*Why don't you tell him?*"

"*Because no one is targeting me. They are targeting a squishy, practically light armoured, walking corpse.*"

"*Ouch... For one, this armour isn't that light.*"

"It's not upgraded like the rest of your knights and guard... It can be almost comparable to leather if someone knows it's just carbon-steel, padded cloth, and where it's weaknesses are."

I ignored the comment. "And for two, I'm not dead yet."

"You might as well be if you have two gods, if we're counting Ciar as one, wanting something from you if its not your life. Then, there is the Black Phoenix, if she was working on her own it's possible that Valrdis might also want your life. So, I believe that makes three gods..." She was not as optimistic as I was. "Shall I continue on with the number of mortal beings who probably want to kill you too?"

"Fine... I'll tell him... later," I sighed internally. "As you said, we need to analyze everything first before coming up with conclusions, false information or worse of all, assumptions with missing information. That, and I have to work up the courage to tell him that his best friends came back as ghosts and didn't visit him."

"Maybe they will later, but if they don't... Well, I'm just glad that I don't have to break the news to him."

"Thanks for your help with this..."

00000

We arrived at the train station an hour or so later, flying through a low cloud that blocked me from seeing the city. There were more than a few knights waiting or preparing to leave as Deigh landed. The station itself was rough at best. Cement was cracked and a few windows were broken and boarded up. If there had been casualties there, the blood had long been washed away and the bodies were eaten by scavengers or monsters. I didn't bother to look around inside, but it did look significantly better than outside through the few windows that remained intact.

It was possible that someone was put on the duty of making things decent. After this trip, the train was going to be used more often for missions and transport of materials as the tracks and pathway from the north to the south had finally been restored – a priority that was placed on the front burner after Orpheal's call.

I looked beyond the station.

The walls of Siofra stood behind it in melancholy. Parts broken while others were left alone. Through the cracks and holes, Elwood Garden poked out of the fog with its massive trees and its own walls, somehow undamaged. How that was possible was beyond my understanding, but it was nice to see some of the city remained as I remembered.

Eventually, the city would be rebuilt and the people who remain will be bustling through its unbroken, cobblestone streets.

I heard my title get called from behind me and turned, seeing the conductor from the train to and from Baiwyn approach. A bit of relief came over me at seeing a familiar face, despite not having much of a connection with him.

The man bowed in front of me. "The train is ready for your departure whenever you're ready, Sire."

"We'll board now, thank you," I answered, somewhat instinctually, and he stood straight with a small nod.

He left, speaking into a conjured orb quietly before dissipating it. A voice echoed across the station that the train was boarding and Deigh and I went to the car I was instructed to head to. Inside was a bit different from the car I was in before, like the one we took south but fancier. It was a single unit, resting car instead of a duo. A bathroom, a bedroom, a dragon bed, and storage were all that lined the inside of the car.

I shouldn't have been surprised to have the more luxurious one, but even after three months, some of the most basic things were different once one was king. None of it I particularly enjoyed or disliked.

All it did was remind and make me grow numb.

Though, at least Deigh got the privacy she complained about the last time we were on a train. She marched right over to her bed, ready for some sleep and rest before the long trip ahead.

There was always the risk that Outland Monsters could attack the train and I didn't doubt that there would be a few fights, but thankfully there were many knights and soldiers on standby for that reason. It gave us as much down time as we could get for the five days ahead. Once the train made it to the farthest point south, they were going to be setting up a base around where Fort Verdant used to be. Then, construction and repair on the wall was to begin.

At least, that was the plan. If Ciar decided to show up…

My thoughts trailed off as my mind became a cluttered mess with random other thoughts, too many to focus on just one. A small pang came from the scar on my chest, and I reached at it, trying to remind my body that there wasn't anything there.

Perhaps it was time for a small rest.

Deigh agreed and I went over to help unbuckle her gear, placing the lose parts in an empty storage bin. Movement came from behind me, and we looked over, finding Owen closing the train car door behind him. A muffled whistle went off outside.

A small smile formed on his face. "Good, you two are going to rest a bit without having me to suggest it."

"I don't need a babysitter," I sighed, unbuckling the last buckle on Deigh's faceguard. She shook once and all the armour from her head and body fell to one side, revealing all her pretty, white scales once more. She nudged me away from undoing her wing armour and I gave Owen my full attention as he hadn't left as we expected. "Something wrong?"

"No. Just wanted to check in on you before heading to my car."

"Considered checked on…" I took off my armguards. "Unless there is something else?"

There was a bit of a sad look, one that I had seen a few times when he thought of the former king and queen, but it went away just as quickly, filling in with a smile at something amusing. "Take the full time to rest instead of a couple of hours. I'll come and get you when we're arriving at the wall."

"You can't tell me what to do…"

"No, but I can advise. You're not needed to do anything except to travel to Seraphina. No people to please, no paperwork. So, relax when you can, there'll be plenty of monsters and planning to attend to once we reach the south wall if you're eager."

"I'm relaxed, have been even before Orpheal called."

"Sleeping periodically and staying up the majority of the night before getting up a few hours later to continue is not relaxing."

"It is when you've had three months to get used to it…" I muttered half-heartedly, setting my armguards in with her loose gear. They made a loud clank as her armour shifted. "Now, how about you stop worrying needlessly and get some rest yourself. You're wasting both of ours away."

"Alright… I'll be on the other side of that door, the next car over, if you need me. Food is in the car behind yours. Nice, luxurious restroom if you want to shower for whatever reason-"

"You're worse than Jakob. Go already. I can find my way around a damn train," I growled in annoyance, crossing my arms. "Besides, who showers when they could be attacked at any moment?"

"Someone who uses the shower to think when they have a lot on their mind and doesn't wish to share with others."

I was left speechless at both the remark, which was true, and him knowing that there was something else on my mind, somehow. I rolled my eyes, trying to downplay it, but it was two seconds too late as he waved, leaving the car.

"We can talk about it when you're ready."

The door closed, leaving Deigh and I alone. A sigh came out. Didn't matter how much I pretended to be fine, he just always knew...

It was irritating.

I took off my pauldron, dropping it in with the armguards followed by my gauntlets, then hung up my armoured coat and cape. As much fun as it would have been to wear all of that to sleep, I wasn't interested in seeing the results.

I rubbed Deigh's nose once more as somewhere between the conversation finishing and me taking off my gear, she had fallen asleep. She was so cute when she slept; made me a bit jealous at how fast she managed to do it. I wandered over to the sectioned off room and found a decent sized bed and sighed again, not wanting to sleep, and closed the door behind me.

00000

Pain came from my arm as I found myself in a forest, exhausted, and slightly blinded by the light coming through the trees. Aetherian was in the body of the Gracidra. I ripped my blade from her chest, doing as much damage as possible. Her purple blood sprayed against the leaves and grass as she fell. Pain came from my chest and right shoulder and I grabbed it, feeling the blood run down my arm and chest under the armour. It eased slightly as the adrenaline started to cease. Deigh came out of the bushes, knocking a tree down that got in the way of her tail. A smile of relief formed on my face as I started walking over to her. The relief ended as the aura came back, freezing my advance for moments too long. I turned to the corpse that was left behind, her blade inches from my chest.

Something blinked into existence and I was knocked out of the way, forced to watch Pyrrha take the blow. The monster's arm went through her chest.

She attacked again, biting into the knight, sending out another wave of fear so no one could interfere – Pyrrha's blood splattering across my face.

Bones cracked as Pyrrha stabbed into the Gracidra's head, her sharp screams becoming breathless. Words came out as a whisper that I couldn't hear, and the monster ripped her arm free. Her teeth tore the knight apart just as Pyrrha's power exploded the monster. What was left of the Dragon Knight fell to the ground, the space silent except for the sounds of her struggling to breathe.

I blinked in disbelief only to find that the area changed to a raging fire in the middle of the night. It was contained as it danced in the middle of a stone circle where dragons laid dead, and ready to be burnt. The dragon that was Pyrrha's, Nora, laid with them. Fire quickly consumed her. The flames blinded me for a moment and when it died, I was in a gloomy tunnel.

The air was stale with the horrible smell of death and blood. Atlamillia was speechless as she looked around and I started towards her. My foot slipped on something and my hard landing found me looking at a forsaken child. Half of her face was gone, bits of brain matter in her light blonde, tattered hair that was dyed in blood. Her single cheek left was stained in tears.

I got up only for Atlamillia to disappear and something reflected off the flickering lights. An arm with a ring, Tetra's ring. Part of Nerida laid nearby as I looked around, frantically, then chased after a false hope – the lights went dark. They came back on as I turned a corner and stopped in front of a wall of rubble. Bodies were stuck or crushed by them or their peers. Evander's body was broken and abandoned.

I dropped to my knees only to be soaked, coughing sharply for air as water expelled from my lungs. Olin was blurry in front of me, surprised by my escape from his water cage. Cyrus abused his distraction to overpower the corrupted knight and struck him. Olin attacked back, recovering faster than either of us thought he would, and I rushed him. Winterthorn sliced through flesh and bone with ease as it entered his back, keeping him from attacking my knight. I removed it in anger just as Citlali came into the room before rushing for Helena. Adrenaline failed to keep me standing and I dropped to the ground.

The darkness didn't stay long as a different light appeared. The warmth casted around did nothing to the freezing needles that stabbed through my body. I couldn't scream as my throat closed and I looked around the cave. Mother turned to me, hearing the silence. The shadow creature got up while she was distracted, batting her into the cave wall. I closed my eyes only for the rain to pour down – no longer in a cave.

The fire was drying it as fast as it fell, repeating the process of wet and dry – the pain of venom coursing through my veins unending. Ciar backed away, wings lowered before turning to me, away from Father as he sent a dark sphere at my broken form. The king slashed a wall of light at it, causing the attack to stop. The monster closed the gap, shoving a clawed hand into him before tearing it out.

I screamed.

Father shoved Winterthorn into Ciar's chest with a gasp then ripped it out, light blasting him back.

The great man staggered, dropping to his knees. Words came from him, words I didn't want to follow as he fell into the mud. The flames dying as the rain fell at full force and Ciar crushed his enemy's heart.

A mutter came from him, searing into my mind, "Who would have thought your kind can live without a heart for a few moments…"

The monster turned to me and went for his sword when a barrier of light divided us, blinding me.

I was left staring into white space, my body no longer aching as I sat up. The space slowly added details of scorched marks and blood smears as ash fell like snow. But it no longer bothered me for some reason, taking away the memories that threatened to break me.

It was a familiar space – even if it was only the second time I had seen it. It made the pain bearable.

The ash was barely noticeable on my white shirt, speckling the black pants as it fell harder. Shapes formed in the fallen ash. Dead trees and plant-life, the bodies of unrecognizable people. Faceless, featureless, just as the ashes of memories not of my own, but of another of a different time were revealed before being buried.

The whispers of the young maiden came to my left and I turned to her. The Black Phoenix stood there; a red magic outlining her black and red form.

I should have been terrified, to get to a blade I knew I didn't have.

But I didn't; I wasn't scared.

I sat there, a huff of almost relief came out. "The first time I was here… It was unsettling. Still is. But I'd be lying if I didn't say the simplicity of it wasn't calming in some way."

The dragon laid down, apparently understanding, and she giggled.

"Yeah, too bad this is just a dream, eh? Just the two of us, not causing the other trouble… just here, in the ashes." I looked away from her for a moment before looking back, admiring her. "You might be terrifying to fight against… but you remind me a bit of Deigh. Much larger and a different colour, but beautiful all the same."

Another giggle was the only reply. She looked at something behind me. I turned to whatever it was to find nothing. Looking back, the dragon was gone, ashes falling to cover where she had been. I stood up.

Where'd she go?

The calming, unsettling feeling of the place became tense. The empty, comforting feeling filled with a different, familiar one as ill intent came flooding in like a wave. The feeling it brought was wrong, corrupting the white, ashen, and dead world.

The need to leave hit much like the wave that came before and I took a step back from some thing that was there but hidden. Black vines came from the earth and I tried to get out of their way, knowing what came with it but they were faster, gripping my legs and stabbing their thorns into my boots and thighs. A hiss came out as I pulled at them only to slice my hands. Blood dripped onto the white, ashy floor.

Something moved at the corner of my eye and I looked, finding Theodora in revealing, Seraphinean armour. The vines pulled me to the ground in my disbelief, my struggle stopping for a moment, and I turned away from her. The vines had to be removed. They only tightened. An ominous presence moved in front of me. I looked up, finding the woman I was trying to leave in memory only a few centimetres from my face. My heart skipped a beat. Her welcoming, bright smile that I had missed turned savage as Ciar appeared over top of her. There was nothing I could say or do as her two-ended polearm was stabbed into my heart by her hand.

I jolted awake, sitting up, and gasped for air as my chest throbbed. My hand clenched at the pain, finding only my drenched shirt in its grasp. The headrush I received from the quick movement caused stars to form in my already disorientated vision. I flopped back into the bed.

What the fuck was that?

No…

No, I was not going to have that be the start of my day. Not all those memories and certainly not with the idea that she… and…

Who?

The dream faded as I tried to reach for it, leaving behind only confusion and discontent at whatever happened.

Not today, Valrdis… not today.

Or… maybe I should start substituting her name for Orithina's if the Goddess of Life did want me dead.

I rolled over, not wanting to go down that road and threw the blankets over my head, the memory of the nightmare completely disappearing as my eyes closed.

Chapter Five: Siren's Valley

Hours had gone by since we left Absalom. Siren's Valley sang out an incredibly, beautiful tune, very different from the one a few months ago. Besides the fights to get out of the kingdom, nothing stirred. It was peaceful. I felt relax in the partially, sunny day. The two things combined allowed me to think over what my parents had said.

There was something else that was bothering me, but I couldn't remember exactly what it was. I knew I had a nightmare on the train, but it was fuzzy. Though, I felt like it had something to do with Theodora…

"Aerrow," Owen called from right behind me, interrupting my train of thought. I jumped to a stand, hand on hilt in a panic. I was not as relaxed as I thought I was. But at least this time, I didn't yell. A smirk formed on his face, barely containing the laughter. "We'll be at the outpost soon."

"Really?" Had we been travelling that long?

"It'll be dusk shortly, we've rested twice," he explained further, and I looked to the west, the sun lower in the sky than I remembered, barely above the horizon. I didn't even notice that we stopped, but it did explain why my stomach was feeling a bit hungry. "You've been distracted since leaving Orithina's Temple and while I would normally leave you to expand at your own pace, there are more battles to be fought. A distracted mind is not for the battlefield."

"I'm…" My tongue caught. He needed to know… but what if it was just a hallucination? Maybe it wasn't, maybe it was possible. I parked myself and Owen followed, sitting across from me as Deigh prepared to help when I needed it. "I have a hypothetical question."

"How hypothetical is this question?"

Good question. I wasn't entire sure where ghosts sat between myths and fairy tales. "So, you know how the Black Phoenix was a myth?"

"Yes…"

"And you know how the Gracidras and his Terror Hounds were fairy tales?"

"Living, breathing fairy tales that killed a third of a town…" He eyed me in confusion. "Where exactly are you going with this?"

"What's your opinion on ghosts?"

A look of surprise washed over him for a second before he went back to his usual, calm demeanour in similar situations. "I've lived a long time, but I cannot say I've encountered one. The closest thing I would consider a spirit of something dead would be pnevallidum. This is with certainty as I had met one that was someone I knew in life. Thankfully, because of my inherent necromancy, she wasn't very difficult to take care of."

That made sense. Pnevallidums were considered spirits in my bestiary, just having the ability to be a necromancer would allow a severe advantage over them. "So, you've never met a ghost? No haunted locations?"

"Your father, mother, and I went into ruins quite a few times on our many adventures before Ruairí died. Your parents swear they had encounters with humble ghosts and poltergeists alike, but I've never had such encounters as far as I'm aware." He thought about it a little longer before shaking his head. "I would like to think that it's possible for ghosts and spirits to exist, but I'm not entirely sure. A priest would know more on the subject. They enjoy the illogical world of the occult."

A small smile formed on my face, though it wasn't out of happiness really. I figured that was where he stood on the subject. He was more practical and logical. The same place where I stood on things. A line had to be drawn somewhere on what was real and what wasn't, even if that line was blurry in some areas. "Well, as you said, you've visited ruins before, but have you maybe visited a tomb or a necropolis-"

"Aerrow, can you stop beating around the bush and get to the point? I'm your guardian, general, and uncle; I've heard crazier."

"I mean, it's not that..." Oh, who was I kidding. The subject was ludicrous. I sighed. "When Deigh and I were in the tomb... we didn't lose track of time."

"You saw a ghost? Did you have to fight it, or-"

"No, it wasn't just *a ghost*..." I played with my gauntlet again as I worked up the ability to say the words out loud. "The... T-the former king and queen appeared as we were about to leave. No, it doesn't make sense and Deigh and I have gone through every single possibility of what could have happened other than that... but... We both saw them, and we heard them."

"They were speaking?"

He was taking this better than expected... not that I should have expected him not to. I nodded. "To me, mostly. But they weren't really ghosts either... If I hadn't seen their bodies, knew who they were, I would have thought them to be alive. They were physically there. I held Mother for the first time in forever and he was…" I couldn't finish the thought as my feelings became muddled and my voice caught. I took a breather. "I don't know what to make of it. Reality, a figment of desperation. A consequence of the venom… spreading the idea to Deigh somehow, we don't know. What we do know is that they had asked me of a request and gave a warning."

"This sounds…" He didn't need to finish the thought as I already knew how it sounded. "In the odds of it being real, what did they say?"

"Normal, parent things: keep doing what I can, protect the kingdom, keep Atlamillia safe… but the way they emphasized on her and then expanded further to keeping the world safe from Ciar… It wasn't just what they wanted. It was more. A mission they couldn't complete, and if I failed, failed to keep Atla safe, then it was going to be much worse than a dynasty ending. At least, that's how it seemed."

"Ciar is a dangerous bastard; I wouldn't be surprised that he could threaten even the laws of nature. What was their warning?"

"That people were out to kill me."

"Well, that's a bit more anticlimactic than I thought it was going to be. That sort of thing tends to happen to kings, whether or not you're loved; there will always be someone that wants you dead. Maybe even try for your throne and use you as you've seen."

"I don't think one of these people is looking for the throne."

"Feeling really vague today, eh?"

I glared at him slightly. He would have been too if he only knew how hard it was to say the next crazy thing that had to come out. "Orithina was the other person they mentioned by name besides Ciar. They implied that she wants me dead, for how long she's been wanting that, who knows. Deigh and I went through it and we think she's been trying to secure it by manipulating fate to her will. In consequence, Atlamillia and whoever has this prophetic sight gets word on it. Then, by some sheer luck and interference from one person or another, those fates never fall through. At least… that's what we think. Feel free to debunk it."

"If they had come to me with the same warning, maybe… but with all the facts I do know, I cannot…" he sighed, closing his eyes for a moment. "Even back before what happened to Aelia, your sister had nightmares. Nightmares of you being killed. I doubt she remembers them; some were horrific. But I passed them off for coincidence since they never came to pass. But thinking back, those things never happened because of Solomon and Aelia, myself, or even some random stranger on the street. Someone managed to take you away from danger as you adventured all over Siofra."

"I never thought anything dangerous could happen…" I shared before disagreeing. "Then again, I never thought I could get hurt back then."

"You were such a handful, you have no idea," he chuckled before growing serious. "That was until the day you left. Your sister had been put down for a nap and woke up screaming unlike ever before. A robed figure in a cave was attacking you. At least, that's how she understood it. It was the scariest thing she had ever seen; she didn't even know the words to describe what Ciar was or what he was going to do to you. We went looking for you, finding Deigh in the courtyard, not sure of where you were. Aelia knew of where you might have gone once we realized you had made it beyond the wall. You know how the rest of it goes from there…"

He went silent again as I waited for him to try to give me an answer of some sort. What that answer was… I wasn't sure if I wanted to hear it, no matter what way it went.

"Knowing what they said, if they were really your parents… it could have been Orithina playing a game, using whoever she could get as her pawns to do whatever she wanted without committing true divine intervention and breaking the oath created. For what reason though, only she would know."

I looked over my shoulder at Deigh. "Looks like you're right. I'm a walking corpse. It was nice knowing you."

Owen made a noise of disapproval, bringing me back to him. "You're not dead yet. It's possible that it's not as it seems. That something else is going on. She's the Goddess of Life, she might just be seeing your future, intrigued by how many times it ends, only for it not to. She may not have any part in it and the warning from your parents, could have been misinformation. Maybe she's manipulating strings and it's accidently put you into those situations, maybe even sent those visions as a way to protect you from the manipulations. There's a lot of different ways for their words to be taken if they weren't specific; both good and bad."

I focused on the bad. "They mentioned her and mentioned fate… Since she's the one who gives the visions…"

"It would make sense for her to be fate itself. Unfortunately, there isn't much to go on with that as Orithina's story doesn't get into that power."

No… it didn't, did it? But was it because she didn't have the ability, or she did, and she didn't want mortals to know about it? A growl came out as I couldn't answer that question. "Even if she isn't trying to kill me… I'm not sure how much I enjoy being divine entertainment…"

"Gotta find a hobby somewhere," he replied cheekily, then grew serious again. "We do know that there is at least one person that wants you dead, and he has many followers. Whether or not there is a god that wants your life for some reason is not something we have much control over. But we can be vigilant to make sure we don't leave Atlamillia to do a job she doesn't want, right?"

I nodded.

"It's good to know this information, even if it could have been a hallucination… But I do wish you would have told me sooner."

"Sorry."

"No harm came of it, luckily. But you need to understand that at least one of us needs to know." He hinted at the two knights leading the way behind me. "We can't do our job to keep you alive and you can't do yours if you're dead. So, don't hide these things, no matter the reasoning."

"I'll keep it in mind…"

"It will be your undoing if you don't allow others to help you."

"I know. I've read enough tales to know how that turns out."

"Good. Don't be them. They're dead in their respective worlds."

"Don't be dead. I think I can do that."

He shook his head and was about to get smart with me when Azarias's voice carried over to us. "Kal Alna Outpost ahead! Food time!"

I looked over Deigh's shoulder and in the valley below laid the walls and buildings of an outpost. Dragon bones decorated the landscape around it like the legends had stated from Valoth Nor's story: *Dragons of Outlands*. It was a bit unnerving to see a giant grave with an outpost directly in the middle of it. Lights had already been turned on, reflecting off the area's features and not a monster stirred.

Perhaps we could get a decent rest here. Even if Outland Monsters attacked, the perks of being in an outpost allowed us to pay for someone else to do the hard work.

Chapter Six: Dragon Tales

The sun had completely set as we landed at the outpost entrance. A golden chalice with gems embroidered into it sat in front of a four-pointed crystal on black flags, flying lightly on towers in the breeze. Guards stood by on either side of the opened gate with the emblem of Vlirrith on their armour. Neither of them batted an eye as we went through.

On the inside, it was almost town-like but perhaps more akin to a hamlet. A trader's building, medical centre, houses for the people who lived there, shops, a couple of inns, even some farmland. The buildings were the same size as the ones in Absalom, but I had a feeling that the farther south we went, the smaller they would become. The thought of only certain buildings being dragon friendly was uncomfortable. It meant that we were being left in the open and become an easier target for someone who cared.

I got off Deigh and we followed Owen towards one of the inns. It didn't take long to get situated into rooms.

Deigh flopped into her bed as soon as I undid her final buckle, leaving her armour strung about the floor. A growl came from her, *"I'm out of shape... I shouldn't be this tired!"*

"I don't think it's possible for you to be out of shape. Not used to the extra gear on the other hand, I can believe," I told her as I started to clean up the mess. *"Want me to get food brought to you?"*

"Yes... I'm starving and tired..." There was a pause before she gave out a noise of disgust. *"And we have to do this again!"*

"A few more times... but soon, we'll be in Seraphina and then you don't have to fly with so much... junk."

"It is junk... how dare you put armour on me!"

"I dare because I want to keep you safe. Outland Monsters are one thing, but Outland Dragons have been more aggressive lately and we're heading right through their territories."

She sighed, *"I know... ugh. Kill me."*

I switched to speaking out loud. "If I killed you, then I'd die too, and I happen to enjoy living from time to time."

"From time to time. At least Owen didn't chew you out as much as I thought he would."

"Well, I told him before something happened," I sighed as I fumbled with the gear. My foot caught and I tried to recover only to trip further. A tail caught me before I could face plant and set me upright. "Thank you."

"You are your own enemy sometimes," she grumbled before turning to me slightly as I put away the gear. "Could you bring me my book while you're up? I tossed the bag just out of reach…"

I looked towards the bag she was talking about and it was a slight stretch away from her. "Are you serious?"

"I'm tired."

"Lazy more like it." I walked over to the bag and brought it to her. "Your book and whatever amusement you brought, *Your Highness*."

"I carried you here, don't forget that."

She did carry me this far…

She pulled out her book and started reading as I left her to sit on the bed. I took off some of my gear, like my gauntlets, the coat, and replaced my pauldron, my less armoured gloves from the good old days, armguards – since you could never be too careful, and my sword belt. Winterthorn was sitting on my side once more and I stretched feeling a bit better. It was nice to not wear so much armour. My relaxed feeling left a bit. Exposure crept into my serenity, the words from the tomb slipping in.

Instead of what I had expected to be the scar acting up, a sharp pain went through my chest where my heart was followed instead. I winced as the remnants of the nightmare came back – which wasn't much.

"I tried to go through your memory, just in case you might have suppressed it," Deigh started, and I looked to her as she turned a page. "But whatever you dreamt of is long gone except for ashes, getting stabbed by something, and Theodora. In what order, correlation, and setting, I don't know."

"Well… that's annoying. I feel like it was important."

"Reminds me of the dream you had when you went almost comatose after the trial. I couldn't see it and you don't have any recollection of having it other than you had a nightmare."

"I don't remember that one either…" I looked down at her book. "How's your progress?"

"I'll let you know when you come back. I'm going to try out the ability once I know you aren't going to be around for a while."

"Why?"

"Because if it works, at least to the degree I'm working with here, I won't have any clothes on."

"O-oh… right… Okay, um… just, wait until after food shows up."

"How dumb do you think I am?"

"I-I'm just saying!" I stuttered, flustered and mildly protective over her wellbeing. "You sometimes get really eager and forget your surroundings. We aren't in Absalom or Asylotum anymore. The only laws are whatever laws that have been placed within the Outpost's walls, and who knows how tyrannical the person running this place is."

"That they would be dumb enough to do anything to insult the king of a powerful nation by attacking his dragon? Oh, did I forget to mention that I'm a dragon?"

"Or it could be some drunk who doesn't care…"

"You're going to be the kind of father that doesn't want his daughter showing any skin, aren't you?"

"I'm sorry if I'm protective… I'm not going to care about what she wears if she's happy. I just…" I gave out a sigh. "I don't want anything bad to happen and I care about the actions that could be taken; what they could do to her… or you in this case. People can be animals if they don't care, men and women alike."

"I appreciate it, but I am still a dragon."

"You're my partner and even if you were a god, I'd still worry for you."

"I know you would, because you're awesome."

Yeah, right. "What do you want?"

"Food."

"Alright, I'll go. Good chat." I got off the bed, the muttered undertone of my words not going unnoticed as she glared slightly.

I left her to her studies and went to find one of the knights and room service. Hopefully, she wasn't feeling too picky tonight.

00000

I sat in the loud pub as a waitress took away my plate. I was ready for bed, but Deigh still seemed occupied, shutting down our link almost entirely some time ago. I didn't blame her. She was prideful and didn't like anyone knowing her mistakes when she made them. That and her obvious insecurities, not that she'd admit it.

I took a drink from my glass of water and listened to the room. There wasn't much being said that interested me. The people around us were just travellers, some of them treasure hunters, others just finding their way, meeting new people for answers to questions about life. All while getting wasted.

I doubted that adding alcohol would help answer the meaning of life, but it wasn't my place nor my business.

Azarias was still talking about the women in Seraphina, a subject that had been brought up by Owen pestering me about that particular duty that I had been avoiding. And while it started off with good intentions, the brunet knight had been going on about the kingdom we were heading to and how interesting the females were for what seemed like forever.

I wasn't sure how interested with Seraphinean women I was going to be, let alone trying to play the silly game of dating no matter how well endowed they were. I had only seen them from a distance and never actually talked to one. I didn't exactly have a preference on the physical appearance like some people at the table.

My interests weren't dictated by appearance. It helped, perhaps, but it was more about personality, which he hadn't really talked about customs or even what they saw in men of any race on the planet. And even if they weren't too different from Absalomian women, the last time I had let someone in, woman or not, while beautiful on the outside, had a lot of secrets with the flaw of letting fear control whether the truth was put forward.

Truth was important, just as important as loyalty and caring for not just themselves and their immediate interests. It wasn't like being queen was going to suddenly make life easier; I needed someone that was going to love the kingdom and her people just as much as I did and nothing less…

I sure as hell wasn't going to find someone like that, without question, on a limited time mission. And even if I did, I wouldn't know – there wouldn't be enough time to know.

My duty had to come first. Love was secondary when it came to the important things, like letting the person you like know that someone was trying to kill them…

I was still bitter but dammit if I didn't miss her.

Loud laughing came from behind me, and someone got frustrated at the reaction. I tuned into it, readying to defend if a fight broke out.

"I swear ta ye!" The frustrated man growled to his company in a very heavy, Absalomian accent. "Tis guy can turn inta a dragon! It's terrifyin'!"

Wait… what?

"How much have you had?" One of the men behind me asked with a hoot. "That shit is just a myth. Not even the tales of Theseus said he could do it and he was the Hero-King! A chosen hero!"

"It's te trut! I saw 'im!"

Maybe ignoring Azarias had some benefits after all…

"I think you got slipped something when you did. Did you harass one of the waitresses?"

"Not tat night… Look 'e-"

"Oh, give it a rest. We're turning in for the night. Word has it that Absalom is going to be hiring guards and workers. Can't get there in a timely manner if you keep chatting our ears off all night."

"Ten be off wit ye, twits. Not sure 'ow much work tere is goin' ta be since te post went out taday."

"I'm sure quite a bit. The new king finally got the train running from the south wall to the capital."

"I knew te capital got focked, but te fock da ya mean new king? What 'appened ta te ol' one?!"

"Had his heart ripped out," the man sighed, and I winced. Chairs moved behind me. "Apparently a monster no one has seen before did it. They're calling him the Kingbreaker."

"'e'd 'ave ta be if 'e took out Solomon. So, 'is kid took te trone?"

"Yeah, three fucking months ago at one of the most interesting coronations I've ever heard of… Where the fuck have you been?"

"'ere, drinkin'…"

"You need to get out more or get a friend that does."

"What's so great aboot bein' out tere…?"

The men left, leaving the single man to grumble about a kid taking the throne and I got up from my seat. Owen, Azarias, and Cyrus noticed, but didn't say anything as I joined the man at his lonely table. I didn't sit down though. I wasn't quite sure what to expect from him and I didn't want to piss him off further before I got what I wanted.

"What's a kid like ye doin' up so late, eh?" The man asked as he took a drink and set his mug down, loudly. He looked up at me. "Unless yer 'ere ta mock me, eh? Wouldn't try it, kid."

"I'm curious to know your account. You said you saw someone turn into a dragon?"

"Say it a wittle wouder!" He hushed in annoyance as he kicked a chair out for me. "Sit or leave."

I promptly sat and moved closer to the man who smelt of alcohol. Cyrus came over, grabbing a vacated chair and the man gave him the stink eye before turning to me.

"Who's red? Broter or sometin'?"

Cyrus gave a physical reaction at the drunk's words like he had been stabbed, but before I could ask, the knight was back to normal in the same moment. I eyed him slightly in confusion before addressing the man. "Travel companion."

"Right, right… kids need a guardian… not as good as a Dragon Knight, but I'm sure yer aware, most are in Absalom… Te kingdom got focked 'arder tan my moter. Almost puts Ruairí's shit ta shame. Must have been tat Kingbreaker… Ya know. Solomon was like, te best? I don't know aboot ye, but I don't tink tat kid's gonna cut it. Big crown ta wear, kingdom in hidin', wouldn't want ta be tat soft shite…"

I sensed Cyrus tense at the remark, and I kicked him lightly under the table. The knight quickly took the hint and sat back, crossing his arms. The man went back to muttering things as he drank, and I attempted to guide him back to my original questions. "Yeah, who knows what the kingdom will be like now that a kid's in charge. Not like he was taught how or something…"

The drunk picked up on my sarcasm better than I anticipated. "Well I don't know! It's a kingdom! 'ow old's te kid anyway? Yer age? 'eard people liked 'im in ta capital but who te fock knows what te kid 'as in min'. Probably fockin' aroun'. Tat's what I'd do if I were a new kin'. Drown me sorrows wit all te girls and drinkin'. Probably get te girls too. Also 'eard 'e wasn't 'alf bad lookin'. Chics love tat broodin', sob story shite. Couldn't tell ye why."

It was sad how far he was from what I was actually doing… Thank the gods he wasn't a king elsewhere. "Perhaps, or he could be doing work as we speak."

"Tis late?!" The man's speech was deteriorating. "Kin' be sleepin' not-"

"Could be trying out that skill you mentioned… who knows, right?"

"Yeah! Te skill! 'e used it! It was terrifyin'!"

Finally… "Who was it that turned into a dragon?"

"Da bloody owner of tis Outpost, te mayor! 'e's like us, an Absalomian. But 'e's like, secret and stuff."

"His secret being that he can turn into a dragon?"

"It 'as ta be why 'e be so 'ighly regarded by te Doge!"

"Who?"

The man went silent for a second before giving me a questioning look. "Ye don't know who… ya don't get out much, do ye, eh?"

"I've been busy… who's this Doge?"

"Te leader of Vlirrit, ya know, te fockin' guy who currently runs tese outposts?"

"The Doge is Aurelio Vlirrith?" I asked and the man nodded.

"Ye, tat's 'is godsdamn name… Weird 'ow ye know te name but not 'is fuckin' title."

Probably because it wasn't an official title… and if it was, it wasn't used during world meetings. "So, you think the owner is running this place because he can turn into a dragon?"

"Well, who else better ta run and protect yer outpost tan two fockin' dragons?!" Did the man know any other adjectives? "Te tings ya couldo!"

"I thought we were supposed to be quiet?" I asked him as the man grew loud.

The man blinked before settling down again. "Right… right."

"That said, no one else but you had seen him turn into a dragon?"

"O'course not! Why da ye tink tem twits fockin' left?! 'e goes and 'ides in te back, te mayor, also ta bartender, anyway! 'e 'ides, bad leg or sometin'. But durin' a raid a few monts ago, wit te eclipse, I followed 'im, 'cause I didn't want ta be fockin' out 'ere wit all tese shites and saw 'im turn inta a fockin' dragon right in front of me!"

"I've heard of dragons turning into Absalomians, but not the other way around… What's to say he isn't a dragon?"

"Cause no one but me sticks aroun' tis place fockin' as lon' and 'e's only been wit 'is partner! Tere isn't anyone else!"

"Do you have proof?"

"Not aboot 'im, but 'e's got a book! I looked aroun'-"

"You were snooping through his things?"

"Don't judge me! You'd be wonderin' what te fock else 'e 'ad if ya were dere, too," he growled before drinking more. It was like his glass never emptied. "Buy me a bevy and I'll continue."

Guess his glass was emptying…

Cyrus left to fetch the drink and the man grunted at some conversation I wasn't a part of. A drink was set down faster than I had expected as Cyrus returned after what seemed only a few seconds.

The man started drinking again and Cyrus cleared his throat. "There, now what did you find in your search?"

"Search what?"

"You found a book," I told him, and a moment of pause went through the man before he lit up.

"Right! Te book! It 'atta ability ta make 'im a focking dragon! It's fockin' nuts!"

"Do you have it?"

"Ye tink I stole it?! I'm scummy, but I ain't a fockin' tief, boy!"

"Er, no. Of course, not… But you didn't happen to read it though, did you?"

"Fock yer right I did. But I couldn't wearn a godsdamn fockin' ting wit it. It 'as requirements and bein' a drunk ain't one of 'em."

"Requirements?"

"Dragon blood level, ting… takes a lot of it. I don't got it ta even attempt te first few skills."

"That's not an issue… what else?"

"'igh magic reserve- whatta fock da ye mean not a fockin' issue?! I didn't even say 'ow much dragon!"

"How high is the percentage?" I asked, pandering to him.

"Forty was what it asked, but you can get away wit tirty-five."

Huh… thought it would have been higher. "Anything else?"

"Why're yer still 'ere? Tat's enough ta kill someone before tere even out of teir moter's cu-"

"So, there's nothing else?"

"Just tat I'pose… ye actually gonna talk wit 'im?"

"Yeah-"

"What're ye, eh? Tink yer just gonna wearn it like yer ta fockin' kin'? Just ask fer it…?"

Time to go. I stood up from the table. "Thanks for the information, sir."

"Yer just weavin'?!"

"Yep."

"'e's ain't gonna tell ye shite!"

I shrugged. "Maybe, maybe not."

"Yer justa kid. What're'ya gonna get 'im ta spill? Whota fock arya?"

"Just a kid."

"Name, or Imma take ye and yer frien' 'ere out back."

I looked at Cyrus with a questioning look, but he was still calm as ever.

What did he give him to drink?

The knight gave a small smirk from his seat, apparently wanting the violence to commence.

A sigh escaped. I had forgotten he was as much as a peace disturber as Azarias was from time to time. I wasn't going to let this break out into a fight and turned back to the aggressor. "Aerrow, pleasure to meet you…"

"Aerrow? What kind of fockin' name is tat? Sounds familiar tough…"

"I do suggest that you lay off the alcohol for a bit, you might-"

"'asn't anyone tolya not ta fockin' tell someone if tere drunk?! Fockin' pissant… Get outta 'ere, squirt." He went back to his drink, muttering to himself, "Tellin' me whatta do… tink's 'e's me kin' or some shite…"

I shook my head and left the man to his drunken ignorance. It was better this way for everyone that he didn't know. Who knew what he could say to people that I didn't want to know about my whereabouts and interests? Cyrus joined me on my next adventure, and I glanced over at him. "What did you give him?"

"Tequila… figured he was the angry kind."

"Why?"

"I wanted him to try and hit first. How many times did he insult you?"

"Wasn't counting…" I looked back at the man as he continued to drink obliviously and turned back to the knight. "It's amazing how drunk someone can get. I'm surprised he hasn't-"

The sound of vomiting cut my sentence short, and my stomach turned. The smell of bile floated over as we went to the bar and I sighed.

"Never mind…"

"So, you're going to ask the bartender about what a drunk said?"

"Couldn't hurt. If need be, I can buy the book from him, or at least, find out where I could get one. If it's true."

"Depends on if the Lord Mayor is willing to talk."

I didn't get to answer as we arrived at the bar and the tender was ready to serve. His accent was not as heavy as the drunk's, but it was clearly there. "Welcome, Sire, Dragon Knight. What y'all have?"

"I have a question; Cyrus might want something…"

Cyrus shook his head briefly, handing over his answer quickly and silently, and the bartender nodded.

"A question, eh? Lots of noise comes trough tis place."

"I heard that you might own a book that I'm interested in," I started, and he raised a brow. "Was wondering if you'd be willing to part with it."

"Depends on te book and how much cash you're willin' to hand over," he replied as he crossed his arms. "So, what is it and we can start gettin' down to business."

"A skill book, allows an Absalomian to turn into a dragon."

"Wouldn't you have tat in your fancy library?"

"That doesn't sound like a no." The Lord Mayor grimaced, and I continued, "How much?"

"A lot. Very few were made and tis is a family heirloom."

"You have someone you want to pass it to then…"

"Maybe…"

"How much for borrowing? I'll bring it back to you when I'm done with it."

"Depends on how long it's outta my possession…"

"Sire, if I may have a word?" Cyrus asked and I nodded. We walked a few steps away. He lowered his voice to that of a whisper, "You can get a cheap rate if you have someone in Seraphina copy the book for you. We can have the book brought back within the next week and he'd probably cooperate more without wasting away our money unnecessarily."

"It's not unnecessary when we could use the ability to fight against Ciar…" I muttered before sighing. "But the idea is good nonetheless."

We went back to the bartender who was cleaning a glass. "Tat wasn't long…"

"Would it be reasonable to have it for two weeks?"

"You wouldn't learn te skills in such a short time, even for a kin'."

"Doesn't matter to you if I learn it or not, just that the book is returned and you're compensated, right?"

"Perhaps…"

"How much to loan?"

"Twelve hundred gold."

"Pardon?"

"Twelve hundred, it's a family heirloom as I said. Plus, you happen ta brin' about trouble if te rumours about you are true. Compensation, right?"

That was five nights at the inn with five meals for us alone… unfortunately, I had nothing to try and haggle the price down. It was going to put a dent in our coinage… but it wasn't detrimental. I looked over at Cyrus who remained silent on the subject.

Couldn't help even a tiny bit… Suddenly, I was missing Azarias's unfiltered help.

Some coin or lose the chance to continue to adapt to fight Ciar…

The choice was obvious.

I gave my answer. "Alright, deal. Twelve hundred for the book and it will be returned in two weeks."

"If it's not, I'm sendin' your court a bill ten times tat prices for damages."

And it's not like Atlamillia wouldn't pay it because if she didn't, it would damage reputation with Vlirrith. They weren't that big of a city state, if one could call it that, but they did have a lot of influence in mercenaries and markets, both good and bad, and that would ripple into the other kingdoms.

I put down the coin in a few of the higher worth ones and he counted them before taking them off the counter. He went to the back room, a limp to his step showing off a hidden injury.

A few minutes of wondering if he was ever coming back, he came out with an old looking book, worn down on its hard cover.

He set it on the counter. "Pleasure doin' business wit ye, Sire. Happy ta be of service again."

Sure, he was… Commerce was, unfortunately, a very powerful tool.

I gave a curt nod and took the book, leaving the bar to head back to our table. I sat across from Owen and immediately felt guilty for borrowing the book for such a price. But the library was too far away, and I wasn't going to get a knight to go searching for it when they could be doing something productive.

"So, where did you run off to?" Owen started, leaning in with apparent interest. "Must have been important if you left during the most important section of Azarias's tale."

This was not interest; he was annoyed that I abandoned him. But my endeavour was a little more important than conversing about visually pleasing women. Not to mention, he brought that hell upon himself for bringing up the subject in the first place. "I got a book-"

"I see that. And how much did that cost?"

"Not a lot…"

"You sound really guilty for something that didn't cost a lot."

"Alright, it was a lot in terms of money, but in terms of knowledge, it far outweighs it. Especially if at least two of us can learn it." I turned to Azarias and Cyrus. "Unless your dragon blood percentage isn't over thirty-five."

Azarias pouted. "Mine's only thirty-two, the same as Cyrus."

That was unfortunate…

He looked at the book in front of me. "What is it exactly for that requirement?"

"The ability to turn into a dragon," I answered, and his jaw dropped a bit.

"What?"

"Figured it'd be a useful ability to learn."

He put his hand on my forehead, lifting the circlet on it slightly. "You don't have a fever… Why the hell are you wanting to use or learn magic?"

"To fight Ciar, or Kingbreaker as some people have decided to call him." The answer should have been obvious, and the nickname caused Owen to flinch ever so slightly. I reeled back my emotions a bit. "He's probably much stronger than before and, unfortunately, we don't know how much more. We have to compensate in someway."

"That is true… but I doubt the ability will be easy to learn…"

"No, but that doesn't mean I can't. I have a pretty good teacher of dragon magic if I need assistance."

Owen crossed his arms. "Cheeky, but don't push yourself. I'm sure there is more than just that requirement to use it. Let me look it over and I'll give it back to you in the morning if I think it's safe… If not, we're giving it back to the Lord Mayor."

"Alright…" I pushed the book across the table. "Just be careful with it… or you're paying twelve thousand gold."

He gave a surprised look back and I turned inward for a different discussion. "*Deigh, you done up there yet?*"

A disappointed sigh came from her, "*Yes… I suppose…*"

"*You seem upset. What is it?*"

"*Well I'm not upset… just not happy either.*"

"*Not everything you planned for?*"

"*I succeeded in my original goal, but I can't figure out how to do this next step… I've been at it forever!*"

I turned back to the table. "I think we should get some rest. We have a long way to go if we have any hope of making it to the next outpost and I don't want to sleep outside."

"That was sudden…" Owen said with a frown. "Everything alright?"

"Deigh has a conundrum and I'd like her to sleep at some point tonight."

"Ah… well, good luck with whatever she's working on…"

I nodded and quickly left. I had no idea what to expect when I got there, but I was truthful on what I had said. Deigh would not go to sleep until she had solved her problem, whatever the hell it was.

Her greatest strength, was her greatest flaws in times like this…

Chapter Seven: Shattered

Atlamillia looked over the documents that were left behind in the late night. It had been a couple of months since she had to complete such tasks and she, admittedly, was leaving it to the last possible minute to enjoy the last bit of freedom she had. She put the pen to the paper and a knock came from the door.

"Come in," she called, not overly surprised at the timing as she signed the document where it needed to be signed.

This was the first time she had been in her study since Aerrow left, her being there with the door slightly ajar meant that she was free to discuss anything related to the kingdom. Silence greeted her and she looked up in confusion, wondering why the door hadn't opened farther to find one very familiar face and the other that triggered a hidden memory. Her body reacted faster than her mind could, getting up from the chair quickly, causing it to fall over. Firethorn was picked up from its leaned form against the desk, drawn, and charged in her hand.

She didn't know who to point it at, her tongue unable to move.

It didn't have to as the one who she had tried with great difficulty to get over, spoke first, his voice was exactly as she had remembered. "Atlamillia, I'm sorry."

The words were like knives as she glared. Her rage overcoming her grief and disbelief. "You're sorry?! You… You left us! You promised me that my last moments with you weren't going to be that trip!"

"I know… but I would do it again without hesitation. It kept the both of you safe."

"So… you really are him," she stated even though it was meant to be a question to know if they were really… She turned to the woman who was her mother. She was beautiful… even more so than the pictures. Just like Aerrow had said she was. Her features were both sharp and soft, her green eyes that would have made emerald green dragon stone seem dull looked at her with held back tears, but not at her outburst. "Why are you here? Why are either of you here like this and not…?"

The words hung as she couldn't finish them.

The former king, Solomon, looked to the blade still held by her. "Are you going to keep that pointed at us and waste the moment we have?"

Moment? What did he mean by…?

The realization hit.

They weren't staying. They were…

She lost her grip on the sword as she dropped her arm in disbelief. It clattered on the floor. "You're… leaving… again."

"Unfortunately." The first word that had come from her mother was from a voice she could barely remember. Shame overcame Atlamillia. "This world is not ours anymore."

She went around the desk, her legs moving on their own and collided with the two beings. One familiar, the other… a faded memory, but her arms knew Aelia, somehow retaining the things she had forgotten. "You can't leave. Not again."

"We know, Little Light… We know."

The name cracked Atlamillia's barrier. Her tears fell. "I can't do this… I'm not ready. You two have so much to teach me. You were always… You can defeat Ciar and anything that comes! Why didn't Orithina protect you?!"

"She did what she-"

"She should've smited that thing! Then you wouldn't have… Neither of you would have!" She gripped tighter at the beings that were her parents. "I'm so sorry. I couldn't protect you."

She broke down and her mother took hold of her, stealing her away from her father. Aelia was so warm. So… alive. She never remembered a comparison to her when she was small, but the woman now was slightly smaller than she was, something she wished she could have grown up with. Familiar strokes of comfort and small hushes didn't help tame the anguish she let out into her shoulder. She didn't want her to go. She didn't want either of them to go.

Solomon stood by, ready as he always was.

Her mother's stroking stopped as she hugged her tightly after a few moments. "I'm sorry I couldn't be there for you… for your brother. But you have to keep going because he's going to need you."

"Need me? He's-"

"Going to die if you don't help him when the time comes," Aelia stated as she put Atlamillia at arms reach. "And while we might not be here physically… we do still love you so very much and we are watching, supporting you the best we can. So, stand strong."

"Stand strong…" Atlamillia gave out a laugh of disbelief. "Held up in this cage, the monster that took you both away is out there, getting stronger and there is nothing I can do about it! What chance do I have if Orithina doesn't want to listen even when all that I have is taken?!"

"Atla," Solomon spoke, a tone she fixated on. "We know how you feel… but you don't belong with us. Deep down you knew that we weren't going to be there, and we tried desperately to make sure that you could keep us for as long as we could-"

"Stop! I didn't-"

"You did. You knew the day Aelia gave you Firethorn. Your mission is to protect, to protect so many. But it wasn't to protect us… I'm sorry that in my ignorance, I couldn't prepare you for that. I thought I would stay as your pillar when Ciar came that day."

"I should have been able to protect…"

He shook his head, drawing her from the queen in a hug she missed more than anything else. "No, I should have done better. I was warned and I failed you."

She felt the man she held start to disappear. "Wait! Please!"

"Orithina has plans… keep vigilant, Little Light," her mother said, coming in to form a group hug. "You'll understand… but you need to continue to protect until your duty is done."

"I can't-"

"You can," her father stated as he gave one final squeeze. "Everything will be okay; I promise."

The body she had in her arms became incorporeal as she fell through him slightly. Her pillar fading again.

"Farther, Mother… please…"

"We love you," Aelia said with a small, sad smile, tears in her eyes still.

Her father nodded. "Goodbye, Atlamillia."

"Good… bye…"

They disappeared and the room felt hollow. Her entire being was empty.

She collapsed to her knees, tears dropping to the floor.

Why did they have to go? They were… they were right there…

A gift or a cruel joke?

She couldn't tell. Both, perhaps.

A gift to finally see her mother's face again, hear her… Hear her father. To hold them one last time…

And then to have them ripped away from her all over again.

A knock came from the door that was still slightly open and she knew that it wasn't them. They weren't there. They weren't coming back. Her voice was solid despite the tears flowing, unendingly. "I'm busy right now."

The door opened regardless, and she looked up, ready to give hell to whoever didn't listen to find Gasper looking down at her in surprise.

She looked away from him, trying to keep her emotions together. "Kid, how many times have you been told-"

"Why are you crying?" He asked, cutting her off.

"I'm not crying… I just… have allergies…"

He closed the door and appeared in front of her, a different colour of green irises looked over her with sympathy. "You said goodbye to your parents for good, didn't you?"

"No-"

"I heard them… your dad and a woman…" He sat down in front of her, cross-legged. "I saw them too. It's okay to-"

"It's not okay! None of it is!" Her hands were clenched into fists. "You don't get it! I was trying to get over them… Get over him being gone… trying so hard because I couldn't be with him… Be with her."

"Your mom? Was that who the beautiful woman was?"

"I couldn't even remember her face other than from pictures and she… just comes in here like that wasn't a sin on its own. What kind of daughter forgets her own mother's face?!"

"She left a long time ago… I don't think she would be mad at you for that."

"How could she not be?! She gave me a duty… One I haven't been able to fulfill once! My whole life is just one mistake! A lie!"

"I don't see how. You're here, still doing duties while Aerrow isn't-"

She looked at him, dead in the eye, her tears still falling. "I almost killed myself the night I found out he died. The night that he broke his promise to come home. I'm supposed to complete a duty... and because of that duty, I couldn't do it. I couldn't be with him where I thought I belonged. Aerrow has no idea of that. The only reason why I'm still here is because she probably wouldn't let me die."

He looked at her with a bit of confusion. "You wanted to die? Why?"

"I was supposed to keep Father safe. I did everything to do just that and he still-" she choked, turning to the floor. The words of being informed of his death repeated in her head from Bretheena. His voice telling her to do what she had to do. "I don't want to be here anymore."

"I don't like being here either," Gasper answered honestly. "I want to be with my mommy and daddy too."

He got up and hugged her like her father had, causing her to choke on her question as she was buried into his tiny, pj clothed chest.

"Mommy told me to give hugs when people were very sad. To hug my baby brother or sister like this when they were a bit older. But... I won't ever get to do that since Mommy is gone with them. It was the second last thing she taught me right before dessert at the little food place by my house. Then, she taught me to say goodbye to her."

"I... didn't know..." she started, and he only held her tighter.

"I know. No one knows but you, me, and Uncle Delram... and that's okay. I might not have a baby brother or sister anymore; you don't have a big brother right now... so, I'll be your big brother and practice what Mommy taught me. And when I'm big... I can teach my baby when they get a baby sister or brother. I won't stop practicing until you are better and Aerrow is home and I know he can give you hugs just like this."

"Gasper... you don't need-"

"I wish I could see Mommy and Daddy again. But... I'm not sure if I would like to see them after I had already said goodbye and then have them go away again. So... I think... you are hurting more than you had before, and I don't want you to die." His tears dropped onto her head as he squeezed. "I don't want anyone else to ever die. Not anyone. Not my heroes, not my hero's daughter... They wouldn't want that. Not ever. I can't let you go where you think you belong because I don't want you to go. Aerrow would be very sad... I don't really get what any promises or duties, or whatever are… but I know that you are needed here. Not for whoever she is… but for the rest of us."

She brought Gasper down and set him on her lap, hugging him tightly as he started to really cry into her shoulder and chest. "It's okay… I'm not going to do anything like that… I told them I wouldn't."

"I know… I heard you and I'm happy. I don't want you to go. You're the big sister I never had… You keep the others from bullying me too much." He wrapped his arms around her. "Please don't ever go away!"

She nodded. "I'll do my best."

00000

She closed Gasper's door, leaving behind the sleeping child all curled up and tucked in. Somewhere during sobbing and crying, he fell asleep on her lap.

So, she brought him to bed… It was late after all and her study wasn't very far from where the kids' rooms were.

She gave a small sigh before starting towards the study to find Holly in front of her, a toy knight in her hands. Atlamillia gave out a slight laugh, "You too, eh?"

"Is Gasper okay?" The little blonde one asked and Atlamillia nodded. "Okay… because I saw you carrying him and… he looked like he was crying."

"He's okay now."

She clenched her toy to her chest. "He must miss his parents… I think we all do."

"Most likely. I don't think that's a feeling that ever goes away, Holly."

"No… probably not… Aerrow misses your mom and that was a long time ago. He showed us a picture once; she was really pretty."

Atlamillia gave a solemn nod. Her mother now, hopefully forever, was in her memory. "She was."

"Can I ask for a favour, Atlamillia?"

She gave a confused look, her head tilting to the side slightly. "What is it?"

"Can you tell Daddy to come back? It's been a week since he left on his mission."

"Delram is on a really important task of checking the tunnels. It would hinder his team if I called him home."

"I know… he said he was putting down sensors and stuff. Will he be home soon? There are only so many tunnels, right?"

"There are only so many, yes… His mission should be finished within the week if the tunnels are in good condition."

Holly smiled slightly. "Okay… good. Can I ask for something else?"

"Maybe…"

"Can he stay a bit afterwards?"

"How long is a bit?"

"Forever?"

"Would he want that?" She asked her and the girl looked down at her toy.

"Maybe…"

"We don't have a lot of knights right now. Everyone's crucial-"

"What does crucial mean?"

Atlamillia gave a small sigh. "Important. Everyone is important for each task right now."

"But why? Why can't we all just stay here! There are no monsters!"

"Because this place is made up… it's not made to keep going on forever like Orithin can. It must recharge like a battery and the longer we stay here, the more energy is used and the longer it will take to recharge for the next time we need it. If we stay here until that battery starts dying… this world will start dying and eventually, a lot of people could get hurt."

"So… because this place was opened for all of us, it's starting to die?"

"Very, very slowly, but yes. That's why we have to secure the kingdom so we can keep this place charged in case we need it again."

"But what about Ciar?"

She blinked in surprise at the name. She knew that Aerrow had told them the day before at lunch as he had mentioned it briefly, but she wasn't expecting Holly to retain it. "I'm surprised you're bringing him up…"

Holly nodded, a worried expression on her face. "Aerrow told us yesterday... but I already knew about whoever this Ciar was before then." She looked to the floor. "It was the night before he told us, or... at least, when he thought it was okay for us to hear after all this time."

"What do you mean?"

"Aerrow... he fell asleep at his desk and the door was opened. I wanted to see what he was doing and heard him muttering in his sleep about Ciar. Then, he woke up from a nightmare with a scream. I left before he realized I was there." Her face scrunched up like she ate something sour. "He never looked so scared before... sounded so... Is Ciar really that scary?"

"Yeah..." Atlamillia answered softly, but hesitantly. She knew that he had nightmares, that wasn't something new, but for them to become night terrors. The only time she had seen him terrified was the evening Ciar appeared below, decimating their ranks. The evening he killed their father. It was something she never wanted to see again. "He's really that scary..."

"That's why we're in here?"

Atlamillia nodded.

"And why Aerrow left... He said he was going to run away if he had to, but... do you think he's going to fight Ciar all by himself?"

"No... no. That's why Uncle Owen, Azarias, and Cyrus went with him, so that wouldn't happen."

She somehow clutched the toy closer. "If he's scary for Aerrow... I don't want anyone fighting Ciar. No matter how strong an army is."

"I don't want anyone fighting Ciar either, but he-"

"Killed the king... he told us." Holly rushed into her legs and hugged tightly around her hips. "Why does everyone have to die?!"

"It's just a cycle..."

"Is it just that? We live to die?!"

She was expecting the existential question about as much as she had expected her parents to show up. "No... There is a purpose to living, to do what you think is right, to share time with others, to protect. Just like what your father is doing now."

"I hate it. I wish Ciar would just go away!"

"Me too."

Holly looked up at her, her big, light-green eyes wet with unshed tears. "Atla…"

"Yeah?"

"Can you sleep with me tonight?"

Atlamillia looked at her, confused. "I thought you don't like sharing the bed, even with the other girls for sleepovers?"

"I… lied. I used to… but then it just reminded me of Mommy. I had a nightmare… Mommy or Daddy would sleep with me when I had one, but Daddy is gone, and Mommy was…" Her expression turned terrified as a memory went across her mind. "M-Mommy was… eaten."

Atlamillia hugged her as the girl started crying. There was no way that she could say no, not after knowing how awful it might have been to witness. The paperwork could wait until morning… not that she was sure if she could go back in there. Two kids, her parents… Tonight was just not a good night for anyone. It needed to go away. "Alright."

Holly nodded, still crying a bit and after a few moments, she settled down, allowing Atlamillia to wipe the girl's tears away. "Sorry, just when I think of what-"

"No, it's okay. It was scary, I couldn't imagine what it was like… I would be crying, too."

"Okay…" She huffed out a big breath. "I'm okay… Can we go now?"

"Yeah, but I have to change first, alright?"

Holly grabbed her hand with the hand that was free of the toy. "Okay. I'll protect you until we are safe in my room, under the blankets. I saw the more scarier thing; I'll defend you!"

Atlamillia smiled a bit at her horror stoked enthusiasm, the process of her trauma turning into something better, not that Atlamillia knew if it was for the better, and they walked down the hall towards the stairs.

Chapter Eight: Seraphina

The sun broke through the clouds for the first time since leaving the mountains. Its light reflected off my page from the book I borrowed and into my eyes. A small hiss of irritation came out and Deigh to laugh at my misery. I looked out at the strange land, taking it as a sign to break for a small bit.

A small river flowed below, and I followed it through its fields and forests to a great lake, one from even high up I couldn't see the other side or the shores to the east and west. Clouds and fog broke above the water of Seraphina Lake and the edges of rock came through. Waterfalls fell into the lake from the breaks in the floating landmass and off the sides leaving me in awe.

My moment of enjoyment ended swiftly on the wings of a large, black dragon as it flew out of the clouds for a moment. Distinct spikes came out of its spine and torso, the large horns placed on its head removed the idea of it being friendly. Its lean form flew back into hiding, deep jagged wings and a long sweeping tail cut through the clouds like a phantom. It was unsettling how it moved, making the flow of water seem clunky compared to it. Even from as far as we were, I knew it wasn't making much noise, if any at all, as it flapped its wings.

Clouds parted more and as more of the rock of the floating isle appeared above, so did the monsters that were attacking a barrier field. About thirty Outland Dragons blasted it with dark streams as they flew by, causing the shield that held them out to sputter, but not enough for it to break down entirely.

We flew upwards, towards the assault, and I loaded up the crossbow with an Outland bolt after putting away my book. A cry came from one of the dragons as it noticed us. Several calls and barks came from within the group and about half of them headed towards us.

Missiletainn flew next to Deigh and I looked over to Owen on the black and yellow dragon's back. "Last minute advice?"

The great general nodded. "Don't hesitate. It's going to feel wrong for killing them, but they attacked first, and we have to defend ourselves."

I looked at the crossbow for a moment. I didn't want to kill them, no, but we needed to get to the kingdom. They weren't going to allow that. "I wasn't planning on hesitating."

"Planning and doing are two different things. They are still dragons and I know you." He looked back at the force that was coming in fast. "If you don't want them to suffer, you know where to aim."

I nodded as we flew past a large building surrounded by an equally large, gated fence below. I looked back at it to make sure no Outland Monsters or Dragons were attacking it. The out of place building had nothing around it, seemingly abandoned, and I looked ahead.

I wasn't sure why it was there at all, probably a research base of some sort. But it was nice to know that we didn't have to rescue it while dealing with the danger coming towards us.

I raised the crossbow to aim at the nearest Outland Dragon and readied myself. A few seconds passed as the distance closed, waiting to see if the dragons were coming our way to truly attack us. There were no negotiations to be had as the closest one started to charge up an attack.

I pulled the trigger. The purple, dark energy attack went to escape the dragon's throat only to be cut off as the bolt pierced through its eye. A painful scream went through the silence, lasting a moment as it fell, but it was long enough for me to hate every millisecond of it. The regret of killing someone flew in faster than it fell to the earth. I clenched my jaw as I reloaded the crossbow, putting away the horrible feelings that gnawed at my stomach.

Owen was right. It… was awful. More than awful, straight up unholy. Unfortunately, they didn't give us much of a choice – there wasn't the option for a sound peace without confrontation.

I turned my attention to the next dragon and aimed for a moment before firing as Deigh set her jaws around the throat of a different one, less distraught about killing the dragons than I was.

But… I supposed that was a consequence of being a Dragon Knight. Sometimes you had to kill to protect – even if the thing you were killing was a living person just as you were.

My dragon fell just as Deigh's lost a head when she released a fireball. Claws raked her armour when one came from below, forcing her to turn her attention to it as it flew up past us, and I had to hold on. It was twice her size, dive-bombing down with dark magic forming in its jaws. We didn't stick around to fight it head-on as she took off quickly towards the floating kingdom, allowing me to reload a third bolt. A dark stream went past my head as she made a sharp turn, turning around about hundred-eighty degrees to fire a ball of white flames at it. It hit the creature's wing and I followed it with the crossbow's crosshairs, firing at it as it fell. Another direct hit and it screamed. It sent out one final blast towards Deigh as she went over it.

Something caught my attention to the right, and I turned to it just as the jaws of another dragon were way too close. A speeding ball of light hit the side of its head, blasting a hole, and Deigh moved out of its falling path. I turned to where the ball had come from and saw a small glint coming from the side of the rock shelf for a moment. The sun had reflected off of something inside.

Another ball of light flew past and the sound of something exploding came from behind me. Outland ash fell as I turned around to see nothing had remained of the presumably large Outland Monster that had attempted to attack from behind. Deigh went towards a monster that was heading for Sage as I got back to work at removing the next Outland Dragon that went to attack us.

It was a nice feeling to have a sniper on our side, but if something took notice of where those blasts were coming from, it probably wouldn't have been good for the one behind the trigger. I kept an eye on the unknown sniper's scope glint as I targeted a dragon heading towards Tempest and fired my bolt. It went into the creature's chest and the dragon dropped out of the sky, crashing into the lake below. A few calls came out from the dragons that were left in the area as they changed strategies.

Two of them seemingly started to sweep the cliff side.

"*They are going to have to be able to defend themselves,*" Deigh told me, sensing my anxiety that they were probably searching for the sniper. "*The others need us here.*"

"*I know… let's try to regroup with the Seraphineans. It could draw off the dragons and centralize the monsters so we can deal with them quickly.*"

Deigh went over to Missiletainn. I landed on his back, grabbing Owen's attention and Deigh incinerated a monster coming from behind.

He looked over at me with a bit of surprise and Deigh took watch for anything that got close so we couldn't be interrupted. "Something wrong?"

"The monsters are all grouped together at the barrier. We should make our way over there and take advantage of it," I suggested, and he nodded.

"It'll take time with these Outland Dragons and Sage not being able to outfly them… but you know this…"

"There's a sniper. They're going to need help if their position is compromised. The two Outland Dragons sweeping there, I think, are looking for them. It's only a matter of time."

"Snipers park in one place and suddenly think they are just so safe…" A sigh of annoyance came out and he turned to Azarias and Cyrus fighting off a tricky dragon. "We could split up if you're willing. The two of us draw the dragons to allow Sage and Tempest to fly to the kingdom. This will allow us to grab the sniper if they need assistance on the way by and attack from below."

"I don't think Deigh minds being the centre of attention, but how are we going to get them to target us? It's not like we can go past them, and they'll find us interesting. They know Sage is an easier target to remove."

"We'd need something they would be interested in," Deigh started as she came up next to us. "Do they have the same interests as Outland Monsters?"

Owen crossed his arms. "What do you mean?"

"Are they drawn to royal blood?"

"Yes… but not to the same degree as monsters are. They have thought and strategy; they're going to notice something is off if they just suddenly smell Aerrow bleeding for seemingly no reason."

"I also vote for not injuring me," I said, placing in my two coins and thought about it more. The dragons weren't monsters, so what we needed were war tactics that worked on people. What made people attack others verses someone else? Atlamillia came to mind on the times she tried and successfully attacked me whenever I teased or tricked her… It could work. "Why don't we force them to follow us?"

Owen rolled his eyes. "Alright, genius, with what?"

"With what we do best: annoy them. If we make us seem like the bigger problem, the bigger threat, they'll forget about Sage and Tempest if they stay out of sight. Then, they'll gang up on us." I looked over at the dragons that were readying to attack. "There's only seven of them, between Deigh and Missiletainn, I'm sure we can bother them enough for them to ignore the two dragons that use the fog hanging around to get to a higher altitude. Tempest and Cyrus can manipulate the clouds to make sure they can sneak to the island."

"I'm in!" Azarias agreed from behind me, and we turned to him in surprise. He was not there a moment earlier. "What? I don't like fighting dragons. They hurt."

"I guess we're going to piss off some dragons…" Owen sighed, turning to me. "This wouldn't be a discussion if it weren't for that sniper… Where are they anyway?"

I doubted it was just the sniper as I knew all too well that he probably could take them all at once if he was alone with Missiletainn. But because he wasn't, we were in the way and could easily be killed in the onslaught. I pointed towards the rock shelf on the lower half of the floating landmass. "Somewhere in there. I saw light reflect off their scope."

"Out of the way of the fighting, but also away from support… Maybe they have a friend."

"I didn't see a second reflection, but there might be…"

"You don't want to risk it."

"They've been pretty helpful, and I don't think it'd be very kind to just leave them, even if their choice in location wasn't the smartest." I turned to Azarias. "Stay out of sight, once we grab the dragons' attention, head to the island from above and wreak havoc on the enemy forces. We'll come from below so pay attention. Have the Seraphineans retreat as we come up so we can do as much damage as possible without afflicting friendly fire."

"You got it! Don't get nommed on!"

"Nommed on?" I didn't get my question answered as he left.

I shook my head and got back on Deigh. Missiletainn sent out the first attack, blocking an Outland Dragon from going after Azarias's and Cyrus's regrouping. It turned to us with a hiss. I gave Deigh the command to pepper away.

She purred in delight, "*They could all use a little extra seasoning, yes…*"

"*Please don't eat them…*"

"*Who do you think you're talking to?! I'm a glutton, not a cannibal!*"

"*Just making sure…*"

"*You're lucky your life is connected to mine…*" she growled as she blasted out tiny balls of fire towards the group of dragons. "*Or you'd be their dinner.*"

The dragons turned on us and Deigh took off, leading them away. She dodged a water-based attack before pelting a dark sphere away with a fire one. I aimed the crossbow at an incoming dragon off to the side and fired. It missed as it maneuvered out of the way. It didn't get much closer as our friendly sniper shot it instead, saving Deigh and I with another headshot. I turned to where the sniper was and noticed that they hadn't moved, but the other two dragons in the area had.

They closed in quickly from above and below, probably well out of the sniper's view. I turned to Owen, reloading another bolt. A dragon was coming in from behind him. I shot it, a bit closer to Owen than what I wanted, but the action did grab his attention and pierced the dragon's skull, killing it.

"Please reframe from aiming near my head," he scolded, but I didn't have time to apologize.

"The sniper's about to have company. Cover us?"

There was a curt nod from him in agreement and Deigh went towards the floating rock. Another shot came from it, taking out a dragon that I was about to shoot when it got in the way. If I were Azarias, I would have probably complained that they were stealing my kills, but I wasn't. I was quite happy not to be the one doing the deed. Happier still if no one had to die at all, but I couldn't dictate the actions of others.

A slight noise came from my side and I turned to it and saw a dragon appearing out of the low cloud. I fired and it screeched as my bolt made another clear hit through its gaping mouth. Deigh moved upwards, out of its continued momentum before returning on course, the entrance way of the cave becoming clear.

The dragons barrelled into it and a sharp, female scream of surprise came to my ears. Deigh, flying a bit too fast to land safely, glided past as a loud sound echoed from inside and a dragon shrieked. I jumped off, crossbow aiming on the dragon closest to the exit, and fired. The bolt went into the back of the dragon's skull as I rolled out the landing. The dragon collapsed and I turned to the sniper who I could hear breathing heavily behind a second dragon corpse. Deigh landed behind me and a large, barrelled gun was pointed at her – a sky-blue haired Seraphinean with a large bun came out from behind it slightly.

"Friendly!" I shouted before she could fire, and the barrel was turned on me. "Don't shoot… please."

"Who the hell are you?" The woman or girl, I couldn't tell her age, interrogated with a Seraphinean accent.

She looked between the two of us with sky-blue eyes glaring – the only hint of a pupil being a slightly darker blue colour in the centre of her irises, the defining feature that all Seraphineans had. Two, feathery wings of the same colour disappeared from her back, leaving me a bit confused.

Could all Seraphs do that?

"Obviously not from around here if you're gawking."

I wasn't gawking… curious but not… "Apologies. No, we're not from here. We're from Absalom."

"Hm. And you just happened to drop in?"

"Quite literally, yes. We saw some dragons sneaking up to your position and figured you would need assistance."

"I could have handled it," she replied as she finally lowered her weapon.

She came out from behind the dragon corpse and walked up to the front of the cave, standing not far from me and barely at my chest as she was a foot shorter. Her interesting black and white Seraphinean armour shimmered with power, seemingly unaffected in my presence… for about three seconds. The armour's glimmer ended, making the plates in her cropped, sleeveless, armoured top and low sitting, plate skirt become useless other than for fashion. Her gauntlets that extended up her shoulder to double as pauldrons had the Seraphinean, eight-winged, golden ring emblem etched into it. They matched the emblem on her skirt's sides. They powered down next followed by her thigh-high boots of the same colour scheme.

If there was a bright side to her armour, the likes in which I had never seen before, her arm and leg gear were still functional as armour. The rest of her outfit however… not so much.

She looked down at herself in surprise, tapping at her small chest like there was a button there only to sigh as she adjusted the black, cropped, turtleneck, lowering the opened chest part and fixing the bunched cloth.

"Still nothing?" The woman, at least, I hoped she was a woman and not some kid playing soldier, played with her skirt before giving out an annoyed tsk, continuing to converse with herself. "For fuck's sake… I wasn't even hit!"

"Your armour doesn't happen to have a magic inhibitor, does it?" I asked sheepishly, knowing exactly what was happening and she glared at me, unamused.

"Why would I want to add that to my armour when it's immune to my presence? It would greatly reduce the damage I could take."

"Well… that's unfortunate." I was a bit shocked it didn't straight up blow up on the poor Seraph. Happy, but surprised all the same.

"What did you do?"

"Nothing, I just shut down technology when I'm near them if its not protected."

"You… but…" She closed her eyes. "Awesome… you come here to help, and then break my armour. You just had to be one of *those* Absalomians."

"It's not like I did it on purpose. I came here because I wanted to help the person who had defended us and was about to be attacked by two, giant dragons since I have something that could pierce their scales easily."

"That's great and all, but I might as well walk around naked." She threw her large rifle over her shoulder, the weapon being almost as tall as she was, and it did not look light. She didn't seem to notice it as she adjusted her slightly side-parted bangs, looking away to the outside world. "I appreciate the help, Absalomian… and I apologize for being rude. I don't generally have people coming in, Outland bolts blazing, let alone helping me, so it threw me off."

I blinked at the sudden switch between the justified anger she had moments before to the calm, emotionless demeanour she had now. "It's fine… Adrenaline and surprise do that. Also, your armour is broken. Nothing wrong about being mad; I'd be mad too being that this is a battlefield."

"It was illogical to put that on a stranger who only wished to help and did just that. I should have anticipated that someone could come along and planned accordingly with the tools at my disposal. You may leave me here to continue defending the kingdom."

"I don't think that's such a good idea…"

"I don't need armour if I'm not spotted."

"The dragons are going to be looking for you now and with no armour, that's not going to go well if you're caught off-guard a second time."

"Then what do you suggest, Absalomian?"

"Deigh and I can bring you up to the rest of the border guard or whoever is up top. That way, you aren't going up there defenceless. Maybe there is someone that can help get your armour working again."

"I don't need a ride, I have wings capable of that."

"It would be safer."

"Safer? On the back of a very obvious dragon?"

"I have armour and can take hits if need be," Deigh said, and the young woman hesitated. "Is there something else other than flying on a dragon you're concerned with?"

"My father... he wouldn't be very happy knowing I was down here..."

"Most fathers wouldn't be," I told her, noticing the issue Deigh had picked up on. "But you clearly have a specific reason to not be caught..."

"I was told to stay home... but I just built Iðunn, and I wanted to use her."

Wasn't that the name of Orpheal's wife? "Iðunn?"

"Yes, that's the name of my gun. Got something against it?"

"No, not at all..." I changed the subject before I was on the other end of her barrel again. "We can drop you off somewhere else instead of the front. Have an idea where that might be so you can head home without being noticed?"

"There is a cave system that leads back to Domrael Hill a couple hundred metres above-" She was interrupted as something blasted the wall next to the cave. Small bits of rubble crumbled onto us. "Looks like your friend needs help first..."

I turned to the outside world as the group of dragons that were left distracted, were no longer focusing on two targets. "We'll drag them along towards the top. There isn't any point wasting time dealing with them down here. Let me know when we're getting close to this cave system. I'll have Owen make a smokescreen so the dragons can't find us for a time. That should allow you to get to your cave unnoticed."

"Not a bad plan for being made on the spot."

"It's kind of my job..." I muttered as Deigh lowered herself for the Seraphinean. I got up with ease and the woman hesitated further. I offered a hand. "I don't wish to impose..."

"Yeah... got it, just... ah, fuck it. What could go wrong?"

Oh, so many things, Seraph... So many things could go very wrong.

She jumped, four wings appearing for a brief second, giving her slight lift and I grabbed her hand, lifting her incredibly light frame with ease. The Seraph sat behind me and looked around, feeling the saddle before turning to me. "What should I hold on to?"

Deigh stopped her flight plan and looked back at us. *"I've never been asked this question before..."*

"And you think I have?" I asked back, just as lost on how to answer as she was.

She turned her attention to our guest. "Him, I guess…"

"That's not very safe. What if you make a sharp stop or turn if there's no seatbelt?" The Seraphinean questioned and I couldn't help but agree slightly to her concerns.

They were all fair points on her side, not ones I've ever had to really consider… Mostly because seatbelts, were for seats in vehicles… which made sense for her to be concerned with. Seraphina had many vehicles, Absalom… not so much.

I turned to her before I was caught spacing out. "I'm not going to be thrown off unless we crash land if that's what you're concerned with."

"How often does that happen?"

"Eh… Three months ago, I think, was our last incident."

"That's not comforting-" She was cut off as Deigh ended the discussion by taking off towards a dragon heading for Missiletainn while he and Owen were busy removing a second one with black tendrils. A squeak came from the Seraphinean as she grabbed around my waist and Deigh blasted out a wall of white fire. The Outland Dragon backed off and Owen looked over at us as the woman behind me got a better sense of Deigh's flying and eased her grip. "Oh, this isn't so bad…"

I looked over my shoulder a bit. "I'll let you know when we're about to make any sudden movements."

"I appreciate it."

"I see you found a child," Owen called, and the Seraph raised her voice, angrily.

"How fucking dare you?!"

"A very angry child."

"I'm not a child!"

Thank the gods she wasn't a child…

"A female friend then?" Owen corrected himself and I knew the implications of the statement from tone alone.

"This isn't the time for this!" I couldn't tell if he was kidding around or being serious, but on both accounts, it was a freaking battlefield! "She happens to be the sniper that was dealing with these-"

A monster caught my eye, cutting me off as Deigh moved out of the way and away from the general, unable to attack due to our friend. Missiletainn blasted it out the sky before coming back into speaking range.

"Anyway, her armour broke. We're going to drop her off at a nearby cave entrance so she can get back to Domrael Hill without her father noticing."

"I know someone with such reckless behaviour…"

"Yes well, sometimes you need to slip the collar to get things done."

He shook his head. "You want another distraction then, so they don't notice her?"

"Just a smokescreen. We'll stick together this time, there aren't many dragons left meaning they'll feel threatened." I turned to the Seraph who had let go and was aiming her sniper at a monster that was moving towards the island. "That means leaving the fight."

She pulled the trigger of her gun and a magic sphere of light exited with a loud, controlled explosion from inside the barrel. The monster died instantly. She looked back at me with a glare. "You can't tell me what to do."

"Want to place bets on whether or not I can tell your father of your getaway today?"

"You don't even know…" She went quiet as she searched my face. What she saw, either sheer determination or dedication, she didn't like as she turned back to her gun, looking down the scope. A minor hint of disgust blemished her lips. "Fine… just don't find or tell my father."

"As long as you go home immediately, you have my word."

"Say that a little more regally and I might think you're royalty or something."

I left it alone and loaded my crossbow. A wave of little flying Outland Monsters noticed our approach as we crept up from below, more than likely sensing us and turned away from the barrier. Deigh blasted them with fire before they could get too close. The Seraph gripped around me again. I looked back at her. "Something coming?"

"No, but we did just pass my cave."

"Sharp turn incoming."

"I figured…"

Deigh drifted to the right, turning our direction a hundred-eighty degrees, and caused the Seraph to brace. Even with armour on, I felt her little frame held a lot more strength than what I was expecting as she squeezed tighter than she had before. Deigh dove and black smoke formed around us but didn't block off the rock side.

A small cave-like opening appeared ahead and Deigh slowed down to a stop. "Is this the cave?"

"Yes." The Seraph let go.

Deigh moved beside it but didn't land as the entrance was way too small for her to think about it. I wasn't even sure if I was comfortable about getting through the crack that was apparently a cave entrance. The Seraph stood up and I followed, just to make sure nothing was going to come out and attack as Missiletainn stopped nearby. Six, sky-blue, feathered wings formed on her back and she undid her bun. A long braid fell past her short battle skirt.

She looked up at me, no emotion laid on her face. "Just in case I forgot, thank you, Absalomian, sir. I hope your visit goes better than this."

"Thank you for the saves, now go home."

"Now go home," she mocked like she was seven, mimicking my accent almost perfectly. It was a bit unsettling. "I swear you're like my dad… I'm probably older than you and you're treating me like a child."

"I was about to say the same thing – the kid part, not the father part," I said, dryly, and a small smirk formed on her face. "What?"

"You're a bit different from others of your kind, certainly softer…"

What the hell did that mean? Didn't matter; I knew what she was doing. She was like one of the kids not wanting to go to bed. "We can continue this conversation on the hill if we cross paths. Now please, your company isn't terrible, but there are monsters."

She rolled her eyes and gave a slight wave to Owen and Missiletainn then flew off, slipping between the cave walls, expertly.

"You didn't tell her who you are, did you?" Owen asked behind me and I turned around, parking myself down again to get ready to leave. "Probably would have made her listen to you."

"Perhaps. But it's also not right to throw a title around just to make people do things," I told him, looking back at the hole, hoping she didn't come back out.

"Know who she was?"

"I didn't ask."

"She wreaked havoc against Outland Dragons and Monsters alike with one blast from a custom-built weapon and had deadly accuracy, yet you didn't ask even for her name?"

"Better not to know. I have no idea who her father could be and speaking openly could break my promise if I said her name within his earshot."

"You say that, but-"

He was being serious earlier… The subject he was bringing up was not one I wanted to speak about, and I passed him a glare. "Owen, we're on a battlefield. This isn't the time to play matchmaker when I'm clearly not interested in looking for someone."

"In a smokescreen, on a battlefield where no monsters are nearby," he argued against my point before lightening his aggression slightly. "You've been avoiding this subject for months and tuning it out when forced within vicinity of the topic. Where else are you going to be this receptive?"

"Not right now…" I growled lowly, "and probably not for some time. So, drop it."

Owen looked ready to bring up other possible people I could match with, the look I had seen before, but he went silent on the matter, turning away after a moment with a nod. "Alright… I'll leave it be for now but know that I only want the best for you."

"I know. But like that sniper said, I'm still a kid really. I don't want to make a mistake and have the kingdom pay for it. It doesn't have that kind of luxury right now."

"If you need someone to speak to, about getting past this and opening up to the idea, I'll be here to help. And when you're ready and need help finding possible choices, I'll do what I can to assist along with so many others back at the castle."

I nodded and looked up as the sound of monsters caught Deigh's attention. The smokescreen started to die and on the other side, monsters were heading our way. "Next time we have such conversations, we should try doing it in a safer location. This is the second time you've done this."

"Third time, actually, did it at the border too. But yes, I agree. Azarias and Cyrus should have made it to the top by now."

"Let's go meet them and give this kingdom some breathing room on this front."

Missiletainn agreed and fired a black stream first, leading the way and Deigh flew behind him. She charged up her flames before slipping past and unleashed them at the monsters that grew closer. The flames covered the area in fire and the squeals of desperation from the monsters went silent. She stopped breathing fire and came to a stop high in the sky, above the island and most of the monsters. I pulled out my blade, putting away the crossbow and she went back into the wave, blasting more fire while I made sure no Seraphineans were in the way. My blade sliced through anything that survived her flames, careful not to accidentally add my own magic to the mix.

She flew swiftly as we passed Cyrus and Tempest on one side helping some Seraphs on flying, maned cats – tyraulias, and Azarias and Sage were on the other, closer to the island, creating shards of rock to kill anything that banged on the barrier.

I looked through the clearing and my breath was somewhat taken away by the view of the kingdom below. Buildings of glass and stone with columns at their entrances laid themselves around green fields. Rivers flowed from a large lake that I couldn't see the other side of, sitting next to a large hill off to the left, far in the distance. A city of glass and metal that looked so tiny from where we were, reflected the sun's light like a lighthouse on the hill.

Magic and technology went through the few buildings that were closer as the crystal-clear water fell off the side of the island, forming a waterfall down into the lake below. Cannons lined the edge of the island, blasting out at monsters as lean, metal poles stood on the outside, a hundred metres off the island. Some sort of technology went through and between them to create a barrier that the Outland Dragons were trying to break through earlier.

A thought dawned on me as I looked at the barrier's glow.

Where had the dragons gone?

The sound of something coming in fast came from behind and above and I turned, putting up a fire barrier to defend Deigh as a large, black orb almost hit us. The shield shattered, both from my instinct to not use magic and the power of the attack, but it gave me the chance to redirect the remainder away with my blade into some unsuspected monsters. I searched for where it had come from and a huge Outland Dragon was on top of us.

Deigh turned, keeping me from being squished just as it collided with us. It rammed us downwards at incredible speeds, forcing me to grip onto her. The island's rock moved quickly upwards, giving me barely a glimpse of Missiletainn and Owen dealing with several dragons at once – blocking them from attempting to help. A quiet shout of our names came from them but was quickly absorbed by the wind and distance.

Deigh grabbed at its throat, trying to throw it off, succeeding in slowing down the dragon a bit. I looked down to find the ground was approaching fast. I carefully put away my blade, almost dropping it as she jerked, claws scrapping her armour and a dark beam went by my head. I grabbed the crossbow and loaded it. My finger slipped, almost misfiring it as she whipped around, throwing the dragon into the ground. She blasted fire only for the dragon to counter with its own blast. An explosion went off as the two attacks collided, causing the lake behind us to respond; huge waves of energy went across it and sent water into the air.

Water rained down on top of us for a moment as Deigh landed not far on a boulder. The dust settled and I stood up, holding out the crossbow as the dragon, the same size of Archelaos, got back up. I looked it over, never having seen an Outland Dragon this close before and realized from the massive horns on its head and spines on its tail, according to lessons, meant that it was male. Rage was in his eyes as he glared back along with something else…

Something else was going on inside his head and I wasn't going to kill him if I didn't have to.

Deigh stopped her aggression, but I kept my finger on the trigger, keeping wary of his actions as my peaceful ways got in the way. "Stop this and leave."

The dragon snarled at me and I tried again.

"I don't know if you even understand me, but I will kill you if you force my hand by not leaving. Please don't make me, enough blood has been spilt."

The dragon looked me up and down before stopping his growling. His tail flicked, but he didn't change his stance. "Poiui eínunt esos?"

Poiui eín… He knew Ancient Dragon?

My mind turned into the lessons of learning the language as the dragon repeated himself and I understood him.

"Who are you?"

I changed my tongue to his. "Aerrow, the-" Dammit! What was the word?

"Vaex means king," Deigh filled in the word I was missing, and I finished my sentence with a small thank you.

"The King of Absalom. Who are you?"

"Zegrinath, Leader of the Megalona Danguis Tribe."

I gave out a look of confusion at the very deep response.

The Megalona Danguis Tribe?

Why were they here?

They were supposed to be peaceful… I was sure that the dragons attacking the kingdom were a horde, not a tribe known for following the truce to the very letter. Not attacking unless the light attacked first…

And if they were attacking Seraphina, what had the Seraphineans done to provoke?

Did Ciar get them to attack?

The dragon looked us over before making a sharp bark upwards. Similar calls came in response and the dragon named Zegrinath looked at me once more. "My people are retreating, Strange King. Too much blood has been spilt today."

"Thank-"

Zegrinath cut me off, switching to my language of Ori with a tone that sent a chill up my spine. "Only because you did not take my life today when you could have, Strange King from the north. But you should know, we did not start this." He turned back up to the sky, to the floating island above. The sun's rays came out from behind the clouds, lighting up the black and purple scales of the great beast. A foreboding expression on his face as his scales ruffled, highlighting red tints. "They did."

"What are-" I didn't get to finish my question as a Chaos Portal appeared behind him in silence, a swirling vortex that was impossibly black and very different from the Daemonias Portals and even Owen's as it felt ungodly archaic,. "Wait."

"I pray to Valrdis that we don't meet again, Strange King," the dragon said before turning, leaving his back open and walked through the portal, abandoning Deigh and I on the shore of Seraphina Lake, alone.

The portal closed as the sun disappeared slightly behind a cloud and I looked upwards. More portals opened as Outland Dragons went through, closing behind them, and leaving only Outland Monsters to assault the island. Monsters that were becoming fewer as the seconds passed.

I unloaded the bolt carefully. "I'm surprised that worked…"

"He either finds you interesting enough to keep alive, or more threatening than he's willing to deal with right now."

"An Outland bolt pointed at your head does that…" I muttered, turning to my thoughts. What did he mean by strange king? The only one acting strange was the Outland Dragon who retreated without much persuasion. "Do you think that maybe he didn't attack us because we didn't do whatever forced him to attack Seraphina?"

"Perhaps… Megalona has always been known for upholding the truce code, even towards Theseus who was not well liked by their kind. Maybe Orpheal can provide an answer to what he meant by Seraphina starting it," Deigh said, looking up at the island, pondering. "I hope that it wasn't arrogance that made some Seraphs go after the tribe."

I hoped so as well…

It was one thing for an Outland Dragon Horde to attack, it was another for a peaceful tribe. And if they managed to damage relations with them in some way, evoking their wrath… I wasn't sure if I could do anything to interfere from them killing one another.

What would happen if the tribe asked that of a horde to complete whatever revenge they were hellbent on getting?

A shiver went up my spine at the prospect. We had come here to help with monsters and Ciar…but I couldn't put my party on the line for this if it had become a far larger problem – both as a knight and for my kingdom's sake.

Chapter Nine: Domrael Hill

We joined the others back in the sky by the kingdom, disposing monsters as we went. After what seemed like forever, the questions that begged to be asked, were finally free of one hindrance as the monsters in part of the northern front had been dealt with. Deigh landed on the island next to a swift river. I got down, my boots tapping on the smooth, dark blue stone that lined the edge of the island. The air was a bit cooler than it was on the ground, but it wasn't too different in atmosphere pressure as I looked around, taking a breather. Definitely thinner, but nothing I couldn't adapt to as long as I was smart.

A sophisticated, metal railing etched the cliff edge with openings for cannon barrels as a fort sat nearby. Seraph Legionaries ran and flew up and down the border, some eyeing us as they went, others not caring. I looked over at Deigh to check her armour. Zegrinath did a lot of damage to it, and despite the constant reassurance from her that she was fine, she was injured underneath, bleeding from claw marks and a bite. She was going to need medical attention. Dragons weren't prone to infection, but I didn't want to take the risk of her getting sick for even a moment, let alone for her pride.

Missiletainn landed next to us and Owen drop down beside me. He seemed a bit concerned and looked us over. It was the first time he had been able to check in since we ended our discussion a couple of hours ago. "You two took quite the beating, doing alright?"

"We're fine," Deigh answered, bopping me on the head with an armoured nose. I rubbed the spot as an ow came out. "He's just worried over paper cuts."

"I could stick my whole hand in this one," I growled as I slightly poked the armour around a wound and she hissed. "Paper cuts, she says."

"Paper cuts can hurt you know!"

I stopped bugging her and gave my attention back to Owen. "I've only got a few scrapes and in need of a shower to get the ash stuck to me off. Deigh took the brunt of most of the onslaught."

"No paper cuts?"

"No paper cuts," I laughed a bit. "I'm actually a good fighter when things are as they should be."

He gave a small smirk. "You are, but don't get cocky – our anomalies will return before you know it."

"Yeah…" My hand went for the back of my neck as a pain stabbed into it, a phantom one though. His lighthearted smile faded, and I cleared my throat, trying to bring back the atmosphere from before. "Orpheal mentioned he'd meet us at the most northern tip of the kingdom… How far do you think we strayed off course?"

"I don't believe too far," he answered, looking at something behind me.

I turned around to see what he was looking at and saw a dark-blue haired Seraphinean that took me a second to recognize as Orpheal, closing the door to the fort. He wasn't in his lab coat and was plated in black and white armour, something extremely similar to Ciar's black, purple, and red set. My heart skipped a beat as my hand dropped for my sword only to freeze. It took a moment to be able to swallow the frozen fear as I tried to rationalize that the armour type was just the best version for their preferences.

It only half worked.

I plastered on a greeting face as the Lord Director walked over.

Orpheal stopped in front of us with his lean figure, his six, armoured wings stretched slightly as he stood over two metres – almost a foot taller than me. It wasn't something I picked up on over communications. "I apologize for the welcoming party, King Aerrow. I hope the rest of your journey was not as exciting."

"It wasn't, but we came knowing what to expect, Lord Director Orpheal."

"From reports I heard; you managed to drive the Outland Dragons away. Have you dealt with them before?"

"This was actually my first time seeing one in person…" I admitted as Zegrinath's words came back. I was going to have to find a way to address it without coming off as rude. "Now that a good portion of the monsters are gone, perhaps we could get started on other projects and discussions."

"Already? You just got here."

"I don't wish to give Ciar and his followers anymore time than they've already had."

"No, I suppose not. But it would be unwise to continue without rest. You've travelled all this way and that can cloud judgement, especially injured ones." He hinted at Deigh. "We can get started first thing in the morning. I'll take you to the embassy now, you can settle in, and if you wish, we can go out for dinner and discuss the last few days. Use it to catch up so we're on the same page and be more than ready for tomorrow's larger tasks."

"Aerrow, the man is offering free food," Deigh almost begged through the link as I went to ponder his offer. *"I've never had food this far south before."*

"Are you going to settle down long enough for a healer?" I asked, knowing that she wanted to explore Domrael as fast as she could, something that was really, really risky of doing. She wanted me back home and safe – perimeter checks and details of missions to be completed as quick as possible was fuelling her need to avoid down time with her *paper cuts*.

"For food I will."

That was good enough for me. I gave Orpheal my answer with a nod. "Rest is probably for the best, get Deigh a doctor… Maybe see a small bit of this beautiful kingdom.

He relaxed ever so slightly. "I'll have my personal doctor, Fyliel, waiting for us at the embassy."

I turned to Owen and he gave barely a nod in agreement and I relaxed a bit. Like Deigh… I just wanted to get back to Absalom. But Orpheal had a point, a point that Owen probably agreed with more than me wanting to rush things along. I looked to Orpheal. "Whenever you're ready, we'll follow your lead – oh, that reminds me. We brought the samples."

"Oh yes, the samples! I'll deliver them to my lab after the embassy. My team will be able to pick up where Dr. Helena McGregor left off. In the meantime, I must check in with General Io before I leave."

I nodded. It gave me some time to figure out where Azarias and Cyrus had flown off to. The Seraphinean leader turned around to leave, and I noticed that like the woman from earlier, his armour was not alight and had a large gash through it. "Lord Orpheal?"

"Yes, King Aerrow?" The man asked, stopping to look back. "Something else come to mind?"

"No just… if you need more time to rest, we can start whenever you're ready."

A small smile of emotion came from the Lord Director as he shook his head, knowing what I was referring to. "That won't be necessary. There isn't much time to rest when work needs to be done. So please, think of some things you'd wish to do or see tonight and over the course of your stay while I finish here."

"Take your time…" Orpheal left, and I passed a look to Owen, lowing my voice. "That doesn't look good."

"He knows his limits," Owen somewhat agreed with me and shrugged. "He'll seek medical attention if he needs it once he's content. That'll probably be after he's made sure you're safe in Domrael Hill."

"Is he like this with all his guests?"

"No, just the ones he feels responsible for. Like a guardian, he treats some of his assistants and many of his students as such. He's a father first, a teacher and leader second."

While it was nice to have a stranger be that kind, it made me a bit worried. "Isn't it dangerous to be like that as a leader when your position could be taken? Someone could easily abuse that."

"He's careful about it from what I've seen, but it's that very nature that has given him the votes needed to be the Lord Director. He cares more about the people in his kingdom than his research which is hard to come by here. Though, with that said, he may forget you're a king at times."

"What's one more person treating me like a child?" I huffed, hinting at the way the knights and Deigh treated me from time to time. "I happen to be an adult; I can care for myself."

"Literally the opposite of what you said a couple hours ago…" he muttered, and I raised an eyebrow.

"Wanna repeat that?"

He rolled his eyes. "Just don't be surprised by the treatment."

I just gave a small nod, my mind going down a darker path than what I wanted it to. Treated like a kid… a son no doubt. All the people who treated me as such except for Owen were dead. I didn't want that trend to continue, especially since Orpheal had a daughter that I had yet to meet. "What should I know about Éabha?"

He didn't seem confused about where the question came from, his expression changing to a softer one. "I can't give you much, I haven't seen her since she was two, maybe three. But through the gossip I've heard, she purposely avoids working with others, even with assignments I worked on. I don't think she likes strangers."

"I see…" It seemed off for the director's next-in-line to be antisocial. "I thought it was important to be social in an oligarchy."

"It is, but I don't know her reasons. She might just be naturally introverted, or it might have been caused by Iðunn's death."

I knew better than anyone how the death of a parent could affect someone… though I wished I knew that Iðunn had died before now. It wouldn't have come up casually, but I should have known just from the lack of Orpheal mentioning her in the few discussions we had. I swallowed down the distaste. "How did Iðunn die?"

"Outland Monsters above the lake below us during a research expedition. Éabha would have been seven at the time I believe… it was an unfortunate accident."

"Another thing Orpheal would have bonded with my father over… I hope he's spoken with someone over the last few months. It's important to do." Owen raised a brow, and I rolled my eyes. "Shush, I know. But this is different. He's clearly a proud man who I doubt would speak freely about it with someone. I have Deigh."

"Clearly doesn't work out entirely…"

"I apologize for my outburst, but to be fair, we were on a battlefield. I'll talk when I'm ready."

"I know… Still want a CT?"

"Yes. I need to check in with the kingdom."

He nodded. "I'll have Azarias and Cyrus find one before dinner tonight."

"You're coming, right?"

"Someone has to babysit the king while Deigh is resting."

"I still better get some foreign food…" Deigh growled. "This dragon needs it."

I shook my head. "You'll get it, don't worry. Besides, while I'm out, you can practice more."

"Ooh, you're right. I can… And maybe, if it works out well, we can go shopping."

"If we have the time," I sighed and noticed the fort door open once more.

Orpheal came out, walking tall if not somewhat intimidatingly as he came over to us. Tempest and Sage landed nearby, their knights giving acknowledgment that they were still alive.

The Lord Director stopped in front of us. "There's a train waiting to take us to the city; it'll be a short trip. I can also provide you a magic inhibitor bracelet on the way if you don't have one, King Aerrow. It will make wandering the city less… interesting."

"That would be wonderful," I answered more exasperated at the relief than what I intended to be. It may have limited my ability to use magic, but that wasn't even a price in my mind. "Now I don't have to worry about shutting down a city block."

"Oh, I think you'd shut down a little more than a block without it…"

00000

"I don't want to go…" I whined a bit as I adjusted the suit jacket and a purr answered. Deigh purred a second time in her sleep, clearly having a good dream, and completely unaware of my complaints. I turned to her with a small smile. "At least one of us is enjoying ourselves."

I closed the closet door and my reflection looked back at me. The scars from Aetherian and the altar around my right eye seemed more obvious in the lighting and I looked away from them to the suit to distract myself from tumbling down that hole.

The black and red cloth that sat on my frame looked fine, but it only reminded me of Theodora, another memory I wanted to leave behind. And just like every other time I wore it; those memories weren't as easy to run away from. It was irritating. I could have just bought a new suit, but it was money that needed to go elsewhere. Then again if I hadn't rented that book… At least Atlamillia could send more if we needed it. I was going to have to tell her about it when I had the chance to call her. She'd make the better call on the subject anyway if buying a new one was worth it.

I grabbed the crown that sat on the dresser nearby and looked back at Deigh through the mirror, holding it out. "You think I should wear it?"

She rolled onto her side, but other than the simple movement, she was unresponsive. All her wounds that had, had thankfully been healed thanks to the fantastic work of Orpheal's doctor. That added with the food she gorged on; she was probably having quite the sleep.

No wonder she was purring away.

I waited a few moments before sighing, "Yeah, Owen would probably get mad if I didn't."

I put the circlet on my head that, admittedly, I had grown used to wearing and it felt strange to not have on when leaving my room. My hair, still wet from the shower, argued to work with it, however. I gave another sigh as I took it off for the time being. I'd fight with it later.

I turned to the box on the table behind me and walked over to it, my shoes tapping on the strange flooring that looked like wood, but definitely wasn't. I set the crown next to it and hesitated to touch the box. Inside was the device I had asked for thanks to Cyrus and Azarias. Owen took the liberty to program a few numbers that he had on his CT and would have to be updated when I contacted someone in Asylotum. But the underlining worry was there.

I wasn't sure if I could use it. Sure, it was tested within my presence without the bracelet that kept my presence from wiping out a good chunk of Domrael Hill, but I was still cautious. Luckily, the embassy was built similarly to the bracelet which was nice to not be stuck wearing it all the time while in my temporary place of residence. I looked at the CT warily. I hadn't actually practiced with it; I was just near it when Azarias showed it off.

The test that somehow proved I wouldn't break it went on for about thirty seconds which finished with Owen ending the call when the knight decided to be silly. He pretended that he was far away even though they were only a few metres apart.

Owen may not have found it funny, but I was quite amused by it.

I broke through the hesitance that I had and opened the box, grabbing the slick device. It was a bit larger than Owen's but also thinner, red instead of black, and didn't need a special case to keep it protected from magic users. It was supposed to be the most durable one they could find that could also deal with my pesky existence. How durable was it though; I wasn't sure nor was I planning on testing it out. It cost twice as much as the book did.

Azarias's excuse? It had a really nice camera.

It was a good excuse… because dammit if I wasn't going to abuse it by taking pictures. Then in my free time, possibly draw them out.

It was nice to think about hobbies again.

I looked at the box in my other hand and read the back. The numbers seemed to be details about the Communication Tablet, but I didn't have a clue on what any of it meant. I went down to the more notable features which were in bold letters, probably for marketing purposes. It was waterproof up to fifteen metres and it had a high magic resistor. It also had a new capacitor crystal, created by Gordin Labs, to convert excess magic and keep the CT charged, which I kind of knew what that meant.

It was never going to die.

That meant I could never use the excuse that the CT was dead.

Haha, ah… That required having someone that wanted to talk to me…

I needed friends.

Aoife and Dani were, I suppose, friends… but they were Atlamillia's friends first. I just piggybacked off her and while we talked, it seemed like we were acquaintances more than anything else… Aoife more so than Dani but trying to have a discussion with Dani from time to time was rough. Something either came up or our schedules clashed. Either way, I didn't find it as easy to talk to her as she had with Atlamillia.

I needed to make a friend my age on my own. Maybe then I could figure out how to be a proper friend with Atlamillia's.

I set the box down, pushed the square indent on the bottom of the screen, and leaned against the table. It lit up to a picture of Azarias and Cyrus, one doing a silly pose and the other, not so much. I shook my head. It wasn't a bad picture, just not what I wanted on my screen. In time it would have to change. I tapped the button again with my thumb and it opened to a different background: the backsides of Sage and Tempest.

I held back the urge to go find my idiotic retainers and looked away from the picture to the bottom of the screen where five, little squares sat, each icon different for each application: options, camera, pictures, contacts, and notes.

I tapped on the camera lens icon and quietly walked over to Deigh who was still sleeping. The screen didn't have much on it, a circle at the bottom with two options above: video and picture. I left it as the picture option and held out the device. Deigh's head slid onto the screen as I aimed it correctly. Once I was happy at her curled-up position, I tapped the button. It made a loud click sound and I scooted away before she could notice.

Now how did one get the picture to be on the background?

Options seemed like a good start.

Tapping on the gear box gave me more than a few settings to pick from and I ignored all of them as I read each one until I came across background. I tapped it and it showed the two backgrounds. Without hesitation, I picked the dragons one. Three pictures were available to pick from and I went with the one of Deigh I had just taken and adjusted it the way I wanted it. I hit the done button before pushing the square indent again. The options disappeared off the screen and brought me to the main screen where Deigh now laid sleeping.

Not bad for my first picture…

I tapped on the contacts square to explore and it brought me to a very short list of available people: Owen, Directors' Demesne, Asylotum, Siofra Castle, and Atlamillia. The last one wasn't going to have anyone answering it for a little while. Cyrus suggested buying one for her as well and sent it to be expressed delivered… meaning someone was going to be teleporting their way across the continent just to get it to her by the morning after tomorrow.

That must have been an interesting job. Not one I would have wanted to have though.

I clicked the button on the side and the screen went black with a soft click. I didn't need to have a review of the kingdom that very moment. If I called at such an hour, which wasn't late for me, Atlamillia would have given me hell over it. Plus, I wouldn't procrastinate a diplomatic dinner.

Not the first one, at least. First impressions were important.

I looked up from the CT, putting it away in my pocket, to my cape that was sitting on a chair.

Naked once again…

I put a hand through my hair and found it to be a bit drier than before. Having thick hair on my head was great, but it took forever to dry.

I looked at the clock on the bedside table. It was about time to go meaning I had to stick on the crown again. Picking up the crown, I wandered back to the mirror.

Stupid thing…

It was light as ever with its weaving Absalomian knot and simple sapphire in the centre of the circlet, but it felt like it was the heaviest thing I would ever have to carry.

A knock came at the door as I finished fighting with my hair and went to it. On the other side was a suited-up Owen, not armoured and no weapon on his side. The rest of the penthouse sat behind and below him in silence. It was weird to see him without a weapon or armour, but I guess he really didn't need them to do his job. I had only seen him wear the suit a few times, with its basic black jacket and white dress shirt, but he was dashing as ever in it. Not so much to say that it was fancy enough for a ball or something, but it was nice enough for a dinner and it was less stuffy than it looked as it was combat ready, unlike mine.

He did a look over before nodding in approval. "You cleaned up nicely, ready to go?"

"As ready as I'll ever be."

"You have your CT?"

"Yes… and two knights I wish to do something horrible to."

"Finally got to see their shenanigans, eh?"

"Unfortunately, oh! But look!" I pulled out the CT and went to the main screen before showing him. "I took my first picture!"

He gave a surprised look. "That's surprisingly well done. If I didn't know better, I'd think you've been taking pictures for a good while."

"It has an automatic focus, so that probably did most of the work… but I'm happy that it looks good."

"She has no idea you took it, does she?"

I put away the CT. "No, so let's go before she wakes up."

He gave a small chuckle with a shake of his head and we left the embassy.

Once outside, the landscape was just as beautiful as it was from the top floor. Streetlights glowed brightly, but softly on top of their weaving, spiral poles. No vehicles of any sort took to the road next to the large walkway as it seemed everyone had gone home. The edges of the walkway were lit up, showing where the edge was so someone couldn't fall off into traffic on low cloud-covering or foggy days. I heard the sound of water within the quiet evening but wasn't sure of its source as we walked away from it and farther into the city. As we made it to the downtown centre, the number of people and the strange vehicles slowly started to increase.

The city from my view in my room was built like a grid, similar to Dawne and the buildings we passed, their shops and tall, spire-like buildings, all made of glass, hardened steel, and other components I couldn't see, were all dark except for the streetlights' reflections and our own. If there were lights inside, turned on…

I turned to look back at the embassy, knowing that the top would have had lights, didn't show that they were on. It was strange, the windows weren't tinted, yet no light came through.

"Unless they are stores, the windows reflect outside light and don't allow indoor light to go through them. They're built so they don't show what's inside," Owen told me as he noticed my confusion. I nodded in acknowledgement, turning forward again. "Since everyone can fly, it would be easy to look into someone's life."

It was an interesting creation. I had seen one-way mirrors before, but this was something else entirely. What else could I learn about this kingdom?

We turned a corner, and the street was lined with bright coloured lights along the buildings. Doors were opened to many of them and Seraphineans with different numbers of wings and colours were about, coming and going through the different doorways, patios, and buildings.

How the noise of all these people was swallowed at the corner was a mystery of its own, but it certainly left me missing the quiet life. I stayed close to Owen as we went by people, sticking to the middle of the road. I felt people eye us as we passed, making me wish I had armour on.

Eventually, we came to a doorway that had bouncers outside of it and a lineup of people in formal attire waiting to get in. There were a few people who skipped the line, walking to the entrance and were either given access to the building immediately or told to wait like everyone else. Owen skipped the line and I followed. The bouncers stopped us for about half a second before looking over at me, letting us through without asking who we were.

"Lord Director Orpheal mentioned you'd be coming, King Aerrow," the man closest to me said before looking to Owen, giving instructions. "Take the stairs to your left and follow them to the top. A host will bring you to them."

"Them?" I asked, but my question was left unanswered as someone got a bit rowdy next to me in quite the threatening manner. Owen moved me through the door as the larger bouncer, closer to Owen, grappled the man. Something metal hit the ground, but I didn't see what it was as I was kindly pushed up the stairs. Owen stopped rushing me forwards after a bit and started walking next to me. I gave him a questioning look. "What was that about?"

"Someone having too much to drink and being way too entitled. There are going to be people uneasy about the current situation and could be carrying weapons, just so happens that one was also intoxicated. Going to have to keep an eye out for that."

It was more of a note for him rather than for me, but I put it in the important folder regardless. Those same people could also be working for Ciar and guise concern for ill purposes.

We reached the top of the stairs to find a host waiting in front of a door. He bowed. "King Aerrow of Absalom and King's General Owen, I presume?"

"That is us," Owen answered, and the tall, four-winged Seraph opened the door with a button to reveal a shiny box of fear and sadness. "Oh, he went for the big room…"

"Lord Director Orpheal planned for the best, General Sir."

Owen turned to me. "You'll like this room, Aerrow. Once, of course, we get to the top."

"Joy…" a small mutter came out of me as he knew exactly why I was unenthusiastic about the experience that was about to take place. I shifted the bracelet I was given under my shirt nervously as we entered the elevator.

Couldn't just take the stairs… or better yet just have everyone on the ground. I mean, why wasn't that an option? They didn't have dragons… build wide or something…

The elevator was faster than any elevator I had experienced as three of the four walls of the box became windows. I watched the island grow small as we climbed and a large building at the top of the hill appeared, showing off its white grandeur with bright lights coming up from the grass. I didn't get a chance to enjoy the view as the elevator stopped, reminding me I was on the thing, and I turned around. The doors opened and the two of us walked out, leaving the host behind.

A completely glass-walled room was what we were met with where the ceiling reflected the star-filled sky with tiny bits of dragon stone. The floor was made of dark blue, Seraphinean stone that, now seeing it firsthand instead of it being a tiny stone, resembled that of marble. A waterfall sat at the far side of the room that flowed along the side of the walls in their Seraphinean stone beds, disappearing back into the wall by the elevator. Only a few tables sat about with a bar off to the right, its tender drying glasses, keeping busy within the quiet room.

I followed Owen through the room and passed a few Seraphineans who were quiet in their own conversations. Orpheal came in sight about halfway as he stood up from his table, wings gone like the sniper had willed hers away. His dark blue hair was brushed from its messy state of combat I had seen earlier into more of a side part that I was familiar with. It wasn't in a ponytail though, instead was down, sitting at his shoulders with his black turtleneck shirt underneath a royal blue suit, tinted with royal purple.

Someone stood up next to him, drawing my attention and I quickly realized that it was the sniper from before, only her hair was down, framing her face with a small braid behind her bangs that created something similar to a crown. Her sky-blue colours complimented the man next to her, the purple dress somehow matching both Orpheal's suit and her armour earlier. The long, slick, and tight design pretended to be strapless with an open chest, straps leading to a turtleneck-like choker, similar to her shirt from before. Long sleeves matched the gauntlets, laying on the back of her hands at one end and stopping shy of her bare shoulders on the other. Silver-white embroidery with blue crystals lined the edges of the sleeves, the bottom of the dress, and around her waist.

Admittedly, if she had been wearing anything else, I probably wouldn't have recognized her right away.

She gave a slight reaction with her already large eyes, widening for a split moment before going back to being emotionless. Luckily, I gave no reaction to recognizing her, solidifying the promise I made and turned my glance back to Orpheal.

Though… knowing that her father happened to be the Lord Director, made it clear on why she was out fighting. Her father had been on the front lines, she probably felt responsible to do the same, even to look out for him the best she could without being noticed.

"Lord Director, my lady," I greeted once we arrived at the table. "I hope we didn't keep you waiting."

"Not at all. We arrived not too long ago ourselves, Sire, General," Orpheal welcomed as he turned to the woman. Upon getting to the table, I realized that she probably felt very small with everyone else towering over her. She certainly broke the hundred-sixty-centimetre mark now, but I knew that wasn't the case when I was standing next to her in the cave. Heels were a marvellous thing. "I'd like you to meet my daughter, Éabha. She practically lives at the lab, so I figured you'd best meet in person before you think something is stalking around."

"Dad…" the girl grumbled barely above a whisper. She curtsied slightly with a small smile of greeting on her face, but it didn't quite meet her eyes. "King Aerrow, General Owen, pleasure to meet you. And for the record, I don't stalk."

I bowed respectfully, choosing my words carefully so I wouldn't fumble. "It's an honour to meet you, officially. I've only heard of you from your father and my general."

"I apologize, King Aerrow." Orpheal turned to his daughter. "I hadn't realized you two had yet to meet. She often avoids communications; it's never occurred to me how many…"

Éabha remained expressionless, though her left hand betrayed her as she played with her dress. I changed the subject before I could get her into further trouble since I hadn't meant to in the first place. "It's no trouble. We haven't had many conversations in the last few months. Though, since we'll be working together often, Aerrow works just fine; much easier on the tongue."

"The same can be applied for us," Orpheal agreed and looked me over once more before a sigh came out. "You're so much like your father."

A mellow pain of grief hit my chest, acting up the phantom pain of my scar, but I kept my hand from reaching for it. I continued to be as neutral as possible with my answer, but some of it slipped out in the first few words. "He was a good example to follow, so I'm happy to hear I'm walking in similar steps."

"Then let's sit and get ready to order so you can continue to do so. You did a lot of work today, and from the train ride – your journey was quite a long one."

Only the farthest I've ever been.

We sat and Orpheal started asking questions, a lot of questions, for us to answer.

Chapter Ten: Zerach

I pushed the screen's end button in annoyance as my sister ended the call on me mid-sentence. Sure, I may have been overbearing on the state of everything, but I also had almost a week's worth to catch up on in kingdom affairs. I set the CT down and grabbed my copy of the transformation book. It was sitting on the desk when I returned last night after a long, long game of three thousand questions. Cyrus or Azarias must have done me the favour of copying the original before sending it back where it came. I was going to have to thank them.

I looked at the time and found that maybe my sister was right on it being too early. There was no way even Owen would be up, let alone those two.

I flipped to the page I had last left off and continued studying.

There were so many ways of using the skill, from summoning wings all the way to a full transformation. It was all so intriguing, but difficult to test without using magic. I didn't want to alert Ciar if he happened to be nearby. Then again, according to Orpheal, no one had spotted him. Whether or not that was a good thing was still up in the air. My thoughts unexpectedly turned to the sniper and I frowned, flipping the page.

She was as Owen had said: quiet and wasn't too happy about being at a social event. She wanted to be elsewhere, probably just as I wanted to be, and for that I didn't blame her. Socializing was exhausting. Way harder than the skills in the book would ever be. I kept reading as Deigh continued to sleep, still in the same place from when I left her last night. Suddenly, a knock came from the door making me jump at the sudden noise.

Who was up at this hour?

"Come in," I called quietly, not wanting to wake Deigh, who somehow slept through it. The door opened to show a dressed and mildly armed Owen. I turned back to my book. "Morning. You're up early."

"Early? Orpheal's chauffeur will be here within the hour to bring us to his lab," Owen replied with a bit of confusion.

I looked at the CT for the time and sighed, the page number I was on was very different from where I started. "I must have been absorbed in this book. I didn't notice the time, sorry."

An amused chuckle came from him. "Did you at least learn anything?"

"Quite a bit, but still not readying to try out one of the smaller transformations. I don't want to test it until I'm a hundred percent on it."

"Still concerned about using magic?" I didn't need to answer as I closed the book and stood up. "You're going to have to get over it in time… practice makes-"

"In time… are those two up?"

He wasn't happy about being interrupted but answered my question regardless. "Up, brought breakfast and are cooking it as we speak."

"Alright, give me a few minutes and I'll meet you out there…"

He gave a simple nod and left, closing the door behind him, and I started to dress for the day with a minor resentment over my fears.

It didn't take long before I was dressed into my old, casual gear with the only difference being Winterthorn on my black and brown belt, the magic inhibitor bracelet, and being thousands of kilometres away from Siofra. Back in my white, long-sleeve shirt, red cape, black pants, and black and brown boots, it felt like old times. My brown gloves sat on the table beside my plate where I was snacking on the breakfast upon it, looking through a newspaper in the dining room section of the penthouse. Nothing was entirely interesting in it other than the Outland Dragons and a screaming front picture and story of our arrival, specifically mine.

Whoever took the picture had skill if nothing else as they managed to get Deigh about to majestically dive-bomb some monsters. I was there too, but she looked amazing.

"Front page news, eh?" Azarias teased as he stole the page from underneath me. "Look at that shot. You're a hero that drove the dragons away. And that angle, bet you're going to have a fan club here."

I rolled my eyes. "Please. The only reason why anyone bothered is because I'm a king. If it were one of the Seraphs, it wouldn't even be mentioned in this thing."

"And that look," he continued, ignoring me, "I think you're smouldering here… that is what the ladies say is hot."

"Wouldn't have a clue…" He could stop at any time…

"Oh, lighten up a bit. How many people get to be on the front page of a foreign nation's newspaper for good reasons?"

"It'd be more exciting if they also didn't tell everyone who is working with Ciar that I'm here so... cover blown."

"You weren't exactly asking to be in hiding..."

"Wasn't asking for a parade either."

"Alright enough," Owen growled, but didn't bother to take the front page from Azarias like I had hoped, allowing him to continue to read. "We knew that Ciar was probably going to find out eventually, so now we just need to be a bit more cautious since that, at the very least, all of Domrael Hill knows. I'm sure that Orpheal and the other Directors have already increased security as they are aware of the danger that he and his zealots can bring."

"Hopefully, they aren't needed. One kingdom in a rough spot is enough I think."

"It is. So, you're going to stick with someone, just like before, alright? No shady places, no being alone. We know Ciar can't handle anything greater than one on one fights well, so we'll keep numbers to our advantage."

"Sometimes I feel like my title means nothing because you're still bossing me around," I muttered before agreeing somewhat sarcastically. "Yes General, I'll stick to one of you when I'm not inside this lovely embassy until I feel like ignoring your order."

"I was so proud of you until that last part."

I shrugged as a buzzing sound came from somewhere. Owen pulled out his CT from his pocket for a moment before putting it back."

"Our ride is here. Time to go see what this grand machine is."

00000

I somewhat enjoyed the trip from the embassy to where we were meeting Orpheal. It was my first time being in a vehicle like it or rather any vehicle at all. The elongated aftrus, or elaftrus for short, looked the same, but longer on the outside compared to other vehicles that were all somehow aftruses. The inside was much fancier too. Seats lining the sides and the wall where the driver sat behind, snacks and beverages, alcoholic and not were in a cooler built into the leather interior. It was a smooth trip, unnaturally so that at times I wondered if I would get motion sickness before my body got used to it.

The vehicle pulled into a giant, walled-off, property at the top of the hill where a massive building sat. I turned my attention from the city to that of the place we were driving into. A large pond sat in a field with trees dotting about off to the left and I turned to look out my window on the right. More trees and other roads led towards mansions, very spaced out from each other with their own fenced-off property. Ahead was the large, white building I saw last night. It wasn't lit up this time, but it still glowed slightly in the sun's light. Movement from the rear-view mirror caught my attention and I turned to see the intricate gates close behind us on their own. The driver pulled the long vehicle up to the front of the large building and we got out.

White, three petalled flowers sat beneath small trees on each side of the doorway, hiding away from the light. I turned away from the décor to Orpheal and Éabha as they came out of the large, glass doors that could let even dragons inside, showing off the building's age to a time when all buildings were designed as such for Dragon Knights to defend millennia ago.

Both Orpheal and Éabha were in lab coats, Orpheal back with his ponytail and still with his turtleneck. A seemingly similar relationship to the style like I was with my own white shirts. Éabha, on the other hand, wore a black skirt, knee high boots, and a simple top. A choker of the same colour as her outfit sat around her neck and her hair was put into a braid once more.

I wonder how long it took to braid that much hair…

Orpheal greeted us as we got to the top of the stairs, "Good morning. I hope your first night was to your expectations?"

"It was. I hope you two didn't arrive home too late last night," I answered him. He shook his head slightly.

"Late nights are something we often do. Come, I'll take you to my section of the demesne. There, you'll be able to meet my partner and a close friend who is also my secretary. Both have been informed to help in anyway they can. For ideas, Naftali will be the one you seek when I'm not around and if it's food or anything out of the blue, Solaria Elicia will be at your beck and call, even if what you need is across the city."

"Thank you…" I looked back at Azarias as I heard him mutter something inappropriate and he caught my gaze before pouting.

We walked into the building and the inside was nothing like I had ever seen before.

Spires that glowed with purple-pink mixed with white-blue energy lined the room like support beams. Large screens showed off the weather, the time in multiple time zones, and someone speaking about what I could presume was news from the partial listening I was doing. A front desk with a woman and a man sitting behind it gave nods towards their two fellow Seraphs before going back to quiet chatter and their screens. Above was a large picture of the night sky, some stars twinkling like it wasn't morning or indoors. They moved incredibly slowly like it truly was reflecting the stars that would have been out at such an hour if it weren't daytime. The floor had a massive, beautifully designed compass that laid overtop of the floating island and the ley lines that crossed the region.

Doors caught my attention as they stayed open without assistance and I quickly caught back up to Orpheal. We left the main foyer through the right into a decent sized hallway with the same spires protruding through the walls, giving the hall an interesting light.

The doors closed by themselves and my astonishment couldn't be held back any further. "This place is beautiful."

"Domrael would be pleased to hear that. He came up with the finished product of the Directors' Demesne two millennia ago. He left it to our line to continue to work at it until science and magic could complete it to his image, which it finally has been. You're the first foreign leader to see it complete."

I went to ask what he meant by that only to remember that Orpheal and Éabha were the descendants of the Hero of Seraphina. "When was it all completed?"

"I technically finished many of the plans over the last three hundred years, but it's greatest and most difficult feature was created by Éabha three years ago to exactly as Domrael hypothesized in his journal. The spires you see have ley line energy running through them and she found a way to get the energy of Orithin through conduits without interrupting their natural flow. This has allowed the building to get a very aesthetically pleasing look while also allowing us to adapt our technology to more magically inclined individuals like yourself."

"It's not that impressive," Éabha stated before I could reply. "I just expanded on previous notes and the latest works of a woman named Theodora Rinn."

My heart skipped a beat as Éabha said her name, but I didn't say anything as she continued.

"She took Dagdian magic and our tech to create weapons. I adapted what she started in hopes of creating less risks for Dagdians to use technology in the future on their continent. Though if I remember correctly, King Solomon also had a hand with expanding some of that research after she presented it to him to create the standardized weapons Dragon Knights use now."

Two blows, one thought. "He did…"

She looked back at me in confusion, somehow picking up my grief that I was sure I hadn't placed in my tone. "Is something wrong?"

"Ah, no." I looked about, trying to rid the feelings. "I just figured that something would have broke by now since you're still developing the tech…"

"Something probably would have even with your bracelet if I didn't scan your magical presence before hand and proceeded to calibrate the entire building to make sure nothing was going to malfunction."

She tossed a small device back at me suddenly and I caught it. It was turned on and the number eight-hundred-seventy-six was on it.

"That's your magic frequency without the bracelet on. The High-Risk magic frequency sits around seven hundred… so your family sitting around the eight-hundred-fifty is a problem. Your bracelet hinders that, dropping it to just below seven hundred for the sake of the kingdom. It would have been lower, but your magic presence is higher than expected."

"So, I'm a bit higher than average…" It would have been interesting to see what would happen if the bracelet weren't collaborated correctly. Probably only a few explosions… I moved the device and pointed it at Cyrus and the number changed to six-hundred-forty-seven. "What's the average frequency of an Absalomian?"

"Six hundred. Dagdians are around six-hundred-fifty in the lower ends and my hypothesis, using you as my evidence, states that Archon Thaloth is around the nine-hundred mark. But it could be much higher due to his constant need to be the greatest magic user the world has ever seen and being incredibly secretive with how much power he's capable of. Dagdians can lower their magic output if they are talented enough so even if someone were to read him using the MFR, he would probably always have it reading lower on purpose." She sighed with a hint of annoyance, "He has a lot of ambition, but what kind of goal is that?"

"I don't know if it's a bad goal. I heard Dagdian magic can do some insane things."

"Nothing that tech won't be able to do in time. Especially with minds like Dad. It's only a matter of years."

"That's impressive… So, you brought this reader to the dinner just to calibrate?"

"The demesne is delicate and sensitive to such high levels of interference even with the ley line energy going through it and your band. Calibrations had to be done in case your bracelet somehow broke or the lab's protections failed. With one system failure, an experiment could go haywire and bring down half this island. Don't know about you, but I happen to enjoy the island as it is."

I gave her back her magic frequency reader. "That's understandable… but may I ask how long that took? This place is massive and seems to have a lot going on."

"Er…" She apparently wasn't expecting me to ask as her confidence left. "I think I finished around four or something… did some final checks this morning before you arrived."

It took that long? Supper finished around midnight… "I'm sorry… if I had been informed, I could have sent someone to help."

"I would have declined the offer, so it's fine. It gave me some time to set up and pass the time with my own research. This place is dead at those hours, so it's nice not to be bothered by people, gossip, and braindead chitchat."

I looked over at Owen for a moment and a small frown formed as the conversation from yesterday came back. I could see why the other researchers talked about her behind her back, but it wasn't right to do so if she just enjoyed being alone. It was sad that she wasn't comfortable to even bother with people, having to be awake at ridiculous hours to be released of the nonsense she couldn't help. If she was happy, what did it matter to them if she played solo on projects?

Then again…

A small feeling hit me that it wasn't as fun as she was making it out to be. It was probably incredibly lonely to not have *braindead* discussions about silly things. I didn't have a lot of time to do that sort of thing back in Absalom and in Asylotum, but even I had my retainers, the kids, and Atlamillia's friends to chat about nothing important.

Who did she have?

"Hey, since no one asked," Azarias interrupted my thoughts and the two Seraphs turned to him. "What's the highest reading of magic you can get?"

Éabha answered, "It's based to the scaling of Orithin's magical resting point of a thousand and the lowest being zero, which is no magic. But not even rocks have such a low rating."

"Anything get that high?"

"Your samples of Ciar, they were recorded by your doctor to be around nine hundred, but that was three months ago. He's probably become stronger since."

"Yep, probably, but what's the highest number? You said Orithin was a thousand."

"It's not the highest – that number just means that things are normal if magic is under it. Orithina though, she clocked in around fifteen hundred according to records."

"Uh, did you say fifteen hundred?"

Orpheal took over answering questions. "Domrael developed the MFR and created the measurement system that is similar to that of sound waves since they follow the same sort of rules of exponential function."

Good gods was I happy to understand what was being talked about. Though admittedly, didn't think I would ever need to use that knowledge.

"If someone was under a thousand, they were considered mortal, over however, they were considered divine. There is a lot of debate on where a line is drawn between levels of divinity since stories dictate that not all divine beings were equal, but it's safe to say that at resting, if one was around fifteen hundred, they were considered at a Divinukos level of divine."

"Wow…" Azarias exasperated and Éabha nodded in agreement.

"Aerrow's magical potential reads eight-hundred-seventy-six now, but it was eight-hundred-ninety last night. So, I calibrated the building to have a magical resistance of nine-hundred-fifty in case of the use of magic brings it up, which will happen to make the Zerach more responsive, and calibrate accordingly from there. The use of magic will cause a large influx, but as long as Ciar doesn't show up with a level higher than what I'm happy with, the demesne should be safe, a bit unhappy about having her core defences working so hard, but safe. Dad's probably going to raise the protections higher if the magic frequency estimates come back to determine how much growth Ciar could have done within the last three months." She pocketed the device and gave a small giggle of unconfined excitement. "Who would have thought that this lab would have two sources of nine-hundred magic levels inside of it at one time?"

"I think it's lucky for everyone that both sources will be inactive for the most part," I commented, indicating towards the building's systems. The words though only brought out a bit of a grim look from Orpheal as he looked over his shoulder and Éabha looked at me in confusion. "I don't use magic unless I absolutely have to."

"Why?" She questioned and Orpheal started to tell her not to poke into other people's business, but she ignored him. "You should excel in it."

I humoured the questioning and Orpheal's sigh barely reached my ears. "I do. I'm just not a fan of it."

"What a strange concept to not enjoy something you're good at."

"That's like saying just because someone is good at sneaking and stealing, or sneaking and killing, they should be a thief or an assassin and enjoy it."

"Everyone has their talents."

"You should be an assassin if you get bored," Azarias said, and I rolled my eyes. "You're good at killing things and sneaking around."

"I don't enjoy doing those things either," I growled in annoyance.

"Someone's grumpy... I was kidding. You know, a joke?"

"I'm going to make a joke by sending you off to find something that doesn't exist and see how much you enjoy it when you come crawling back looking like a fool."

"You'd have to make it real convincing to make me believe it exists at all."

Challenge accepted, just needed to wait for the right opportunity. Or... I could hold it over his head and he'd never know when...

"What's with the devious look? Hey! Stop plotting!"

"No."

A pout came from the knight at the answer as we came to another set of doors that slid open. On the other side was a similar design to the main foyer with the ceiling a bit lower. Instead of being the kingdom on the floor, the whole map of Orithin was on it with a hundred thin lines covering it, matching the ley lines. Though it seemed like only the main ones were depicted instead of all of them.

"Welcome to Gordin Labs," Orpheal said a bit excitedly in the silence. "This is where we'll finally solve the Outland Monster epidemic."

That was quite the line... I wondered if he rehearsed it.

"Doctor Gordin, I've informed Naftali to move the Zerach as requested to the main lab," a woman's voice called from the back of the room.

I turned to the voice to find a white haired and winged Seraphinean standing behind a desk wearing a black, lowcut, long sleeve shirt against her incredibly pale skin that made Orpheal and Éabha seem tan. Very pale irises looked me over and if it weren't for the darker coloured section of the Seraphinean pupil, light grey in her case, I would have thought she didn't have irises at all. It was a bit unnerving, but a kind smile was on her face, welcoming us to the lab. And like many other Seraphinean women I had seen since arriving with the exception of Éabha, she was very well endowed and tall.

What Azarias had said in the outpost several nights ago was accurate, and admittedly, attractive. Not like Theodora but…

I escaped the less than appropriate thoughts, leaving them behind, as Orpheal acknowledged the woman with a nod. "Thank you, Solaria. You've met most of our guests, yes?"

"Yes," a playful laugh came out, amused at the Lord Director's preoccupied mind. "General Owen and Brigadier-Commanders Azarias and Cyrus, a pleasure to see you good and well after two years… and this new face must be King Aerrow." She bowed lowly. "It's an honour to meet you, Sire."

"A pleasure to meet you, as well, Lady Solaria," I answered as a small hint of nausea hit me. I wasn't surprised, something that had been happening at least once a day since leaving Asylotum, but it did disappear slower than what I was accustomed to, forcing me to swallow a bit of bile. Just had to hit when I was doing something important…

She gave a perplexed look. "Are you feeling alright, Your Majesty?"

"I believe so?" Where was this coming from? It's not like I made any visual expression of my slight discomfort.

The secretary came from around her desk, four wings closed, and walked up to me. Her eye level met my own. "You seem to be imbalanced."

"Um, I think I'm fine, Lady Solaria…"

She gave a nod, but it wasn't at my answer. "Ah, you're still recovering from Asylotum and its effects."

"P-pardon?" It was minor at best, affecting mostly my appetite and maybe my durability, but those things weren't exactly visible and only people who knew me would know about how much I ate in a day.

"She has a very keen sense of health and is also the lab's main medical specialist," Orpheal explained before I went on the defensive as Solaria continued to look me over, somehow not entering my personal space. "She knows when people are sick before they realize it. They're sent home to take care of themselves and not get anyone else sick."

"I see…" This was his secretary?

"I suggest not doing anything too strenuous over the next couple of weeks to recover. The same goes for your general. It will help make the last symptoms of imbalance disappear," Solaria said before taking a step back, putting her hands behind her long, yellow skirt. "You have a long life ahead of you if you take care of yourself."

"I appreciate the advice and vote of confidence… May I ask how you know about the affects of Asylotum? I haven't told anyone here about it."

"I'm capable of sensing imbalances in people, such as sickness, or in General Owen's and your case, the imbalance of Orithin's presence. It's a simple deduction of how it could have been caused."

"Huh, that's interesting."

She gave another small smile before turning to Orpheal. "I apologize for keeping you longer than anticipated. If you need me, I'll be here."

"Thank you, again, Solaria," the Lord Director said, and the secretary walked confidently back to her desk. "This way to the lab, it's a bit farther in."

Probably for security purposes…

We left the woman as another door slid open to a second hallway with many ways to go, but Orpheal led us straight ahead. My curiosity got the better of me. "Orpheal, how does she do it?"

"Seeing imbalances? I'm not sure. She was always a good medical personnel before, but didn't enjoy being a doctor or a nurse, so as a friend since childhood, I hired her as my secretary. Her secondary abilities are a good asset to keeping this lab and the people healthy. But as for her sensing, she didn't have it when we were kids or even well into our adult lives."

"What changed?"

"She became pregnant and developed it."

That's a thing a woman could develop while pregnant? "Her kid must be really lucky to know when they're going to be sick."

"Perhaps, but the infant died a few days after birth."

"Oh… that must have been…" I couldn't even imagine how awful it would have been. "I'm sorry. I shouldn't have imposed such a question without her here."

"It was over thirty years ago, so I'm sure she wouldn't mind. I know her well enough to know that if you have any questions I cannot answer, she won't be upset to answer. She's a good woman, like a sister, a great friend, and a fantastic worker. Though, there are times I wish she would drop the formality at work, but she insists it as her duty."

That was good to know that they were such good friends. Both of them could confined in their losses between the loss of a child and losing a wife.

Éabha scoffed ever so slightly as she stuck her hands in her pockets. "Aunt Solaria is just wanting to make sure you're respected."

"I am respected…"

"You are also always on the line of being challenged by the other directors…" She changed the subject with a sigh. "There's one thing you should be made aware of that Dad didn't inform you of, Aerrow, is that Naftali looks about a step from the grave. He's fine for the most part, but just a warning. He has a weaker system and so he doesn't keep on weight well. But he's a genius."

"He must be if you're saying that," I tried complimenting, but she seemed oblivious to it.

"He's playing with multiple treatments and eats a lot, so don't be surprised by how much. Personally, I think the calories go straight to his head and skip going to other places."

"As long as he's healthy, I'm not too concerned about what he looks like."

She looked back at me with a hint of judgement. "We'll see if you can standby your statement."

Rude… but fair.

It's not like she knew me well enough to know I meant what I said.

A sign reading *Main Lab* caught my eye, ending the conversation. The sign sat overtop of a large set of doors next to a red, shielded light that was turned off. A second sign was placed on the doors with a warning: *If the light is on: DO NOT ENTER.*

Safety first was never a bad thing in my books… but what could they be doing in there where the light would have to be on?

Orpheal entered, following the rules, as the doors opened automatically. Inside was a massive, round walkway with a guardrail on the outside. Lab stations lined the walls with different types of devices like fume hoods and washing stations placed in between them, making it seem like spokes on a wheel. The centre of the room was below the walkway with what looked like to an adjustable platform that was raised. A strange device sat on the platform that was like nothing I had ever seen before.

Large and rectangular, polished metal plate covered what laid inside, but it was far from slick looking. It was bulky and many wires were attached to dozens of ports that connected to machines around the walls of the lower section. A console laid partially visible from the upper ring with several screens and earpieces, none of them turned on. What they were for, I couldn't tell.

Movement drew my attention away from the machine and a very frail and short, six-winged Seraphinean looked at the huge and strange device on the top of the platform. Skin clung to his bones and heavy bags sat beneath blue-yellow eyes. The golden-blond, thin hair that was on his head was messy, but somehow through the appearance, he was actively looking between the device that was only a few centimetres shorter than I was tall and a tablet in his hand. His golden-yellow-coloured wings reacted to his excited motions.

It was as Éabha had stated, he looked just about dead, but there was a lot of life behind his eyes.

"Your timing is impeccable as always, Orpheal. I was just finishing up the last little bit of kinks so we could get started right away," the man said as we got to the stairs leading to the centre that was about a metre and a half lower than the walkway.

"Good work, as always." Orpheal turned to me. "This is Naftali."

The man looked over for the first time, a smile on his face as he left behind his tablet, trading it for a cane I didn't notice, and with its assistance, came over to us as we reached the bottom. "My, you're a tall one. Taller than your father, but definitely leaner. You must have got that from your mum."

I blinked in surprise. "You knew my parents?"

"I've been the head of the biology department and Orpheal's lead assistant and advisor since he became Lord Director. Your parents were frequent visitors then." He held out a hand and I shook it without hesitation, knowing it to be a greeting for Seraphineans instead of simple words or gesture like in

Absalom, but not too firmly. The individual bones within his hand were practically visible. "Tall and strong, good, good. Perfect for a king and for the one who is going to make this all possible."

"I hope this goes as well as you three believe it will. I have no idea what I can do to help with this… machine." I turned my attention back to the large device that looked like it weighed a ton.

"The Zerach, an amazing feat of biological engineering and magic to deal with Outland Monsters and Outland Dragons. Or really any other Outland Creature. The device is not as heavy as it looks, made from a carbon alloy. It's just large due to all the parts for easy access. In time, if the prototype finally starts working, we'll have smaller versions of it. So! Shall we get started?"

"Yes… but there is something I forgot to bring up last night. It might have been for the better though since the head of biology is here," I started as he reminded me of what happened yesterday. I didn't turn my gaze away from the machine. It was haunting in some way, in others, marvellous. "Yesterday, I met an Outland Dragon during the battle who had some words that concerned me. Words I would have dismissed, but knowing the history of their tribe… I feel like it's worth mentioning."

"An Outland Dragon spoke to you?" Éabha asked and I nodded, turning away from the machine. "How and why?"

"In Ancient Dragon, and I had an Outland bolt aimed at his head." It wasn't entirely important, but that was the how and why. "He retreated as I had forcibly asked him to. But what he said before doing so stuck. He stated that the Megalona Danguis Tribe did not start the attack, but Seraphina had. Did something happen between the tribe and the kingdom that I should be aware of?"

A look of surprise went across everyone's faces before Orpheal answered after some thought. "Nothing that I'm aware of. You, Naftali?"

"No projects have gone anywhere near the mountains. Many in our lab have wanted to go to just the lake, but I've forbade many of the trips because of the monsters' intensity lately."

Orpheal gave a curt nod and turned back to me. "I'll ask Solaria to send out a request for an immediate gathering of the other directors for later this afternoon to see if they might have done any excursions and their logs. If what the dragon said is true, which knowing the tribe it probably is, means someone crossed a line and brought risk to this kingdom."

"You don't think it could be a lie though?" Éabha questioned her father. "A false claim to attack and put the idea into an ally to cause discord within our alliances and kingdoms?"

"Outland Dragons have a reputation to not lie as it ruins their pride and honour of being creatures of Valrdis, the Goddess of Truth. They will attack head on with probable cause and don't swindle their words for doubt and deception. They consider that to be dabbling in the territory of Orithina. Mindless hordes even have their purpose for specific reasons, kill and/or eat generally, but that's their reason."

"There's always a first…" she sighed and Orpheal gave her a stern look. "I'm just making sure I catch all the angles like you taught me to."

It was a good thing to bring up, as there could always be a first. But with that specific tribe and the feeling I had, I couldn't agree with her. There was something amiss, I just wasn't sure what it was or who was at fault. All I could hope for was for it to be resolved peacefully with no more bloodshed on either side.

I didn't want to kill anyone else.

The Lord Director gave a simple nod, not bothering to continue the unnecessary scolding, and turned to his assistant. "I leave them in your hands, I'll be back shortly."

Chapter Eleven: Go on an Adventure, They Said

A couple of hours went by and as Éabha had stated; I did have to use magic. Except what she didn't account for was for me to accidentally melt her strange device.

She screamed in surprise and panic for a split moment that changed to anger, cursing up a storm at my carelessness. Naftali started laughing, which only angered the poor Seraphinean further, causing the biologist to laugh even harder, tears forming in his eyes. Orpheal came in as she turned her anger from him and back to me as I tried to apologize, making it rather poor timing. It was shutdown quickly as he didn't find the whole thing as amusing as Naftali who needed to sit before he fell down, still laughing. Something about Éabha never giving out such a reaction being his reason for breaking down, but it only left me confused.

It was probably for the best that Orpheal had come in when he did, the things she had said to me before would have easily grounded her, if not kicked her from the lab – but it was still unfortunate timing. Not that they weren't deserved. I made a very stupid, impulsive decision in the midst of panicking about using magic and taking off the magic inhibitor.

I tried apologizing a second time, Éabha's expressionless demeanour setting in once more with a monotoned reply that it was fine. The device wasn't hers to begin with. She was just more concerned with her life. She apparently had never seen white-clear fire just appear so close to her, something that I was more than accustomed to. Her father let her off the hook after her explanation and I apologized a third time.

I stood by, watching my party, Orpheal, and Naftali work on the device as my role was done about five minutes ago. Staying out of the way, an unexpected squeak came through the link.

"Everything alright?" I asked after a moment of no follow up from Deigh. I went to check on her senses but was shut out. *"Deigh?"*

"I'm fine… but you can't see."

"What was the squeak-"

"I did it!"

"Did what exactly?"

"I mastered the transforming ability!" Her excitement was more than a little contagious and a smile formed.

"Nice job!"

"And now I know why you people wear clothes... It's cold!"

Well... yeah. Clothes did wonders in that department. *"There should be something in the closet that you can use... or steal one of the blankets on the bed."*

"I might just do that..." I could basically feel her bound towards the closet only to stop.

"Something wrong?"

"Well... I'm kind of, er, wary, to look at a mirror."

"Deigh, I'm sure you look-"

"But what if I'm not?! I could be... well, that might not be possible but, you know. What is the standard for beauty?"

"Deigh, I'm sure you look fine," I repeated fully, *"if you need help-"*

"Absolutely not!" I heard the closet door close as I had forgot to close it earlier leaving her to look at herself, blocking me from seeing anything, which I suppose was reasonable. *"Gods, females are strange looking... but not terrible I suppose. Tempest might have had a point with his art discussions."*

"Are you happy with your-"

"No. Yes. Maybe. I don't know," she growled, the swings in mood hit me harder than I was prepared for and a headache formed. *"I can't tell if look alright or if- Ugh! My wings and tail are back!"*

"That might be because you're not able to concentrate-" She wasn't listening as she continued.

"They're so tiny and cute! But gods! Go away! I'm trying to figure out if these things are supposed to look like this!"

What looked like what? *"Deigh-"*

"I can't let anyone see until I know for sure! Maybe there is something in the back of the book for adjustments."

"Deigh, you look fine." My words had little weight since I had no idea what she looked like. *"And if not fine, then perfect. You don't need to be so concerned."*

"You're not here and no, I'm not letting you see! Is it good? If you were a girl, it would be easier to compare… I wonder if there are any suggestive magazines somewhere in the embassy."

"Deigh, you can't go comparing yourself to Seraphinean models – they're body type is barely comparable to an Absalomian."

"But what else can I compare it too?!" Her emotions were mixed with pride and worry. *"I'm so happy I succeeded in only a few months, but dammit!"*

"Deigh, I'm sure that-" I didn't get to finish when suddenly, a sky-blue Seraphinean appeared in front of my face over the railing. I gave a small shout of surprise and banged the top of my head off the railing as I jumped. The conversation between Deigh and I ended swiftly as she shut me out and I rubbed the painful spot with a hiss. I turned my attention back to the girl that scared me half to death. Luckily for her, Orpheal was too engrossed in the Zerach to notice.

Her blank expression became slightly confused as her frown looked like a strange smile upside down. "Did you not hear me the first two times saying your name?"

"Ow, no…" The rubbing was helping the discomfort as I looked at where the railing was before looking back at her. "What are you doing hanging over the railing like that?"

"Getting your attention, Airhead."

"Airhead? Really?"

"Your head is like the void, there isn't anything else to add."

"That hurt almost as much as this railing did."

"Maybe you should pay more attention to your surroundings. That way, you don't hurt yourself and actually hear when people are calling your name."

"Sorry. I was distracted, listening to Deigh," I apologized, and she gave me a very confused look, her brows furrowing.

"Your dragon?"

"Yes. She's doing her own revolutionary experiments."

"So, instead of splitting your concentration between here and her; you completely spaced out with her. Smart."

"It's not like I'm needed right now or in danger," I growled back, and she rolled her eyes, standing up straight.

I turned to her as she crossed her arms, proudly. "You have the attention span of a bee at times, don't you?"

"You think you're being clever, but a seven-year-old already used that insult on me."

"The kid must be smart, but I still have claim on Airhead and many other insults to come."

"Must have a lot of pent-up irritation if you've got more to give to someone you don't even know, let alone a king."

"Someone needs to tell you the truth of your irresponsible ways since being nice clearly doesn't work. Not to mention the horror it must be of being condemned to remain silent. I pity your knights and subjects on that regard."

"For the record, it's not often when I tell my knights or subjects to keep their thoughts to themselves, usually only when it's incredibly inappropriate."

"Is that so?"

"I don't have the luxury of ignoring them. Even the kids' concern over my actions from time to time is valuable to me and I listen when they bring it up. That includes my air-headed times…"

"The Airhead isn't dense."

"And I'll take the compliment where I can get it…" I turned back to the machine, hopefully to end the verbal assault I didn't ask for.

Why was she bugging me anyway?

She seemed so happy not to communicate casually before, but here she was, doing it with a stranger. Insulting and being mean but attempting to be social. I held back a sigh as she shifted uncomfortably behind me. Her words weren't as harsh as they were yesterday – almost teasing in nature, which was strange for someone who didn't seem to care. Yet she didn't leave when I tried to end the conversation. She talked to me more than I had expected her to, and while as sharp as her tongue was, she didn't seem to want to leave me be.

Unless she did care a bit… her curiosity fuelling her boredom. A small huff came out, "So, you're bored too?"

"I didn't say I was bored," she replied so matter-of-factly, I almost believed her.

"Soooo, you're purposely trying to get a reaction from me, because?"

"Because I was bor- erm. Because I could."

Bored. Because she was bored.

She reminded me of someone. Not of the knights, nor my uncle. She reminded me of Claudius. The thought made me somewhat homesick. I attempted to remove the feeling by creating a conversation which, was surprisingly easy for me now that my thoughts associated her with the little white-haired child. "So, what do you do in your free time?"

"Stuff. I'd ask what you do, but from all the information I've gathered from our few discussions, you don't get much of that since your dad died."

"No, not generally."

"What did you do before then?"

"Stuff… depended on the day and how much of a masochistic mood I was in."

"Like duties that come with your princely title, or did you like going out and doing whatever you wanted?"

"Both basically."

"Bet you had someone to spend that time with."

"At the time, six kids constantly getting into trouble."

"I didn't think you were-" she started; her tone filled with surprise that I quickly ended.

"No, no. They're not mine. I was practically their babysitter though."

"Ah. But did you have someone else?"

"What do you mean?"

"Like a special someone, a romantic interest."

"I…" My hesitation broke through as Theodora came to mind and I gritted the thought away. "I don't have an interest, no."

"Oh, I sense a story here."

"Except there isn't because I don't have some special person," I told her carefully, keeping my tone in check. "There were no little excursions of flirting and using it as an excuse to avoid duties."

"Alright, apparently I hit a small nerve," she started as I heard her get closer, leaning against the railing behind me. A small peek told me she was mimicking my stance of disinterest. "But as king, aren't you supposed to be looking for someone? It's not any of my business really, but from watching you yesterday, it's reckless to go into battle when you don't have an heir to your throne. That is how your kingdom works, right?"

"It is, and if anything were to happen, gods forbid, my sister can take the throne."

"So, you're not looking." A statement over a question.

"Not right now, no. I'm not invested in something like that when there are other concerns that need to be addressed."

"Or it's because of this story you refuse to tell and probably the crushing weight of your dad being murdered."

Every word that came from her stabbed my heart and I wasn't even sure if she was aware of it. I didn't give her the satisfaction of her conclusions being right, keeping my tone the same as before. "You're incredibly blunt, eh?"

"I'm just trying to figure you out. But you aren't giving me much to work with. Not to mention, you're not like other Absalomians I've met… So, you're interesting and difficult to understand."

"Glad to be your observation rat…"

"Well, no… but yes, kind of. Maybe more like a Fiery Pig, they're an easier rodent to experiment with." She poked me on the head, and I turned to her. A small expression of sadness appeared on her face and her tone changed to one of understanding. "I'm sorry about your dad. I bet it isn't easy since you have to literally take his place. I understand somewhat, but for me, I think it was easier to deal with death as a kid verses if it happened now… I don't know how it would be like if I lost my dad."

"Perhaps for some people it is…" I answered sombrely. My mother as a child and my father now… both hurt just the same.

There was silence for a moment before she had an excited look in her eyes. "I know what you need. It might help a bit with the grief, enough for you to at least start looking for a girlfriend. You probably have a few people harping on you, yes?"

I looked at her suspiciously. "What is it?"

"Well it's not going to be me that solves this particular problem. Though, it would be the quickest solution to just marry the closest ally… but that would be difficult to pull that off since I certainly have no interest in courtship right now either… Anyway! Where I was going with this. What helps me when I get sad-"

"I didn't realize you had that feature."

She gave me an unamused look. "Oh, I see how this is. Look, I was going to help you, but I'm not a program. I have feelings and you just hurt them."

I sighed, not getting pulled into the guilt trip, crossing my arms. "What is your suggestion, Éabha?"

She froze slightly, not expecting my ability to be stern. She looked over my posture before continuing what she wanted to say, more carefully this time around. "You need to go out and see new things. Expand your horizons."

"With the possibility of zealots running around? My knights are needed here, not to be concerned with me."

She lightened up again. "Yeah, so let me be your bodyguard instead. I can show you some interesting places."

I narrowed my gaze, growing cold and wary. "Why?"

"What do you mean: why?"

"Don't take this personally, but just because you're Orpheal's daughter doesn't mean you get automatic rights to trust. Why are you even bothering to assume I need assistance at all?"

"Because I know people don't get over losing a parent in three months. Also, because I can? It's fair not to trust me, I don't know your history on the subject, but you can't gain trust if you're not willing to open yourself up to the possibility. I'm doing it by offering my hand, will you do the same?"

I wanted to sigh at her reasoning, but I didn't express how correct she was.

No… I suppose I couldn't learn to trust someone if I didn't open up to the idea. But… the last time I trusted someone for casual purposes on my own – they almost got a lot of people killed and almost destroyed a kingdom on top of it.

"I'm the last person who should be saying this but, you need to relax a bit and have some fun. Tension and stress are deadlier than any monster. Can't lead if you're dead, right?"

"I don't know…" The inner child in me wanted to go, without hesitation, to explore this strange land with this stranger. But the rest of me knew better.

"Plotting an excursion, Aerrow?" Owen asked suddenly behind me, and I turned around in surprise.

"No, not entirely…"

"You have the right to be wary, but Éabha isn't plotting anything malicious."

"And you know this how?"

"Yo, I'm like, right here," she pointed out, dryly.

I ignored her as Owen explained himself. "She's looking for a friend, even a blind person could see it."

The girl tsked. "Hey, I'm not-"

"Orpheal and I thought maybe you two could go out for a bit since there's nothing else for either of you to do right now."

"You did?" I looked behind him to see that the Lord Director was gone. "Where'd he go?"

"To the meeting he set up," Éabha replied, checking her nails as I looked back to her. "No wonder you need babysitters."

Wow… Rude…

I turned back to Owen. "You seriously think I want to go with her?"

He shrugged. "You said you wanted to explore."

I frowned. I didn't mean quite literally, especially with someone I barely knew. "I don't know…'

"Think of it this way then, you're free of your retainers for a couple of hours."

I haven't had that honour in forever. "What's the catch?"

"You check in every hour using your CT and if you're even a minute late, I'm sending the Seraphinean Legion to find you. So, don't get into trouble and set an alarm through the options. Stay on the grounds or in the main city nearby, in high public areas where lots of people can keep an eye on you and no alleyways. The alleys here are nothing like in Absalom."

"Good gods above, anything else?"

"Keep each other safe, by all means necessary."

"So, if he becomes some brain-eating ghoul, I have permission to blast his head off?" Éabha asked and he shook his head. "But then I wouldn't be safe."

"If such a ridiculous thing happened, then you can tie him down somewhere and call me or your father with your CT. Orpheal did give you my contact information, yes?"

She gave a nod, not overly pleased with the answer, but I wanted to go back to the first thing he said. What did he mean by tying me down? She didn't look strong enough to overpower me, not to mention she was a foot shorter. There was something I was missing… but… if she really were that strong, she could make a decent sparring partner. Ciar was part Seraph, maybe she fought similarly.

Éabha brought me out of my thoughts as she sighed, "Okay, fine… But did Dad say anything about using my lab?"

"Yes. No explosives."

"Son of a… What's the point of having a lab if I can't use a living torch to blow things up?!"

"I'm not a tool, you know…" I told her and she shrugged.

"Depends on your point of view." She looked Owen. "Alright, we won't use my lab, but I need to go there and switch out my coat and grab some gear."

I turned back to my uncle and questioned him one last time. "Are you sure this is fine? You don't like me going out on my own, let alone with a stranger."

"You also need to go or you're going to slip your collar when I really don't want you to. But you are my king, you do what you want. I've just given my suggestion."

My tongue worked faster than my brain did. "We'll come back if something seems amiss."

"Use that gut feeling and head of yours, and it will be fun."

"What does Orpheal say to all of this?"

"The same. Just don't do anything that will make him your enemy."

I could do that. I didn't really know what could make him my enemy, but I knew I wasn't a delinquent either. I didn't wish to continue the conversation out of the idea of not escaping the clenches of my knights and hopped over the railing. The action scared Éabha slightly and I started to leave. "Come on, before he changes his mind."

"You don't even know where you're going!" She called, and I stopped in front of the doors as they opened.

"Not a clue, so let's go."

I walked through them and they closed only to open again as she came running through and started walking beside me with a glare. "Unbelievable… and here you were thinking I was the child."

"I didn't say a word."

"You were thinking it."

Well now that she brought it up…

I didn't say anything as she led the way to her lab down the hall, passing a few people who I guessed were students with their books. She dropped off her lab coat, revealing a simple, long sleeve shirt, and put on a white coat. She grabbed her sniper rifle, folding the barrel in half, collapsing it into two barrels before folding it one more time so that the barrel was underneath the stock of the weapon. She clipped it over her shoulder then picked up a hilt from the table which she activated, and a small blade came out. It disappeared after a moment, back into the hilt. She attached to the outside of her leg, just below her skirt.

I didn't disagree with the extra weaponry, especially if one of the zealots showed up. My hand subconsciously made it to Winterthorn on my side. I looked behind her to see her armour on a stand to the side and several projects about the benches. She didn't seem to notice me looking around and led the way out, turning off the lights behind her.

The walk was decent, but silent, like she had nothing left to say. We went outside and I looked about the property as we walked the road the elaftrus took earlier. The gate neared, reminding me of the pond to my right. Shaded bushes and a few trees were along its edge, giving the pond a hint of added beauty to it. The three petalled, white flowers grew below the foliage. Éabha cut in front of me and started towards the pond and I followed without a word. The grass under my boots seemed no different from home as we went across the lawn and stopped at the bushes. She knelt in the grass just in front of the flowers, gracefully.

I eyed them from my stand not too far, but not too close to the wingless Seraphinean as I wasn't sure of what her personal boundaries were.

"They're pretty, aren't they?" She asked me as she looked up for a moment before turning back to the flowers.

I gave a nod. "What are they?"

"Trilliums. They generally grow in forest areas, more north at the mountains, where its cool and shaded during the months of Penquinus and Hexsexus. But somehow, in Seraphina, they only grow here, on the top of Domrael Hill all year around. No where else in the city or the island can they be found. They're a mainland plant, somehow growing out of their comfort zone and no one knows why."

Her tone towards the flowers made it seem like she wasn't talking about them but something else. "You must really like them."

"I do. They're my favourite flower, and not because it's the kingdom's national flower."

"Absalom's flower is the rose, a white one specifically. They happen to be my favourite too. The castle courtyard had red, white, and black roses covering the bushes that lined the walkways. They even grew in the harshest of Cheimoiemses."

"Roses growing in Cheimoiems? Doesn't it get really cold in Siofra since it's pretty far north?"

"It does when the lakes freeze over, but they don't seem to mind. They're a strange breed, similar to these trilliums. Only a few places in Siofra, like the city's gathering spot and Elwood Garden could grow them. But I'm sure other places could grow them as well throughout the kingdom, I've just never really gone to see where."

"You say could and had, why?"

"Well... I don't know if they're still there. Monsters destroyed the capital and much of the castle, and while they seemed fine when I left, three months have passed. No one has checked the castle grounds for that sort of thing."

"Oh…" She went silent as she played with the petals of one of the trilliums in front of her. "I'm sure your roses are doing okay. If they can survive northern Cheimoiemses, I'm sure some overgrowth won't do them harm."

"Probably…" I knelt down next to her to get a closer look. Three leaves laid behind the white petals. "I've only gone into a forest twice in my life… but I bet there would be flowers similar to these in one of them."

"You think so? I'd like to see a whole bunch of them. Lines and lines, not in small patches like this where they are confined."

"If the Zerach works as intended, you might be able to see the forest near by. It's to the east from here if I remember correctly."

She scoffed. "Yeah, right. Dad hates me leaving this stupid cage. I'm lucky to go into the city and go shopping without a chauffeur or him every few months. With him is rarer than not as he doesn't really do trips like that."

The bitterness in her tone was evident even if she was trying to hide it. "He just wants to make sure you're safe-"

"Yeah I know. He doesn't want what happened to Mum happen to me. Unfortunately, I'm an adult now and he still treats me like I'm seven."

I understood where he was coming from. I, admittedly, did the same thing to Atlamillia for the first month and a half of being in Asylotum. Then, she threatened to kill me if I didn't lay off. I tried to bring up an optimistic point of view instead of suggesting what Atla did; it was an effective method, but not one I would consider to be the best. "He let you go out into the city today; I think that's some growth."

"Only because he knows you're capable of taking care of whatever comes our way, being a Dragon Knight and all that. He doesn't want to know that I can defend myself."

"Have you told him?"

"Yes, and I've shown him. But he's apparently deaf and blind." A small chuckle came out and she glared at me. "Of course you'd find this amusing, you can do whatever you please. You have no idea what it's like to be stuck in a couple hundred hectares of property for most of your life."

"No, I don't. But I prefer to be stuck in my comfort zone than go out and explore like I used to. You may have been able to defend against dragons, but monsters are so different from them. They don't speak, they can't be reasoned with. They kill because they can. It's dangerous out there and don't even get me started on people who are probably worse than any Outland Creature. Unfortunately, now as king, I not only have to deal with monsters, but people I may not enjoy speaking to, and I have to leave my home."

"People are the worst," she agreed with a small laugh. "You sound jealous."

"A bit I suppose. But I also understand why you might not prefer the life you have. If your efforts yesterday said anything, you enjoy living on the edge, in the chaos of it all, and you do well in it because it challenges you. You don't belong in a cage. Much like these flowers, you're out of place here and that probably makes it hard for you to make friends." I turned to her as she caught my gaze. "Is that a correct assumption?"

"Something like that…" She looked back at her flowers before looking at me again. "You're weird…"

I sighed. It wasn't the reaction I was expecting but should have. "Please, enlighten me why this time."

"You're not much older than I am. You're what? A couple months older? Yet, you seem to understand my frustrations even though you just met me compared to people who have known me my whole life. Not to mention you haven't stormed off in irritation at my horrible mannerisms towards you."

"You're blunt, but it's not bad. Now Azarias, he has no filter at all. As for understanding, I've just experienced and learned a lot of things, most of the time the hard way, so I'm more empathetic. Plus knowing a bit of the background of the person I'm attempting to communicate with helps with seeing how they see things."

"You snooped into my history?" It was more of a statement than a question.

"A little bit. Just that you're often alone, meaning you probably don't have many friends and you have a lot of pressure coming from your father who's the Lord Director. Even the pressures of the Seraphinean Hero from two thousand years ago probably comes to your mind from time to time. That sort of thing creates walls as people judge you on those particular things and not the things you want to be noticed for."

"You didn't need much information to understand the hero pressure, huh?"

"No. In this case, we're similar."

"Well since you know just sooo much about me, I want to know something about the snooping king from the north."

I eyed her. "I'll answer depending on the question."

"Where did you get those scars?"

"Oh…" I touched the one under my eye as the memories of that night flashed by, causing it to sting. I looked away as a sigh came out. "I don't really want to talk about it."

"This is so unfair on how one sided this is… but I'll have you know; you don't know everything about me. Just some surface level shit."

"That I can believe. I've only met a few people that were ever truly so simple."

"Oh? And what are they like?"

"Doesn't matter. They're in prison for the rest of their miserable lives."

She blinked in surprise. "And that took an unexpected dark turn… Hey, instead of reminiscing in the past; how about we make new memories? Something fun?"

"You sound like the kids back in Asylotum. What troubling idea do you have?"

"Well it's dark and brooding if you want to continue sulking."

"I'm not…" I rolled my eyes, unable to lie out of it. "It's annoying how you're seeing through me. I'll have you know it takes a great deal of effort and years of practice to create a mask."

"Your mask isn't terrible. You're just easy for me to read as I'm really good at reading people. Especially people who I know a bit about."

"With the number of insults you were flinging earlier, I was concerned that you lacked any empathy at all."

"You should hear what I say to the people I dislike. So, do you want to go?"

"You never said where."

"Well… it's not in the city… and it's not really public either. But it's technically within city limits."

"And that ticks off two boxes that Owen would not approve of… But he did say be kids. Kids break rules."

"Kids break rules…"

"You're not secretly a cultist for Ciar, right?"

She laughed a little, shaking her head. "No. I don't have the time or the patience to play sheep to some god-complex maniac."

"Okay…" Even if she were, Deigh would know exactly what was happening and be able to warn one of the other dragons in the embassy. It was nice having so many different ways to communicate with the knights. "But I'm not leaving the kingdom if that was your idea. There is a line I must draw."

"Alright fine, we won't leave…"

"Trust me when I say that it's not worth it."

She gave a small pout and I pulled out my CT. "What are you doing now?"

"Changing the lock screen from these two," I replied as I took a picture of one of the trilliums and started for the options.

"Didn't think you'd be into flowers… not very manly or Absalomian-like from my perspective of them."

"It's what I like, plus, I'll be able to show the kids back home what a trillium is. They love flowers and since its on a CT, they can't pick it."

"Kids and flowers… definitely not what I pictured the King of the Dragon Kingdom Absalom would be like."

I didn't have much to respond with as I stood up. It might not have been what she had expected with her gusto macho words that were intended to be mocking and somehow weren't inaccurate to the dragon kingdom I ruled. But it's who I was… I wasn't going to pretend to be anything else.

She followed suit and started back towards the gate with a mutter, "I'll find out one day why you didn't like being in your cage before or why you don't like magic now…"

She was still on that? Well, the answer was never, but I humoured her. "Maybe…"

We left the Directors' Demesne, heading towards the island's edge and along the property's beautifully designed walls that had square-like vines,

Seraphinean meander, running along the capstone siding. A large rock protruded from the hill and she went behind it, disappearing. I followed her and on the other side was a large, ancient bush, but no Éabha.

Where'd she go?

She poked her head out from the side of the bush with a large grin on her face. "Thought I left, didn't you?"

"No…"

"Come on, it's in here."

In where?

I looked at the bush she disappeared behind again and sighed as I went to the side of it, squeezing my way through. I tripped into a large space inside the rock and was caught by two sky-blue wings as she leaned against the wall, expectedly.

"Turns out Dad was right, you're really clumsy."

"Thought you said you didn't know much about me."

"I lied, sort of." She shrugged. "Basics, like how you crave adventure, but you also hate it because of… something… Dad never told me what that reason was, but it had to be something traumatic to destroy a personality trait."

I changed the subject as I got on my own two feet and her wings disappeared. "Can all Seraphineans do that?"

"I hate it when you change the subject… Do what exactly?"

I continued to keep on the new subject. "Make your wings disappear. Your father can do it and so can you."

"Only some people can."

"How many wings do you really have? I've seen two, four, and six."

"I'm a six-winged Seraph, just like Dad."

"Must make it a bit easier to navigate through small spaces without the extra appendages."

"It can. It also makes you fit in better with other people when you're in crowds. There aren't many six-winged Seraphs outside of the demesne, but many with four and two. I sometimes pretend to have the same number of wings as them when I sneak out."

"Meet any new friends like that?"

"Did I meet any new friends while I was out, Aerrow?"

Right… She really was a loner… I looked around the cavern and down a tunnel that seemed to go deep into the island. "So, where does this lead to?"

"This leads to that cave entrance you dropped me off at."

"That's quite a ways." Six hundred kilometres plus as ways…

"It could be if I were walking. There are other places in here too. Much closer since I know you can't fly."

"Is that where you wanted to show me?"

"Well I didn't bring you down here for tea."

"Funny…"

"Yes, I wanted to show you one of the places down here. But I don't want to venture away from my path. There's a lot of tunnels and I haven't marked them all yet. I don't feel like dying down here with you, no offence."

"None taken. I wouldn't want to die down here with me either. My imagination tends to run wild."

"Considering you're terrified of elevators, I'm not shocked that you're a big baby."

I wasn't sure how she came to that correct conclusion, but I defended myself all the same. "I like to call it self-preservation, thank you."

"Whatever makes you feel better." She pulled out her white CT and frowned. "Hey, you better call your general before we head in. There isn't a signal down here, or at least, a good one, until we get to where I want to go. That will be long after your timer goes off."

"Good idea." I pulled out my CT and called him, putting the device to my ear.

He answered a few moments later, "Hello…"

"Hi."

"You're calling five minutes early."

"We're about to go through this loud store, lots of music coming from it. We might get lost in it or worse, miss the alarm. So, Éabha figured I'd check in with you before hand."

"Really don't want me to send the Legion after you, eh?" He fell for the lie. "Alright, off with you. We have lots of work to do yet, going to need you to do your part again tomorrow. I'll give you more details tonight."

"Thanks, talk to you in an hour."

"Remember, it's supposed to be fun."

"Yep, lots of fun." I ended the call and pocketed the device. "Alright, we have an hour to get to your secret place."

"We can make it."

I, for some reason, doubted it as her confidence wavered in her statement. I didn't waste time arguing though as she led the way through the tunnel, and I reset the alarm.

The walls of the tunnels were blue and ancient like the rock above, seemingly carved by some long, lost river. But along with the river, the moisture was long gone, leaving a very dry tunnel system. Nothing stirred amongst the rock, small, blue-white lights powered by magic lined the walls, most likely Éabha's as they had the same magical presence as her. They made the space bright and very obvious on where she hadn't gone before. The tunnels without lights were left almost as black as Zegrinath's Chaos Portal. Surprisingly, the amount of space within the tunnel was wide and high, making the entrances that I had seen so far to be complete shams to what was held within. Deigh could have moved through them easily.

My childhood memories of being an explorer came to mind once more and I couldn't help but smile a bit as we went. If things had turned out differently, I'd be urging Éabha to help me explore the rest of these almost ruin-like pathways and corridors. It carried the same atmosphere as that of Elwood Garden and Orithina's Temple. Ancient and mysterious. A history lost to time.

It was thrilling.

I reeled myself back before I got out of the pen I had made. Exploring was good for the soul, but so were set boundaries of where to go and where not to go. To follow Éabha's direction on not going into uncharted areas and not leaving the kingdom were those two rules right now.

A dark passage appeared as we turned a corner and it seemed darker than the others, leading deeper into the floating island. A weird sensation came from it, causing me to stop. I hesitated to continue down the much brighter path as I looked into the abyss.

There was something down there… but I wasn't sure of what nature.

"Come on or Owen's going to come and find us," Éabha called, drawing me away from the darkened space.

If there was time, I wanted to check it out either on the way back or another time. Owen mentioned to follow my instincts, and they were telling me to check whatever was down that particular way.

I hurried after the Lord Director's Daughter and we continued down the tunnel of light.

Eventually, a different light appeared at the end of the tunnel and the giant cavern opened up into the side of the island. A pool of water, fed by an underground waterfall, was emptied out by its own as it overfilled its space and through the cracks in the blue stone. The water fell of the side. Soft grass grew on the hard rock, giving away to some luminous moss that also grew on the ceiling. Out through the open cavern was the forest I had mentioned earlier far, far below us. Part of Seraphina Lake could also be seen along with some mountains beyond it and a small speck of Akirayuu Ocean farther past.

Moments went by as I continued to look out, unable to speak before she broke the silence. "Pretty, right?"

"This is amazing…"

"It's the perfect spot to just get away from the kingdom and look at what the world has to offer without risking Outland Monsters trying to kill you. We're still technically in Domrael Hill and the barrier blocks our presence here."

"Even if it wasn't… I could see why they'd have a hard time getting in here…"

"Yeah, now the only thing missing here are trilliums. Then, it'd be perfect."

I turned to her. "Have you tried planting a few?"

"I couldn't… They're a delicate plant and I would just end up causing them to die."

"I'd offer to help, but I know nothing about botany."

"It's okay. Maybe one day they'll start growing down here for no plausible reason. I won't put my faith into the false hope, but it's a nice thought."

"Doesn't hurt to hope for tiny miracles." I told her as I pulled out the CT before I forgot. There was a signal now that we were technically outside. How the CT's signal worked was still a mystery to me. "Like being released from this stupid call every hour nonsense."

"Lucky for us, it only took forty-five minutes to get here, even with your curiosity pitstop to venture off elsewhere."

I rolled my eyes as I turned off the timer and called Owen.

Chapter Twelve: It'll Be Fun, They Said

The cave and the scenery were beautiful still even after the minutes had gone by with nothing remotely to do; just sitting at seemingly the edge of the world was everything I needed right there and then. Deigh was viewing what I was seeing as I opened the link between us completely. While she wasn't sitting on a cliff edge like I was, she was sitting on my bed in her new form, swinging her legs back and forth, pretending to be there. Whatever her form looked like; however, she had still refused to show.

A breeze went by and she shivered, turning off what I was feeling from her side. A small smile formed on my face at her reaction, a smile that didn't go unnoticed by the Seraph nearby.

She played with her gun, leaning against the side wall. "Why are you smiling?"

"Because."

"I mean sure, but logically speaking, expressions change through thought; something more than just, 'because' crossed your mind."

A small laugh came out. "Can't just leave it be, eh?"

"Curiosity is a fatal flaw of mine… So, what is it?"

"If you must know." I turned to her slightly. "Deigh got cold with the breeze."

"Cold? She's not even here."

"No, but I am. And I can confirm that the breeze is a bit chilly." Especially to someone who wasn't wearing clothing.

"I mean… not really. Are you cold?"

"A bit." I shrugged slightly. "But if I need to, capes work well as blankets. This view is worth it."

"There is so much I don't understand. Can you explain to me how Deigh feels what you feel? How you communicate?"

I frowned slightly as I thought about her question. I wasn't entirely sure how to answer it. "I'll do my best, but its something that just… is, for an Absalomian and an Absalomian Dragon."

She put away her weapon, silently waiting for me to speak.

"Absalomian Dragons are born, sort of, when an Absalomian is born. But that connection between them is there even before birth."

"How? Where do the dragons come from?"

"Good questions… They are kind of bestowed to the mother by a divine egg carrier called Dragazon who is said to work as a solitary being, neutral to Orithina's and Valrdis's territories. This is thought to be the reason why Absalomians, being creatures created by Orithina, are able to be born with or learn dark element magic and a female not of Absalomian origin, is capable of having an Absalomian child. After the mother receives the egg, it must then be protected, usually by the parent dragon. If the egg is broken and the dragon dies, so will the baby and vice versa."

"When does the egg get bestowed?"

"Uh… a couple of days into pregnancy, I think…"

"That is like, the greatest and most accurate pregnancy test to ever exist."

"Yeah, I guess it's not terrible. Until you have to make sure that egg, while incredibly durable, is not left where it could get broken for nine months. And while I have no idea on what being pregnant entails, I bet it could get really tedious. That… and say if someone did something horrible to a woman-"

"You mean rape." I looked over to her in shock and she shrugged. "You beat around the bush, wastes time."

"Some people are more sensitive to that matter… but yes, that. It leaves the female with a great decision. A fetus would technically be in an embryo state, that egg – while in a similar position, has a developing dragon inside. Dragons are considered to be a gift from the gods, from Orithina and Dragazon… It's not a simple decision."

"Explains why you don't have the death penalty in your kingdom."

"Yes… do you?"

"It's arbitrary, but yes. It creates free test subjects for the kingdom. Before it was because of heresy and sacrifice to Orithina, but now it's for science."

That… Yeah… That was really messed up.

What Éabha believed about how evil or great Seraphina's justice system was, she wasn't sharing other than blunt basics…

But to me, that was a bit beyond twisted. Even if it was for science. They were still people, no matter how awful their crimes were. A simple, straight up beheading or an injection would be more appropriate if they had to keep the death penalty.

Though, my opinion didn't entirely matter. Not even as a leader of a foreign nation. Different customs, different histories, and the idea of giving people over for science or the gods was so ingrained into not only Seraphina's society, but several of the other kingdoms for millennia at one point or currently practiced – my views would be seen as strange and wrong.

I was going to have to ask what rules not to break after the discussion was over in case diplomatic immunity didn't cover.

"So, what happens with that situation?" She asked and I shifted back to teaching.

"She could destroy the egg or bring the child to term, raise them, or put them in an orphanage so they can be adopted."

"Alright. Fast forward nine months with a happy family, how does baby and dragon work?"

"The dragon is like most babies: clumsy, needing food and shelter, but they are pretty okay on their own for small bursts. Baby Absalomian, however, needs a lot of care. Depending on the whelp that is born with the child, certain needs are sometimes required. Ice dragons don't like heat for example, so neither will the baby."

"And you have a very hot, fire breathing dragon, so you don't like the cold."

I nodded. "Luckily, dragon lines follow similarly to genetics from parent to child. So, for my family, we've all been light and fire elements and thus, the dragons have only ever been light and fire. Sometimes, sometimes dragon genes wander, but never into an opposite element."

"And there are six elements based around your species, right? Fire, water, earth, air, light, and dark?"

"Exactly. Seraphs, I believe are only light-based element users, right?"

"Yep, we're element locked. But at least we can learn natural magics that Dagdians use." She went back on topic. "Alright, so the dragon is a fire type, the little bundle of scales and the little bastard gets cold easily, what else?"

I raised a brow, feeling like the name was directed at me, but I let it go. "From there, the baby and the whelp grow, at slightly different rates. Dragons take longer to reach their full size, usually between fifty to a hundred years and don't really start talking until somewhere around five and ten-years-old. Absalomians generally finish between sixteen and twenty-five and start talking between the ages of six months to a year and a bit."

"Did you stop growing?"

"I honestly thought I did, but in the last few months, I had another growth spurt of three inches at some point. I'm pretty sure I'm done though; being a hundred-eighty-eight centimetres is taller than average for my race," I answered with a small shrug of thought and continued trying to answer fully before she could ask more questions. She was worse than the kids. "But the link starts to develop around the ages of three and seven. It depends on the development of both the whelp and the child and how often they sync up with each other. Sometimes this helps with their development in different skills like talking and walking and so on."

"When did you and Deigh start syncing up?"

"Personal question but... I don't know. Young, before I remember as she's always been there... but it was definitely before the age of five since she was very vocal."

"That's a specific age..."

"Yeah well, there's a reason why I know-"

"Why?"

I avoided the question. "Deigh and I have known each other's wellbeing for as long as either of us can remember. But we didn't really have conversations through our link until after... a-after a month of so after my fifth birthday."

"So, you communicate with feelings, then words... what else?"

"Being able to know where the other is, is the next skill that is developed. But this can be hindered if one of us is really sick and injured badly; anything that affects cognitive thinking. At this point, a kid and a dragon are able to share senses, individual actions, trivial things like hunger, pain, and even taste – but Deigh and I don't do that last one... We tried it once when we were eleven, one of the worst decisions we've collectively made. Sometimes, if I'm eating chocolate, she'll sneak in because she can't have it physically, but I'll never go near the things she eats."

"Collectively, so you don't think exactly the same?"

"A dragon is a person, just the same as Outland Dragons are, or you and me. They are exactly like us with their own feelings, concerns, temptations, likes and dislikes. Deigh's prideful, stubborn, gluttonous; I'm stubborn, a trickster, a bit of a pushover at times. Some traits crossover like our stubbornness and wanting to do what's best. Headstrong at times, we get from our parents even though dragons don't see Absalomian parents like you and I would. Deigh still gets the same skills and traits as I would. Some things though also differ like siblings would. She's a fearless death machine while I'm a bit of a wimpy death machine. I try to avoid physical conflict while she craves a good match. I like bantering and she doesn't. But catch her on a bad day and her tongue is sharper than her teeth."

"Got your feelings hurt by her, hm?"

"Many, many times. She's cruel when she wants to be."

"*And you love all of me,*" Deigh said, and I nodded as I continued to speak out loud.

"And I love every aspect of her, flaws or not. She's a piece of me just as I'm a piece of her. We're one unit."

"Hmm… I guess that makes sense since you would die if she died and vice versa."

"It's a brutal symbiotic relationship. An Absalomian can get sick, and the dragon can be completely healthy. This can drive a dragon insane at the thought of watching their life slowly come to an end… It doesn't happen often since dragons seem more accepting at the idea, but it does happen and it's frightening to watch…"

"Frightening and sad probably…" Her tone turned sombre, and she looked out at the open space. I wasn't sure what she was thinking of, but it didn't seem like it was pleasant.

"Did I answer your questions well enough?"

"They weren't very scientific, but dragons are almost divine beings themselves, a gift from Orithina and this Dragazon. Perhaps it is just magic on how you are able to always have someone with you, no matter how many people disappear from your life. Absalomians live such long lives compared to everyone else; I suppose it makes sense that you will always have a companion."

"Sometimes…" Her body language had long changed from curiosity to learn more to depression; the exact cause of it though was in the air. "Is there something you wanted to talk about?"

"No… was just thinking more on your link with Deigh. It's interesting. You are interesting…"

"You've said that a couple of times now."

"And I'll probably continue to say it. You're so different from everyone else; I can't help but want to know more about you, your kind, everything."

"I'm sure any other Absalomian can explain these same things to you if you ask them."

"Perhaps, but admittedly, I don't think anyone else would have had the patience to deal with all my questions like you have. Not to mention that the answers are more conclusive when they're from the king of the people I'm learning about. You're supposed to know all these things, right?"

I gave a small nod.

"What's it like to be king?"

The question was a bit unexpected as I wasn't prepared at all for it. It wasn't like I was expecting someone to ask me that. Favourite colour, food, maybe even if I liked wearing sweaters or something… but not that.

How could I answer such a question?

It was a lot of things… most of it not great. It wasn't what I had wanted with my life, nor was I prepared for it… I looked out at the view, watching birds fly far below. "Stressful, I suppose… Very stressful."

"Why? You have all the power you could ever want. If I were you, I'd probably be fucking around, literally, with anyone I wanted and maybe drinking, or whatever people do to have fun… Just having a time with no rules to obey. Drown out all the feelings of losing Dad if he died anyway I could."

"That's what a drunk said at the Kal Alna Outpost," I huffed out a laugh and she sighed. "What? It's true."

"I was just thinking of what a guy would do in such situations… not specifically me… I'd probably blow up a mountain… maybe drink. Alcohol numbs my mind in ways nothing else can."

"I haven't been able to get drunk from the few times I've partaken so… I wouldn't know." I turned back to the original topic sensing that if I hadn't, she would have pestered me about it later. "I could have done all those things, perhaps... But that wouldn't make a very good king, now would it?"

"Probably not, but I doubt many would condemn you for wanting that. You're young, definitely within the age of wanting to fulfill sexual needs, depressed."

"Not depressed, first off. Second, not even interested in that... other thing..."

She gave me a skeptical look. "Yeah, huh..."

I sighed. "King Solomon did a lot for the kingdom. As his son, it's my job to fill his place to provide what he gave, especially with the state of how the kingdom is now, and with Ciar being on the loose; there's too much to do to mess around. To sit like this at the edge of everything, watching the light of the sun fade... None of these thoughts would be on my mind until my duties were done back home. I came to this kingdom for duty, not desire. If I had it my way, I would be hiding, staying with my people in Asylotum. But I can't send my knights to certain death to deal with Ciar who has all the time in the world to figure out how to get into the realm. Sure, we could hide there, thinking he'll die of old age – but we don't even know if he will. Perhaps he is some immortal being and that's not a risk I can take."

The memories of Ciar attacking that night in the storm came back and a scowl formed. My hand brushed the old wound on my chest as I felt the sword inside me all over again.

"To be content in a false hope of never being hunted because he assumes that I'm someone I'm not, allowing him to hunt those who are exactly who he thinks they are... but I can't. I swore an oath to the king to protect my kingdom and any other kingdom across Orithin as a knight then, as king now, should the need arise. And it most certainly has. Once Ciar's gone, the duties will lessen with time, and then maybe... I could sit on top of a mountain for fun." I stopped talking as an awkward chuckle came out. "Oops, I rambled. Haven't done that in a while, sorry."

"Well, you did. Do you feel a bit better now that you've voiced some of your thoughts?"

"Ah..." I thought about it. "I suppose a bit... It doesn't resolve anything, but-"

"But it helped to talk."

"I suppose..."

"It's important to de-stress since, clearly, having a dragon partner isn't the same as talking about your internal conflicts to someone else."

I was left without anything to say as I pouted slightly, looking back out to the forest.

"So, you're a cheesy, loyal bitch."

"Is this what Hell is? Because I don't think Ciar gave me a good enough demonstration."

"Teasing aside, it seems like you're doing the best you can instead of being a typical, young adult, despite being terrified to leave your cage."

"I didn't say I was terrified," I growled, looking back at her with a slight glare.

"No, but it was heavily implied." She gave a look that I couldn't read. "Being a good king sounds stressful. But from observation, our few conversations, and listening to your knights – they care a lot, meaning you're doing a good job. So, chill. You'll make your knights worry more if you stress yourself to the point of getting sick."

"I'll keep that in mind…"

"But just so we're clear, I'm so glad I don't have your job."

"Yeah, Atlamillia says the same thing."

"Your sister, right?"

"Yeah."

"She's smart."

"She is…"

"You must miss her."

I nodded. "Greatly."

"You could call her," she suggested, and I gave a short and sweet answer.

"Nope."

"No? Why not?"

"Because she won't answer if I did."

"Rude."

"Says the Lord Director's Daughter who called a foreign king a baby, a bastard, and a bitch, in that order."

"That's a lot of b words… I'll have to change that up a bit."

"So excited…"

"Oh, I bet…" She stopped her quick responses with a pause and genuine emotion came from her. "Are you okay?"

"What do you mean?"

"Well just from what I've managed to fish out of you, there is clearly a lot more running through that void of yours."

"Didn't realize you were a therapist."

"I'm not-"

"I'm fine. Rambling helped."

That was a lie and a half.

It helped at first, but now all it made me think of was Ciar and subsequentially, Theodora, not within the safety of the sanctuary. For all I knew, I sentenced her to death.

I needed something to distract myself before I fell off the cliff edge. "Wanna break another rule?"

"Another one?"

I turned to her, trying to place some excitement in my voice, but it didn't work very well, "Yeah, there is a tunnel that we passed; I want to know what's in it."

"Oh, so one of my rules." She pondered for about half a second. "Yeah, sure. Why the fuck not?"

"You're quite vulgar."

"And you're not, but you don't see me bitching."

"What would your father say?"

"My dad's not here so fucking fight me!"

"Not the most lady like…"

"Never said I was."

This was true… She did not once say that she was noblewoman-like. I changed the topic a slight bit. "So, what do you do for fun if not fancy parties?"

"Well… I do like having tea with some of the staff, Aunt Solaria and Dad when I can… And when I'm not working… I guess make weapons, play games. Oh, and I like fighting, trying out new and old ideas from books."

One of those past times really perked my interest. "What kind of games?"

"Gory, hard, competitive ones."

"P-pardon?"

"A video game, you know, a thing you play on a screen?"

"I know what it is…" I turned back to the open world. "I just didn't realize they got gory…"

"Aw," she teased but I didn't dare look over at her. "The thought turning your stomach?"

"No." A bit… I had seen a lot of graphic things, the last thing I wanted to see was that on a screen for personal entertainment.

"Have you played one, Princess?"

"Definitely not. I used to draw sceneries on my free time when I wasn't babysitting. Seraphinean Tech hates me, remember?"

"Brother, you are missing out."

I didn't get to object against any of it as an alarm went off on the CT and I pulled it out of my pocket. It didn't seem like it had been an hour…

I called Owen, who started to answer only for something to explode in the background. I pulled the device from my ear as the call ended and looked at it for a moment.

What the hell was that about?

A sigh came out, not sure if I should head back or not to check. I put the device away, the signal still saying it had service.

I hoped he and the others were alright…

"Dad has a habit of making things go boom," Éabha started, apparently knowing exactly what happened. "Don't worry, they're fine. I would have been notified if something was really wrong."

"How exactly?"

She pulled out her CT, her screen showed off statuses of rooms in different colours. Most of them were green, one was orange, and two were black. "I created a program to let me know if one of the labs in the demesne is critical or offline when I have a signal. These are the ones found in Dad's wing, the main lab's not great, but not injury threatening."

"I see…"

"Come on! Let's go do something fucking stupid. It'll be fun, they said."

"That is what they said." I got up from the edge and walked along the rock wall before dropping off the side, back into the safety of the tunnel. Éabha gave me a look. "What?"

"You are accident prone according to Dad, yet you just did that?"

"It was fun."

"Gods above… alright. Lead the way, great genius of our time."

"Sarcasm is noted and unappreciated."

"Sounds like a personal problem."

I just shook my head and led the way back through the ancient cavern.

It didn't take long to make it back to the dark cavern and she summoned a light in her hand then stuck it on the wall. A small explanation came from her of it helping us get back if things got complicated. She took the lead as she was the light-bearer and the feeling that I had before grew. There was something important down the tunnel we travelled… I just didn't know if it was a good feeling or not.

The tunnel seemed to end after a long while of walking with a small light coming from the one side of the T. I looked towards the light and found a hole in the wall, showing the outside world. Turning to the other side, the feeling was down it. It had been getting stronger as we went, but now it made me hesitate. It was uncomfortable, not quite wrong but was. It also felt somewhat familiar, but I couldn't figure out from where. Éabha went ahead but was more cautious than before, muttering that she had a bad feeling. We walked a little farther down the line to be met with an entrance way to a darkened cavern.

She brightened the light as I looked behind us, feeling like something was watching. There was a glimpse of what seemed to be a wisp that looked like that of a figure. Suddenly she backed into me, not allowing me to have a good look. Her light dropped from her hand and it landed silently on the floor. I turned away from the wisp to her; her hands covering her mouth in shock. I moved her to the side as my instincts kicked in and took a closer look inside.

Strange runes covered the walls that had a dried liquid from long ago plastered across them. About ten, see-through beings, wispy-like, came into focus about the room when I looked at them, but seemingly disappeared when I looked at the wall behind them. I turned back to them, seeing that they weren't paying attention to us as they wandered, but with no purpose. Like they were stuck in circles.

Unable to leave this cave.

I went to ask Éabha if she was seeing what I was when I noticed that along with her, the weird beings were all looking in the same direction: the floor.

I followed my gaze to find a familiar circle with indents around it and a huge, dried, mummified, Seraphinean corpse laying on its front in the centre. Its eyes were closed as its mouth was opened in a silent scream. Its neck was at a strange angle as its face looked up at us. Éabha started to panic and I moved her behind me, going to say something comforting only for the CT to go off, scaring a scream out of both of us.

I took it out and saw that the timer was done, but there was no signal. I pried my eyes from the device to the dried corpse but noticed that the wispy beings that I could somewhat see before, disappeared at the noise as if frightened at the broken silence. My voice broke the emptiness, lowly. "We have to get to a signal, quickly."

"The opening at the other end..." she muttered, almost instinctually.

"Let's-" My tongue froze as the corpse seemed to twitch.

"Did it just move?"

I couldn't answer. Maybe those strange beings knew better...

The corpse's eyes opened, showing a purple light in empty eye sockets and my voice cracked. "What the hell...?"

The corpse groaned loudly as its limbs creaked and cracked. It slowly got to a stand, making me almost drop the CT. It looked down at us, its head was two and a half metres in the air, a jaw hanging from its slightly crocked head. It twitched before screaming out a hellish death sentence, the magic presence I was sensing doubled. A mixture of necromancy and something else.

The creature continued to twitch in a disturbing manner as it took a step forward and I took a step back. Creaks and cracks continued to follow the pops, turning my stomach. If some nonexistent, weird hallucination wisps weren't interested... this thing was not worth it. I was not fighting-

It moved into a stance to charge.

"Fuck me..." I turned to Éabha, giving her a bit of a head start as I pushed her. "Run!"

She turned around and we ran back to the T conjunction just for her to scream in surprise. She came to a sharp stop instead of heading up the way we came. I ran into her, almost knocking her over as I grabbed her arm and looked up at what blocked her path. A purple barrier with black lines ran through it at random, stretching across the tunnel's entrance back towards the surface. I went to attempt to barrage it only to feel the chaos energy. My eyes went wide in recognition.

It was a Necromantic Barrier, something that was indestructible and painful to even touch, especially to light element users such as us. If my studies were correct, it was a trap that armed itself with the activation of an undead guardian... I just never thought I would have ever come across one.

I looked to the opening in the wall, hoping to climb out that way to find the same barrier in place, blocking any escape. Another death scream came to my ears and I turned to the large corpse rushing at us faster than its lardy body should be able to, still twitching. Its two wings still had some feathers on the mummified appendages, dragging and scraping along the walls and floors. Its limbs trying to fall apart only to form back into place. I pulled out Winterthorn, stepping in front of Éabha, and blocked its trample. It pushed me back slightly as it collided, sliding my boots across the stone.

"What the fuck is that?!" Éabha asked as I heard her assemble her gun behind me.

A grunt escaped as I tried to keep it at bay, "A guardian-"

"For fucking what?!"

"Go under it's legs."

"Excuse me?! He's naked and still has his-!"

"There's more room back in the cavern," I urged, realizing what I was asking as it pushed back harder. I growled, trying to fight back, but I couldn't keep friction to hold it in place. "Unless you want to feel what that barrier does, it's going to crush both of us into it if you don't move now!"

She didn't argue further, sliding around me, under my blade and through its legs, thankfully without touching anything. It slipped to the side, causing me to fall forward just for it to catch me with a backswing. It was stronger than it looked as it sent me off the ground and into the barrier across the opening several metres away. A sharp scream came out of my mouth at the barrier's touch, it's magic stabbing through my back, and my sword dropped to the floor. I followed after it, dropping to my hands and knees. The pain subsided once I wasn't touching it, allowing me to catch my breath. I looked up, wondering why the guardian hadn't attacked further and found it chasing Éabha back down the hall. Another growl came out as I picked up Winterthorn, the CT ringing and left ignored, and I chased after the guardian.

It made it back into the room, a few paces ahead of me as the CT stopped, and I leapt, stabbing my sword down into its back. It screamed loudly, spinning around, trying to get to me. Suddenly, sickening, popping noises came from its shoulders. Its arms were no longer unable to reach me. I let go of the blade before it could, dropping to the floor. It turned its head a hundred-eighty degrees, the vertebrae in its neck cracking as it did, looking angry. It grabbed Winterthorn and whipped it back at me. I rolled out of the way and the blade bounced off the rock wall.

I went to retrieve it and loud explosions came from behind the creature. It turned its head back only for Éabha to roll under it, her sniper now a double-barrel shotgun, and she fired into the back of its knee. The leg was blasted out from under it as I picked up the blade, tossing the inhibitor bracelet to the side. I went for its head, lighting my blade into a pillar of white plasma and sliced across its head and chest, cleaving it into two, disgusting halves. The creature dropped and I backed away from it.

What the hell…

If I didn't puke, it was going to be a miracle… but at least it didn't have any smell at all.

A sucking noise entered my ears and I gagged. The corpse started to form back together in front of me. Éabha shot its head into paste as it was passing by. The pieces started to mould back together again.

This wasn't working. "Éabha, get back."

"Get back?" She looked back at me in disbelief. "We need to tear this thing apart! It has a guardian shard in it!"

"I know, but it's too big to shotgun and hack it. It will just reform long before we find it. It has no stamina, we do." I was so happy that I didn't have to explain how to kill it.

"We can try…"

I grabbed the Seraph by her shoulder, pulling her back as she shot it once more. "You're not fire-proof, give me a few moments to find it."

"That crystal is though, what are you going to do once you get it?"

"When I find it, I need you to be ready. I'll throw it at you and hopefully, it won't start forming around it. But you need to be away or you're going to get burned. Take the CT as well, I can't afford another one right now if it melts."

She didn't seem very happy about it as I handed her the device from my pocket. She took several steps back before running down the tunnel.

I lit my blade on fire again and continued to hack at it to give her more time to get as far down the corridor as possible. I didn't know how hot it was going to get nor how far it would travel, but the closed space meant it was going to get very, very warm – more than what the Seraphinean was probably comfortable with. A lot more.

Her voice echoed down the tunnel, "I think I'm good here!"

"Let me know if you change positions," I replied, raising my voice as I concentrated on the abomination in front of me.

The guardian got tired of being cut into different pieces as I was just about finished wasting time, and threw its arm at me, pelting me in the side. I recovered quick enough only for its hand to grip around my ankle, trying to keep me in place. Memories of the Gracidra dragging me into her realm came back in a flurry. A battle cry came out as I got over the fear and stabbed down into it. The arm exploded into liquid, removing it from my ankle. I turned to the monster and my blade reacted, solidifying the white plasma form. I rushed it, stabbing it once I arrived, and heard the arm reforming behind me. I unleashed the contained energy.

It exploded into flames, screaming as it tried to hit me, and I jumped out of the way. I went in again, stabbing and releasing the quickly charged, stored energy, causing the rest of it that had reformed to explode into bits. Fire encompassed the mass and the room, raising the temperature and I looked around for its life source. A purple glow came from the dimming fires as the creature attempted to reform in its charred husky state.

I grabbed the crystal. "Éabha!"

"Ready!" She shouted, and I charged to the hallway, tossing it towards her before hiding back behind the wall.

A rifle went off and the shards of what was left of the crystal came flying back into the room. The flames stopped writhing, quickly going out as its fuel burnt off. I put out the flames with a simple thought, allowing the room to cool. I looked around the corner as Éabha inspected the entrance way and gave me a massive grin. "That was insane."

I went over to her as she put Iðunn over her shoulder. It vibrated slightly on her shaking body, but I couldn't tell if it was due to adrenaline, fear, or excitement.

Possibly a combination of all three.

I looked her over. "Are you alright?"

She gave a nod. "Yeah… You weren't kidding when you said it was going to get warm. Good thing you gave me the CT."

"I have to call Owen back before he freaks out even more than he has… I'm sure Deigh told Missiletainn that we were busy, but…"

"That windowed area should do."

I gave a small nod, and we went to the other end of the tunnel at a brisk pace. The CT went off as soon as it got signal and I answered it. "So, you know how this was supposed to be fun?"

"Aerrow! I am this close to sending the Legion to find you! What are you doing?!" Owen was not happy.

"Breathing… doing my best to not throw up. The usual."

"I said I would protect you, but I'm starting to think that I should just kill you."

"That would be treason, Uncle."

"A justified treason at this rate when all I got from Missiletainn, according to Deigh, was that you were busy. What were you doing and why didn't you answer?"

"We were dealing with something…" I looked down the line. "I only just got signal-"

"Where on Seraphina could you lose signal?"

"Er… underground… Look, you said to have fun."

"And you just implied that you didn't…"

"No. This was terrifying-"

"And not okay. That thing was the stuff of legends and its not fucking okay," Éabha shared as she leaned against the wall, processing everything. "Awesome, but not fucking okay."

"In Éabha's words, it was not fucking okay." I looked outside; the barrier gone. "Where are you right now?"

I could practically see the confusion on his face. "What do you mean?"

"Are you near Orpheal?"

"No… I'm not. What is it?"

"I need you to come here when you can; we have a problem. Deigh can direct you and we'll meet you at the entrance. Keep this out of Orpheal's range, please."

"Okay, weird request, but consider it done nonetheless. Are you at least safe?"

"Yes, traumatized, but safe."

"This should be a good story to hear. We're on our way whenever Deigh arrives."

"*I'll be there in about five minutes,*" Deigh told me, and I shared the information then ended the call.

I looked down at Éabha who seemed disappointed and still shaking. "Sorry. I know this place is important to you, but this is really important. Owen is going to keep your father out of the loop for now to keep your little escape safe… Are you okay?"

She nodded. "I appreciate you keeping it from him… You didn't have to."

"No, I did. I brought you down here and if I hadn't, you would have never known about that guardian and it wouldn't have ever woken up."

167

"What is the problem exactly? You told Owen that there was a problem. Didn't we take care of the guardian?"

"Yes… but the guardian wasn't what I was talking about. What it was guarding, is." I led her back into the cavern and hinted at the floor. "That is what it was protecting."

"And certainly not your bracelet…" She pointed to the wall on our left.

I walked over to it and found what was probably my inhibitor bracelet. It was just a pile of cooling goop as I picked it up a bit before dropping it. "Oops…"

"You know how much of a pain in the ass those are to make? And, to top it off, you're stuck in these tunnels until I sneakily go find you a new one and bring it back after I calibrate it."

"Sorry… but, as weird as this sounds, I don't regret using magic." I turned back to her as she continued looking around. "The question is now, why was it protecting that circle altar at all?"

"And a bunch of corpses…" she added, looking at something farther still to the left.

I turned to where she was walking towards and a small offshoot of a room was barely visible in the dim light still left on the floor. Something seemed to be laying on the ground, just past its entrance. I went over to her and inside the small room was a pile of bodies in all forms of decaying states and mutilations. She poked at one nearby with Iðunn, more curious about the corpses than I ever would be.

Suddenly, instead of the cave, the tunnels and the castle halls appeared in front of me. The bodies weren't Seraphineans anymore but Absalomians and dragons. The smells, the blood, the screams that would have filled their harbouring safety, the echoes I heard in the city. The wisps brought me out of the hallucination a bit, their strange essence fading and made the cavern seem less suffocating.

My stomach couldn't handle it any longer and I quickly left the cavern that was both as it truly was and Siofra's tunnels meshed together.

"Hey, where are you going?" Éabha called but I didn't answer her.

I managed to make it back down the hall at the open rock wall, somehow, and threw up. The memories of stepping into the ripped apart man and the girl emphasized out of all the memories, making me sick again. Tears threatened at the corners of my eyes as I tried to hold back the thoughts of losing all those people. Losing Tetra, Evander…

Father.

Why were there always bodies?

There…

Here…

There had to be two dozen people in that mangled mess… all killed by that guardian.

A small shriek came from behind me that turned to an uncomfortable giggle causing me to panic as I snapped around. Éabha in the hazy distance, was still in the cavern messing around. She held an arm that had come off; it was dried and withered. She dropped it and it hit the floor with a loud, echoing crack.

I threw up again, the memories fading slightly.

These weren't my people…

My people weren't going to be put through that again…

I couldn't let that happen again.

…

What was this place?

Chapter Thirteen: Apology

I sat in the silence of my room as I read my book, trying to distract myself, waiting for Owen to give me some idea of what that place was. It was somewhat working, but I couldn't get the image out of my head.

The bodies, the dried blood, the undead guardian – whatever those wisps were that didn't come back. Why was any of it there? Why was the guardian defending an altar? Why was it collecting bodies of the fallen?

What was that altar?

There were so many questions with no answers.

It had to be of some importance. The strange language on the walls that I recognized, like the writing that was on Aetherian and the walls on the temple but couldn't place. The runes were the same as the ones found in the cavern in Absalom. All of it was the same, up to even a body and a trap left behind. Why was someone killed there before and why was someone killed afterwards? Perhaps it wasn't the same here as it was in Absalom, but it made sense if it was.

But that was also impossible to determine from my desk or without the proper technology. Especially with how open that cavern was and how old that mummified corpse had to be. The blood stains on the walls and ground were long dried and contaminated with the blood of the victims. There wasn't going to be a point of reference to determine any similarities… or even how those people got down there at all.

A knock came from beyond my open door at the main entrance of the penthouse. I got up from the desk and walked to the sound. My hand went for the handle only to hesitate as it trembled. I tsked in annoyance, trying to calm my nerves and my stupid head.

Ciar wasn't on the other side. Why would he be?

I grabbed the handle and opened it. On the other side, Éabha was shifting her weight back and forth, a bit of colour on her cheeks like she was embarrassed.

Surprise caught my tongue, "Uh… what're you… 'i?"

She raised an eyebrow, her coy nature gone. "Is this how you greet everyone who comes to visit you?"

"Sorry, you just surprised me. I wasn't expecting you."

"Who were you expecting?"

Ciar. "No one, I guess."

We stood in an awkward silence before she stood on her toes, trying to look over my shoulder then set back down on her heels. "We just gonna stand here all day in the doorway, or…?"

"R-right." I opened the door farther, clearing my throat, and stepped out of the way. "Come in."

"Why thank you." Sarcasm dripped from every word as she walked in and I closed the door behind her. She took off her boots and looked around the space as I somewhat eyed her. I was curious to know why she came and cautious due to my own paranoia. "Wow, this place is huge… Two floors. It's like a castle or something and that's just the top floor."

"Have you never seen something like this before?"

She shook her head, still awed. "A loft for bedrooms… workspace, common room, even a dining area… I had no idea this was even up here with all the facilities already in the embassy."

"It's not terrible. Has its advantages and disadvantages: like the glass floor of the loft let's Owen know when I'm up well into the night."

"You've been here two nights. How and why are you up late enough for him to be mad at you?"

"Habit, I guess… um… This is where I'm supposed to offer you something, but all I have up here is water… and I guess a lot of empty furniture."

"I'm okay for refreshments, but I appreciate the offer." She wandered inside more, still looking around before sitting down on the couch. "So, I guess because of our fun adventure yesterday, Dad was informed and dropped everything to go see that weird place…"

"Owen told him about it after seeing the bodies, but as far as I'm aware, the story is that Missiletainn was flying overhead and sensed dark magic and asked Owen to investigate. The guardian being killed was covered by Owen's own necromantic inherit skill and he obliterated it by accident when turning it off."

"So, Dad has no idea that we were down there?"

"No."

"I see… Well, I should be glad that it never came up, but…"

"You want to continue working on the Zerach. Yeah, me too."

She passed me a confused look. "How come you're not down there with your knights?"

"I was told it wasn't necessary for me to go."

"I suppose that makes sense. You were pretty shaken about the whole thing, even after we left. Why is that?"

"Oh, I don't know," I started, pretending to ponder as I sat heavily in the chair next to her. "How about the two and a half metre, one hundred-forty kilogram undead, Seraphinean monstrosity that was trying to kill us."

She eyed me, not totally believing my words. "I figured you would have seen worse."

"Well… I have. Just not that."

She was silent on the matter as I set my head back, staring at the high ceiling. A sigh slipped out as I thought back to the questions from before with the strange altar. The thoughts turned darker still, the tunnels of Siofra dancing at the edge of my mind.

To Ciar.

The back of my neck stung for a moment before registering the chair and shifted its remembrance to my chest.

"Are you going to be okay?"

"You keep asking me that. What do you mean this time?"

"I don't think you were shaken because of some dried-up corpse. You only went all weird after we found the bodies in the room. So, it was something else."

It was a whole bunch of something else. "Owen was just concerned about another trap, nothing more."

"Then why-?"

My hand dropped from my chest to the arm of the chair. "You ask a lot of questions."

"I want to know more things. Books only answer so many questions and none of them are going to tell me about your reaction to what happened."

"There are just some things better left not said."

She seemed annoyed with my answer as she huffed. More silence followed only to be broken by her once more. "What's the scariest monster you've ever met?"

"Ciar."

"Besides him…"

I didn't need to look at her to know her eyes rolled at my simple and obvious answer. I thought on her question more, running through the monsters I had met and killed. There were quite a few of them. "What kind of scary are you looking for?"

"Something trauma-inducing scary."

"I guess that eliminates the Archvesper for me… But I'm sure Owen would disagree…"

"He's an arachnophobe?"

"It's pretty funny when it's not a monster and he catches one nearby." I laughed a bit though I was surprised that she knew what the Archvesper was.

"So, then what's yours?"

Adamant, as usual…

I turned to my nightmares for assistance. "Probably a toss up between this demon called The Effigy and the Gracidra, if I can't choose Ciar."

"What are those?"

"You probably wouldn't know The Effigy, but have you read any Norian Tales?"

"Why would an intellect who enjoys real life horrors, read fairy tales?"

"Cause they're fun?" I could feel the deadpanned look she was giving me and just moved on. "The Effigy is a shapeshifting jerk that feeds on fear. This allows it to get strong and weakening their opponent physically while also torturing them by taking what they're scared of most and shoving it in their head. According to the entry, it can speak to you in your head and often takes the shape of someone you care about."

"But it didn't do that for you…"

"If it had, it probably wouldn't have been as effective."

"So, what did it do?"

"Turned into me and then said I was going to get everyone I cared about killed."

"And you believed it?"

I didn't reply and switched monsters. "The Gracidra is a monster created by Orithina to hunt demons. The Hound Empress and her Houndmaster, the Gracidras from the Norian Tale – Little Blue, slaughtered a third of a little town called Baiwyn in the southwest of Absalom."

"I hate that you keep doing that, but fine… What makes her different?"

"She has her hounds drag people into her pocket dimension while they're sleeping. This dimension is a foggy and dark thorn maze. Once inside, she toys with them, hunting them down until they are no longer amusing to her, and kills them. She then eats their insides and has her hounds put the corpse back where they found them."

"That's disgusting."

"It is and the dread that comes from finding someone dead is just as horrifying. But I don't think it compares to when she's hunting you. Her existence causes you to panic when she's nearby, makes you freeze when you're trying to calm down, and can induce hallucinations." A small sigh came out, "Can't say I had fun in her maze."

"Did she catch you when you were sleeping?"

"No. Thankfully, Owen and Missiletainn took turns to make sure that didn't happen. But she did drag me away while we were heading to the Gracidras's den to gather survivors as we thought the fight was over."

"So, you were off-guard, but in armour. If she relies on trickery, she couldn't have been that tough."

"I wish, but she had half of those people who had died, powered up on dragon magic that she didn't need to be tough originally – she had every advantage. So, when you realize the power she has over you and try to fight against the hopelessness, you hear her. The hum that has been following you but can't tell how far away it is. Looking through the dense fog, trying to get the upper hand to see if you can strike first when suddenly, she's got the tip of her bladed arm caressing up your spine just to show how pointless the armour on your back really is."

Éabha gave out a giggle of discomfort, my storytelling on point. "That's awesome. Not for you, but…"

"You and I have very different opinions of what is awesome."

"I like scary monsters, from a distance usually, but I can still appreciate them."

"You and Azarias have that in common."

"He clearly knows how to enjoy life."

"I'm more of a read-a-good-book kind of guy myself. Oh, that does remind me. There is a bestiary that I'm sure you could find in a bookstore with those monsters and many, many more if you're interested in finding worse things than what I've experienced."

"Oh? What's it called?"

"*Outland Monsters: Types, Abilities, and How to Kill or Avoid Them* by Theseus Fionn."

"Your ancestor wrote it? What a lengthy fucking title…"

"I know…" I chuckled slightly. "But it has more than just Outland Monsters in it. Sections include demons and supernatural creatures, and so far, they all seem very real."

"Useful for you?"

"Very. It's the only reason why I survived the Gracidra in the first place."

There was silence for about three seconds as she changed the subject, seemingly not wanting to spoil more of the book. "So, what's Deigh like? I've only met her once, but not really."

"She's a bit of an excitement seeker, but she mostly enjoys eating as many new things as possible."

"Food is life."

"Food is life…"

"Where is she?"

"Sunbathing on the roof."

"Like a cat?"

"Most likely… Did you want to meet her?"

"I do, but not right now. I don't want to disturb-" A loud grumble went across the room, cutting off her sentence. I stopped staring at the ceiling and looked at her. She caught my gaze before blushing, looking away and leaving me a bit confused. "Don't look at me like that! It's just a stomach doing stomach things…"

"You get embarrassed surprisingly easily…"

"I've never done this before."

"Done what?"

"Invited myself over to someone's place."

"Really?"

She nodded. "Yeah… so this is kind of strange, a bit exposing too."

"Heh, I suppose it is. I've never thought of it like that." I looked at the clock on the wall. "It's nearing lunch, you have any good spots in mind?"

"Huh?" She looked back at me in surprise.

"Well, I'm hungry, you're hungry. You're probably still more curious than a child over who knows what, and I wanted to apologize for ruining your cave and plans for today."

"So, taking me out for lunch is your solution?"

"As Deigh puts it: food is always the answer."

"Do you believe that?"

"Not even a little, but it's all I have to offer and it's better than sitting in this place on a nice day."

"Didn't think you liked going outside since your hobbies that I'm aware of are all indoor ones."

"There are just some habits that die hard, enjoying the outdoors is one of them. The number of times I've snuck out of the castle to enjoy some outside time is impossible to count. I don't think the knights will mind if we go out for a couple of hours following the same rules as yesterday. Sticking together and being watched by dozens of other people but someplace still relatively secluded so we're not caught in the open. Someone is bound to notice something is off if a zealot or Ciar show up."

"I would hope so."

"So, you have somewhere you'd like to eat?"

"Yeah, I have a spot and it's a patio… unless you want someplace dragon friendly…"

"Deigh will find her own food when she's hungry. This is an embassy after all."

00000

People chatted around us at their own tables as the patio umbrellas blocked out the blinding sun. The two of us had our meals already and I was diving into what Éabha suggested. It was a chicken curry as I wasn't a big fan of red meats, and it was quite different from what I was used to. Unfortunately, I wasn't enjoying it as much as I wanted. It felt like someone was watching, not that it was much of a surprise. It was what we wanted after all. Even though I certainly didn't stand out like I had in Absalom as much as red-burgundy hair seemed more common, it was stupid to think that no one would notice the black sheep in the crowd.

People were going to look in our direction, be it they caught my eye colour and thought orange was strange or intriguing, or the fact that I was the only one on the patio without a set of wings. Or at least, started off without having any. There were a couple of Seraphineans that made their wings disappear after a bit, but they were already welcomed by their Seraph brethren. Éabha looked up from her food for the first time in about five minutes as she looked around then back at me.

Suddenly, her four wings disappeared, and she rolled her eyes. "People, am I right?"

"People…" The feeling left slightly, and I went back to trying to enjoy my food. How she knew I was uncomfortable about being watched; I didn't know.

"So, what's with the cape?"

"Eh?"

"You wear it even when you hadn't planned on going anywhere, why?"

"I like it?" What kind of question was that?

"You just wear it casually?"

"It's not weird to wear capes in Absalom. Dragon Knights, as you saw Azarias, Cyrus, and Owen wearing them when we first got here; guards, adventurers – lots of people wear capes."

"Does your sister wear a cape?"

"Not often… but that doesn't mean that I'm not justified to like my cape. I don't question why you're carrying a rifle."

"Says the guy carrying a large blade that could count as a two-handed weapon. At least mine isn't obvious," she scoffed as she pointed at Winterthorn with her fork. "Is it because you're attached to your cape?"

"And what if I am?"

"No need to get defensive, I'm just curious. It must mean a lot to you if you've only had the tears repaired so it wouldn't fray but couldn't bear to have material added to it to completely fix it."

"It does have great significance… yes. It was a gift from my mother even though I wasn't big enough to wear it at the time."

"I'm guessing it was the last one she gave you before she died."

"Yeah…" I shoved food in my mouth though my appetite had left and swallowed. "So, weapons. You build them?"

"I built everything you saw the other day."

My astonishment came out as my eyes widened slightly. "That's impressive."

She shrugged. "It's not that impressive when it clearly had a severe flaw. It's been something I've been trying to get around for a while now."

"You mean not using a magic inhibitor. It takes away defence, right?"

"A significant amount since the defences need magic to be useful and if you add greater interferences to the inhibitor, it requires more power and lowers defences. Eventually it just spirals until becomes nothing more than basic armour. The power needed to keep up with requirements is just gobbled up."

"Besides magic, what else does the armour need to work?"

"Electricity, which the mechanics don't do well with magic."

"Have you tried fusing the magic like you have with your weapon?"

"Yes, it's the reason why the armour worked in the first place. But then interference shows up and that balance is destroyed. It was a miracle that Iðunn didn't stop working when you showed up." She gave a small sigh before perking up. "There is an idea I've had that included a capacity crystal, but large ones are hindering and can become an interference themselves. This becomes a problem when you need a lot of power, like the armour. There is the option of just using my magic, bypassing the need for electrical components, but it would be a waste and risky in the long run if I don't have a capacity crystal charged, even with the newer ones. Or worse, it becomes a mainstream for legionnaires, and they run out of charged capacity crystals in the field."

"Yeah…" I could see how that would be a very bad design flaw. I had seen with my own eyes how even the armour of the Dragon Knights at home, while made to deal with magic interference, sometimes failed. The knights were able to deal with it, but the Seraphineans weren't as hardy, nor did they have dragons.

Her eyes brightened as she got excited again. "But I've been working on something much more interesting."

"What is it?"

"A high firing rifle that mixes the weapons research from Theodora and Domrael's capacitor crystal designs. It's also brought up the many issues that I've had, but I don't want to go and break it either since it's pretty small in size. It took a lot of time to make it the first four times."

"Four times? You rebuilt this rifle four times over?"

"In the last month… yeah. It keeps malfunctioning every time I try something. The first time almost killed me."

"How on Orithin did you manage that?!"

"You hold it pretty close to you and when I tried it… it blew up."

"Éabha…"

"But I now have a testing range thanks to it and I'm not dead. The price to pay for better working conditions!"

I just shook my head as I thought over her problem, back to playing with my food. Her armour and her strange concept weapon both had the same issue, but one was significantly smaller than the other… "You just started to bring about your armour issue a few days ago, right?"

"When you broke it, yep."

"Then maybe… Now I know I'm probably the last person that should be suggesting anything, but how about working on the armour first and work backwards. You might be able to see something there that you couldn't see on the rifle because the parts are too small." There was silence as I looked up from my plate to see her staring at me. "Did I say something wrong?"

"No, I'm just flabbergasted that I didn't think to try it and you took no time at all to suggest the idea."

"I do have some decent problem-solving skills," I stated, a bit cheekily as I grabbed my glass for some water.

Suddenly, a wave of negative energy came into my senses. I snapped my attention to it, up to the top of a nearby, low sitting roof behind Éabha slightly. I set the glass down. Someone in dark clothing stood there, seemingly doing nothing. I narrowed my gaze.

Were they pointing-

A glint of a scope came as they shifted, purposely aligned so Éabha couldn't be in the shot.

I started to get to a stand, realizing what was happening a bit too late. A bolt struck the upper left part of my chest. A scream escaped as it exited slightly out my back. I staggered, tripping over my chair as people started to scream and panic. The ground was hard as ever as I landed. Éabha came around the table as I tried to sit up, my breathing constricted slightly. Pain shot through my veins, the bolt coursing its magic through my body with ease. Harsh coughing tried to break through what obstructed my airway as I was leaned against the patio wall, out of sight and nearby. Blood came out, running down the side of my chin and covered my sleeve.

The bolt must have hit my lung… and who knows what else.

I didn't dare remove it and neither did Éabha as she applied pressure with a rag a waitress left behind. Blood covered her hands, an affect of the bolt to hinder clotting, as her calm expression was cracking. She looked towards where the bolt had come from as someone else came over to help. She quickly told them not to leave my side.

"Éabha, wait-" I tried to stop her from leaving, blood getting in the way of the full warning. She ignored me as six wings appeared on her back and she left swiftly. I peaked around the wall to find the culprit leaving.

"*I'm on my way with an antidote,*" Deigh said through the link and I got up, painfully with the help of the wall. "*Wait-*"

"She's going to get herself killed," I growled, starting after her and abandoning the Seraphinean who was trying to help with a small thank-you. Éabha dropped to the ground a building over, looking towards the alleyway with her rifle.

I got to her relatively quickly using the unfortunate fact that I was used to the world of dizziness, bleeding, and pure determination to stop what was going to happen. I put a hand on the corner and followed her barrel to a cloaked figure that matched that of the zealot I had met in Siofra. They had their hands up in surrender – a surrender I didn't believe for a second. Éabha looked at me in surprise for a moment, but it was more than enough time as he summoned a glowing ball from the air, Dagdian magic reaching my senses. He clicked a button with his thumb.

It was a magic bomb.

I pulled Éabha around the corner, out of the alleyway and covered her as we hit the ground. The bomb went off, causing a loud ringing in my ears. The building next to us exploded outwards, sending debris and glass flying, some of it hitting me. Traffic turned into a mess. A pole was hit way too close, dropping right next to our heads. The screams of people registered as the ringing started to die. The dust from the bomb and the building was settling along with other debris and I waited a few moments before rolling off her. I leaned against my arm and side, resting a bit on my back slightly, trying not to stab the bolt back out again. The cuts and scratches from tiny wounds bled onto my sleeves with ease as nothing blocked their paths.

The world was much fuzzier than what I was comfortable with as I started coughing again.

Éabha sat up before looking down at me in disbelief and shock. "Why'd you do that?!"

"Because it was a zealot," I muttered out with a rasp before a groan escaped my lips. My arm holding me up almost dropped me as a pain in my side registered in my head. "They… they don't like being cornered."

"You didn't need to be a shield! You were shot and-" She stopped giving me hell as we turned to the new aching spot, just under my ribs. The white cloth of my shirt was shredded and quickly dyeing red and dripping onto the sidewalk. A large shard of glass covered in blood was sitting on the ground between us. "Oh gods…"

"I've had worse…" I grunted out, trying to be optimistic as I put pressure on it to the best of my ability. A hiss came out. It hurt. "Are you okay?"

She gave a small nod, her colour starting to come back, and I gave out a slight sigh of relief that my breathing could handle. I winced as the bolt's magic entered my back.

At least only one of us got hurt today, and it wasn't the squishy Seraphinean.

Deigh dropped down on the street as the sounds of sirens came to our ears. Éabha looked up at her, startled at her arrival. Deigh shook her head as I gave her a cheeky grin and she turned back to Éabha. "Give this to him, I'll check the alleyway."

The girl didn't argue as my partner passed her the vial of liquid and walked over us. She opened it for me, and I sat up with a lot of difficulty, taking it from her, and downed it.

A gag came out at its repulsive taste. "This stuff is so gross!"

"Then perhaps don't get shot with an Outland bolt next time," Deigh growled back at me before tsking in disgust. "Perfect, they're gone."

"Where'd they go?" Éabha asked, innocently.

"There, there, and over there…"

Éabha went pale as I dropped back onto the ground, my arm giving out quicker than I anticipated and landed in a warm liquid. "Aerrow?!"

"A medic would be…" I started shallowly; blood dripped back down my throat cutting off the rest. An unhealthy cough came out and blood splattered onto the pavement, adding to a growing pool of red. The movement caused a sharp pain to rip through my side again and the world grew dark.

Chapter Fourteen: The Garden

Atlamillia looked at the box that she was delivered in the garden. It wasn't a big box, but a small one, and she knew what laid inside. It was innocent by nature, a better way for her brother to keep in touch... But she honestly didn't want to always be available, especially lately.

It had been several days since the late King and Queen showed up in her study... and she still hadn't decided if she should say anything to Aerrow about it.

They wouldn't have been able to meet with him; he didn't have the capabilities of necromancy nor did he have any residual Godling traits. If they were restless spirits or more prominent, maybe... but they weren't. They had a set time limit and then they were gone.

What if she brought it up? How would he react?

Probably not well... They didn't say anything about him either... just that he was going to die without her.

She gripped the table in front of her. There were some things better off not knowing... for both his sake and hers.

Besides... how would she even explain why they came to her without telling him about what they knew? No one alive except for her and Lucilla knew what her training had been for and as far as she was concerned, she hoped no one would ever have to.

"What's with the world ending look?" A voice said suddenly beside her and a small yelp of surprise came from Atlamillia. "Oops."

"Good gods! Where did you come from?!" Was the only question she could form on her tongue as Aoife looked up at her sheepishly, moving her brunette hair behind her ear.

"The garden entrance, you know, like a normal person."

"When?!"

"Erm... just now? Kinda? I called your name, and you didn't respond." Her grey eyes looked down at the box. "Ooooooh! What is this?!"

"It's a-"

"This CT is the newest model! You can't get this outside of Seraphina for like another month! How?!"

Atlamillia couldn't help but laugh a bit at her enthusiasm, "Aerrow sent it, or one of his knights thought to do it for his benefit… He forgets that some of us have been doing these jobs for a long time and thinks he must do it himself. It's like help isn't part of his vocabulary."

Aoife crossed her arms. "Just because you don't agree with how he does things doesn't make it dumb you know. You two just have different opinions on matters, not that I blame him. He doesn't want to see anyone else hurt."

Atlamillia shrugged. She understood that but being on the other end was aggravating from time to time. She could threaten him all she wanted, but that wasn't the case for everyone. She could only imagine how Owen and his retainers were dealing with it. With a lot more patience than what she had, that was for damn sure, but who knew for how long. Aoife brought her out of her thoughts as she looked at the box, muttering to herself.

"These are a freaking fortune!"

Atlamillia nodded. "Oh, I know. I got a letter from Azarias attached to it saying that Aerrow spent a lot more money than he had meant to on the way there. Something about a book… I'm going to be sending them a care package soon."

"It's a good thing he has you," she answered, somewhat listening as she continued reading the box, off in her own little, excited world. "It has the capacitor crystal that turns your excess magic into battery for itself to reduce magical interference! So awesome…"

"I didn't realize you were such a technophile."

"I'm not really… just… ah, an enthusiast for new things?" Aoife twiddled her thumbs, coming back to reality. "I'm kinda like a bird, it looks shiny and cool, but I don't have a clue on how most of it works. Just what it does."

"That's a lot more than what I know about Seraphinean technology," Atlamillia admitted. "I know what a capacitor crystal is… but as far as the components of how the rest of it works… I'm a prodigy in magic, not technology, electronics, or invention."

"But you're really good at adapting to situations…" Aoife pouted. Atlamillia didn't need for her to explain what she was talking about. "You completely mopped the floor with Dani and I the last time we fought."

"You're doing really well. You only just started learning basic magic and fighting techniques and you're further than most would be by now."

She wasn't listening to her encouragement. "You know how long and hard we planned out our attack? Days! And then you just destroy it and us for the fifth time in a row."

"You made me think about what to do if it's any consolation?"

"Not really… It just shows that I… really suck at fighting in any form. It's really annoying since if I wasn't, maybe I could have helped back in the city. But nooo, I suck and Mór was more interested in keeping us alive rather than fight monsters… Like, what's the point of having a dragon, a literal death machine, if she doesn't even like fighting?!"

She wasn't being serious about being upset, frustrated a bit, perhaps, but not upset.

Atlamillia pondered on her words a little longer. Mór didn't like to fight… "There might actually be a reason why you're finding it difficult to fight in any type of scenario."

"Eh?" The girl gave her a confused look, her sass and excitement gone and replaced with curiosity. "What do you mean?"

"Well, our dragons are just an extension of ourselves in a way. We have our differences, of course, but our skills are based on the same fundamentals. Lucilla and I are powerful magic users, hers being more in favour of fire while I'm more comfortable with light. We have the advantage in range, but we can work well in close combat. We're just not as physically strong."

"Yeah… but I'm not exactly sure what you're getting with this."

"I guess another example to what I mean would be Aerrow and Deigh. They have a nice balance of close and range combat with physical weapons while also having magic as an option for quick, adapting tactics. Both stay nimble, making them hard to pin down even if one of them is a dragon that is over eight metres long. They hit hard, leave, and then hit again. Sometimes they both get too focused on the risks and forget that they can't fight forever." She leaned against the table. "Owen and Missiletainn on the other hand are the opposite with the same well-balanced range and close combat. They are a bit slower, but a hell of a lot tougher. They go about locking their opponents down and decimating them in chaos long before their enemy can attack – their physical attacks are saved for larger things that take more energy to destroy, and they know how and when to retreat even in high-stake situations."

"So, your brother makes stupid decisions if the stakes are high, and your uncle stays the same. What about Dani? She doesn't seem like either of those."

"Dani... is a strange hybrid of them. She's fast and agile, attacks quickly where the strength of her attacks don't necessarily matter, and then retreats before she can be hit even though her durability is scary. Diarmaid happens to be that heavy shield that can swoop in and protect her or anyone else around. Between the two of them, they could make Aerrow's reckless abandon much less reckless if they happened to work together on the same battlefield – especially being an air-fire hybrid. The only better combo would be if she were a water elemental user, and they could fuel each other's magic."

"Alright... so where does that put Mór and I? We haven't really figured out what our fighting style is and... my offensive magic is trash."

It clicked, and Atlamillia felt bad about not noticing it sooner. "Aoife... I have an apology to make."

"Why exactly?"

"I... might have been teaching you incorrectly. The mock battles and lessons that I gave were offensive tactics and strategies because that's what you wanted, and I went with what I thought was best without actually looking to see what you were good at."

"You might have skipped over the part of telling me what I'm good at."

"You're a support – the pinnacle and probably the most important part of an army or party. It's why Mór doesn't like fighting. She knows she doesn't excel in it despite probably being able to take out this castle all on her own. As a light user myself, I should have been teaching you lockdowns, healing, and other assorted tactics to take out your enemy. Not having you cleave around a weapon a good portion of your weight."

A small feeling hit the pit of her stomach at her words as Eadric came to mind. He, too, was a support. He wasn't a fighter, and he was going to-

She stopped her thoughts on the memories before they could present themselves.

Aoife sighed, thankfully not seeing the internal struggle. "But how does that work if I'm alone."

"You get a beat stick, or something similar. Maybe a gun, though it would waste magic to use... I suppose during practice you can use one of Argona's Fangs for the time being to practice magic use in weapons."

"That would be cool, and my aim is probably the only thing that is good. But what kind of beat stick should I try? Like a mace or a morning star?"

"If you want to try those, sure."

"No! I want to try the flail!"

"Er…" She flinched as the idea of Aoife using a flail didn't end well… "Don't take this the wrong way, but you'd kill yourself with that."

"How could I take that the wrong way? It shows that you'd care if I died." She started bouncing up and down a bit. "Alright! I can do this! I can beat the shit out of things with a morning star and heal people!"

Her happiness was a little more than contagious, back to her usual self, and Atlamillia couldn't help but smile at it. "I'm still working on healing myself and other light abilities, I'll see if Helah will mind having an extra student from time to time."

"We're going to learn together with the Matron of all people?!" She settled into a more casual mood like she wasn't the most excited person in Asylotum. "Yeah, I'm down."

"It won't be as often as our little mock battles; there are things that Helah wants to teach me one on one, but I'm sure with her guidance, you'll make a fantastic support."

She nodded happily before looking at the box. "So… you gonna open it?"

"I suppose I should… I won't have to have Jakob or Bretheena coming to knock at my door at a quarter to four to tell me Aerrow called and is waiting in the communications room if I do…"

"Hehe, I guess you weren't kidding about him being overbearing. Does he even sleep?"

"I think? Holly said he does, but I honestly don't know."

"He's as bad as Dani when she gets going… Kind of wish he would have let her go with him for that *extra* support and all that."

"Maybe… but at the same time, I'm kind of glad he was very blunt about who could go with him. The less people that Ciar can get a hold of, the better. Maybe he'll chill out before Owen has to talk to him… though it might get through if he yelled at him…"

Aoife shook her head, but the smirk on her face said that she was amused by the thought. "How is that hunt coming along anyway? It's been three months and still nothing?"

Atlamillia sighed, "Nothing. Ciar just up and vanished like he did thirteen years ago. Plotting most likely and I doubt he'll be gone for much longer."

She frowned as Atlamillia looked over the device she had taken out. The icons on the bottom were written out on what they were, no picture was on the background like she had seen on Aoife's CT. She was going to have to figure out how to do that after she addressed what was going through her friend's mind.

"What is it?"

"Well… I know about the mission because you told me, but… it seems a bit reckless for Aerrow to go, isn't it? He just became king and not that his people need him here all the time as he… gods that book he wrote has more instructions in it than ever necessary… The point I have to ask is, why did he go and not say, you? Not that I want you to ever go anywhere far but, aren't delegations done in times of turmoil through an envoy?"

"He's paranoid that if Ciar came back, he would use me as leverage to get him in the open, or worse, kill me. That is something I don't blame him for. He hasn't been well long enough to teach anyone how Ciar fights efficiently or has had much experience to confidently say that that is Ciar's fighting style." She set the CT down. "And, as I'm sure you've overheard many times between us, he refuses to teach me anything about Ciar, purposely blinding me to keep me from being his envoy in the first place… not that I wanted to go but like I said earlier… it's annoying that he doesn't trust me."

"And your training does require you to be… well, here."

"Yeah, Helah can't come with me on a trip to Seraphina, not with the temple being a possible target like it has been for monsters. If Ciar gains powers through the dead, the royal tomb is an obvious target."

Aoife gave out a growl of frustration. "This is all fucked up! He's damned if he stayed or if he went. And he went… hopefully the other houses don't get on your ass about it. Dani is worried about that the most, she wanted me to tell you that."

"That's what the Dragon Knights are there for if they do start being loud and if Aerrow's trip is longer than expected since the majority, if not all of them, are loyal to the king and the king alone… Thankfully, the houses were persuaded to give him a month and a half as their extension before they can start bitching…"

"He made some friends before leaving at least."

"He did… which is why those houses have expressed their approval for even longer if necessary and agreed that this mission for the device will be worth the minor absence. Speaking of fussy, you said Dani is concerned?"

"Her parents have sent her a lot of requests and missives… She's gone to see them now."

"Is that why you came to see me?"

"I haven't seen or heard from you in days and got a bit worried about you. But partially yes… I was hoping that if Dani didn't return, you could rescue her."

"I don't think that would be-" Atlamillia started before being cut off by another familiar voice.

"Princess Atlamillia, I hope I'm not interrupting." They turned to see Brigadier-Commander Delram Tadhg knelt just off the patio in the grass. She signalled him to stand just like every other time they had formal discussions relatively alone. His mind had never been able to distinguish that while in armour. His formalities were always set at their highest with her even though with Aerrow, he was incredibly casual. Though, it never hurt her feelings. They had only become acquaintances three months ago, on the cusp of friendship if she could call it that. "We've placed all the sensors and examined all the tunnels. They are all online and the war table has been programmed for your viewing pleasure."

"I'll make sure to tell Aerrow the next time I speak with him…" She hesitated on dismissing him as his body language was still somewhat formal. "Is there something else?"

"There were more than a few of the intelligent Outland Monsters inside the less protected tunnels. What they were doing in there is still unknown, but I have a guess and it's not a comforting one…"

"What's the guess?"

"Reconnaissance… only a few of them engaged with us while one always seemed to slip away, going where, we don't know. We've tried trackers on them, but they were always ripped off by it or something else. None of the dragons could track them either, slipping into holes or small Chaos Portals. I'm sorry."

She kept her repulsion to herself as her face remained neutral. Reconnaissance for what purpose? What was the end goal? Clearly for Ciar since he was the only one who had some sort of control over them... but what could they say as they couldn't speak? Were they reporting back to a theoretical Outland Monster that could strategize? "Then it's a good thing we placed those sensors down. Thank you for such a hard mission... has the Eastern Team returned?"

"Yes. They also reported the same phenomenon."

"Anything else?"

"No, my lady."

"Then you and the teams can take a well-deserved rest for the next little bit. With the tunnels under watch now, we can really begin Phase Two which is where we're going to need the knights the most."

He nodded, saluted, and started to leave to give the message to the other knights.

"Oh, and Delram?"

He turned around. "Yes, Your Majesty?"

"Holly misses you, a lot."

He gave out a hearty laugh. "She always does... I'll find her after I report to the knights."

He went through the garden's entrance way, heading for the door back into the castle. Atlamillia turned to Aoife who had patiently waited for her answer. "I'll see what I can do about Dani if her situation escalates... but Aerrow worked really hard to get House Raghnall to cooperate. I don't want to tear that down, but..."

"I get it, it's a complicated situation with everything at such high tensions. You are, after all, asking for the houses to give up most of their guards for Phase Two."

"We wouldn't have to, but a lot of knights died or were injured beyond recovery for service because of Ciar and his onslaught in both the city and the south."

"You could hire a company from Vlirrith. Dani stated that her parents and a few others have done it... for whatever reason."

"Hiring armies would be good on the surface, but Aerrow doesn't want them to levy us into submission. Had one meeting with delegates and was offered a lot of things, all for a lot of gold. I personally think that they are scummier than all the houses horrible traits combined... Both Aerrow and I think Aurelio Vlirrith is plotting something... Whenever he shows up in a meeting instead of having someone else take it, he sounds like he's bargaining."

"That's sketchy..." Aoife commented before eyeing her. "How are you handling everything?"

She frowned. "What do you mean?"

"I wasn't kidding when I said I was worried about you. You just had your first birthday without your dad. The first of Hepseptus was a little more than a month ago and you haven't talked about it even though everyone knows you didn't handle it well." Atlamillia went to argue but Aoife wasn't done. "I think this is the first time you've been outside since Aerrow left, not to mention the kids have been wary to bother you... Did something come up?"

The memory of her parents in the study flashed by, but she shook her head. "No... no I'm alright. Just been busy."

Aoife didn't believe her; she could read her like a book, but the girl simply nodded. "Okay... but if you need to talk to someone, about literally anything, I will gladly starve just to make sure you had someone to listen. Okay?"

"Where's this coming from?"

"Just a feeling... I'm sure it means nothing but, you're my friend and if it's a quarter to four in the morning and you're not sure of what to do or... you know, the darker shit is running through your head, I don't mind."

Her gut was more correct than what Atlamillia wanted it to be... and it made her both upset and grateful to have met the lighthearted girl. "I... I'll let you know if I need to talk."

"You want to process it on your own, I know." Aoife smiled warmly before giving her a welcomed hug. "And there are more of these whenever you want."

She hugged back; a lot more emotionally than she had wanted to give. A well of emotions wanted to burst through, but she wouldn't allow them. The hug lasted a few more moments before breaking.

It wasn't like her father's hugs, or her mother's, or even Aerrow's... but Aoife's hugs were just as cherished.

She swallowed down the grief. "Thanks..."

Aoife grabbed the CT. "Alright! Time for some much-needed fun! Let's take some pictures!"

"Heh, okay... but what happens afterwards?"

"Afterwards... we have a late lunch... because I'm willing to bet you haven't eaten yet."

"Ah... no... I suppose I haven't."

"Dani's right. You and your brother are the same. You forget to eat when you're emotionally stressed. I'll make sure you don't starve just as Dani pestered the two of you before he left."

Atlamillia sighed, shaking her head. Suddenly, the CT rang out in Aoife's hand and her happy tone turned to concern. "Your uncle calling is never good."

"No... it's not," she agreed and took the device that was handed to her. She answered the call and brought it to her ear like she had seen Aoife, Dani, and many others do so many times before. "Hello?"

"Oh good, it did arrive," Owen's voice commented from inside the top part of the CT more calmly than what she liked.

"What is it?"

"I figured that I should let you know that Aerrow was being... him, again."

She groaned. "What did he do this time and how long is he going to be in the hospital?"

Aoife looked at her in confusion. "Hospital?"

Owen sighed, "Not as long as the doctors want him here. A magic bomb went off in an alleyway a few metres from him that took out part of a building, sending glass everywhere. This was, of course, after that same assassin tried to kill him with an Outland bolt."

"Someone tried to assassinate him?! Who?!"

"A cultist. They are a lot bolder in their home turf… that or their leader being called the Kingbreaker gave them more of a drive." The title sounded like he had swallowed acidic nails as it came out. "Aerrow's going to be fine despite the loss of blood from the anticoagulant affect of the bolt. They're just making sure that they remove all the glass and heal him the best they can while he's here. If it goes well, we're heading back to the embassy tomorrow night. It's too risky for him and the other patients here in case another one of those bastards want to commit murder-suicide again."

"I see… How do you know that none of the doctors working on him aren't working for Ciar?"

"We don't. Cyrus hasn't taken his eyes off of him in the operating room and I'm in the observatory just outside with Azarias and Éabha. Orpheal has been fetching us whatever we needed so we don't have to leave. Right now he's out getting us some much-needed food."

"Éabha?" She had only briefly been told about the small Seraphinean Aerrow had acquired who was following him around like a cat. "Why are they there?"

"Three guesses on why Aerrow was being a hero." The voice was so deadpanned it almost made him sound dead inside.

"He was shot and Éabha gave chase, right?"

"Full marks…"

How could she get it wrong? From the bits that she knew… the Seraphinean seemed like the perfect foil to Aerrow's stupid hero complex, whether she knew it or not.

A girl's voice came quietly from Owen's side that she didn't know. "He could have just stayed by, it's not like I can't take care of myself.

"Zealots are scary, he was concerned for you," Azarias commented. "And they had a bomb."

"He's the one that let the guy get the bomb off by distracting me! Someone could have died because of him."

"A zealot did die, remember?"

"That's not what I meant!"

Atlamillia sighed, quieting the argument from the girl she presumed was Éabha and Azarias. "Anything else I should be made aware of?"

"If he called you again this morning at his usual time, then no, you're informed of everything," Owen answered her, sounding just as impressed as she was, but the argument seemed to have settled.

"Nothing on this altar then?"

"Nothing as of yet."

Great... "Thank you for taking care of him..."

"You know it's never trouble. If it were you instead of him, I would be here all the same."

"I know... but I should still say it."

There was a bit of noise on his end before he said anything more. "Ah, hospital food... you'd think I'd be used to it by now."

She couldn't help but giggle before sighing. "Okay. I'll let you eat... Hope it tastes good?"

"It's hospital food in Seraphina... it's blander than cardboard."

"Hey... not all of our food is bland," Éabha said, but it wasn't as confident as she had been earlier. "It's just a preference a lot of people prefer here."

Owen just sighed again, saying goodbye, and ended the call. She looked at her CT screen and tapped the red button on it.

Aoife, unable to hold back her curiosity, asked her question. "Is everything okay?"

"Besides our king being a colossal tool and that whole 'not knowing when to retreat' I said earlier being proven once again... everything is fine." Atlamillia shook her head. "I don't see what Dani sees in that idiot."

"She likes the heroic types; can you blame her?"

"A bit. What's so great about having a relationship with someone who has an unconscious wish to die?"

"Life insurance?"

Atlamillia looked at her friend in shock. "Okay... wow. That was dark."

"That's the only answer I got other than she wants a good guy and heroic types tend to be selfless, the opposite of her suitors."

She went to argue but it fell flat. "Yeah... I suppose that's not a bad reason... Um... pictures I guess?"

Aoife nodded, going along with the much-needed distraction, and they went about the garden before heading out into the city, exploiting the bit of free time Atlamillia had.

Chapter Fifteen: Gone Fishing

Azarias opened the door to the embassy's penthouse and Cyrus walked in, wary of anyone who could have come in unexpected. I followed in afterwards, barely waiting for him to give the clear and Owen wasn't far behind me, locking the door behind him. I flopped onto the fluffy chair; the night buildings were shining through the windows for a moment until more lights were turned on. Papers laid about the table in front of me and I grabbed one, reading it to be of an altar, but not of the one that was found in either cave.

I turned to Owen. "Any luck on figuring out what's in the cave?"

"You just got back from the hospital after spending thirty hours there and you're already trying to do work," Owen scolded with a growl. "You need to rest, not work. Doctor's orders."

"I'm fine-" I tried to insist but he wasn't having it.

"No. You need to rest. The only reason why Orpheal cleared you to leave was because it wasn't safe for you to stay there any longer."

I gave out a small sigh, knowing about the zealot that had tried to traverse the hospital and got caught. Unfortunately, they killed themselves before they could be captured. How though, I wasn't sure, nor did I want to know. "Just tell me what you know."

He glared slightly but obeyed the order. "Literally nothing."

"What about the text on the walls? It's like the text in the temple."

"They seemed to be nothing more than scratches, despite the similarities. But if it is text, it's too eroded away for me to make sense of it as I'm not familiar with it. Solomon would have though, that was his area…" A sad sigh came out of him as he couldn't finish his sentence. He pinched the bridge of his nose and I looked away in shame at the thought of Father's death. "I honestly have nothing else I can tell you. There is nothing for you to do. Nothing on the zealots, nothing on the altar, and the Zerach still has issues that require you, but it's too risky right now to head over. Perhaps tomorrow afternoon will have higher security in place, but that is a serious maybe."

I set the paper down, not realizing how stressed he was over everything. "Sorry. I shouldn't be rushing things and should have realized how difficult everything is. It was selfish."

He gave out another sigh, different from earlier as he sat on the couch. "It's not your fault entirely. You're just trying to do your job and help with ours, but it does get in the way."

Yeah, it probably did…

"And that's not even mentioning how bold the zealots have become. Who would have thought they would attack in broad daylight like that, with Outland bolts no less?"

A small scowl formed. "It was a possibility that I should have considered…"

"Considered or not, knowing what that zealot gave away with their attack – we were thinking about them wrong. They're an organized chaos and that is incredibly difficult to prepare for. There are things going on that we have no idea of both with the zealots and this kingdom. We cannot risk trusting anyone in the Directors' Demesne. They are too suspicious and keep too many secrets. None of Orpheal's people except for Naftali and Solaria… Gods, these scientists are shrewder than anything else with trying to overthrow each other and one wrong move could get you killed. Especially now that we know that someone gave permission to that zealot to enter the demesne and follow Éabha from her house."

"Wait… why would they watch Éabha?" I asked, looking over at him in shock and confusion. "She has nothing to do with any of this and as far as anyone was aware at the time, we knew each other for two days. We literally only conversed over the course of a few hours."

"They wouldn't have known that she was conversing with you unless someone told them which places everyone but those closest to her on the list of suspects which is… a daunting list of people."

It made sense… she didn't talk to anyone outside of Solaria, Naftali, and her father, and I doubted any of them would risk getting her hurt if they were Ciar's cultists, leaving everyone else that we had passed on our two outings. These people were just plain difficult. Even if they weren't part of Ciar's following, they could be using assets available to take out competition. But how would they even get the information that Éabha and I could possibly be something akin to friends just from us walking through the embassy and the front lawn?

My thoughts wandered to the other issues. There wasn't anything about the altar either, no one seemed to know what it was for and it didn't look like there was any recorded history of the matter in Seraphina. Then there was the Outland Dragons that was just as mystifying as the first two issues.

Orpheal's and Owen's discussion came to mind back in the hospital that apparently the meetings they had were fruitless. The directors were quick with their answers either knowing nothing about the tribe's anger, or they weren't talking.

… There might have been someone that would know at least about one of the problems presented.

But… that required going against Owen's wishes, even if it was for every intention to make his job less stressful than it had already become.

A small sigh came out as I struggled on what to do.

I didn't want to be anymore of a burden, but I couldn't send him just in case they knew of the title he carried, and he wouldn't let me go if I suggested it. I doubted Zegrinath would even speak to Cyrus or Azarias. They didn't know his first language and if one of them accompanied me, I doubted it would end well for anyone involved as it would be seen as an attack. The only thing that was an issue to the horrible plan was where the tribe called home. I knew vaguely where it was, but that was a lot to cover and Deigh and I did not have that time to pick and guess.

Owen might've though…

Dammit…

I could stay and we get no answers, or I could go and risk getting Deigh and I killed.

But there was so much to lose, and our time was running out, that I was certain. I wasn't sure why I felt it as so, but I did. The feeling, once I addressed it, was getting worse, knotting my insides almost as much as my dilemma did on what to do.

"Is there a map of the kingdom and area?" I asked, making my decision.

Owen gave me a strange look. "Possibly… why?"

"I want to lay things out, maybe there is something we can't see."

"That's a pretty good idea." He left, heading to find a map.

He came back not too long afterwards with a large map of the kingdom and a good portion of the land and lake around it. Domrael Hill was expanded on the back. Cyrus got me a pen. I started marking X's on where we came from, the building that we passed on the way by as a way point, the northern side that we met Orpheal and the heaviest side of the attacks before flipping the map over to mark the embassy, the Directors' Demesne, and where the cavern was. No relation came from them, not that I was really looking for one, and turn to the general to get the information I was really looking for. "Is there anywhere else notable?"

"This block here is where the attack happened," he started, taking the pen from me, and marked it on the map before turning it over. "This X here is an old research station that was abandoned a couple of years ago, the three of us helped patrol the path between there and the city from monsters and dragons to ensure the equipment wasn't damaged."

"Which is why it wasn't being attacked like the kingdom was – no one's there?"

He nodded and circled a mountain to the north that stood out somewhat on its own compared to the other mountains around it. "And the Megalona Danguis Tribe lives here. The only things that relate are the dragons that attacked the north, which is closest to the mountain, and the caves with the altars were close to the borders of a capital city if it was made after Domrael Hill became the capital two millennia ago."

"So, if it was made before, it's a coincidence that it's nearby..." That was something interesting that I hadn't considered. Another question to ask if I could talk to Zegrinath if he knew of these altars. "Alright... well, that was worth a shot. I'll turn in for the night now, call Atlamillia to see how she's doing... Before I leave though, is there anything else?"

"I don't think so..." He passed me a surprised glance. "You're actually going to get rest?"

No. "I'll try, but if I don't succeed, I have a skill to learn."

Owen relaxed greatly. "Thank you..."

I simply nodded before heading up the stairs to my room. I closed the door behind me as Deigh laid out the armour quietly, waiting for me to buckle up the rest of hers.

00000

The air was cold as we flew towards the mountain that was well within sight in the dark night. Monsters seemed to be few and far in-between, mostly attacking the upper part of the island kingdom we had left behind. They didn't seem to notice or care about our low flying to keep from the eyes of those who may have been protecting the border or interested in murdering me. If they had, they certainly hadn't kept up.

Monsters disappeared entirely as we reached the space around the mountain like an invisible wall kept them at bay. We descended closer to the mountain, but nothing gave indication that anyone, let alone a tribe, lived there.

"*Maybe this is the wrong place,*" Deigh muttered quietly, the stillness was unsettling.

"*They should be around here somewhere... The lack of Outland Monsters suggests it.*"

"*Perhaps... but we can't spend all night out here. Owen is really worried and so am I.*"

I knew they were. I tried lightening the mood a bit. "*It's probably not that strange for a king to be shot at, at some point.*"

Deigh did not find the cheekiness amusing. "*There's being shot by a normal bolt, and then there's being hit with an Outland one.*"

"*Good thing I moved when I did.*"

"*You should have ducked. Do me a favour and do that next time, or better yet, you sense a bolt, you hide.*"

"*Great ideas. If it weren't for that zealot, you would have never thought of them.*"

"*You're unbelievable at times, you know that?*"

"*Aw, love you, too.*"

She went to start giving me sass when something moved in the darkness. We went silent as she slowed her flight path to a stop. I looked around. Nothing moved, but we both felt something was watching. Five, large Outland Dragons appeared, seemingly out of nowhere, and surrounded us as their throats glowed a purple light.

I skipped Ori and went straight to Ancient Dragon, hoping to stop the assault. "We're here to see Zegrinath!"

The dragons stopped their attack as one drew closer to me. Deigh grew rigid, her scales standing on end, but didn't attack despite every sense of her wanting to do so. Orange irises practically glowed against black eyes as the dragon looked me over with a snarl, showing off her teeth and fangs that were much larger than Deigh's.

"And who do you think you are?" The dragon growled threateningly in the same tongue. Her voice didn't make her sound very old, but her physical assets made her question effectively intimidating. "Coming to our territory, demanding to see someone while clad in armour. We should kill you here for even breathing our tongue, Creatures of Light."

"I apologize for the unfriendly appearance, I would have sent a letter asking if we could meet, but I didn't think a messenger would have delivered it. My name is Aerrow, the King of Absalom."

"A king? You're nothing but a child."

"I didn't plan on being king so soon, but life isn't fair that way," I growled out slightly by accident at her scoff and changed my tone before I pissed her off further. "Zegrinath mentioned that the Seraphineans started a conflict with you, and you retaliated. I want to know what they did."

"You aren't even of their kind, yet you come here on their behalf? How stupid and cowardly the Creatures of Light have become."

"Not on their behalf. I'm trying to get down to the truth and the only one who is going to tell me that, is him. He knows who I am, ask him to see if he wishes to see me. If he doesn't, we'll be on our way, or you can try and kill us… but I'm not really looking to die tonight; I've already had two close encounters this week and would like to leave it at that."

"Bold of you to make humour of a situation even when you are most certainly at our goddess's gates… Can't say I've come across a Creature of Light that has done that before." She turned to one of the other dragons and they left, disappearing back into the darkness and the dragon looked back to me. "We shall see what Zegrinath wishes, but don't expect any quips to save your life. You're amusing, but not *that* amusing."

I remained silent. I didn't want to push it.

The seconds turned to minutes, each moment becoming more tense than the last. The three other dragons came in and out of sight, patrolling while their leader barely moved from her spot in the sky. Her attention fully on us. Then, her head turned slightly.

The dragon that left, came into sight next to her, speaking quietly in a lower female voice, "Cindreiss, Zegrinath will see them."

My nerves relaxed a bit as the leader gave a small nod. "Continue the patrol, just in case he brought any friends… I'll escort them in."

"Is that wise? They killed many of us the other day."

"Only out of self-defence," Deigh stated, barely shy of bitter spite. "We didn't come here to kill anyone, and you attacked us first…"

"We just came here to talk." I tried to calm down the venom that was about to form between the three of them, hands raised.

The dragon named Cindreiss looked me over before looking back to her companion. "Zegrinath trusts them enough to see them for whatever his reasons. If they do attack, feel free to eat them."

"As you command."

The other dragons disappeared, leaving Cindreiss to eye Deigh. "Follow, Orithina's Spawn."

"*I would have never thought I could be insulted like this,*" Deigh commented as she followed the Outland Dragon at her slow pace. "*I'm a living emblem of our kingdom.*"

"*That's probably why she trusts us even less… She knows exactly who Argona and Theseus were.*"

"*That doesn't mean that's who we are. I'm a bit more prideful than what Argona was said to be… and you're a squishy, little pushover.*"

"*Well don't tell her that or she'll definitely eat me.*"

"*Yeah, probably.*"

Our discussion ended as we went through a cave entrance and down a large, dark tunnel. The tunnel ended after a few minutes to an abyss with a dim light and around us were Outland Dragons doing typical dragon things. It was something I should have expected but didn't. They were eating together, sleeping on warm rocks, discussing things, all communal or on their own – just like any other community.

Lava pooled unexpectedly at the bottom of the hollow space, giving light to the mountain interior as a waterfall flowed down the left wall into the darkness.

I didn't realize that there were still active volcanoes in the region, but perhaps it wasn't an active one at all. It was possible that it was something else that I wasn't aware of. Outland Dragons wouldn't live in a hazardous environment, especially not a volcano. They weren't fire resistant, at least as a whole. Like Absalomian Dragons, only a handful would have been.

Cindreiss flew out of the large space and into another tunnel lit with purple flames of dark-fire magic. The tunnels went farther down into the earth before levelling out. The space opened again as green and blue dragon stone glowed on the ceiling and walls, reminding me a bit of the tomb except there was no mosaic here. The floor was that of crystal, melted to create a smooth surface, but along the walls, the geodes were left to continue growing in their full, unrefined glory. Two tunnels went farther in but were as dark as the entrance way into the mountain.

Cindreiss landed, directing Deigh to do the same. She followed, and I got off. My boots clunked against the floor, the sound echoing unnervingly in the silence. I highly doubted that it was a trap, but in the case that it was, I didn't stray too far.

Claws clicking came to my ears on the crystal surface from the right tunnel and it wasn't until Zegrinath's snout was graced by the dragon stone light that I realized he was there at all. The glowing orange eyes, much like Cindreiss's appeared next, followed by purple and black scales that glowed with excess power. His red tints weren't visible as the scales weren't raised in defence and fury like the last time. A small gesture came from his wings and Cindreiss bowed, leaving the three of us alone.

Zegrinath spoke first in the silence, "I should eat you for forcing a retreat."

"I'll be honest with you, this is the third time since arriving that someone has threatened to eat me and it's getting old," I replied, my mouth moving faster than my brain, switching to Ori as the words were harder to find.

Deigh corrected me. "Only the second time. Cindreiss only threatened to kill you."

"Close enough…" I sighed and a minor hint of amusement was displayed on the large dragon for a moment. I got my act together. This wasn't the time to be making remarks, even if my tired mind didn't want to filter things through and I went back to Zegrinath's native language. "I appreciate you hearing me out."

"I was a bit surprised when I heard you, of all Creatures of Light, had requested to see me," he started before lowering his head down to me, all amusement gone and replaced with a suspicious glare. He switched back to Ori. "Why did you come to my home, descendant of Theseus? You should know your family is not well received in this mountain, so why?"

I matched, happy that the conversation was in a language I was more familiar with. The last thing I wanted to do was translate something wrong like I had with the Cleansing Gift. "Well, I'm not my great grandfather, for one. And for two, I knew the only person you would see would be me."

"Because I told you of such a minuet detail, you just had to fish for the truth... Strange King you are indeed."

"Yes, and I have a few questions, but I wanted to start with what you were talking about. What did the Seraphineans do? I have spoken with the Lord Director, both him and my general have talked to the directors and none have said or shared anything about offence to your tribe. They said that they've retreated from even leaving their island for the last three and a half months."

"Yet, you do not believe your allies?"

"People lie or say nothing at all to keep friends when they've done something wrong," I stated bitterly. "I trust my general and the Lord Director due to some recent events... but no, I do not trust the people under him. Are they lying or are you creating a pointless strife with nothing to gain?"

"It's a shame that it's not your allies you turn your trust to, but an enemy."

"I have no quarrels with tribes who only want peace. My enemies are those who wish to harm my kingdom and my ally kingdoms with no just reason such as hordes and monsters. The Megalona Danguis Tribe has never been one to attack with such animalistic purposes. I've only been told good and remarkable things about your people and the few that exist on Yasuquinn, so I know that there is a reason behind your attack. I do have to apologize though for my actions and the actions of my knights against your people. It was in self-defence, but that doesn't mean it was right." I took a small breather. "I hope knowing why it happened at all, there can be a way to figure out a solution to right what was wronged. Hopefully to never have this happen again."

Zegrinath pulled his head back, still looking down at me. There was a moment before he gave a small nod. "I sense you are telling the truth. But I suppose I shouldn't have expected anything less from you, Strange King."

I looked up at him with slight confusion, mostly at the nickname more so the words that came before. "I don't know what you mean... You have every right to distrust me."

He didn't answer, blowing it off as he continued with what he had to say. It made me realize why Éabha hated it when I did it. "By Valrdis's Law, you came seeking for the truth, and so, it would be wrong to deny you of it. The Seraphineans came to our mountain and took our children. We do not know how or why, but even through all the precautions, they did it three separate times in the last three months and the whelps' scent led back to that rock in the sky."

Three times?! "They were just gone?! Nothing to even…"

Zegrinath shook his head, his eye contact went to the geodes next to us in agony. His voice wavered a bit from it's deep and rooted position, threatening to crack as it softened, "None. The latest napping was two days before we met and they took my only child, Tad'Cooperith. My mate was driven with grief to find him – it led her to go to the kingdom, to demand for his return. She was killed before the rest of my people and myself could arrive. We don't even know if she was able to speak before she was blasted from the sky. The first casualty, and she was not the last…" He turned back to me, anger and grief were not hidden in either his face or voice. "I will not rest until my son, and my people's whelps are home. I will not be convinced that they were killed just like Vothedissith was until I see their bodies with my own eyes. This, Strange King of Absalom, is why we attacked four days ago. We want our children back."

Tears stung my eyes which took a great deal of effort to hold back as I looked to the floor.

How could anyone do something like that?

It didn't matter if they were from a different place… a different people… They were still kids!

And for what purpose? Seraphineans were known for two things, religious rituals, and science… and only one of those had the use for living subjects. Especially ones who wouldn't even be able to fight back let alone fly away.

"That's…" I was a lost for words and Zegrinath filled them in with a few feelings that I was trying to sort out, and what he most certainly felt.

"Disgusting? Disgraceful? Pathetic? To come here without valid cause and not fight us head on but to slip in the shadows where we are supposed to be safe from your kind. Yes. It is all those things and more."

"I'll find out who did this and bring them to you. Find your children and bring them home. This is far from anything I could have imagined… Children don't belong in the crossfire, to think otherwise is monstrous. They are supposed to be safe with their home."

"I'm glad that even a Creature of Light has this sense of morality as we do… You have received your answer, what were your other questions?"

Right. I had almost forgotten… and frankly, even asking now felt inconsequential compared to the subject that was presented. I cleared my throat, going ahead with them and treaded lightly. "This probably has no matter to you, but a… friend and I stumbled across an altar inside the island. It's an old altar. Really, really old; older than any records we've managed to find and a similar one was recently found in Absalom. Both used a living sacrifice at possibly the time of its creation or when it was in use, and recently, someone was murdered to activate the one back in Absalom. I don't know what it did, but it was trapped to keep anyone from seeing it. The one in my kingdom had been destroyed and buried under rubble, but here, they had an undead guardian protecting it – something a Seraphinean wouldn't be able to do naturally. Both had markings on the walls, scratches my general said, but humoured that they could be words as they looked like something on the walls of Orithina's Temple in Siofra. Unfortunately, Owen doesn't have any idea on what they could be. He mentioned that my father might of, but he was killed three months ago."

"And you believe that I would have the knowledge of these altars and scripts?"

"I was hoping that, yes. Outland Dragons live a long time, if not forever, which is far longer than any Creature of Light does. According to our books, your people hold onto past stories far better than we do of times far before our records."

"You were brave to come here, it's good to know that your bravery isn't forged with complete stupidity."

I wanted to make a remark, but I stayed silent as the leader thought over what I had said.

"There are many altars that have been created, lost to time, to deities and monsters alike. Did these altars have six indents, something that a stone would fit into?"

"Yes. The one in Absalom still had its stones. Each one seemingly from a different kingdom."

He narrowed his gaze to almost a glare. "And one of your people removed them?"

My throat went dry. "Y-yes. Elias and Mazaeh thought that the stones were interesting, not thinking that desecrating an ancient relic was a bad idea."

"A terrible idea at that. Probably the worst mistake they'll ever make, and I doubt that they even know it," Zegrinath growled in irritation. "Those altars are seals. They are not made for worship. Six of them were made across the world and were meant to be left alone, forgotten, and hidden from your kind and mine."

"You clearly have not forgotten."

"Valrdis is very open about answering questions that my kind asks, so long as we do not disrespect her wishes such as finding and desecrating seals. She's a very vengeful goddess, but her sister is worse. If your people lived so closely to those locations, Orithina should have told your leaders about the great devastation that could happen if those seals were to be broken and left unprotected for them to be so readily available."

"Except they weren't so open... at least at one time," I muttered, pondering. "The one in Seraphina seems like it was inside an underwater river, long dried since its rise to the sky millennia ago. Absalom's was sealed in a mountain until something recently, knowing that it was there, broke through the rock. This allowed, at the time, two teenagers to find it."

"That... is very peculiar..."

Wasn't it ever... "How do these seals work? What are they sealing away?"

"The seals are to keep the Daemonias Realm from spreading its taint into our realm."

Taint? How? "Valoth mentioned that the Daemonias Realm was a different universe; that it housed demons, but he didn't say anything about the Daemonias tainting ours. Just that the demons were interested in getting in."

"Valoth probably didn't think it was important to say as the seals prevent their contamination despite demons managing to slip through the cracks. They are not perfect in repairing the damage caused by the two goddesses' fighting, but they do their job."

"He mentioned that Valrdis and Orithina broke space during the First God War..."

"What the god said was accurate."

"He is a god then?"

The dragon nodded. "I'm sure you could tell that he isn't one of your Light races if you were face to face with him."

"He looked like a Dagdian, but his presence was like my father's one moment and hidden the next… It would also explain how he knew about other places, written stories over millennia."

"He's not always on Orithin. His power is being able to leave this universe to others – he helps when and where he's needed."

"It'd be rather useful if he was here helping now…" I sighed, turning back to the original subject to someone who was. "What else is there about the seal?"

"I know how they came to be and only that a Creature of Light of a specific region can be the only ones that can remove the stones of that region. They cannot be tainted by the Daemonias… but even though that the stones were removed, this should not be enough to break the seal. Weaken it, perhaps, but simply placing them back into their position would effectively protect it."

"So, there was something else done then…" I didn't like the implications of what he was presenting. "Anything else?"

"Unfortunately, that is all I know of the seals. I do not know of what lays inside the Daemonias other than demons or how that realm can taint ours. But clearly there is something in there that our goddesses do not want in this universe."

"Maybe the scripture says more."

"If they are the seals, you already know the Language of the Gods."

My head, once again, tilted in confusion. "I recognize it, but I have no idea what language it is, if it's a language at all."

"How do you spell your name?"

"A, e, r, r, o, w…" I trailed off on the last letter as he bit his left claw, causing black blood to drop onto the crystal floor. "Ah, what are you doing?!"

Zegrinath didn't respond with words as he wrote out the same letters as the letters on the walls, Aetherian, and the temple, but much clearer and across the floor, stopping after the sixth one: △◇▽▽△◁. "You may know how to speak our tongue, but it seems like you have forgotten how to read it. This is your name in Ancient Dragon, the Language of the Gods."

"This… this is the same letters on the walls, on Aetherian… and it was Ancient Dragon the entire time?!"

"Possibly a bit eroded, depending on how well that seal was preserved physically, but yes."

I was so mad at myself, my words stopped working. I knew the language the whole damn time, but I didn't know it because I hadn't practiced. And I didn't practice it because it was associated with dragon magic – which made me forget how to read it and then forget why I forgot it in the first place.

At least, my speech retained… a small blessing.

Deigh patted me on the head, lightly, but I flinched as I already knew the words she was about to say. "There, there. You just have to relearn it and that won't take long to do. You can thank the trauma later for helping you meet Zegrinath."

"You're not helping me here, Deigh…" I sighed and she stopped trampling over any sense of pride I had. An amused look appeared on the Outland Dragon's face once more and I stood up straight again. "You have helped a lot. Thank you."

"I only helped because you saved my people from further loss and didn't take my life when you could have." His expression darkened. "But I suggest you take this information and do what you can then head home before you're caught in the crossfire."

"Crossfire?"

"My people and I are not letting this go any further and are preparing. We will be back, and it will not be as diplomatic as our last visit. I will break that shield and we will slaughter all who get in the way of finding our whelps."

"Wait, hold on-"

"You have seven days come daybreak before we start our search. If you are not gone, we will kill you and your knights should you intervene. Do you understand, Strange King?"

"I… yes…" Would I do the same? For my kid, yes… I'd burn every barrier in my path for them. Somehow underneath how awful the visual was, it seemed justified. There was a line… and that would cross it. I needed to give a chance to the kingdom. "If you get a scent before then, please give the kingdom a day before you assault or even in the middle of it – if I find them, we'll need a way to get them to you."

"I will allow twelve hours after I sense Tad'Cooperith and cease our assault, after that…"

It was fair game…

I wasn't optimistic on the survival rate of the whelps on top of being able to find them in such a short time. If a kid got kidnapped in Absalom, the first twenty-four hours were crucial. Anything past that… kids were usually found dead. Someone had kidnapped dragons three separate times – if it was for science, that meant they needed more test subjects…

Tad'Cooperith was the latest bunch, so there was still a chance.

But it had been almost a week…

I held back a scowl at the dreaded thought. "I'll do everything I can to find them."

"Strange King, I wish to believe you, but unless you hold that promise; I will only see it as worthless breath."

He knew the odds…

I jumped onto Deigh's back somehow under the weight of an entire nation possibly being destroyed. "I'm not leaving the south until I figure out what happened to them."

"You have been warned."

"Yes, but I'm tired of seeing people die, physically and emotionally. Yours is no exception."

Chapter Sixteen: Fire Sugar

Reeving, upset, and tired… all of what was said ran through my head the entire way back. Zegrinath had Cindreiss's party escort us most of the way, keeping Outland Monsters at bay, but part of me wished they hadn't. It was a feral part of me that I kept in check.

I took a small breather, driving the less than moral thoughts away. I couldn't let my emotions dictate my actions, even if it were against monsters. It was how mistakes and accidents happened and both the whelps and Seraphina couldn't afford that. Calm and cool like the freezing air was going to be my reference to be, especially when I had to confront the directors.

I didn't know what their reactions were going to be like, whether they would cooperate or be difficult – anything that could cause an act of spite was on me. But… surely for their kingdom, they would… Oh who was I kidding? It took forever just to get some of my houses to cooperate on the same goal and some of them had seen the destruction that Ciar and his zealots had brought. What would the directors do in the face of an if? If the tribe broke through. If the dragons made it to the capital… Just a bunch of ifs… but I had to confront them regardless. One of them had to know of something, even if it was just a whisper.

The attack on Megalona Danguis Tribe wasn't done by one person, that much was clear, but it certainly wasn't that of a random civilian either. It was calculated and being in such a high-profile kingdom, everyone was connected if they were doing something precedented… Even if it was immoral. Research and creation were the pride and honour of Seraphina, anything different or new would raise someone's reputation and to do that, a director would know about it for praise, funding, or even job opportunities.

It was just a matter of who wasn't talking or needing a trigger to jog the memories if it slipped their minds.

Maybe Azarias and Cyrus needed to be more persuasive…

Gods I hoped that wasn't going to be necessary…

The Outland Dragons left us near the island, but stayed low like we had earlier, the dark of night still holding strongly. We flew quickly after a curt goodbye and thank you. The sooner we got back, the less likely Owen would catch us, and the sooner we could sleep and get started. I really wasn't interested in being lectured about how stupid the idea was and the risks since I already knew them.

Deigh flew up the side of the rock before reaching high into the sky, high above the buildings and in a layer of cloud where she was camouflaged. The embassy came into sight and we slipped inside, back up the elevator to the top floor. In a matter of minutes, the darkness of the room was all that there was, both of us out of armour and ready for bed. Well… I was, Deigh passed out almost as soon as I got the armour off her.

She was growing again to be as tired as she was.

I stared at the ceiling, unable to sleep like she had. I wanted to get to the bottom of everything… but it just wasn't feasible at three in the morning.

Eventually though, sleep did take hold, plagued with nightmares, just like usual.

00000

I took a shower after waking up a little later than I had intended; a couple hours later than when I usually got up. My body needed a full five hours, and I was begrudged to oblige. I doubted the others would have minded though. As far as they knew, I was sleeping in.

Deigh and I walked out of the room, dressed but not in a condition that I would have preferred. The shower was supposed to help with the nausea from Asylotum's affects, but all it did was ease it for the moment before it came back. I looked over the railing to see Owen in the common room, alone, and reading what seemed to be a book of a play.

"Are Azarias and Cyrus not up yet?" I asked him quietly, descending the stairs. I got to the bottom by the time he decided to look up from his tale, a neutral expression on his face. But, knowing him my whole life – he was far from neutral. He was angry.

"Azarias and Cyrus left to go find CTs for themselves."

"Did something happen?"

"I don't know, *Sire*. Did something happen?"

How did he… "What are you talking about?"

"You weren't where you said you would be," he growled, his anger was barely contained. "I set a security system around the penthouse in case someone tried to break in, and it turns out it was activated when you came back in this morning. So, mind telling me where the hell you went?!"

"Out, nothing danger-"

He interrupted me, standing up. "Not in armour it wasn't. For fuck's sake, Aerrow! There are people trying to kill you and you keep taking stupid risks!"

"This one was necessary," I said with a bit of understanding. I knew what I did wasn't optimal, but he didn't understand...

"If it was so necessary then why didn't you talk to one of us?! We're supposed to be protecting you! Your companions in this shitshow of a quest! And yet you can't even bother to trust anyone let alone us! Do you have any idea how infuriating it is to the rest of us that you treat us like we're children?! Not just because you have this stupid complex that borderlines ego that you *have* to protect everyone, but it's also the fact that it makes everyone around you feel inadequate! Solomon gave me the task to protect and help you; and when you run off to who the fuck knows, without trusting me enough to tell me where – that doesn't fucking let me do what he asked!"

I went to defend myself against his words. I wasn't treating... It was to protect-

"Yes, but you just proved his point," Deigh muttered and that defense I had shattered.

I did prove him right, didn't I? I had no idea and now that it was placed in front of me...

I looked away, angry and disgusted at myself for being blinded by my own fears. "I'm sorry..."

He crossed his arms. "You've been a real prick, and while we all understand where it comes from, it doesn't hurt any less."

No, it probably didn't. "Sorry... If I'm being out of line again, please tell me right away. I don't want you to feel or be treated like that because I do trust you. You're my uncle and I've never not trusted you with my life..."

"I'm glad to hear that... I honestly thought that you lost the ability to trust at all."

"No... just the ability to show it," I sighed, a pit formed in my stomach at the prospects of the direction I was heading. "If you'll let me... I'll lean on you more, work on not letting my fears control me... I don't want to become my grandfather."

"You're more than welcome to let us help you," he said, "but don't expect it to be kind all the time..."

"No, and I don't wish it to be. Gods know I need all the help I could get if I managed to piss you off."

"Now you're giving me too much credit," he chuckled slightly, but the undertone was a lot louder. "So, where the hell did you go if it was so necessary that you had to leave without us knowing?"

"If I had told you before hand… you probably would have locked me in my room…"

"There's the lack of trust again…"

This was going to be a hard road to get off of.

"Yes, it will be… but I know you can do it with practice," Deigh agreed, laying in the corner, still tired.

"Have any suggestions?"

"Just remember what your father told you the night before your knighting. Learn from mistakes and grow from them."

"I know it was dangerous, the duty of a king is not always the safest path. Your father told me that when I was promoted by Ruairí as King's General. Some things just have to be done alone… but you and your sister are all the close family I have left if you ignore the children that are my pupils." He ruffled my hair like he used to years ago. "I only want to help and if you need to go on your own, then I'll let you go – but I want to know about it."

"As long as you promise not to lock me in a room if it's super stupid." I grinned slightly, moving his hand off my head, lightheartedly.

He shrugged, innocently. "I promise not to lock you in a room."

"Alright then."

"But that doesn't mean I won't lock you in an area like this penthouse if need be. There are some things too stupid to let you do on your own."

I went to open my mouth to counter before closing it in disbelief. Loop-holed… again.

Owen shifted his weight. "Location?"

"You can't get mad…"

"I promise not to get mad for you telling me."

He was testing my ability to trust… but it was respectable. "We went to the mountain where the Megalona Danguis Tribe lives."

"I'm sorry. You did what?!"

I crossed my arms. "You promised that you wouldn't get mad."

"I'm not mad; I'm furious! Why the fuck did you go to the tribe, on your own, without telling anyone?!"

"I wanted to speak with Zegrinath. He's the only person who could give us some answers. So, we went without telling you because we knew he wouldn't have spoke to anyone else or if anyone came with us."

He furrowed his brows. "What did you ask?"

"Why they attacked and about the altars. And while he knew about the altars, which will allow us to find more answers, the attack is the matter that needs to be addressed now. We need to gather all the directors; I need to speak with them, or this kingdom will fall."

"Fall? What do you think they'll share now even with that overhanging threat if they wouldn't speak about it before? The dragons have already been on their doorstep once, what makes this any different?"

"If they hadn't before then perhaps, they will talk now… but if they don't with words, they might react when I ask them where the whelps of the tribe are. Since you know them better, you should be able to tell if someone is hiding something."

His anger disappeared in a single moment. "Someone kidnapped whelps?"

I nodded. "Zegrinath warned us that he's preparing to raid the kingdom in seven days, starting today."

"Seven…" He broke off, leaving me to see his mind whirling in a million different directions and possibilities. "No… that's not enough time for… One of the directors would have definitely known about this… How long ago were the whelps kidnapped?"

"There were three kidnappings in the last three months. The latest one was a week ago, Zegrinath's son was taken then."

"The odds of him being alive are…" A noise of disgust came out. "Whoever did this, timed the first one and the last one to our arrival."

"Yeah…" I didn't notice the overlap. "We need to find them before they attack. And even if we don't before, I promised Zegrinath I wouldn't leave the south until they had been returned."

"Even if you didn't, I would have pressed the matter of finding them. Those dragons will destroy this kingdom, killing millions of innocent people if nothing is done. Even I can only kill so many. If their first assault miraculously fails, they will be back with more than just themselves…" He pulled out his CT. "I'll call Orpheal to set up a meeting immediately. In the meantime, you should get something to eat."

"I'm really not hungry, it's a bad morni-"

"I don't care, you're eating even if you throw it up."

"Is there anything else I could-" I stopped asking my question as he passed me a look. "Right… right. I'll… be over there… eating…"

"When you're done, we'll fly over, and you can do your duty while I do mine."

I nodded, even though I wasn't sure if he meant done eating or done throwing up. It was a good plan despite that small, missing detail and my need to do something hating it. But it too, needed to be worked on. It wasn't a secret to where my workaholic nature came from either. I went into the dining room to figure out what to eat, a choice of leftovers from an earlier breakfast or cereal. I went with the cereal as the others probably wanted the bacon more than I did.

It didn't take long to make as it was about three and a half steps, and I sat at the table, still nauseous. I shoved a spoonful of cinnamon wheat squares into my mouth as Owen finished speaking with Orpheal, hoping its sweet yet somewhat bitter taste would make me hungry.

It didn't. Introducing food to my pallet somehow made me feel worse meaning that the nausea was strictly Asylotum's lingering effects and not stress. Annoying for sure, but it did mean it would go away sooner rather than later. Hopefully.

He sat across from me. "Orpheal's setting up a meeting in the Directors' Boardroom as we speak; he'll call back when he's rounded up everyone."

"That's good," I answered, swallowing. A small sigh came out as I couldn't enjoy the food. I changed the conversation to a problem that I had in the past and would most likely have in the future, hoping for a solution. "I have a question for a future self."

"I might have an answer for a future nephew," he answered in amusement. "What's your question?"

"How do you enjoy food when things are stressful?"

"Asylotum bothering you today?"

"Very much so… so when something else does, what do I do?"

"For when stress takes your appetite, I find that sometimes, you don't enjoy it, but endure the experience as you think about what would happen if you don't eat. Tends to change the perspective and you feel a lot better about eating."

I raised a brow, not convinced, but stored it away to try it when that time came. It wouldn't help me now as the food that went in would not ease the queasy feeling I had, but that didn't mean that it wouldn't hurt later. It was always better than not dying.

I looked up and found him looking me over, making me frown. "What is it?"

"You look a bit paler today. Let me know if the symptoms don't let up, okay?"

I nodded. Movement caught my eye to the left, and I looked out the window. The day was relatively nice looking out as a Seraphinean Legionary was patrolling the city on the back of a tyraulia. The cannons on its saddle were almost identical to the sketches I saw in the book I was reading three months ago.

Watching the creature fly about made it look quite majestic, but certainly not something I would want to fight against. Phoenix back home was a pain when he was riled up and he was about a metre long and weighed about five and a half kilos; the tyraulia was four times as long and probably over thirty times his weight. The golden coat with its two sets of massive wings of the same colour, the feathers practically glowed as it flew.

It was beautiful to watch.

"It's quite the majestic creature, too bad they only like warm places," Owen commented, observing my distraction. "It'd be a nice unit to have other than dragons; great in smaller spaces and can fly."

"I wonder what it would be like to fly around on one of those."

"Not as smooth as you think it would be. It takes a lot of training…" He trailed off and I glanced over at him as he narrowed his gaze. "But it's a bit curious for a legionary to be flying around with one in the middle of the city, far from the base."

I turned back to the soldier and the creature. "Is it just me or is it getting closer…"

Deigh walked over from her corner, curiously, before a panic ripped through the link. "The cannons are charging!"

"Deigh hide!" Owen shouted as dark magic erupted from him. He flipped the thick, hardwood table and forced the two of us behind it.

The cannons released their energy as Deigh left. The dark shield had barely formed a wall in front of the window and the energy exploded into the room. Glass shattered as the beam was directed around the barrier. The table creaked as Owen struggled to keep the blast out of the way with a grunt. It ended after what seemed like an eternity, things still smashing and shattering as I peeked around the edge of the table and Owen stood up. Tendrils broke from his fading walls, flying towards the tyraulia faster than it could fly away.

The tendrils grabbed the creature, wrapping and dragging it towards us, crushing its cannons. The Legionary screamed as the tendrils pierced through the armour, shutting down its protections, and I winced at the woman's pain. The ability stabbing into you probably wasn't pleasant, but being a light element-based creature, it must have been agonizing.

Owen brought her and the creature to only a metre from the massive hole in the wall where panes of glass used to be. I looked up at him, being completely hidden behind the table, and he glanced at me slightly. "Stay here."

"Are you-" I started quietly, matching his volume of barely a whisper only to receive a glare and I listened to his instruction. "Be careful."

He walked around the table and I turned and found a hole to look through. The general was precise as he removed the Seraph from her mount, bringing her into the embassy and let the tyraulia go. It flew away in terror, not that I blamed it.

"Who are you?" Owen asked cautiously, keeping his distance and the woman in the helmet gave a slight smirk.

"For Lord Ciar…"

Nothing needed to be asked about what she meant as a dagger was dropped, covered in blood. She wasn't too far behind it as Owen released her.

The armour around her legs was let go, allowing the blood that pooled inside from a wound in her thigh to splatter onto the floor.

Owen gave out an uncharacteristic growl before sighing, containing his anger. "You can come out now…"

I stood up and looked around, avoiding the corpse on the floor. The kitchen area, it's glass cupboards and dishes were shattered. A cool breeze went through the room, the shattered windowpane was embedded into the walls and table that weren't protected by the barrier. Metal framing was exposed, some of it bent out of shape or melted.

A reminder to breathe came from Deigh as I let out an exasperated noise, breathing heavily as I registered what just happened.

That was… I didn't even know what to call it.

I turned to Deigh, trying to calm myself as she came out of our room. Shrapnel and glass decorated the entire open area, pieces of it were even embedded in the walls on the other side of the penthouse. "Are you alright?"

She gave a nod as the sound of Owen stepping on glass came from behind me. I turned to him as he looked outside. Sirens started to register from below with the sounds of people screaming in the distance.

"What are you doing?"

He looked back after a moment. "Making sure she didn't bring company."

"I don't think she would have needed it if we didn't see her in time…" A scoff came out. "I used to think that weird cannon thing was really neat when I saw it in a book."

"Now?"

"Now not so much… How did she get a military tyraulia?"

"She either stole it… or my guess, she is part of the Seraphinean Legion. Someone told her you were released from the hospital and were here."

I tsked in disgust. "Now what?"

"We get you someplace safe."

"But what about the meeting?"

"The meeting? Aerrow, we're lucky that charge cannon didn't obliterate us." He hinted at Deigh. "She could have been killed if she didn't get to your room in time."

"Those dragons are going to attack this kingdom; we can't just hide!"

"Yes, and while finding the whelps and their promise is important, so are your lives. We need-" He didn't get to finish as a bunch of embassy security burst through the door that was surprisingly intact compared to the scorched wall.

"Your Majesty! General Sir!" The security head didn't get much further than that as she looked at the gaping hole behind us. "Gods… What happened?"

"She happened with a tyraulia…" Owen answered, indicating the body next to him. "Lock this place down, now. Anything or anyone suspicious, inside and in the surrounding area, is to be reported back to me and my knights; work with law enforcement."

"Yes, General sir!"

"Be cautious," I warned, turning slightly to the woman on the floor before turning back to them. "If there are any more cultists, they might try to hurt others, work in pairs."

"As you command, Sire."

They gave another salute to Owen before leaving, a few of them sticking around to guard the breach.

I lost my grandeur stance and leaned against the table. It creaked under the excess pressure, but other than that, held strong. A sigh fell out. Adrenaline was running dry and the imbalance that Solaria mentioned returned harder than expected. A sense of dizziness set in along with my stomach wanting to throw up despite having barely anything to empty. Unfortunately, I had a feeling that I wasn't going to have time to settle its wants. I turned to Owen. "We should leave a message for those two in case they come back before us and have one at the front desk."

"Where are we-" He didn't get to finish his question as his CT rang in his pocket. "Speak of Valrdis…"

"Orpheal?"

He answered it with a nod. "Orpheal, is it set up?"

There was silence for a moment as he listened before nodding again.

"We're on our way now."

He ended the call, and I asked my question. "I'm not overstepping?"

"No… for now it would be safer for you to be with me in the demesne until we figure out a new location… Plus that other, inclosing problem."

He didn't say the obvious in front of the bystanders and I gave a nod in agreement, walking over to Deigh to check her once more as Missiletainn came through the new entrance. Thankfully, the attack didn't go farther than the main area. Owen left a message with security and we went through the main entrance, leaving the same message with the secretary there. People had crowded around the embassy as law enforcement kept people back and we flew over them, faster than any of them could react.

Chapter Seventeen: What About Dragons?

The green grounds of the Directors' Demesne came into view at the top of the hill. We quickly flew over the gate, the guard not bothering to stop us, and we landed at the building's entrance where Éabha was starting to head inside. She looked up at us in confusion as I got off Deigh, cautiously as the affects still hadn't let up. Somehow, I was still dizzy – an issue to address to Owen once the meeting was over.

She gave a small wave. "Uh… good morning? I thought Owen was kidding when he said you were leaving the hospital."

I shook my head. "I was released last night in secret, only a few people knew about it."

"And you're moving about despite being a bit paler than I recall… Oh! Does this mean we get to work on the Zerach after the meeting?! I mean you probably shouldn't be moving around a bunch as I remember Dad saying you were kept to max on healing while you were there, and it was messing with your sensitivity but…"

I shook my head sadly, stopping her untethered thoughts. I felt really bad for turning down her enthusiasm. "Probably not, there are a few situations that I…" I stopped to correct myself, looking at Owen. "We have to attend to before the Zerach can be worked on."

"Oh… Then what brings you to the demesne?"

"I'm the one who called the meeting-"

"You called it? You're capable of ordering people?"

Ow… "I'm not a push over all the time."

"Then what-?"

"You'll find out, there isn't time to lose," I stated strongly, and she read my expression quickly before regaining her maturity with a small nod. We went inside as she led the way, and I cleared my throat a bit. "I also need to apologize for the other day. I didn't think you could handle yourself, the exact same thing you get mad at your father for, and I'm sorry."

"I forgave you a while ago. I was annoyed, but I also had never faced a zealot before and it's nice to know someone has my back." She looked up at me and frowned. "Did something happen this morning at the embassy?"

"Owen gave me a piece of his mind for my behaviour-"

"No – you have a cut on your neck. It looks like if it were any deeper, it could have been dangerous. I highly doubt Owen did that."

"No, he didn't..." I rubbed the left side of my neck to feel crusted blood and it stung a bit. It must have been caused by whatever made the hole in the table. I folded down the collar of my shirt, opening the tie a bit so it wouldn't rub against the wound. "Something happened, but I'll explain later."

"Why not now?"

"Because you'll ask a million questions."

"It hurts my feelings when you treat me like a child..."

Her words weren't in the same category as the conversation from earlier. "You ask more questions than a child, plus, you're pouting."

"Oh, come on! You pout too."

"Yeah, but I'm older."

"I'll be eighteen at the end of next month!"

"That still doesn't change the fact that I'm still older."

"That still doesn't change the fact that I'm still older," she mocked, once again mimicking my accent with scary accuracy, before blowing out a sigh, giving me a look that I got from the kids when they were begging me to let them do something. I ignored it and she growled. "Gods you're stubborn. Even Dad falls for it most of the time."

"You keep forgetting, there are seven kids back home who try that on me all the time."

"I don't forget. I'm just testing to see how many times it'll take until I fucking succeed in getting what I want."

"The universe will end before then."

She rolled her eyes but remained quiet as she kept her insults I could feel, to herself. She looked back at Owen before stuffing her hands into her coat pockets. Large, glass doors sat at the end of a hall where a large table that seated six on two of the four sides sat in a boardroom. Everyone of the seven directors of Seraphina were there. Three men and three women sat on the longer sides, separated with a chair between them. Some of them had their four and six wings out, others had no wings at all. Orpheal was amongst the wingless, sitting at the head of the table, separated from his peers.

Before we even got to the doors, I could tell that most of them were bored, twisting in their seats while others were on their CTs. The only exception being Orpheal who sat there, waiting patiently, and more still than I had ever seen him be – not even fidgeting. He didn't know why Owen asked him to gather the directors, but he certainly knew it was important. He noticed our approach first, getting to a stand instantly, and we went inside. Missiletainn stayed outside to guard the door.

Éabha took a seat next to her father as I muttered not needing anyone to stand, and Owen and Deigh stood on each side of the door, keeping their eyes on the directors. There were no windows or spires, just the long table and a large screen that sat at one end of the table, opposite to Orpheal. I walked in front of the screen and kept standing as I looked at each one of the directors that sat there: annoyed or intrigued. A bit of both, vastly all intimidating, but I kept my anxiety in check. I stood tall, using my lessons to the fullest to be commanding like my father had been.

We weren't going to catch something if they thought I was a joke – whether or not if they knew anything. I turned to Orpheal. "I apologize for asking this meeting-"

"Yeah, some of us actually have work to do," Iason Marcaigh sighed, interrupting me as he set his CT down, still on. "I don't know how your kin-"

I cut him off, "My kingdom works about the same way yours does – needing people alive. Unless you've somehow conquered death."

The rest of the table sat up straighter in curiosity and concern. Iason was left with his mouth slightly ajar at my response.

Kalla Raith filled the silence. "Are you threatening us, King Aerrow?"

"I'm a little more direct with my threats, Director Kalla. No, what I want to bring up is only accusing whoever is responsible for threatening this kingdom and its people. So please, listen and don't feel insulted if you are not to blame."

Vígdís Verdant flicked her dark green hair over her shoulder. "If you're talking about some Outland Dragons; the dragons happen to attack the kingdom from time to time, just as they attack yours."

"Do you know the difference between a tribe and a horde, Director?"

"Well I wasn't born yesterday."

"Then I can presume everyone here has the competence of at least a two-day old child such as yourself." I received a glare, but she kept silent as I continued, feeling more confident about my position despite being nauseated and dizzy. "The dragons that attacked the other day are from a tribe, a peaceful one, and someone from this kingdom kidnapped their whelps."

A round of surprise came from many of the directors, including Éabha and Orpheal, but a different look of surprise came from Ellis Conchobhair. I passed the notice to Deigh.

"In three sessions, children were taken from their homes and brought to this island for one reason or another. They are going to attack this kingdom in seven days if those whelps are not returned."

"You're really concerning yourself with some whelps over an alliance between-" Vígdís started to quip again but I talked over her.

"Yes, I am. And while some of you might not have morals, people's lives are at risk in this dangerous game that someone started to play; yours and mine. Whoever is behind this has already got several of the dragons of the tribe and Seraph Legionaries killed due to this disgusting act. Why would I risk my people, my knights, or myself if my allies couldn't bother to protect their own people first?"

"You wouldn't…" she muttered, and I gave a hint of a nod.

Ohad Heiðrun broke the silence. "King Aerrow, how did you come across this plot? How are you so certain to accuse anyone in our kingdom of such… distaste?"

"Because I did risk my life for this kingdom to speak with the leader of the tribe. He told me what was going on since one of you has been lying," I answered with a slight growl.

"I thought you said you weren't accusing us of anything?" Embla Achia asked in a higher pitched voice than what I had remembered her having, tears in her eyes. She was clearly scared, and I cut her out of being behind anything. Just from her tone alone, it was clear that she wasn't guilty of hurting anyone. "Why would anyone want to hurt someone let alone children?! And they're coming to attack our home? Seven days is too short of a time to prepare for a planned assault with our resources strained… Dear Orithina…"

"I know, it's why we came in the first place to help with the onslaught you were already dealing with. But with this new development – we're not going to be able to stop them," I told her softer than my tone had been, and she relaxed ever so slightly. I addressed the rest of the table. "I'm not saying anyone is directly involved, but you may know someone who could have snuck into the tribe's mountain. It's paramount that we find them, not just to save your kingdom. Some of them have been here for a week and others for three months, away from home."

"Poor things…" Embla commented softly. "Why so many kidnappings."

"I don't know."

"It's still an if they can break through," Iason stated, and everyone turned to him.

"It shouldn't matter if they do or not!" Éabha spat out. "The fact is that they have to at all!"

"You're not old enough to understand war-"

"This isn't war! This is going to be a genocide if we can't find their kids!"

"If. If they break through and *if* we can't stop them afterwards. There is a lot of land between the north border and us. It's our territory and it will be just them verses us; no monsters other than the few that get through before we repair the barrier-"

"*If* we can repair the barrier," Ohad commented. "They may have planned for that and the only thing they're waiting on is another horde or tribe to arrive as backup *if* they can't break through."

Vígdís scoffed. "Honestly, I think we should let them try, it'd give us more data to build better and understand Outland Dragon physiology with such a body count available."

"At the cost of our people?!" Kalla exclaimed, her tough barrier of detachment breaking. "What the hell is wrong with you?!"

"Nothing because I don't mean at the cost of them, that'd make me an accomplice to terrorism… We can evacuate their attacking area and have them come in."

"And what if they don't come where you expect them?" I asked somehow over the noise and it quieted. "We know for a fact that they are coming, but what if more are kidnapped? They won't hesitate to come sooner – nor can we assume that they will come from their mountain directly to the north end of the island. I've met their leader, he's not a directionless animal, he is on a mission and he knows what he's doing."

"Why would he give you time to warn us then and prepare?" Ellis asked.

"Because I spared his life. He's giving time for me and my party to make the decision to leave before he decimates this island…"

Iason gave out a small grunt, leaning back in his chair. "Honourable… I'll give the monster that. But this might not even be an issue if you had killed him."

"Perhaps, but this also brings up something else. The timing of two of the kidnappings were perfectly matched to when we were supposed to arrive – the person responsible knew when we were coming, it can't be a coincidence. Who better to deal with Outland Dragons than people with dragons and a sure knowledge that we could kill them without issue? This would make room for more whelps to be taken since there would be less adults to guard them, especially if one of us had happened to kill the tribe leader. They could turn any preparations on the dragons' side worthless and force a reckless attack, a gateway to let whoever kidnapped those whelps have many more test subjects, and it wouldn't be just whelps the next time."

There were no expressions that had deviated as silence reigned supreme – either not knowing at all, too afraid to speak in case they were found guilty for, at the very least, treason, or thinking about how anything done could be undone by a vile agenda. I looked over at Owen, hoping he could help.

Owen gave a nod in understanding and came forward slightly. "Perhaps if no one knows of the whelps, then maybe one of you can explain how a traitorous Seraph Legionary knew that His Majesty was at the embassy and not at the hospital like the news stated, and tried to kill us with a tyraulia charge cannon?"

Orpheal's stillness ended as he looked between the two of us in surprise. "You were attacked at the embassy?! That should've been impossible and with one of our tyraulias no less!"

I gave a small nod. "It was an experience to say the least… but if it wasn't for the general, it would have succeeded."

"It shouldn't have happened at all," the leader continued in anger and contemplation. "No one at the hospital would have known about your release since I'm the one who released you and had the paperwork delayed… no one else outside this room could have known."

"That was my conclusion as well," Owen agreed, staring daggers at the table. "The only people who would have known about his release and where we would be are all sitting in this room."

A look of disgust came from Ellis for a single moment while the others in the room became even more perplexed, but it was enough. I walked over to him slightly but kept a safe distance away to let Owen take care of him if he tried anything. The Seraph shifted, leaving a sweaty palm print on the table. "Director Ellis… do you have something you wish to share?"

The man said nothing.

Suddenly, a surge of light magic came from him, but before Owen or I could react, a flash of light radiated from him, blinding everyone in the room and pushing us slightly away from him. Minor screams came from others, Owen's more painful than the surprise of the Seraphineans as I recovered, slower than what I would have liked. I went to draw my sword when something cold and metal was placed against my forehead, lifting the crown slightly and caused me to freeze. The light pulse died as my eyes adjusted and I looked up to see a silver barrel. I followed it to the hand of Ellis who held the gun to my head.

My heart skipped a beat at the thought of his finger twitching in the wrong direction. Dark magic secretly and swiftly made its way into my senses, but the tall man expected it as I doubted he could sense it. He lifted his other hand slightly in response; a glowing magic bomb in it as he looked to my left, stopping the power in its tracks. "This is active Owen, I let go and everyone here becomes paste."

Owen growled as the magic disappeared, a bit of blood was running down the side of his chin. I wanted to ask him if he was alright, but Ellis started talking again.

"Now if anyone moves even a muscle, magical or not, the kid gets his head blown off." No one moved from what I could tell as he turned me around so he could face the rest of the room, leaving me blind to them if I didn't have Deigh.

"Ellis," Orpheal started as the director in front of me tensed slightly. "There is no need for-"

"Your mouth has more than a few muscles; I suggest you keep it shut."

"You have control-"

"Save the speech because if you do say another word, your little girl is also in the line of fire."

Orpheal stopped talking as Deigh's view confirmed Ellis's threat. Éabha was standing behind me.

I could feel her scales bristle at an idea. *"I can set him on fire."*

I didn't get to answer as Ellis was already ahead of her.

"You can try something, Deigh, but can you breathe fire faster than I can pull the trigger? Missiletainn?" Neither gave him the satisfaction of answering as he looked around the room, keeping me at arm's range, daring me to move. Luckily, I wasn't stupid enough to think he couldn't see me in his peripherals. "Now, here's how this is going to work. You're staying here and we're going to take his royal highness with us. But don't worry, he won't have to worry about anymore assassination attempts."

Where was he going to go?

Who was us?

What was he-

"Aerrow! Ohad-" Deigh started only for a screaming Daemonias Portal to appear next to me, scaring the majority of us from the screams.

I went to ask what she meant by Ohad when it came to a sharp halt as a painful prick entered the side of my neck where the cut was. A cool liquid poured from it and the world became fuzzy.

"Aerr-" Deigh's voice was cut off as the link shut down.

I staggered, my legs not being able to keep me up as drowsiness set in.

A set of arms caught me from falling too far. I looked up in anger to see Ohad dropping an empty needle, a surprised smile on his face. "This usually puts someone out in a matter of seconds… This will be exciting to have you as our guest."

"I'm not going anywhere," I growled out a mutter, pushing him away, and getting to a difficult stand. The only saving grace was that I was used to the visual impairment making it much easier to adapt to whatever he had injected me with.

The gun wasn't pointed at my head anymore as Ellis hadn't expected me to get up, and a bright light filled the room behind me before he could shift, blinding him. Owen's magic came into my senses again as I attacked, kneeing the man before disarming the gun by twisting his wrist. The gun was sent flying to the other side of the table as Ellis screamed out in pain. He backed away a few steps as black tendrils wrapped themselves around his legs. He grabbed where his other hand used to be, blood leaking from underneath. I turned around carefully to see the hand in the grasp of a different tendril, carefully being brought over to Owen, the ends of the wrist shredded at a molecular level.

"Thanks for the hand," Owen said too happily towards Ellis and struggles came to my right.

I looked over and saw Deigh had Ohad pinned to the ground, claws threatening to rip him wide open. An unsettlingly growl came from her, "Where are the whelps?!"

Ohad was quiet and she took that as an invitation.

"You drugged my partner, give a reason not to attack you."

He remained silent and she put pressure on her claws, poking his skin through his clothes and he screamed.

"Deigh, that's enough!" I ordered her and she removed the tips from him. I walked over to her, though it was becoming incredibly difficult to stay awake. "He won't talk if you kill him."

"I will never talk, and our lord will kill you," Ohad told us, and I turned back to him.

"I highly doubt it will be before you talk when you have the pleasure of meeting Cyrus and Azarias."

He did seem to know their reputation as his eyes grew wide in fear. I turned away from him as the doors opened behind me. Security came into the room and arrested the men, leading them out.

Owen came over, tossing a deactivated bomb in his hand. "It was so kind of them to give us such an expensive gift."

I sighed with a small smile, shaking my head at his attempt, feeling my legs ready to give out again. I stumbled as I tried to compensate, and he caught me. My response had a heavier accent than what I wanted. "Tanks…"

He quickly grabbed a chair and I sat down; my head felt heavy, the rest of me, a bit warm. "Are you doing alright?"

"I don't know…"

He looked over his shoulder. "Orpheal, assistance!"

The Lord Director came over immediately, pulling another chair over and sat on it, sticking his hand on my forehead then put two fingers on my neck, pressing on the wound a bit and I winced. He was not a gentle doctor. "He has a bit of a fever, most likely from the imbalance Solaria warned about… but his pulse is slowing down…"

"Maybe a sleepin'…" My words stopped as I closed my eyes for a moment and felt myself fall. Ciar appearing in the abyss. I jolted awake, a gasp escaping as Owen caught me again.

"Easy there…" His tone was calm and soft, my grip on his arms eased. "You're going to be okay."

"You'll just need to sleep it off," Éabha commented from nowhere, scaring me. I looked up at her as she observed the needle in her hand. "How many purple concoctions do you know of Dad?"

"Just one…" Orpheal answered, taking the needle from her carefully. "They must have got Solaria's Night from our medical section."

"What's tat?" I asked, trying my hardest to stay awake.

"Solaria invented it," Éabha answered. "The amount they had can put out most Seraphs in barely a few seconds, just like Ohad stated. But I guess Absalomians are a bit more resisted to its effects… That's interesting."

"Tat's… great." I just wanted this to be over with. "So, I'll be fine?"

"I'll keep an eye on you, double check the contents of the needle, but yes, if there are no surprises and as long as you take it easy to recover from Asylotum," Orpheal stated. "You think you're capable of standing up? We need to get you someplace safer."

"I tink I can…" I started, feeling slightly better and did get to a stand upon his request, faster than he and Owen were expecting. My legs denied me of farther action as the moment was gone in an instant. They turned to mush and fumbled as the world grew dark for a second. Éabha caught me before I could land on her. She helped put me back in the chair as I gave out a sigh in annoyance. "Never mind…"

"Did you know you're heavy?" She asked me and I looked up at her, not surprised.

"Yer just small…"

"Oh no, I could easily carry you. I was just saying that you're heavier than what your form suggests."

My words slurred. "'ow? Yer barely over a metre-n'a-'alf, maybe tirty kilos? Imma little more tan twice tat."

My struggle was apparently amusing to her as a small giggle came out. "Seraphs are strong, despite our easily breakable bodies. We should arm wrestle when you're not passing out, see who's stronger."

I just shrugged, not having the will or energy to try and disagree. I turned to Owen. "Where're we goin'? Is tere someplace else where…?"

He looked at his CT, many messages were on it though I couldn't read what any of it said. "Cyrus is getting a hideout situated, one where we can train if you want when you wake up and have rested properly."

Did Aerrow want to train?

That was a question for future Aerrow. Current Aerrow was having a hard time creating sentences…

Why was I referring to myself in third person? I looked up to Deigh, expecting an answer only to remember that she couldn't hear me in my head and I certainly couldn't hear her response.

Orpheal stood up. "Let's get you onto Missiletainn. If anyone is wanting to hurt you outside, Deigh would be targeted and you're not going to be able to hold on while she escapes if you can't even stand on your own."

I looked to the floor in disdain. "Okay…"

Orpheal and Owen got me up and Missiletainn lowered himself to help. I held myself up surprisingly well as Owen stayed on, making sure I wouldn't fall off. We left, Orpheal and Éabha walked between the two dragons as they chatted, their words weren't coherent anymore as I focused on staying awake. I wasn't much use if something did happen, but I was too scared of waking up somewhere I wasn't familiar with. At least if I were kidnapped, I would be aware of it – if barely…

The word kidnapped repeated itself dauntingly.

I was almost kidnapped… why? "Why did tey want me for."

"I don't know, but we'll get to the bottom of it," Owen answered, reassuringly, and I looked back at him, surprised that he heard me. "I won't let anyone take you, okay?"

I gave a nod, looking away, trying to keep how terrified I was at the prospect of it being expressed, but it was rivalling the fear that Ciar put in me. It should have been impossible… But the thought of being kept alive… toyed with until I wasn't of use… Possibly trapped within myself.

It was worse than dying.

He placed a hand on my shoulder, squeezing it. "They won't-"

A loud explosion blasted out, cutting him off and scaring me. I snapped my attention away from Missiletainn's black, purple, and yellow scales to the front doors of the main foyer. Two vehicles were up in flames and Deigh rushed ahead with Orpheal; Éabha and Owen called them back with no success. Missiletainn and Éabha went after them as Deigh pulled out something from the fires of the farther vehicle while Orpheal spoke the words, cessarfidh igteine, Dagdian words of power that I couldn't understand. Almost immediately, the fire went out and Orpheal pulled out Ohad, or at least, it was the outfit he had on with the blood marks of where Deigh had poked him. Half of the director's face was blasted off with a giant hole in his chest.

Orpheal placed the corpse on the ground before turning to Deigh who shook her head.

I looked away from the scene in disgust, knowing what happened. "Dammit!"

Chapter Eighteen: Caged

I groaned, a headache was well established, and I sat up, waking up from a dreamless sleep. I should have been content, not having nightmares, but I didn't feel rested. My head tapped the headboard as my senses of Deigh set my concerns at ease slightly. I certainly wasn't feeling great on top of being exhausted, but at least I had the normalcy of her being there.

I looked around a bit, trying to recall what happened. There was barely a memory of getting into bed. At some point, I knew I almost fell off Missiletainn when trying to get off him in the room I was in now, rescued by Owen. He then helped me with my pauldron and sword belt after I struggled with them and told me to take off my boots and cape… But other than that, I was wearing exactly what I was in before, feeling gross, and remembered nothing else, not even how we got to the safe house.

How long was I out for?

Scanning the room, it seemed to be a few levels up as the windows showed the roofs of other buildings, but it wasn't as high up as the embassy. I got out of bed, feeling a bit nauseated, and looked outside. Wherever the safehouse was, it wasn't near the Directors' Demesne, let alone anywhere I recognized. I turned from the window, finding a new set of clothes waiting for me on the table, and the bathroom door open.

A smile of gratitude fell on my face.

Owen was a saint.

A purr came through the link like a warm blanket, "*I'll tell him you said that.*"

"*Deigh…*" Gods I missed her. I started to walk to the bedroom, finding a towel waiting inside. "*What did I miss?*"

"*Owen is finishing plans with Orpheal on how to continue working on the Zerach as it has become a top priority besides finding the whelps. I'm sure the subject of defence will come up again in no time – they keep going back to it without fail. Domrael Hill and Rath Hill are close to the border but aren't being evacuating as they would be easier to defend. However, other places that are along the border have been given word to leave; they're moving inland.*"

"*I don't blame them…*"

"There's been a lot of tension as they're trying to spread resources accordingly... Azarias and Cyrus on the other hand are taking a much-needed break from almost pulling an all-nighter and are sparring in the other room, waiting for you to get up. It's so much more entertaining than listening to these two."

"You're bored? You could be helping them..."

"I said my piece a while ago and all they're doing is recycling problems with no answers... not to mention the amount of apologizing that happened is astounding."

"At least we retained his friendship even if I wasn't the nicest person in his boardroom... whenever that happened."

"Yesterday. Orpheal would have been over earlier, but between making sure you weren't drugged with something else, getting details on defense, and us going through different avenues to collecting more information on the corrupted directors – this has been the first free moment to settle out thoughts everyone's had."

"Yesterday was when all that happened? What time is it?"

"Don't know. Pretty sure your CT is still in your pocket."

I followed the hint and found the CT where she said it was and sighed, starting to undress. I pulled off my shirt before actually looking at the screen. It was ten to three. *"Seventeen hours?!"*

"More or less; between not following Solaria's advice and her concoction, you were out cold. Didn't even mutter in your sleep."

"I don't recall me talking in my sleep."

"Sometimes you do, more recently for a ton of reasons, but you aren't loud."

"Do I even want to know what I say?"

"Names generally. Two of them are pretty common, two other names a little less, and one name that you haven't really said in the last few months, only starting again when we left Asylotum."

"One of them your name?" I asked as I turned on the shower, and a purr of pride came from her. *"You must be pleased."*

"Sometimes, other times you make me worry."

Then I guess the other names were probably that of my parents, Ciar, and… her.

"Being in Asylotum kept your mind occupied where you wouldn't think too much of her after the first month. But since being removed from most of your duties, Theodora has come up again, yes."

"Before Orpheal leaves, can you ask if Solaria has a forget person concoction?"

"I'm not doing that… You'd hate losing those memories even if they hurt."

Perhaps, but I'd probably be able to start dating, much to Owen's and the kingdom's pleasure. I left the conversation as it was and got in the hot water.

00000

I walked out of the bedroom; a pullover sweater kept me warm as the t-shirt underneath just wasn't enough after the shower. Deigh was viewing the sparring match on the other side of the glass wall between Azarias and Cyrus. Steps came from above and I looked up to the right, seeing Owen coming out of a room, pretty high up, and easily being that of an entire level that could have been a floor, but was only a loft. The walkway was glass with two metal rods being the guardrail and a Seraphinean sized, metal, spiral staircase connected the two floors.

He looked down at me. "Good morning, sleeping beauty. I see you found your way around the room."

"Afternoon… and I did. Thank you…" I walked over to the couches as I heard him descend the stairs and found papers scattered across the tea table between them. They weren't the same ones on the altars, but the backgrounds of people. "Anything that gave reason for those two to join Ciar?"

"Unlimited research is the going theory. They both found the rules restrictive and tried to bend them whenever they could," Owen said as he arrived at the sitting area, tossing a small box at me. "This is for you."

I looked at the box in my hand. No markings were on it and I opened it, finding tablets inside, two different types. "What are these?"

"Anti-nausea pills and pain killers. I grabbed them from the medical centre in the Gordin wing. Figured you'd might want them when you got up. The pink ones are for nausea, same dosage as before for both."

I had never been so happy to hold medicine. "Did Deigh tell you that you're a saint?"

"She did... but I don't mind hearing it more often."

"Well I thank you, Saint Owen." I popped one of each and dried swallow them, not wanting to wait to find water somewhere. A small sigh came out. "What's all over the table?"

"These are all the people that worked for Ellis."

"That's a lot of people..."

"Ohad has just as many, in that box there." He indicated at the box next to the couch. "Both had families, but they apparently kept their allegiances a secret. Ellis's wife is a priestess at the local church and hearing that he was worshiping a false god... well, you can imagine how she took it."

"I'm guessing not very well... and that means there hasn't been any leads to follow on yet. Deigh told me that you and Orpheal were discussing plans to defend the kingdom."

"It's looking really bad right now," he admitted. "There was nothing in their labs, their research here held nothing of suspicion and the people closest to them have been clean in person, hence the paperwork here."

"A different location then..."

He nodded. "And knowing that Ohad could summon Daemonias Portals, that could be anywhere."

"Probably not far. They would have to be able to get to their location and back to Domrael Hill without suspicion meaning only one portal. Do we know the maximum distance a portal can go?"

"Only a rough estimate of it being far using the portals made a couple of months ago. But we also don't know if skill is correlated to distance like it is for Chaos Portals and Teleport Glyphs."

"No... I guess we don't. What about the portal that was made? Did it lead anywhere?"

He shook his head. "It was closed before anyone could investigate."

"But... it should have stayed open longer than that. It was open when we left the boardroom, they couldn't have closed it since they couldn't use magic when they were detained."

"It closed not long after that according to security. There were also the murders meaning that there is at least one other zealot if not two still on the grounds. It's most likely someone higher in the food chain of command, but there could be more."

"So, we learned nothing from this other than someone on the grounds has more authority than them and they might not even be a crazy zealot on top of it," I sighed in frustration. "Could just be a regular, functional being who joined the cult for the same reasons that these two did."

"We're steps behind them in finding the whelps, but a step ahead in keeping you safe."

"Believe me, I'm more than thrilled to know that... but it's only going to be a matter of time before those whelps are dead, and/or they find this place."

"I've placed wards on the underground exit which would keep anyone out if they happen to find it. Right now, Orpheal is the only person who knows where we are. So, it'll be easy to pinpoint the cause if a zealot does find this place."

That was a fair conclusion. One solid point in a vast of unknown variables.

"It's a precaution over distrust," he reassured me and continued. "After dealing with all that... Orpheal and I came up with a way to get that Zerach here without someone noticing since we have to get it functioning in case the whelps aren't found in time."

"I doubt you're going to have someone fly the damn thing... it'd be kind of noticeable."

He gave a chuckle. "Not to mention damage the fragile thing. No, we're going to Teleport Glyph it here. Orpheal knows how to use glyphs so he can also get Naftali and Éabha here as they don't. The idea of using a trolley and a Chaos Portal was played with instead of just appearance, but apparently the machine isn't stable enough to introduce that much of a foreign element to it."

"So, it might get damaged when it arrives... hopefully nothing horrible to fix, we have less than six days to get it working." While the idea was a bit risky, it was smart all the same. No one could track a portal or a glyph, just who used it and its radius distance. "And the embassy?"

"The embassy is fine along with its residents. No one else came out as suspicious and no one else got hurt... Though, a lot of suspicious packages have been delivered. They have been disposed of accordingly. Any mail that is not suspicious will be delivered through Atlamillia if its from home and as far as I'm aware, no one in Seraphina is wanting to send safe mail to you, but if they wanted to, it would go through Orpheal – the mail is being delivered to the demesne."

"Good but… gods… That's so excessive if not a bit confusing. Do they want me dead, or do they want to kidnap me?"

"We've determined that there are two groups of cultists. The ones dedicated to Ciar and Ciar alone are the ones that want to kill you and just destroy everything around them. They are being called Prime Zealots thanks to Azarias. Then there are the ones that follow him for their desires, experimentation or whatever he has to offer, this grand group until further notice wants you alive. Our lovely knight has yet to think of a name for this group since its too broad to know everyone involved."

A small laugh came out, though it didn't stay. "So, Primes and… let's call them Boffins cause it's a fun word and we only know of scientists for this group… they're competing?"

"Ciar more than likely has ordered his followers to kill you on sight, or at least, subdue you. The Boffins… that is a fun word, anyway, the Boffins are fighting for your survival. There haven't been any cases of clashes in public yet, but I wouldn't be surprised if the city started to have an increase in murder."

"I used to like being wanted… Anything else?"

"Cyrus looked into the reports over the last bit with local authorities while Azarias spoke with the military and special investigators for any correlations with the whelps. Both found related incidents where several Absalomians have gone missing that were living in or visiting Domrael Hill. They tended to be the kind that could go missing and have no one miss them, but it wasn't foolproof since some have been reported. They have been working together to solve the open investigation, but even with Cyrus and Azarias, there wasn't anything found."

"Absalomians don't just up and vanish without clues… they have dragons."

"The dragons also went and disappeared with them, there has been a theme of hellish screams in parts around the city, but that's the only correlation between the incidents."

"No bodies either?"

"None. It's been going on for about four months now and previously, other races have been taken as well – but that has only been speculated as there isn't an actual connection between any of them and those disappearances have been going on for over a year. So, in reality, it could be different people. There, unfortunately, hasn't been enough information and for what end, if they are all by the same serial offenders, your guess is as good as mine."

"We should focus more on how it lines up with Outland Dragons since they were only three months ago and that lines up with the missing Absalomians to a degree…" I thought about it a little longer, trying to figure out why they would want those subjects. The fly back from Megalona Danguis came to mind as, unlike the trip there, there were no Outland Monsters on the way back. It would be something that a zealot, Prime or Boffin, would have to worry about. Creatures of Light… "Maybe it's not about the dragons entirely, but something to do with the Outland Monsters."

"We know Ciar can lead them to any target he wants, why would he, or anyone else, be interested in researching what is already known?"

"Because I doubt his zealots have such a luxury. They can direct them, put up portals for monsters to smell or sense Creatures of Light on the other side, or lead them with their own person, but we have yet to see them command their own armies like Ciar has. If they had been able to, the zealots in the kingdom would have had assistance when confronted. Instead, they were killed or committed suicide."

"So, why kidnap Outland Dragons?"

"Outland Monsters avoid them, even the group I was escorted with didn't have a single monster to contend to."

"And the closest thing that could be comparable with them and a Seraph would be an Absalomian…" Owen crossed his arms in thought. "But they are different types of dragon DNA. Not to mention the obvious fact that dragon blood, Outland or not, if it isn't diluted into something – is toxic to everyone, including us. Even your blood is toxic and it's only fifty percent."

"I don't know… I'm not a biologist. Perhaps it's the magic. Something about the elements. Absalomians are capable of learning at the most, five of the six elements if they are pure to one element and are incredibly dedicated. A Seraph wouldn't care about those who could use light, but an Outland Dragon is like an Absalomian and can learn as many elements except for light if they are pure dark elemental. Dark elemental magic is their birth element, it wouldn't matter who they grabbed. What would happen if a light-based creature became capable of wielding dark magic?"

"They could boost each magic exponentially on their own and without being limited to attribute. You then add the compatibility of Dagdian magic... That would be a horrible combination to fight against if they survived that abomination against nature."

"And with Ciar... who knows what he can give them. Clearly something that is of value, like a mirage dragon."

"Like a mirage dragon... unfortunately, we don't have enough information on what they could be doing, or any idea on what could be done since none of us are intellects in those fields. Orpheal and Naftali perhaps, but speaking to them about it could lead to risking them further or risk our edge if they speak to others about it."

"You think they'd do that?"

"Scientists, inventors, creators in general bounce off ideas from others, even if they are trying to be secretive. It happens from time to time and it gives them a sight that they couldn't see before. But in this case, it would be unwise to have them accidently bounce off ideas, even vague ones, to someone that could be working for Ciar. Naftali may not be the type to do this, but I know that Orpheal has frequently blown secret projects with your father."

"What about Éabha? She seems to have quite a bit of knowledge and she doesn't talk to anyone really."

"Do you really want her to risk going through other people's research? Because from my understanding, she's bold enough to do so without permission to get answers and while Orpheal has authority, their government is a directorate, not a monarchy. She's ranked by the other directors and could get into serious trouble if she were caught."

"She would be the one to look through every outlet... but is that so wrong right now? This kingdom is under threat and as she so kindly stated yesterday, it's going to be a genocide if those whelps aren't found."

"As said by the other directors yesterday, it's *if* they get through... she'll still be punished regardless."

I sighed, annoyed at how small minded it all was, but understood it on a degree. Her fatal flaw was well acknowledged by the girl and even if we asked a single question, she wouldn't stop. Not for anything except the truth and that could lead to some dark, dark roads such as secret projects, good or bad, that the other directors were working on. "So, how are we going to find out what the Boffin Zealots could be doing with Outland Dragons?"

"Look into the research and theories of all the directors to get any idea on what could be happening."

I raised a brow. "Can we do that? That seems pretty private if the Lord Director's Daughter can't do it."

"We can't do it... legally."

"Then why bring it up?"

"I was going to hack into their databases."

"You know how to hack?"

He nodded. "I can't do it from here, but in the demesne I can. I was actually heading that way before you woke up."

"You were just planning on taking everything they have without filtering any of it? That could be a millennium of work and for all we know, there is nothing you could have found useful in any of it."

"I didn't say it was a great plan, but it's possible that there are answers somewhere and that is more important. Luckily, you were up before then and I got to bounce ideas off you."

"Lucky you... So, you're still going?"

"With filters in mind. It'll still be a lot of work I'm sure. A long time before I'm done since there are four other directors to look into, and if push comes to shove, we can still ask Orpheal about his work, hack into it to make sure he isn't hiding anything if he has nothing to share. But I don't think that'll be necessary. And it shouldn't be too hard to look through all of the data I bring back when you're going to be here with nowhere else to be for a while."

I didn't want to do that at all, but I had really no other options for helping out the tribe or the kingdom. There certainly wasn't an excuse I could use to get out of it. "I'm caged to this building then, eh?"

"Unfortunately, but once things cool down, I'll take you around Seraphina and we can go get you whatever you want."

"I think I want a hat, it's cooler here... maybe a scarf." A sheepish laugh came out at the prospects of wearing such fashion while still in Kalokairtas. I looked back at the sheets on the table. "Have you gone through all these already?"

"Just about. Ellis's finished files are in the box under the table; Ohad's not done."

"Alright, I'll go through them… You go do illegal things. Don't get caught. Éabha told me that they have the death penalty here and it's to be a lab rat."

"You think this is my first time doing something like this?" He asked with a cheeky grin, one I hadn't seen in a long time. "You're so innocent. It's only illegal if you get caught."

"I hoped it was… but I was clearly mistaken since you have a whole motto," I sighed.

"The number of times I used it during my old adventures with your mother and father… Admittedly, some of it might have been more illegal than my phrase could cover…"

"Good Orithina…" A thud came from beside us. We turned to the noise and on the other side of the glass wall was Azarias getting to a stand, dirt covering where he hit the wall a couple of metres in the air. Cyrus was on the other side of the room, walking intimidatingly towards the other knight with a sword in his hand.

"You have those two to go find food or whatever else you need to stay sane…" Owen told me as I didn't look away from the less than friendly skirmish. "Or you can hide in your room and study more if you get sick of them, but you need to rest today – no ifs, ands, or buts, Doctor Orpheal's orders."

"If that's what the doctor ordered… Cyrus seems to be in a bad mood," I commented. "Did something else happen?"

"He's frustrated that he hasn't been able to stop these incidents."

I looked back to my uncle. "He wasn't even there; how could he have?"

"That's why he's angry. He had been elsewhere. The guardian, the outing you had with Éabha, the two directors, even the Seraph Legionary, he would have been able to fry that cannon before it would have gone off." He explained, his cheery grin long gone. "He doesn't show it, but he cares a lot and worries about you. Don't tell him I said this, but you remind him of his little brother."

"He has a brother?"

"Had. He blames himself for not being there when he was killed, and now he's worried that it'll happen again."

"His brother was killed? How?"

"Cyrus comes from a criminal, black market family. He wanted nothing to do with it, but as you've seen, he has picked up a few tricks from those days before he left at nineteen. His brother, your age, stayed behind as things were getting dicey between the other families. Cyrus left and became a Dragon Knight – when he went back to pick up his brother, he found that his parents were alive, but his brother had died during a home invasion the night before. They blamed his death on him abandoning the family."

My jaw dropped slightly. "That's terrible! Why would a parent do that?!"

"They, like many others, are terrible parents who blame their children for things out of their control. They depended on their sons to take care of them when they couldn't be bothered to do the same in return."

"What happened to his parents?"

"They're in Dawne Institution along with many other criminal families… Cyrus got his just deserts, but he still blames himself after ten years. He stopped showing a lot of his emotions and expressing himself after that day. His brother was everything. His light, hope, the reason why he became a knight in the first place…" Owen looked to where the two knights had been sparring. "He eventually became close with Azarias and began to move on slowly. Being his best friend, Azarias brings out the best and worst in him. But it still wasn't enough to close the book… Then, Solomon gave him someone to care for, a piece that he had been missing… He's scared that you'll end up like his brother. And when you stopped asking for help, shutting everyone out…"

I had no words as I looked at Cyrus who was taking out his rage on Azarias who was taunting him. No sound came from the room as to what the brown and green, armour-clad knight was saying, but it seemed to push buttons.

"You wondered why he continued to be your retainer after you attempted to dismiss them? It wasn't because Azarias wanted to stay, Cyrus wanted to keep you safe from yourself. So… keep that in mind. And again, don't tell him I told you."

"I won't… What was his brother's name?"

"You'll have to ask him. I've shared more than I should have but thought it would help you pave out the road you want. Get you to talk more with him. He'd probably like it even if he's a bit reluctant."

"I'll do that, gods know I should have done so a long time ago." I waved at him. "Good luck."

Owen waved back and left. He opened the door next to a set of stairs that left downwards and close the doors behind him. A tendril came from under the door, locking it from the inside.

How convenient…

I looked back at the battle that was happening as Azarias got the upper hand, locking Cyrus in an earthen box. It didn't last long as it exploded and Cyrus sent another blast of air, sending his poor partner flying. I hadn't realized how much pressure he put on himself…

Azarias let him release that stress.

Then to add the behaviour I've been displaying…

I really needed to work on being less of a selfish jerk about the choices I made and fast for them.

I sat down on a couch and started to look through the papers. I turned my attention slightly to Deigh. "How long have they been at this?"

"Over an hour… and they seem to just keep going."

"Have they taken a real break?"

"Nope." She looked back at me. "You're going to ruin my entertainment, aren't you?"

"I'll give them another half hour…" A dreaded feeling entered in unexpectedly and it wasn't because of the time limit or the whelps. "Then I have a new task for them, I just hope it's nothing at the end of the day…"

A hint of concern came through the link at my sudden shift. "As do I… but I'm proud that you're showing that you trust them by letting them go without you to the seal that you're worried about. Oh! Right, completely forgot to tell you."

"Tell me what?"

"You know those books you got a while back, your bestiary, the history book, and the treasure hunt one?"

"Yeah?"

"Well, the treasure hunt book was called *The Seals of the Light Army*. I think it might have to do with these seals."

"But the book is back in Asylotum…" I sighed as I pulled out the CT. I had to ask for assistance anyway. "I'll send Atlamillia a message about it… hopefully she gets it."

"It would be risky for her to send it, considering we don't know if there is another copy running around."

"I know, which is why I'm messaging her instead of calling. She can look into it for us when she can while I get to sit here for the next century, trying to figure out where some whelps are, who is doing what to them, all hopefully before the island is blasted into pieces out of the sky."

"Hehe, oh, it won't take long to go through this paperwork."

"It will if you don't help."

"I can't believe you'd volunteer me."

"Such a shock, devastating really since you have places to be."

"You're a jerk at times, you know that?"

"Says the one who does this to me all the time," I said, putting away my CT as I finished my message and continued reading over a file to find nothing of use and went to the next one.

They all seemed clean on paper. No reason to go to Ciar and no holdings of a place for such research. It quickly became a dreaded thought that it was a waste of time to go through all of these people… but I wasn't going to follow the lazy path. Not when there could be something. Those whelps depended on it.

Suddenly, the door to the training room opened and a groan of pain came to my ears from Azarias. I looked up to see the two knights coming out of the hall, covered in dirt and sweat.

A giant smile appeared on Azarias face as he noticed me. "You're alive!"

I gave a simple nod and he frowned.

"And now you want something from us… what is it?"

"I need you two to go on a field trip."

"And let you leave this place?! Hell no!"

"I'm not leaving. Under practically every circumstance. Owen talked to me yesterday about how awful I've been treating everyone, not telling, or trusting anyone with missions I thought only I could do and how it affects everyone around me… something I didn't realize. I'm sorry… I'm working on it so that I don't do that again and let you guys help more. And while I do, I hope you two can tell me when I'm straying from a good path again because I know I can't do it without help."

There was silence from him and Cyrus as they both, in their own way, judged my words carefully. A sigh came from the brunet. "Well, I'm glad he said something, and you finally learned that lesson, even if its going to be a rough road, but I think we all agree that we don't want to leave you alone either."

"Yeah… but this trip will need both of you to do a video call with the CT… I'd like to go with you, but I was told that I have to rest and it's way too risky. Plus, I know you two can do it."

"What is it you want us to do?" Cyrus asked as Azarias seemed unsure.

"I need you to go to that altar and show me the text on the walls, poke around to see if there's anything weird. I'm going to translate the runes to get a better understanding of what that place is."

"You know the language?"

"Ancient Dragon; just worn down and slightly warped… but it's the language. I'll have a letter translation by the time you get there as I'm a bit rusty, but I can read and translate it afterwards."

"You want pictures too?" Azarias asked and I nodded.

"Yeah, just in case something shows up in the picture and not in person. None of us are necromancers so if there are any ghostly or necromantic magics hanging around, a camera should be able to pick it up if its strong enough – at least, that's what the rumours say."

"Owen said something similar even though he doesn't need help to see that… yet he's somehow skeptic of ghosts."

"And you're terrified of them despite not ever seeing one," Cyrus added, and Azarias gave a dramatic grunt in agreement.

"Why shouldn't I be?"

"Because even if they are real, most of them can't hurt you."

"You've never been attacked by one, I know the stories! Ugh, whatever…" He turned back to me. "What about the investigators?"

"Kick them out and tell them it's our crime scene. We don't know who is on our side and just in case we find something important, I don't want to show our hand."

"And what if they don't leave?"

"I'll let you decide about what should be done… my suggestion is call Orpheal, but I know you two have a special protocol of things and… well, you two just warmed up."

"No, that was a full workout. They can be our warm down if anything happens… speaking of anything happening; what happens if you're attacked while we're not here?"

I raised a brow. "Do you actually believe someone would attack a random building in the city?"

"No, but still, humour me."

"I'll remain unless I have to leave. This place seems pretty big, easy for even me to hide in and I haven't even been downstairs."

"Lab, kitchen, and dining room. It's the ground floor. There is an exit downstairs, leads outside. The main exit though is on this floor and leads to an underground tunnel with a hidden entrance. There is a cabinet in the way of it."

"This building only has two and a half floors?" It seemed like it could have been four Absalomian floors at least just from the one I was on, eight Seraph floors.

"Yep. It's a safehouse. Outside it looks like a shitty apartment building." Azarias hesitated as he thought on his answer a little more. "Okay, not shitty. It's in a decent neighbourhood, but it doesn't hold a candle to royalty standards of living."

"And the ground floor door is locked, yes?"

"Locked, warded, boobytrapped, and seized. No one is getting in. The only way that door works is from the inside by pushing on the obvious seal in the middle of the door."

I gave a minor sigh of relief that I hadn't realized I had been holding. "Okay…"

"Concerned?"

"A bit…" I admitted my anxiety as it boiled to the surface, the fears that came from yesterday. I didn't hold them back like I usually had in attempt to trust them more with my feelings. "Someone might accidently come in here, or worse, someone finds out. I've never been held hostage before, nearly kidnapped as such... I... I'm a bit scared of it happening a second time."

"You don't count Olin's attempt or the Gracidra?"

"Not really. We knew what Olin wanted to a degree and monsters are just as predictable... But this wasn't the same. It was different..." I turned back to the papers of Ohad's contacts, clasping my hands together. "We don't know what they wanted... What they could or would do... Nor do we know what it takes to stop them. We don't even know who they are, just that they are an associate of Ciar which... could mean anything and they could do anything with or without his regard. It's kind of terrifying."

A hand was placed on my shoulder and I looked up to see Azarias with a happy grin. "We won't be long then if you're that worried about being alone."

I just nodded and he started walking away, Cyrus following him. I let them be as I turned back to the work as Deigh's completed pile grew.

"Oh, Aerrow?"

I looked up in confusion at the cheery knight as he practically hung over the railing on the floor above. "Yeah?"

"Nice sweater, purple looks good on you."

"Uh... thanks."

He left and while it was a strange compliment, it did bring a small smile to my face as my concerns fell slightly. Cyrus was lucky to have him as a friend, and... so was I.

Chapter Nineteen: Od Symalum

I finished copying down the alphabet of the dragon language from the picture Atlamillia had sent me and set the CT aside, waiting for Azarias and Cyrus to call me. The list of insults she strung together about me forgetting such an important language put Éabha's mouth to shame. But it was well deserved. As prince, I was supposed to know it perfectly, as king, even more so.

The CT gave out a beep and I looked over to see my sister had sent me another message. I picked it up and read that she couldn't get to reading that very moment or over the next few days but didn't explain further.

I frowned and messaged her back, asking what came up.

Seconds turned into a minute of silence before she replied with, 'don't worry about it'.

Like I wasn't going to worry about it now with such a vague reply. I wanted to press the issue... but stopped, erasing my message I had started to write. I had to let it go if I wanted to get out of my habit of control. Even if I didn't, drilling for answers would have been fruitless as she could easily just leave her CT in a tower on silent and never answer.

It sucked not being in person... but it was for the best – being locked in my own tower so far away. She could handle whatever the issue was without me, she had been doing this for a long time... and it was about time I believe she could do whatever was needed of her to do.

I messaged back, telling her that it was alright and good luck.

I set the CT down, struggling to leave it be and distracted myself with the last few files left of Ohad's list of people.

Nothing stood out. The names, their properties, or their affiliation of how they got into Ohad's circle, nothing even muttered treason. I looked at the final file before tossing it in the box, an exasperated sigh coming out.

None of these people were of any use on paper. There was no paper trail, squeaky clean. Over the next few days, Owen, Azarias, and Cyrus could go and speak to those that worked with the two dead directors if they hadn't done so already... but who knew if there was a trail to follow there.

There was something missing.

Someone was hiding in plain sight and I didn't have a clue who.

Could have been Orpheal, Naftali, or Éabha, though that seemed unlikely… or was it more? Was I just wanting to believe that they weren't followers of Ciar, trying to hold on so I wouldn't lose any more companions…?

I didn't want to go through another situation like Theodora again.

My hand ran through my hair as I thought about the possibilities…

I didn't know what to believe, who to trust outside the people I came with… and yet I was supposed to know what to do when a direction was needed. I didn't even know what I was doing half the time, and it was affecting the people I did trust, or at least, should have. My head gave out a pang, but the medication wasn't through with its cycle, leaving me to suffer with it. The pain was somewhat relieving… a reminder of some sort.

I couldn't let the anxiety control how things were viewed. To let it go down a path that the kingdom had wanted to leave far behind. The fear dictating its overall objective and consuming it.

That was my grandfather's legacy… It wasn't what I wanted.

I may not know every consequence to every action, but I did have people who could help me discover what they could be if I asked. Give me options to how things could turn out, for the better or the worse. Owen, Azarias, Cyrus – maybe Orpheal, Éabha, Naftali, and Solaria here; Atlamillia, Aoife, Dani, and my council back in Asylotum. Even Óðinn if I was feeling daring.

What the hell did these cultists want?

Why was Ciar like this? He looked like a person in every aspect yet acted like a monster. Where was the Seraphinean part hiding underneath the demonic being of the Daemonias? What was his goal?

No one answered except for the soft purrs of Deigh through the link caused by her dream. I looked over towards the open door to my room. I couldn't see her, but I knew she was curled up, cozy, and not stressing over matters that we couldn't control nor answer.

A sigh escaped. If I kept it up, my downwards spiral would eventually destroy her sweet dreams, and I didn't want that.

I took a more constructive approach to ease my mind.

Maybe I could look at a map of Seraphina, something in more detail than the one in the embassy. It wouldn't have been as detailed as it was outside, the preferred amount of detail, but I couldn't leave. It was risky and someone else could do it instead, even letting Deigh wander around the island was too much if someone were somehow able to make whole dragons disappear. This was going to have to be a task left to the knights… a massive task since the kingdom, while not as large as Absalom, was still vast. A lot of things could be underground, seemingly unmarked, and away from railways and covered by trees. If only there was some technology that could see the whole region from the CT… even the whole planet.

Ah… That'd be cool…

A king could dream of putting a camera in space.

Maybe a space program could be implemented once Outland Monsters were more under control. It would have made sharing resources and people more reasonable.

The CT rang, showing off Azarias's name as the caller. I had yet to put contact pictures as the adding his CT number was a last-minute thing on the way out the door. I answered it and it showed his face way too close to the camera. "A little close…"

He adjusted it with a grin on his face, showing a bit of the cavern behind him. "You stayed!"

"Yes…" As if he had any doubt. "What took so long?"

"We had to fly back to Domrael, and these guys took fucking forever to leave."

"I hope that was the only issue with them."

"That and we had to wait for Orpheal to tell them to get the fuck out. And to top it off, they moved slower than a kid heading to bed!"

They were probably just as intrigued about the site as I was, most likely for a very different reason though. "So, what's it look like in there?"

"Oh, dark. The lights are on down here and they have a CT signal booster, so that's nice." The video bounced around as he moved, and the scene changed from his face to that of the cavern as he switched from the front camera to the back. The dried blood was still covering the walls, but it seemed like the undead guardian was cleaned up. "We got: no corpses. That's always a pleasant sight."

He walked over to the small space where the bodies had been stored. Nothing remained other than a sigil on the floor. I looked at it longer but couldn't figure out what it was. "What is that marking?"

"Hmm, I'd tell you if they left behind their notes... Cy! You know weird magic shit!"

A mutter from the red knight came from the distance, but I couldn't hear what he said. He appeared on the video, knelt, and looked at the floor.

"Seems to be a preservation sigil. It's a necromancy ability," Cyrus commented as he stood up, looking around. "The guardian was most likely ordered to place the corpses in here according to these sigils."

Azarias moved the view I had to the walls and ceiling that were also covered in sigils. "But why? Why not just throw the bodies out the hole?"

"Probably fodder to create more guardians. For what purpose? I couldn't say."

"Well the only active necromancer we know of is Ciar," I said as I took some notes. "Unless you have objections."

"Yeah, I got one," Azarias started as he scanned the room with the camera again while I tried to find anything else suspicious. "He didn't have guardians when he attacked Absalom. All the undead he had, were the people killed there and Archelaos. It would have been stupid to not bring a few along to siege a kingdom. Most people don't know what a guardian is, let alone what to do with one when they come up. He would have had a massive advantage against local soldiers until the main force of Dragon Knights came to the south wall."

"You can have a guardian be used offensively?"

"If you target yourself or someone else as its object of protection, yep. But the guardian will fall if that person dies – like another necromancer trying to turn it off or change its master. It's crystal overloads."

Risk and reward... so if the creator of the guardian wasn't Ciar, who set the guardian up? "Is there any information on who the guardian was? If there is a way to tell how old it is, maybe we can pinpoint who made it."

"I'll have Sage ask one of the people up top," Azarias said as they left the small back room. He had the video on the floor which showed no signs of sigils or of words. Just abandoned slots where something was placed a long time ago. "The carvings on this are exquisite... water must have been flowing here for hundreds of thousands of years to get these kinds of-"

"Azarias," Cyrus growled, apparently not interested in the geological make up of the cavern. "Focus on the unnatural..."

"Right… Aerrow, you said that the one in Absalom had something like this, right?"

I gave a nod. "Yeah, the exact same. Stones from each kingdom were supposed to be inside those slots that you like so much."

"Explains the lack of erosion there… Though… I'm still wondering how some stones are supposed to create some spooky seal. To seal what anyway?"

"The Daemonias, but Zegrinath suspects that there might be some other thing inside."

"And we're just going along with what an Outland Dragon said? I know he's from one of the few good tribes but, I wouldn't go about and trusting him at the drop of a hat."

"I don't entirely either, but he has no reason to lie about this and it's the only lead we have. It's not like it hurts to follow it."

"Until we set off a trap or something… I'm NOT sticking my hand in a hole in a wall, alright!"

"I… I'm a bit confused. This isn't a fantasy, adventure story – it's real life."

"Wasn't it Valoth Nor that told us that every story has truth to it? Traps are real!"

"Fair enough… Alright, say that we ignore Zegrinath's help; when I was down there, I was drawn to it. There is something there, a purpose to it. My instincts tell me that the seals breaking is a really bad thing."

"And your instincts are pretty on point when it comes to area disturbances and whatnot… Are you seeing anything we're not?"

"I don't think so… there doesn't seem to be anything interesting about the circle other than it's creation."

"What? You don't find all this blood interesting?"

"No."

"Azarias, the walls," Cyrus stated forebodingly, and my imagination went straight to bleeding walls. "The script here seems more prominent."

Thank the gods… No bleeding walls.

The video moved from the floor to the walls with a bit of a stutter as it lost signal for a moment. Script was written on the walls, some of it harder to read than others, and I started scribbling down the different words as Azarias patiently waited. He stood as still as possible to allow me to make sure I was writing it down correctly. Noises came from the background as Cyrus took photos around the room. After gathering most of the words on the wall that I could, I let Azarias be free to do as he pleased while I translated, looking away from the screen.

The words weren't overly helpful. They weren't in phrases and just seemed to be words of power such as the elements: ⟨△ ⌇∧ ↯ ⊔, ⟨◇▽ △∧△, △◇▽△, and ▽ ↯▽▽△; fontis, nerqua, aera, and girra for fire, water, air, and earth.

⟨△∧⟩ and ⊔⌐△∧⊠▽↯⊔ which was foux and skotbris; light and dark, or it could have meant order and chaos. It was hard to say which meaning it had since it was in terms of magic, and not in general speech. For all I know, it was both simultaneously.

▽▽△⌐⟨△ or drakco came up as well which surprised me a bit. Then I realized that Valrdis had her Black Phoenix Dragon and the Outland Dragons while Orithina had given Absalom her dragons. Then there was Dragazon. Dragons must have had some significance to them when they created the seals.

If they had… there was no reason for Zegrinath to lie. He had pledged it under his goddess, the Goddess of Truth, but it never hurt to be skeptical.

⌐△∧△◇ and ∧▽△ ⌇△∧◇▽; Zotae and Thanatem… Life and Death, those were capitalized meaning they were proper nouns.

Maybe there was more than just some realm of demons trying to corrupt our own. Life and Death gods had to work together to invoke such words on the walls. I doubted it was an easy feat to have such opposites placed within the same seal.

I looked to the screen as a flash came from a camera and the room lit up, but not as much as some hidden script did as Azarias skimmed by it. "Wait, go back to the centre."

"Oh? You done translating?" The chipper knight cooed happily. "What's all the chicken scratch say?"

"Later. Go back to the centre; face the back wall."

"Want me to stand in the circle too while I'm at it? Cy, if he wants me to be sacrificed, don't do it."

"Don't tempt me…" a growl came from somewhere in the room and Azarias sighed.

"And here I thought we were friends." The video moved to the floor as he walked before showing the back wall. "Alright, I'm in the circle of death and misery, looking at the back wall… There's nothing here."

I looked carefully at the wall and found that he was very correct on his statement of nothing being there. The wall was blank minus the words I had already wrote down.

But I swore I had seen something… "Cyrus, can you take a picture somewhere in that direction?"

There was silence for a moment and then a flash. The wall glowed out words for a split second, but it was enough for Azarias to start freaking out in both glee and fear in a bundle of words I could not comprehend.

"Turn off the lights in the cavern," I told them. "Make it as dark as possible, then try again."

"Aw man… It's gonna get real dark. They put a tarp in the doorway… I don't wanna be in this place with no light and freaky invisible writing."

I just shook my head at the antics as Cyrus told him to suck it up. One by one, the lights were turned off and the room got darker and darker. And then, it went black on my end. From the noise though, it seemed like they were still turning off lights. A handy thing to know that the camera's lens was only so good in dark places.

A thud came from their end, followed by a quiet apology from Cyrus before a light flashed again, but the view was off centred.

An oops came from Azarias. "Ah shit… it's dark in here. Okay, round three."

The flash went off again and the words were highlighted much better than before, but they were gone quickly. I frown slightly. "The flash is too quick…"

"I got this," Cyrus told us, somewhere in the darkness.

Suddenly, a bolt of electricity struck the ground loudly, causing Azarias and I to scream. I readjusted my grip as Azarias walked around the steady bolt that stretched from the ceiling to the floor. I almost dropped the CT at how close it was to the camera.

"That's bright…" the brunet complained, "but it works. Here you go, Aerrow."

He lifted the CT so I could see the glowing walls, not as centred as I would have liked, but the seventy-degree angle wasn't terrible. I scribbled down the text that was lined out like a passage:

> ᒐᐃ ᔅᘔᐎᘔᐅ ᐁᐅ ᔅᐃ ᔅ ᐃᐊᘔᐎᐱ ᒐ. ᐊᐃᘔ ᒐᐃᐊᐃᐱᐅ ᐃᐁ
> ᒐᐃ ᐅᐃᐊᐱᐃ ᐁ. ᐃᐁ ᒐᐃ ᐅᐃᐊᐱᐃᐱ ᐊᐊᐃ ᔅᘔ. ᒍᐃᐎᐃᐊ
> ᒐᐁᐃᐎ ᘔᐊᐊᐱᐁ ᐃᐁ ᒐᐃ ᐅᐃᐊᐱᐃᐱ. ᐎᐁᐃ ᔅᐃᐎᐃᐁ
> ᒐᐁᐃᐎ ᘔᐊᐊᐱᐁ ᐃᐁ ᒐᐃ ᐅᐃᐊᐱᐃᐱ.

There was a second passage that I wrote out and came to realize that two words repeated throughout it. I went to start translating when the screen caught my eye and found that the glowing words were also on the other walls. I asked if Azarias could shift the feed around only to find the same two words were repeated over and over again: ᐃᐁ ᒐᐃ ᐅᐃᐊᐱᐃᐱ.

"Hey, Aerrow? This place is creepy, and Cyrus doesn't like it… Can we leave?"

I didn't answer him as I translated the two repeated words only to have my heart skip a beat.

What was this?

What did it mean?

What did those two goddesses almost unleash?

Why were the words making my whole body grow cold?

"Aerrow?" Cyrus's voice cut through my thoughts, bringing some sort of warmth back into me and I turned back to the screen in surprise. The lights were on in the cave, the bolt was gone, and both of their faces were on the screen. "Is everything alright?"

"I…" My tongue couldn't form words, paralyzed.

"You don't look so good…" Azarias commented, and I turned back to the sheet on the table. My whole body was slowly thawing out of its rigid state, but the words threatened to take hold again. I didn't feel good about any of it… "Come on now, use your words. What's the creepy text say?"

"I… I didn't translate it all yet…"

Cyrus's voice was softer, "You clearly didn't have to."

I shook my head. "Od Symalum."

"Od Symalum?"

"It's what was repeated all over the walls, the ceiling, the floor… it's just two words, but it feels like I was thrown into the Theseus Sea in Cheimoiems, like I know the implications…"

"What does it translate to?"

"The Calamity," I answered as I looked over the words in front of me. "What kind of threat is given a name like that by the most powerful beings in our universe?"

"A calamitous one," Azarias answered cheekily, and I glared.

"This is serious. It's a name, a title – something I have no idea who or what it is, but somehow do and it is far from alright! This seal was created to keep that thing out. If Zegrinath was telling the truth, there are six of them and it took six seals to keep Od Symalum out. Six of them with the power of dragon magic, every element, and invoked both Life and Death. The seals were only known to keep the Daemonias Realm out, to keep out its taint… But this Calamity, is that taint, I know it. It's trying to get in to corrupt and destroy everything! The seals were locked away, disappeared, and forgotten to keep whatever that thing is from getting in and someone is finding them, breaking them… There are only four seals that we know of left. That person is only four seals away from unleashing it!"

Chapter Twenty: Gravity

There was silence from the two knights as I tried to go through years of lessons and history, anything to try and figure out what Od Symalum was. But nothing came. Just like the seals, it seemed like the over looming threat was forgotten. Yet I was drawn to that place... That name made my soul ache...

I knew nothing about it, yet I felt like I had.

A mutter from Azarias came through, asking about what they should do, and I didn't know. Not in the grand scheme of things, at least. I quickly mentioned to continue taking pictures of the words and then come back with something to eat. I wasn't hungry, but I knew I should eat, and the thought would lessen their worries a bit.

What was there to be so scared of when none of us knew what the threat of Od Symalum even was? Perhaps now, after all this time, it could be defeated.

My entire being disagreed by instinct.

"Alright, we'll finish up and come back. Don't have a panic attack while we're gone."

I was well past panicking, but he knew that. "I'll... translate more of the text, distract myself..."

"Good. Just do that... uh, grab a throw blanket from downstairs and read?"

Cyrus stole the device. "We'll find out what The Calamity is before anyone decides to end the world. We have the resources, you're a king with connections to whoever you want. There will be others like Zegrinath who know pieces. It will be fine."

The confidence was staggering, but as defiant as it was, I couldn't shake the horrible feeling. It didn't seem like it was enough. The dread that I felt when Absalom's seal was broken washed over me.

We didn't have a lot of time...

How much was not a lot?

Not forever... but not tomorrow...

Soon.

I took a breather. "I'll see you when you get back."

He made a grunt of an agreement, back to being his normal, little to no word self, and I ended the call. The sheet in front of me had a lot of untranslated text... I had work to do.

What was the full warning?

Hopefully, something useful.

I got to putting letters that made sense onto the sheet, but it was quickly disheartening as each word that came before the named thing was nothing important. It was just a warning stating that breaking the seals would release The Calamity, which we already knew.

Kánite denon afitus. Prosocave Od Symalum. Od Symalum élani. Zotae sfragillum Od Symalum. Thanatem sfragillum Od Symalum.

Do not touch. Beware The Calamity. The Calamity comes. Life seals The Calamity. Death Seals The Calamity.

It just repeated over and over for each element and other words of power all basically telling this thing to go away. It was practically an exorcism... And it was done six times over.

The Calamity's Gate is sealed.

I stopped writing the next line of text.

Why was this a proper noun?

What was this gate? Why would The Calamity have one?

Where?

How was this gate any different from the seals?

I grabbed a new sheet of paper and wrote down Od Symalumtoi Pýta and started back on the other translations. The process became easier as the letters when on. Before reaching the last few lines, I was translating the words without writing them down at all. It was nice to be back up to where I should be... but none of the scripture was helpful. Just a whole lot of sealing measures.

I sat back in the couch and stretched. I needed to figure out what this horrible thing was... but I didn't exactly have a library at my disposal. Someone did though... but she was busy with something. I grabbed the CT anyway and opened the messaging for Atlamillia and started typing, asking if she knew anything about The Calamity, Od Symalum, or a gate – to get back to me as soon as possible. The faster we knew about what it was, the faster we could figure out who could be breaking the seals.

The message was sent, and I got up.

There was one other thing I could check. It hadn't let me down yet… Maybe since Theseus wrote about the seals, if they happened to be the very same ones I needed to know about, then maybe he knew about what The Calamity could be. I went over to my room and went through my gear to grab my bestiary. I left behind its case and quickly left, hoping I was quiet enough to not disturb Deigh. She had stopped purring in her sleep a while ago… But she didn't seem like she was having bad dreams yet. Another reason to not freak out about the possibility of someone wanting to end the world.

Who knows? Maybe the warning was far louder than the problem that the seals held.

My subconscious did not agree.

I skipped to the table of contents for supernatural creatures and briefly went across the names, looking for anything that held the word: calamity. Calamity Puppies was on that list and I turned to it, quickly realizing that it was not what I was looking for. As dangerous as the puppies were… they were adorably anticlimactic. Though, knowing that a litter of stray puppies in a box could quickly turn into a slaughter of half a dozen families was a bit unnerving.

I went back to the table of contents, the image of the cute, fluffy creatures turning into mangy, razor teethed, and clawed monstrosities were seared into my brain. This world was weird, and it made me want to go elsewhere. Like a planet with no magic, or monsters on its surface. Just… people.

But then I wouldn't have Deigh…

That world sounded painfully boring, even for me.

Demon, death puppies it was.

The list continued, but nothing else read along the words of calamity in the supernatural section. Maybe it was a demon.

I went to the demon table of contents. The list wasn't particularly long… Valoth did mention that only higher classed demons would ever attempt to enter Orithin. So, that could have been the reason. But out of all those upper demons, or Archdemons as one of the entries had called them when I had read from the bestiary before, none of them were named calamity either.

Maybe it had a different name now than when the seals were made... That meant going through all of them...

The things I did for my people.

I got started, carefully reading each entry – each one making me wish I hadn't. If I didn't have nightmares about any of these things once I was done, the world might have been ending after all.

The door unlocked from across the room, causing me to jump and grab the closest weapon I could find, ready to defend from my seated position. The door opened and two wild knights appeared on the other side. A growl came out as I lowered my weapon. "You two almost gave me a heart attack! I thought you were a monster or something!"

"A monster? Why?" Azarias asked before looking to my hand. "Wait, were you going to fight a monster with a throw pillow?"

"A distraction..." Yeah, okay so maybe my weapon of choice wasn't great. But thrown hard enough, even the fluffiest of pillows hurt... sort of. I set the pillow back on the couch before moving the book to a safer location on the table, leaving it open to a strange, demonic creature with large eyes and mouth. It screamed that it was a jerk, but I hadn't read as to why it looked like an asshole. I cleared my throat and stood up, a little more regally to compensate the pillow. "So, did everything work out alright?"

"Pictures, food," Cyrus summarized thoroughly as he held bags and Azarias continued.

"And we got you those fish shaped crackers you like so much. Figured that over the next few days you'll need a happy snack."

I couldn't hold back my surprise and a small smile formed. "I appreciate it."

Cyrus went to head downstairs with the food before stopping. "Why did you think we were monsters?"

"Um... W-well... I was reading scary things... making a list of possible candidates on what The Calamity could be and informing myself of the horrible things that come from the Daemonias if nothing else."

"Oooh, let's see what you got!" Azarias exclaimed all too happily as he skipped over only to stop dead in his tracks when he looked down at my book. All happiness left as he grew rigid. A bit of a scowl formed.

"Do you know what this is?" I asked him and he remined silent for a few moments, his expression growing colder than Cyrus's.

He looked to nothing in particular. "You two can eat without me. I'm not feeling great."

I didn't get to try and ask about the sudden shift as he walked past swiftly, heading up to his room. Sage was ahead of him, leaping onto the loft and disappeared into the knight's room.

Azarias stopped for a moment, looking down at me from the loft. A dark shadow was casted from his bangs, covering the upper half of his face. "The guardian, by the way, has been dead for about thirty to thirty-five years... Your description matched that of a missing person's case from around that time. Also, that *thing* is not what you're looking for."

"Azarias-" I winced as I was cut off by his door being slammed shut. I turned to Cyrus just as he was trekking downstairs. He either didn't know what that was about, or he knew exactly what that was about and wasn't going to answer my questions. I turned to the book and sat down again.

Freegdred was its name. A wish maker... but only to those who were worthy of its assistance. It could come on its own, but it was generally summoned using a ritual. It would answer the call most of the time, but sometimes, it would ignore it when it was busy and the person on the other end would receive a different demon instead, usually not something pleasant. It would only grant a wish with good intentions for others. A heart of gold was the only way to appease the demon and a bargain could be struck.

Sacrifice was common or exotic foods. If the Freegdred was not appeased, it meant it sensed impurity. Greed being a major factor, any sense of the wisher using the wish to better themselves in some way would cause the demon to only see itself. It would then eat the wisher alive, along with anyone else involved including those within the wish unless the wisher had asked for it to kill someone, then that target would be spared.

What a jerk...

Why would Theseus include the summoning ritual?

Did someone really think they were so pure that they would even call such a thing? Maybe if someone was desperate... really that selfless...

The catch was probably that the person would offer themselves to the demon for whatever their wish was...

I would do that for my people… but I also didn't think it would be that simple, and I didn't have a pure heart of gold.

I sighed as I turned the page to some gruesome slime thing of fangs and teeth.

I set the book down. That was enough of that today. Before I lost all of my appetite.

I looked up at Azarias's room. Why did he know of this demon? Had he or someone he knew wished for something? Did it turn out well or did the creature eat them?

I wanted to go up and ask, but I wasn't sure if it was the best time… I'd ask when he had some time to himself.

Heading to the first floor, I could hear Cyrus moving about. At the bottom of the stairs, its space was just as large as the upper floor, the rooms though were a lot more open. The only things that gave a difference between the rooms were different floor materials, a few pillars, and bits of furniture laid about. A large lab space with several lab counters, instruments, and devices were put away in their appropriate spots and out of the way, leaving the counters for the most part bare. An island counter also doubled as a half wall, separating the space from the dining room mixed with a second common room which sat next to a large kitchen with its own island counter for a smaller eating space. It was an impressive place, though I had a feeling the lab wasn't made for anything dangerous from its openness.

The smell of food entered the air as Cyrus pulled it out of paper bags next to a large envelope that I guessed were the pictures. I wandered over, joining him at the island counter after washing my hands. "Do you know what that was about?"

"Yes," he answered simply, but didn't elaborate as the silence dreaded onwards.

"Alright…"

"It's a sensitive subject, something only he can share."

Seemed to be the only way to get information today… A bit annoying, but I understood the reasoning, and it was worth a try. Though, it did make for a good opportunity to speak with Cyrus about his brother. The only problem was… how to bring it up without mentioning Owen. Maybe approaching it from a different angle… "You were going pretty hard on Azarias for a simple practice earlier."

"Perhaps." He set the food out and sat down across from me. I started eating, the food made me realize that I was starving.

"Is there something bothering you?"

"Just keeping sharp."

He was making it incredibly difficult. "So, sending your friend high up the wall was just casual practice?"

There was silence and the knight shoved food in his mouth, less than pleased.

"You know you can come to me when there is something wrong. Whether it's something I've done or if you were swarmed by a group of girls again."

A curt laugh came from him. "I do not get nearly as much attention here as I do in Absalom. Azarias on the other hand, has had a few Seraphs come to him. Apparently, brunets are rare in this kingdom."

"And this upsets you?"

"It's relieving to have a point be proven."

Most likely the point of being swarmed is not as great as it looked. "So... What's with the aggression?"

More silence.

"Perhaps the latest surprises?"

"Something like that..."

"I apologize for the instability of it all..."

"The instability of it is fine. Random events do not concern me."

"Then what does?"

"Your inability to stay out of danger when I'm not there."

The shock from the bluntness was not hidden well on my face. It was a little more than what I was prepared for. "You can't dictate when someone or something decides to spring things up."

"No, but I should be there regardless of what you do. But one after another, you've sent me on a different task, or I was elsewhere."

"You can't always be there... It's impossible."

265

"So far I haven't been there at all."

"You were there when Olin attacked."

"He wasn't much of a threat."

"But he was still a threat and you stopped him before he could hurt me. That still counts."

He sighed in irritation, "You're worse than my brother…"

"You have a brother?" I asked, careful to make sure I didn't say *had*.

"Ruben… was my brother." The name was cautiously said, barely above a mutter. "He died a long time ago."

My curiosity to learn more was met with instant regret. Just saying his name sounded like he was being impaled a hundred times over. "I'm sorry."

"No need. It's something I should have brought up as it affects my duty." He set his utensil down. "You remind me of him. Air-headed, wanting to do what's right despite the risks, hiding your own issues with a small smile saying even the smallest things count in a positive light. He was foolish too, thinking he could carry the weight of the world on his own, letting others do what they needed to do. It was both selfless and selfish behaviour, one I knew would get him killed, and I wasn't there to defend him when it did."

"And you think being there these last few times would have helped the situation? Being there for him?"

"Perhaps."

It probably would have gone a very different direction if he had been there. Unfortunately, we couldn't go back in time to prove it. "You don't always have to be there… it's not going to be possible to always be there when something comes up. And by the sounds of it, your brother's death was not your fault. He made the decision to do what he did, letting you do whatever you needed to do. I don't know the circumstances… but if he was like me, then he knew the odds. He was probably protecting something he cherished, and I doubted he had regrets or ever blamed you for not being there in the end."

"The only thing he protected were monsters who didn't love him back."

"He might have known that too, but just didn't care."

"What do you mean?"

"Exactly as it sounds. He probably didn't care that whoever he was protecting didn't love him. He still loved them and would have felt as you do for not saving them. Failure, regret, trying to figure out where you went wrong. Sometimes, no matter what, there wouldn't have been anything you could've done. It happens regardless, and you lose. But he managed to overcome those odds, even at the cost of his life."

"How could you possibly-?!" He started angrily before calming down in realization that I wasn't just saying things like some priest. They were the feelings I didn't share with the outcome of the battle at the south wall. "Perhaps he would have… but our parents are not as noble or great as the former king. They should have been the ones to die that night, not him. They deserve death."

"I'd like to think that no one should have died that night, no matter how awful they are."

"Oh, you innocent, little king. You have no idea how awful they are…" he said with slight affection. It was a bit strange coming from him, but I couldn't say I minded it. "It's rude to ask a king of something as a guard or retainer, but I will ask anyway. Will you please stop putting yourself in danger for people, especially for those who do not care?"

I figured that he was going to ask me that at some point, unfortunately, my answer had been made long ago, even with working against the habits I had developed. "I'm sorry, but I can't. I can't standby and watch even if they don't care or are ungrateful. I promise that I'm working on not carrying everything, but I can't do nothing when I can do something."

"I knew that would be your answer… Fine, but please, ask for help when you need it. Azarias and I are both available at any moment. It's not a bother to us, so don't ever think it is and go off on your own, not even to protect us. You've done it with the Terror Hound, and it is exactly what Ruben would have done. I don't want what happened to him, to happen to you. You've had too many close calls and it's only a matter of time."

"I'll do my best…"

"That is all I ask. I want to protect you, from yourself if I must."

There was silence again as we started eating. My tongue couldn't hold back a lighthearted comment after I swallowed. "So, this is what it's like to have an older brother… Already being bossed around."

"I'm sure Atlamillia would be quite thrilled to know that you feel her misery."

"Please, I'm the best."

"You're something at the very least."

I rolled my eyes at the remark and continued eating, not instigating the carefree feeling knight in front of me. It was strange to have Cyrus be so open, to speak so much. But I was happy all the same. Better bonds, better synergy, and the understanding for when the time came for battle… Whatever and whenever battle came… "Hey, Cyrus?"

"Hm?"

"Can we have a light spar afterwards… I'm supposed to be relaxing but, we've barely practiced together."

"A light spar then, but only if you finish the food on your plate."

This was going to be something to get used to…

00000

I put up Winterthorn just as the training sword came down hard and a grunt came out at the blow. I reflected it only for Cyrus to use my momentum that I had turned on him, back on me, shouldering me in the chest. The air was knocked out of me and I lost grip on my sword. I took a few steps back to recover.

"Retreating already?" He asked curiously and I looked at him with a bit of disdain. This was the fourth time he had done something similar, only this time I lost my weapon. He wasn't beating me in a sense, just bullying me and testing waters since he also didn't entirely know who he was dealing with.

"I thought this was supposed to be light sparring."

"It is, I'm not using magic." I went to retrieve Winterthorn only for him to blow up the sand in front of me, forcing me to retreat. "Find a new weapon."

"Seriously?"

"This is the best time to practice with something else."

I crossed my arms. "I fail to see how…"

"You know that not all fights are fair, learn to tip it in your favour no matter what you have."

A small sigh came out and I turned to look at the rack nearby. Several weapons sat on it, typical melee ones like spears and axes, then there were a couple of ranged ones such as a bow and a handgun. I went over to it, deciding what to pick. A gun would be useful in its own right of sheer power of not needing to be healthy to use, but it did require magic and that was not something I was going to use. He was using a sword, so a spear would have the advantage… but what would be more interesting? I picked up the bow and the quiver of arrows, snapping it onto my belt and turned back to him.

If Cyrus wanted to fight me, he'd have to get closer and with the rack right there, well, he told me to make it to my advantage.

I grabbed a couple of arrows from the quiver and notched one of them, pulling the string with my left as the faintest of smirks formed on his face, clearly interested.

I tilted my head slightly, tauntingly. "I wonder how fast you are?"

"You think a ranged weapon will stop my advance?"

"I don't know, will it?"

He took the bait and started towards me. I released the arrow, preparing the next one almost immediately and fired it. He took advantage at the fact that I aimed at his armoured chest and easily dodged the first one only for the second one to scrape his cheek, deflected mostly by his armour. He took a step to the side and halted with a slight glare.

A small grin formed on my face as I prepared the third arrow. "Just because I don't have Seraphinean weaved armour doesn't mean I don't know that the armour protects vital areas with an energy field. How do you think I win against Owen?"

"Fearlessly aiming at my face is a bit much…"

I shrugged. "Maybe… but unless the gold light in your armour disappears, I don't have to worry about accidently killing you. Still confident that you'll make it here?"

He didn't reply with words as he charged again, his heightened aggression speaking quite loudly. I aimed and fired, grabbing a few more arrows as he had to backtrack his step a bit before progressing. He hit the fourth arrow away with his sword while the fifth one scraped his leg.

He closed the gap between us, forcing me to use the bow as a deterrent from his sword hitting me. He tried to shoulder me in the chest again, but I sidestepped, the bow becoming a baton and I swiped upwards with it. A growl came from him as he was forced to take a few steps back to rebalance from the chest blow, allowing me to grab the spear from the rack and attack. He got his sword up to deflect, allowing the pointed end to go in one direction, but the other end of the shaft came from underneath, knocking a leg up. I charged into him and knocked him over. His training sword went flying as I turned the head of the spear and rested it under his chin.

He contemplated before leaning back onto the ground. "Should have expected you to use the rack…"

"I did kind of tell you when I challenged you to get closer."

"You did and I will not lose a second time."

"And why's that?" I asked cockily only to receive my answer as an electric shock went through the spear, leaving as quickly as it came, and I dropped it with a slight yelp. I took several steps back, rubbing my hand that tingled a bit as the pain died. "Ow… Sore loser much?"

He set up, a neutral expression on his face, but a hint of a glare told me he wasn't overly pleased. "Yes, and I won't hold back next time…"

"Let's go ag-" I started to challenge him right there and then, a bit thrilled to learn something new, only for the side of my head to give out a pulse of pain. I grabbed it as a small noise came out. The training room grew a bit dizzy.

"What's wrong?"

"I think I over did it…"

He got off the ground and walked over to me, making sure he could catch me if I fell. "If you feel like puking…"

"I won't do it on you," I agreed with the phrase he didn't finish. "Just need to rest… properly this time."

He gave a nod, and we left the training room for my room.

Chapter Twenty-One: Tunnel Lights

Atlamillia was ecstatic that Aerrow didn't push the subject. She looked at the war table, pocketing the CT. He had the right to be worried, but it was nice to know that he believed in her. That, and she knew he had his own problems to deal with... like relearning a language that he should know fluently. Her frustrations with her brother died quickly; the war table was much more important and immediate. There were hundreds of lights on the table that decorated the landscape that was her beautiful kingdom... but five had gone out.

She touched the table where one of the lights, now a darkened circle, sat and it opened a rectangle of static. Offline. She pressed the button under it for a recap of what happened to get the same results as the last four: some monsters that didn't stick around, and then rocks falling, collapsing the tunnel.

She put her hair up in a loose ponytail, subconsciously removing her ability to pull her hair out. It was far from good. It was even passed bad. Phase Two was ready to start at her command, and Phase Three, which hadn't even been addressed to the public, let alone anyone outside the immediate court and crown circle, was already getting hindered. Perhaps it was good that the public didn't know. Such a hindrance would have definitely shaken the populous and the houses with the mention of the delay.

She looked up from the table to her entourage and general just as a sixth light went out. "This needs to be dealt with immediately without hindering Phase Two. Suggestions?"

There was a moment of silence before Ronial spoke up, but he didn't look happy with his idea. "I have one, but it will possibly affect the following phase."

"Adjustments can be made to a plan not in motion."

"If that's the case... We can effectively protect the tunnels with the knights available as well as fully commit to Phase Two by pulling them back, choosing only a handful of tunnels to make sure that the full tunnel is secure. The sensors were placed near the entrance and about halfway down. By the feed, they are collapsing perfectly on top of the gates meaning whatever is doing it, knows we have sensors not watching the gate as they keep our knights located there and the entrance busy."

"How many knights do you think are required to protect a tunnel?"

"It would be limited to at least one earth element knight at the gate, halfway down, and at the entrance if the tunnel is a shorter one. If not, two in the middle which…" He pulled out a CT and tapped it a few times. "Which is a little less than a tenth of the knights…"

"How many?"

"Ninety-five of them are available for one shift at a time. And if we divide them with an average of three and a half, three different teams over the course of a day… we can realistically protect about twenty-seven of the tunnels."

Her mouth felt dry at the number. "Twenty-seven? That's it?"

"That's like…" Elias started, and they turned to him as he looked at the map. "Not even seven percent of the tunnels across Absalom… For Phase Three to work, we need tunnels across all the provinces and advantageous points. Twenty-seven is too little."

"It would be easier if Aerrow came back and used that dome like the last time," Mazaeh commented. "He could get rid of the monsters in an instant and we wouldn't have to worry about Phase Two, let alone Phase Three."

"But then Ciar would just bombard it with boosted monsters," Ronial explained, shaking his head. Ideas were being written across his face just as quickly as they were being wiped away. Atlamillia hadn't known much about Ronial, but to watch him work as she did now, it was plain to see why Owen and her brother thought he was perfect to be her general. "That shield wasn't like King Solomon's. It can't handle that much stress and the knights can't defend on that many fronts if Ciar prepares an onslaught… It would be the same outcome as before except we definitely wouldn't have a king left to lead. Aerrow was lucky enough to survive the last time and that was a last-ditch effort of spite by Ciar."

"You'd think he'd get enough of a thrill from killing two royals; and all of this is because he thinks Aerrow is a Godling?"

"Unfortunately," she sighed. Her words threatened to expose the real reason Ciar came in the first place… but none of them needed to know if Aerrow didn't. "But with the Zerach, once it's completed and brought back here, Aerrow can use the shield and the machine to take care of the advantage Ciar has against us."

"Which we don't know how long that will take," Bretheena informed. "Our options are leaving the tunnels as they are, possibly leading to casualties, or losing some tactical ground in some areas."

The table turned to Atlamillia as she was the only one who could give the order. An order that she didn't want to give as neither option was good. Another light went out and she tsked. "We'll pull back the knights and fortify areas of most prominence. Two tunnels per province for the north and south, two tunnels for intended targets like major cities or a fort. One of the tunnels must be in Siofra as Fort Hammond is there."

"The castle tunnel was excavated this morning, so that is an easy one to pick," Ronial shared. "Though, it is possible to give one of Aesear's tunnels to another province since Orithina's Temple has theirs."

"I suppose that seems fair… Which province do you think should have the honour?"

"Um, you wish for my suggestion?"

She gave a nod. "You've seen every detail about this, and you've been communicating with the provinces and house leaders. I've left a lot of the diplomatic issues to Aerrow over the last few months so I'm not as up to date on the drama as I'd like to be."

"Well… my suggestion is to go with the province of Drixula. They got hit the hardest and from my understanding, Governor Wyrtha Kastor and major houses Sigeweard and Suerius have been rather… shall we say bitter, about the crown not acting immediately."

"Good gods some things really don't change… They only care because their estates happened to be trampled. They don't actually care about the towns and cities in their districts," she spat out and Ronial gave out a quirky little laugh.

"They're not much better towards the other houses either from the meetings and parties I've attended when I was still living at the Jósteinn Manor a few years back. May I ask if the crown has assisted?"

"We have, sort of… Aerrow gave a bit of compensation when he was going around, but he specifically told them that there would be more done once the walls are repaired so we didn't have to rebuild their fancy fences a second time." She gave a small sigh, "But… I suppose it would shut them up for a time if they got to have one more tunnel than the other provinces."

"I would also suggest letting them pick which one." He looked at the province south of the capital's province. "But out of a selection. There are a lot of tunnels, and only a few of them are worth anything for our purposes."

Atlamillia looked at the map.

The north tunnel was probably going to be one of the larger towns, possibly Graemerae. The south was obvious, that being the tunnel where Fort Verdant used to be. The other would be the capital of the province, Nervalia.

"The large mountain fort, Fort Heirobha, would be a good option. It's close enough to the wall, but not so close that it would be overlapping, plus it would give us the magic sensor range," she suggested. "The other would be in House Curtis's territory and the minor house Hildebrand around Lake Hudvíkin. There is really good farmland there that is able to grow the longest, if not all year around – if they don't pick it, we should prioritize it when we can. It's far enough from the wall and from the last report, it wasn't hit hard. People can go home sooner and start growing again, start the rations up in case Cheimoiems hits hard this year so we don't have to keep using Asylotum. As for the third option… I'm not quite sure. There isn't a lot of strategic resources other than the province produces a lot of the crops there for the kingdom… Wait, doesn't House Hugberaht have that weapon's manufacturer… what's its name?"

"Vragi. Yes, the minor house has a partnership with them."

"Then that will be the third option. Whichever one they don't pick will be the next wave of tunnel systems we'll protect unless some other problem arises. Crops will be good, but if we have to, Asylotum is already open and available – it would just be nice to not use its power in case we have to hide back in here for longer than a few months. We need that factory, if not now, then as soon as we can."

"Your choices aren't really choices," Bretheena said looking to her from the map. "But it would give them the idea that they are choosing."

"That's all they need. If we play nicely in the playground, it will force them to play nicely back." Atlamillia looked over the map again. "I'll have Jakob send out missives to ask the houses of Drixula to come immediately after we decide the remaining tunnels. Ronial, after this, I would like you to pull the knights and put them in those tunnels, start the set up for routine patrols. I'll send Mazaeh your way with the final three tunnels."

"Of course, Princess Atlamillia. So, the first extra tunnels should all go towards the capitals of each province…"

00000

Atlamillia only gave out a sigh after the house heads had left the war room. It had been, well, a nightmare to get them to decide. A long, long nightmare. They eventually went with the factory over the lake and fort, but the houses all seemed to be pleased with such a privilege that the other provinces didn't get.

"Still hanging in there, Atla?" Mazaeh asked and she gave a small huff. "Yeah, same."

"Like… I know it's late… but shouldn't they just, cooperate so we can all just fucking do what we want to do? Not argue and make everyone's life miserable?" She asked and he shrugged.

"I don't know, maybe it's a noble thing. They had certain angles that they wanted to achieve, good and bad, not caring about how long it took. They are leaders too, I'm sure they care a bit about their districts and wanted to have the best possible outcome."

"Hmm… maybe." It had more merit to it than she wanted to admit. She had done similar things for the sake of the kingdom and royal court. "You should give those notes to Ronial and hurry back. It's late and depending on how well these plans go, you might be needed for assistance or fill in from time to time."

He nodded, folding up the list of tunnels being protected and left. She looked down at the table again. There were more than a few lights gone. She just hoped that the tunnels they decided to protect, could be protected before their light went out. She left the war room alone and was met by Aoife waiting silently outside against the wall.

Atlamillia gave her a confused look. "Shouldn't you be home? It's late."

"Maybe…" her friend started. "But when you got summoned in an emergency, I wanted to stick around to make sure that you had someone to talk to afterwards."

"I can handle emergencies, you know. It's kind of one of the things I was brought up to do… not to mention, I have just about anyone in the castle to rant to if I want…"

"Yeah, and so did Dani. She still preferred to talk to someone outside of it all. Apparently felt better to have an outsider to discuss issues with."

Atlamillia shouldn't have been surprised by her intentions, but she was, and a small smile formed. "I appreciate the concern, but really, the emergency has been dealt with for now. But I might take you up on that rant offer a bit later, just to see."

A small giggle came from her. "Okay… so, it's nothing too bad?"

"It's... bad. But it's not going to end the kingdom." It wasn't the full truth to the problem since if the plan didn't work, the kingdom would almost certainly be stuck in a world destined to collapse after some time. But she wasn't one to jump into a fit over a scenario that *might* happen if they were completely negligent. "Speaking of Dani, have you spoken with her?"

"No..." Aoife's lighthearted nature went sombre. "What do you think she's doing?"

"I don't know... I'll have a missive sent to see if Eudoxia happens to know."

"And what if she says nothing or lies?" she asked, crossing her arms uncharacteristically. "I've only met her once and... no offence to Dani, but she's a psychotic bitch. She's only nice to who she feels worth the effort."

"I am, unfortunately, well aware of that. Got quite the rant from Aerrow in one of his lower times when he was puking his guts out. It's amazing what he lets out when his guard is down."

She raised an eyebrow. "He can rant?"

A small giggle came out of Atlamillia at the reaction. "Of course, he can."

"Don't laugh! Have you met your brother?!" Aoife exclaimed before shaking her head, settling down. "This only proves my point. What if Dani is trapped?"

"That... is a good question. There wouldn't be much I can do if Eudoxia flat out refuses to answer the missive other than bring it up with Aerrow who is on the other side of the continent, in the real world. Not that we can tell if she lies... But there might be someone who can."

"There is?"

"Dani's brothers. Out of the four of them, which one is more caring for her wellbeing and less under the thumb of Eudoxia and Tyriel?"

"I mean, they all care for her deeply, but the younger two, Bryce and Rórdán will probably be more under watch since they are at parent approving ages unlike Endymion or Deòrsa."

"Endymion is the eldest of the brothers, right?"

"He's our age, a year younger than Dani... I thought you would know this stuff?"

"Just confirming… it's been a long day." She gave out a sigh. "I'll have a message delivered to him while Jakob is distracting the head through Bretheena. If their stories line up and Dani isn't there, we'll know that Dani is missing… if they don't, I'm sure Eddy there will tell us exactly what's happening in the Raghnall home with her."

"When are you sending out the request?" Bretheena asked right next to them. Aoife squeaked in surprise at the sudden appearance, but Atlamillia had expected her to appear at the sound of her name.

"When the hell did you get there?!" The poor girl asked, breathlessly, and a small smile formed on the retainer's face.

"I've been here the whole time."

"No, you weren't!"

"There is a nice beam that supports the ceiling along the walls like an offing. The perfect place to see who comes and goes from a room where Atlamillia is inside."

"But… I would have seen you come down…"

Atlamillia attempted to comfort her, but even as the words came out, they fell flat. "I haven't figured it out either, but have come to accept that she's around most of the time…"

"Sure…" Aoife adjusted her shirt. "Um… when are you sending out those fancy messages?"

"Right now. They should both have answers in some form or another by morning." Atlamillia turned to Bretheena. "That is if you don't mind staying up a little longer."

"I'll pass along Jakob's and we can head out as soon as possible."

"Alright, don't start a fight…"

"He starts them, but I'll do my best to keep the peace."

Atlamillia sighed, accepting that that was the best she was getting and turned to Aoife. "So, by morning then."

Aoife nodded a bit uncertainly. "I should head out, go to bed if I'm going to knock down some doors tomorrow. I want to be somewhat awake for that."

"Did you want to stay here for the time being? You'll know when I do about Dani's situation and you wouldn't have to travel back home at such an hour."

Aoife gave a happy smile that Atlamillia solely missed. "I would love that."

00000

A knocking came from her door, waking her out of a depressing memory of being with her father in the city; one she wasn't quite ready to abandon yet. She rolled over, throwing a leftover pillow over her head. "Go away…"

"Atla, breakfast is getting cold…" Juno called back, and she groaned.

"Then go eat… I'm not hungry."

There were a few grumbles from the other kids before a collective thumping of them running away. She sighed. At least they listened this time. The outside world started to disappear again, fading back to the fountain in the city square. The twilight light of the eclipse glazed the space in its off colour. She went to turn to her father only for the dream to disappear as her name was shouted excitedly, scaring her half to death. She snapped her attention to it, rolling over just in time to see Aoife land on the bed, overtop of her, still in a nightgown.

"What the-"

"Morning!" Aoife greeted ecstatically. "The kids said you wanted to see me?!"

"I…" She looked over to the door that was closed, but she could only imagine that the kids weren't far. She sighed again and looked up at the cheerful girl. "They lied to you to get me out of bed."

Her eyes grew wide before looking at the door. "Those little shits…"

"Mmhmm…"

Aoife looked back down at her, confused. "Hey, are you okay? Why are you crying?"

"Huh? Oh…" Atlamillia wiped the tears away that she hadn't noticed and rolled back over. "It's nothing, just a dream."

Aoife released her from her cage she had formed and flopped onto the bed in front of her. Her hair a bit of a mess, but not in a bad way as the bit that was hooked around her ear went across her nose. "Wanna talk about it?"

278

"Not really…"

"Okay…" There was silence between the two of them for a moment before she looked at the comforter. "Can I get under the blanket? It's cold out here."

A small laugh came out and she nodded, barely keeping her eyes open. Her friend moved into a ball for a moment before sliding underneath and gave out a shiver. "That's better… no wonder you don't want to leave, this is basically Athnuracha right here."

"It's a nice space…" Atlamillia adjusted her arm, moving it closer to her face. "Sometimes I don't ever want to leave…"

"Then stay a little bit longer," Aoife offered with a small smile and grabbed her hand with reassurance. "You miss your dad… that's who you were dreaming about?"

"Maybe…"

"Then I'll protect you for a little bit longer from those monsters, okay?"

She went to argue but found herself unable to. The dream of the memory was right there… She nodded slightly as her eyes closed. "Okay… Goodnight, Aoife."

"Sweet dreams…" the girl yawned slightly and Atlamillia drifted off again.

00000

A light knock came at the door, waking her up a bit from the warm thoughts of her memories. Her eyes opened slowly, still not ready for the day. There was a soft light coming from the balcony doors where the curtains hadn't been closed properly. The light stopped behind that of a figure that curled up slightly in front of her. She looked ahead and saw her so-called protector out cold, still holding onto her hand and her hair in the same place as it had fallen. The only indication that the girl had moved was the movement she had made that reminded Atlamillia that she was there at all.

A smile formed on Atlamillia's face. Aoife looked so peaceful, much less energetic than she was normally. It was more of the fragment of calmness she gave out once in a while. She closed her eyes as she breathed in deeply. She didn't want to disturb the wholesome peace she had found.

Another knock came from the door. Her illusion, breaking.

But alas… She didn't have the privilege to just enjoy the warmth and safe haven of the moment.

She opened her eyes and found a pair of grey ones also starting to wake. The light brown hair that had relentlessly fought to stay in its position was finally moved as Aoife's free hand flicked it over her shoulder.

A slight moan came out of the girl, "'ornin'…"

"Morning…" Atlamillia greeted back softly. "Did you sleep well?"

"I haven't slept this good since… ever…" She stretched slightly before squeezing her hand and her eyes went wide. "Oh! I hadn't meant to fall asleep…"

"It's okay…" Atlamillia giggled slightly before curling up and accidently bumping her knee against hers. "Oops… sorry."

Aoife bumped back with a cheeky grin. "It's so nice in here… Pillows just melt away everything… A dangerous weapon against a protector's duty."

"It really is…" They laid in silence before another knock came from the door. "Persistent, aren't they?"

"Well… you are reigning regent right now."

"Right…" She called over her shoulder, not wanting to get up, "What is it?"

"Lady Eudoxia and Lord Endymion have given their replies and they conflict, Princess Atlamillia," Jakob answered through the door. "Lord Endymion has requested you to help… how did he put it according to Bretheena… Ah, yes, formally, to lessen the tensions between the Raghnalls."

"Lessen tension… I'm going to lessen the number of bones they have…" Atlamillia growled before sitting up. "Send word that I will be formally visiting the Raghnall home for business this afternoon."

"It's almost noon now, Your Highness."

She looked down at Aoife who gave a surprised look before shrugging. She turned back to the closed door. "This evening then… for supper."

"Of course, Princess Atlamillia. I should remind you that His Highness is expecting you to explain the empty void you left him with. Your uncle has stated that King Aerrow mentioned it briefly over breakfast this morning about the lack of communication but didn't wish to come off as overbearing."

That was new… She wondered who yelled at him. "I'll do that once I've been updated on the details. Thank you, Jakob."

"Do you wish for Ramsey to make brunch for you and Lady Aoife? She is in there, yes?"

A slight blush of sheepish embarrassment felt warm on her cheeks. Why was she embarrassed? She didn't know, but here she was. She looked slightly down at her friend, trying to hide the emotion. "Are you hungry?"

Aoife gave a little nod, hiding most of her face under the blanket for some reason.

She turned back to the door. "Please."

"It will be ready shortly."

There were steps that moved away from the door and she let out a held breath.

"Was it okay for me to be here?" Aoife asked shyly and Atlamillia gave her a confused look.

"Why ever not?"

"I don't know…" She squeezed her hand, reminding Atlamillia that they were still holding hands. "It was by accident, but aren't you a bit concerned that someone might think we-"

"Then they are clearly bored," Atlamillia cut her off. "Besides, even if we actually did anything, I can date and screw whoever I fucking well please."

Aoife's concern went away with a giggle as she sat up, letting her hand go. "It astounds me from time to time on how bold and blunt you are."

Atlamillia shook her head. "Let's go eat some food while I devise a way to save Dani without violence… Gods, I sound like my brother."

"You do a bit…"

There was a small sigh that came out of her as she got out of bed. She had to prepare for the day and call her brother back once she made sure she had everything he was looking for and had the details about what he was missing back home… That was going to be a fun conversation… long too she didn't doubt. But one thing was for certain, she didn't need to tell Aerrow about Dani. The last thing she wanted him to do was worry about someone he couldn't help.

Chapter Twenty-Two: Deliverance

A loud bang came from downstairs, jolting me out of my studies. I looked towards the closed door. Silence followed as if nothing happened. I hesitated to get back to reading, turning to the time. It was still early, before Azarias and Cyrus would be up. Another bang reached my ears, causing Deigh to wake up in alarm, and ready to go. I threw in the bookmark, closing my book.

What on Orithin was that?

We went over to the door as I grabbed my blade and opened it, quietly. Outside, the main room and the training hall were dark, the windows showed only the lights of the city, slowly dimming as the sun was starting to appear from beyond the horizon. Nothing moved and I started forward, taking only a few steps before someone dropped from above, landing impossibly silent. I withheld a scream of surprise to not give away my position, drawing Winterthorn. The tip was on the intruder's throat before they could draw their own weapon.

"Whoa! I'm sorry if I upset you! Please don't skewer me!" Azarias whispered out a plea and I lessened the stance, realizing who it was. The blade was removed, and he took a step back with a breather. "Geez, don't you know that kills people?!"

"Were you investigating the noise as well?" I asked quietly and he nodded.

The three of us silently made our way across the room and to the stairway, Azarias taking the lead. The lights were off on the bottom floor, but the sound of someone fumbling in the darkness came to my ears, telling us that there was someone in the safehouse besides us. We descended the stairs, the noise of the intruders not lessening. Azarias made his way around the side while Deigh went to the other as I made it to the bottom. The sound of something heavy was ran into. I turned on the light, ready to attack only to be met with Orpheal, Éabha, and a much healthier looking Naftali in the lab space. The Zerach was set in the centre next to the scientist.

I was going to have to ask how he was doing after I found out why they were here so early.

"See, I told you I could find the light without magic, Dad. You owe me a shopping trip," Éabha declared and I lowered my weapon. She turned to the sword in my hand. "You really need to work on your greeting protocols."

"We thought you were intruders," I growled. "But I suppose we should have known better with all the noise… What are you three doing here so early?"

Orpheal frowned in confusion. "Did Owen not tell you we were coming?"

I didn't get to answer as the door unlocked upstairs and I looked up the stairwell. Owen came through the door, a bit tired looking. He turned to me as he sensed someone watching him.

"Good morning, Aerrow. Sorry I'm late…" He trailed off as he noticed Winterthorn. "Something going on?"

"Did you happen to forget to tell us something before you left?"

"No, I don't think… Oh…" His expression told me I had nothing to explain. "Well, you now know that Orpheal was bringing the Zerach over this morning."

"Fuck this…" Azarias sighed, putting away his sword as he walked past me and started to march loudly up the stairs. "I'm going back to bed…"

"What fell in his breakfast?" Éabha asked, innocently enough, and an answer came from him someplace upstairs.

"I haven't had that yet! You are all psychopaths! Who willingly wakes up at this hour?!"

I gave out a sigh of my own and turned to the three Seraphs. "I apologize… he's grouchy when it's early."

"Can't be pleasant all the time…" Orpheal muttered before looking proudly at the Zerach. "One Outland Control Machine, delivered. Though… we are sorry for the noise."

"It's alright… just wished we had some warning, Owen…"

"Good night, Sire," the general called from the top of the stairs and I shook my head.

"Looks like we aren't starting on this right away…"

Naftali gave a small shrug. "That's alright. I want to run a diagnostic before we work on it. She's never been teleported before and could have a few loose screws. Don't want to blow her up in here… It will take a few hours to go through everything."

"Take as long as you need…"

"And we have to make sure the lab's machines are calibrated correctly," Éabha explained, adding to Naftali's list. She looked around. "I have to admit, I wasn't expecting this low hazard lab to be this nice when Dad told me about it."

"Er… thanks? I'll leave you three be. I'll be upstairs." I motioned, putting away Winterthorn. I started to head up the stairs only for Éabha to call my name. I turned around, letting Deigh head back to bed to see the lively girl at the bottom. "Yeah?"

"Later, like a lot later, I have something for you and a preposition, but you'll have to remind me."

"What's wrong with now?"

"Well… I forgot it, and Dad needs to wait for his teleport to work again."

"Got too excited to start working again, eh?"

She crossed her arms, looking away from me, annoyed. "No. You're just assuming things because we woke you up."

"I've actually been up for a while, but good try though," I told her with a small smile. I could understand where she got that since I was still in pjs as I hadn't planned on leaving my room so soon.

She seemed surprised but didn't say anything else as Orpheal called her away and I left her to her work. Back in my room, Deigh was curled up, but not quite asleep yet. I looked to the book on the table before deciding against studying more. I changed and left, closing the door quietly behind me, heading back to read more about demons and what could be the creature that the seal was talking about.

The minutes quickly turned to hours as I went through the text, carefully going over each entry and getting nowhere on what The Calamity was.

Atlamillia had yet to answer me from last night, making me a bit concerned for her. I lightly tossed the CT across the couch in frustration for not knowing and closed the book. Not only did the demon entries not mention it, but there also wasn't a demon that could be powerful enough for the goddesses to need six seals to keep out.

Horrifying?

Yes.

Traumatizingly enough that, like last night, I was going to continue to have nightmares for days to come?

Absolutely.

But I was kind of a baby… so that was something to consider.

I looked over the script on the pages and through the photos that were printed out. No answers were found as there wasn't text that I had missed and no hidden magic within the pictures. I set them down. Maybe there wasn't anything to be said…. Nothing to be told about what it was only that it was… Perhaps it didn't have a name that the gods knew about and just called it that.

I shuddered at the thought.

Something so horrible that they didn't stop to ask for its name.

But there was something to consider that maybe the name wasn't for a creature, but rather something else. Maybe it was an adjective made proper… which was strange but not unheard of.

But an adjective for what?

Who would want to break the seals at all? It didn't matter what was on the other side… only that it remained there and out of our realm.

"Whatcha looking at?" Someone asked in front of me suddenly.

I jumped, looking up to see Éabha way too close. My body sat back quickly from my pondering position, my heart skipping a beat in panic. My voice cracked, "When did you get there?!"

"About ten seconds ago to freak you out apparently, Airhead."

"You need a bell."

"Because you space out?"

"Because you walk unnaturally quietly," I stated, clearing my throat. "Just about ready with the Zerach?"

"Almost. I came up to get you for breakfast."

"Breakfast?"

"Yeah, you know, the thing that gives you energy for the day? You need it especially when you're using your brain." She flicked my crownless forehead and a small ouch escaped. "Owen's called you twice, so I figured I'd come and get you… you've been sitting here for hours, barely moving."

"I was working…" I told her sheepishly, though I was a bit surprised that he was up already. Probably shouldn't have been, but I thought maybe he'd sleep more after spending hours over the past two days with solidifying plans and what not for the dragons…

Gods that was in five days…

She looked down at the table covered in papers and pictures. "I see that. Od Symalum… what's that mean?"

"It means The Calamity in Ancient Dragon, or the Language of the Gods as Zegrinath explained it."

"You did mention you knew Ancient Dragon… It's pretty impressive to know more than one language."

"Not really. Ancient Dragon is supposed to be known by the royal family."

"Do you know Dagdian?"

"Not even a little bit. I haven't conversed with many Dagdians in my life, nor can I use their magic so there is no reason for me to learn it for even basic power words. Do you know it?"

"I think knowing the broad spectrum of physics, chemistry, biology, and many different mathematics is enough languages for me. Any Dagdian magic I can use; I don't require the language to do. Being a genius has its perks."

That was fair… Now if only I could ask her biology expertise to figure out why whelps were being taken. "So, food?"

"You didn't tell me what you're working on."

"Just scriptures from the cavern… It's nothing you need to worry about."

"Yes, clearly," she said sarcastically. She stood up straight and looked down at me accusatively when I didn't reply to her instigation. "Fine, keep your secrets. It's not like I'm a genius and could help or anything."

"I know you are, but in this case, I think it's better to keep you focused on the more immediate problem and out of trouble, right?"

"You're no fun."

"Gods forbid that I be responsible and not put my ally's daughter in danger by riling up her fatal flaw."

"I'm your ally too, you know… and I can keep my curiosity in check for the sake of the mission."

"Can you though? What if I told you some wild theories and exactly where you could possibly find answers but weren't allowed to go get them?"

"Ah… maybe?"

Yeah, right. We weren't asking for Orpheal's help with our theories either and he had the ability to walk away… Speaking of. "Naftali's looking better today."

"I didn't think you'd notice," she started, looking thoughtfully back at the stairs. "He's apparently found a working solution, but it's still incomplete. He's missing something but hopes he can get it soon, just takes some time to prepare."

I frowned slightly at the tone that dropped a bit. "You're worried about him."

She gave a hint of a nod. "I am. He wasn't doing well. He has his ups, but his downs have been more frequent – I honestly didn't think he was going to be able to finish the Zerach, especially with this added development. It set him a bit on edge after finding out."

"But you said he was perfectly fine a few days ago…"

"It's not like I would have told you the truth about his condition, I just met you then." She scowled slightly before sighing. "But it wasn't exactly a lie either. He's got a lot better since he was told that you were coming, hope probably being the leading cause. But four months ago, he was hospitalized. I don't know the details about it, but he came out more diligent than ever, obsessed even… I think he was given a life expectancy."

"That must have been terrifying for him… not knowing if you're capable of seeing your life through."

"From the few fights he's had with Dad, without a doubt. But now that he has a working cure to his illness. He's got high hopes that he won't be needing his cane in the near future."

"That's great!"

"It really is. Now I just hope that the Zerach doesn't give more complications, or his treatment might start losing potency… The thing with him is that he's healthier when his hopes are high. If they get shattered…"

"I think that's the same with everyone, you get better faster in an environment that is positive and not depressing."

"Exactly, so getting the Zerach done for him is one of the reasons why I've been so focused on it… now more than ever so that it's before shit starts hitting the fan. But I'm going to be sad when I find out that I'm not going to be needed as an assistant for him anymore."

"Oh, I highly doubt you'll never be asked for help again," I reassured, and Owen called both of our names from downstairs. I stood up and walked past the wingless Seraph. "Come on, I'm sure Owen made you something to eat as well."

"Uh, why?"

"Because he's nice." I turned slightly to my bedroom door before descending the stairs. "Deigh, food."

00000

I watched the monitor in front of me, pushing a button every time the metre that was displayed was raised into a box, capping its output. It descended back down. It was a tedious job, but someone had to do it. And who better than someone who was incapable of doing anything on the machine in front of me. A noise ripped through the room and the monitor in front of me started to fuzz up in white noise. The bar I had been watching climbed rapidly at the spike of energy. I pushed the button quickly only for the bar to barely move from the box and was forced to press it repeatedly to keep it under control.

It was swiftly becoming apparent that pushing the button wasn't going to work for much longer. "I don't wish to alarm anyone…"

"Cut the power!" Orpheal ordered and Azarias shut down the power source by pushing the emergency stop button near him.

An angry growl came from Naftali as he made the motion to throw his cane, but the walking device didn't leave his hands. "That should have worked! What the fuck are we missing?!"

There was silence about the room, and I felt bad for the man, even more so now that I knew that this project might have been his last one. He had to make it work, not just for the kingdom.

I tried thinking about it. The machine was made for Outland Monsters, but I doubted that bringing one to the device would be the answer when we couldn't get it to stabilize on its own. Maybe there was too much magic interference…

I voiced my thoughts for everyone. "This is similar to how the communication room and the printer acted when there was too much magical interference. Is it possible that this could be the case?"

"No! It's impossible!" Naftali spat as he turned to me. "We built this thing with magic in mind right from the beginning! Outland Monsters give out magical presences and having you here is supposed to allow it to adapt!"

"Yes... but Éabha's weapon she's been working on was created with the same idea in mind – but it's still having problems. Is it possible that maybe this can't be-"

"This isn't a tiny weapon! Models show that it is possible!" He took a slight breather, leaning against a counter as one of his legs buckled. "There has to be a way even with the magic. There has to be."

"Actually, Aerrow, you bring up a good point," Éabha started. "And my solution... might actually work with this."

I turned to her; my surprise not hidden. "You figured out a solution?"

"I did, using your advice by trying on the armour first. It was a bigger object and much easier to tweak and diagnose problems. I got it working last night." She turned to the rest of the company. "We can try the capacitor crystals on the Zerach to help deal with magic absorption."

"The number of crystals required would just cause more interference," Orpheal told her, and she shook her head.

"Not if we change the main power supply to the capacitor while also having ley line conduits as the power's route. This will allow more natural energy in the air to run it without needing a back up or an external power source making it more portable. As an added bonus, the conduits will also protect the electrical components if we build them inside out. A natural magic inhibitor without an actual inhibitor. The only downside is, we're going to need a much larger magic to electrical generator than the one I built... and being that it's a prototype, that could lead to trial and error depending on how much generation is needed. I know there isn't a lot of time but..."

There was silence in the room as Orpheal and Naftali looked at each other, running through what I guessed to be calculations. Orpheal turned back to Éabha after a few moments. "You're a genius, you know that?"

She blushed under the compliment but didn't say anything as Naftali shrugged, frustration gone. "Yeah, screw it. It's probably going to work, but in the off-chance that it doesn't, blowing her up a sixteenth time won't hinder progress – we'll all be dragon food anyway."

I was a bit dumbfounded at the remark. "You've blown this up… fifteen times?"

"We've been working on her for a while now. So that's not a bad number."

"How long is a while?"

"Eh… six months? Maybe it's been five and a half?"

That was more than twice a month… I turned to Owen. "Is this place really safer than the embassy?"

"It had its biweekly blow up a couple of days ago, remember?" Owen said, half-heartedly. "We're fine, statistically speaking."

"*Want me to start packing?*" Deigh asked and I kept myself from saying yes. "*Alright… Personally I think you've put too much faith into thinking this won't blow a hole in the floor.*"

"*I probably have… but here we are.*" I turned my attention to the people in the room. "We should take a break for now, get the necessary equipment figured out and ready – have other resources put towards finding the whelps."

"The materials are going to require heading back to the lab… Oh!" Éabha gave me a minor glare. "You didn't remind me to go get your thing."

"I feel like I just did…"

"Not directly… Anyway, can I ask you something, upstairs?"

I gave her a look of confusion before nodding, and she skipped ahead, bounding with endless energy up the stairs. I followed her, less energetic. I barely made it to the top before she started to pull me to the farthest part of the level, away from the stairs.

When she stopped, I asked my question. "What did you want to ask?"

She shifted from side to side, sheepishly. "I… I-I was wondering if I could upgrade your armour."

"Upgrade it?"

"Yeah, with the new technology you helped me make. I tested it already for you with the thing I wanted to give you, so it will definitely work…"

"I barely helped with that… I'm a bit speechless if I'm honest since you've clearly gone through a lot of trouble to get specifics."

"I guess… but I also don't want to leave you without armour to do it."

"That won't be a problem. I have training armour that works just as well."

"Great! Oh… I also would appreciate it if you didn't tell Dad. He might think I'm bothering you."

"It's far from a bother, if anything, I'm honoured just as much as it probably is for you to be able to work on something like this."

"Oh, it is, but that doesn't mean he'll see it that way…" She glared at the staircase for a moment before turning back to me. "So, you'll let me upgrade it?"

"Just don't blow it up. It's fireproof, but it can still be shredded. I'll put it in a Dagdian bag so you can take it without being noticed by your father."

"Noted… and another thing. Would you mind terribly if I also copied the design?"

"Uh… no? It's only a tad unique compared to other Dragon Knight armour so I can be a little more careless. Or at least, that was Owen's comment on my design choice."

She giggled. "I can see why he'd think that. Okay! Great! The coat is so cool…"

"Do you just want the coat or-"

"All of it. The coat, boots, pauldron, gauntlets, guards. I'll have it all modified and upgraded in a few days."

"In a few days? Aren't you going to be working on the Zerach?"

"Yeah, but I only need to start it off and I want to make sure that you are as prepared as possible in case the Outland Dragons break through. Dad and Naftali can finish off the rest of it the day after tomorrow if it goes to plan. If they need help, I'm sure Aunt Solaria can join in which leaves me all night and all day tomorrow to play with it!"

"As long as it doesn't get in the way of other tasks…" I told her before a small smile formed on my face. "Thank you. I'll get the gear now."

"Yay! Oh, and I guess I can tell you about the thing I wanted to give you since I doubt I'll be able to bring it over today…"

"What is it?"

"A power-shield, the first and only one of it's kind. It's powered through excess magic. I took the idea I used to build the circuit powering the model of your CT so you can be as stupid as you'd like. Like using yourself as a shield for an explosion without the risk of death. You'll have to probably work with it in order to get a good handle on how to use it to the fullest, be it extension or simply putting it away, but I know you're not completely incapable."

Though I was impressed that she was the one who had invented the self-charging CT, I wasn't going to boost her ego after that last comment. "One of these days, I'm not going to have the patience to tolerate all these insults."

"Maybe when you're like, a foot in the grave, and dying of old age. I'll be long dead by then, so I have no worries."

"Ah…" It was a surprisingly dark and depressing thought. I changed the subject back to her device, leaving existential mortality behind. "So, the only one of its kind, eh? What about you though? Wouldn't you, or even your kingdom, benefit from your shield bracelet creation too?"

"Perhaps… I originally made it as a thank you for saving my life, but as you guessed, I grew curious about other applications. Unfortunately, it only works as intended with someone who is over an eight-hundred-fifty magic frequency. Anything lower than that drains magic after its initial charge is used up which is not useful for a shield and you'd be better off without it. So, it is yours and yours alone."

"Oh… well I greatly appreciate the gift, Éabha."

"I'm just happy to help keep you alive, other people are going to need your reckless abandon I'm sure."

I went to make a remark when a CT rang on the couch behind me. We went over to it and I picked up the device I had abandoned, the screen showing Atlamillia was calling. I turned to Éabha. "Sorry, I have to take this. I'll have Deigh bring out the armour for you. If Orpheal-"

"I'll tell him you're busy," she finished, and I nodded, answering the call.

"Atlamillia, where have you been?!" I started picking up all the sheets on the table in no order and wandered to my room, shutting the door behind me.

Chapter Twenty-Three: Homesick

Deigh left the room with the equipment in the bag as I dropped the papers on the table.

"Hi…" Atlamillia said, her voice less than impressed with my concerns through the CT.

I parked myself at the desk. "Do you have any idea how worried I was about you?"

"There was a bunch of things that happened at once…" she answered. "It's mostly taken care of now. So, you don't need to worry."

I was more worried for her than whatever came up as she sounded tired, but she did distract me from it. "What happened?"

"Outland Monsters collapsed another collection of tunnels."

"A collection? How many is a collection?"

"About five in the west end, four in the east."

"Wait, you said another collection."

"Another seven tunnels collapsed yesterday."

"That's sixteen tunnel systems…"

"Yes… I've rerouted the knights to keep a handful of the remaining tunnels secure. Unfortunately, we don't have enough knights to secure them all and only have faith in hopes that they are left alone."

A sigh came out. "I really hope this is just a coincidence and Ciar isn't trying to get me to come out of hiding…"

"You're hiding? Why?! I just talked to Owen the other day and he said nothing!"

Guess he left that up to me. "You know how I was shot?"

"Yes…"

"Well the following morning, after getting back from hospital, a follower of Ciar's in the Seraphinean Legion blasted the penthouse using a charge cannon on a tyraulia. It ripped a portion of-"

"Are you alright?"

"We're fine. Luckily, Owen and I were in the dining room talking when we noticed her approach. He was able to put up a wall to deflect most of the blast. After that incident, we went to the Directors' Demesne and I was almost kidnapped."

"For the love of the gods, Aerrow!" She practically screamed in my ear and I winced, pulling the CT away. "You're supposed to be in friendly territory!"

"I know… but we knew that Ciar had vermin in Seraphina. It was just unfortunate with the timing and that two of them were also directors."

"Two of them… Alright, you're going to tell me every tiny detail from the time you talked to me about being shot, all the way to what you were doing the second before you picked up the CT."

"I don't think you need to be-"

"Spill."

"Is this what it's like when I pry over everything?"

"Yes."

Guess the receiving end did suck. "I hope you're comfy, it's a long story." I explained everything that happened in the last two and a half days from the trip to the Megalona Danguis Tribe to Owen giving me hell and the latest revelation in the Zerach. I took a small breather. "And now Éabha is going to be upgrading my armour so I have a little more defence."

"Good, because it sounds like you're going to fucking need it," she said without missing a beat even though she had been sitting in relative silence for the past half an hour. "So, the biggest issues you're having are the seals, some missing whelps and their lovely tribe ready to barrel in, and two groups of the same cult wanting you in some way or another."

"I miss being wanted by only a bunch of kids…"

"I miss you taking these monsters out and dealing with them… They're driving me nuts."

"Well, now you have some stories. That should entertain them for a while."

"Yeah and give them more fodder to this genius idea that they came up with to help you," she growled before growing silent for a moment. "While I can't help you with two of your problems; I'll look into your seals and any other possible references to Od Symalum when I can…"

She shivered slightly as she said the name and I agreed. "Yeah, I don't know what that thing is, but my reaction to reading it was about the same. It's uncomfortable in some horrible way."

"I'll see if Helah might know something more, if not, there is always the library I can send someone to go to."

"Don't be shocked if you find nothing. Zegrinath knew nothing of what the seals were for except for the Daemonias Realm itself…"

"Oh, I know. The gods are real fucking advanced when it comes to writing shit down…" If sarcasm were a physical weapon, she would have just destroyed a city. Her mood was just as sour. "So, no leads on your whelps?"

"None… as I said, they could be anywhere. A single portal radius… which we don't know how far that actually is and time is running out."

"I would have to imagine its not far from Seraphina if its on the mainland. Seraphineans love their tech too much and setting up an entirely new area secretly would be a pain."

"A pain, or a genius idea of deception. If being here has taught me anything, it's that Seraphs are incredibly determined."

"I don't know if all of them are as determined as your new friend. Are you sure she's capable of other modes other than workaholic and adrenaline chaser?"

"She loves learning new things…"

"So, no… You make the weirdest of friends."

"She's not… that weird. Blunt, oblivious to emotional regards of her words at times… Okay, she might be weird, but she's happy and that's all I care about. Plus, I'm sure she and Claudius would be two peas in a pod if they ever meet."

"Glad to know I wasn't the only one to think she was just a slightly grown Claudius."

"Heh, no…" I sighed as I thought about the kids… even though I didn't get to hang out with them as much since becoming king; I did enjoy the time I had with them. I missed Elwood Garden, the castle, Siofra… "I want to go home…"

"I know… but you're needed there."

"And I hate it! I'm stuck in this stupid building in the middle of the city somewhere. I don't even know where I am and I'm here with no leads to solve anything! I can't even open a window let alone go outside. Deigh can go through the underground, but it's not the same… I'm losing it a bit here and it's only been two days."

"I'm sure if you ask Owen in a few days, he can escort you around the block or something for a bit. But you need to give it some time. You have patience, unlike me, so you can make it until then. The Zerach might be done by then and maybe it can help find the whelps if your search expands off the island."

"Perhaps…" It was a nice thought. But since we hadn't even been able to stabilise the thing to stay powered without threatening to explode… I wasn't feeling confident that the machine was going to be ready for dealing with Marsutsepi classed monsters, let alone something substantial. I changed the subject. "How have you been?"

"Things have been fine here except for the impending doom of being locked in here-"

"I didn't ask about the kingdom, I asked about you," I interrupted, but not rudely so. I did want to know everything about the kingdom, but I was more concerned for her. "Have you been eating? Taking time for yourself? Hanging out with your friends? Sleeping?"

"Jakob forces me to eat when I forget, and I've been decently sleeping I suppose…"

"What about taking time-"

"Once in a while. When you get back, I'm going to disappear for a week. Find that place I've been sensing if it hasn't been found yet and raid it like a tomb robber."

A small laugh came out at her enthusiasm. At least she was in decent spirits. "Any nightmares?"

"Afraid of being killed?" She asked and I shook my head, not that she could see.

"I'm not asking for me."

"Oh, Aerrow, do me a favour and stop doting. I'm fine and your monsters are doing great. You need to focus on what needs to be done there and staying out of trouble… maybe find a girlfriend."

"And how am I supposed to do that last thing trapped in a modified apartment building?"

"I don't know; you're the creative one out of the two of us. Stare outside and window-shop or something."

"Are you insane? Why in the world would I do that?!"

"Cause you're desperate."

"Not desperate enough to creepily stare out a window!"

"It's not like they can see you so think of it not being creepy and for the greater good of the kingdom. If you spot someone of interest, you can figure out if they go through your area often."

"I think I'd rather be the bad guy…"

She sighed in annoyance, "Fine, have it your way…"

"I will because I'm the king."

"Whatever… look, I have to go. There are some things to work out-"

"Yeah… I know… but I appreciate you getting back to me."

"Of course, just make sure you stay your level-headed self, don't make stupid decisions, and try not to feel too homesick."

"I'm not sure how to do that last one…"

"Just think about what the kids will do when you get back."

I shuddered. They would never leave me alone. Ever. Again. "Not feeling that homesick anymore… I'll talk to you later, then?"

"Maybe I'll have the kids come do a call with you next time, eh?"

"That would be nice if you have the time."

We said our goodbyes and I ended the call, leaning back in my chair. What a nightmare this all was… and there wasn't much I could do about it, as usual. At least the kingdom seemed to be in a decent position, despite quite a few tunnels collapsing.

Atla got ahead of it, for now, at least.

Now if I could get ahead in finding the whelps… maybe I could get Azarias and Cyrus to scout out areas, not trespass, but an aerial view around the island…

That wasn't a terrible idea. And while they did that, I could go through all the horrible reading of the research Owen brought back. Hopefully, it wasn't a lot. I had yet to ask him about it.

I got up from the desk, pocketing the CT, and walked to the door. I opened it just as Éabha was about to knock on the other side. I looked down at her in confusion. "Something wrong?"

"Why do you always presume something is wrong?" She asked and I shrugged.

"Because usually there is something wrong, am I mistaken this time?"

"Not... entirely. The parts that are needed for the Zerach are going to take more time than initially thought after looking at the blueprints. So, we won't be able to reformat it before the dragons show up."

Great... Hopefully they were going to attack somewhere far from Domrael Hill until then. "Anything else?"

"Uh... well... yes. There is one other thing..." I waited patiently for her to figure out what she wanted to say before she sighed, "Never mind..."

"What is it?"

"It's just a stupid idea. It's not important or appropriate right now."

"It's clearly important to you."

"Sort of... Alright... I was wondering if I could stay over tomorrow or something... Show you some cool things, forget about the troubles of possibly the genocide of my race for a bit since neither of us can really do anything about that right now."

"I thought you wanted to work on your projects too. You can't do that here."

"I do, I really do. But Deigh mentioned she wanted to show me something but in exchange, you needed something fun to do."

"Fun? This really isn't the time for that considering, I wouldn't even know how to have fun right now," I replied apologetically and internally sent out a message to Deigh, wondering what the hell she was thinking. "I'm sure Deigh will show you whatever she wanted to show you without bargaining."

"I mean... maybe..." She may have been hard to read at times... but she wasn't very good at hiding disappointment. "I kinda figured. It's why I said it was stupid, there's too much happening so..."

Dammit… with what she said, knowing that going through the databases wasn't going to be done solely by me and that I also wasn't a slow reader, even if there were years of logs; it probably wasn't going to take five days to go through them. I sighed, "It's not stupid to want to have fun with someone… You can come over tomorrow and stay if you want-"

"Really?!" Éabha exclaimed excitedly as she practically danced in place. "We're going to have a blast! I'll bring snacks and… stuff… Hmm, what do you bring to a sleepover?"

Sleepover, eh? Well, I guess that was implied when she said stay. Orpheal was probably going to be too busy to waste time to come and get her anyway. "I'm not sure… I've never had a sleepover before."

"Then it will be a learning experience for the both of us! Hehe… this is great!"

My homesickness left slightly as her excitement was contagious and a small smile formed on my face. "Maybe do some research on the subject first. That way you get the best results?"

"Good thinking! I'll do that before I go to sleep tonight."

"Make sure you actually get sleep…" I muttered as she started to list things off that she needed to do, not hearing what I said. I planted a hand on her head, ending her jittering. "Oh, good. You do have a cease button, Sparky."

"Did you just call me Sparky?!"

"Yes… and I think it's accurate. Relax, you literally have the rest of the day today and all day tomorrow to get ready so it's the best it can possibly be."

"But what about-"

"You're staying over, yes? We have all night to do whatever you have planned for this… *needed fun* sleepover." I removed my hand and she continued to stay still. Her excitement was barely contained behind her big, sky-blue eyes. "It's not like I'm going anywhere."

"That's true… I should get going. Dad is waiting for me."

I nodded and she left, leaving me to wonder if this sleepover was a good idea at all.

00000

I waved goodbye to the Seraphs after they had finished gathering the last of the details for the Zerach and watched them disappear in the bright light of the

Teleport Glyph. Now that they were gone, other projects could be discussed and put into motion.

I turned to Owen. "How successful was your mission?"

"Yeah," Azarias growled, "where the hell were you all night?!"

"Gathering intel," the general answered, not very impressed before turning back to me. The gaze directed at the knight was gone. "And it was very successful, quite a few logs to go through, but not as many as there could have been. I'll show what I found upstairs."

A small sigh escaped, but I wasn't sure if it was one of relief or mild annoyance at the number of logs that were waiting for us to go through. The three of us followed Owen upstairs and parked ourselves on the couches, Cyrus opting to sit next to me, across from his friend. Owen went to his room and came out a moment later with a tablet and sat in the vacated spot next to Azarias.

I answered the question that was on the brunet's tongue before he could ask it. "Owen had the brilliant idea of hacking into the remaining directors' databases to see if they had details around Outland Dragons – hoping that we could find a reason why the whelps were taken in the first place and if any of the directors left could also be traitors."

"And I'm guessing the sarcasm is because his actions were illegal…" Azarias confirmed and I gave a nod, though it was only half the reason. "Are there any other tasks that can be done besides reading logs?"

"I did think of something earlier that might be able to lessen resources on Seraphina to finding the dragons, but it will be a little more difficult to do between the lack of our own resources and well, babysitting me."

"It's not so much as babysitting you but protecting you," Cyrus corrected, and I shrugged.

There wasn't much of a difference in my head. "Still has to be someone here besides Deigh in case something does happen, but the mission I thought of is a partner job for the same reason. Since there aren't any leads on the whelps, scouting is the next step."

"Scouting would do wonders to speed things up," Owen pondered. "And since we can't directly ask for assistance without giving away our hand… just asking for some scouting maps and tips from the Legion and local law enforcement won't. We might even be able to find out not just where the whelps could be but congregations of where Ciar's followers might meet."

Finding Ciar was also optimal, something I hadn't even considered being a possible outcome to the missions. "Finding their meeting spots, maybe finding Ciar – get people to talk about the whelps, whoever else has gone missing, and what other projects they could be doing. The only problem will come with leaving the city boundaries and anything underground... If we can't find anything, the search will have to expand and I'm not sure how grand an idea it is for you three to leave the kingdom."

"Yeah, that would be a problem, especially if the dragons attack in the same area or early. Then there is the amount of ground that could actually be covered when we take turns doing expeditions..." Azarias agreed with a small sigh. "Sage would be perfect for ground reconnaissance, but when it comes to having to go farther out, it takes a lot more time to get to and from locations if we can't go by train. Eventually, those trips are going to last more than a day."

"And those scouting missions could turn disastrous if you're caught unprepared – someone could see a pattern, attack, and force our hand if they take the route of ransom..." The good idea was quickly turning into a risky operation.

Cyrus leaned on the armrest. "It's a risk that is worth taking. Two birds, one stone."

"There is also the fact that we aren't new to dangerous missions, both Outland Monsters, Dragons, and people," Owen reassured. "The only problem that comes up is if Ciar rears his head and getting away isn't an option."

My chest gave off a soft, but painful pulse and I rubbed it. "About that... what is the status of Ciar's samples?"

He gave a small frown, looking away from my hand. "They're still trying to construct the DNA sequence, it's going faster with the equipment here, but a lot of it has to be manually constructed. Removing impurities has also been a challenge since the samples are over three months old."

"And the venom?"

"Also going faster, but when I asked Naftali about it yesterday – they might have hit a wall. He was having his people try a different method to get around it."

"So, the only real escape from Ciar would be to outfly him or a Chaos Portal until an antidote or vaccine is made."

"Or killing him," Azarias added cheerfully. "He can't hurt anyone if he's dead."

True enough. "If you think you can take him without dying, then do so, but…"

"Be careful, we know…" His happy demeanour lost its motivation. "Oh, who are we kidding? We don't even know how much it takes to kill the bastard, especially after all this time."

There was an uneasy silence that fell over the living room. It was exactly as he said. We didn't know. It had been three months since anyone has seen him and, in that time, who knew how much stronger he could have become. He was strong the first time around. What would happen if we did get the upper hand? The last two times, he fled to heal… I doubted it would be any different if we had managed to fight him to that point again. He knew his limitations, long before we would know, and he'd escape before it was a liability.

I shook my head, trying to clear the horrible thoughts that started to form. "Let's just stick to the plan of running away until we have a better idea of what Ciar has become and for now focus on scouting mission steps. We need maps, local information, teams…"

"I can head to a barrack to get maps and feedback about the surrounding area off the island," Owen offered. "Someone has to go to the local precincts, gather intelligence there."

"We should split that into two halves." Cyrus suggested. "Azarias can go first, that way he can bring back some food for supper and anything else we might need, and I can take the night shift."

"That frees up time for me to juggle other barracks if need be…" Owen turned to me. "Do you have any objections to the plan?"

I shook my head. "None and if it goes well, we can get started tomorrow."

"Éabha is coming over tomorrow, isn't she?"

"Yeah, probably in the afternoon. Though, I'm not entirely sure how this sleepover thing will go…" A sigh came out as my hand dropped to my lap. Playing around was the last thing on my mind.

"I'm sure it will be fine. We'll stay out of the way to make it as authentic as possible because it's an important experience for you as a young adult, won't we, Azarias…"

"Why are you singling me out for?!" the brunet exclaimed. "And besides, shouldn't we be supervising this? Leaving two young adults of the opposite genders alone always leads to trouble – the kind we don't want."

"Yes, we should, but also…" Owen didn't finish, but he didn't seem to need to as Azarias made an 'oh' noise, some unknown discussion taking place before shaking his head.

"Fine, out of the way, but not out of reach if you need us…"

I raised a brow, suspiciously. "What was that also about?"

"Oh, that? Well, if you tried to make supper and no one was around…"

"My cooking isn't that bad…" I growled, not believing his answer to be the truth, but left it be. "It's just not complicated."

"You're not making peanut butter sandwiches…" Owen declared, and a triumphant laugh came out of me.

"On the contrary, Uncle. They would be glorious peanut butter and *jam* sandwiches. Royalty's greatest creation. Why would I make something so basic for a guest as a simple peanut butter sandwich?"

Azarias's hand met his face while an aggressive sigh came out of Cyrus beside me.

"I can't let this be…" the red knight mumbled, standing up.

"Can't let-" I started, passing him a confused look only for him to grab my hand, dragging me off the couch. "Ah, hey!"

"You're learning how to cook some basic meals."

"I thought we were having take out-"

"Azarias can bring back groceries instead to replenish the stocks."

00000

I poked at the pasta I managed to cook. It was alright, slightly overcooked as it was a bit mushy. The tomato sauce with some vegetables was slightly bland, but edible, and not something I looked forward to doing again. Cyrus was gone and while Azarias was devouring it by the spoonful, I doubted he would have been as enthusiastic if he hadn't been starving.

He swallowed and pointed the utensil at me. "Are you going to eat or what?"

"I ate some but… this sucks." I pushed the dish away, finished with it.

"You can't be good at everything, but it's not that bad."

"Compared to every other meal I've ever had… this is like dirt and I've eaten enough dirt to know."

A laugh came from him, "What you're experiencing is what happens when you make food for yourself. Your food will never taste as good compared to someone else making it for you, especially if it's made with love and your food always is."

"Remind me to never cook a meal for myself again…"

"Okay, but what if you're on cooking duty and we're in the middle of nowhere?"

"Guess I'll go hungry."

"You really don't like your own cooking…" He shoved another spoonful in his mouth with a shrug. "Still beffer than my firsf fime."

"You were probably a kid the first time you cooked, so I'm not that surprised." I thought back to last night, a similar set up but this time I was alone with Azarias. Maybe now was a good time to bring up what his reaction was about. "Hey, can I ask you something personal?"

He swallowed his bite, the coldness I saw last night coming back. "Depends on the question…"

"Last night…" I hesitated further, still unsure, but went with it, curiosity cracking my better judgment. "Did that demon have something to do with why it's just the three of you in your family?"

"Not exactly… Kris's father pulled a disappearing act as soon as he found out that Larissa was pregnant. To this day no one knows where he scurried off to after telling her to break the egg or he was gone… You already know what her answer was."

"Wow… was not expecting that…"

"Neither was she, but I noticed that since being in the castle, Cyrus has been more forward than he usually is… And she might be interested." A small growl came out. "And I can't stand that thought!"

"Er, why? Cyrus is your best friend. Wouldn't that be a good thing for your younger sister to be with someone you know and trust. Good for Kris?"

"Exactly! He's my best friend, but she's also my sister – I don't want it to go sour."

"You really think it could? How long have they known each other?"

"Eight, nine years… okay it's highly unlikely but I don't want him to boss me around because I'd be the 'younger' brother!"

I was left a bit stunned before we both started laughing a bit. Like he would actually listen to whatever Cyrus said in a casual setting.

He stopped after a short bit, his thoughts drifting elsewhere. "But I guess that doesn't answer what you were asking…"

"You… don't have to answer it. It was insensitive of me. Sorry." I stood up, noticing his dish was empty. "If you're done, I'll take care of the dishes."

He didn't say anything as he gave a small nod and left, heading upstairs, and muttering about sorting through the information he brought back that we both knew didn't need to be any more sorted out.

I washed the dishes, putting them away after drying them, and turned around to be met with prying red eyes in a dark cave. I backed up, running into the counter painfully behind me in a panic. I blinked and the cave was gone along with Ciar, leaving me alone. I looked around, frantically only to realize it was all in my head. A tsk came out in frustration, bracing against the counter. A bit of water left behind touched my skin which only brought me to Siofra's blood covered streets. The tunnels.

"*Aerrow,*" Deigh's voice broke through the memories, softly.

"I'm here," I growled out, quietly, grabbing the dish towel and dried both the counter and my hand.

"*Maybe you should-*"

"I'm fine, just startled myself."

She didn't push the subject further. "*I'm going to catch a few fish. I'll be back soon.*"

"*Happy hunting…*" I muttered, looking back into the darkened part of the floor, rubbing the back of my neck.

Only the Zerach sat there now and while significantly less scarier than Ciar; it was still a bit unsettling to see. It was a great machine, but it was lifeless. I set the dish towel on its railing and headed back upstairs, turning off the lights behind me.

It didn't take me long to get from the first floor to my room, my book where I had left it that morning. A small sigh came out. It had been quite the day, but it was productive in a way, so I couldn't complain – even with whatever the hell that was about a few minutes ago.

Yet a frown formed; instead of feeling accomplished, there was a daunting feeling that I couldn't place. The CT had found its way into my hand and I stared at it.

Why did I want to check in with Atlamillia? It was late and she would only get mad if I did call her... So, why-

A knock came from the doorframe and I jumped slightly in surprise, turning to it. Azarias stood there, leaning against the frame, his arms crossed, but little energy came from him. "Hey."

"Hi..." I put the CT back in my pocket and straightened my stance. "What's up?"

"You wanted to know what happened to my family? How it relates to Freegdred?"

"I don't want to intrude on personal-"

"And I want you to know what happens when you fuck with things that you shouldn't play with." He pointed at the couches in the other room. "Care to find out?"

I nodded hesitantly and swallowed the discomfort. He seemed hollow, nothing like the man I had known him to be. It was more than unsettling. I walked out of my room and we sat across from each other on the couches. The silence went from seconds to almost a minute as he thought over what ever was going through his head.

Then, he spoke. "You read the passage on what Freegdred is?"

I nodded. "A wish maker with conditions."

"My parents... Gods, still to this day I don't understand their mindset when they got a hold of the summoning ritual." He gave a small sigh before continuing, "They summoned Freegdred and from looking at a journal left behind from my father, they wished that both my sister and I would be well off, rich and famous – that sort of thing. It was heartwarming to read at first but knowing the outcome of what happened... Freegdred saw greed in their hearts."

"How could asking for your children to be well-off be greedy?" I questioned.

"The journal wasn't shy in explaining a lot of it. They were in debt, a lot of debt between gambling, deals – even had a contract with, er, never mind..."

"Cyrus's parents?"

He nodded. "He told you, did he?"

"Last night... So, your parents were in a lot of trouble."

"They were. The fame and fortune from child prodigies would have not only given them the extra money, but also protection through security and public presence... Freegdred could see that when he heard the wish after being summoned into our world and decided to kill them. But was it before or after they offered an exchange? I'm not sure."

"That's an odd detail to think about. From my understanding, the demon just sensing the greed should have just attacked, not listen to a bargain."

"It might have, but the deal would have been definitely something to ponder about," he almost spat out, the conversation bringing back emotions that he had been hiding well up until that point. "Freegdred likes exotic gifts, food especially, so when I read later on in the journal where they had..."

He choked on his words and I let him decide if he wanted to continue. After a moment, he cleared his throat.

"My father, at least, was going to offer Larissa as a gift to it since he didn't think she was worth anything even if she got Freegdred's blessing. The demon could do anything it wanted to do to her and Rhea."

"They were just going to offer her up? How old were you when they...?"

"She was eight, I was ten... but that's not even the worse of it... I was running late that day from playing with my friends in Elwood Garden and came home to that massacre. Freegdred had already started to advance on Larissa, Rhea was trying to defend her."

"Wait, why would Freegdred attack Larissa and Rhea if they were the ones that were offered?"

"Why do you think?" He asked, emotionlessly and it took me less than a second for it to dawn on me.

"They tried to offer you instead, switching the deal around... Gods..."

"Freegdred was able to kill both of us along with our pathetic parents, but he didn't get any further than knocking my sister and her dragon into a wall when Sage and I attacked. One thing my parents knew for certain was my potential as an earth element user – I was, and still am, a prodigy in massive, hard hitting damage and imagination. Sage and I used our power to kill that fat, ugly bastard before he could kill us."

"You killed a Heftvarys level demon at the age of ten?" To say I was astounded was putting it mildly. "That's insane."

"At the time, I had never used such skills before, such violence, but put under that pressure... I couldn't run with Larissa and Rhea and there was no way I would have been able to get help. So, I did everything I could to stop it... and we did."

"Just knowing the fight with the Terror Hounds and how the Effigy bled... that must have been quite the blood bath."

"It was. After Sage and I killed it, the four of us were left in the hallway completely shocked of everything that happened for, I don't know how long before neighbours noticed the door was wide open. I think someone came in for a moment, saw the mess and then called the guard." A small laugh came out of him, "Their faces when coming in, seeing the demon like that will forever stay with me. The face of, 'I don't get paid enough for this shit'. They quickly helped us then called in the Dragon Knights. Owen was the one who answered the call."

"You met him way back then, eh?"

"Almost twenty years now, and he's still the same. He talked to us like we were more than just traumatized kids. By the time he arrived, the guard had thought that Sage and I had killed everyone there, not just the demon. They even separated us from Larissa and Rhea. Owen put us back together again. He wasn't even close to suspicious, it showed his experience, something that the guard didn't have."

"That and I doubt the guard deals with demons very often."

"No, no they certainly don't. Being a Dragon Knight definitely makes you deal with that sort of thing more often than I'd like to admit."

What a horrible thought... "So, Owen explained what happened then?"

"He did. He explained everything to us from what the monster was, how it got there, etc. Eventually, he asked us if we knew why our parents would have summoned such a creature. We didn't know, of course. It wasn't until exploring our parents' things that we got that answer, also with the help of Owen."

"He left quite the impression on you."

"He did. Seeing him come to my house on Missiletainn, wearing his black cape and his armour before it had Seraphinean tech… He was both awe inspiring and terrifying. But when he found out that Sage and I had killed the monster, he was surprised, said the usual, 'you're so brave to kill a monster' and it stuck with me. Brave, but only for Larissa and Rhea, that's what I told him. Eight years later, I signed up for the Dragon Knight Trials and Owen substituted in for the commander that was judging my trial. He wanted to see how much Sage and I had grown, and then he twisted the trial, forcing us to fight him because the monsters were not nearly as strong as the demon was."

"I think I remember that trial. Owen left the booth and eight-year-old me didn't understand why he left…" A small chuckle came out as the memory stepped forward. "It's nice to know that he wasn't only brutal with me…"

"He was a monster, just as terrifying as I thought he was eight years prior, especially with Missiletainn as his back up…"

"I can't remember who won, but I'm going to say you didn't win that fight."

"I still can't beat Owen to this day so, you'd be right. He destroyed our asses, but we did have to make those two actually work for it a bit. And then he passed us."

"I guess that's when he took you as his protégé."

He nodded. "Me and a real, brooding jerk that I had trained with a few times at the training grounds. He was quite the character before the trial, but after he came back – Cyrus was someone completely different, and I couldn't leave him be after that."

"He must have hated you for that."

"He almost killed me… on more than one occasion, but that's in the past." He went back to being solemn. "None of this would have happened if my parents never summoned Freegdred… A part of me is glad that it turned out the way it had… but it haunts me still that they could have done something like that, thinking that they could get away from their problems and that's why I don't talk about them. Why that demon – will forever be hated for taking them away for an arrogant mistake which I could only guess caused them to have a psychotic break. They loved us, so how could they give us up if they were sane?"

"It must be difficult to both love and hate your parents. Love them for what they had intended before what they actually did."

"It is… so, I try not to think on it, hoping that one day, their memory will just disappear. I have Larissa, Rhea, Kris, and Ramekhan now as my blood relatives and can be there for them like our parents never could… So, if you don't mind, I'd like it if you never brought up the subject again. That, or hit me hard enough for the memory of them to leave."

"I can't do that," I laughed slightly, and he gave a dramatic sigh.

"Lame… So, what did you learn from this?"

"Don't play with things from a different world and that you are one hell of a big brother."

"Damn right I am. Now let's get you some tea or water because you have not had nearly enough liquids today."

"Good gods, now I have two of you…"

Chapter Twenty-Four: Dinner with a Demon

Atlamillia ended the call and shoved the CT in her pocket as she stood up from her desk. Aerrow… was a walking hazard. If she didn't die due to stress because of him, it would have been a miracle. She looked to the clock in her bedroom. It was almost time to head to the Raghnall home for her dinner date. She didn't want to go, but for Dani, she would. Her request at this dinner would be simple and would more than please Eudoxia and Tyriel…

Was it throwing Aerrow under a dragon a little bit? Somewhat… but it's not like she was putting words in his mouth.

She went over to the vanity and looked over the emerald green, off-shoulder, slim floor gown she was wearing, slightly adjusting the fabric on her arms. Had she been in Absalom all Kalokairtas, she would have tanned a bit more than the pale colour she had now just by being outside to training. But the sun that lit up Asylotum was not the same. It didn't truly exist, just as the moons of Ori and Val that lit up Asylotum weren't real. They pulled the tides or were warm under the light, but they were functioning as a mortal thought they would. Had it been a few thousand years earlier, the knowledge of UV rays and outer-stellar objects wouldn't have crossed their minds.

She knew though.

She knew the moons blocked many harmful things the chaos of space could throw at her massive world, or the UV rays and plasma that the sun threw on solar winds which hit Orithin's magnetic field that created the beautiful auroras across much of her kingdom. But none of that happened in Asylotum. Why would it need to? It was just a land that needed the basics of what would be considered normal.

She sighed, realizing she zoned out as she struggled with creating a small bun. She looked over at her partner that was amused at her struggles, laying on her bed. "How many times must I ask you to not allow me to space out before you actually listen?"

"An infinite amount. You don't allow yourself to leave reality enough."

"Nothing good comes from it," Atlamillia growled as she tried the round bun again. It wasn't cooperating. "You didn't happen to learn that transformation ability that Deigh has learnt without my knowledge, have you?"

"I have no need to learn such a skill," she replied as she stretched a bit. "But if you want me to learn it for the sake of doing your hair, I will."

"For someone who doesn't have a need to learn it, you don't need much prompt to go out of your way…"

"To make your life easier, I would die for you if it didn't kill you. Some little cosmetic skill has no comparison, you know that."

She did know that, and frankly, she didn't deserve Lucilla just on dedication alone. "Well, don't die any time soon… okay?"

"I don't plan on it… as for your hair, you might want to ask for some assistance since I cannot at this very moment."

She turned to the mirror, looking at the bedroom door's reflection. "Bretheena, can I have your assistance?"

The door opened almost immediately as the strawberry blonde came in, wearing a simple blue gown and her hair down for once. Her long bangs covered the left side of her face in both a beautiful and intimidating manner. Exactly who Atlamillia needed as her escort tonight. "Having hair troubles?"

"Yes… I just want a simple, round bun, and it's being difficult."

"I can do that," she laughed a bit and took the top half Atlamillia was struggling with. In a matter of a minute or so, Bretheena was putting in the final bobby pin, securing the rose bun in place. She grabbed the hand mirror on the vanity and angled it so it could reflect into the larger mirror to let Atlamillia see the impressive work. "Is this alright?"

"It's beautiful, thank you."

"All ready to go then?" She asked as Atlamillia turned around to face her.

"I believe so."

"Do you have a plan ready to let Dani leave without conflict?"

"Yes, just don't look surprised when it's brought up."

Bretheena raised the eyebrow that was visible. "What could you have in mind that would surprise me?"

"I'd discuss it, but we're running late." Atlamillia looked over at Lucilla. "We'll be back relatively soon."

"I'll be ready to attack upon request," the blue dragon replied too casually, and she curled up. "Oh, and you might want to say goodbye to the little monsters unless you want them to follow you."

Atlamillia sighed. The children were a nightmare, any time that something came up that wasn't expected, they were knee deep into business not of their own. Like a surprise outing. Where would those kids be at such an hour?

Courtyard probably. Knowing Gasper and Lyric, they would want to be near the dining room while pretending to be patient. They would also probably be practicing their studies if they were restless.

Poor courtyard, it never got a break from chaos.

By the time Atlamillia and Bretheena got there, the sun was starting to get lower in the sky, giving it a slight red tinge through the windows which would become a brilliant hue in time. It would be a nice day tomorrow.

The sounds of children laughing came to her ears as they went through the courtyard door, so much quieter than the one Siofra Castle had. On the other side, the flowers seemed happy with the children all standing in a circle of awe as Aoife showed off the light orbs that she had been working on, letting them dance around and a small smile formed on Atlamillia's face. Aoife could have been a performing artist with the lights and dress alone. The single shoulder, teal gown was form fitting on the girl, making her incredibly elegant and nobler than what Atlamillia had known her to be.

It was like her personality, a juxtaposition.

Aoife looked over at them and the orbs disappeared. The girl flushed slightly. "You look so pretty in green… why haven't you worn this before?!"

"There haven't been many opportunities for this…" It was somewhat a lie. There were many times where she could have worn it, but being that it was the last gift her father had bought her while they were out in the city… It took a while to bring herself to wear it. Now she hoped that it would bring her some luck tonight. She looked at the girl, her head tilting slightly in confusion. "Why are you wearing a gown?"

"Going to put the etiquette lessons Dani and you have taught me to help save our friend from hell," she answered calmly, settling into a persona that Atlamillia had rarely seen. It made her miss the old Aoife a bit, but she also enjoyed the calm air it gave. "The kids were going to sneak out when they noticed you were missing and saw me in a dress."

"We were not!" Claudius argued and the other kids looked up at him, destroying the lie he attempted to make. He looked at them before sighing. "We really need to work on your skills to lie when caught…"

313

Atlamillia shook her head. "Larissa knows that we'll be heading out, so you guys need to be on your best behaviour... We'll be back a little later tonight."

"But you might need a hero to rescue you," Gasper started, and she shook her head. "No fair..."

"I want to know what Dani's parents are like..." Juno sighed. "There are so many stories... is it true that Dani has brothers?"

She nodded. "She does, but they are a bit older than you."

"Oh..." The disappointment from the 'oh' was staggering.

"I believe your food will be ready shortly, so, go wash up. I heard Ramsey made something special for you tonight." Their faces lit up in glee and they started heading inside with the minor exception of Gasper who waited for the others to leave before coming up to her.

She gave him a confused look, but before she could ask, he hugged her. "Good luck."

Surprise formed before a small smile as she remembered his little vow from the other night and ruffled his hair a bit. "Thanks."

He looked up at her, perhaps a bit paler than normal and she frowned. He mimicked her look. "What is it?"

"Are you feeling alright?"

He had a confused expression for a moment then turned away in embarrassment. "It's a bad day with Asylotum... like how it is with Aerrow and Uncle Owen."

"You should've asked Larissa or Helena for medicine..."

"But then the other kids will laugh at me. Juno has the same element and doesn't get nearly as sick."

"You can't help it if you're not feeling well, Gasper. Plus, if they tease you about being weak, tell them that only powerful magic users only feel bad in Asylotum if they aren't compatible. And if they don't believe you, tell them to ask anyone in the castle."

"Even you?"

"Especially me. I've dealing with both Aerrow and Uncle Owen for the past three months."

"Okay," he laughed a bit and then let her go, running inside after the others.

Aoife and Bretheena gave her questioning looks, ones she didn't leave in suspense, and quickly explained. "Gasper has decided to take up the role of being my big brother while Aerrow is gone."

"That's... a bit weird, even for him. Why?" Aoife asked.

"He was going to be one before the attack on Siofra... So, he's filling the void." She looked over to the door that was closed. "I think he feels like he failed before he even started."

"Poor kid." Bretheena sighed, "I hope he knows it wasn't his fault."

"I think he does... but for right now, he's practicing so that when he's older, he can teach his kids. And as sappy as it is, it would be cruel to deny him of that."

A small giggle came from Aoife and Atlamillia barely had time to prepare as the girl attacked her in a massive hug. "You're so cute, you know that?"

"Stop it; I have a reputation..."

"Not with us you don't!"

She sighed and hugged back slightly. "Happy?"

"No."

00000

The Raghnall manor was like the other manors in the area, there was nothing special or different physically, but the atmosphere... Atlamillia wanted to crawl back to the castle. She didn't know why she felt as she had; it wasn't exactly a sense she had often, but it was there. She knew she was greatly unwanted. Under any other circumstance, maybe she might have been. Eudoxia did want to raise her family status like the power-hungry, ambitious woman that she was... but she also wasn't stupid. She knew why Atlamillia announced that she was visiting with little warning.

"*Your plan may not be enough...*" Lucilla voiced her concern and Atlamillia gave a small nod. "*I'm not there, but I feel like an Outland Pit would be more appealing just from feeling what you are.*"

"*I'm tempted to see if there is much of a difference... Can you do me a favour?*"

"Of course."

"Think of two other plans in case this isn't enough. I'm not going to be able to concentrate with a sound plan if this is going to be throughout all of supper..."

"No... I guess you wouldn't. This feeling is not something either of us are used to..." Lucilla gave a small sigh. *"I'll think of two other options for you, but for now, I really need to silence most of the link. It's setting my scales on end."*

"Do what you must," she told her, and she felt her partner close off most of her senses except for the basic ones.

She looked over at Aoife and Bretheena as they reached the door to the manor. Bretheena looked neutral in expression, but Aoife looked like she wanted to throw up. Her complexion was a bit pale, and she was biting her lip slightly on the side, something she rarely did.

"Are you okay?" She asked her.

Aoife nodded as Bretheena knocked on the door. "Yeah, I'm fine. This place is just tainted with pain and control…"

"You sound like Aerrow," she tried to joke, but it only half worked as the small smile that formed, didn't last.

"I've always been good with sensing the well being of places and people… but since practicing magic with you and Dani, they've just got better and more… potent. Dani's terrified." She turned to her, more serious than Atlamillia had ever seen her be. "We have to succeed; I don't care the cost."

"We'll get her home," Bretheena stated quietly, her head tilting as she heard something they couldn't. "Relax and pretend to be happy."

There was only a moment between the words coming from her mouth and the door opening to a man in a full suit. He bowed before them. "Good evening, Princess Atlamillia and guests. Lady Eudoxia is waiting in the dining hall. This way."

"Thank you," Atlamillia told him as they followed him, protocol and etiquette taking over the horrible feeling the house brought. "I have to apologize; I have never been to the Raghnall home before. What is your name?"

"Grier, Your Highness. I'm the family butler for the past seven hundred years."

"That's a long time…" Aoife stated out, her calm, noble demeanour coming back.

The man chuckled. "Yes, it is. Many Raghnalls have come and gone through the years and I have a feeling that one more may be leaving tonight."

"You are surprisingly open with someone who could be considered an enemy in these circumstances…" Atlamillia said, and the butler nodded.

"Perhaps. But I want what's best for my family and knowing what goes on in these walls… Lady Eudoxia has been very vocal about her displeasure of Lady Dani being on her own, especially after the attack in the capital. It scared Lady Eudoxia and Lord Tyriel when she didn't contact them. They thought the worst as I had… But their iron grip is not what Lady Dani can bare…." Grier looked back at her. "I do hope that you can ease the pain from both sides."

"We'll try… but as far as we're supposed to be aware of, Dani isn't here."

Grier gave barely a laugh. "Yes, I suppose that is the truth we're stuck with, isn't it?"

There wasn't any more discussion as she practically felt the tension up ahead. Two great doors sat at the end of the hall they turned into and Grier opened them once they arrived. On the inside was a large dining hall with a table to match that could seat fourteen people at a time. Eudoxia sat at the head on the far end, and her husband, Tyriel, sat next to her. His ashen blond hair was tied back into a small ponytail, neatly, as his light blue eyes, that were similar to Dani's, judged them. Grier led them to their seats on the opposite end of the lady of the house and left with a bow. Atlamillia looked to the house leader and found the gaze was unexpectedly intimidating, more judgmental, and unsettling than her husband's. Her green gaze looked not just at her, but through her, but the expression on her face was neutral, if not slightly happy.

It was a terrifying mask.

"Princess Atlamillia, it's a pleasure to see you after so long. I didn't see you at the meeting the king had before he left," Eudoxia greeted, gracefully but also with inquiry. "It was unexpected."

"I was with Matron Helah," Atlamillia told her, not that it was any of her business, but she needed to create some sort of foothold.

"The Matron, so late?"

"It was a late training session."

"Oh, I see. I figured your lessons would have finished before the Anoxiver Festival."

Atlamillia gave a nod in agreement. "They did. These are advanced studies in elemental magic."

"I'm happy to hear that our leaders are keeping diligent as ever despite everything. You're looking well. Much better than when I last saw you at the coronation – what an experience that was, wasn't it?"

"It was, but I hope nothing like it occurs again."

"No, I hope it doesn't either. I've never seen you lose your composure as such. Eadric must have been important to you."

The words should have sounded consolidating, but the way she said it, or rather implied, were like nails on a chalkboard. It set her even more on edge, but somehow, she kept it out of her voice. "He was giving up his place on the council to be my retainer before his death. Finding out that he was murdered trying to save my life was unexpected and there wasn't much time to process it. So, he was important to me, yes."

"As a retainer or as a partner?"

"Excuse me?"

"Just a bit of an unexpected reaction for someone that, as far as many of us knew, you didn't have an attachment with. Unless it was a ruse."

"He was my friend, a new friendship that came to be just before Absalom was attacked. It's not really a surprise that the rounds of gossip hadn't reached outside of the castle by then."

"Gossip, rumours. They usually tell the truth to some regard."

"And they did, up until a few days before the attack. I really didn't have any personal feelings for him in that manner." Food was brought into the hall and were set in front of the five of them. She waited for the servants to leave before she continued. "Lady Eudoxia, why are you bringing up rumours and, admittedly, strange accusations?"

"Dani has been seen in the castle for the last three months, yet our king informed me that he hadn't noticed her there once. Was he lying?"

"Not on purpose," Atlamillia answered, cautious of how she worded her phrases. "She's my friend and has often been invited to the castle to help with my training or tea. King's General Owen has also offered his services to helping her grow which also brought her to the castle."

"Yet the king didn't know?"

"They did talk, frequently in fact, but I don't believe she once introduced herself as being your daughter and it wasn't something that ever came up in discussions between the two of us."

"It's clearly common place that you make friends in circles far below your stature…"

She felt Aoife and Bretheena tense at the comment, but thankfully didn't show or speak their insults. Atlamillia grabbed the reins again. "They are far more valuable as friends than many of the nobles. You should know that all too well, Lady Eudoxia."

"I'll admit, the yes-men of our classes are quite boring… but there are many who aren't."

"I'm aware, I happen to be friends with one… speaking of, where is she?"

"Here, safe and ready to resume her duties as heir to the family line."

"That isn't what was informed to me by my butler this morning." The statement was far from innocent as the undertone she added was more questioning of Eudoxia's loyalties to the crown. It wasn't unnoticed by the woman.

"This is because she came home this afternoon. I was so sickened with grief at the thought of her being like those back in Siofra and to finally have her show up, home again…" The words were genuine, but they were also off. "I can't bare the thought of her running off again."

"It seems strange for her to come home suddenly…" she said in a pondering tone, and the woman across the table sneered slightly.

"Are you implying that she never would come back?"

"No, not at all. She was just in the middle of training and she's not one to just disappear without telling anyone that she would be gone for more than a day or so. She sends messages if something unexpected happens either through letters or CT. We were worried something happened to her."

"Oh… my apologies, Princess Atlamillia, for the accusation." Eudoxia relaxed slightly. "You seem to know her quite well."

She gave another nod. "We've only been friends for a few months, but having trained and learned new things together, I feel like we've grown quite quicker than most would in such a short time."

"Then you wouldn't mind sharing how she fits in at the castle if she's been there all this time. She's not as open with her mother, unfortunately, so its hard to read if she's uncomfortable or not."

"She's quite in place when she visits; she's well liked. You've raised her well."

"Excellent, I'm glad."

Atlamillia turned to the plate that she hadn't realized she had mostly finished. She may not eat when she's emotionally stressed, but dammit if she didn't gorge on food when it was any other stress. She looked back to the woman across the table. "Would it be possible to let her stay at the castle for the time being?"

"She just got home. Why would she want to leave again so soon?"

"She might not, but as house leader, you must see a request from the princess for her assistance to be a prosperous one. If not just for the princess but for the king."

"Perhaps… but I feel like the conversation should include her and my second eldest… I wouldn't normally have him in such discussions, but he has been acting heir since her disappearance."

"Of course, it's a family matter after all. And with your house spare, I can bring about a matter I've been meaning to discuss with you."

She raised a brow before calling Grier.

The butler came in from the door he exited from with a bow. "Yes, Lady Eudoxia?"

"Please retrieve Dani and Endymion – tell them to be properly dressed for our guests and dessert." She turned to Atlamillia. "That is, if you are wanting dessert, Princess Atlamillia? It's a family special."

"I've heard from Dani that it's quite delicious if it's the one I'm thinking of."

A small laugh came from her, one that set the mood to a less tense one. "She's always loved it, so this is no surprise. Grier, if you could then?"

"Of course, my lady."

The butler left and there was silence at the table, letting them finish off the rest of their meals. About ten minutes later, a knock was placed at the door.

Tyriel took initiative, speaking for the first time since they had arrived. "Come in."

The doors opened, showing Dani in a simple black gown that made her seem like she was a ghost with how pale she was against it. There was a look of surprise that briefly went across her face at seeing the three of them at her dining table, but it was quickly brushed into being emotionless. Though, Atlamillia could see the relief in Dani's eyes. Relief and worry.

Beside her was a tall, incredibly attractive young man that took Atlamillia off-guard. She knew it was Endymion from his light-blue-hazel gaze that was both calm and curious, the same look that he had the last time she had seen him a couple of years ago at a ball. But he had grown a lot in two years from being an awkward kid in the corner with his brothers to how he managed himself now. Like Dani, he shared the black hair of their mother while not as pale as Dani, he was pale against a similar coloured suit to his sister.

She stared a little longer at him than she had meant to as she turned back to Dani, a bit warm as she noticed that Endymion, who had also looked her over for about the same length, turned towards his mother with a small greeting. Dani noticed her unexpected infatuation, giving a small smile that would have been a laugh if the circumstances were different. The conversation between the two of them and Aoife came to Atlamillia's mind about what her reaction would be meeting him again after two years and now she owed both of them lunch in town.

But this wasn't like then, she could feel the daunting aura that had filled the hall. It felt like a funeral – it was just a matter of who was being buried…

There was another reason why Eudoxia had called Endymion here, but she didn't have a clue why.

Endymion and Dani sat next to their mother, across from their father and Eudoxia started up the conversation as dessert was brought into the hall and only after Atlamillia had had a taste of the sweet, creamy tart. "So, what did you wish to discuss, Princess Atlamillia, now that everyone is here?"

"Besides Dani being very valuable at the castle? It has come to mind, and I'm sure yours, that Dani could be a potential candidate to be the king's queen. She is already friends with most of the staff if not very familiar with everyone in the castle, but she's also spent quite a bit of time with the king as it is despite not knowing of her origins."

"So, you think it would be better for her to be at the castle, live there if not nearby?"

"It would certainly give her the advantage of who could be his queen, especially once he comes back from his mission and will be solely focussing on finding a suitor to continue the family line."

"This would be most wonderful, and judging from her reaction," Eudoxia said, sounding surprised as she looked over at her daughter who was slightly flushed at being the centre of the discussion around her crush. "It would also be in her interest as well."

"So, you agree that she should stay at the castle."

"Not entirely." Her doting look grew cold as she looked to the other end of the table. "It's not just your family that has to keep growing. It's the duty of my children to provide and continue the family line, just as it is King Aerrow's and yourself for yours. What happens if he chooses someone else? Her time at the castle, while benefitting for you, would be worthless for her and our family. She would have wasted months away, hiding in a castle, where she wouldn't be seen for potential suitors and they could all be gone by then. Rumour has it, many of the house heads are pushing for their lines to thrive, arranged marriages in the off chance that they are left similar to your family. A head without an heir and a spare also without an heir. No one to follow up the line if only two people were to perish. I cannot let such a risk take hold."

"She would get tons of exposure to many suitors as they come to the castle: Dragon Knights, nobles, even foreigners in the event that Aerrow chooses someone else to be his queen."

"None of that time will be spent with grooming and arranging ties for security."

"Mother, you can't just bargain-" Dani started only to be silenced with a single glare.

Eudoxia looked away from her daughter to Atlamillia. "Family lines and future growth are what truly matters. I cannot risk this family being in the same position as yours…"

"My family's position isn't-" Atlamillia started to argue but she wasn't done.

"But perhaps there is something that can be done for both of us."

She held back the hesitation to the proposal that reeked of discomfort. "What exactly are you suggesting, Lady Eudoxia?"

She didn't answer her directly as she turned to Endymion who froze under the look she didn't understand. "Endymion, what's your opinion of Princess Atlamillia?"

"I... I don't understand what you're asking, Mother," he answered with a lower tenor pitch.

"Just a general opinion. You haven't seen her in a while – you two didn't talk at the coronation it seems."

"No, we didn't..."

"Seeing her, listening to her words, how does she seem to you?"

Endymion turned to Atlamillia slightly before looking back to Eudoxia. "She's well educated, cares for family matters and her friends. Many of my circles say she's well versed in court and is incredibly talented with magic. Many of the knights are terrified to spar with her, so they often deny her requests if they aren't willing to put their pride on the line."

"Would you put your pride on the line?"

"It would be an honour to spar and learn from her, not shameful to lose."

"She's also quite beautiful, wouldn't you say?"

"Ah, well yes, of course, but..." he started and looked over at her again, uncertainty clear as day. "This sort of discussion is rude to have in front of-"

"Then, it's settled."

Atlamillia grabbed the conversation again as both his and Dani's eyes went wide in a realization that she had yet to fathom. "What is settled?"

Eudoxia looked over at her, the glint in her eyes was one of victory if not slight cruelty. "For both of our goals to be met. If you wish to have Dani, you must promise that if Dani is not the king's chosen queen, you, Atlamillia, will marry Endymion."

"Mother!" Dani exclaimed, standing up from the table. "You can't just force-"

"I can and I will. Princess Atlamillia, we both have families to attend to in the most optimal way possible and an arranged marriage is very optimal. You get a partner if Dani isn't chosen, allowing both of our families to grow, and if

Dani is chosen, our families grow. Either way, we both win. Dani gets to be in the castle, spending time with all those you have said she would, and time with the king. If she doesn't win his heart, then at least the sense of structure is there with the spare who could have an heir before the king does…"

"How is this beneficial exactly?" Atlamillia questioned, strongly. "What if I have someone in mind already?"

"We all know you don't. Dani has told me that the only males worth the time are two Dragon Knights and you have no feelings for them," Eudoxia answered making Atlamillia very aware that she had known she would come to Dani's rescue. She had schemed it all out before hand. "And… this deal secures the future if something were to happen to our king while he's out of the kingdom. You get a husband and consort without needing to look for one."

"Mother," Endymion started, and she turned to him, but unlike Dani, he didn't back down from the glare. "Forcing someone into an arranged marriage is archaic. You said so yourself when you said that we could choose who we wanted."

"And two of my children are adults with no connections to anyone worth your time until now. You would be doing your family and the royal family a service, a failsafe in a world of uncertainty. You've always said you wanted to have an important purpose… being betrothed to the princess of our nation in case something happened to our king is probably the most important purpose there is."

"Is there no other way you would let Dani go upon Princess Atlamillia's request of being an asset to the kingdom?"

"Not when it only benefits her. She knows more than anyone that being selfish leads to instability within the houses that help structure our kingdom… What I'm offering is a solution that comes with extra bonuses." .

There was silence at the table as Atlamillia tried to figure a way out of the proposal. She came to help Dani; it wasn't even for her. But if she said that, told her that Dani hated every part of this house except for her brothers, it would have caused an uproar and the girl would probably be chained to the basement until there was nothing left of her… metaphorically or literally, she wasn't sure. Eudoxia was more than a wild card. She was something else entirely, and her actions could not be predicted. *Lucilla, please tell me you have something.*

"*I don't… She took the ideas I had and shredded them when she brought up your family. You don't have that luxury of being indecisive and Aerrow dying before he returns is more than a possibility just from the incidents he's had while in Seraphina.*" Atlamillia looked from the dessert that had long lost its appeal to the woman across the table. *"She doesn't need to know the details to know that Aerrow's life is not secure, she sees it."*

"I haven't shown anything."

"You didn't say anything that agreed to him being secure... So, you didn't have to. It was implied that you could very quickly become queen."

"For Orithina's sake..." She looked to Dani, the look she got from her friend was telling her to just leave, abandon her there for the sake of her own freedom. But she couldn't do that. "If... Endymion approves of this... Then I accept your proposal, Lady Eudoxia."

"I-" Endymion started, most likely ready to argue but her answer had caught him off-guard as it came out more conflicted and his mother took advantage of it.

"He does. Grier will prepare Dani's things and perhaps, soon hopefully, Endymion and you can spend some time to better know one another – a chance most betrothed partners rarely get."

"Yes... Of course..." Atlamillia stood up from the table, eloquently. "I thank you for the dinner at such a short notice, Lady Eudoxia... But I must head back to the castle now to check in with the council. This new... opportunity, will surely be wanting to be known by them as soon as possible."

"You truly are the perfect princess, just as everyone says." She turned to Dani and Endymion. "You're both excused."

Both children left, Endymion swifter than his sister, passing only an apologetic look to Atlamillia on his way by and the door was only shy of being slammed open by him on his way out, though she didn't know who he was mad at. Atlamillia, Aoife, and Bretheena caught up with Dani who didn't stop to turn to them until they were up a flight of stairs and down a corridor, far from the dining room.

Grier walked over to them and stopped with a slight bow. "Lady Dani, what shall I retrieve?"

"Everything," Dani answered, her voice hoarse and strained. "Have someone help you deliver it to my place... you know where it is."

"I do..." He looked to the rest of them, his words seemingly made for Dani who hadn't turned around, but more so for them in his stead. "Please take care."

He left, his shoes tapping the floor as he went towards the staircase and only when he was out of earshot did the black-haired girl turn around. She was crying.

"Dani," Atlamillia started but was silenced as Dani shook her head, knowing what was going to be said.

"No, this is all my fault. I'm so sorry. I should have never returned, I should have ignored her missives and stayed far, far away."

"No one can fault you for wanting to ease your parents' pain." Aoife tried, but she wasn't using it as an excuse.

"She's a monster and I should have known that something like this would have happened. Now Endymion and you are…" She choked on her words and Atlamillia drew her into a hug. "I'm so sorry."

Atlamillia tried again, though even as she said the words, they felt like glass shards. "It's alright, Dani…"

"You should have just left me here."

"There's no way I could have done that."

"This is far from a price that should have been paid! You're going to be forced to marry someone you barely know because we both know that Aerrow doesn't even know what he wants and could easily die…" She trailed off as she looked over Atlamillia's face. "He has already been…"

"A few times… yeah. He's in hiding as we speak."

"You couldn't lie against what that bitch already knew…"

"No, I couldn't… but if there is an upside… I'm engaged with your brother; can't say I was expecting that," she joked lightly, and it brought out a small laugh from the girl that was also filled with distraught.

"You could definitely do worse. He's one of the kindest people I know, and he's not a push over in a spar.'

"Smart too I bet."

"Yeah…" Her tears came back. "Gods, I'm so sorry, Atla…"

"Let's just get you out of this hellhole and back home, okay?"

The girl just nodded, unable to say more as Atlamillia turned to Aoife, feeling her gaze on her. The brunette had a look that was distant yet hurt, but before she could ask, it was gone. Aoife's gaze was on Dani, a small glee dancing where the pain had been a moment before. "Let's go celebrate your rescue with reckless spending, a small party."

"A party? At a time like this?" Dani asked, confused.

"You get to leave this place forever and you can get your brothers to see you whenever you want without having to be sneaky, that's worth celebrating. What do you most want in your home, Dani?" She urged and there was a small moment of thought before Dani went red at an idea. "Okay, no. You can't have him, something reasonable."

"That is reasonable!"

"He's a continent and a dimension away. Pick something else. Snacks, expensive shoes…"

"I shouldn't be spending-"

"I'm buying it, so shut up, and pick something."

"Well… It's pretty lonely in my house…"

"A pet then?" Atlamillia suggested. "A pet is always a good start to a new chapter in life, helps with depression I hear as well."

"A pet would be nice… Yeah, let's go to the animal shelter, get a puppy or five," Dani answered, carefree a bit as she seemed to linger on the idea. "Just a bunch of puppies to curl up to."

Aoife laughed, "You can have a single puppy. Two max!"

"Okay… Thank you, Aoife…" Dani turned to Atlamillia. "I'm still-"

"Apologize one more time," Atlamillia sighed, "and I'm going to lose it. Let's just get out of here and get you a couple of puppies."

Dani nodded and the four of them left the corridor in silence, allowing Atlamillia to think. She was not as okay with any of what happened tonight as she had voiced. In fact, she was devastated.

She hadn't planned on getting with anyone… She dreamed that, yes, one day she could have a family… But she knew better than to source one out. Her life wasn't looking great for the long run and she didn't want to put that weight onto anyone else – not her brother, her friends, and certainly not onto a fiancé or husband… And if she had completed her life's mission and lived, she didn't want her life to be dictated by something as political as the mess she crawled into.

She felt someone looking down at her for a moment as she descended the stairs in the main hall and found Endymion by the railing of the floor above. He disappeared behind the banister, continuing to wherever he was heading, not noticing that she had noticed him. She caught up with the others at the bottom, holding back a sigh.

All she could feel was pity for him.

Chapter Twenty-Five: Dragonbane

Missiletainn flew out of the underground cavern into the early evening air. It was a bit of a relief to Owen. Being underground, even if it was on a massive, floating island, was never something he was fond of. Sure, it was dark, something that he preferred, but it was smothering. Plus, spiders tended to enjoy caves, and that was all he needed to hate damp, dark places. His skin crawled and he let out a small wave of dark energy to expel any critters that could have dropped on him in the journey from the safehouse.

Outland Dragons, Monsters, demons… he had fought them all… but none of them were spiders. Crawling, curling up when they died…

He paid attention to the open air for monsters as Missiletainn flew up the side of the rock wall. They weren't as many of them as there were a week ago, but enough to concern him. They banged on the barrier repeatedly, loudly. The Seraphinean barrier could hold it, without question, but how long was it until something substantial came along?

They managed to get back to the top of the island, the spiralling towers of glass and steel reflecting the low sitting sun that was sinking slightly behind it in the distance. The city was beautiful against the open sky and rock, hauntingly so. The glow made it seem like the whole city on the hill was on fire, the light reflecting into the massive lake that sat in the circular valley. The soft ripples of Infinite Spring almost brought the illusion to life. A train moved along the track, swiftly down the hill and out of the city centre from a station that laid next to the military base where they had to go. He couldn't see the base from where they were, but he knew it was there. Another train moved from Domrael Hill, heading towards the lakeside somewhat. It disappeared and reappeared out of the forests that surrounded the water, travelling towards Rath Hill.

The hill was the second largest on the floating kingdom, second to that of Domrael, but the history behind it made it more than just the city it was now. Ruins of a castle from the monarchy that used to be sat at the top of it, still visible after two thousand years. They were preserved and protected by the Directorate that took its governing place. Underneath the crumbled walls and towers laid the royal crypt.

He had never been to it, and as far as he was aware, neither had Solomon or Aelia – so he didn't know what it looked like inside, but he could imagine it was similar in aesthetics to the older parts of Rath Hill. It was a protected place, even more sacred than that of the Absalom Royal Tomb if that was possible.

The fall of the castle was before his time, but he knew the story behind it, the legend that created Seraphina's emblem and that of the Gordin family's. It was just a pity that it was created to cherish a love Domrael couldn't have or save. Like one of the tales and stories he preformed on stage dozens of times over.

He turned away from the desolated shadows to that of the bright city they were about to enter. The past, at least that far back, wasn't going to help anyone, let alone find some missing whelps.

Owen turned back to the distant ruins again, eyeing it before a building blocked his view.

But finding some whelps wasn't his only mission, now was it?

Domrael Hill's city lights glowed below as Missiletainn flew by the embassy. The top part where the penthouse laid had a sheet blocking where the damage had been done, and at the base had a blockade to keep people away from the zone. Neither of them was entirely surprised that it hadn't been completed due to security issues, but he kind of hoped that it would have been. The safehouse was nice, but if they could secretly go back to the embassy – there would have been a lot more places for Aerrow to run around and entertain himself instead of being in a small complex, left to look over some logs, training, and whatever books he brought. It's not like there were many people in the embassy, just security and staff as far as Owen was aware, and that meant there would have been more people to protect him.

But alas, that wasn't the case… He was going to have to see about the progress and determine from there if it as worth it. Perhaps another day if his schedule tonight became more than just a visit to Fort Nekarios.

The beautiful fort came into view as soon as he thought out its name and Missiletainn landed in front of the large, rounded building. He didn't need to land to know why it had such an old, and almost foreign name to the Seraphs' culture. It was named after the ley line that sat underneath, coursing its power through the cement. Even over a dozen kilometres off the ground, the ley line somehow still ran through the land. He got off Missiletainn and while his own magic couldn't feed off of the magic line, it still made his body tingle slightly.

It had been a while since he had walked over a major ley line.

He looked from the ground to the building. It was rounded at what would have been edges, glass for windows but clearly reinforced with a second floor above for sniping, and a third above that that held a landing pad for whatever machines and flying creatures the Seraphineans had needed to land: airship, mobile turrets, tyraulias, cetaykoses, even a dragon. The turrets that lined the landing pad could be seen from the ground for a moment before the overhang blocked them as they reached the fort doors.

Two Seraphinean Legionaries saluted them to which Missiletainn and him acknowledged back out of respect, and the doors opened automatically for them. Inside greeted them to an open space, much to the Seraphinean aesthetic design with three spiral towers in the centre, a new addition he hadn't seen the last time he was there a few years back. They glowed their blue-purple, pink, and white hues – letting them know that they were ley line spires just like in the demesne. The light reflected off the water that flowed down them in a fountain. It gave the bright room of beige, black, and white a welcoming feeling, but it was far from fashion.

The great room had the second-floor line the edges, hiding watchmen, sharpshooters, cameras, and turrets; all ready to defend before a pin could hit the floor. Both of them had only seen it in action once before, and it had ended just as quickly that they, in their youth, didn't even have time to activate a chaos field.

He looked beyond the four-metre-tall fountain to see that the desk at the back had attendants and turned to Missiletainn slightly. *"You want me to deal with this? We might have to go down some of these corridors and I know you're not a fan of them."*

"Best not to be separated. We already know the corruption has spread to the Legionaries and that Absalomians have been kidnapped. If it's as you brainstormed, you're a perfect subject."

"Fair case, just don't start complaining about having the walls closing in on you."

"Maybe if you learned that dragon skill yourself, you'd understand the concern about being in small spaces."

A retort was starting to form only for an old name to grace their ears to the right. "Can't say I was expecting the Dragonbane himself to show up in my fort tonight."

They turned to the voice and found an old friend in a silver, Seraphinean armoured uniform. Grey-black under-armour was the same as the others, but the old general's rank allowed her freedom to have the glow of energy throughout the piece to be orange instead of the white, yellow, or blue he was accustomed to.

"Haven't heard that name in a long time." A small smile brushed his face as a chuckle came out. "How have you been, Io?"

A grin formed on her laugh-lined face as she moved her medium, silver streaked, magenta hair behind her ear then crossed her arms as she stopped not too far from him, eight inches taller than he. Her eyes, the same colour as her hair, were ever so lively and inquiring as always, looking him up and down. "Good, but certainly curious to know how you barely changed since I first heard of you nine hundred years ago."

"Oh, you know, good genes, healthy, childish lifestyle."

"Probably not having kids helped. Dear ol' Solomon, rest his soul, aged when he did. A little bit at least."

"Yeah… yeah, he got a few streaks that aren't dissimilar to yours."

She rolled her eyes at the remark, but didn't take the bait, seeing right through him. "Feeling the weight of it all, huh? Kids, even royal ones, somehow always do that."

"Well, admittedly, this is the first time I've had to be in this position. Even with the knights I've helped raised over the centuries."

"Now you know how the rest of us feel," she jabbed and then frowned. "I'm sorry about everything, from Solomon to how your mission here has gone… It's only been three months, but it feels like it's been an eternity with how busy everything has been. There hasn't been a lot of time to connect."

"A quick call next time wouldn't hurt," Owen joked slightly before matching the mood that wasn't shifting. "It's been about the same in Absalom and Asylotum. Busy, monsters, missions – there hasn't been much time to really think things through. Well, when I wasn't puking my guts out, I suppose."

"Asylotum still a problem at your age, mm?"

"Cheeky…"

"Who would I be if not cheeky?"

"Tolerable."

She shook her head. "What can I help you with today? It has to be pretty important if you've left Little Dragon's side."

"It's important, yes," he agreed, not surprised at the use of Aerrow's old nickname, and Missiletainn continued.

"Orpheal has told you about the whelps?"

"He has and we have teams looking on the west side and making their way back east since it's a good place to start," she confirmed, shifting her weight. "That and others preparing for the worst. I've personally been dealing with the matters as of late over the disappearances and others that I'm sure you're both aware of."

"The Absalomians?"

"Yep, so you did get that information. I have a couple of divisions also looking into it for a broader spectrum since we aren't limited by province borders."

"How's that coming along?"

"It's not… There has been a few bits and traces here and there that all have been inconclusive. Whoever is behind it is meticulous and frankly, possible knows the system as much as the three of us would…"

Owen didn't like the tone she had underneath it all. "Something's bothering you besides the lack of evidence."

"Just a feeling that there is something and they are connected to something much more dangerous in the long run."

He looked to Missiletainn for a moment before deciding to lead her in the right direction to what they had come up with. His partner gave a curt nod, agreeing. "How about we talk somewhere more private. The whelps are a sensitive subject and the details of everything could bring in more information than prying ears need to hear."

"Yes, let's." She motioned for them to follow her and they did, heading towards one of the corridors of the base.

Once inside the much smaller corridor, the colour pallet was about the same as the larger room, but it wasn't wide enough for a smaller dragon to spread its wings, let alone Missiletainn's almost fourteen metre wingspan. Instead, he kept his wings as tight to his body as possible. Owen shook his head at the dragon's attempt to try and make himself smaller and turned to Io, bringing up some small talk to pass the time and distract his partner. "Any other strange occurrences around Seraphina that you might be able to share?"

"Probably nothing you're not aware of, like the undead guardian."

"I only got a few details on our large friend…"

"Probably because unlike what Orpheal told me, you're not the one who dispatched it." She side-eyed him. "He's never dealt with such things before, but I have."

He shrugged. "I could have killed it."

"That would have been a very different mess to analyze. The remains I received were charred and incinerated, nothing that could be used to visually identify what the person used to be. Luckily, he had bits of DNA to confirm the face and body it ran around with to the man who had gone missing thirty-two years ago. So, unless you learned fire magic since the last time I saw you…"

"He shares the same trait as his father," he told her vaguely as the braces in the walls and ceiling protruded were also posts for Legionaries to stand guard at every other one, listening. "Discovering new places, finding trouble, even if he's tried to kill it off, it still lingers."

"I see, so how'd he destroy the guardian if he has his mother's lineage? Last I heard, he didn't practice much which would make light magic difficult to purify."

"He doesn't and isn't able, no. What you saw was raw power and nothing more… but luckily, he wasn't alone when it activated. They were looking around her hideaway when he sensed something in an unexplored part."

"The underground tunnels are quite numerous and expand the whole island. I'm not surprised that she would go exploring to get away and hadn't found the guardian until now," Io stated, catching onto who he was talking about. There was a moment of silence as she pondered before making an 'oh' noise, changing the subject slightly. "Right, we've also checked and keep checking in on places of interest for a certain someone. No one is going to be getting any corpses to add to the fire."

Surprise briefly made to his face as he looked ahead. "So, the Tomb Keepers of Rath are accounted for?"

"For now, yes… But it's difficult to be sure since some of my legionaries could be traitors and for all I know, I sent them on ahead to prepare a buffet of power if there is anything that resides in what's left."

"It's still worth the check ins, everyone and their mother knows what is found at the ruins if they were born here. It could easily be targeted without the extra protection. That is if they haven't gone through there already."

"Glad you agree." She stopped, moving in front of him and the door opened next to Owen. "You haven't seen my office since I got promoted."

He raised a brow. "Promoted to what? I thought you got the highest possible rank and were supposed to be retiring."

"Eh, that was the plan, but here we are. I was promoted to the rank of Lord Director's General."

"That's a new rank…"

"Orpheal dug through records to find it because the rank of authority for being a Grand General apparently wasn't good enough for me, whatever the hell that means. So, he went all the way back to when the kingdom was a monarchy. There was a title similar to yours, right hand of the monarch, but the actual name of them has been lost, so we improvised."

He shook his head, amused, while Missiletainn chuckled, and they went inside. The office wasn't too different from her old one, just slightly bigger and many more books on the shelves, insulating the room even more than it would have without them. Missiletainn was much happier to be out of the *small* corridor and sat elegantly in the corner, prepared for anything.

Owen and Io sat down at her desk and she got straight to business. "What is it that you were suggesting about the whelps?"

"Nothing but theories… which is why I came here for some information and maps of the area. Locations of interest that might need further looking into."

"I'll oblige… after you tell me your theories…"

He wanted her to figure some of it out on her own, not wanting to play his hand in the extremely small chance that the woman devoted to Orithina was actually corrupted by Ciar. But he knew better than to do that. She was a busy person with a lot on her mind. She didn't like being left to hang and possibly head down the wrong path. He wasn't going to give her everything but hoped that they could come to the same conclusion that Aerrow and he had come to. "The going theory is someone or a collection, specifically our friends, are trying to find a way around the Outland Monsters instinct to kill cultists or whoever is behind the kidnappings."

"It would definitely save the trouble for a zealot to avoid being eaten and still drag monsters through Daemonias Portals. But… that doesn't sit right… Why would they go through all that trouble just to have the possibility to avoid being eaten?"

"I also doubt it would work for anything more than a Typoregula monster since they took only whelps. They don't have the same scare factor that a healthy adult has on Outland Monsters. Monsters aren't biased on what dragon blood they get, even if it's their distant sibling species."

"And to tie it in with Absalomians, if they were kidnapped for the same cause, homeless Seraphineans, even a few Dagdians... It doesn't make sense." She leaned forward in thought before looking at one of the files on her desk. "Unless they were trying to repeat history..."

"History?" Missiletainn and he asked at the same time, and she slid the file over to the edge of the desk.

Owen took it and opened it to find reports of excavations of two locations, one with a petrified corpse of some sort of person, but they were mostly bone and the other was mummified leather, immortalized in a bog. He set the pictures aside as they were far from helpful and looked over the notes of the anthropologist. "Wait... these people aren't of any race of this world..."

"Not of any now, no."

"These magic signatures, even after so long..." He looked up to her. "What or who are these people?"

"We don't know. We only found two of them, and as you can see, their conditions are far from optimal. The skeleton was fossilized in Siren's Valley while the bog girl was encased in an ancient bog that now sits under a modern bog near Infinite Spring. What we do know is that they are hundreds of thousands of years old... maybe even a million years if the carbon dating and the radioactive isotopes are correct. They died horribly and violently from our investigation, but what's left of the magic was what intrigued us the most... even if their genes are simultaneously incomprehensible and unique at the same time."

"Let's start with the genes first and then move to the magic," Missiletainn suggested, and she complied.

"They have traits from all the races that live on Orithin now, including Outland and Absalomian Dragons, meaning they were completely contaminated in their isolated landscapes or..."

"They came first..."

The history of Orithin, or rather its races, weren't easily found or sorted. It left many to wonder if perhaps the missing link... wasn't missing at all and the legends had more truth than fiction. Unfortunately, neither of them was exactly an expert on the subject. In fact, most of the information Owen knew came from Azarias from when he studied such things.

Io moved the discussion towards magic. "As you read, they have both light and dark attributes. Their magic so incredibly powerful that its remnants remained in and on their bodies for so long that it rivals that of conspiracies of the goddesses' battle locations across the world." She set her chin on folded, propped hands on the desk. "The people responsible for the whelps, could be responsible for the kidnapping of innocent people. The timing matches since these excavations were leaked four months ago to the media."

"A month is more than enough time to prepare if someone was dedicated enough…" Owen concluded, and she gave a small nod. "But why the sudden jump to conclusions?"

"Because shortly thereafter, the bog girl went missing from our lab, right from under our noses," she muttered, shamefully. "If someone were to perfect magic fusion… they would be able to rival Ciar with ease just from the information we have on him. I don't know how much stronger he has become in the last three months… but he could be beaten this way."

"Or he could amass an army, or someone could, depending on what else they do to those people they have taken. The whelps if they reverse the process for them…" The thought turned his stomach before it changed to suspicion. "Please tell me that this excavation is nothing more than that."

She narrowed her gaze. "What are you implying."

"You're not going to attempt such things, right? Breaking the natural order-"

"Absolutely not. I've had predecessors that were insane enough to think that they could. Their experiments ended in death. Light and dark magic cannot reside in the same host unless it's been manipulated by a god to will it so. And the only known successor of that was the Fallen Hero of Dagda, two thousand years ago, and even that is probably a myth since no one even knows if he existed."

"And if he did, he wasn't an elemental user, just could use both sides of Dagdian magics…"

"Exactly. It's a different story entirely if we add the pure forms of light and dark elements. And if we ignore that, if someone wanted to create some sort of hybrid between Outland Dragon and … whatever Creature of Light, the host cells would reject the infusion. It's been studied over and over again to understand why Outland Dragons don't intermingle with Absalomian Dragons despite both having the ability to reproduce." A slight frown formed on her face.

"I should also iterate that my pride and feelings were hurt for suggesting that I would do something so unethical."

"I know, I know. I'm sorry. I know you wouldn't reach that far normally, but as you said, times are more trying than usual between Ciar and now the tribe's promise to invade."

"Well I'm not desperate, I assure you. My Legionaries will fight this exactly as our goddess made us, with the odd modification if we lose some limbs in the process."

"How is that leg doing anyway?" He asked, trying to lighten the conversation slightly. He was happy that he hadn't slighted her too badly, but he had to be sure. And he was positive she knew that as well.

"She's doing alright. Got a modification for the prosthetic last week. Not only is she stronger now, she's also lighter and feels like it actually is a true limb with how responsive it is. Even better than my actual leg."

"Well, the other leg's nerves are nine hundred years old." He received a glare as he looked at the file a moment longer before setting the pictures back inside. "So, what are the odds of these bastards being successful?"

"Depends on if they have the resources, brains, and are extremely desperate… It's not just the magic combination that would be terrifying. I've run my own simple models in the off chance that if it did work – what would happen. These are obviously far from accurate and need to be taken with a grain of salt, but if they are correct… combing an Outland Dragon with an Absalomian is the best chance one can have. They have a greater chance of just surviving due to the similar DNA sequencing and still be small enough to control. Then, add the Outland blood mixed with a high enough dragon percentage Absalomian, they could have their healing factor increased. I don't know what state of mind they would be in, if they would be more Outland Dragon or themselves, how the natural instincts of each race would interact with the other… but if they have enough rational thought to have basic controls of that of a thrall…"

"Taking them down would be a challenge without Outland weapons… add just being manipulated and controlled with Dagdian magic… Gods, that could give the experiment a full range of tactics if they were versed in such things."

"I don't think such a thing would exist to have both a well strategized mind and be influenced as such by Dagdian magic. But a thrall is plausible if, and that's a huge if, that this new being could be created."

"Dagdian magic is limited by the target's will, so at least that's a good thing."

"And being that there are no mind control machines despite all our best efforts, the only thing we do have to worry about is a thrall appearing," Io replied, somewhat amused at the thought of a mind control device before growing dead serious. "You, Little Dragon, and your knights need to watch where you step. These people are dangerous if they are trying to do exactly what is in this file and you are all fine targets."

"I know…"

"I'm not going to provide you escorts to ensure that my legionaries, if they are corrupted, cannot do anything more than what has been done. So, when you do what you're about to ask me next, you are doing it alone."

"I appreciate the warning. As for what I'll be asking, I need maps of the area and surrounding area of the kingdom, train routes and times, patrols, possible odds and ends."

"I can provide some of it including train passes, but if you want updated information about the edge of the kingdom and surrounding areas, you're going to have to head to a border fort. We haven't been able to pass information well through the CTs due to monster inflation and interference. That, and a horde showed up yesterday."

"And I doubt they are leaving…" Missiletainn guessed, and she sighed. "The barrier's power has been waning as of late. Too many variables pounding on it that the power grid can't keep up, even with new ones. We're trying to strengthen it in areas that are harder to defend, but it's leaving weaker spots that the tribe will definitely exploit if their kids aren't found."

"And the horde is sensing those same points…"

"Yes, and one of them just so happens to be where a fort is sitting."

Owen gave out his own sigh. He hadn't wanted to get into a battle. "Alright. I'll head to where they are most focused. Their leader should be there."

"Should be. There have only been patrols and scouts hitting other places and not reaching any of the other border forts."

"Which border fort are they attacking?"

"Fort Rodina, it's currently northwest of here if they are still following orders." She got up and Owen and Missiletainn copied, following the old general to get the information she could provide them.

00000

The pounding of the Seraphinean barrier only reminded Owen of when the Archvesper pounded on Solomon's. It was different, since the Seraph's barrier was mostly electricity with magic upgrades interwoven into it over the last few years, but it didn't make him feel any less upset. It was a small thing that reminded him of a dreadful time… but it also told him that his friend was alive. Seeing the mechanical barrier now was just a mockery of what had gave him fortitude. Because like the barrier they were nearing, his best friend was dead.

A small tsk came out as he pushed the grief aside. It wasn't the time to get sentimental for something he had spent time and time again to accept for not only his own sake, but for the kids his friends had left behind.

But he'd lying if he said he had completely got over Solomon's death.

It took a while to get over Aelia's… so it would take just as long if not more so for his childhood friend and the stupid things they used to do. It was just as sudden as hers, but even more shocking to see Archelaos as an undead. And because he wasn't a practiced necromancer, his hand had been forced when it came to who could finally put that husk to rest.

It should have been him, but instead, it had to be left to his partner's son.

"Ciar will not go unpunished, I assure you," Missiletainn growled, listening in on Owen's thoughts. *"He will pay very, very dearly for using my best friend like a puppet."*

"Revenge is not a suitable colour for a knight…"

"I'm not a knight; I'm a dragon and we are very unforgiving by nature."

"Don't I know it…" he sighed, not being able to disagree. There were very few people that could be forgiven by the general unless their offence was bad enough. Ciar was not in that circle of people and his crimes were far beyond the limit he had. *"Let's focus on the tasks at hand and deal with these monsters. We've been out long enough."*

"Yes… and while we're at it, let's send a little message to anyone watching not to pick a fight with us."

"We're going to paint a target on our backs…"

"Perhaps… or we'll scare them to the point that they never rear their disgusting heads again." It was a calm tone he used but calming in the way that the world would hold its breath and brace before a deadly, colossal storm.

It was a thriving, morale boost to a natural being of chaos that Owen was.

Owen scanned the area, picking a place to start. The flying air base glowed in the dark sky as the sun's light had finally went behind the island and horizon. Its frame was rounded like the ground base, but it wasn't as tall. It was wider as the propulsions of the engines that kept it afloat could be switched and twisted to move it wherever the Seraphs had wanted it to go like the massive, flying fortress that it was. Smaller monsters were fighting against Seraphineans and tyraulias on the other side of the barrier. A few of the turrets blasting at dark masses in the sky that strategically weaved and attacked the base while others worked on the barrier's support towers.

It made the decision on where to go first a simple one.

Missiletainn charged up a dark ball and casted it out into an Outland Dragon that thought he was being sneaky near a barrier tower. Scales came off his hide and he turned to them, his spines aglow slightly as he charged his own power.

The attack was never released as Owen manipulated it inside of the dragon, twisting it up and threading it through the dragon's organs before letting it rip the dragon apart. Black blood oozed from the dragon's eyes, nose, and mouth from what Owen could tell before the dragon died in silence, unable to make a noise as the attack had been practiced to perfection.

The dragon's head hit the side of the barrier on the way down, grabbing the attention of the Outland Dragons, Monsters, and Seraphineans around. The Outland Dragons that weren't being targeted by turrets grew rigid while the Seraphs relaxed slightly as Missiletainn left the protection of the barrier.

It was still for a moment in the immediate area, monster and soldier trying to figure out what to do next with the sudden appearance of the new arrivals. It ended as an Outland Monster attacked. Owen barely looked at the grotesque creature of flight and fangs as he activated a small barrier of his own. The monster ran into it and the barrier folded in on it before dicing the thing into tiny pieces.

It was a visual warning that preceded Owen's voice, one that he knew the leader would hear over the sounds of battle. "Party's over, Horde. I suggest you leave, or you will perish."

The Outland Dragons, almost at once, made the active decision to ignore the warning and went back to attacking, a few leaving the towers alone to gang up on Missiletainn and him. A small tsk came out as he reached for his crossbow and loaded up an Outland bolt.

Some things never changed.

Missiletainn flew upwards, drawing the dragons away from the other Seraphs while also getting the high ground, giving him, and Owen all the freedom in the world to do as they pleased. He plastered one with a dark sphere as Owen fired a bolt towards another one.

The bolt hit a hind leg, missing Owen's original target to end her life swiftly as she cried out in pain. He fired another one, this time not missing her head. The dragon dropped just as he prepared another bolt only for a dragon to get past Missiletainn's defences, grappling his partner.

Owen felt the attack of another dragon from below and he grabbed the attack just as it started towards them, stopping it midair. He sent it back as Missiletainn held back the jaws of the massive dragon he was dealing with and blasted a sphere of dark energy down its throat. Owen used the extra source, like the dragon he killed earlier, and mimicked the internal attack, easily overcoming the dragon's own attempt to take the magic – killing it instantly.

Tendrils of dark magic formed around them, preparing for another assault. He wasn't going to let them get close a second time and if they weren't going to stand down… then he was going to force them, permanently.

"Esos eínunt évus makrýongus tria apex spímum, Drakcooletis," a low, angry voice growled, coming from below them.

By the time Owen looked, the massive Outland Dragon was in front of them, keeping his distance from his shield. Neither knew what the dragon had said, but they knew of the name in the phrase, and who it was directed towards. Owen wasn't expecting to be called it once today, let alone twice in two different languages. "You know who I am…"

The glare that came from the black beast was a bit of a surprise. The words that came out of him were vile and spat out in broken phrases between Ancient Dragon and Ori, but the message was clear enough. "Esos killed od orba tode my kin at od gate. Esos murdered my brother kat tois family, monónum-handedly. Tode course eggo know esos."

"The gate… That was centuries ago." The old memories before he was the King's General came back. Solomon, Aelia, and him returned in time to see Absalom's Gate under assault by a dragon horde. He glared back at the dragon, just as spitefully. It wouldn't have been until after the fighting when he was able to reunite with the others in the capital. To pass the message to Ruairí and

Solomon of what happened to King's General Lomám, only to find out that the king had known all along from one of his spies that had been watching them and the battle from afar. "Your hordes attacked our kingdom. Your brother killed my mentor! Him and so many others."

"I'm glad esos remember, Drakcooletis... Now prosecro to your goddess kat pay gim what esos did!"

"I'll pay for defending my home when raiding and murdering innocents for the sake of a disgusting game is justified. Now leave or you'll join your dead brother."

The dragon gave out a roar of sheer rage before charging, not using magic. Missiletainn remained relatively still, not bothering to move and steady. The larger dragon collided, readying to bite out Missiletainn's throat only for the smaller dragon to use the momentum, flinging him away, downwards.

Owen drew Eclipse and its golden blade went black almost instantly. He remained neutral inside, giving a small exhale to remove any of his anger as he dropped off the side. This dragon, while awful, wasn't to blame and he had moved on from his mentor's death a long time ago. The Outland Dragon below recovered swiftly, but not swift enough.

Tendrils gripped onto the dragon, digging into his scales, and slightly slowing Owen's descent, keeping the dragon still. It took him less than a moment to reach the Outland beast and shove his blade into his skull, not giving the monster a chance to react. The energy released from the blade caused the dragon's head to explode. The tendrils that had both kept the creature from getting away and slowed his landing ripped the rest of the creature into pieces at a molecular level, raining blood in every which way, much of it splattering against his armour. Missiletainn caught him before he fell too far along with what remained of the body.

Owen wiped his face of the blood, bitterly, as a mutter came out, "Hordes never change... their arrogance doesn't let them learn of consequence..."

A small noise of agreement came from Missiletainn before heading towards the next thing that had to be killed to protect Seraphina and all the innocent people that resided within. And in this case, all were innocent to an Outland Dragon Horde. He just wished it didn't always have to resort to their deaths.

But, as each moment passed, he knew it was a fruitless wish. Outland Dragons fell with ease to him and Missiletainn. Even without his partner, the title

343

Dragonbane was earned repeatedly as the dragons practically threw themselves at him.

Why they did it, thinking that they could defeat someone clearly stronger than their leader by more than a little bit, Owen didn't know, but it didn't matter. His duty came first and if they didn't want to leave, that was on them. He had given them more than enough warnings.

By the time the fighting had ceased, and the Outland Dragons and Monsters were defeated in that area, the moons in the sky had risen and were crescent and gibbous shades of red and blue, respectively. Pretty, but they didn't hide the gleam of blood that covered them. Even if it was black, it still reflected when it was wet and poor Missiletainn was bathed in it. Though, he doubted he faired much better since he couldn't even see the red glow or the white plates of his armour.

He looked at the Dagdian satchel that sat attached to Missiletainn's gear. It had everything they needed from the two forts and with success came the reward of finally heading back to the safehouse.

00000

Missiletainn and Owen arrived at the door where their bed laid just beyond it, leaving behind a few ash piles of what used to be spiders on the ground that had clung to his armour on the way back through the tunnel. Owen's skin crawled. He knew he got them all, but he felt like they were inside his armour. If he had the time… he was going to vaporize the whole tunnel of their very existence. The thought of how much energy that would take reminded his body of the day he just had and dropped like a mountain on his shoulders.

A sigh escaped. He didn't know what time it was, but it was well into the night and from the lack of sleep last night…

He was getting too old for this.

A small laugh came from Missiletainn but didn't disagree with him as Owen unlocked and opened the door with a tendril. On the other side was a mostly vacated living room with a single light on coming from a tablet that sat in his nephew's hand. It was somehow being held there by it and the arm of the couch, miraculously balanced between the two. Aerrow was passed out, his head resting in the space his arm had created on the couch arm, next to the CT he had been reading. Owen walked in farther, seeing over the second couch that documents were spread out on the table in front of the young king, seemingly read.

A small, quiet laugh escaped at the sight. His nephew might have been a king now, but he was still a kid too, staying up far past his bedtime when he should have quit for the night. Missiletainn left Owen to go clean up, the blood and ash dried to his black, purple, and yellow scales still reflected in the light slightly. Owen wandered over to Aerrow, taking the tablet from him before it could drop at a slight movement.

He looked at the file that was being read and found it to be only a few pages into the work he recognized as Embla's before turning it off. A door opened next to him and Deigh wandered out. Her head tilted to the side slightly, a signature action of the Fionns that meant they were confused. It always made him think of a puppy whenever they did it.

"Why are you covered in Outland Dragon blood?" she asked, sleepily and quietly.

He gave a simple answer, barely above a whisper, "Border patrol needed some assistance... Sorry for being so long."

"He was worried about you since Cyrus came home first... You should have called."

How ironic for him to be getting the same message he gave to someone else that night. "I honestly forgot, but I'll do it next time."

"Good, or else."

Owen turned to the sleeping redhead on the couch who looked surprisingly peaceful. It was a nice change of pace from the times he had seen him sleeping out in the open. Unfortunately, he couldn't be left like that or he wasn't going to feel great in the morning.

Deigh saw his intent and intervened with almost a plea. "Leave him be. He isn't having a nightmare for once."

"But he's going to hurt himself if-"

"I'll move him later if his dreams don't shift, but for now... please."

A small sigh escaped as he nodded in agreement. "Alright... I'll check again in a few hours. In the off chance that something happens, I don't want him to be undone by a sore back and pulled muscles because he slept like this."

"That won't happen."

Owen pulled out the maps and other documents he had asked for from the satchel he had detached from Missiletainn earlier and set them on the table. "Just in case he wakes up before I do."

"Oh, he probably will."

He looked at the white dragon in the dark a little longer before giving a small goodnight and headed to his room. He needed to get out of his gear, clean it and himself, all before he could head to bed. Hopefully, he too could get a good night's rest without nightmares.

Chapter Twenty-Six: From Hell to Glory

I lazily scrolled through the logs on the couch. Or at least, that was the attempt to force the idea of calm. It only half worked. The days were counting down, and while Azarias and Cyrus were out and about – I wasn't content with sitting and looking at logs. It didn't feel like it was helping. Even Deigh was able to give more help than I was, scouting the rock side of Seraphina and the lake below with Missiletainn, keeping within the barrier but also away from any possibilities of zealots attacking them.

Owen's voice came from downstairs as I heard him going over the Zerach with Naftali on the CT. It would have been nice even to help with that, but from the numbers being discussed, it sounded like they were doing measurements.

A sigh came out as I went to a different entry, finishing up with the one I had. It was boring and thankfully, there wasn't a lot to go through. Well, not a lot in the grand scheme of things, but hopefully my job could be finished and bring to light where the whelps were. If not... then the other avenues were all that we had to go after with no leads.

I turned back to the writing, removing the option to even think about the dark road my head was trying to go down. It was bit difficult to understand the details, but as a whole, it made sense. Embla's work didn't seem to have what we were looking for. She wasn't a biologist, so even getting hints on what the whelps could be used for wasn't something the logs were providing. She wasn't even a weapons manufacture or an inventor. Her lab seemed to focus on environmental and geological histories of Orithin, even off the continent. There were some biology reports, but it was more impacts of how Outland Dragons affected their environment like any other civilization did.

It made me think that Azarias would have enjoyed reading it just from his reaction to the seal.

I reached the bottom and found it to be the last log of the director. I closed it with a huff of annoyance. It cleared the director for now, but it had taken several, precious hours away from possibly figuring out a plot from the other three directors. I looked at the directors left. Perhaps Vígdís would have information to help figuring out missing pieces if she didn't take them.

A bright light glowed on the floor, just above my view of the screen and a sense of resentment came as I knew what it meant. I looked up to see the light of the Teleport Glyph formed completely and then disappeared, leaving behind

Éabha with her bags in hand. I turned off the tablet and set it on the table, sitting up instead of sprawled out – the opposite to what I wanted to do.

"You need a break; you've been at it since five this morning," Deigh scolded quickly. *"It's four-thirty."*

"Well it's not like I'm going to send her away, but-"

"Missiletainn told me the only reason why Owen hadn't forced you yet was because Éabha was going to force this break."

I kept myself from rolling my eyes at the conversation that was barely seconds and greeted the Seraph like I wasn't having a debate with my other half. "Hello, Éabha."

"Hello…" she started, setting her bags down on the floor, some much louder and clunkier than the others, and leaving me to only guess what was inside. "This is a first…"

"What is?"

"You're greeting people properly… I don't like it."

"Sorry to ruin the normal for you. I'll do my best to avoid being decent the next time just for you," I retorted and stood up from my seat. "Did you do everything you wanted to do?"

She nodded. "Yes, and the parts for your upgrades are being made as we speak. They should be done by tomorrow, allowing me to use them tomorrow night."

I couldn't tell if she was happy or not. "Exciting?"

"Very."

"So, what's all of this?"

She looked down at her bags and a sadistic grin formed on her face, one I didn't think was possible for her to make. "The greatest fun you're ever going to have, or your greatest nightmare."

"I'm going to have to disagree on it being the latter… but I don't know if I'm as keen on finding out now."

She went back to being emotionless. "I figured. You're like clockwork; easy to get a specific reaction with hardly any effort."

"It's just that there are some things that I don't overly enjoy."

"Because you're a big baby."

"Is this what sleepovers are about? Tormenting the host?"

"I mean, I read that there should be pillow fights... but I'm not sure how much fun that would be. So, I went with this inst-" She didn't get to finish as the couch pillow I threw, hit her in the face. It dropped anticlimactically to the floor. The silence only lasting a few moments before the most emotionless, deadpanned tone I had ever heard, came out of her. "I can't believe you've done this."

"That... was so satisfying," I laughed, unable to hold back a grin. It was one of the best reactions I could have ever hoped for. I grabbed the other pillow. "Alright, you may throw the pillow back, and I won't catch it."

"Nah, I think I'll hold onto this one and throw it when its least expected, since catching doesn't mean blocking," she growled, setting it on top of an open bag. "Now then, where should we set up?"

"Uh... I don't know. Depends on what we're setting up?"

She didn't give me an answer as she looked around the room before landing on the blank wall where my room sat behind. "That will work. But we're going to have to shift furniture around; we can't play with this setup."

"Play what?"

"You would think after me keeping things vague this long, you'd get the hint that it's a surprise."

I resisted the urge to sigh and dropped the pillow back onto the couch. "Where am I moving things?"

"You don't have to, but I appreciate the offer. Have one of the couches facing this wall, the tea table can be placed in front of it."

"Just the one?"

"The second one isn't really required, so unless one of your knights decides they want to watch, they can move it then," she replied as I got to work, moving the table first.

I stopped moving it as she stared. "Something wrong?"

"Aren't you supposed to be, I don't know, kinglier?"

"What do you mean?"

"Well, kings have servants, right? And I'm pretty sure they don't comply with mediocre tasks on a whim. Throw pillows… you know what I mean?"

"I understand… but I also don't need to be waited on hand and foot. I don't need people to do tasks I'm more than capable of doing on my own. As for the pillow thing, I'm a king, so I can do as I please."

"You're a child."

"Still older than you."

"Really?" She rolled her eyes. "So, since you're sooo capable, does this mean you can do laundry?"

"Yes… being a Dragon Knight requires you to know that basic thing especially if you're out on missions…"

"Alright… but can you clean?"

"I'd like to believe so."

"Can you cook?"

The memory of last night came back and I looked to the table that I sat down in front of me, sheepishly. "That one isn't my strongest skill… but I'm working on it."

"What have you made?" Her curiosity peeked.

"Toast, basic sandwiches. Some sort of pasta dish last night that Azarias deemed edible as he devoured most of it. I hated it. Though, I did make really good brownies on my first try back in the castle with minimal supervision from Ramsey."

"That's baking…"

I shrugged. "It involved an oven."

She sighed, "I guess it's more than what I expected… but there is a solid difference between cooking and baking. Just so you're aware."

"I am now," I said, though I wasn't sure how important it was to know and got back to moving furniture. "Can you do any of those?"

"Those what?" She asked as she set up some sort of box on the floor.

"Mediocre tasks."

"Yes… but I also have people that do them for me."

"So, being the Lord Director's Daughter is similar to being a lady of a house, princess-like."

"I never really thought about it that way, but yes… I suppose there isn't much difference other than the span of our powers and duties."

I finished putting the couch where she instructed and stood behind it, curiosity taking hold. "Why do you act differently from your social class if there isn't much of a difference?"

"Bit of a strong question, don't you think?"

"You already asked me it; it's only fair."

She plugged in the box to another box using a cable of some sort, picking up the second box and set it on the table I had moved. Eventually, in the silence, she shrugged. "I don't know… I generally do act like what is expected of me, especially with the other leaders… You just make it seem less important. I apologize if-"

"No, I didn't mean… I don't care if you're being informal. I was just asking because I was curious," I told her, ending the unnecessary apology. "I much rather have people be their usual selves over customs and protocols. So, you were right when coming to that conclusion. If I only got formalities and niceties, I wouldn't get to appreciate certain, brighter personalities hiding away."

"Awe, why thank you!" She was way too cheerful. "But I don't think you'll be thinking that for long."

Maybe brighter wasn't the word I wanted. Dark and sadistic perhaps… She set down two controller-like devices on the table next to the box and I turned to them, curiously. "What are these?"

"I'm almost envious of your oblivious existence…"

"Rude…"

"Eh… before I tell you; I want to give you that shield."

Right… I had forgotten that she made me a shield… though I wasn't exactly excited to try it out.

She went over to her bag and pulled something that seemed like a silver amulet with a sapphire embedded into it, encircled by a weaving motion of metal. It took me a second to realize that it matched the Absalomian Crown.

She held it out to me. "It would have taken less time to make as it was supposed to be a hospital gift… but I was informed halfway through that you're ambidextrous and you left the hospital earlier than expected. So, I had to engineer it to make sure that when you used it, when a grip is summoned, it's formed correctly. I also made sure that while it's powered up, you're not actively using magic. It's a passive so it won't announce itself to say, monsters when you're using it."

"So that's what you meant by how you intended it and why it wouldn't work…" She gave a nod. "Thank you."

"No problem, like I said, you're probably going to need it."

I took the object from her. The amulet was more like a treasure than an accessory. It had a decent weight to it, even though it was only about five centimetres in diameter; the gem itself being about half of it. "How does it work?"

"Instead of making it have a generic strap that can break, it creates one by reading the surface area it needs to cover." She took the jewel and placed it on the back of her arm. An ice blue band went around her arm like a bracelet. Pulling the object off, the band disappeared only to reappear when she stuck it to mine. The colour was no longer ice blue but pure white. "Different sizes of arms, different band sizes. Plus, you can wear it over your large gauntlets. It works the same under clothing as well since having it over your preference of long sleeve shirts would be annoying."

"So, it's a protection bracelet…"

"It acts like a bracelet when its not being used. It becomes a shield when you want a shield, whatever kind of shield you can think of."

Whatever kind I could think of…

I held out my arm like I did have a shield and it activated to the design I wanted. A grip was created, allowing me to grasp the large and extremely wide shield in front of me that was a slightly translucent, and white and red in colour. Éabha punched it hard, forcing me to brace against her hit, but the shield didn't waver. I changed the form to something a little more practical if I wasn't taking on a horde and within an instant, it had my kingdom's emblem. The colours changed accordingly so it laid on a silver background in a robust, triangular shape and gold edging. She gave me an amused look that turned to slight surprise when the shield turned into a circular, yellow one. Eight, white wings came form the edges, matching that of the Seraphinean emblem.

She shook her head, playing off the amusement she found at my antics. "Having fun?"

I created a simple dome around me before nodding, the grip disappearing from my hand, but not abandoning my location as it moved slightly when I shifted my weight. "Yes... this is amazing. The applications for it are infinite. Like it could be used as a form of communication or something."

"Er... yes... I suppose it'd be good for making shapes for some strange form of communication... but that's not what I had intended for Guðmundr..."

No, I doubted it was, but where was the fun if you couldn't get creative? Wait. "Guðmundr?"

"Y-yeah... I... I named him..." She went a soft pink as she looked away in embarrassed. "You don't have to keep the name. It's stupid anyway-"

"No, no. It's a great name. You just don't often hear of shields being named in Absalom. It surprised me a bit. Guðmundr... It's a perfect name for such a magnificent shield." She smiled, her sheepish look to hide, gone. I turned to a more serious question I had about Guðmundr. "Is there a limit to how much he can take?"

"You need a bit of concentration, so if you went unconscious, the shield would stop working. He does need magic, so if you ever reach a max limit, he wouldn't necessarily work or work efficiently. But as for brute force, I shot him at point blank range with a charged shotgun blast, penetration rounds, and explosives. He didn't break... So! If you can hold the force from say, close explosions, you shouldn't be sent flying as he will disperse the force, but I can't guarantee total clearance from that. Forces can only be diverted so much and then it's up to how much strength you have."

"I just need to make sure he can handle Ciar... Ciar uses a blade, a dangerous one, but if the shield can take the hit, the blade won't be as dangerous. Especially if Guðmundr doesn't emit magic."

"Yeah... a draining blade." She crossed her arms slightly, pondering with her hand at her chin. "Dad told me that someone had got a hold of that technology from his lab. It wasn't even close to being done. But I guess it doesn't matter now."

"Do you have any idea on who could have taken it?" I asked, making the shield disappear and she shook her head. "No one suspicious?"

"None. Everyone in Dad's lab is loyal to him. His circle is small, and he would notice if someone were acting strangely. He doesn't even take trainees within his main research labs to make sure that someone doesn't steal his, or his employees', work."

"Maybe one of the other directors?"

"Maybe. But it's possible that they are already dead. The two traitors were cooked, remember?"

"Yeah, I remember…" I left the dark, morbid memory behind. "Sorry for asking."

"No, it's important. Ciar stole Dad's tech and tried to kill you with it," she stated, and I noticed she was staring at the scar under my eye. "And you didn't exactly get out scratch free because of it."

"No…" My neck tingled painfully at the thought of that night and I rubbed it, trying to remove the ghost pain. I turned to the boxes she had set up. "So, did you have some sort of thing planned with these boxes?"

She didn't seem pleased about the subject change but for the first time, she didn't push it. "Yep! I bring to you a video game console and projector."

The projector was probably the device on the table… but the box on the floor seemed bland at best. Black and rectangular, the only thing that made it seem like it was a machine at all were two buttons on the front of it, one of them with a red light in the centre. "Are you sure this is a good idea? What if I break it?"

"I calibrated it with a few add-ons in the internal hardware to make sure that you couldn't," she said like it was no big deal and went around me, pushing the button with the red light on the box on the floor. The light changed to around the button, a pale yellow, and the machine came to life with a soft hum. "Can you close the curtains? The projector won't work well in the light."

"Sure." I went to the task and went over to the massive, windowed wall.

Outside was bustling with people in the day of the lively city and I hesitated for a moment, yearning to be out there, enjoying the sun while searching for the whelps. I held back my disgust at the idea of having fun, the need to break for a time, and closed the impossibly large curtains. With the curtains drawn, only a hint of the light came through and I turned away from the desires to the very dark room. A soft light came from Éabha as she brought up a glowing orb which directed me back to the centre of the room. The projector was turned on, creating a blue square on the wall and she dismissed her light.

She passed me a controller, a soft yellow light coming from its centre. It's buttons on the right were placed like a plus shape, also glowing the same colour: A, B, C, and D. Directional arrow keys were in a similar spot on the left and two sticks were outlined in the light on the bottom, making the controller seem symmetrical, but not quite. She sat on the couch and I joined her, realizing quickly that she didn't have the other controller in hand.

I looked at her in confusion. "Are you not going to play?"

"No… I'm going to sit and watch, help you when you need it."

"Is that fun for you?"

"Generally I prefer playing, but in this case… I think I'm going to enjoy every moment."

"Sadist…" I muttered, turning to the wall as the light darkened.

Smoke started to rise as a glow, similar to embers, appeared at the bottom of the projection. Lightning struck, causing me to jump. A moment passed as I realized the sound had come from the projector and therefore the game. A stifled laugh came from the Seraph, but I paid her no attention. Lightning struck again, the sound of rain coming closer, and a dissident melody started to build. The title of the game formed, and the rain turned out to be blood as it painted the letters.

I looked over at her in dismay. "Death Tolls… This is a horror game."

"It might be…"

"Why does the first game I ever touch, have to be a horror game?"

"Gets you straight into the experience of the emotional grasp that the artform brings. Like a book… but visually there and it makes you work for the story."

"But why horror?"

"It's one of my favourite games. The graphics are revolutionary. It's a three-dimensional, action-adventure, role-playing game. The first of its kind to break the normal pixels on a two-dimensional plane. Though, I have to admit, the models are pretty polygonal… it's the first step to making even more realistic games to better tell stories… or just, massacre everything in sight. Video games are great."

"But a horror game…?" I sighed, "Fine. I'll play it, but only because it's a favourite of yours…"

"You're so nice."

I might have been too nice…

I hit a button on the control as the game told me to hit any button and I was brought to three save files; two of them being empty and the other with almost a hundred hours logged into it. The very thought of spending that long playing a game, let alone a horror game, was unbelievable. Not just unbelievable. It was… insane…

I went with the empty file on the bottom, figuring out the controls quickly, and pressed A to make my selection as the screen directed. A scream echoed throughout the room and after my heart settled; I wondered what Owen thought downstairs. I waited for a moment, listening, but neither the general nor Deigh in my head said anything. I turned back to the game.

It went into a small scene, the blood still raining onto familiar cobble streets of the city I recognized as Siofra. The massive stone buildings, the winding streets. Elwood Garden was in the far distance, exactly how the city was before it was destroyed. But instead of the wet stone that I could practically smell at the thought of rain, despite only seeing the scene, the red and green rocks were strictly red and dripping. I swallowed down the discomfort of all too familiar connections to when the city was attacked.

I passed a side glance at Éabha, hoping discussion would take away the memories. "Someone took some inspiration…"

"They… oh! Oh gods." She stole the controller from my hands and pushed a button, freezing the visual. "I completely forgot and that this and…"

I knew she meant no harm, shaking my head. "Éabha, it's fine."

"I'm so sorry." She looked like she wanted to hide in a hole. "I got excited to share and didn't even realize how you would have reacted to the game after what happened."

Apparently, my reaction was more visual than I had intended. "It's as you said, a game. One that they clearly put in a lot of work to make it so easily recognizable; it's like a time capsule."

"You did guess it really quickly; it doesn't even tell you where you are until after the tutorial… You don't have to play it. I don't want it to bring up any horrible memories – I don't know how similar this game is to what happened in your home despite having no connections to it…"

"There might be similarities, but it's also fiction. Like, look at all that blood just raining from the sky, it's almost silly," I told her with a bit of dramatic flare, showing off the frozen, falling blood. "Plus, it's your favourite game so I'm curious to know why."

"Only if you want to." A small smile formed on her face, but it looked forced.

"Let's see what this horror show has in store." I took the controller back and pressed the same button she did to resume. "Welcome to the grand tour of Siofra. My name is Aerrow, and I'll be your tour guide as I used to live here. Please pardon any screams that may occur on the journey, I've been told I'm a baby and I have no idea what will happen."

Éabha giggled and I settled down a bit. The joking helped a surprising amount, but it did take away from my experience of the tone it was trying to set.

"I've actually been down this street. That walled off area is Elwood Garden, and from here... if you follow the road north, you'll find the castle."

"Both of which are places you can explore, but the game is set in a different version of Siofra," she shared and then said something unexpected. "Outland Monsters don't exist in this world."

"Oh, really?" What was used as the monsters if not literal monsters?

"Just horrible demons and different monsters. Ghouls... a lot of creatures coming from that book you told me about, and some other obscure ones from another book recommended to me about monsters from other worlds. But no Outland Monsters."

I raised a brow as I watched the scene scan over Siofra, the castle highlighted in the distance with its large towers and the emblem sitting on the tallest. I was proud to have my city feature in a game, but it was also making me strangely homesick. Even though the game itself wasn't as realistic as my memories, it held the charm and feel that the city gave off somehow. "A book on monsters from other worlds, eh? That wouldn't happen to be written by Valoth Nor, would it?"

"Ah, yeah... Why do you know that?"

"No reason..." If I was honest with myself, I wanted to get my hands on it when I had the free time to enjoy it. It would be interesting to learn about creatures or monsters from different places, how they were similar or different. "Why is it raining blood?"

"The demons are causing it. It's thankfully not any of your citizens' blood." The aching memory left slightly. "But it still looks the same so it's kinda gross, but besides that, it doesn't hurt you."

"Alright, so what exactly am I supposed to be doing here?"

"Your job is to go through this desolated place and shut the demon door before some horrible monstrosity comes out and kills everyone left."

"So, this all takes place in the city?"

"And a little bit outside. I don't know how detailed it is though. In an article from last year, the creators visited the city and thought it would be the perfect place for a horror game because of how old it was and just the designs of the setting fit the theme more than Seraphina did."

"I mean... I suppose it's kinda creepy... Definitely not as many lights. It's also not as bright all-year around because of how north it is."

"Really? Hmm, yeah, I suppose... I've only seen it through this game and if it's similar than I could see why they picked it. But even though I've never been there, just looking at it through the game, it's so beautiful and different compared to Domrael Hill. It has something that this city doesn't."

"There is a difference for sure, I'm just not sure what that difference is... You might be able to pinpoint it though if you'd like to visit when it's repaired," I offered as a lone, four-winged Seraphinean, or at least, that's what I guessed they were supposed to be, came out of an alleyway. The visuals were quite polygonal, but it was better than what I had expected. The screen shifted so my view was a little bit behind the character, telling me to move the left stick. I did as it suggested, and the very sleek man moved in the directions I prompted. No answer came from Éabha next to me, and I looked away from the projection to her. "Unless you don't want to."

"I would love to, but I don't know how much Dad would be into the idea."

"He would definitely be invited-"

"He never leaves the island," she interrupted with a slightly annoyed sigh, but I wasn't sure who she was mad at. "But maybe once things settle down, he might consider. Also, if you stand still too long, a monster will kill you."

"Shut up and play the game... got it."

"Not quite what I had in mind, but it's close."

I moved the tall Seraph around the street, not quite sure on where to go. It didn't take me long to get the picture of where I was not invited to go as a horrible, almost melting shamble of flesh and fangs came out of the darkness of a house I wanted to explore.

And doing exactly what I would do in that situation, Mr. Hero ran... though he didn't scream at the surprise like I had.

Each moment that I thought I could happily explore, more monsters appeared to ruin it all, usually in traumatic, awful ways. A few times in surprise, causing me to freak out a bit, completely immersed. I attempted to fight once I figured out that I could, but the monsters each had their own way to destroying the character along with my dignity, all while Éabha seemed to enjoy watching me be tortured.

Though, as awful as the game was for me, it was the most relaxed and happy I had seen her be. So, I continued onwards, dying horribly.

After dying so many times, I had, admittedly, gradually became more and more frustrated with the game, not that I wasn't enjoying the creation a bit. I definitely saw the appeal and why Éabha liked it, but it was a stressful thing. I wasn't sure if it was hard, or if I just sucked at it... Monsters would hit me once and my seemingly long health bar would drop to almost nothing.

It made it difficult to progress through the story I had managed to come across. And the worst of all, Owen, who had been hiding on the ground floor all this time, switched out with Missiletainn to get food with Deigh. The dragon left behind had laughed every time I got scared for a few minutes before heading up to his room, his gut unable to handle how funny my misery was.

So, instead of saving me from the game, my so-called uncle left me to be eviscerated by his dragon with the parting prod for me to fight on, egging my pride to succeed.

And dammit if it didn't work.

I took a breather as I managed to fight and beat some creature that was as majestic as it was horrifying. It had four long legs with hooves, a swift tail, and some person melted into its back, dragging long arms across the floor. It was a demonic thing for sure as it was skinned and had a skull as a head. It was painful and disgusting, but... it fell.

Unfortunately, I was so concentrated on removing it; I didn't read what it was called and only caught a glimpse of its name: nuck- something. Whatever it was, it was not of Orithin origin. Orithin didn't have whatever that creature was that the man rode upon. It looked cool though, a useful animal creature for riding on.

Suddenly, my break from hell ended as a stone-bat creature – not unlike the creatures that attacked the arena during the trial, but still different enough, labelled gargoyle, came from the sky. It killed me instantly as I didn't have much health left from the last fight.

The game over screen appeared and when I hit the button to continue, like the hundreds of times before, it put me back before the fight I had just finished.

My sense of accomplishment drained completely.

"Oh… I guess you didn't save after you beat it…" Éabha stated the obvious and I set the controller down. "All done?"

My head met my hands as I leaned forward. "If I don't stop here; I'm going to toss the game out the window."

"At least you're not acting on it. But I'll give you credit, I thought you would have rage quit two hours ago."

"This game brings out a side of me I didn't know I had."

"Irrational anger?"

"Yes…"

"Aw… it's okay. The next time you want to play, you can use a handy tip I'm going to give you."

"Couldn't give that to me hours ago?"

"No, but only because you did really well for your first time playing this game, let alone any video game. I almost want to say you're a natural at it."

I sighed. I didn't want to play another game again. But I had to believe that they weren't all as awful as that game was. I turned to her. "What's the tip?"

"If you pay attention to the music," she started, grabbing the controller, and started to play the game, bringing the nameless hero over to the demonic creature. "Each attack and defensive action are in beat to the music. Most of the music is easy to follow, so once you get the rhythm, like any real battle, it's a little easier to attack and counter. There are a few enemies that are odd, but it's because the music that plays for them is just as odd."

The character moved flawlessly out of the strikes, and attacked without the random tapping of attack buttons, hoping to hit like my version was. They were meticulous and without being hit once, she dropped the monster and killed the gargoyle before it could even reach the character. She saved the game and put the controller down.

"There, so you don't have to repeat that battle."

"I could have done that…" I muttered before she smiled slightly.

"Probably a lot faster if it was real life. Wanna play something a little more fun and less masochistic?"

"Please…"

Chapter Twenty-Seven: Writing on the Wall

Atlamillia held back both frustration and interest as Commander Kail gave out his report from the latest excursion around the greater Asylotum area. The investigation had to be called off in order to ready the next phase of getting back to Absalom and to deal with the tunnels. It wasn't so much the exploration of the strange land being stopped that pissed her off but rather that they had come across something and they weren't able to look into it further. There was a powerful magical presence behind a wall that had scratches on it and of course like good Dragon Knights, they came back as soon as possible to complete the new duty at her command.

The rock wall of a mountain side was several hours away from the city and while she wouldn't have cared too much about scratches, the markings on the tablet were familiar. Ancient Dragon marked the wall, but the pictures didn't show everything that was written and from the erosion, it made it all the more difficult to read. Perhaps this was the place she had been sensing for almost three and a half months.

She looked up to Kail. "There was nothing else suspicious there at the site?"

"None, Princess, at least from our brief visit. I apologize that we couldn't search it further."

"Don't apologize for following orders I gave; we have more pressing matters than some markings on a wall." She gave a slight smile. "Just means that this place has more mystery than previously thought and can be looked into later."

He gave a small nod. "I've already uploaded the data that we've collected for your convenience. Is there anything else you wish for my team and I to do before we head to our new assignments?"

"No, you're free to go. Thank you, Commander." He gave a bow and left her study, closing the door behind him. She sat back in her chair and a sigh came out from Lucilla. "Something the matter?"

"It's just strange to be receiving reports in your study or even in the war room when these sorts of things are usually discussed in the throne room," her partner answered, uncomfortably. "It shouldn't matter as the information is being given, but the practice and negligence seems odd."

"I'm not sitting on the throne or going anywhere near it," she answered more firmly than she had intended. She looked away from Lucilla. "Sorry, I just think it's a bad idea. I know no one would care if I did sit on the throne, it's technically my place for right now but…"

"The risk… I know. Pretend I said nothing." The blue dragon stood up, poking her forehead slightly with a claw, lifting the Crowned Princess circlet on it slightly. "Come on, Helah is going to be here soon for practice. It'll keep your mind off the grand issues and focus on the easier to reach ones."

"Let's just hope that Aoife practiced – that's what I'm more worried about."

00000

Atlamillia faced a target on the back wall of the training grounds, concentrating on the words of Helah as she described the mental state that both she, and Aoife should be in. It was a simple exercise… or at least, it should have been. The simple conjuring of whatever magic they could produce without a conduit. An added bonus mark if one could have it be substantial enough to hit the target twenty metres away.

It didn't have to be lethal, even a heal would leave markings behind on the targets that were designed for such things. But here they were, struggling to produce anything. It made sense for Aoife to have trouble, but Atlamillia had been training long before she could remember and even in the graces of Asylotum, she struggled.

No light magic. No fire. No power at all could be formed in her palms or even around her as an aura of some sort.

She, a prodigy, couldn't produce any sort of energy or magic without a conduit. And to add to the mess of it all, she couldn't stop thinking about the deal she had made the night before.

Betrothed to someone she barely knew. Endymion wasn't hard on the eyes, far from it, nor was he a bad person, but she didn't know him. He didn't know her. What she was… and he certainly didn't know what the hell she wanted since she, herself, had no godsdamn idea. Her mission had always been her forefront goal, anything past it like hobbies, family, marriage, being a ruler, hell even sex, were all just compromises to the mission.

A disgusted sigh came out.

How could an amateur like her brother, who had his head in the clouds all the time, with barely any practice of magic at all, do such magic skills with ease while she couldn't with all the blessings bestowed on her and fully concentrated on a good day?

It was humiliating.

The insult to her injury came at the production of a little, bright amber orb in Aoife's hands. The girl's eyes went wide in excitement and turned to her to show the orb only for it to vanish. The disappointment on her face almost made Atlamillia want to give her a hug.

"Did… Did you see it?" Aoife asked, sounding disheartened and Atlamillia nodded. The disappointment disappeared in an instant with a happy grin. "I did a thing!"

"You did a thing," she agreed with a bit of a laugh. Her unwavering enthusiasm was contagious, as always. "Congratulations."

"Yes, congrats, Aoife, but you still have a long way to go," Helah told her before crossing her arms. "So, enough talking."

"Yes, Matron!" Aoife got back to concentrating immediately after the words exited from her mouth.

Atlamillia sighed, silently. Her energy was boundless, while she was using all hers to even get a fraction of what her friend had accomplished.

The minutes turned into an hour more of training and concentrating on the same task to which Atlamillia had not been successful in once. Aoife, on the other hand, had managed to excel further than both Helah or her could have imagined in the short period of time. Her amber orb was able to change to a more translucent colour and was much larger, allowing Helah to assess it as a minor heal.

Atlamillia stopped practicing and walked over to her friend and her orb of magic. Helah noticed and before she could react, the matriarch stole one of Argona's Fangs from her belt and sliced the side of her thumb with it. "Helah?!"

"Whoopsie, I hurt myself by accident." The matron handed her back the dagger with a small, childish grin that fit her unageing fifteen-year-old body. She looked to Aoife whose orb had disappeared after the act. "Can you fix it?"

"Like hell it was an accident, we watched you do it," Atlamillia growled out a mutter. It was the same act she did every time she was testing out the potential with any ability. Maybe not injuring herself since that could only assess healing, but the persona kept running. It pissed her off. She was over two-thousand-years-old. She should act like it.

Aoife swallowed before nodding and concentrated on her healing orb again. She made it more compact, the amber glow more condensed like amber itself, and moved it over to the wound. The bleeding stopped and a good portion of the cut healed within a few moments, leaving behind a red, irritated line where the skin was closed. The orb ceased to exist, and an exasperated noise came from Aoife as she took a breather, apparently holding her breath. A pout came from her. "Dammit, I couldn't heal it all."

"No, but this was very good for your first try." Helah looked over at Atlamillia, fondly. "You were right when you told me about Aoife's specialties. She is a naturally gifted healer. It's been a while since I've had the pleasure of training one."

Atlamillia crossed her arms, admittedly feeling left out. "And what does that make me?"

"I've been training you for years. With Aoife here, perhaps we can explore avenues that we haven't thought of to boost each of your potential."

She uncrossed her arms. Her point made a lot of sense. They were hitting walls with her training and now that Aoife was officially on-board, perhaps those walls could be overcome as new ideas came up.

"But that's enough for now. Atlamillia, you're coming along but I sensed quite the block in your thoughts today that was hindering your progress." She frowned. "Has something happened that might be the cause of that?"

"No… just distracted with my lack of progression," she lied and Helah nodded.

"Then next lesson, I hope you clear out those negative thoughts before hand. You don't need me to lecture you on why."

"No, Matron…"

Helah's gaze looked behind her and her eyes went wide. "Oh… my… Orithina… PUPPIES!"

"What are you-" Helah was gone before Atlamillia could turn around and found Dani at the training grounds entrance walking beside her new family members.

The first one was a small, golden retriever puppy, barely a few months old. Her golden fur was completely puffed out, apparently considered normal for the breed, and her tail wagged at a million kilometres a minute. A small ball in her mouth that only left when she was sleeping or was asking for it to be thrown.

The second dog she adopted was a massive, monstrosity of an Absalomian Shepherd, a breed that was used for hunting Outland Dragons frequently once upon a time but were still used once in a while by the knights for various of other tasks. His head sat five feet in the air and was just as fluffy as his puppy companion after taking the three of them, her two knights, and Jakob to wash him the night before. A few scars riddled his body from the days when he had been in the wild and somehow, the seven-year-old dog had ended up in the shelter with no one, for obvious reasons, wanting to adopt him. He had a tough exterior for the reaction of someone fearing him – but then they came along, and that barrier was shattered as soon as Dani laid eyes on him. It was more than apparent that the dog had bonded with her friend in the stand-offish love kind of way as Atlamillia had yet to see him leave her side and was incredibly well behaved.

So, he, along with the puppy, were instantly adopted.

The matron was buried in the fur as she hugged the large dog, barely taller than he was. His paws were about the same size as her face. The small golden retriever whimpered a bit at the lack of attention before noticing Aoife and Atlamillia and ran over. The large dog looked confused at the affection from the woman before letting out a huff as Aoife picked up the golden ball of fluff after the puppy had dropped her ball. Kisses swamped every exposed pore in a matter of milliseconds.

"Shamrock! Sto-pah! My mouth!"

The puppy stopped licking her, seemingly understanding the grief, and waited patiently to be petted. Aoife patted her and the three of them walked over to Dani where Helah had not yet unwrapped herself from the dog that had terrified the kids at first. It was a bit strange for Atlamillia to witness. She had never known the woman to like animals as she had never seen her near them, but certainly wouldn't have thought she would have loved something quite that size. The dog could probably be rode into battle.

Dani had a sheepish smile on her face as Helah escaped the dog's red-burgundy and silver coat. "What's his name?!"

"Ardyn," Dani answered and scratched Ardyn's head. He looked to her like he was asking for help when Helah went back to smothering him. A small sniffle came out from the coat. "Is everything alright, Matron?"

"I used to have an Abby Shepherd when I was younger. The same coat... same red eyes. Theo was his name."

"I can't imagine where that name came from," Atlamillia mocked and Helah escaped the mass of fur to glare through some tears.

"He was a great dog!"

"That you named after your crush that you basically stalked."

"I did not stalk! I'll admit that I was obsessed with him, but I did not stalk him. Theseus and I were friends!" She was back into the fur. "Plus, he was the one who gave me the puppy so, shush you."

A small giggle came out as she was finally able to tease her mentor after so long. "Well, Ardyn seems very confused by your actions."

"That's because he's never got the love he deserves until this wonderful woman came along. No, you did not, did you? Big, smart boy would put half my priests to shame with your problem-solving skills. Yes, you would." She started scratching a spot and his leg involuntarily started moving in happiness. "And if she doesn't, I'll make sure you are very happy back at the temple."

"You're not stealing my dog," Dani stated, surprisingly firm before getting a bit red with embarrassment. "Ardyn and Shamrock are part of my family from my friends so…"

Helah simply nodded. "Can I visit him?"

"Um… yes?"

Aoife leaned over to Atlamillia. "Could she even deny the matriarch of that to begin with?"

"I'll be honest with you," Atlamillia started, petting Shamrock's head a bit. "I have no idea. Helah kind of just goes and does what she wants."

"She does seem to be that kind of person… Wait, she had a crush on the Hero-King?"

"Yeah… it's a bit weird being his great grandchild. After all these years of being her pupil, some of the stories I get are… well, let's just say I shouldn't know about. Ever."

"Gods, I can only imagine."

"No, I don't think you can… and she can recite them with detail."

"I bet she'll be sharing all your stories with your kids too later in life, being immortal and all that."

Atlamillia frowned, a foreboding weight entered her chest. "Yeah…"

Aoife noticed immediately and Atlamillia looked to the puppy in her arms. "Are you okay? I know you were lying earlier since you were probably thinking about what happened last night. It's not exactly something one can brush off."

"I'm fine, wasn't thinking on that." Atlamillia gave a small smile. "You should ask Helah more about your training before she does steal Ardyn away."

"What are you planning on doing then?"

"I need to look over some things that the knights brought back from their last mission." It was another lie as she just wanted to clear her head, alone, but Aoife didn't seem to care if she knew, smiling happily back.

"You should tell me about anything cool they found. Asylotum is such a weird place."

"That it is."

Atlamillia left the training grounds, leaving behind a very distracted Helah and Dani as they had started talking about what was best for the Absalomian Shepherd in terms of diet.

The halls were surprisingly quiet as she made her way up to her study, Lucilla joining her there. A communications tablet sat on the desk and she walked over to it. It wasn't too dissimilar to her personal one, just significantly bigger and heavier. She leaned against the desk as she looked over it before tapping on the application she needed. If it weren't for Aoife, she would have been incredibly lost on how the device worked at all. She went over the logs that Kail's team submitted with further detail than he summarized, and it was a surprisingly humorous document to read. Sarcasm, satire, and wit were all over it.

It was clear that the person who wrote it, didn't want to originally, but they had fun, nonetheless. Unfortunately, their name wasn't written on any of the logs, so she didn't know who to thank for such a great read. It was incredibly disappointing. It was an official report, yet she had never seen anything quite like it before.

She got to the pictures that were accessed in the side bar that dropped down from the icon on the right. She opened them and looked them over, making the pictures larger as she zoomed in, but the quality was as she had deducted earlier. The writing was too degraded to read from the pictures.

She wanted to know what was there. Their purpose.

And she wanted to be left alone to think.

A devious thought came to mind. It's not like she was going to be attacked by monsters or something in Asylotum. She could get away from her retainers that stood outside the door. It was easy enough as she hadn't ditched them in several months. She went over to her partner and placed the tablet in the bag on her saddle before looking over her supplies. There was enough there for a day trip. Some snacks and rations that were replenished every morning in the off chance that she needed to disappear. Extra clothes too which was never bad, armour.

She looked at Lucilla. *"Already for an adventure?"*

Lucilla gave an enthusiastic nod, the tip of her tail wagging excitedly. *"It's been too long."*

"I'll meet you in the courtyard," she told her before turning to the study door and headed out. On the other side were Mazaeh and Elias with Tatian and Manuel, exactly where she had expected them to be after following her from the training grounds. But they weren't alone as she knew Bretheena wasn't far, Scarlett's tail poking out from the balcony awning. She addressed the knights first as Lucila left for the meet up. "I have a new mission for you two."

"Something come up?" Elias asked and she shook her head, his shoulders visibly relaxing.

"No, but I'm concerned about the status of the new plan for the tunnels. I want to know how it's going from your perspective and if it needs to be altered further."

"You want an update; we can do that. How in-depth of an update do you want?"

"A report from each province segment should be fine. There are six of them, so six statuses. Between the two of you, you can get three reports each and with you being there, perhaps you can give me a better insight of the state of things, both in the tunnels and above ground. Sometimes the knights like to soften the blow and I much rather have it as it is to prepare accordingly."

"That might take a while if you're concerned with time…" Mazaeh told her, and she shook her head.

"I know, but time isn't something too concerning if we see things in the early stages. We don't need to be blindsided a second time."

"We'll send a message your way if we're not able to be back before midnight," Elias told her, and she gave a nod. "Stay out of trouble. No more deals and all that."

She snubbed him off. She hadn't told him about what happened the night before, but she wasn't surprised that they knew since they got into everything. The council was informed therefore, somewhere along the way, they knew. Unlike the two knights however, the council was quite happy for the backup plan, happier than what she wanted them to be if she was honest. "Keep that to yourselves. Very few people know as of right now."

"And you want to keep it that way, we know. Don't want Aer to be pressured into anything."

"Exactly, so if you know what's good for you..."

"Sealed lips."

Mazaeh lightly tapped Elias's shoulder, beckoning him. "Come on, you're getting east and south."

"Bastard, why do you get Aesear?"

"Because you talk too much and didn't pick."

The brunet growled as he trudged after his friend. Their dragons followed not far behind as they continued their bickering, Elias mentioning that his parents had been begging for him to go to their house to pick up a few things, and she turned to the lip above her. "Bretheena, I also have a mission for you."

The lip wasn't a wrong assumption as Bretheena appeared over the side and dropped down in front of her, silent as always. "A scouting mission?"

"Kind of. Could you head to the library back in Siofra Castle and see if there are any books or grimoires on basic conjuring skills? I'm at my wits' end trying to figure this out and I need a different approach."

"You have basically asked everyone here to help you with this skill with no success, so a book might do it," she agreed before frowning. "But I don't want to leave you here alone..."

"I'll be fine for a few hours in my own home... Besides, Citlali sent a message saying he'll be arriving in an hour or so if he's on time. I'm sure he'll be using up a lot of my time to get his money's worth."

Bretheena gave a small laugh. "It's been over a month since he's been on that mission... I'm curious to know what he dug up."

"I'll give you details if he finishes before you get back. The library sprites should make navigating the library easier and since the castle has the tunnel again, you won't have to deal with monsters while you're at it… hopefully."

"Which is always nice… Be careful while I'm away."

"Always am."

Bretheena gave a small nod and left swiftly, letting Atlamillia to do what she pleased. She waited a few moments before making her way towards the courtyard. She had to give her retainers some time to leave the castle area before she could slip away unnoticed.

After her walk, the plateau courtyard was open for her and Lucilla to head to the opposite direction of the gateway. She mounted and they left, staying somewhat low as they weaved in and out of the natural terrain before gaining some air, out of the city limits and away from prying eyes. She pulled out the tablet after a few minutes to make sure they were going in the right direction. It was in the southern quadrant and from her map of the place, about an hour out if they flew at a faster speed than casual. The same direction as the tug she had been feeling.

She looked down at Lucilla. *"You up for that?"*

"The only reason why I'm not flying as fast as possible is because I don't know what to expect at the other end."

A small giggle came out. *"Just don't go too fast if you get excited. Best not to get stuck between dimensions or something."*

"What a terrifying thought…"

It was, wasn't it? The odds of it were slim since surely Orithina would have thought about the speeds of the fastest dragons. Then again… she didn't write anything down or tell any leading family in any of her kingdoms about seals holding back a horror from some other place, so, who the hell knew. Certainly not either of them.

00000

Lucilla dropped onto the stone floor of a large canyon that laid between two mountains as Atlamillia double checked the armour she placed on during the travel. They looked around the foggy, arid space blocking much of what was around them in the ominous place. A long-dried riverbed sat under Lucilla's claws, the sediments and rock layers were not shy of its past with different colours of red, green, and purple. A faked past, but it was a nice detail all the same. There was definitely a magical presence in the far corner of the pocket dimension, but she didn't have a clue as to what it was or why it was there. It was familiar though. Very, very familiar. She tried to home in on the presence when a voice echoed out, scaring them half to death.

"What is this place?"

She turned to the noise to see a silver-purple dragon coming out of the fog, towards them on the valley floor. On her back was a much more familiar face that was both unexpected and a bit unwanted as he looked over the chasm walls. "Endymion?"

"Hm? Oh… hi…" The sheepish look on him told her more than enough. How had he forgotten that they were there despite clearly following them? "Ah, so… this is a bit awkward."

She glared, not dancing on the issue. "What are you doing here?"

"I wanted to apologize for my mother and upon reaching the front gate, Selene noticed you leaving and so we followed, hoping to catch up…" That was a lot more truthful than she had anticipated. "So, now we're here… wherever here is."

"The middle of nowhere…" she sighed. She wanted to do this alone in case the scripture, which was a good tell sign, was divine in nature. The sort of thing that if she played with or investigated, would draw attention and suspicion if she weren't alone. "You should head back to the city… This place is still undiscovered territory."

"And yet you're here, alone. That's pretty dangerous considering you're sort of acting ruler right now."

Wrong choice of words on her part. "So, you're going to be my acting guard? Forgive me but I don't need your protection. I can take care of myself."

"I know you can. I'm aware of the stories but that doesn't mean you should be alone. Just in case there's some sort of trial or whatever this place is supposed to be."

"A trial?" How'd he come to that conclusion?

"It's a presumption, but the magic here is… I don't know how to describe it. But it feels heavy, like it could be hiding something, somewhere here, purposely set up for someone who would follow its signature. Someone that's not me that much is certain."

That wouldn't be unheard of... Orithina was very good at manipulating fate and could have set something up for her, or Theseus from days past, or even someone completely unknown to do... whatever laid beyond the sealed wall she and Lucilla had yet to find. This was the place she needed. "I suppose that's a fair assumption... but I don't know your skills very well and if it is made for someone specific, I don't want you to do anything stupid."

A small chuckle came out of him, his question was rhetorical, "Not a fan of heroes, eh?"

"No. They tend to be idiots. I should know, my brother is one of them."

"I'll try not to be very heroic then, but luckily for both of us that if I do, I have a special skill that allows me to be protective and not get hurt."

She raised a brow. "What exactly do you mean?"

"You know, natural enhanced abilities like my sister's ability to combine her types without much thought. Mine lays within air manipulation. I can make the air become an unbreakable shield by compressing the molecules in the area. Plus, I have blink."

"Blink..." That was more than surprising to hear. "You're capable of the minor teleport?"

He nodded. "It's significantly quicker and I've managed to develop it to three consecutive uses before it becomes difficult to use."

"The only other person I've known to have it was a knight in Baiwyn, so this is a bit surprising to know that you also have the ability."

"I mean, it's basically space distortion. A high tier air magic skill that is like necromancy where only certain people have it. So, this doesn't surprise me as most people tend to stay quiet about being able to use it."

Probably because it could be used for crime and it's terrifying if used offensively. Most Absalomians have some sort of resistance to being torn apart by magic like light and dark when it came to molecular separation due to their dragon blood, the more the better – but blink was something else entirely. It was a rapid displacement with little to no signature of magic left behind. "Well... that's good to know..."

"So, what are you doing here, Princess Atlamillia?"

"Looking into a finding further." She didn't need to tell him every tiny thing... and as helpful as his skills could be, she didn't want him here all the same.

"He's not going to leave," Lucilla told her what she already knew before elaborating. *"But it wouldn't be a bad thing to have someone here with us just in case. Plus, this is a good opportunity to get to know each other better."*

"I guess..."

"Atlamillia and I would appreciate if you two could watch our backs in case it gets dangerous," she expanded out loud to Endymion and Selene.

The young noble gave a small nod before looking behind him. "I believe the strange place you're looking for is over there. We saw some strange markings on the wall when we landed."

Lucilla marched past them, going to the direction he hinted at, and Selene caught up, walking next to her. It wasn't a far walk of silence before they came across the wall that matched the one in the pictures. Atlamillia pulled out the tablet again, going through the information before putting it away and getting off Lucilla. The wall was as she predicted; the words were Ancient Dragon. They were slightly eroded but being able to see it with her own eyes, it wasn't hard to read.

"So, the markings are words," Endymion said next to her, scaring her slightly. She hadn't heard him walk up to her. "At least, you seem to be able to read it."

"I can. It's Ancient Dragon."

"Ancient Dragon? Isn't that a dead language?"

"To the people of light, for the most part. Several Outland Dragon Tribes and Hordes still use it though."

"Huh, that's actually really cool. What does it say?"

"Pértra edic laïono od Vasígnum tode od Divinukos. Eísammeo ai esos eínunt áxigna."

He looked at her, completely dumbfounded. "Uh... what?"

"Beyond here lies the Realm of the Divine. Enter if you are worthy."

"That... is quite the statement."

"It is." She crossed her arms, looking at the wall. "Which makes me wonder what lays inside."

"Not that there is a way to enter but... even if we could, I don't think it'd be a good idea."

"It's just a warning to the weak. A bold message with no bite. I've seen it many times before," she told him honestly with a shrug. "There might be a test, as you said, but we should be fine."

He shook his head. "I have a bad feeling about this. I don't think we should tempt fate."

"Then don't follow, but I need to find out what's beyond this."

"Princess, I don't think it's a need but a want. You need to eat and breathe; this place says it's the Realm of the Divine."

"Exactly. I can't have the knights come here and get hurt or killed by such things. As a descendant of a chosen hero and of the royal family, I have that divine right without question." The only thing she didn't have was a way to enter that realm. It called to her. She couldn't leave without finding out what was there, for herself more so than her excuse.

A sigh came out of him, "And you say heroes are stupid…"

"Did you just-"

"Yes, Princess Atlamillia, I did. With that said, I'm not going to leave you to die out here in the middle of nowhere or in there if we manage to get in. If stubbornness runs in your family, the gods know I've heard all about it from my parents and my sister; you simply won't leave this be."

She rolled her eyes, but didn't bother to argue with him, turning back to the wall. He could stay if he wanted, follow and help, it didn't bother her any as long as he didn't get in her way. Now the question was, how the hell were they going to get in? She placed her hand on the cool stone, the leather etching the letters. Orithina clearly wanting someone to get in…

Her thoughts turned darker as she went over the information Aerrow had given her about the seals. How they were probably created. They consigned with how the gifts worked, the demand of the user's essence, not just magic. Just like so many other divine dealings… She pulled off the glove on her right hand and extended a claw on the worn one, slicing across the pale skin on her palm.

A hiss came out and Endymion panicked. "What in Orithin are you doing?!"

"Opening this wall, hopefully."

"Through blood?!"

She placed the blood-pooled hand onto the wall and wiped it across the text. The wall glowed slightly before fading into nothingness, showing behind it a large and dark tunnel into the earth. A small sigh escaped, "Of course it would be blood…"

"This isn't the first time?!"

"Well, not this exact thing but… I'm well versed in divine natures and blood carries the life essence of a person… So, it makes sense that it's highly valued as a currency for divine recognition."

"This sort of thing is the reason why Pegasus still has sacrificial offerings…" Endymion growled like she was the one enabling the religious acts. "And seriously, if this sort of thing needs to happen again, might I suggest the back of your arm instead of your hand. There are significantly less nerves there and it's easier to bandage."

She looked at him dead in the eye as she gripped her sword's hilt, her conduit, and healed the wound with little to no effort. Her words that formed on her tongue afterwards were dry and complacent. "What bandage?"

"Right… you're capable of healing…"

She put her glove back on the healed hand and looked to the entrance. The power that came from it was like how she felt when she came to Asylotum for the first time. Almost like breathing unlike she had ever breathed before, only amplified by ten. Like she was going to die without its embrace. It was a bit unnerving if she was honest, but she didn't share the thoughts with the young noble duo. She didn't beckon him or announce that she was going in, simply doing so and Lucilla quickly caught pace with her, not questioning her feelings on the subject.

There were just some things that while Lucilla could feel them like her own, they weren't exactly something she could help understand what they meant. A barrier between the two of them that as far as she was aware, other Absalomian-Dragon partners didn't have, but something they lived with. A benefit or a curse, it was up in the air. Her father explained that it would take a lot for them to slip into expiration shock if they were separated, but at the cost of her not being able to share certain things.

"Princess Atlamillia, perhaps a second…" Selene tried to protest but trailed off as neither she nor Lucilla slowed their descent.

Endymion gave a huff of acceptance. "Come on, I don't want to explain to the king, Dani, or Mother that the princess was killed due to arrogance."

"I heard that," Atlamillia called up and a scoff came from him.

"Too bad that you couldn't hear reason as well."

She didn't say anything else to instigate him further and looked down the tunnel. The light from above was blocked out as Selene and Endymion moved inside and left the tunnel even darker. She lifted her hand slightly and conjured a ball of blue light. The ball floated above, near the ceiling, and created shadows on the earth and walls. The temperature dropping surprisingly quickly as they moved forward before balancing out as her breath showed, telling her that her battle skirt and armoured, short sleeved coat were not appropriate for the environment. Caves were weird.

Suddenly, a pulse of energy went through the tunnel, sending a chill up her spine.

What the hell was-

"Princess-" Endymion started, startled, but didn't finish.

She turned around. The floor below his feet was glowing and a white light to blind her. The ground below her disappeared as she fell into a white void with a scream.

Chapter Twenty-Eight: Fight Club

A grin had plastered itself on my face a while ago, and it only seemed to grow as the game went on. It had wavered once when one of the artificial intelligence players did something unexpected. The game was neat. The players had to develop their country and spread it across the world through conquest, alliances, score, and/or cultural influence… But it wasn't so different from the years of lessons about running not only a nation, but conquering land, and warfare. It was something I never thought would be viable since the kingdoms had never gone to war against an entirely different nation before, but caution and paranoia of the possibility dictated what studies I had.

Turned out, I was a fantastic conqueror, and using the history of my kingdom, I filled in the weaknesses that could have cost my in-game nation its existence. Now, it was a massive empire with overwhelming technological advancement and wealth against the only nation left on the continent. Pefror had been a pain in my western border since the very beginning. Picking wars, forcing me to split my armies, taking my resources, and plundering my cities… But not anymore. It stopped picking fights a few in-game years ago, but only because it couldn't breach my walls.

After so long, the advancement I had obtained by taking and adding the other nations and countries to my own. Their researchers to the culture, engineering, social economics, and the sciences of biology, chemistry, and physics; the infiltration spies that had tried to stop my hand were now used to create chaos in Pefror, destroying the hope that its citizens had in their government. I certainly had no trouble getting through their walls after the hell I put the neighbouring nation through.

Now they were going to be swallowed into the great Empire of Truara.

The swoop of taking the towns, cities, strategic resources, bases, and basic structures was a swift one, lasting only a few turns. The siege on the capital was over in almost a few seconds once I had strategically placed the breaching artillery rockets, cavalry, infantry, and airships in position, and on standby. The rockets blasted, the bombs dropped from airships, and then my cavalry and infantry came in hard, taking what was left with little difficulty.

Had it been a real city with real people where the population of innocent lives were considered, I probably would have done it in a different way. But this game didn't consider citizen death a factor, and so, I had free reign to do whatever I deemed necessary… And that was just about everything I had to show the AI how insignificant it was compared to my might.

A cackle came out of me, a bit unexpected as the triumph of finally destroying my enemy was more than satisfying. To destroy the pain that Pefror was and ceasing its taint on the Cruylia continent and the map, even more so.

I noticed Éabha look over at me before turning to the bottom right of my split screen.

"When did you…? Nope." Her demeanour dropped along with her shoulders and controller, having the held device land in her lap.

"Nope?" I asked in confusion and she pushed the button I had come to know as many games' pause button. I looked back at the screen on her side and she scrolled to the bottom, selecting Surrender. "Wait-"

"Nope. Not doing it."

"What do you mean-"

"You're beyond my skill level. I can't compete and I had to input cheat codes halfway through to ramp up the difficulty for you."

"You cheated?!" I exclaimed, turning to her as my screen screamed victory.

"I had to, or you would've been stampeding right through the whole map an hour ago," she explained, sitting against the back of the couch. "Besides, if it was that big of a deal, you would have noticed, and I'd have to be forced to fix it."

"I mean, I did notice that Pefror was still being a colossal jerk for most of the game despite not getting much bigger…" I glared. "So, it was your fault that I lost my crabs for thirty years!"

"Might have been… but hey, you overcame it and got them back."

"My people almost starved and rioted for that stunt!"

"And look at that, you conquered half the world, congratulations."

Her lack of caring bothered me, but I let it go as it was just a game, and I had, indeed, won. "So, I'm guessing you don't want to play this again…"

"I think I'll watch the next time you play. You might be able to beat the AI on the highest difficulty, which is them cheating all the time."

"Why do they have to cheat?"

"Cause the AI is dumb, and so, this is how it was compensated." She set the controller on the table, standing up, and stretched. "Ugh! I've been sitting too long…"

"Only a couple of hours." The familiar voice of Owen corrected, causing both of us to jump. I looked behind us to find that Owen, Cyrus, and Azarias were sitting on a turned couch behind us and were snacking on popcorn and jerky. "But it was fun to watch. Good job, Aerrow."

"How long have you three been there?!" I asked, my voice cracking.

"Long enough to see you get your ass handed to you by that gargoyle creature," Azarias answered too casually, shoving another piece of jerky into his mouth. It was a mean comment, but it did explain why neither of us heard them come in. "It's a nice break to just sit and watch after a whole day of working… you should do this more often, it's healthy for you."

"Maybe…" I had gotten distracted by the flashing lights and forgot about the whelps. Suddenly all the fun I had was drained out.

"I bet millions of people could get the same entertainment if there was a network that could allow one to show off the game."

"The CT network is growing and has been tested to do exactly that. The term we call it is streaming," Éabha told us and I raised a brow, a bit surprised. She caught the glance. "What?"

I gave her my honest opinion. "Yeah… I don't think it will catch on, but if it did, congrats."

"You're not the most technological person around, being that you are a ruler of a nation that has issues with Seraphinean Tech, so, I can see why you'd think that." She gave a small shrug. "But that doesn't mean you can't support funding for such projects even if you don't believe in it…"

"Perhaps once Absalom is in the position again to throw money around. Bad investments and all that."

She made a face as I stood, restless and back in reality. Video games were great, but it didn't feel right to continue without progressing in something. I looked at the curtains to find that the crack of light that had been there, was long gone.

How much time did we waste away?

I didn't get to check the CT as a small, excited noise came out of Éabha, surprising me.

"I have a great idea!"

"Why don't I like the sound of this?" Cyrus asked and she snubbed him off, turning to me.

"We should train."

"Are you sure that's a good idea?" I asked, playing it off like I wasn't greatly interested. It meant I could figure out if she had similar techniques that Ciar used without the others getting angry with me for not taking the break that this sleepover was supposed to be. Well, other than Deigh as I felt her ready to give me hell. Surprisingly, she waited for the others for their answer. "I thought sleepovers were supposed to be less violent than pillow tossing?"

"That's for regular people, we're the elite with the ability to do just about anything we want."

"Speak for yourself, I'm not allowed outside…" I muttered. "But I wouldn't mind sparring with you."

"We could learn from each other!"

A scary thought came into my head. "Yes… but if I hurt you, your father would have my head along with my kingdom."

"Probably but there might be common ground between the way I fight, which is a variant of Seraphinean and self taught, and Ciar's style."

I gave a look over to the others on the couch, choosing my words carefully. "Maybe there is a connection."

"He is half Seraph; his zealots are all over this island. He probably grew up here meaning his fighting style would be soiled in Seraphinean influence. It would give you some good practice since you're probably wanting to do something productive after all that playing." She was reading through me too well and I didn't deny it as I turned back to her. "In the off chance it's not similar, we can play a guessing game of where this guy learned how to fight. You've probably memorized much of his form and pose, right?"

"I wouldn't say memorized but had it seared into my brain…"

"So, you could mimic what he did?"

"I mean, maybe… He was a foot and a half taller than me when we had fought so the reach would be significantly different-"

"The tactic though is still the same and that could help the rest of us get a better understanding. Maybe even evolve it and use it against him…" Her mind was moving at a million kilometres a minute, ideas unsaid could be seen through slight changes in her posture and face. She turned to the knights. "Please let us spar!"

They seemed to be contemplating as I looked over at them. "Is that fine? I know we don't have a healer or a doctor, but this would be a missed opportunity."

"I have Fyliel's address should we need a doctor and can't get to Orpheal just in case he does want to kill you," Owen answered, apparently agreeing with my comment about hurting Éabha being a bad idea. "It would be a small Chaos Portal trip away. So I suppose the spar would be in the best interest of our end goal."

At least that was a bit comforting.

Suddenly, all three of them looked to Éabha, a variety of expressions from surprise to glee were on their faces. I turned to her as Azarias started to say my name only for the rest of it to be silenced by the sound of the throw pillow colliding with my face. It fell into my hands that hadn't made it to defend.

The girl was pleased with my dumbfound expression. "Ah yes... sweet revenge."

"I... alright." My objection fell flat, and a sigh came out. "I guess I should have remembered that that was coming at some point."

"Probably should've... want to have a second round?"

"I don't think the pillows could handle a second round after the practiced first..."

A small pout came from her, then she shrugged. "Later then, with expendable pillows."

I couldn't tell if I was glad that we weren't going to have a true battle with pillows or disappointed but dropped it before I could find out. The pillow was set back onto the couch and I turned to the knights. "Could you come watch? With your experience, this spar could bring about tactics for fighting Ciar and... maybe referee so she doesn't accidentally kill me."

Azarias was more than enthusiastic as he basically leaped from the couch. "Time to gear up! It's trainin' time!"

00000

I put on my training armour coat that was black instead of red. The lighter gear of basic gloves and armguards went on next, reminding me of the days before being king. I pushed the thought away before it could bring up feelings I didn't want to deal with.

Guðmundr sat underneath the guard, but over the gloves where I would have had the inhibitor bracelet if I was allowed to leave the hideout. I activated the shield, out of curiosity, and he formed a simple, round shield before disappearing as I lowered my arm. It was neat that he worked, now the trick was remembering I had him in the middle of a fight. I walked to the training room where I could see Éabha in her armour, it glowed a bit as she stared at the weapon rack. Azarias was talking with her as his hands moved as they always did when he was into a conversation, but it didn't tell me what they were talking about.

"Hey, Deigh, what kind of..." My question trailed off as I realized that she was already sleeping. I stopped, turning to our room slightly before going back the way I came. I looked inside, finding her curled up in her corner and I shook my head. We were just talking about playing it safe and she was already out cold. How on Orithin had she managed to sleep so quickly was a skill I wish I had. I turned off the light and closed the door quietly with a whisper, "Sweet dreams, Deigh…"

She didn't respond, not that I expected her to, and turned back to the idea of getting somewhere with something. I was happy that the others were allowing me to train instead of resting. But I had to do something to help with one of our problems, and that meant I couldn't be left unprepared again against Ciar or whoever decided to show up.

"Quite the scary look on your face," Owen's voice came to my ears and I snapped to it in surprise. He leaned against the stairway, not in armour but certainly refreshed from his trip earlier as his hair was wet and in something far more casual with a black hoodie and slacks. "Something on your mind?"

"Not really." I gave a small shrug, lowing my hand from my chest, and walked towards the training room entrance. "This training will hopefully make up for it."

I felt him eye me a bit before a slight sigh came from him but didn't push the subject further. We went into the room in silence, the door hiding the laughter that came from Azarias over a joke neither of us heard.

Éabha turned to us with excitement before it became a frown. "You don't ever show skin, do you?"

"I'm sorry?" I was a bit more than confused. "We're supposed to be training, that requires armour. It's supposed to cover-"

"Yeah I know," she sighed, disappointed. "It just makes it difficult to practice healing."

"If you led with that earlier, we could have done training afterwards."

She pondered with a shrug. "Since we're already here and you brought your sword, let's make the most of it."

"Wait, you want me to use-" I didn't get to finish my question as she closed the distance between the two of us on wings, bringing down a broadsword upon my head.

My hand drew Winterthorn, barely in time to block the surprise attack that was too unsettlingly close to Ciar's first attack on me. Owen quickly vacated towards Cyrus who was sitting on a bench where Éabha had been a moment prior. I tried to shift her blade, but it wasn't budging, forcing me to put my free hand on the grip as her strike was winning against my block. I slipped under her guard, shoving my shoulder into her exposed chest from her flying position. The black and white armour glowed as it took the blow, but she backed off regardless, keeping herself off the ground with four wings. I tightened my grip on the hilt, feeling a tremble of fear trying to take hold. My neck and chest stabbed, but I couldn't let go of Winterthorn.

It wasn't Ciar, but the uncanniness of the first attack wouldn't let me decipher the difference.

"That shoulder check would have really hurt if my armour didn't take it, not bad," Éabha complimented and the tension I felt eased ever so slightly.

Ciar didn't talk nearly as much.

She set the blade that was a couple of inches longer than she was tall to her side, both tempting me to think she was wide open while also setting herself for whatever attack she wanted to make if I didn't bite her bait. She had every advantage being that she had more field and height, even if she was a foot shorter than me. Her reach was more than compensated compared to my limited range, being stuck to the ground, or jumping. And jumping was just a stupid thing to do to engage.

The only trick I had up my sleeve to limit hers was a fire dome, but I certainly wasn't going to do that if I ignored the magic signature I would put out. We were inside an enclosed room and inside a building. I didn't want to hurt her or the knights and my uncle that were nearby, watching.

"Aw, you're not going to come at me?"

"It would be what you want, wouldn't it?" I commented back, forcing a cheeky grin to hide my insecurities. "All you'd have to do is simply fly away whenever I got close."

"Hehe, yeah… it'd be almost boring to watch you run after me." She looked at her gauntlet like she was looking at her nails in disinterest.

"You're such a sadi-"

She didn't let me finish a second time as she was moving again, striking with her blade swiftly, forcing me to defend. A ball of light formed in her free hand and I ducked out of its path. With my blade out of the way, she moved forward to continue her blade's path. I kicked up a wad of sand as I disengaged, predicting her overeager aggression.

She cursed, getting out of reach again to rub out the sand. "That's not very honourable… I thought you were a Dragon Knight."

"There's a line of honourability that crossing will get you killed," I growled, adjusting myself to be less rigid despite every part of me disagreeing with the fact that she wasn't him.

It wasn't something I had really noticed before, but her just simply being in one spot, not quite out of combat, was almost identical to how Ciar positioned and poised. None of the other Seraphineans I had seen had the same elegance while assessing what to do next or seemed to move to the same, unheard beat.

The sand attack didn't last more than a few moments and she attacked again with a grin. She struck hard, magic encasing the weapon to keep it from breaking as I deflected it, but it was a fruitless attempt. She attacked again, using the momentum I had given with the deflect to attack my exposed side. I activated Guðmundr and broke the attack, dropping the flat of my blade on her shoulder as she bounced back. She was knocked to the ground and I closed the gap that formed. My sword went to secure the victory as she got to a stand, but it was a pre-emptive thought and nothing more.

Light magic came from her suddenly and my charge gave no time for me to defend, my boots slipping in the sand. A ball of light formed, seemingly out of nowhere and hit me directly in the chest, blasting me away.

I hit the glass wall; the breath being knocked out of me before I hit the hard, sandy floor a few feet below. I started to get up and noticed Éabha had sent out another light sphere. I dodged to the side, barely getting to a stand when she appeared above me, knocking me over by grabbing my wrist and using the broadsword to sweep my feet from underneath. Her sword came down onto my exposed chest and the memory of that night came back for a moment.

Winterthorn blocked the attack as my body moved when my mind couldn't, throwing it wide and sent Éabha, who was standing over top of me, off balance. Using my other hand, I further threw her off and unable to correct as I grabbed the leg next to me. I lifted it into the direction of her fall, pulling myself up in the process. She landed with a slight grunt as I got on top of her, keeping her pinned between my knees and a hand on her shoulder, my sword at her throat.

She seemed surprised at first before a large smile formed on her face between the heavy breathing. "Hey, Aerrow?"

"What?" My question was more of a growl as I tried to connect with reality that the fight was nothing more than training. I reassessed the match and found it didn't seem like it was for sport. She barely held back just as my blade had been restrained from touching her skin.

She didn't seem to notice, however, as a giggle came out, "Nice tie."

I looked at her in confusion before noticing the intense magic on the back of my neck and skull. A light field was under my knees. I looked behind me to confirm what I thought was there and came face to face with a massive vine of light, one that if our fight had been to the death, would have obliterated my head into nothing in a last-ditch effort even if my sword had gone through with its path.

The movement of looking behind me caused a sharp pain in my sword arm, making me remove Winterthorn haphazardly to the side to not drop it on her. I grabbed the painful spot between my coat and guard and looked at it. Blood was on my glove and the culprit of the act laid beside us: the blunt, training broadsword.

"Oh, and you stabbed yourself or… maybe I stabbed you? It's a bit hard to say."

"How the hell did that happen?!"

"Well, you jumped onto me as I went to defend, not expecting you to do that and, you just… didn't notice I guess." It was surprisingly casual the way she explained it, but I wasn't entirely satisfied.

"What did you think I would do if you thought your blade needed to go there?"

"I don't know, get up for a better advantage?" She tried moving then gave a small sigh. "You know, I could practice that healing skill if I could get up... So, could you maybe get off of me?"

"R-right..." I stammered, forgetting that I had trapped her and sat on the ground next to her, keeping pressure on the wound. It probably wasn't that bad, but it was better to be safe than sorry.

She sat up as Azarias cheered with a book in his hands, coming over. "That was such a good match!"

"It was something..." Owen somewhat agreed, bringing a first aid kit with him and Cyrus trailed behind them. "But was it helpful?"

"There were a lot of similarities-"

"We can discuss things after we deal with your cut," Éabha interrupted, apparently eager to heal, but didn't hop to it like I had expected her to.

In the pause, Cyrus picked up the broadsword and scanned it before sighing. "I'm going to go clean this."

"You're not sticking around for the show?" Azarias asked and he shook his head. "Fine, just don't take too long – we have things to learn still!"

Cyrus left without a word. I looked to the Seraphinean in front of me, paying attention to the silence. She seemed almost nervous as she looked at my hand covered wound. I turned to the book in Azarias's hand, catching part of the title on the spine: something Healing. I looked back, not needing to know the rest of it. "You've never actually done this before, have you?"

"I... well, I read about it. Seen Dad and Aunt Solaria do it... Mum a long time ago," she answered as Azarias and Owen joined us on the ground, Owen opening the medical kit. "At least wait until I try before setting things up!"

"Maybe if you had tried out healing with one of your lab pets before hand, I might have." He looked at her with slight disdain. "I don't like knowing after the fact that you're using my king as your Fiery Pig."

"It's not like you asked either. Besides, how hard could it be?"

"Those words are usually something I say before getting into further trouble..." I muttered out and Azarias handed her the book. "Seriously, it's okay if you don't think you can do it. We can ask your father if it needs more than a bandage or -"

"I want to learn how to heal and if Dad found out, he'd flip."

"Hence why she didn't practice before hand," Azarias shared. "We were talking about it before you arrived, which is why Cyrus left for the moment. Turns out he doesn't like seeing people he cares about being tortured."

I raised a brow. "Who would?"

A scoff came from Éabha, "I'm not going to torture him. I already told you both that I have the fundamentals down!"

I turned to Owen, slightly confused on how we went from healing to torture. "I don't know enough about the learning process but is torture really something that can happen when practicing healing? It seems very counter productive."

He didn't answer me directly as he eyed Éabha a bit who looked from him to the book, apparently knowing what he was going to say. "If you're really bad at it…"

"Which I can't be…" she muttered. "It runs in the family."

"Sometimes gifts skip."

"How about we just try it," I suggested, trying to ease the growing tension. "It's not like she can mess up so badly that I die from bleeding out with a small wound like this. It'll be fine. Éabha has probably seen Solaria and her father heal people many times and I believe she can heal a bit of it, if not all of it."

"You could run a church with that much faith," Owen growled. A sigh came out. "Fine, I'll let you two do your trying, waiting here with bandages… Azarias, have your CT ready to call Orpheal."

"Yes, sir!" Azarias agreed way too cheerfully, pulling out his CT.

Éabha glared at him. "Traitor."

"Look, I like you and trust you – but he's also my boss and you're going to be practicing on my liege and nation's ruler. Priorities are necessary."

She didn't argue with him and opened the book to a page already marked before hand, reading it over quickly before turning to my arm. "Alright, I think I have this…"

She did not have it.

She formed the healing orb like the book showed, and what I had seen Atlamillia do countless times before, but it was only useful as a soft, white-blue light, and it stung. A lot. I held my tongue, but not the recoiling flinch and she apologized, trying again.

The second time was more successful as the stinging ended and I relaxed my jaw. The bleeding stopped, but she wasn't satisfied with her progress and jumped to the end of the book, skimming, or according to her, reading it. A proper healing orb that Helena would have used formed in her hands and executed it with perfection, healing my arm and a bit of my fatigue, on purpose or not, that was still in the air.

She closed the book, triumphantly. "Little disappointed that it took three tries, but it turns out healing was a lot more difficult than I gave it credit for."

"I mean, it's healing. That's a hard skill to learn even for the most inclined individuals," I told her, and she shrugged. "That book is a thousand pages; I doubt that any of it has rambles and fluff."

"No, it's very technical. I read the whole thing twice last night and just read a couple of chapters now to hone the skills necessary for that outcome."

I went to argue on how insane that was but simply shook my head. She was a genius, and she did prove that fact by learning an advanced skill of healing straight from failure of basic clotting in about ten minutes. "You're something else, Éabha."

"Thank you. I'll take that as a compliment."

"As you should, it was one."

She stood up as Owen finished packing up the first aid kit. "But I should apologize for not saying something before. Sorry."

"Run it by me first next time. Not Aerrow and not Azarias or Cyrus," he said. "Because caution and thinking ahead clearly only comes with age."

We all gave a different line of disagreement to his claim, all of which he ignored.

"Let's keep this training to a minimum of injury this time, eh? I'm going to go get Cyrus."

"We'll try," I told him as the rest of us got up, and he left with a curt nod of acknowledgment.

It didn't take long before he got back with Cyrus who had cleaned the weapon only to find out that we had cracked it, giving us a bit of trouble for the rough housing. A small apology came from the both of us, though I was left more surprised over the fact it hadn't snapped entirely seeing the massive crack.

Éabha's strikes were harder than Owen's or even my father's when we had sparred, but not as much as Ciar's. She placed a shield using her own magic to try and protect it, knowing that the clashes would have broke against Winterthorn.

She might have been small, but she was stronger than she looked, just as she said she was.

I picked up my sword off the ground where it had been left and sheathed it, removing it from my belt. I hadn't meant to use it in the little spar to begin with, just didn't want it to be too far from my side. Owen took it from me, unprompted, and traded it for a training blade. I happily accepted it, not questioning him about giving me my preferred weapon choice and turned to Éabha. "What weapon are you going for?"

"Maybe another broadsword. We didn't get to discuss it earlier because I wanted to heal, but the way you reacted to my attacks did tell me that you were familiar with them meaning I do have more to share."

"That's because Ciar used them before... was that a Seraphinean style?"

"For the most part. It's about overpowering your opponent and making sure they can't get an opening, for attack or recovery. For having only gone against it twice, I'm surprised that you had learned to defend and counter against it so fast and without magic."

"I'm a fast learner..." I cleared my throat slightly, trying to listen in on the other side of the room between Azarias and Cyrus, but they were discussing battle strategies quietly while listening in on our conversation. Owen was silent between the four of us. "Was anything you did in that spar something unique to you?"

"I'd like to think a good portion was... Like the lure in before blasting you was something I came up with on my own, but even then, you seemed aware of it at the last few moments – the only reason you couldn't stop was because of the terrain."

"Sand is rather slippery, yes. But Ciar did so something similar. Though, I must admit, you hid your magic a lot better than he did."

"Perhaps the same source of learning?" Owen suggested and Éabha shrugged.

"I don't know. I read some of Domrael's journals and he mentions that sometimes pretending to be open, leaves your opponent vulnerable and gave some details on how to use magic as that instrument. But those journals aren't available to anyone outside of the family circle, so it's possible that the idea was picked up from somewhere else. It's not like it's a hard strategy to come up with."

That was true, the tactic was universal to bring your opponent into a false sense of security – I've done it many times without magic. But the form and execution of the attacks were awfully similar, like they had both studied from the same art form or teacher. I sighed, letting it go. Similar didn't mean the same and there was a level where if I dug too deep, I'd find nothing but lost allies and a world of paranoia.

"So, we can spar and practice with Éabha and get decent results, that's good to know!" Azarias called and I looked to him. He looked ready to go with a spear. "Let's do that for a bit, then a certain someone needs to break."

I pouted. "I don't need to break."

"Your drug supply says otherwise."

I went to counter before sighing. That was a fair assessment to figuring out my health. "Éabha and I can share what we have for a bit... then we should stop, not just for me. You guys have been working hard all day."

"Yep, we did! Once we're done, Owen will have supper ready for all of us while we clean up!"

"Oh, will I now?" Owen challenged next to us and Azarias's pedestal was knocked over.

"Er... well, maybe if he were a gracious and merciful god that would be willing to make something for us to eat? Sparring is calorie consuming as we mortals get hungry but will have to clean up first..."

He sighed. "I suppose this god could make you something... just this once."

"Thank you, Lord of Darkness."

"Dramatic much?" Éabha asked, a bit rhetorically.

I shrugged. "That's how he is."

"Alright then... Let's get to it."

00000

I yawned, taking another antinausea pill after changing into a loose, red, long-sleeve shirt that was borderline a sweater and some pants. The shower was quite nice to my body that, by the end of the training and learning, was incredibly needed. Azarias was right, I was not ready for that much practice for a full on second spar, not that the second mini spar held anything back. Éabha and I had our hides handed back to us on a silver platter at the single moment we had the upper hand. That and I got a bit cocky… which didn't help matters on how quickly Azarias and Cyrus ended things.

There was some noise coming from the living room where Éabha was laughing at something, apparently all cleaned up after using the guest bathroom downstairs. I went to join them when the sound of my CT came to my ears from the gear I had yet to put away. I went over to it in confusion and a bit of shame that I had forgotten that I had put it in my pocket out of habit. I dug it out and read a number but no name.

A frown formed and I answered it, warily, "Hello?"

"H-hi, Aerrow… um," a familiar voice spoke, shy and soft as ever. "It's Dani… Atlamillia gave Aoife and I your CT number last night. But if you don't want us to have it, we can delete your contact information."

"No, it's fine. It's nice to have my contact list grow with people I know." A small giggle came from her that came to a quick end, seemingly distracted. I leaned against the table. "Something the matter?"

"Have you spoken to Atla recently?"

"Yesterday afternoon I believe… did something happen to her?"

"Oh, nope! Nothing happened since you last talked."

"Okay…" That wasn't suspicious at all.

"But then again… did she mention possibly leaving for a bit?"

"No, she didn't." The frown came back. "Is she missing?"

"She sent her retainers on quests and took off someplace, didn't tell anyone where she was going."

"It's possible she's hiding somewhere in the castle. She did that once in a while back in Siofra and once a couple of months back in Asylotum. She likes to meditate and practice where no one can interrupt her."

Dani gave a small sigh of relief. "Okay, I was a bit worried that maybe she went to that place she was sensing on her own."

"I know there were knights scouting for such places, but I think that was halted for the tunnels."

"Yeah, they came back. She mentioned that she was going to go through their notes but didn't say they found anything... How long would she disappear for when she went to meditate if she didn't go to the solarium?"

"Hours, sometimes not coming out of hiding until well into the night... but if she's not around by morning..." I couldn't finish the thought. I knew she could take care of herself, but now that Dani brought up Atlamillia, a horrible feeling washed over me. "Can you do me a favour?"

"Anything."

"Could you check the far towers, the ones where they seem sketchy, and no one likes being around? She doesn't have that sort of sensitivity and probably would have thought they would be the perfect place to practice. If she's not there and isn't back by midnight, please call me."

"I'll let you know, regardless of if she's found or not."

A small relief came, but it wasn't nearly enough to satisfy the worry I had. It felt like something was wrong, I just didn't know how or why. "Thank you."

"So... um..." she started hesitantly, the heels of her shoes hitting the castle floor coming through as she walked, presumably towards the creepy towers. "Since we haven't talked in a while... erm, h-how's Seraphina?"

"The kingdom is beautiful, just wished that the circumstances weren't the exact opposite."

"I'm sorry... Perhaps once Ciar is dealt with, maybe you could go back for a proper visit."

"Like a vacation?"

"Yeah! Leaders do get those once in a while. It's not good to work all the time and you could bring whoever you wanted."

"I could..." The idea was more than absurd. But it might have seemed that way because of everything happening and the controlling habit I was trying to break. "It might be fun to try."

"I'm sure it'll be quite memorable, in a good way."

I laughed a bit. "It'd be really nice to draw out a sketch of Infinite Spring here. I only saw part of it on the train ride to Domrael Hill and from the border. It looks so calm, and I can only imagine what it looks like from someplace high."

"Gorgeous I'd imagine."

I gave a nod in agreement. "So, how have you been?"

I heard her shift something in the background, stopping her walk. "Oh… fine, I guess."

"That was convincing."

"Some family stuff came up. But it's fine now. Got to see my brothers."

"I bet they missed you."

She gave half of a laugh. "They always do."

"Did you make well with your parents?"

"Something like that… I have to go. I just saw Lyric sneaking around."

"Ah… alright. If there's something wrong, you can tell-"

"Yep! I know. Just saw Karros – I think they're after the cookies Ramsey baked, so I have to catch them in the literal cookie jar. Bye! Good luck!"

The call ended abruptly, leaving me flabbergasted at how the conversation ended. I shook my head. Dani was strange sometimes, but this was a new bar. There was something happening back home, but it wasn't the kids sneaking around at ten at night. I was going to have to ask Atla about it when I could. Hopefully, she was fine.

I set the CT in my pant pocket and turned to the armour, the only thing I could really deal with at that very moment. "Let's get you taken care of, eh?"

Chapter Twenty-Nine: Between Worlds

A small pain pulsed on the side of Atlamillia's head as she started to awaken. She didn't remember passing out, just that of the white void. A slight groan escaped as she sat up from the hard earth that she landed on. It was a bit blurry at first, but as her sight focused, the ground revealed some dimly lit grass underneath her. It was an interesting outcome, since there wasn't grass anywhere near where she was before. A moan came from nearby, and she snapped to it, ready to defend herself only to find Endymion using a rock to help sit up. She went to ask if he was alright, but her voice stopped when noticing the sky that surrounded them was very different from anything she had seen before.

It was almost black with swirls of colours or strange cloud-like streams that moved slowly, glowing and distorting, creating a twilight hue. The grassy plain they were in was surrounded by a large, ancient forest that wasn't dissimilar to Elwood Garden, holding all its secrets within. She looked around further, finding it was just the two of them. Lucilla and Selene were missing. She called her partner silently only to get no response. There wasn't even a sense that she existed at all.

Atlamillia got to a stand and looked around for movement from familiar blue scales that never came. Panic crept into her chest. "Lucilla! Lucilla, where are you?!"

"Selene?!" Endymion called, also getting to a stand, fear poking into his voice. "Selene!"

She turned to a darker part of the forest, somewhat feeling her partner in that direction. "Lucil-!"

"Princess Atlamillia," Endymion said suddenly, cutting her off. She ignored him. Lucilla was more important than whatever he had to say. She went to attempt again but was hushed by his warning tone. "Atlamillia!"

She turned to him with a glare. "They have to be someplace around-"

"Listen."

She did as she was told, a bit unnerved at his tenacity. In the unsettling silence, things, large things, were moving about the forest around them. Branches broke behind her and they turned around to the noise, but nothing appeared. "Don't suppose it's a person making that noise, do you?"

"No… I don't." He looked down at her, visibly a bit angry behind his light blue-hazel gaze, but he kept it to himself. "We need to figure out where we are and how to get back… Do you know anything from your knowledge of divine trials on what could have happened and how we get through it?"

It would seem like a trial, the entrance way basically spelt it out, but what she had anticipated was not what happened. She went through all the lessons and books she had experienced. None of them though were what came to mind first at his question, but rather the trial her father had asked for her help to create. The only problem was, she didn't witness the trial in its full completion. She turned to the noble and elaborated. "This scenario reminds me of a few elements of different accounts… but in order to be sure of it, were you at the Dragon Knight Trial during Anoxiver?"

"Yes." His answer was quicker than she was expecting but continued.

"Then between the two of us… we'll get out of this without issue."

"You have yet to inform me of what you dragged us into."

"I didn't drag you anywhere, you followed me, remember?"

"Whatever… what exactly is this thing?"

"Depends. What were the exact details of the trial my father and uncle created?"

He gave a hint of a glare which was reasonable to a degree, but she wasn't apologizing for being wrong about the warning. "Groups went into the labyrinth with a Dragon Knight as their escort mission. They were to judge the mission and supposed to be completely useless unless they needed to step in. The trial runners were to make it to the end of a moving, ever changing maze without their dragons where a mildly challenging fight was to take place. If they went the wrong way, the monsters in those rooms were significantly tougher, but it would open up a shortcut to put them back onto the right path without the maze changing for a time in their section. The first group to get out of the maze got a bonus reward."

So, it did follow the algorithm of several trials. Luckily, this trial they were stuck in wasn't as tedious as an escort mission. But that didn't mean the monsters were going to be a walk in the park. She gave a small sigh, the panic she had before left a tiny bit. "Lucilla and Selene are safe then, just out of the way, and waiting for us probably where we left them."

"You know this for certain?"

"Yes. This is a trial created by Orithina to judge our worth. If we have our dragons, it wouldn't be able to judge our strength alone, which is way more important to her than our dragons' abilities since they are flying reptiles of death."

"Wouldn't it be important to know if the dragon is just as capable as the Absalomian?"

"She already knows. It's the likes of you and I that are in question."

"Great... getting judged in a trial I would have never thought of participating in. Ever."

"Yeah well, get used to it if my brother doesn't marry your sister," she growled, bitterly.

A small tsk came out of him that bordered a growl, but it wasn't aggressive, only annoyed. "What the hell is that supposed to mean?"

"I'm sure you're not completely oblivious to the Cleansing Gift I have. I have it and other gifts with possibly many more to be obtained for a variety of reasons down the line – most of them come with weird shit like trials."

"I'm aware of your gift, but I just assumed..." A sigh came out as he crossed his arms. "So, you're what my mother calls a pawn in the grand game of control."

She winced at how accurate it was and nodded. "In a sense, but it's nothing more than residual gifts left by my great grandfather. So, whether I like it or not, stuff like this happens from time to time."

"That may be so, but according to Mother, that's all Orithina needs to implement anything like this."

A frown formed on her face as Endymion looked around, a whole lot calmer with the situation. She would have expected him to act a little more freaked out about everything, but he was clearly well versed. Eudoxia knew an awful lot about divine dealings... It somewhat unnerved her as to why she would. As far as she knew, the Raghnalls were not of any significance in Orithina's Light, teachings, or even the gods she had studied and were associated with Orithina and Valrdis.

More noises came from the forest, reminding her that they couldn't stay out in the open any longer. Only Orithina knew of what monsters laid around. It was doubtful that any of them would be demon hunters; most likely some Outland Monsters since Orithina hated her sister. And as far as she was aware, the best way to test worthiness was to pin them against things created by the person one hated most. But that didn't mean there couldn't have been prototypes of Orithina's creations within the realm that was their prison until they could leave – one way or another.

They made a silent agreement on what direction to take, following an incredibly faint sense of where their dragons were into the darker part of the forest with little to no natural paths. She noticed the grip he had on his rapier was tight underneath the rose and thorn guard, the Raghnall emblem, but ready for action at a split moment. She kept her guard up as well but stayed relaxed all the same. She was used to monsters, her promised fiancé on the other hand, she didn't have a clue.

She took a second glance again at his belt and realized that the blade was a lot closer to her than she had expected. He was left-handed as well? He noticed her staring and she looked away to the bushes beside her, passing it off as her looking beyond him to the trees and brambles.

If he was going to ask her what she was looking at, he decided against it. It was probably for the same reason why she didn't break the silence to ask more about him or even his choice of weapon.

A rapier was an interesting choice due to its thin blade and most knights didn't take the weapon into battle for fear of it breaking. The confidence that he radiated with the weapon on the other hand shared a different story. While she didn't know about his experience with monsters, she knew he had been training for the trial next year. Whether he wanted to do it or was forced, he seemed to have made his choice in weapon.

Movement reached her ears from her right. She drew Firethorn, but the action was far slower than Endymion's as he was in front of her, thrusting his rapier into an Ardyn sized, rat-like Outland Monster directly into its eye. The blade was brought into a ready position, waiting for the next monster as the first one blew up with air manipulation, turning to ash. She didn't give him compliments or even a thank you as the silence held the noises of things moving in bushes they couldn't see through. Something caught her eye below and she turned to it. Large vines and roots moved quickly towards him, leaving her very little time to act.

Vines of light were summoned, knocking Endymion out of the way of the plants' grasp, causing him to hit a tree harder than she had meant to. Blue fire escaped her blade as she sent the stream across the plants, slicing them clean. A strange scream came from the direction her flames disappeared to. She commanded the light field below them, the vines of light chasing and constricting anything within it. The roots and vines that seemed like part of the forest struggled against her grasp. Endymion took the opportunity to plant his rapier into one of the roots and a surge of fire magic came from him. Red fire went thought the plants, following their pre-made paths, burning them from the inside out. The scream came back, followed by two dozen more of the same noise.

She sent a look over at Endymion who had the same idea as her and a grimace went across his face. A long cut was stretched across his cheek. He sheathed his blade while she released the light vines but kept her field underfoot as they took off towards the direction of their dragons.

They needed an open space, not a small area that anything could come from anywhere and where branches could become just as dangerous as the monsters if they weren't careful.

Endymion took the lead, slashing out strips of air to destroy any large branches and bushes in the way. She kept an eye out behind them. A few rodent monsters were chasing them, and she sent back a wave of fire. The bushes and monsters seared and burned at the flames touch, quickly incinerating the monsters.

They broke out into a clearing, half of which was a swamp. A small look of disgust went across her face and she turned back to where they had come from, making their ground. They had to get across the swamp, or at least go around, but they couldn't do that with monsters that moved faster than they were. No roots were underfoot now that they had escaped, allowing her to remove the light field, giving her much more freedom to attack, hopefully whatever controlled them. Nothing moved in front of them. No noises as they stayed ready, but not quite ready enough to make a real plan yet.

She searched for Lucilla again through the link and the lack of a second mind made her feel incredibly isolated, even more than being in some trial realm. It was so unnatural, even for her. Her heart skipped a beat at the thought of being forever separated from Lucilla. In times like this… they could have burnt the whole forest down, but neither her nor Endymion could fly. She, and she was sure he, were pretty fire-proof, but they still needed to breathe. All the air magic in the world couldn't save them from a lack of oxygen from the smoke that would have come from the living matter if they completely consumed the area in flames.

Her kingdom, vast, had had similar fires where towns and cities hundreds of kilometres away, could be affected by the smoke. If either of them decided to burn down the forest, they would be right in the middle of it.

It made the feeling of never being with Lucilla again all that more horrible. The feeling to curl up into a ball, and accept death crept closer at the edge of her mind. She turned to the person who definitely had not wanted to be part of this mess and was suffering just as she was – hoping that it would distract them both. "Endymion, I apologize for not heeding your warning."

He looked at her with a surprised look for a moment before turning back to the forest. "This really doesn't seem to be the time to apologize."

"It's not… but if you're feeling anything remotely to how I'm feeling – not being able to sense our partners, this break is appropriate to let you know that I was wrong."

His grip tightened around his sword. "This isn't new for me, but if you're feeling like I felt for the first time then it's best if you leave whatever comes to me and keep yourself calm and safe in your head. Maybe plan on a way of getting through that swamp instead."

Her eyebrows furrowed. "The first time?"

"Stay within your comfort zone. You could go into a state of shock or terror with the absence of Lucilla, even expiration shock. We're not going to survive this trial if you lose yourself."

She didn't like how he avoided her question, but the annoyance did give her something else to focus on. They were going to deal with this just so that she could pry him with questions later.

A small splash came from behind her. She turned, quickly sending out vines that stopped a large tongue in its place a few feet away from attacking them. She looked beyond the tongue to a massive frog-thing reefing on its appendage. Fire was sent up the vines as she gave it a wave of fire from her blade, slicing the monster in two.

The monster dispersed into ash, leaving her to see the rest of the swamp. No bridges sat, that was certain, but there were rises in the swamp that could count as land. Unfortunately, they were also spread out farther than either of them could get to with a running jump. She turned to the bank. There were a couple of logs that they could use to connect, but they were so large that even the smallest ones, she wasn't sure that Archelaos would have been comfortable moving. The closest one was massive but sliced down the middle into two halves.

But perhaps muscle wasn't required.

She turned around, her plan forming, and was met with a gruesome sight coming out of the forest. Five, green, red, and purple plant creatures with five petals covered in teeth as their faces slithered out on roots. It reminded her of the monsters that had bulldozed through Siofra months before, just less bulky as they were more sunflower-like, standing at two and a half to three metres tall, looking ready to devour anything in their path. Other plant heads grew from their green and black stems, saliva drooling out of their mouths and onto the grass, causing it to shrivel up and turn black wherever it fell. Roots and vines grew from their stalks and their heads turned on Atlamillia and Endymion, hearing them take a step back away from the strange Outland Monsters. They screeched, the same noise that they heard earlier exited their mouths and was followed up by more of the screams from the forest in the distance.

Endymion looked to her. "We can take these if you're willing, but I don't know how long we can keep it up after that. Do you have a plan?"

"Yes, but it'll require a lot of magic to pull off, and alone time." She pointed to the log thirty metres away. "We're going to make that our portable bridge."

He glanced behind her and his jaw dropped slightly. "Are you out of your mind?"

"There isn't any other option," she growled, crossing her arms. "Well I suppose there is the other option of swimming. But if this place is remotely alive, there will most certainly be leeches in that swamp at the very least and if that wasn't enough of a turn off, probably more of those frog monsters."

He grimaced, turning back to the moving plants.

She drew her daggers. The plants were slow, but who knew what range they truly had. "What will it be?"

"I'll use air magic to help lift it, but you're going to have to be able to direct it on top of lifting. Can your vines do that?"

"With concentration, yes."

"Then let's give you some."

She formed a light field underneath them. Vines came out from the field, rushing ahead, and met the monsters. The monsters attacked back, grappling her vines with their own, slowing their approach and occupying them. She rushed ahead of Endymion, hearing him not far behind, and went to the left side. The two, less stationary heads struck, and she slipped to the side of one before moving to the other side of the other. Her daggers went across their stems. Blue fire licked their edges, allowing the heads to be consumed by the flames that spread upon contact. The saliva combusted before exploding, causing dirt to fly up and in her face.

The monster lunged just as she managed to brush the dirt from her eyes and her vines caught its petaled face only a few inches from her own. She didn't give it much time, moving onto the next one with a small bound around it. Her vines dug deep into its body, crushing it to death.

Endymion also finished the one on the far right as air sliced through the plant and dashed between its pieces, fire wisps burning the saliva before they could touch him. She took the effort as a warning to keep the monsters' bodily fluids off her and sent flames ahead and under her steps. Her target turned to her and was met with one of her daggers as two light vines cut off its other two heads. She released the fire stored inside, setting the flammable substance within its body ablaze. With no where to go, the stem exploded downward and part of its body blew apart, setting the middle monster somewhat on fire before it could turn to ash. A rapier caught her eye as its user finished off his second one.

He taunted the final one by slicing off one of the mobile heads with an air slash. She threw her dagger into its stem to draw it back to her. It reeled back and she used the dagger as her conduit, letting her light vines wrap and constrict its movements. He came from above it, avoiding a stream of saliva that was thrown in his direction and cut it down.

It dissolved it to ash, and she stopped her light field and vines once she found it safe to do so. The rapier's blade reflected off the light in a particular way that she found to be odd. If it were metal, it would have gleamed like that of a regular weapon. He handed her the dagger. She took it as he sheathed his weapon, stopping her from examining it further. The sound was the same as Winterthorn, Eclipse, Aetherian, and her weapons.

Her question was falling off her tongue before she could think it through. "Your blade is made from primordium?"

He didn't give much of a visual response as he looked to his rapier for a moment then walked past her. "It is."

"That seems a bit fancy for a minor house, no offence."

"It's a family heirloom. I don't know where its origins lie, just that it was supposed to go to Dani."

"But she left…" Still odd to have such an expensive and almost mythical weapon in the hands of the heir.

"She never liked rapiers. I always joked with my brothers that that was the reason why she left."

Atlamillia caught up with him as they wandered over to their log. "If the rapier is supposed to go to the house heir, what weapon does Eudoxia have?"

He stayed silent, the only sound was movement from the forest in the distance and their steps on the ground that was hard and wet in no particular pattern.

"Has to be something extraordinary if the rapier is less. The craftsmanship is amazing."

"It's… extraordinary, if not horrifying." He paled slightly. "I'm not supposed to talk about it."

"Even to the princess?" He shook his head and she sighed. "Alright. How about what it is? Could you at least tell me that?"

He gave a nod. "It's a two-handed, long whip sword. My rapier, Trisa Orra, was made from the leftovers of Mother's sword. At least, that's the legend."

"Must be old to have a name in Ancient Dragon and not Ori," she commented, keeping the uncertainty out of her tone about finding out about the whip sword.

She had only heard of such things and had never actually seen one in action before. Then there was the fact that the name of a rapier was in a dead language of Absalom. The Raghnall House wasn't as old as some of the other houses, so it wasn't around when things were named in such ways, meaning that the weapon and its parent were possibly older than Winterthorn. That, or it was named by someone who knew the language, and that was interesting in its own right.

The time the kingdom had started to move away from Ancient Dragon was a little more than four thousand years ago, choosing to speak Ori which was the same language as the other kingdoms. The moment when Winterthorn had been named and bestowed to the head of House Fionn, the largest of the kingdoms back when there were several kingdoms – petty or not – roaming around, was a historical bookmark to that switching time as it also made her house have the High King of the Kingdoms of Absalom title. It was given to her great, great, great grandfather. Not that anyone knew what Winter meant, but it kept its name regardless.

So, Trisa Orra was either older, or one of the royal blacksmiths made it – which were only a few families even then. By the time Theseus was running around, there were only two families that were fluent in the language, and they died at Lake Gloinne, two thousand years ago.

"The name actually means something?" Endymion asked and she nodded.

"Rose Wrath, whether it was one word or two originally, that I couldn't tell you."

"I'll be honest, I think I liked not knowing the translation better," he chuckled slightly.

"Too girly for you?"

"Perhaps a bit. But it's a rapier, sophistication is implied. Maybe it'll make me seem more like a gentleman."

She rolled her eyes as they stopped in front of the log. "You could have the most brutal weapon named Fluffy Bunny and still be a gentleman. A weapon isn't going to help you if you're an asshole."

"Imagine the humiliation of dying to something called the Fluffy Bunny. What a way to go…" His light laugh trailed off as he looked at the tree they were supposed to move. "Gods this is a massive thing."

"It is…" The tree's split trunk had to be three times as high as he was tall, and standing next to him as she did now, she knew he stood almost a foot taller than she was… And here she thought Aerrow was tall, but Endymion had eight centimetres on him. Screams came from the forest, causing her to jump as they were closer than she had expected them to be. "You think you'll be able to move it?"

He gave another nod as he looked down at her. "Hopefully, just be ready to grab it… if it's hardwood, I may not be as supportive as I'd like to be."

"Leaving me to compensate…" She was a bit nervous knowing that. She looked to the edges of the swamp and her doubts grew of them being able to make it around. The tree bridge across the swamp was their only way if they wanted any sort of relief from monsters. "I've never tested how much my light can lift."

"I'll keep an eye for monsters, so don't worry about them." He pulled out Trisa Orra again and moved back, guarding her from anything that could come from the water or forest.

A large force of air magic came from him and she embedded a dagger into the tree. She was going to need a second conduit in case she lost connection with the log and if she had any hope of moving it farther than a couple of metres. She backed away and readied her vines along the trunk. Her feet anchored into the ground; the tree was lifted by the air pushing from underneath. It crept towards the raised land in the middle of the swamp. The weight that fell on her vines hit hard and almost caused her to buckle under the strain after a couple of metres from the log moving over the water's surface, not wanting to disturb it.

She closed her eyes for better focus, clearing her head of the screaming monsters and danger that were coming in fast. Her heart skipped a beat at the thought of trusting someone she barely knew with her life. The thought of him failing and being attacked.

She removed the thought and followed years of training. She had yet to have a reason that he couldn't do his job and she wasn't going to give him a reason that she couldn't do hers. Her dagger conduit connected to the dagger in her grip, sheathed on her hip. She could sense the magic that was below her vines, in the earth and the disgusting water as they moved the log across the gap. Then, there was land on the other side. They lowered the log, and she opened her eyes again, finding their efforts a success.

Unfortunately, there was no time to celebrate or relax as Endymion ran past. "They're coming. We have to move this now."

She gave a curt nod, not that he could see it, and rushed after him. They stopped in front of it, and she had to admit, she didn't exactly think through how they were supposed to get up almost six metres with monsters on their heels after using that much energy. Normally, she could have made it up with a bound or two, but not after what she just did and what she had to do as soon as they got to the other side. There wasn't a good way-

"Pardon the intrusion," Endymion started and picked her up. She didn't have time to protest as he jumped, using air magic to make the leap, and they landed at the top. He set her down and they ran to the other side. Her thank you was short but acknowledged.

They dropped onto the gross, wet land with a splash and they didn't wait to start moving the log again, taking a few moments to rotate it around them and setting it onto their little island and the next. She released the vines and the pressure of it relaxing was a mistake on her part as she shouldn't have. A wave of dizziness hit her, and she braced against her knees. Her breaths felt constricted in her chest and she loosened the collar of her armoured coat and shirt.

She hadn't felt like this in a long while, not with magic…

No. Not that long, was it?

Three months ago, when she killed the Black Phoenix... She couldn't pass out here.

"Are you okay?" Endymion asked, crouching in front of her. Sweat dropped down the side of his face, but he seemed fine all the same, looking over her with concern. She looked away and went to stand, but her pride caused her to trip over herself. He rescued her from falling in the mud and sighed. "We're safe for now. Take a rest until you get your colour back and then, you can macho that log to the next landmass."

"For how long, I wonder..." she muttered but didn't argue, sitting on a rock not far. Her head hurt, but now that she was sitting, her body was feeling the stress less so. It infuriated her. "I shouldn't need rest; I'm supposed to be stronger than this."

"Princess Atlamillia, you're a princess, yes, but you're also seventeen and without your dragon – that changes things," he told her as he sat on another rock nearby. A huff of relief escaped his lips. He was more exhausted than he looked. "Expecting so much is fine if you're not thinking the goal will be life and death if you don't make it."

"I wish that was the case..."

"You should be congratulating where you are succeeding and not getting aggravated where you aren't. You moved most of this thing by yourself, picking up where I couldn't. That in itself is a feat for our age. If my mother saw where you were in your magic skills, she would be furious at me for not keeping up."

A small laugh escaped at the thought. "Your mother is ambitious and wants her children to be the best. There's nothing inherently wrong with wanting you to shine your potential, but if she saw this... I'm afraid she run you to your graves if she thought you could compare against someone who has residual Godling powers."

"Without a doubt," he replied, almost bitterly before looking up at the sky. "Where do you think this place is?"

"A pocket dimension... maybe between dimensions. Hard to say."

"What do you think makes the sky like that?"

"I don't know..." She looked up and watched the colours swirl almost hypnotically. "It's kind of pretty how it lights this world up though, isn't it?"

"It is... just wish I knew what caused it... Maybe we're in a nebula."

"That would be nice… I'd like to see that in person if this isn't it."

"A nebula?"

"Yeah, that and space in general. Just get on a ship made for space, see this world from Ori or Val… maybe even farther. See the other four worlds that are in our solar system and beyond." The thought pained her.

"Maybe we'll be able to have a project that will allow space travel. It can't be that far off with the creation of the CTs and even a device that could control Outland Monsters and if it is, we live far longer than anyone else. Time isn't something we have to concern ourselves with."

"Perhaps, it's a nice thought." A thought that she couldn't put her heart into. She was stuck on Orithin, no matter what inventions come to pass. She stood up. "I'm feeling better now. We should take this carefully since we don't have to worry about monsters getting on."

"As you command, Princess Atlamillia."

Chapter Thirty: Darkness of Light

They got onto the log and she looked out across the swamp. They were almost halfway there, the next island seemed to be it, but it was daunting. How long would it take to get to the other side? How long had it been since they entered? They were limited to how much magic their bodies could exert at a time, and while she knew she could do it, painfully if necessary, she wasn't sure about Endymion, nor if they would be in shape to fight monsters that laid beyond the swamp. Outland Monsters were going to arrive, that wasn't the question, but rather when they were going to sense her and then Endymion. How long would it take for them to get to the bank and how many?

She dropped down from the log and tried sensing for Lucilla again. She was closer, but she still felt hollow. A surge of anxiety entered her chest. What happened if she was wrong? What if Lucilla wasn't safe and the distance, the mask this world put on her, made her believe that she was at the end? She was all she had to console in. Without her…

"Princess Atlamillia?" Endymion asked and she turned to him in surprise. She had forgotten he was there. "Are you ready?"

Atlamillia gave a nod, focusing on the task at hand, not the what ifs. The vines set themselves along the log. Her partner in hell lifted the log with air magic while the vines kept it in place, helping it stay off the ground and water. Though, now that he wasn't distracted by monsters, lifting the log was a lot easier on her end. The log was quickly rotated around them and set it lightly onto the new island. Her vines disappeared and the drained feeling came back. She lit a small fire in her palm, and it glowed a bright blue before being put out with a simple close of her hand. There was something wrong. It took no effort at all when it should have with the amount of magic she was using.

"Something wrong?" Endymion asked, almost breathlessly and she didn't know how to answer his question.

There could have been something, or maybe her paranoia of not being with Lucilla was affecting her judgment. "Let's hurry across this place."

"Alright, do you need help getting up?"

"If you don't mind…" It was more than embarrassing, but she didn't have the right to deny his chances of living for pride.

He got them up to the top of the log and they walked across, looking around. The swamp noises seemed to have died as they went, creating an eerie silence. He put a hand on his rapier and his words were barely louder than a whisper, "There is something terrifying here."

"More than what we've seen?" She asked with a confused look. Last she checked, most Outland Monsters were pretty fucking terrifying.

"Yeah, the monsters that were on the bank behind us are backing away."

She turned around and saw that they were indeed cowering. Her nerves got the best of her limbs and she started to move faster. They couldn't be attacked in the middle of the swamp, especially not by something scaring other Outlands Monsters. Something moved underneath the log, brushing against her light vines, not even fazed by their touch even though she knew that it burnt its skin. She took off running. "We need to get off!"

Endymion chased after her, catching up with ease. Something went through her vines, blasting through the log. They were thrown, practically launched off it, and she used her light vines to catch them before they could hit the hard ground. They eased them down and she rolled it out and turned around as their half of the log was coming down on top of them. She activated her vines again, gripping onto the log before it could crash down on them. A grunt came out under the weight and she barely was able to throw it to the side. Her vine grabbed her dagger before the log was swallowed by the swamp and she took it, drawing Firethorn for battle with-

Nothing was there.

Endymion gave out a growl as he got up slowly next to her, holding his head. "What the hell was that?"

"Something big…" She looked at him as he lowered his hand to find blood smeared at the side of his head and hair. "How did that happen?"

"A piece of wood hit me, sorry."

She put her weapons away. "Keep an eye out for monsters while I heal this."

He didn't argue with her, taking out his rapier as she formed a healing sphere. It was simple to do with a conduit to help her, and she started working on the wound. Something caught her eye behind her but didn't get to check it out as a massive splash came from where they had come from. She stopped healing, getting most of the injury except for some of the surface level damage.

They prepared for an assault as a plant head appeared out of the water, three petals instead of the five they had been seeing and it screamed at them.

Water dripping came to their ears behind them. Atlamillia turned around as water covered vines hammered down on top of them. Air magic tried to break the attack, but it wasn't enough to stop them from slamming into them. A sharp pain tore through her body as the water felt like it was trying to rip her apart, breaking any hold of a scream she might have gave. She came to a stop at the edge of the water. Lesions and almost burn marks appeared on her skin under her shredded sleeves. She coughed out water. Blood speckled the ground and she started to get to a knee, her arms threatening to give out.

A water element Outland Monster of all things had to be in this hell.

She wiped the side of her mouth, wincing as she found her skin to be sensitive, and looked around. Endymion was also getting up, coughing, and grabbing his rapier that he dropped. A splash came from behind her, and a surge of water magic sent a wave of fear through her, almost causing her to freeze as she slowly turned around.

A terrifyingly massive, deformed skull of something as long as she was, came out of the water. It's skull mouth, that was lined vertically with a row of teeth, opened slightly to a breathing rhythm showing pink flesh inside only a metre away. Hollowed eye sockets were a swallowing blackness and black-red plant vines formed through cracks in the skull.

The horrifying sight was a distraction, not allowing her to notice a vine had crept around her leg. It tightened painfully, picking her up violently, and causing her to hit her head. She grabbed at the vine, her gauntlets' claws digging as fire magic ripped through it. More vines grew, fixing the tears she had made and climbed up her leg, crushing it above the armour. A small noise came out of her that quickly turned into a scream as the vines attacked further with water, piercing into her skin, and quenching her fire. It went black for a moment as she lost consciousness.

Her breath was shallow as she opened her eyes. The view, dizzy and spinning from being upside down and saw the gaping maw that was so close by. A sphere of water was forming inside of it. She went to grab a weapon only for the vines that had crept all over her to tightened, restricting her from moving. The water that laced across her skin seared and caused an agonizing scream to escape. She tried to break free, but her concentration on using magic was hindered. Suddenly, the vines' attack stopped when something severed them from above and the water sphere that the horrific thing had released, flew over her.

She hit the ground hard and the vines that encased her fell off slightly. The monster screamed. She looked above her and through the blur, saw it was on fire, and being torn apart by air slashes. She struggled to sit up and Endymion helped pulled off the lifeless vines with a hard look on his face.

He looked behind her for a moment before grabbing around her. "Close your eyes and don't move."

"What are you-"

"Don't even breathe; I've never done this before."

She did as he asked, holding her breath, and closed her eyes. The moments of waiting for something to happen were short, logically, but in her head, not being able to see, to move, were agonizingly long. Her senses of magic increased at the lack of stimuli, filling in the gaps and tried to keep her alive. Water magic surged all around them, growing stronger. The want to bail on Endymion's instructions almost came to fruition, her instincts to live trying to take hold. She wanted to tell him to hurry up, but she remained still, her heart skipping beats as the magic was more than enough to kill them.

Then, a rush of air magic formed around them, blocking out the water element entirely.

The sound of water went past her head as a strange feeling tingled her limbs. They dropped a bit, like they were in the air slightly before the air magic came back, turning her stomach. It disappeared as the lighting changed behind her eyelids, only to form again and underneath her now was dry land and grass. The urge to throw up overcame the pain as he released her and she turned away from him, puking what little she had left in her stomach.

Atlamillia heard him give out a sigh of relief as he stood up for a moment before sitting on the grass again, apparently not able to stay standing. "We made it…"

She coughed, unable to throw up anything else and took a breather. She looked up and saw that they were no longer in the swamp but in a clearing that, if it hadn't been in a hellhole, would have made for a nice place to relax. "What…?"

"I used blink to get us out of there," he answered. "And because it chased away the monsters in the area, I think we're safe to rest for a bit."

Thank Orithina…

No, wait… She put them in this fucking mess!

She sat back against a tree, away from the bile that laid off to the side and turned to the noble sitting across from her. "Thank you for rescuing me, but would it have killed you to do it earlier?"

He laughed a bit at her joke, but it sounded like it hurt to do so. "Sorry, it had more than just that skull head. The three petalled head was also part of it along with a second one."

That made sense on why he wasn't as free as she had last seen him. "Are you okay?"

"Could be worse with clothes and footwear forever soaked if we both weren't fire elements." He gave a small smile. "It wasn't entirely interested in me compare to you... Are you okay?"

"I'm alive..." She gave a small wince as she moved the wrong way. "Fuck... If I knew that there weren't going to be more monsters, I'd heal..."

"It'd be nicer if that water field that's been made could boost your light magic as well as our fire..." he agreed. "But you should heal up regardless. You're bleeding enough to draw in monsters if they are feeling bold and opportunistic."

She gave a small nod and started healing a little bit while he got around to drying their footwear. If the water field stayed up when they continued on their way again, it would mean they had a lot of fire easily at their disposal, until it was doused at least. But that was a problem if they came across another swamp, right now she was just glad that there was something going a tiny bit right for them. She searched for Lucilla again and found her even closer than before, actually being able to feel her vitals, but not her thoughts. A small sigh of relief came out as her healing became easier and the anxiety relaxed.

They were almost there. They just had to leave, perhaps even were able to run from any fights that came their way – avoid another swamp monster and not have any more close calls.

About twenty minutes went by before they started moving again and healed. The forest was relatively quiet, the water field neither growing nor dying out as they went farther away from the swamp. It made her anxious as the ground hadn't shifted to tell them that there was wetland nearby.

How far did its power go?

Endymion shrugged to her question that she didn't realize she asked out loud and abused its power just as she had, forming another fire ball and threw it at a monster that tried to get in the way. She slashed out a stream, keeping a good pace as they went towards their dragons. His movements, like hers, were quicker than before, her magic doing them wonders.

They broke through the forest to end up in an empty field with a gateway in the middle that looked very similar to Asylotum's. The archway lined with dragon stone shined brightly with the sense of their dragons coming from the other side.

"Oh gods… there is a light at the end of the tunnel…" Endymion sighed in relief next to her. "We beat the trial."

She gave a nod as they started towards it. "And once we get through that gate, we'll get a reward for completing this fucking thing."

"A reward?"

"Power, weapons, sometimes a relic or even a wish."

"Sounds like we just completed a dungeon in a game," he commented. "Why don't people do these trials if it has the same rewards as a roleplaying game?"

"There are some people that seek them out… but most people are sensible, and these trials are made for the powerful that are supposed to be worthy… not your average treasure hunter."

"I think I get that now being inside this-" He stopped talking as a pulse of water magic came from behind them.

They turned around as the trees were smashed through by a water sphere. Atlamillia quickly dodged to the side while Endymion went to the other. The sphere landed, creating a crater where they had been before. Out of the broken forest came the creature on a massive, red-black stalk, walking out on a pair of scaly legs and webbed feet. It roared loudly and they turned tail and ran. They were almost out; they didn't have to fight that horrible thing. Atlamillia met up with Endymion on the other side of the crater, but as they got closer to the arch, familiar vines came out of the ground, covering it.

She sent out a wave of fire from her sword to slice through them, but water blocked the attack. His attack was right behind hers, but like the attack before, it didn't matter. More vines built up and before long, it was a massive, impenetrable pillar of vines that tried to grab at them. They stopped running, getting out of its reach. The earth vibrated under her feet as the monster charged at them, spheres of water escaping its maw as the two heads that Endymion had mentioned earlier, came out of it like hands. They dripped saliva like that of the smaller plant monsters from before.

A frustrated growl came out of Endymion beside her as they regrouped from dodging the attacks, speaking the words that were already on her mind. "That bastard managed to follow us all the way here?!"

"At least it's out of the swamp, its water attacks will be limited." She looked to the ground and saw it bulge, vines moved underneath, breaking the earth as they raced towards them. "We're not going to be able to stay stationary for long, so keep moving and deal with the smaller heads as your familiar with them. I'll take the main head and create a light field to hopefully tether this monstrosity down."

He passed her a glance with concern. "Are you going to be able to get up to it? It's nine metres in the air."

"Who said anything about it standing?" She asked rhetorically. "Use your fire liberally… it'll make its water attacks easier to deal with."

"When you're ready, Princess Atlamillia."

She didn't say she was ready, but acted, forming a light field below them and dashed towards the monster. Line vines grabbed at vines underneath the earth and above, gripping and slicing through them. They collided with the main source of her anger and she used her body to control the vines with better efficiency, clenching her hand into a fist as the vines wrapped around the stalk. They constricted and she set them on fire. The monster screamed, fuelling her revenge for what it did to her.

It didn't have the advantage of sneaking anymore and she wasn't going to let it get a hold of her again.

The vines dragged the monster to the ground but couldn't crush it further, and Endymion moved ahead of her, going after the left, three petaled faced head. She went after the skull head as it tried to make a water sphere and shoved a massive vine down its throat. Fire lined Firethorn as she charged it with light and fire. Her vines reacted to the charge and were set on fire. The saliva combusting inside its body was incredibly audible.

Plant vines came out of the skull, forcing her to stop her advance for a moment. Her vines tried to grab at them, but the monster started to move at her distraction. She focused them back to holding it down and backed away, using the extra room she had to her advantage. In the midst of the retreat, she noticed Endymion dodging the streams of poisonous saliva that the two heads were throwing at him, not letting him close as the plant vines tried to keep him still.

She had to finish her head before it grabbed him.

The vines that had tried to grab her converged on her retreat and she sent out a cross slash of fire. The attacks cut through the vines, not being able to keep the water on its surface to douse her flames. She dashed though them before they could regrow fully. But some of their water attacks still attacked her through the regrowth, trying to slow her down. It worked to a degree as she tripped, but recovered barely, her foot slipping through a vine that hadn't tightened around her ankle.

Her blade charged with fire magic again as she jumped onto its face to close the distance and stabbed her blade into it, breaking through its skull. The energy was released into a blue, explosive stream of fire and blasted the monster apart. She landed her drop with grace as the ash fell around them. The vines that covered the arch dissolved and she turned to Endymion who was killing the final head. He gave her a wave and she let her shoulders relax slightly. The water field started to disappear as she met up with him.

A sigh came out of her, "Let's leave this place before something else shows up."

"Think we can leave?"

She gave a nod and started leading the way with a brisk job. "Hurry up if you don't want to be stuck here."

She stopped in front of the arch as Endymion moved next to her, looking beat up, but not as bad as he could have been. She walked through the gate. A white light blocked her vision and when it died, they were left back in the dark tunnel. She looked around and found Lucilla laying down next to Selene, a small campfire between the two of them. The blue dragon noticed them but didn't have the chance to move as Atlamillia collided into her with a hug.

She squeezed the best she could around her partner's neck. She never thought this connection was a privilege until now. "Never leave me again."

"You left us," Lucilla growled, not as enthusiastic as her. "You have any idea how long you've been gone? We've been worried sick!"

She looked up at her dragon in confusion. "It couldn't have been more than a couple of hours, right?"

"Ah no, she's right..." Endymion shared, and she turned to him as he looked at his CT. "It's a quarter to eleven... time must have been moving differently there."

She looked at her CT, confirming the time and saw that there was no signal and put it away. "I'll have to contact one of my retainers... but there is still the matter of what's at the end of the tunnel."

"You disappear into a hole in this forsaken cave, have been gone for hours, and you want to continue?!" Selene spat out, her silver and purple scales stood on end. "You may be the princess, but you have no right to put my partner in danger! Look at the two of you; you look like you came back from hell itself!"

"I didn't expect there to be a trial, let alone something like-" she tried to defend but Selene wasn't hearing it, furious.

"No, you didn't expect it because you didn't think! We tried to warn you and you didn't want to listen!"

"Look, I'm sorry, but it's not my fault that you decided to play hero and follow us." Atlamillia couldn't hold back the bitterness in her tone which pissed off the dragon further.

"We didn't want you to-"

"Selene," Endymion sighed, and his partner stopped verbally assaulting her. "She's right. We followed her despite her asking us to stay out of it. I was mad too with how it turned out, but she shouldn't have to apologize for our actions."

Selene was silent for a moment, but it was more than obvious that she was still angry, wrapping her tail around Endymion protectively. "You could have died though..."

"Could have, yes. But we didn't so it's alright."

"Alive, in one piece, and ready to go collect the reward for going through that place," Atlamillia agreed, trying to move the conversation along. She just wanted to go home, but she wasn't doing it empty handed after that.

"A reward?" Selene's anger dropped with almost recognition.

"Apparently the gods like to make people work for things," Endymion explained out loud to his dragon. "I know it was scary, but if we're going to continue being in this position, that means we're going to have to get used to this."

More was said, but the conversation went internal between the two and Selene's glare disappeared to that of slight pity. She looked down the tunnel with a slight growl. "I understand... Eudoxia is never wrong, is she?"

"What is Eudoxia's fascination with divine dealings anyway?" Lucilla asked them, picking the question right off of Atlamillia's tongue – already sifted through the time in the other place. They remained silent on the subject and she sighed, putting out the fire. "Never mind…"

Lucilla and Atlamillia started down the tunnel, not bothering to wait for the two, quiet nobles. An orb of light formed in Atlamillia's hand to light the way.

"It's not that we can't tell you, it's just that we don't entirely understand either," Endymion answered with a bit of resentment. He caught up to them with Selene not too far behind him as Atlamillia looked over at him. "Mother has always liked the idea of the divine helping out mortals and vice versa."

Atlamillia glanced over at him in confusion. "A fantasy?"

He shrugged. "Maybe… but she talks about it to us a lot, first to Dani and then to me. It went along with our lessons well."

"Which was how you know about trials."

"It was a guess using her explanations, yes."

Atlamillia still didn't like how well informed he was on just some explanations. Even she wasn't knowledgeable in everything, clearly, and she had been diving headfirst into these sort of things for years. Between Father's collection and Helah's teachings at her disposal, she was still left clueless. She turned inwards as she reflected on the few hours they had spent in that place.

She thought she would have done better. Succeed and defeat all the monsters that opposed her, without help. But if it hadn't been for Endymion, many times over as physical help and emotional, she would have died. She wasn't ready for the trial or any others like it that could come in the future.

And she should have been.

She should have been able to function at full strength without Lucilla and protected him, not the other way around. She was supposed to be stronger than what she was, but yet she was hitting limitations. The words he had said to reassure her came back to only haunt her now.

She was only seventeen. She had been seventeen since the first of Hepseptus, a little over a month and a half ago… Yet it meant nothing in the grand scheme of things. War was war. The innocent and the weak, the farmers and civilians, children would be placed on the front lines if need be to protect a nation should the knights and soldiers fail. And she was supposed to be the one who was drafted first – to protect those people.

But she was useless when it counted.

Perhaps at the end of the tunnel, the reward that laid there was her answer to why she hadn't been where she was needed to be.

The tunnel turned and when they got around the bend, another archway laid at the end. It laid dark until they got closer where it activated. She didn't hesitate walking through its threshold and when the white light died, she stood on a small island floating in a realm that was the same as the trial.

The colours of the strange sky were all around her as the others came through the portal. But like Asylotum, she felt welcomed here. The lush grass was a vibrate, deep green, and short – covering the whole island except for a large maple tree in the centre. Its leaves were rich, royal purple on one side and golden-yellow on the other.

Under its massive branches stood a two and a half metre tall, white knight who was covered head to toe in glistering armour that the strange colours of the sky reflected off. Gold trim etched out parts of the armour and under armour, a cape in the same colour of purple lightly blew in the breeze. The emblem of Orithina sat on their chest plate, a golden-yellow ring that had eight rays of light extending through it and out like the sun in equal length around the ring. The knight's massive claymore, also white, had its tip in the ground in front of them. The golden pummel of blade sat at their chest. Their hands clasped overtop of it, showing the purple grip, as they stood there, unmoving like a statue.

She had never met a knight like this before, but she knew who, or rather, what they were. Apparently, so had Endymion.

"A Divine Knight of Orithina… Is this another trial?"

The Divine Knight answered with a gesture rather than words, moving only one of their hands, beckoning for something to appear in front of the tree. A pedestal rose from the earth and the hand was placed back. Atlamillia went over to it, seeing the pedestal like it before and found half of it to be blank while the other half held a white, dragon stone relic.

She turned to Endymion who had stayed a couple metres away. "Take the relic. It can be used to enhance your magical potential or that of a weapon."

He frowned. "What about you?"

"A relic isn't going to help me," she answered bitterly. What she needed was a blessing of some sort, and it was clear that the pedestal only showing one reward meant that the trial hadn't thought her worthy of anything.

Something she agreed with.

He stared at her a while longer before stepping forward. He picked up the relic that had an Ancient Dragon word of power etched into it which faded and replaced with other words before switching to a different word. An endless cycle that was signature to relics. "How do I use it?"

"You hold it to yourself or a weapon and, like magic, you will it into whatever you want."

"So, I don't have to use it now?"

"No. You could hold onto it indefinitely, sell it perhaps. You don't have to use it for power but instead a longer life span, even healing a disease. But the choice is yours. It's limited however, so it won't be used up by something beyond it."

"Then I'll keep it for a special occasion… You never know when I might need it if this is what I have to look forward to in the future."

She simply nodded and they started to head back only for a deep, male voice to echo through the space. "You have a power unclaimed, Princess Atlamillia Serenity Fionn of Absalom."

She turned to the knight in confusion. "A power?"

"This is why the pedestal is empty. A blessing of power of your choice. You may then choose to take it or leave it behind."

Atlamillia walked back to the pedestal. Her wish for power was easy to choose. She wanted to be stronger, surpass her limitations that her being forced upon her. She placed her hands on it.

The wish was instant, a surge of light, fire, and dragon magic entered her. Her magic, she activated it without the use of a conduit, like she had always been able to do it with ease. The orb of brilliant light changed to that of a purple fire, hotter than any other, even hotter than Aerrow's and Deigh's. A smile crept on her lips as the fire turned to plasma, something she had never been capable of doing before. She could do anything she could put her mind to.

Kill Ciar.

Take back her home.

Wipe Outland Pits off the face of the world.

Take the throne like Theseus should have.

Her smile wavered at the thought. Why would she think that? Theseus was long gone; her brother was the king.

"Be the Divine Leader of Absalom," a familiar, young woman's voice whispered in her ear. "Mortal boundaries matter not to you now."

A ruler who would never grow old. Forever strong and sharp. Watching the other kingdoms grow and fall should they stay on the path of their mortal, prideful ways.

She could be that ruler. But what of...

If she was like this, was Aerrow even her brother now?

"He is an abomination. He was never your brother nor your family. He, along with the other mortals who stress you, force your hand... You do not need them any more to rule."

How could she say that? Even if he was as she said, Atlamillia had grown up with him. He was her family and all she had left by blood. Her Uncle along with the houses helped rule her nation even if they were a pain from time to time. Removing them would cause a riot. Her uncle would never approve such actions.

"You remove them by Divine Decree. None of your mortal subjects would care with that reason. You are a voice for me now, no one would object to you. And if they wanted to, they would never succeed."

"I don't want this..." she muttered out, but the young woman continued.

"But you do. Deep down you want it to be simple and my gift will do that. You will become more powerful, exponentially so. Take whoever has potential and devour them as your own." The voice softened as Atlamillia's heart skipped a beat. "For Absalom, for the light, you do what you must."

Endymion asked her what was wrong behind her, but she couldn't answer.

The woman started speaking again. "You struggle because you are scared. It is only natural. The crossroads of mortality and divinity... But once you pick the correct choice, the divine right that this trial has finally made available to you after years of struggle; it showed you that you cannot be what you need to be at the rate you wish without me. Once you accept my divine gift, the reason for it will be clear."

"*But at what cost…?*" She asked and the voice created a form that she, nor the others, could see except perhaps the knight. The woman wrapped her arms around Atlamillia from behind, creating a feeling of security.

"Depends on who you ask, but to me? Nothing at all. You will secure your dreams, fabricate them into reality and do as you please. You could connect with your parents through this gift. I know you miss them."

The thought of seeing her parents, being able to connect with them whenever she wanted, caused her heart to ache. A tear fell that was wiped away by the invisible woman.

"I did everything I could to protect them… but only so much could be done against him… You can get the vengeance as soon as you found him, found them both for their deaths. For your suffering."

Ciar was to blame for their deaths… but he wasn't alone in the act. Aerrow had led them to Ciar. He was the one who got them killed. She couldn't stop him from doing that with all the warnings she had gave them.

"You tried as I had… but your power alone is not enough. It will never be enough if you go down this path without me. Accept my gift, and you will never worry about mortal problems again. They will only submit to you, and those that rise, can easily be snuffed out."

She could have all the power she could hope for… Hear the goddess she prayed to for as long as she remembered whenever she asked to speak to her…

Yet she couldn't bring herself to betray Aerrow for a throne that was never hers. She couldn't abandon Dani, Endymion, and her retainers and caretakers. Aoife…

If she gave up her mortality, she'd only see them as puppets… She couldn't do that or bare the thought that that would be all she'd see them as. Not to her friends, not to Aoife, and especially not to Aerrow.

The voice had only salted her hidden wounds to try and go against him. To secure the throne as hers and nothing more. And what would she do that was any different from what he was doing? He was doing everything he could for their kingdom. He was stronger without divine help, a more suitable ruler than she ever would be, with divinity or not.

All for his kingdom.

His kingdom. Not hers.

"Do not make a choice out of fear," the voice persisted, but her decision was made.

"*I'm sorry.*" She had to do it the way where she wouldn't lose herself and the people she let into her life. For Eadric who would do things he was not inherently capable of, just for her. If he could do it, damn it all if she couldn't figure out how to be successful in the abilities she had. "*Forgive me, Orithina.*"

"Dear child…" a sigh escaped that was filled with disappointment. "I only wanted to make it easier for you."

"You choose to reject the gift?" The Divine Knight asked beside her and Atlamillia nodded.

The power left immediately with the embrace around her, taking with it all her strength to stand. She dropped to her knees as the knight blocked her head from smashing into the stone on the way down but wasn't able to catch her. Not that she had expected him to do so. "Thank you…"

"Zimrikiel," the knight answered her unsaid question and turned to the arch behind her. He stood up. "You stand on holy earth of the worthy. As a Champion and Divine Knight of Orithina I deem you unworthy to be here. Leave or I will make you."

"I only came to bring Princess Atlamillia home, Champion Zimrikiel," another familiar voice replied. She turned around to see Citlali walking over to them. "Please forgive my intrusion, I meant no offence."

The knight said nothing, putting himself into his statue-like posture. She got up with a bit of difficulty; her energy was long gone. Endymion came over to help, and she let him as Citlali stopped in front of her. He was armoured in red Seraphinean armour like he had just come back from his mission, but other than that, had remained the same as he had before, dark brown hair in a ponytail and green eyes alert as ever.

He gave a small bow. "My mission was successful, but it comes with concerning news, but not so concerning that it must be spoke about now. Come, I'll escort you and your friend back to the castle."

She didn't have the energy to ask what he meant or even how he got there and climbed onto Lucilla. Citlali joined her without permission, but she didn't tell him to get off. They left the knight and the world behind, a dreadful feeling that she had made a mistake sinking in. One that would cost more than what she was giving for the gift of divinity.

They got to the surface where a fake, star-filled sky spread out above them. She pulled out her CT to find more than a dozen messages were waiting, asking her where she was. She replied to each of the people with a few words of text before putting it away. Lucilla took off and her eyes closed in exhaustion, passing out.

Chapter Thirty-One: Dress-Up

I woke up, checking the CT on the side of the table to find that its screen was free of notifications. It was expected as I had already received a message from Dani telling me that Atlamillia was home, but I had hoped to find some sort of explanation for whatever she had been doing. Anyone I asked, being the three girls, either didn't know or didn't want to explain past that she looked like she had got into quite the fight with something. All Atlamillia shared was that she was tired and had went to see Helena before heading to bed.

It was typical of her, but it bothered me regardless. Where in Asylotum had she gone to get into a fight?

The restless question faded as I thought back to the rest of my long night, last night. It had to have been long if I was still laying in bed, not very motivated to leave its warm embrace. During the time, the rest of us were cleaning up, Owen had made corn chips covered in cheese and leftover chopped vegetables and ground beef from the other night. Admittedly the tomato sauce I had made, made for a much better dipping sauce than it was on the pasta. We snacked on it while Éabha showed off the other game she brought. It was a much more relaxing game and wasn't anything like I had expected.

It was a little farming, exploration, role-playing game that seemed pretty innocent, at first. I had made a character from a selection of different clothes and styles from its pixelated options. I went about the game's setting like an unsuspected victim until its colours started to show. Some of the individual things that at first glance meant nothing but as it went on, the ghostly wails when it rained and the horrible monsters in the forest just outside the farm's land showed that there was some corrupted and twisted undertone wrapped within the story. Something I should have expected from Éabha's preferred games.

Despite it's messed-up nature, it was a single player or two-player game which allowed us to explore the valley together. The experience went well into the night and messed with my head a bit as I had dreamt about it. It was weird, but it wasn't my usual nightmares, so I certainly didn't hate it.

It was a nice experience and probably my favourite game out of the three. To simply just enjoy life and grow things on a farm. The only concerns you had being your crops and the occasional monster that would come at night but couldn't do any harm while you were inside. It was like a safe version of my adventurous wants and it fulfilled a small part that had been left to rot for so long.

Though, there was a part of the game that neither of us really got into: making friends with the town nearby. We did it, as giving gifts made the game a bit easier in the long run as they gave gifts depending on how much they liked us. Then there was the feature that we definitely didn't explore and that was a romance with the locals. That took a lot of gifts and time, similar to how real relationships worked, but simplified dramatically.

A small chuckle came out at the thought of wanting to go back to that little farm. But play time was over for the time being, at least for me.

Dawn of another day.

Seventy-two hours remained…

I got out of bed, turning on the small light on the desk so not to disturb Deigh and got back to work. Some time before heading to bed, Cyrus and Azarias had placed their collected intel of their scouting mission on my desk. I looked it over, comparing it with the maps I had, trying to decide if any of it was worth a second look over.

Places were crossed off that were definitely free of whelps, circling other places. The circled places could have more information, and even if the dragons weren't there, some of the locals could have more to say. Perhaps local legends or even of strange locations of interest that could give away to underground facilities that couldn't be seen from above. Or perhaps they were as innocent as they looked. As I continued looking over the information, it was quickly dawning that between the patrols, there wasn't enough ground being covered in a reasonable amount of time.

The island was massive. The tunnels below could be almost as endless, connecting to places and chambers that we had no idea what could be hiding inside. Trains could only take the knights so far. The Legion was on the west side moving east, sweeping across… but it was possible that the cultists had been warned and the whelps were long gone. Maybe they weren't and the Seraphinean Legionaries were true to their vows. What if the whelps were caught between our searches and theirs? There wasn't enough time to search everything without pulling all-nighters and I was not going to ask my knights and uncle that. I wasn't going to condemn them to a suicide mission.

I held back a growl of frustration at the directions every action pulled in. There had to be a way to find the whelps and stop the dragons from destroying the kingdom without sacrificing so much.

There were people that had known about the whelps, but the only two that we knew of were dead. There was no shame with whoever was behind their kidnapping and they had no qualms about tying up loose ends. But… there was another option though, one that if I remembered correctly, was a bit immoral and incredibly dangerous. But it wasn't that steep of a price if a necromancer was around, and it just so happened that Owen was one. He could just call one of their souls and we could interrogate them to tell us everything.

Then again… the bestiary was quite helpful on telling me that horrible things could come instead of a soul if the summoning was done wrong… Not to mention Azarias's warning.

I sighed as I was right back where I started, not knowing what to do, and I set the page down, turning to maps. I was going to have to ask Owen about what the best action was to take, whether a séance was worth a try. It's not like we couldn't kill whatever decided to come along, but he knew best. He was, after all, the most sensible out of all of us.

I looked around the desk to continue working on the director reports only to find that the log CT was missing. A note had replaced its last position. I read it quickly before tossing it in the paper bin. Owen had stolen the tablet while I was on the farm to work on his director. It was annoying that he didn't bring it back, but it wasn't worth waking him up over. Just meant more time was spent reading to catch up.

I grabbed the grimoire to study more on the transformation skill. The bookmark where I had left off was almost halfway. It was definitely more than possible for me to practice the magic at how far I had come along with it, but I wasn't confident about using a tiny bit of magic, let alone something that required a lot of it. The risk was too high, and I continued reading.

There was more to learn other than partial transformations like being able to transfer my own knowledge of magic into the dragon form to enhance their physical attacks and forms. Then further still with a full transformation and enchanting my apparel so it wouldn't be destroyed when using the skill.

That was a very useful skill to learn in theory first.

I felt Deigh get closer, and I withdrew my attention from the book. She tapped the top of my head and I looked up at her with a smile. "Good morning. Did you sleep well?"

She nodded. "It was longer than I wanted, but it was needed. What's got you in a peppy mood?"

"I just started reading more of this book. Came up with some fun things to try."

"I think you lost a bit of time; you've been reading that book since I got up."

"Did you not just get up?"

"No. I left, headed downstairs, ate breakfast, and came back up to tell you that Owen's a bit worried that you might've still been asleep."

"Oh." How did I always get absorbed into things? I set the question aside as a great mystery and turned towards the whole reason why I was behind in work in the first place. "Did you show Éabha what you wanted to show her?"

"If you listen carefully, you'll hear your answer."

"What are you…" I went silent as I heard the small girl excitedly squeak about shopping from the other side of the closed door. "Did you transform in front of her?"

Deigh excitedly nodded. "She wants to go shopping with me so I could have my own clothes and explore more of this place where a dragon wouldn't be able to. Show me some tricks about sneaking around for espionage and the sort. Tempest is jealous that I completed the feat before him. He now owes me a shark when we get home."

"It's wonderful that you're happy about beating Tempest and going shopping, but you're not going on any espionage missions," I stated firmly, getting up from my seat to face her. The idea of her going out on her own scared me, but I kept it to myself. "Even if no one would know who you are, that is the last thing I would ever want you to do."

"It would get things done faster; we don't have-"

"I don't care. Unless its an absolute last resort. There is no way I will agree to let you go. I don't want you to risk your life out there alone."

Her scales bristled. "Just because I would look different doesn't mean I am different. I can kill someone easily."

"It doesn't matter. In that form, you are more susceptible to damage, especially if you aren't aware of it. If someone knew, they could just use an Outland bolt and kill you instantly. If they knew of the skill, they could lock your ability to return to your original form with one of so many abilities out there. They could kidnap you like they tried with me." My fear accidentally slipped but I continued anyway. "The warnings in your book explained those things and I'm sure that Ciar, or any of his followers, are dedicated to knowing those exploits if they are going off of the past with Theseus and Argona."

"But…" She couldn't argue as she looked away in disgust. "I just want to help."

"I know, gods I know… but we have to be careful too. Taking unnecessary risks like that won't help anyone but our enemies. We have to leave the sneaking around and intel gathering to the others. You're powerful, yes, but even with all my years of training, it wouldn't apply to you well. I have my own technique just as you'll have yours and unless you're the exact size and build as me, your style is going to differ. If you try and use me as your reference in a life and death situation, you're going to die just like if I used this dragon skill and followed your lead."

She gave a small nod, but it was easy to tell that she was a little more than upset.

"We can practice together after your trip, get you better accustomed to your other form and when this is all over, we can do things that are fun. Like shopping and trying new foods in new places."

"Trip? What trip?"

"Éabha wants to take you, right? You deserve to splurge a bit and you can have fun. I might not be able to go with you physically, but I can help if you want me to. The two of you can go shopping and get a couple of outfits which you definitely need. Something nice and maybe something more fit for combat until we get you a proper armour set. Whatever you want, you deserve it."

She turned back to me, slightly happier than before. "But what about everything else? I can't just go out when you're stuck here."

"If I need a break, I'll join you through the link for a bit. As for this mess, there isn't much for you to do that you haven't already done. Azarias and Cyrus are going to be gathering details around the Directors' Demesne and cleaning up loose ends. Owen, I believe, is going to be on his CT gathering more information from other Seraphinean bases that we can't easily travel to and any of his other contacts."

"I still don't think it's very fair that you're stuck here."

"Go and have fun. I had my break yesterday and you made a certain someone more than a little excited to do things with. You two should enjoy the day of doing… whatever it is you two want to do, if those dragons attack and kill us all, I'd be much happier dying knowing you two got to explore and adventure at least once."

"Yeah well, stop thinking about death, and focus on living," she hissed in annoyance. "Like what happens if someone is following Éabha again?"

"Then they should still be waiting for her to leave her house. That was where she was last seen in public... Actually, maybe I'll have Owen go with you, without Eclipse. If he doesn't have his sword and Missiletainn stays here, watching me, he would have the perfect disguise of being one of Éabha's chauffeurs."

"So, even if she is seen by one of those creeps, they wouldn't be suspicious of her outing... and if they get close enough for us to notice, we can grab them instead of them attacking us."

I gave a nod at the growing plan. This outing was becoming lucrative by the moment. "That would be very helpful if we have a zealot to question... just be careful doing that if you do."

"Always."

"No, you're not."

"Alright, this time I will be. We'll have fun and take advantage of the situation if its given. Orpheal can teleport us back to her place after dropping off any of the parts that are ready for the Zerach. Owen can then teleport the two of us back here after the trip that way no one would think it's suspicious until its too late." Her plan was a solid one.

"Perhaps we'll be fortunate today."

"Oh, I do so hope that a zealot does something brave... Alright, you should deliver the plan while I get ready in here."

"It was your plan for the most part, shouldn't you have the honour?"

"Because I don't want you to see what I look like until I have the perfect outfit."

"That's... fine, but-"

"Are you really going to ask Orpheal to teleport a dragon into his home?"

Fair point... "So, what exactly are you going to be wearing?"

"Éabha has already offered to let me borrow some of her clothes, but I'm sure you don't mind me wearing yours until we get to her residence, right?"

"I suppose not... though they might be a bit big on you..."

"What do I care? I'm a dragon. You people are the ones that insist on wearing clothes."

I sighed, "You probably don't need shoes since you're not going anywhere but to her place and my boots would be far too big... Pants and a sweater should be fine."

Her tail thumped loudly on the ground, missing her regular wagging pattern. Her excitement wasn't contained to just herself and leaked into the link. I smiled at her excitement and started for the door.

"I'll let everyone know of the plans while you get ready. If you need me, I'll be downstairs until you give me the clear that you're gone."

00000

I uncomfortably looked over the research of Director Vígdís with the tablet on the couch. It was borderline immoral. The theories she had come up with were in a large log, but from what I could tell, they were just ideas and not practiced. Many of them involved Outland Dragons directly, the same kind of ideas that Owen and I had brainstormed, but there wasn't a solution that she had come up with to use the blood without killing someone and still receive benefits.

She was looking into a different approach, specifically the power increase that an Outland Dragon got when they had consumed Absalomian Dragon blood, even suggesting that an Absalomian was enough to gain the effects. I didn't like Vígdís very much, just like her theories, even her notes made her sound arrogant and narcissistic. I wanted to believe that they were all just theories and fantasies, but who knew if she had acted on them and I just hadn't come across them yet. If she recorded them at all.

One thing was for certain, I did not feel sorry about calling her a child the other day. Not after reading some of her logs.

A small message came from Deigh, telling me that they had arrived at the shopping centre. I turned my attention to her senses and found her getting out of an elaftrus, one I had been in before, but it was much larger than what I was used to. Owen closed the driver's side, wearing a suit with the Seraphinean emblem on the back of the jacket...

A neat connection came to mind: the emblem for the kingdom was also Éabha's family emblem. I had realized they were the same, but I didn't connect the dots. I was going to have to ask someone about why white wings on a ring were used instead of blue ones which would have matched the Gordin line.

Owen adjusted the little capped hat on his head, keeping it low, and making him look nothing like the general. His acting skills were quite useful in ways I didn't think of. He stood a bit taller than Deigh as Éabha bounded around the vehicle, wingless and chipper, her eye level about five centimetres from hers. I turned back to my tablet, weirded out. It was strange seeing things at such a lower height, especially Éabha who came to my chest normally. But it did tell me that Deigh's Absalomian form was around a hundred-sixty-five centimetres, making her slightly shorter than Atla and quite a bit shorter than Dani. The only three girls I did know that were shorter were Éabha, Aoife, and Helah.

"How would you feel to know that Atlamillia is taller than you in this form?" I asked her only to get scoffed at. *"It's not a bad thing to be average height."*

Deigh swept her obvious envy into a place I couldn't see. *"You're supposed to be ignoring anything that could disclose what I look like."*

"Alright, alright." I left her be but kept the link open on her other senses, continuing to scroll and read.

Outside felt nice. There wasn't much of a breeze, but the sun was warm. The feeling only lasted a few minutes before it disappeared as she went inside. Then, the bombardment of questions from Éabha came. A small laugh escaped at the enthusiasm only to remember that this was also Éabha's first time going shopping with a friend.

Where to go first? What kind of clothes should they get? What should they try on? What adolescent mischief could they get away with?

Owen tried to help answer them, giving a sense of direction to the chaos of ideas. It made me feel bad for putting him in that position. The trip was probably going to take all day, possibly well into the evening and while he didn't protest to the job in any form. I wonder how long it would be before he started to regret taking a job I would have done if I wasn't trapped. Perhaps in a bit I could call to see how he was doing.

My CT went off on the table in front of me and I set the large tablet on my lap, picking up the device. It was a message from Azarias. I opened it and read that they had cleared Director Embla's division and were on their way to Vígdís's lab. I wrote a quick reply, telling him of the work I had come across so far and for them to be cautious. There was a simple acknowledgment back and I set the CT down. I changed my position on the couch to that of laying down on my side and put the larger tablet on the table, so I didn't have to hold it while reading. There was a long way to go, the least I could do for myself was be comfortable doing it.

The long way to go held more subjects within the director's logs. Weapons, biological enhancements... the theories went on seemingly forever. Some had been worked on, but they weren't as awful as the theories I had read earlier. Still not remotely on the moral side, but it was considered legal if I was correct. There was nothing illegal about working on Outland Monsters to see how their power fluctuated through different experiments. But even if they were soulless, the experimentation notes that were made with great detail turned my stomach. I kept my feelings out of the link to allow Deigh to have the best time she could while she picked out different things to try on.

A small sigh came out. How could someone be comfortable about torturing something for days and weeks at a time until it died? It would have never given up, but perhaps that was what appealed to Vígdís. It would never give up the idea to kill everything in the room, yet it would also never understand that it wasn't ever going to escape. It wasn't ever going to end its suffering.

They felt pain... I knew they did as they reacted to being attacked. But it was different to kill one on the battlefield. One that wasn't helpless to defend itself. The poor, little creatures that were captured and tested on for so many theories and hypotheses, without remorse. They were living beings in a sense, right? Perhaps not to the director who may have known better than I. It also didn't help when it seemed like Vígdís also enjoyed the pain she caused from time to time from how her writing or voice changed in the logs that were so very wrong.

I shifted, staring at the ceiling far above me before changing my position back to sitting. With regret, I picked up the large tablet again. I needed to go through the notes and logs... The whelps depended on it if she was their captor... and if she was, only the gods knew what she was doing with them. Probably something that even a god wouldn't have thought of. I hoped that she wasn't their captor, even if it would have made the search come to an end and the kingdom wouldn't be under threat... Ciar would probably be more civilized.

I dug through the notes further.

Another hour went by from when I switched positions and was now pacing as I read for some sort of physical activity. A distraction really to keep me grounded when in reality, I wanted to jump out a window. The experiments switched from monsters to that of people some time ago. The past ideas and theories as well as new ones, like attempting to fuse the power collected from fallen Outland Monsters with Seraphineans, were very practiced on now. And they had not gone well.

Whether or not those Seraphineans were given death sentences or not, the notes did not say. They were numbers… no names, just numbers, and a variety of descriptions of how mentally, physically, and emotionally sound each of the subjects were. The logs, the voice recorded ones, now had screams in the background, which were only vaguely worse to the written ones that shared those same details. For some reason or another, the lapsing of what happened in Siofra hadn't comeback to mind since the logs started like I had expected them to, but I was grateful all the same.

The less flashbacks, the better.

I closed the recording that ended with the woman giving a small chuckle of amusement in her secluded office that muffled the screams in the background. Despite her failures, it seemed like she was getting closer to her goal. I looked to the overall file it was in as it was going by time and not by file and found the biological weapons section. I scanned the details that were written; the category it was placed in was a file called airborne. The idea of a leader of Seraphina doing such research set me on edge. I kept reading the extra details.

The specific airborne weapon she was looking at targeting a selection of Seraphs but would leave other Seraphs in the same space and exposed, completely unharmed.

Why was she trying to harm her people?

I scrolled and found a second recording at the bottom and tapped on it. It started where the last one ended, the cold chuckle was followed by a new voice in the background, but the words were too quiet to hear. I backed it up and raised the volume before playing it. A door opened and closed from somewhere within the room.

"We need to find a new way of segregating the six-wing Seraphs from the eight-winged ones, Doctor Vígdís," the newcomer said, not using the last name like she was familiar with the director. A loud crack of Vígdís moving near the mic caused me to wince.

"We'll find it," the foul woman answered. "I won't allow that bitch to get ahead of me any longer."

"Don't you think that this is going too far? She's-"

"Once this is complete, we won't need to control Outland Monsters like Orpheal is trying to accomplish secretively with tech he clearly stole from me. I'll go beyond him. We will mass murder all those monsters, and anyone else who gets in the Verdant family way."

"It's not *our* family's wish. It's yours! You can't just take control-" A sharp scream ripped through the comment before growing silent.

"Seraphineans are the closest race to the divine. It's why we were so religious in our past, how we are still so religious even with science. Only those intelligent enough can see that it's our destiny to be divine! We shouldn't have to grovel in our floating island any longer," Vígdís stated as something dropped heavily onto the floor. "A new era, and you're going to assist in it, Five-Thirty-Eight."

The recording ended, leaving a dreadful silence to fill the empty building I stood in.

What the hell did I just listen to? Who had she been targeting? Who was the one in the recording that was attacked? Verdant... that was Vígdís's last name. Was it someone in her family?

A million questions ran through my head as I looked at the log date, needing to sit down. It was dated to a few weeks before Orpheal had asked for help the first time.

I scrolled to the top and reread some of the first logs from fifty years back. Her logs had become increasingly irrational compared to the first logs... starting when? I scrolled down the list that really started to turn sideways and checked the date. Three years ago...

What happened then?

I looked over the titles and sighed. Whatever it was, I wasn't going to find it with the files I had. At least, not what I had read so far. The later files and logs may have more information, but I was running out of them. Maybe that wasn't a bad thing. This director was out of her mind and there wasn't much I could do about it without stating that we hacked into their system. That would have been a great way to get kicked out or arrested.

I grabbed my CT and sent another quick message to Azarias and Cyrus to make sure that they both knew of how unstable Vígdís was. How careful they were going to be or how quickly they wanted to set her off was up to them; I just hoped that they played it safe rather than get into trouble.

I checked in with Deigh who, thankfully, hadn't noticed my turmoil over the last few hours and found that she was happily looking at boots. "*Hey, what are you looking at?*"

She didn't give much of a reaction other than a slight purr, "*You already know.*"

"Well, yes. But what do you think of them?"

"They're cute. I'm just having a hard time deciding between them and another pair I found. Shoes on the other hand, I'm not a big fan of."

"No?"

"In fact, I much rather have no shoes at all, but Owen and Éabha both said that I should have some sort of footwear or someone will get suspicious. Then there's the fact that most stores won't allow you in unless you have something on your feet."

This I did know, but I supposed it was more of a subconscious, common sense rule instead of a conscious one. *"What about sandals?"*

"They are worse than shoes."

That wasn't much of a surprise since I didn't care for sandals either unless I was going for a swim. Guess we both preferred boots. I changed the subject slightly. *"What about the rest of your trip? Everything you had hoped it would be?"*

"We need to do this all the time," she answered excitedly and for a split second I was happy she was enjoying it. Then, I thought about it a little longer, the crushing reality of it all.

What had I done? She was going to spend so much money. Money that we did not have the luxury to spend. But... for this single time, at least she was enjoying herself. *"I'm glad you're having fun."*

"I am, but you sound exhausted. What have you been doing all this time?"

"Reading notes, listening to logs. Nothing you need to worry about," I lied, though I had a feeling that she didn't believe me. *"So, are you going with those boots or no?"*

"I can't decide!" she exasperatedly growled, picking up a second pair and forced me to have my full attention on her end. She held out both pairs for me and for Éabha in front of her to see. Both were white with red accents and heeled, but that's about where the similarities ended. The first pair was tall, easily over the knee, with thin heels similar to that of a stiletto while the other had shorter, thick heels and went to about halfway up the calf with a little, red rose on the outside of the ankle. To say it astounded me that she had probably already tried and managed to walk in them was an understatement. "Which pair?"

"Short," I replied just as Éabha did.

"Long."

Deigh sighed, "You both have very different answers…"

I defended, "*I think the short ones would be more comfortable, less flashy.*"

Éabha had also defended her choice, but I was more than certain she had no idea that I had as well. "The long ones are awesome. They make you look elegant, like you're about to head into battle."

"You could get both," Owen suggested, coming into view. He looked alert as ever, not giving any impression that he wasn't enjoying the time out. "You could switch them around for outfits and location. Everyone has at least two pairs of shoes for that reason."

Deigh looked to the boots. "Is that alright? Aerrow was just making fun of me for possibly spending too much money…"

I grabbed the CT to message Owen, letting him know of the very thing I was about to tell her, and a little extra note that came across the link. "*It's fine, it's like he said, everyone has an extra pair at least. And besides, how often will you get to go shopping like this?*"

"*If you say it's alright…*" A beep went across her ears as Owen pulled out his CT.

"Aerrow says it's fine but also mentioned that you're hungry."

"I am?" There was silence as she thought it over and sighed again. They headed for the checkout. "*Look at what you've done to me. I got caught up and forgot to eat at lunch time!*"

"*Well, that's what I'm here for,*" I told her with a small laugh which she didn't agree with.

"*Don't play dumb, you haven't eaten since breakfast either. What's your excuse?*"

"*I'm not hungry.*"

It was the truth. I wasn't hungry, and frankly, wasn't sure I would be for some time. I looked at the tablet that still had more lab records to go. She didn't get to argue with me as she was left to pay for the boots when Owen's CT rang. I didn't pay attention to the conversation on the other end as footwear was placed in the box and I went to the next log. Then, a sharp scream of surprise came from Deigh.

I snapped my attention back to her, never hearing anything like it before as the shrill of fear caused my heart to stop for a moment. A black chaos wall was placed in front of her with Owen holding Éabha in a protective stance. He released her but the field stayed up. Movement came from behind Deigh as employees from behind the counter left in a hurry.

"What's going on?"

"Someone just tried to kill Éabha," she answered, looking upwards to see the ceiling was also chaos. *"I should-"*

"You won't fit in there well and it would blow any disguise you wanted to have," I countered, wishing she could as well, or even better, be there with her. *"Let Owen handle it..."*

"There's three of-"

The conversation ended as a spear of light went through the field, almost skewering Owen.

"Time to leave," Owen ordered and handed Éabha the bags he had. "We can't fight them here."

"Who are them?" I asked, but Deigh didn't have an answer as an evacuation announcement went over the speakers.

Owen took them to the back of the store and through a door which led to a much smaller hallway, connecting to other stores on that floor. The words from him were calm and precise, "Stay close and in the pool."

My concentration was split as my CT rang, causing me to jump. I looked to it and Cyrus's name and photo were on the screen. I answered, a bit confused on why he opted to call me instead of Azarias. Before I could say hello, he was speaking.

"Vígdís just snapped and confessed to illegal experimentation during our discussion. Azarias would be telling you this, but he's heading to the Gordin Medical Wing."

"What happened to Azarias?"

"She found him annoying. He'll be fine, just bleeding. A lot."

I didn't like how calm he was speaking or how he was constructing his sentences. It sounded forced and his phrases weren't his usual mannerism. "How much is a lot?"

"Exterior carotid artery."

"I don't know what that means."

"She slit the artery in his neck," he clarified, swallowing. "But as I said, he's fine."

My heart skipped a beat. "That's not fine!"

"I'm aware but he told me to tell you through Sage." He gave a hint of a sigh. "He will be fine... help wasn't far."

For the love of... I took a breather only for it to stagger as Deigh's side of things got a lot more active in the claustrophobic hallway. "Bleeding knight on one end of the city and an assassination attempt on the other... You wouldn't happen to know what that is about?"

"I do." He sounded relieved, in his own way, for something else to talk about. "Vígdís's test subjects. She has loyal pets and she let them out to kill Éabha. She considered her a rival."

"So, that's who she was talking about in her logs... But why now? Why not in the demesne?"

"Orpheal's lab is too guarded, and she motivated a zealot to head to the shopping mall to guise her attack. Owen has been informed already..."

"So that's what that was... luckily, he's in a tiny hallway as far as I can tell. Should any zealots show up along with her pets, it'll be very difficult to do anything. I just hope these pets of hers aren't as good in close quarters. They seemed highly skilled in light magic."

"I have no concern with the fight. He's in the most advantageous spot he could possibly be in," Cyrus stated, somewhat distracted.

I instigated the thought. "Something else come up?"

"Before she was detained, she mentioned that Orpheal had stolen her work about Outland Dragon blood."

"It could have been a way to plant doubt... a last word." Then again, she had mentioned that before in her log. What exactly does she think was stolen?

"Perhaps... She mentioned it was deleted from her research. This could be a case where the same idea comes to mind in multiple people, and she assumed it was stolen." He paused for another moment then continued. "I'm going to go through her logs to determine if there is something missing. Looking at her notes before, she posts at least something once a day."

"That might take a while… her Outland Dragon logs alone go back years."

"I did see that." I heard some keys clicking in the background. "I'm going to be here so if I don't return, you know where I am. I'll keep checking in on Azarias… He should be healed by late tonight or early tomorrow; I don't know the damage she did."

"Do what you need to do," I told him, understandingly. He didn't want to leave his friend behind, and I appreciated and respected that about him. "Keep me up to date on anything else."

He gave a small noise of agreement and ended the call.

I turned to Deigh's side just in time to see a deranged, broken-winged Seraph crawling on the ceiling. It was quickly knocked off by a tendril as Owen addressed the horrifying act. Three Seraphineans, all mangled and seemingly devolved into wild animals, were immobilized in tendrils before Deigh. Owen looked back at something down the hall, behind her. She turned around as he glared. A robed zealot came out of hiding as their camouflage spell faded and were only a couple of metres from Éabha, trapped by the general.

"Did you really think that would work?" Owen questioned, moving forward as Éabha moved next to Deigh. "Why did you come after Éabha?"

"For Lord Ciar!" The zealot declared. Owen resisted the urge to shut her up with force, the amount of dark magic in the air barely held back in Deigh's senses. "For the glory of the new god!"

Suddenly, there was a slight change in his expression and a chaos shield was formed, ceasing all light in the area as a small explosion went off outside. The walls dropped and the light returned. The zealot was in pieces in front of them, leaving nothing behind but blood and what looked like bones embedded into damaged walls.

I turned off most of the link in disgust.

Why were Ciar's followers so dedicated to killing themselves and everyone else with them?

00000

I listened in silence as Owen explained everything that happened after I stopped participating on Deigh's point of view. Law enforcement relieved him of his duty of holding the tortured people turned pets, allowing him to bring Deigh and Éabha back to the Gordin abode using a Chaos Portal. Orpheal, hearing about the incident from Solaria, who saw it on the news, was bombarded with the incident between Vígdís, Azarias, and Cyrus, and proceeded to lock Éabha in the manor. The lab was, without a doubt, too dangerous for her, but it unintentionally grounded the girl to the situation I was stuck in. Owen and Solaria, switching with Orpheal for taking care of Azarias, did their best for the situation and transferred several of her projects to the manor lab – keeping the girl's secret from him that she was working on my armour.

After that, Orpheal was free enough to Teleport Glyph Owen and Deigh back to the safehouse, not allowing Owen to portal in case of an emergency. A message was passed along that Azarias was resting and in stable condition within Gordin Medical Wing. Tempest was outside of his room guarding and giving Cyrus the ability to check on his friend while Sage guarded Cyrus in Vígdís's lab where he was still going through her logs. Missiletainn had left a while ago to watch the Gordin manor to allow Orpheal the room to breathe and deal with his duties and not have to worry about someone targeting Éabha.

Whether or not the whole set up made me feel better was still in the air. The situation was as optimal as it could get. Everyone was being watched and protected with perfect communication between everyone. But I didn't want that. I wanted my whole team back in base and I wanted Orpheal and Éabha to be happily going about their lives without everything crashing down on top of them in the ways that were probably the worst situation for either of them.

But that wasn't reasonable.

Azarias needed a proper doctor, we couldn't help him in the safe house. Vígdís had possibly just jeopardized Éabha by giving what I thought to be our common enemy information if that zealot shared whatever the director had told her, lies or truth, who the hell knew. Éabha was stuck in her house that was probably much larger for her to wander than my place was, but that didn't mean she was content. She was pretty clear on not being happy when stuck to the grounds of the demesne, and now she was stuck to a fraction of it.

Orpheal was now down half of his directors as there hadn't been time to pass a vote on who the two new directors were going to be. Just as well since he had lost another one. But that left the government of Seraphina in a very difficult situation. At least for the night, it was balanced the best it could be all around.

Owen went silent, finishing the tale and I sighed, "So… that's it?"

"Unless Cyrus or the Seraphinean Legion come up with something, yes. As far as we're aware, Vígdís wasn't working for Ciar. She had managed to find a zealot with the intent of making sure Éabha was killed in case her experiments failed. But given her insanity and ego, she boldly claimed that if she had the opportunity, she would have joined him without hesitation."

"That doesn't surprise me. Her theories and experiments were disgusting at the best of times. I'm actually glad no one had recruited her in time. The things he could have used..." I shuddered at the thought, turning to the tablet that sat on the table between us. I had finished the rest of her reports not long ago. Thankfully, she wasn't behind the kidnapping. "So, back to square one and separated on top of it."

"But alive... meaning we can still find those whelps, take care of Ciar and his spawn, and learn more about those seals."

"I guess..." I growled, unable to hold back my frustration. I knew he was trying to be optimistic, something that was usually my role, but I was tired. Tired of things just going wrong and tired of not being able to help. I was doing my best to keep in mind to not get in the way, to not solve every problem – but I really, really wanted to just go with Deigh and drag out any cultist to give us information, one way or another.

It was a dark and disturbing path that was so very tempting to take. The only things that held the impulse back was the promise I made to Owen to smarten up and my morale compass that the mission would lead to more than a few cultists dead in their suicidal ways.

A disgusted sigh came out. "I should go look over maps again, see if there was something we could look further into. How long do you think the rest of the materials for the Zerach will take to be completed and installed?"

"Not for a few days at least. Éabha won't be able to help directly now if a problem arises. So, that will add time if something comes up."

Because of course it would. We didn't have that time.

I stood up from the couch. "You should rest... You've had a long day."

"I'm actually going to look into the logs left, make some food in an hour or so once Deigh is done eating downstairs," he started before looking up at me with a bit of hope. "Do you have a preference of what you want?"

"I'm not hungry, but thanks for asking..."

His look turned to concern as I left for my room and closed the door behind me.

Chapter Thirty-Two: Let It Out

I swung Winterthorn with control, purposely throwing most of my might into it in order to practice form. To perfect a steadier position with my movements so I wouldn't be taken by momentum. Azarias and Cyrus had, thankfully, come back earlier that morning...

Or was it technically still night?

I supposed it didn't matter. Three-thirty was the time I was going to give Owen if he asked when I was able to speak with him about the plans moving forward.

Would he ask if I had slept?

Most likely. The answer was yes, technically. I was up when they returned and greeted them before they went to their rooms for a much-needed rest.

Cyrus had nothing to report on his investigations into the matter of stolen work and was inconclusive. No logs were missing on the surface, so it was impossible to tell if one of her logs had been deleted. I returned to the maps, thinking long and hard about the situation Vígdís had placed in front of us. It wasn't unreasonable to conclude that a similar project could have been thought up by Orpheal without even knowing that she had the same idea, just as Cyrus had mentioned. It's happened before with multiple inventions and discoveries that were the same but brought to the attention of everyone else by different people – in fact, it happened more often than not after looking into it more.

The thought process, the research, and even studying eventually left me more than restless. Too restless to even sit still.

I dropped my stance and sighed. It was about noon and the practicing for the last couple of hours had not helped my restlessness. If anything, it had encouraged it.

I wanted to leave. Go searching...

Anything to be productive and help.

I turned my frustration on the training dummy I had been practicing on, cutting it down with a single swing by accident. I froze at the action, looking over the act. The dummy wasn't seared in anyway, meaning I hadn't used magic, which was both great and not. I rarely turned to violence to release tension if ever.

It scared me a bit.

"Need a new sparring partner?" Owen asked casually behind me and I jumped, turning around to see him in armour. I hadn't heard him come in. "Or is that one not dead yet?"

"It's…" I looked down at the broken two pieces on the ground in front of me before turning back to him. "Sorry."

He gave a shrug, apparently not as concerned as I was about letting off steam the way I had. "There are more. So, interested?"

"I… yeah… why not?"

I readied my blade, changing targets only to be forced on the defensive. Shards of chaos came from a pool under him and were sent at me in quick succession. I deflected two of the shards before having to abandon my position as they became overwhelming. Another pool of chaos formed underfoot, and I quickly left it, bringing the fight closer to the general. I didn't want to repeat a similar, successful strategy on his part. I brought down my sword only for a tendril to block it and I retreated once more so he couldn't disarm or catch me.

Shards formed again in my peripherals and I activated Guðmundr, blocking one side while I deflected the others with Winterthorn. The shield dropped as I charged again, this time, he drew his blade. I attacked head on. Winterthorn clashed against Eclipse just as the golden blade turned black, absorbing the power from the heavy blow instead of its primordium structure. I switched the angle of the blade, quickly to the momentum of his guard as he released the energy. The barbarian blade went over my shoulder. The power had allowed me to disarm him instead of the other way around.

He rubbed his wrist as he moved backwards. "You're getting much better. Though its quite clear from that strike that you're a bit frustrated."

"Only a little bit," I admitted as his pool formed underfoot again, forcing me to back off.

"Go on."

Didn't really feel like talking.

I went to charge in again when I heard the sand behind me move. My shield went up and Owen's blade clipped it as it went back to him. I froze.

Ciar had done the same trick in the vaults. "H-how did you do that?"

"It's a dark magic ability, like magnetism," he answered, looking over his blade before turning back to me. "As long as the object has been imbued with the same power, I can call it back to me if it's in range. You can thank Ciar for giving me the tip."

I tsked, not angry at him for learning such a useful ability, but at my reaction to it. It was the same reaction from when I saw Orpheal's armour. When I was fighting Éabha.

Panic.

Fear.

The need to run away as the old wounds burned and stabbed.

It was infuriating!

I abused Guðmundr's ability to form into any shape I wanted and got a bubble. Was it stupid looking? Probably, but it allowed me to close the gap without the chaos field trying to grab me. Owen gave me a small look of surprise before sending tendrils and spikes to try and break it. None of it worked, allowing me an opening to close the rest of the gap with a leap, striking down and breaking through the tendrils that haphazardly tried to block. A wave of clashing forces came as my blade hit his, forcing me off him. I didn't give him the chance to recover as I went back in. Swiftly striking with heavy blows, he carefully blocked each one with a blade or chaos spike that lasted as long as it took to form.

It pissed me off for no rational reason. Just like not breaking through completely, I wasn't able to do anything outside the fight. I was tired of it. Tired of hiding. Of wondering if Theodora was fine on her own. I wanted to get over her, but that wasn't happening quickly. Ciar at every blank thought. Each miss between the strikes was just a reminder of how I didn't defeat him.

How I failed to protect the king…

"Even if he was alive, we'd still be in this position," Owen stated, catching me off-guard.

I hadn't noticed I was voicing my thoughts out loud. It ended my attacks as he defended the final one. I took notice that the unending knot engraved on Winterthorn's blade and the eyes of the dragon guard were glowing white with magic. I backed off. The blade darkening back to its normal form as I stopped putting magic into it, regaining control again. "Sorry. I hadn't noticed I was speaking out loud, taking my frustrations out on you like that."

"I purposely provoked you for that reason. You haven't been talking to anyone about-"

"There is nothing to talk about."

"Really? So, you're barely eating, barely sleeping, for no reason?" He waited a moment for me to answer, but I didn't. All I did was look to the sand, unable to look him in the eye. "Your judgement is going to be affected if you don't share. Not to mention your physical health will start to deteriorate. Unless you want to be the first of your line to snap."

I didn't want to have that legacy, but I also didn't want to sit around, talking about things we already knew. Dammit. It's not like he was wrong. I was thinking about doing things I would never do. Aggressively letting out my anger and frustration. Even saying thoughts without any regard that I was saying them.

There were better things to do. More important than… No. He would just say that being a sane king was more important. An insane one would get things done for a time then would be put down, either through self-infliction or assisted means.

"If it helps, Solomon and Aelia also didn't enjoy talking things out. So, they trained, talked it out with few words while swinging a weapon of some kind; depended on the day. It was a more extreme way of releasing stress and anxiety, but it helped them."

"And you think that I would be interested?" My words were just shy of vile. "I don't enjoy being violent, attacking things, let alone attacking my uncle."

"I know, but you've also never been placed in this situation before. It doesn't hurt to try it out if you don't want to do it the old fashion way."

A frown formed. Like that was happening. I looked down to the sword my father once used, and it lit up slightly as I tightened my grip. I turned back to him, a feeling of regret growing. Violence wasn't an answer to anything… but maybe this once, placing my frustrations into action could help. "Fine, but don't think I'll go kindly on you."

"I expect much worse than what you've done so far," he replied, dropping the chaos field and readied his sword. "So, you hate hiding?"

I struck at him which he defended with a grunt from the strength behind it; I wasn't holding back. "I hate being stuck here."

"This building?"

"This building. This city. This position of hiding from zealots." Each item on the list had its own blow, each one defended in some form. "I'm sick of them. I'm either a target or a play... thing for their sick experiments. It's all their fault and I can't do a damn thing about it!"

"Like the whelps..."

"I can't help them either! I promised to help Zegrinath to find them. And here I am, hiding! This kingdom is going to be attacked in less than two days and I'm stuck here when I should be out there!"

"Azarias and Cyrus are out there right now, looking," he said, but whatever hope he was trying to give, only pissed me off more.

"It's not enough! Azarias shouldn't even be out there! I told him to stay and rest!"

My strike was a bit much for him as he dodged instead of blocked, and I stopped attacking. It was easy to strike out my anger, but it wasn't helping, nor did it feel right. All I was doing was lashing out at my uncle like a child throwing a tantrum. I sheathed Winterthorn and he lowered Eclipse.

"He shouldn't be risking himself like that," I said softly, and he shifted his weight.

"And you should?"

"Well..." I so dearly wanted to say yes, but it would have been hypocritical. "No... but he was hurt really bad yesterday. He could have died if he weren't in the demesne. I'm just being hunted... In the city but being out there, the unpopulated parts of the island, there wouldn't be bystanders that could get hurt if conflict arose. I know a part of this lack of care is caused by the need for control, but it doesn't make it any easier to rationalize it as a bad idea. But Azarias got hurt on a mission where that shouldn't have happened, it makes me feel like I shouldn't risk any of you – not that you can't do it, but because I don't want to see any of you hurt."

"I know. You want to bring this whole mess to a swift end any way you can without risking others. But this isn't something you can control nor is it your fault. Azarias was playing a risky game on his own accord, knowing that he was taunting an unstable woman. That was on him, not you. We also know that Prime or Boffin Zealots don't seem interested in either of them because they aren't considered a threat. They haven't done anything to prove that, and it makes them perfect for doing scouting missions."

"And what about you? You killed almost a whole horde by yourself with Missiletainn. I doubt the cultists are going to be leaving you be after that stunt."

"Perhaps not, but I also have my field always active to defend against surprise attacks because I'm aware that sort of power would be noticed and paint a target on our backs. We're prepared for the worst and we know it works. You saw it work on that zealot that was invisible."

I had, hadn't I?

He had been playing this game for a lot longer than this problem ever began. A small sneer formed at the thought of him needing to defend himself in such a way for the sake of missions. It must have been exhausting.

"These people are annoying... but they aren't the real problem. He's worse and it won't matter what protections you have if you're alone. He's killed so many, allowing these people to band together to try and hurt even more innocent people. It wouldn't be like this if I-" I couldn't finish as my throat closed in on itself. My mind wandered back to that night. The mistakes. A dull pain hit my chest from the memory and my hand went to the spot were the scar laid underneath the armour.

He looked to my hand, a grim expression on his face. "This is far from your fault."

"Really?" A cold tone spat out. "Because it certainly doesn't feel that way. I had two opportunities to kill him and fucked up both times! The first time got our king, your best friend, killed. And the second time he got away through a portal because I couldn't keep the barrier closed. He's killed both of your friends because of me and its only a wonder why you don't hate me for it."

"I don't hate you because you didn't kill them. Ciar did regardless of what events took place before. He made that choice to poison Aelia. He made the choice of ripping out Solomon's heart while I was forced to watch, just as unable to help as you were because of that demon." His jaw was clenched as he sheathed his blade. "We all made mistakes that night... but we cannot dictate the actions of others and claim them to be solely our actions and the reasons why things happened. All we can do is learn, move on, and finish what they started by killing or detaining that bastard."

"I don't even know if I could do that..." I admitted, dropping my hand. "If I see him again, I don't know if I could confront him. I honestly don't think that my anger, my determination to protect our people and the people of Seraphina will overcome the fear of him."

"It's alright to be scared-"

"Scared? I'm terrified of him! You say that our mistakes are only half the problem, but I'm terrified of making another one. Someone I care about has died two of the three times I've screwed up against him and who knows how many countless people I don't know have died because I couldn't finish him in the vaults. All the people who died because of his zealots because I couldn't bring their deaths to justice by ending his reign. I don't want someone else to die because I make just one more mistake. I don't want to die and leave Atlamillia all alone with a kingdom she does not want to rule and that monster probably wanting to finish his collection. If I confront him, even with all of this in mind. As a reason to take him down and push forward, I don't know if I'm going to be able to do it without freezing and panicking if the smallest of things that remind me of him do just that."

"I believe that if the time comes, you won't hesitate," he said in the silence that followed. "You didn't when you saw him the second time after all these years and you didn't in the vaults."

"How could you believe that I won't this time?"

"Because you've been left to overthink since leaving Asylotum. But in the off chance that I'm wrong, Azarias, Cyrus, and I will be there this time from the beginning. You will not be alone, and we know that he will be."

"No, just an army that would die for him at the drop of a pin."

"Irrational suicide… but we know he doesn't work as a team with them. He probably thinks nothing more of them but sacrificial pawns to his goal. His arrogance will be his downfall."

"I hope so… because we don't know how much stronger he has become. What allies he's gathered. We could have had a huge advantage in technology, but I went ahead and banished the only person I know who could have thought of a way to get over the difference between us and him within the last three months."

Owen was silent on the subject, knowing exactly who I was talking about. I went over to the side of the arena and sat on the ground against the wall. He joined me and patiently waited for me to figure out my thoughts.

I didn't really know what to say, so I asked instead. "Have you ever had your heart broken?"

"A few times."

"How did you get over it?"

"Well, I never married or found a partner, so you could say it was a battle I never won," he started, and I looked over at him in disbelief as he had a distant look on his face. It faded when he noticed me. How was I supposed to get over someone if he hadn't? "But I also think that I never needed one. Not everyone needs to have a romantic relationship to be content with life. Just a family close to your heart."

"Too bad that I can't follow that path. It'd probably be easier…"

"Dating is, admittedly, a real pain in the ass. You're going to find there are many types of women out there who are just right, but they might find you insufferable. They might find you just as wonderful and you're going to find them unfit for what is required of them. It's also time consuming and impossibly difficult to even think about relationships when you have someone on your mind already."

"It would be easier to not get over her. But we both know that it would be wrong to pardon her of what she did. It would create instability within the kingdom."

"To your governors, lords, and councillors, yes, it very much would. It would give them the sense that you could do whatever you want without consequence and head down a road of corruption. If she manages to redeem herself, perhaps you could pardon her of the crimes… They could ignore the decision if she is an asset – even allowing her to be part of the council again under the right circumstances. But they would not be happy to see that a traitor to the kingdom could become queen."

"I figured…" I sighed. "The time we had together was short, but I miss it. The little walks, our chats, the night in Baiwyn she got drunk and mad at me for not being more assertive. That was a whirlwind of emotions in a single conversation, but it was one of the only times she let her guard down. She was easy to talk to, we were on the same page a lot… At least, I thought we were."

"Which is where it falls through. Even if you lied, saying she was completely free of her crimes, framed; you know that she's not fit to be queen. Your queen needs to be honest with you, not sweep things under a rug when she gets scared. Trust is one of the qualities you have stated to be one of the most important things to you. Theodora has shown she cannot be trusted to take responsibility for her actions. Knowing and saying nothing is worse than committing the deed. She could have lied about it, but at least she would have told you and you could have acted. Instead, your life was spared because those two imbeciles hired the wrong assassin for the job."

"That still doesn't help me get over her. Éabha suggested going out, making new memories – dating in general... but you just said that dating with someone on your mind is nearly impossible."

"Nearly, but she's right. Making new memories with new and old people, exploring more on your own, will make the pain dissipate," he agreed. "Though I'm surprised that she was the one who gave the advice."

"She's a bit socially awkward and has trouble with considering how some things she says, while brutally correct, could be hurtful, she is also a genius. I think it balances out somewhere that gives her that insight."

"She's a good influence on you at the very least. I doubt we'd be having this conversation any time soon if she hadn't spoken to you first."

"No... not like this at least... Scaring myself certainly had a hand in it too." He laughed a bit as I looked up at the ceiling. "Do you think Theodora's alright?"

"Most likely. She's a dangerous opponent, both physically and mentally."

"I didn't exactly leave her to the Outlands in a good mindset..."

"She's a strong, independent woman with a powerful dragon. In the off chance that she-"

"Don't..." I begged, cutting him off as the imagery of her body being ripped apart, like the people in the tunnels had been, went through my head. "Don't finish that thought... please."

"She's fine," my uncle stated with great confidence. "Maybe angry, frustrated since she's also ambitious. But she's most likely fine. Probably exploring the world as we speak. Soul searching tends to happen when something like that happens."

I nodded, placing my arm on my knee, and propped my head up.

"Did talking things out help?"

Another nod came from me that was genuine. It had helped me calm down, think things out easier. I was still scared of Ciar, heartbroken, upset that I couldn't do more to help find the whelps and protect the kingdom... but it wasn't overwhelming. Not like before. Somehow there was a sense of acceptance and ease that I didn't have before. Just like when the ghosts of my parents had come and gone... It didn't feel great, but there was a sense of clarity in it. A sigh escaped. "I'm tired."

"I can imagine, emotions are exhausting," he said and put a hand on my shoulder. "But you're doing alright, and things will get better in time. It'll take work, but it will get better. And if you're having a real hard time finding someone because the women around you aren't right, then I can invite some candidates to the castle."

"Hopefully, it doesn't come to that. If Dani is accurate, I'm sure some of those poor women would only be there because their parents forced them to."

"No, that's accurate. But, you know, a fancy party never hurt anyone – and how everyone is in one location, you can have your picking from every corner of the kingdom."

"What a weird concept, a party of bachelorettes…" The idea was off-putting. "I don't want to talk about this right now."

"Alright."

I looked over at him. "Did you want to continue sparring? I'd like more practice with Guðmundr."

"I'll gladly spar with you; help hone skills. Maybe test new ones."

Maybe…

We got up and I drew the blade on my side as Owen, once again, didn't bother to draw his, and beckoned me to come at him. I did with a lot more composure than before. Shards formed in a pool underfoot and I brought them down with more fluid motions with less power behind them.

It wasn't necessary.

He noticed the shift in my attack pattern and adjusted accordingly. The pool this time became that of a box, surrounding the two of us in an ominous black and purple space. The only light being some purple that ran through the walls, moving like waves, and Guðmundr. Owen's Seraphinean tech weaved armour went black, hiding out the red tints that had glowed for a moment – leaving barely a shadow of him left, one that I wasn't entire sure was truly there at all.

I tried looking around but had no way of seeing where he had gone. A small noise of something moving through the air came to my ears and I formed a bubble shield again. Tendrils and shards appeared almost immediately after the formation, bouncing off harmlessly on all sides. The tendrils became numerous, forming faster than I had been able to find Owen, and engulfed the shield. I looked at the wall that blocked me from them. The squirming, black abyss was disturbing. I swallowed the discomfort. He had never done something like this against me before. How was I supposed to get out of this?

I tried to move, but the shield was held fast, and I rolled my eyes in realization. It wasn't as bad as I thought it was. It just looked awful. By disarming the shield, the tendrils would move like clockwork. But it was also a bit dangerous as I didn't know if he had decided to get me off the ground. It wasn't something I was interested in, falling from an unknown height. I willed spikes to come out of the bubble to create a spiked ball, pushing and destroying tendrils in the way. The ones under my feet propped the ball upwards, telling me that I was still on the ground.

It was all I needed to know.

I dropped the shield, causing the tendrils to lose their grip and I dashed a few steps and activated it again, spikes included as they converged. I dropped it again before they got too comfortable, and sprinted out of the horrible mess, slicing the tendrils that had gathered with relative ease. The sand under my boots proved that the whole battlefield wasn't entirely chaos.

A shadow moved to my right and I got out of the way as a sword glowed in the darkness, going past my right. I smacked it out of the way with the shield as it pulled back and rammed into the shadow that appeared briefly. Owen grunted as he fell hard, causing the box of chaos to dissipate from above. The floor went back to being unsafe as he shifted the magic around, but it let in light and allowed me to see.

More shards were sent from the wall, forcing me to retreat and defend as he got up. I didn't want to risk being in the dark again and changed the shield to that of a large body shield and charged at him. A tendril went around it and I changed the shield again, blocking it and then changed it back when more shards were threatening to make me a pincushion. A small sense of satisfaction came over me. I was getting quicker and more accustomed to using Guðmundr for both defensive and offensive purposes.

I turned the shield into a spiked one as the shards stopped and smashed it into him. The spikes hit his chest armour, causing it to glow as the tech took over and blocked the damage, but not the force. He hit the ground and the chaos pool under him while his sword went over his head. I brought my sword downwards for the victory but was stopped as chaos shards locked Winterthorn into place, causing me to lose my balance. He swiped a leg out, knocking me over with ease as he dropped the shards. My body hit the ground uncomfortably as he got up. Tendrils got a hold of me, locking me into place.

I struggled, the thought of using magic went by but I decided against it. Simple fire magic wasn't going to work this time, even if I wanted to use it, but the dragon skill would have. But I couldn't do it. The thought of being caught off-guard by Ciar sensing the surge of magic overtook the necessity to be victorious in a spar. I dropped my sword in surrender.

A small look of disappointment came from Owen as he released the ability and then helped me to a stand. "That was a perfect opportunity to test out that skill."

"I know."

"So why didn't you?"

"Because he doesn't want Ciar to show up," Deigh stated from behind me.

We both turned to her, but what I found was not the dragon I had known for so long, but a girl. Medium length, white and red hair in a white, silver, and red dress. A mix of formal and casual with its short skirt and a design that made it look like it had a cover on top of it to make the back much longer. The bodice was similar to that of a corset with the front having lace running through to tighten it with no straps to hold it up. She had no shoes or socks on, not even a shawl to cover her bare shoulders. The only accessory she had was a simple white choker with a small red rose that sat on her incredibly pale neck.

She put her hands behind her puffy skirt as she shifted her weight back and forth sheepishly. A voice I recognized came from her lips. "Do I look okay?"

Okay wasn't what I would have described the girl that was clearly Deigh. She was someone I would not have recognized at all, let alone have the courage to speak to if it hadn't been for her voice, her bright orange eyes, and our link. My surprise expression turned to that of a soft one with a reassuring smile. "You look beautiful, just like I said you would."

She blushed, easily seen as there wasn't much to hide it. Even her red tints gave no assistance as she tried to hide behind her long bangs. She twisted back and forth, making her skirt twirl. "Okay... I was really worried that you wouldn't find this form suitable for being your partner."

"Why ever for?"

"Well, if the Argona in your family tree was a dragon-"

"There is no need to compare yourself to her, but if you must, you blow her out of the water."

"Oh, stop it. No, I don't. She was beautiful and had a regal atmosphere even in the picture. Not to mention her body-"

"I can't believe I'm having this conversation…" I facepalmed, causing her to stop as my face grew warmer by the second in awkward embarrassment. Owen stood by with an amused look on his face but didn't assist as I looked over for help. I turned back to Deigh. "Just because some people are… more well endowed than others, doesn't make them pretty. Everyone is different from body types like Argona and most Seraphs to more like Éabha or Helena… What matters is what is on the inside."

"But you happen to like those kinds of women."

"A preference and nothing more, it doesn't make or break my decision. Besides, why do you care so much about that?"

"I care because your opinion is the only one that matters to me," she said firmly though she sounded slightly embarrassed. "I want to be perfect for you, not average in anything… which is what I am for an Absalomian in both height and body according to the lady in the store. Though she did say I could be a model because my physique is amazing."

"See, not average. And even if you were, you look just as beautiful as you do in your original form," I encouraged, though I was sure I wasn't supposed to be having this conversation, let alone with my partner. The thought stuck around a little longer as I analyzed it. She only understood that what was *perfect* for me would have been women I was attracted to. I wasn't female and therefore, she didn't have anything else to compare to. I gave her a warm smile, hoping to push past her insecurities. "Your choice in clothing suits you as long as you like it. You look great."

"Thank you. I really do like it. I don't like pants, so Owen suggested a combat skirt like your sister. Éabha offered to make me a weapon to use in this form that, like my clothing, won't be destroyed when I change back."

"Managed to get that spell working, eh?"

"It took me three tries… not the best record, but they were only test materials."

At least she thought ahead before doing that. "I'm happy that your trip was successful, despite the ending."

"I had a lot of fun and when things die down, I'd like to go with you."

"When things die down… Speaking of dying," I started, turning to Owen as a thought from before came back. "I had a thought earlier that might help us find the whelps."

"I don't like where this is going…" he sighed but let me continue.

"I think we should try and summon one of the directors' souls and ask them where the whelps are."

"We are not doing a séance. Absolutely, under no circumstances, are we doing some ghostly ritual and summoning anything from Athnuracha or wherever the hell their souls went off to."

"It would speed up-"

He scowled. "It's a really bad fucking idea. Period. You never know who you might summon and more often than not, it's a demon."

"But you're a necromancer; you should be able to do it without much help."

"An unpracticed necromancer. There is a reason why I don't play with necromancy and occult magic. It's dangerous and if not done correctly, can kill you or someone nearby."

"I'm sure there is a normal way where we aren't needing high level skills. What's a demon to us anyway?"

"It won't be like The Effigy. The demon will most likely not have a physical form and be able to possess anyone involved. It's not like we can just stroll down to a church to get it out of whoever it decided to possess, nor can we call a priest here. What happens if it possesses you and starts using magic? Not only would we have to try and fight you without killing you, but you'd also announce yourself to Ciar and any zealot around where you are."

"Oh." I didn't know that it could be so dangerous. That was great information to know. "Calling upon a ghost through séance when unexperienced: bad idea."

"Very, very bad idea even when experienced."

"Shame," Deigh sighed as she walked lightly over to us, practically on her toes, and we looked down to her. "It would have been quite useful if it didn't have so many risks."

"Back to the logs, I guess… and maps," I muttered with irritation. I turned back to Owen. "While the whelps are top priority, there is something else I'd like you to do."

He gave me a confused look. "What is it?"

"Ciar's venom. I know you gave me an update recently, but I was hoping you could check the lab and see for yourself how the progress is."

"Worried that there might be a rat in the team… If you think you'll be alright on your own for a while, I'll get you a full report."

"Thanks."

Chapter Thirty-Three: Harvest Valley

I left Owen and Deigh in the training room and went to shower. All the training made me sweaty and gross. It didn't seem like a very long time that I was in there for, but when I came out, wearing only pants to cool off before putting on a shirt that would most definitely stick, Owen was gone. Him along with the tablet I had planned on looking at while he was out. It left me a bit dumbfounded at how fast he had left since I knew he would have cleaned up before hand. He was the King's General, so maybe it wasn't all that surprising at how fast he could get ready. I looked around, trying to decide what to do since the only thing left was to wait until Cyrus and Azarias got back from their scouting. It was empty, even Deigh was gone.

"I went for a treat, using that ability makes me hungry," she explained, and a small laugh escaped. I was happy to know that she was eating.

I didn't get a chance to reply back as I heard something get placed on the floor behind me. I turned to it quickly to find Éabha staring. About three seconds went by as neither one of us moved or said a word. She looked away from my face to my chest.

"Huh, you should go shirtless more often," she stated, almost emotionlessly, but there was a hint of surprise behind it. "Not a bad view."

"You don't need to stare!" I spat out, embarrassed as I realized that I wasn't wearing one, I put on the one in my hand. It stuck in some areas like I had wanted to avoid, but there wasn't much I could about it.

"Oh no! A girl is looking at my sexy abs! Better cover up because it's scandalous!" Her sarcasm was drier than a desert. "It's only weird because you are sexually and socially awkward and are taking my words in that manner. I'm only stating the obvious, not flirting, Airhead."

"N-no… no, of course not." I was exasperated… but I should have known better to think anything else with her. I cleared my throat as she rolled her eyes and continued to eye me. "Um… what exactly are you doing here anyway? I thought your father locked you in your mansion for the time being."

"He did. So, I learned the Teleport Glyph ability."

"You… what?"

"I ignored Dad and learned how to teleport so I wouldn't be caught. What is so hard to understand about that?"

"No, I got that…" I backtracked, trying to lighten her mood. "So, you learned to teleport? That's a really hard ability to learn… Wait, how did you teleport here? You need to know where to teleport, so you don't kill yourself."

A look of pride went across her face. "I knew where you would be and used it as my homing position." The expression changed to annoyance. "As for the skill, I fucking know its hard. I had to use Domrael's journal as well as the damn ability book in Dad's office at home just to learn it and it took me all day."

I went to question her logic behind it all, but then stayed silent. She learned it in a day like she thought that was such a long time. The dragon skill to turn into an Absalomian wasn't as difficult and it took Deigh three months. Something that was said to take years to perfect. But to Éabha, she had perfected it to the point of just needing a person and the general idea of the area and somehow didn't kill herself. "That's… I don't think impressive covers this…"

She looked pleased and surprised at my answer. "You actually believe that I did it all in a day?"

I nodded. "I saw you learn advanced healing in ten minutes. How could I not believe that you learned this skill just to spite your father's wishes? It is something that you would do, at least, that's what I've come to understand about you."

"I can get pretty petty, huh…" she muttered, coyly. "This's weird though; I've never had anyone just accept my achievements without proof other than Dad. Even Aunt Solaria has a hard time believing me if she didn't watch me learn something and she's taught me a few times in different skills over the years."

"There is usually a first for everything," I chuckled lightly before getting serious. "But I have to bring up the problem to this. You left without telling your father. He's going to lose his mind."

"I don't fucking care. I cannot be locked in that empty place any longer."

"He's trying to keep you safe while he's dealing with governing…" She wasn't listening and I sighed, shaking my head. It had only been a day, but it seemed like it had been building and she had had it. She needed the space to spread her wings and that part of her most definitely drove Orpheal up the wall, especially in times like this. "At least let me message him-"

"No! If you do that, he'll come and get me! Then I'll never be able to do anything ever again!"

"But he should know. Perhaps tell him that it's safer here than it is at your place."

"I already tried that. He doesn't want to listen. Just… if you have to tell him, tell him later. He's not even home anyway – won't be back until late. I doubt he'll have time to check on me. With three directors gone, he's busy, just like you said. I'll head home before he notices."

I wanted to argue more about it, but she was clearly upset despite knowing the pressure her father was under. "Is there a particular reason why you don't want to stay home?"

"It's just shitty there… nothing to do. Your armour is being calibrated and I can do adjustments from here with my CT if need be. But the process is going to take all night so equilibrium with the tech won't break if you have a magic spike when you use a lot of magic. I don't want to risk it exploding when you need it most."

"Yeah, that'd be bad…" She didn't want to talk about why she really didn't want to be home. "What's in the bags?"

"Hm? Oh." She turned to the bags at her feet. "Some snacks to make sure you're eating and Harvest Valley if you want to play with me."

I nodded, quite happy to be invited back to the farm, and started to readjust the furniture while she plugged things in. It wasn't long before the two of us were sitting, snacking, farming up a storm, and fighting monsters. There was an immense amount of work to do in the game, but I loved it. It was simple, time consuming, and after letting things off my chest with Owen; I was enjoying it even more than I had before. Maybe it was a blessing that he had took the tablet. I wouldn't have been able to enjoy the fishing I decided to do after planting my final crop in my bag.

"You're in a much better mood today," she said in the silence and I looked away from the projection to her, confused.

"What do you mean?"

"You're smiling more, not brooding. I honestly thought you enjoyed brooding since I haven't seen you this happy… ever."

"Ah, no… Sometimes it's fun to brood… but no. I got some things off my chest earlier today. It was surprisingly helpful to my conscience."

"You talked more about Ciar and your duties that you mentioned briefly the other day?"

"Yeah, and some other things."

"Like that special someone?"

"That was a good portion of the conversation as well…"

"She seemed to get you good when she broke your heart," she commented, and I nodded.

"She did, but I was just as cruel. Unfortunately, it came down between my duty and my desires when it happened, and I chose duty."

She looked at me, surprised. "That's rough, buddy…"

"It wasn't pleasant… no." I turned back to my fishing as I felt her curiosity build. "I could share if you're still interested."

"I'm not going to say no, but I don't want to bring up bad memories."

A small chuckle came out. Bad memories were a good portion of my everyday life.

I decided to go ahead and tell the curious Seraph about Theodora. Our first real greeting and how cold I was to her to our little misadventures. The story wasn't a long one, but it did hurt a bit to finish on how things ended. It made me miss her a little more, but I kept those thoughts to myself. I would, in time, find someone else back in the kingdom. She was going to be a wonderful woman that I could trust and love more than I loved Theodora.

I turned to Éabha as our characters went into their separate cabins for the in-game night. "Do you think I made the correct decision?"

"Duty wise, yes definitely. Trust is important and you have a kingdom to rule and all that. Though I have to admit, banishment was a bit harsh, emotionally for the both of you. What was the other option you had to give her?"

"A dungeon cell."

"Never the fuck mind. Nope. Exile is way better. She goes off and starts anew, you start off a new phase in life. You never have to see each other again. But if she really, really did love you… she's probably still trying to get over you just like you are of her. She might even be pissed off for a while yet…"

"You don't think she could have died?"

"If she's the same woman as the one who wrote the notes I read; that girl is fucking fine. She knows how to survive, even if she's upset. She may have even got over you a few days after leaving the kingdom."

That hurt more than it should have.

"Oh, lose the face. It's normal for a girl to get over guys faster. Generally, within a few days. But that kind of love can take months."

"I'm not sure if that makes me feel better."

"Doesn't entirely matter how you feel about it. The girl is gone. You seem to have a direction, so just follow it."

"You have quite a bit of advice for this sort of thing."

"I read," she stated as she killed a monster in the forest and gave a slight cheer. "Awesome. That's worth a pretty gold piece. We can sell this for a larger inventory."

"And here I thought I was going to be forced to this small bag all game."

"Nope... So, you're feeling better about things? For real?"

"Overall, yes. My problems haven't vanished, clearly, we're both inside instead of being out there. But I'm fine... Why?"

"I was wondering about the scar on your chest. It seems to be inline with the one I saw on your back for a moment before you turned around."

"Oh... that." It probably wasn't that much of a surprise; it was rather large. I resisted the urge to touch it as a phantom pain came from it. "I got it the same day I got the ones around my eye."

She waited in silence for me to make the decision to tell her, hesitantly.

A small sigh escaped, but I decided to tell her. "The one under my eye was caused by Ciar breaking my sword. Not realizing that Aetherian was damaged, I charged it and it exploded, sending shards of it back at me. After that, Ciar got the upper hand, similar to how you did, and pinned me to the ground with his wings... Then he stabbed me through the chest with his power draining sword."

Her eyes went even wider before looking away. "So that's how you knew of Domrael's tactics... Wait! That scar is from – you have all sorts of organs and arteries there!"

"Believe me, I know. My father saved me using a large healing ability after Ciar ripped the blade out..." I hesitated slightly as the memories came flying back. Somehow, I left them behind with a swallow. "The one above my eye was from collapsing after putting up the barrier to protect the kingdom and blood loss. It nearly gave the court doctor, Helena, a panic attack since she thought I died from smashing my head against the altar."

"That was the night your dad died," she concluded with realization and I nodded, continuing my fishing to push past the grief, unable to speak. "I'm so sorry. I should have known that the first time you avoided talking about it."

"You didn't know." I gave a small huff, the pain slowly leaving. "Can I ask some questions about you since we're on the subject of personal topics?"

"You have every right to ask whatever you want. This is twice now that I've been oblivious to your feelings."

A small laugh came out. "Alright, but if you don't want to talk, just simply say so."

"You got it."

Her switch into an indifference was unnerving. "Are you okay?"

She passed me a look of confusion. "Yeah? Why wouldn't I be?"

"You seem upset today."

"Oh... well that's just because Dad being... him. You know?"

"Sort of... But I figured you would have liked using this time to be alone, not having anyone bother you."

"I... I don't entirely like being alone... I've spent a lot of alone time in that house. Never had the opportunity to enjoy time with..."

"A friend?" I suggested and she nodded.

"I've never had a friend, a real friend..."

"Why not?"

"I was homeschooled for most of my life. Part of it being my fault in my arrogance and the other being... a freak."

I looked at her, this time being the one incredibly confused. "What are you talking about? You're a genius but that certainly doesn't make you a freak."

"I don't think you can make that call without knowing something first."

I paused the game, setting the controller down, and gave her my full attention. "Know what?"

"I lied about something you asked me a while ago," she started, standing up and turned to me. She summoned her wings again, but this time, it wasn't her usual four or six. Eight, sky blue wings sat in their full regal grandeur before resting slightly. "I'm not like my dad... and because of two extra wings, he suffocates me in fear that I might disappear. To be called upon some great quest just like the very few eight-winged Seraphs before me, never to return home. There hasn't been an eight-winged Seraphinean born in almost a hundred years and from my understanding, they were all blessed or something... But I... I-I wasn't."

"And that's why you're a freak? Because you didn't have some blessing even though you have eight wings, just like your ancestor did?"

Her wings curled slightly in what seemed like irritation. "Eight-winged Seraphs are supposed to be almost divine beings, Orithina's soldiers on Orithin or something. Stupid superstition, but one that everyone on this island believes because there is truth to it. Adaptable, ungodly beautiful, and smart. Given gifts that a Seraphinean wouldn't have normally or had to work for like Seraph End. But I wasn't given any of them from what I've been able to figure out. The directors know these legends, know the secret I keep from most of the staff in the demesne, from other people, because I don't need or want anyone else on top of them to call me a freak. I'm not to their standards or the tales..."

"I couldn't tell you what these standards are that they compare you to, but I do know what I've seen and so take this as factual and not flirtation because you are, in fact, beautiful nor are you a freak. You're not like any other Seraphinean I've seen and certainly not like any Absalomian. You're smart. Like really, really smart, and far smarter than your peers to the point of them wanting to kill you to even attempt to get ahead. You're also adaptable on the battlefield and in games."

"Being smart in a few subjects is not all encompassing like Domrael was. He knew everything about everything." She sat in a huff on the couch, blushing slightly still from my words earlier. She didn't bother to hide her wings as she glared at them. "We're supposed to be tall and well endowed, or hunky if you're a guy, to show to others that we are perfection from physically to sexually to raise chances of making more eight-winged Seraphs. But that's just not how I happened to turn out. I'm nothing like Mum or Dad. A bit like the runt of a litter except I was the only one born. I'm a disappointment to Dad and probably Mum if she was still here. Sure, I learned quicker than the kids at school or the other directors and scientists in the labs... but that doesn't make up for everything else I lack."

I understood why she felt unsure. She had a legacy to carry, and she felt like she failed just by being different. "I get it. I got the same treatment from those in the castle, still do from time to time and while I could list things that you should work on, like conscious empathy thinking or the fact that you get really mean… none of that really matters. I see nothing that makes you a freak even if you're a bit different. I'm different from your stereotypical Absalomian, does that make me a freak?"

She looked to the floor. "No…"

"Exactly. So, you're a bit different. Maybe you're exactly as you need to be and it's not you who is wrong, but everyone else that thinks you are," I deducted, and she looked back at me in confusion.

"I don't understand. How could they all be wrong?"

"They're following a script of what should and shouldn't be. People aren't programs, machines; they're not even formulas. They can't be sculpted and drawn out. They're supposed to be different and unique with some similarities to help with bonding. It's wrong to expect things from someone just on appearance, legends, and myths that just aren't them. Even following scripted destinies and whatever can be faulty."

"How can someone's destiny be faulty?"

"I've had a few run-ins where I was supposed to be killed. But here I am, not dead. The point is, there are some expectations that are expected from us, like my duties as king and your duties as the heir to your director line. That's not something we can avoid, but we also have to be ourselves in the process, not whatever everyone else thinks we should be. If we can't be our own person, then we can't develop our talents to the fullest potential and be who we are supposed to be. Whether or not it's by divine design. Going by what everyone else says, going with the motions, not gaining some sort of footing, you're going to be swept away in a tragic tale of misfortune and misdirection.

"Your father, I'm sure, knew this and felt like you could thrive better if you were on your own and homeschooled instead of being picked on, diving into studies you took interest in. But he may not have realized that in doing so, you felt cooped up and caged. The expectations of his fellow coworkers dropping down on you as soon as you entered the scene with your first major breakthrough. Each thing you did, probably magnificently so, was never good enough for them when it should have been even though they couldn't do it. This is speculation, so I could be wrong, but what I can say for certain is that your father, and certainly your mother, are very proud of you. They don't think of you as some runt or failure. They love you for you and nothing less."

She stopped glaring at her wings and turned to me, teary-eyed. "You… you really think that? That he did what he could to make sure I could develop my own skills? Not because Mum died or because he thought I… was useless?"

"I'm sure that a small part was due to her death, such as not letting you leave the island."

"But… if that's true, why did he leave me alone after he pulled me from school?"

I frowned. "What do you mean?"

"There was an incident when I was a kid, about a year after Mum died. The kids were being mean, like they always were… but it was different that day. Seraphinean girls start puberty around the age of eight, so when I didn't, they noticed. They called me a boy and cut my hair in class – the teacher did nothing." I winced at the thought of how awful that must have been. "That was the last day I ever went to school… but it was the first day I noticed that Dad had been avoiding me. He could barely talk to me, look at me. He'd set up lessons and disappear… he was doing it before, but because I was at school, I never noticed. And when he was giving attention to all his students… I wondered if there was something wrong with me. I wanted what we had before Mum died because I loved him so much and looked up to him… But was it all fake? Was he forced to like me because of her? Is it still like that now?"

I held back a sigh, keeping neutral despite wanting to be disgusted at his past actions. "That wasn't your fault, Éabha. He wasn't avoiding you because you were worthless and didn't need his attention nor did he fake his love for you for your mother."

"Then what is it? Why would he do that if he didn't think-"

"He probably couldn't look at you because of how much you look like Iðunn," I explained before she could spiral. "It wasn't right, not even close, but my father did the same thing for a short bit before being punched in the face by Uncle Owen when my sister and I told him. When did he start giving you attention again?"

"After I broke down in front of Solaria… But it could still all be an act…"

"I doubt that greatly and I'm willing to bet that he hasn't forgiven himself for doing that, but he also wouldn't tell you unless you asked. He's a proud man, just like his daughter. He doesn't want you to think he can make mistakes for your sake. So, if you want to know the full truth, all you have to do is ask him. You're good at reading people, you'll know if he's lying or not."

"Maybe… Wait… Owen, you mean your general, he punched his king in the face?"

"I wasn't supposed to see it, but I walked in on them getting into an argument… He's got a really mean right hook."

"Oh, my gods… I knew he was bold but…"

"They grew up together, if there was something that needed to be said or done to one, the other wouldn't hesitate."

She laughed a small bit, probably picturing the image then grew silent as she twiddled her thumbs. She looked like a lonely kid, far from the brick wall she had established.

"Éabha…"

"Yeah?"

"What your dad did was wrong, but it wasn't because of you. Those people that bother or pick on you, they don't matter. You're perfect the way you are and beautiful both inside and out. You're talented in specific things and that's okay. If you're happy in those pursuits, then you should excel in them to the highest caliber you want to go. If you want to branch out, then do it for you and no one else. You have eight, ungodly, beautifully majestic wings that are nothing like I've seen – use them to get you to new heights that you want to explore. They were made for flying, not for people to grab onto and hold you down."

She gave out another laugh as she wiped a tear I didn't notice fall. "Gods, you're a cheesy fucker, aren't you?"

"I'm stating it as it is… cheesy or not. It's the truth. At least, the truth I believe in and know that you need to hear it."

"I pity Theodora for not being truthful to you. You would have blasted her ego to the moons in compliments like this…"

I sighed. "I was just… never mind."

"No, I'm happy that you appreciate me for who I am. It's very confident boosting for someone so insecure to have a king of a foreign nation speak so highly of me. But that doesn't make it any less cheesy."

I gave her a small smile and picked up the controller. "You ready to start playing again or do you have any more secrets you want to share?"

"No. I only have this large, feathery one…" Her wings disappeared which made her seem so small on the couch in comparison. We played for a few minutes before she started up conversation again. "Hey, Aerrow?"

"Yeah?" I asked, looking over at her slightly.

"Thanks for not being a prick."

I gave her a minor look of surprise before passing her a reassuring smile. "Anytime you need a monologue, you know where I am."

"I might need one in the future; depends on if it sinks in the first time. I'm a bit stubborn."

"I didn't notice…"

We played a little while longer, how long, I wasn't sure as the game seemed to make time meaningless, but the snacks she had brought were long gone. I checked the CT for the time on instinct. They weren't wrong, as usual. It was getting late, and the others were going to be back soon. Éabha had been here longer than I thought she was going to be. Not that I minded her company, but I was worried about her getting into trouble or Orpheal freaking out.

I paused the game. "I'm going to let your father know that you're here now if you're not going back soon. He might get mad, but it's better than him getting home and you're not there."

"He's going to be furious…" she grumbled before sighing. "But I guess I should be happy you didn't tell him right away… Ugh, it's not like I went on some magical adventure."

"No, but you did disobey my instruction to stay home," a stern voice answered her behind us, causing us both to jump. I got to a stand, drawing my blade only to stop halfway when I realized that it was Orpheal sitting on the other couch that wasn't moved. A very pissed off Orpheal, but Orpheal all the same. "Good evening, Aerrow…"

"Good evening, Orpheal…" I replied unsettlingly back as I let go of my blade. "How long have you been here?"

"About ten minutes. I figured it would be kind to let you finish your day while I recharged my ability before I take a certain someone back home." He turned his calm, scary demeanour to his daughter. "You are so grounded when we get home. Your grounding will cease in the event of something coming up or when the parts of the Zerach are completed and are needing to be installed."

"But why?! I didn't walk here or even get a ride-" Éabha tried to protest but was interrupted, still uncannily calmly by her father.

"I'm aware of how you got here. Congratulations on your new skill, but I told you to stay home. Instead, you came here."

"Yes, because-"

"We can discuss this at home as we have all night to do so. Pack it up. Now."

A string of incredibly quiet insults came from her that I could hear but was positive her father could not. She was about as happy as he was... But I hoped that the two of them could work it out – now that she had been given light on what I thought were his reasons for everything... hopefully they could.

Chapter Thirty-Four: The Eye of the Tyraulia

Atlamillia waited in annoyance for Helena to finish her healing session since the one last night wasn't enough.

"You're still refusing to tell me where you got these injuries from, eh?" Helena inquired for about the tenth time, but like the other times, Atlamillia was silent. She didn't need to be given shit for doing something reckless nor did she need the fifty thousand other questions that would come with it. "What about you, Eddy? Going to share?"

"Princess Atlamillia has asked me to be quiet on the subject, Dr. McGregor," Endymion answered politely as he was being healed by a student of hers.

"Asked or ordered?"

"Asked and I'm not going against that request."

Helena leaned closer to Atlamillia's ear, whispering, "Were you two doing something naughty? He is that betrothed boy, right?"

"We were not!" Atlamillia snapped. She should have been embarrassed, but all she felt was anger at herself for a dozen of reasons, one of them being towards the boy who was being loyal to her, but it only served to piss her off further. She couldn't tell if he was genuinely being nice or if it was because they were betrothed. She got off the medical table, swiping her cloak on her way out the door. "Focus on healing him. I'm sure Eudoxia is wondering why he didn't come home last night."

"I'm not done with you-"

"I'm fine and have other matters to attend to."

"If you start taxing yourself, you're going to regret it," Helena growled out, apparently not in the mood for her shit, but she simply didn't care, opening the door to let herself out.

"What's one more regret?"

She put on her cloak as a knight on the other side closed the door to the medical wing behind her. The hall laid along the mountain side, large windows letting in natural light and a view of a depressing city below that could barely be seen through the grey. It was relatively early, but the cold chill was swept into the castle due to the torrential rain outside. It rained in Asylotum since it had its own weather system. It wasn't easily forecasted using normal weather patterns however – but meteorologists had managed to figure out how to predict forty-eight hours ahead. She had received the warning of thunderstorms for that afternoon, but she still wasn't prepared for it.

Unlike the castle in Siofra, the castle she walked through was more primitive – not insulated properly since Asylotum didn't have the snowstorms that Absalom endured a good portion of the year. The lack of proper upgrades in renovating left her horrible mood even worse since she wasn't just grouchy, but cold. The cloak didn't keep out the dampness in the air nor did it help her stay cozy. She wanted to go curl up in a fire since she doubted being by one would do anything.

A new thought occurred to her as she wandered to the window, away from everyone and stared out at the rain. It was perfect for training. Stressful conditions of being a fire-light elemental all within the middle of her opposite elements with the added bonus that nothing could attack her. Maybe Orithina was still helping her along even though she couldn't accept her gift.

"I'll keep you updated for when the thunderstorm moves along..." Lucilla told her, but uncertainty was in her voice.

"Something wrong?"

"I don't want you getting hurt. You might be limiting yourself by practicing too much."

"I don't have much of a choice now that I've given up-"

"Exactly. You are a mortal being with mortal needs. You need rest." It was more of a statement over a generalization.

"I'm fine."

"No, you're not. You are exhausted physically, magically, and mentally. I let it go this far and you almost died in that trial-"

"I said I was fine," she growled before closing the link between them. A mutter for seemingly no one but herself came out as she continued on her way towards her study. "I know what I'm doing…"

The walk was cold, quiet, and empty. The children were in their class and she wasn't sure where Aoife or Dani were, but was happy that she hadn't run into them. She could only pretend to be in a decent mood for so long and she didn't want to spoil their delightful moods.

She peeked over her shoulder and found that, unlike her forcefulness to see Helena earlier, Bretheena had disappeared completely. She was admittedly grateful to be left alone, but to where the woman had run off to was another matter.

Maybe she got into another fight with Jakob. It seemed to be the only way to distract her, and she knew that her other two retainers were either sleeping or preparing for the day as they got back late.

She got to her study where the paperwork for the day had been laid out, but no other sign of anyone else being there remained as the lights of the room were off. She turned them on, lighting the fireplace easily to give her some sort of warmth back into the room. The dry wood crackled, trying to spit its sparks beyond the hearth and she turned to the mantle where a few trinkets sat: an old, wooden Dragon Knight doll, an endless Absalomian knot on a stone plaque, and a creeping ivy. She didn't know who they originally belonged to or how old they were, but there they sat, little treasures, immune to time.

The door opened without her consent as she walked to the front of her desk. She looked over to see Citlali come in and she leaned against the desk, not amused, but knew that he was going to show up at some point in the day. He stopped a few paces from her, giving a small look over before looking her in the eye. "You should be resting."

"You want your money or not?" She asked, a bit bitterly but true to always he wasn't bothered by her tone, staying relatively neutral and casually respectful.

"I'd like my employer to keep giving me work. She can't do that if she's dead."

She rolled her eyes. "Details of your mission?"

"The routine or the oddity first, Princess?"

"The norm, then the oddity, please. Have the monsters changed much? New Outland Pits? Any varieties?"

"Some of the monsters have been powered by the same malice that Ciar uses. Using the magic scanners at the abandoned bases and my own recordings of monsters' magic levels with a MFM before and now. There has been a significant change in Typoregula and above class monsters, though surprisingly, any monsters that are on the lower Typoregula scale and below has no change at all."

"He's probably saved his power for anything worth his time…" Atlamillia pondered.

"It's a brash strategy at best. Your soldiers, guards, and knights are aware of the danger that the higher classed monsters can be."

She eyed him. "What do you mean?"

"If I were him, I would have made the lower classed monsters be a threat. A hidden dagger that could abuse the lowered guard of your defenders. Giving powerful beings more strength is a wasted opportunity."

"So, that means he either acted brashly as you said, or he doesn't have a tactician."

"At least during the time he was north if he's not strategically inclined."

"Do you know for certain that he's not near Absalom?"

"The last of the readings of when he infused his powers to the monsters was shortly after the shield dropped. Any other inflictions of his magic have been recorded towards Seraphina over time, but they were faint. Was it him or one of his followers? It's hard to say."

"And of the Outland Pits?"

"No new ones have been made on or near the surface. Noelani couldn't sense anything within your borders."

"It must have been difficult to only travel on your vigorid. She must be tired."

"She enjoyed the Kalokairtas heat of Absalom without the cold nights that our home is famous for."

That was probably because most of Fiery was a desert; Absalom actually retained most of its heat.

"She would love to see the princess if you have the time to visit the stables. She still has that pebble you gave her and plays with it from time to time."

"She... does?" She didn't think vigorids had such complex thoughts being that they were snake-bug hybrids. But she guessed that was her failure of assuming – something she had been doing quite a lot.

"She does... Princess?"

"Yes?"

"You seem more troubled lately, not that I have been back for long, but speaking with others around the castle, it's quite apparent."

"Just concerns over the future, nothing more."

He crossed his arms, not believing her. "Is that so? It wasn't something that led you to that place with the Divine Knight?"

"What was the worrisome issue you wanted to share?" She asked, dodging his questions, but the look on his face made her think he already had an idea without needing to ask at all. Just as he knew back then in the library. He didn't want to know, but he was guessing more all the same.

He took a seat in the chair beside her without an invitation, his presence both gave her a sense of calmness and anxiety. His expression hid his thoughts. "Perhaps it's not strange, but from my understanding, the king and you are the only Fionns alive, yes?"

"Yes..."

"Are you sure?"

What the hell was he trying to get at? "I'm positive. There are a few crypts empty in the tomb, but only because their bodies couldn't be recovered for one reason or another. Why?"

"I spotted someone on the western coast," he started, looking up at her. "Their physical appearance from afar: red-burgundy hair, orange eyes. Reminded me a bit of the late king and the current one from the moments I caught a glimpse of him."

"That's impossible. It had to be an illusion spell."

"No, Princess, I don't believe so. Outland Monsters seemed particularly interested in him, and his movements were similar to King Solomon's in a way. Unfortunately, by the time I was able to teleport for a closer look, he was gone and the monsters with him."

"He didn't have a dragon though," she stated, looking for confirmation and Citlali gave a small shake of his head.

"Not one that I saw... If it wasn't a living relative, is it possible your tomb was broken into?"

"Absolutely not." Her answer was meant to be strong, but it wavered, and she bit her lip. It shouldn't have been but... They had only been concerned about keeping Ciar from taking power from the dead inside. Who's to say someone didn't sneak in and steal a corpse puppet. "I'll have Helah check the tomb to make sure…"

"That would be best. I don't know enough about necromancy to advise you, but I'm more than certain that the dead can still talk if one is ambitious enough. Family secrets, things they've seen from the other side, they've seen while alive. Things that no one alive knows."

She hated the implications of that thought. "Did they look like they were a shambling corpse while they fought?"

"No, very alive, but they also had armour – so caution is my advisement."

She nodded.

"I've also taken liberties to investigate this more on my own within circles I trust and vaguely so. Perhaps this person is a lost family member finally come home or an impostor."

"Any lost member has been gone for more than five hundred years. They have no right to be called family if they've cowered away when this kingdom needed them at the time of my father's coronation." Her words were just shy of venom. "Please keep me informed on the development. Perhaps it is someone who's studied closely to the family fighting art and are wanting to cause more chaos by posing as someone dead."

He gave a small nod in agreement and she pulled out his payment from the small Dagdian bag on her belt, giving it to him.

"This covers the job and some extra to pass the time during your break until I can get your next assignment."

"Thank you, Princess. It's always a pleasure working for your family," he said, almost amused as he took his payment and put it in his own Dagdian bag. A small smile formed on her face for a moment that he didn't miss. "Maybe I should compliment you more often to force you to smile once and a while; your subjects would appreciate it."

"I doubt it has much weight to it," she growled, rolling her eyes as a knock came from the door and before she could tell them to come in or wait, Elias barrelled in. His hair was a complete disaster, more than usual, and a couple of books sat in his arm.

"I'm so sorry, Atlamillia. I didn't realize the time and-" He stopped apologizing as he noticed that he had just walked in on their meeting. "Oh, hi. Um… welcome back?"

"Somethings never change…" Citlali commented, standing from the chair. He gave a wave of goodbye as he started to walk out the open door. "I'll let you know if something happens. If you need me, I'll be about – trying to find the warmest place in this castle."

"If you find it, let me know…" Atlamillia told him, somewhat jokingly, but not entirely, and he gave a small agreement before leaving. She turned to Elias. "Something come up?"

"Er, no, just… late for the shift retainer care…"

"Shift?"

"Yeah… um. We figured that we should be doing more of a rotation to protect you that way you can still send us on missions and not have what happened yesterday… you know, happen."

"Close the door," she spat as she couldn't hold back her anger and he did so promptly. "I don't need twenty-four-hour protection."

"We know but-"

"There's no but. What happened was a fluke, nothing more."

"You never explained to us what happened so how are we supposed to know that?" he asked, surprisingly boldly. "We promised Aer we'd protect you. We can't do that if we don't know the threats."

"There is no threat!" She took a small breather to lower her voice. "I went ahead and did something stupid but enlightening. That's it."

He frowned, waiting a moment to see if she would break before sighing when he knew she wouldn't. "Fine… but we're probably going to keep this up for a bit anyways. You might get a benefit from it."

There was no benefit in never being left alone. "How exactly have you implemented your new setup? Do you just switch at times?"

"Mazaeh and Bretheena are shopping for CTs as we speak, protective cases so that they won't break. Oh, Bretheena told me to give these to you." He presented her with the two books he had. "They're tomes for conjuring."

She took them. "Thanks… so you are all going to have CTs… great…"

"Communication, plus with the next phase starting soon, we thought being around to listen in on any mishaps would be beneficial."

He clearly didn't want to stay on the subject further. "How are the tunnels?"

"The plan is working well. Some soldiers have also been recruited to protect them as spares to lessen the stress of the shifts."

At least no one had to order that development. "Do you think we could have more tunnels protected through the use of regular soldiers?"

"No… that I don't think we can afford." He sighed, "The monsters are fine for the knights but having soldiers without assistance is like handing the bloody things a free meal. They aren't the typical drones. The ones that we saw were intelligent which a soldier wouldn't have the specialties to fight against."

"Son of a bitch…" she muttered out; he gave no response to her outburst. It was good news that they were aware of the problem, but the coincidence wasn't just coincidence anymore. Ciar was exploiting the tunnels, or at least, someone was. "Thank you for the report, Elias."

"It's no problem and if you need more investigating done, one of us that aren't on duty can go."

"Perhaps…" It wasn't a bad system they've created as it also meant that if things got hairy, two of them could rest at a time and switch out when needed. But she highly doubted it would ever get that far. She opened the first book and was a bit surprised to find it written in Ancient Dragon. One of the sprites must have helped in finding it as she knew Bretheena didn't have a clue on what was written.

"Good gods, it's all chicken scratch."

"No, this is Ancient Dragon."

"Will something that old help?"

"Maybe… maybe not." She read over some of the words before sitting behind her desk. "I recommend taking a seat; I'm going to be racking your brain for assistance if some of these directions get strange."

"Don't know how helpful I'll be, but sure. Glad to help in anyway I can." He sat, happily so as she read. There were a few moments before he broke the silence again. "So, are you going to tell us about what-"

"No."

"Maybe we could help with whatever is bothering you."

"If you can figure out why some of my magic skills are lacking far behind others, I might tell you what happened."

"That's actually easier to answer than you think. You're seventeen, there's a reason why the Dragon Knight Trial is available to only those going to be eighteen that year or older. You're not fully developed magically… at least, that's what my school taught me."

"School… what do they teach at school?" She inquired as she turned the page, finding only advice that she had tried and failed on multiple occasions. It was an interesting point he had brought up and not one she had considered. She had always thought and been taught that the trial was set for a year after becoming an adult so one could experience adulthood and take the time to consider doing such a dangerous job. "Do they talk about the Dragon Knight Trials often? Magic development along with biology?"

"There is a course that students can choose to take as an elective. They talked about the process of skills and development in preparation for the possibly of being a guard, soldier, knight, or teacher. You don't reach a natural maturity of your capable skills until around eighteen, and that varies from person to person. Some are early, some are late. Once you've reached this level your skills can only grow from there for years and centuries at a time if you practice – but not everything is available to you until you've matured magically."

"I see… and from your understanding, where do I sit?"

"Atla, that was two years ago since I took that course. I don't remember everything from it."

"But you know some clearly, so with your best judgement?"

He squirmed as she looked away from her book to him. "Well, in some areas you're more than advanced. This would mean you developed early… but with your inability to simply conjure magic without a conduit suggests that you're late… like really late if not inadequate to using magic well. I've seen you use magic, so don't think that I mean you suck. But if I'm honest, it's like you've locked to a rigid system and you're just not capable of releasing magic naturally through it."

"I've been training for a long time… I suppose it's not unreasonable to think that system limited my growth."

"Yeah, you're missing the raw chaos of it. You're kinda stuck in this order of how things work and then on top of whatever pressures being a princess entails, it just works against you…"

"Chaos, eh…" She knew how to get that raw potential out… but it was going to take a while. She turned back to the book and read exactly as he explained, just in fancier terms. "So being in less than desirable circumstances, practicing, is what I should be doing?"

"That is a way… but you shouldn't force the matter. I know you can do it with time."

"I don't have time."

"You do have time," he tried to argue, but he didn't know what she knew. None of them did. "You need to rest on top of the practice. That is what that class taught me. Proper rest allows your abilities to grow without hurting yourself, just like exercising and-"

"Has the thunderstorm started?"

"Uh, yes but… I think it will be over soon. How did we get here?"

She didn't answer him, not wanting to, and switched back to the book and asked him to demonstrate one of the strategies it suggested.

00000

She wished she were numb to the freezing rain that pelted her skin. Her outfit was not appropriate to the torrential downpour that hadn't ceased in the hours she had been outside. The light of day was long gone with only the training grounds' few lights remaining. They didn't glow very brightly on the walls leaving most of the wet, sandy space in a depressing hue, but she didn't care.

The cold. The rain. None of it mattered or was a negative view to her. She was getting somewhere; she could feel it. She had managed to use the cleansing gift through her sword which had substance to it and had managed to do it consistently. The lack of armour was just proof that she was doing it through that single conduit, and it was controlled.

Now after hours of being tortured by the weather, practicing what the books had suggested and through Elias and Aoife helping her early on, she felt the natural flow of magic she had been missing. Now all she had to do was figure out how to get it out just as naturally.

She needed to form a sphere of light and she was going to throw it at the training target. That was her goal. Or at least, that was the plan to signify the end of her day's worth of training. Now she wasn't so sure if she could take that extra step. Her head hurt and she was exhausted from the use of so much magic and concentration without a break. But she couldn't break now. She had to keep going. If not to send that target a gift, at the very least she could create her orb.

"Atlamillia, you've done enough," Lucilla tried to protest for the millionth time, not outside like she was. She sat by the entrance way, watching her in paranoia. *"Please stop."*

"You know how much progress I've made. If I stop now, I might not figure this out again for who knows how long. I can't give this up."

"At the cost of hurting yourself and if I tried to force you, you'd only get hurt more so please, just stop. Come inside and get warm-"

She blocked her out and focused on her skills. She didn't need the distraction. Several minutes went by as the pathway started to build itself in her mind and body, connecting and flowing. The raw energy that was trapped inside wasn't so trapped anymore. She almost had it.

"Atla," Aoife called from behind her just as she was about to form it, startling her. She turned around and saw her and Dani with hair matted to their faces from the rain that fell around them. Their clothes quickly becoming as soaked as hers. "What are you still doing out here?"

"Training." She hadn't meant the answer to be so short, but she found it difficult to have the air to speak.

"We know but…" the girl trailed off and Dani picked up where she left off.

"We're worried. It's not good for you to be in the rain and cold. Especially not for hours like this, your body isn't made for this weather."

Atlamillia knew that which is why the rain made for such a perfect training environment. She noticed movement from behind them and saw Citlali leaning against the doorframe with Lucilla not far. Both were barely lit by the lights at the entrance. She tsked. "Glad to know Citlali doesn't listen when you don't throw money at him."

Aoife gave an uncharacteristic snarl, coming forward. "This is not about listening! We thought you had come inside hours ago and when we found out you hadn't… Atla, this is suicidal!"

"It's progress," she replied neutrally only to be retorted at.

"At what cost?! There is no progress worth this torture!"

"It's not torture. I'm fine and I've managed to actually get somewhere."

"You have?" Dani asked, more curious than angry and Atlamillia nodded, turning inward.

"Watch."

"Atla, there is no need-" Aoife tried again, sounding more worried than angry, but she wasn't listening as she connected the dots internally.

She wasn't going to just summon a light. No. She was going to give it substance equivalent to that of the Cleansing Gift in a condensed form. Something she could use without having to say a prayer to Orithina for a smaller group of monsters. Something that Aoife might be able to expand on further. It might have been risky to try it, but this was the only opportunity that was capable of producing such a thing. As she willed it, light formed in her ungloved hands. It gave off a warm embrace that even she wasn't expecting to be so strong. The magic brought over her two friends, seemingly drawn to it.

"This is... wow..." Dani was left speechless.

Aoife gave her a bright-eyed look of glee. "I don't know what this is, but you did it!"

Atlamillia couldn't hold back a blissful smile. All of her hard work, years of practicing, hours of training in the pouring, freezing rain. It finally paid off. She did it! She didn't need Orithina's-

A sharp pain ripped through her head and body, causing her to lose concentration on her sphere. Dizziness made her lose her balance as the two girls became four. Her breathing was difficult, her chest constricting.

"Atlamillia?" Dani asked as she came closer, catching her sway. "Are you-"

She didn't get to finish as Atlamillia started coughing, trying to get air and succeeded a bit. She pulled her arm away and found blood covered a good portion of the white sleeve she had coughed into. The rain tried to wash it away, quickly taking most of it. She grimaced, but her discontent of the outcome of progress wasn't given a chance to express itself further as blood blocked her breathing more. She coughed harshly and her body revolted at the action. Her legs gave out as she slipped from Dani's loose hold onto the wet sand.

"Get Helena!" Dani screamed over her shoulder as Aoife knelt next to Atlamillia.

A warm feeling of healing magic came from the brunette and she stopped coughing a tiny bit, finding it slightly easier to breathe, but nothing more. She knew this feeling once before; she went farther than she had meant to go.

"It's not working…" Aoife started to panic. "I can't fix this!"

No, she couldn't. She wasn't skilled enough yet.

"What am I supposed-?!"

"Aoife, it's alright," Atlamillia muttered out, trying to reassure her. "It's something that's happened before; I'll be- ah!" The few words were more than what her body was willing to spare the energy for as another sharp pain ran up her spine.

"You idiot! You shouldn't have been trying so hard!"

Perhaps she shouldn't have, but it wasn't because she was writhing in pain. The looks on her and Dani's faces were far worse. They were terrified. She went to apologize only for a sharp noise to escape instead. The darkness taking hold as her name was screamed by Aoife.

00000

"We were about to leave when the knight said she was leaving behind her gift." Endymion's voice came to her ears as Atlamillia started to wake. "She went back to the pedestal to receive it and there was a magic influx for a few minutes. I think she was talking to someone, she muttered about not wanting something and didn't respond when I asked what was wrong. Eventually, the knight asked her if she wanted to reject the gift and she said yes. I don't know what the gift was… but after her answer, the magic disappeared, and she lost her ability to stand and was pale."

"That sounds like she was offered one of those residual gifts locked away…" Bretheena pondered. "But why would she give that up?"

Atlamillia decided to answer her, opening her eyes to find her friends, retainers, Citlali, Helena, and Endymion standing and sitting about a separate medical room. "Because it cost my mortality."

They all turned to her in surprise as she sat up a bit, much to the protests from Helena as she rushed over. She waved her off and Aoife asked the big question. "You were offered to be a divine being? A god? But… why? Why would you give that up?"

"Because she doesn't want puppets and pawns," Citlali answered when Atlamillia couldn't find her words to explain the horrible proposition of what it would come to. "Most gods don't see us anything more than opportunities to further their goals. I'm sure that somewhere down the line, taking the throne by force would be inevitable."

Aoife looked at her, horrified. "Is… that true?"

"I don't know," Atlamillia lied and internally she was grateful that Citlali had offered his own explanation. "Maybe, maybe not. But it doesn't matter now. It showed me that I have so far to go and because I gave up the easiest path… I have to compensate."

"Compensate for what?!" She snapped, surprising everyone in the room. "At what point is it fine to push yourself to the brink of death for power?!"

"It's not about power. It's about protecting people I care about."

"Well I don't know about everyone else, but I don't want to be protected by someone who is just going to die! You mock heroes doing stupid things and yet you did just that. Something stupid for protecting and you know what? I don't agree. There's no victory. Residual gifts or duties, or whatever! I don't care! If you just die after protecting against some threat, Ciar or some other asshole down the road, it doesn't matter – no one wins! The people left behind; what about them? I don't like heroes because the people they leave are left knowing that the heroes don't get to share that protection! We can't celebrate together if you're dead."

Atlamillia was left surprised as she had never thought about it that way. She mocked the stupidity of a hero's actions, having a death wish, but she never thought about it from the perspective of the protected. But it was her duty to protect, that was the whole point of her going so far… It just never occurred to her about what happened afterwards. It never came up because even simple future thoughts and the planning of it hurt too much to think about losing it all should she perish to succeed in her duty.

"Atlamillia… if you die just to protect us; I will never forgive you." Aoife looked on the verge of tears, but Atlamillia didn't need to see her face to feel the weight of her words.

Something in her heart ached at the thought of the girl never forgiving her. It hurt more than she had expected it to and if she were honest, if anyone else had said it, it wouldn't have had the same effect. Her head was nodding to her promise before she knew it. "I'm sorry…"

"Don't be sorry. Tell us what we can do to help you not die."

"I…" A small huff of amusement came out at her gusto. "Okay… Citlali?"

"Yes, Princess?" The Fiery asked, stepping forward.

"I need you to find more places like the trial around Absalom while keeping track of whispers. I'll keep training normally, but I know that there are trials and places of divine interest out there… Time is limited, and I can't tell you why I feel that, but it is. The more help, the better, safely this time as well."

He gave a nod. "I'll be ready to depart in a couple of days."

"Thank you."

Chapter Thirty-Five: The Spiffing Seraphs

Owen took another look at his scouting map as Missiletainn landed next to Infinite Spring for a drink and rest. They had been out for hours, searching, scanning, and determining if the area had anything of value. He activated a field of chaos above them, blocking out the sun for some shade. They shouldn't have been surprised by the heat, it was after all the later half of Octius – the peak time of Kalokairtas, and they were near the equator of the planet, but yet here they were, surprised by the hot day.

They were just about done their scouting, the planned part at least. There was a place just outside of the area that caught both of their interests. A faint magic coming from a bit farther in the woods.

"*I wonder if it has to do with the bog girl,*" Missiletainn shared as he straightened up, swallowing the last gulp of water in his mouth. "We aren't far from where she was found as we've travelled this far."

"No, we aren't… but it's a concern that we might get in over our heads."

His partner gave a hint of a head movement that was equivalent to a shrug for dragons. He wasn't bothered at the sense, just as Owen wasn't. It wasn't a powerful source, just one that piqued their interest. "If it's zealots, we'll deal with them. If it's not, then it might just be a cave."

A sigh came out of Owen. "I'll be a bit disappointed if it's just a cave. That's all we've been finding. Nothing but trees, rocks, and rube Seraphs."

"Mighty tough Seraphs with guns pointed at the wrong people… It's almost like they don't know that we, personally, have helped this kingdom from being overrun by monsters for years."

"They might not," Owen humoured. The conversation was rather pointless, but it was nice to talk, or rather complain, about something other than trees, rocks, and caves. "Prideful and arrogant; it's hard to say what they know and don't. We can't change that about them nor force them to help us, just like how they can't force us to help them if the barrier, gods forbid, did get breached."

"I won't help them, but you would."

"Only because I vowed to do so…" His voice was strained with regret. His conscience wouldn't be bothered if they had got what they so dearly wanted

– but that vow he took years ago stuck. "But that's a turmoil for a different time. You have a long enough break?"

"For now, yes." Missiletainn stretched like a cat. "I'll get more of a break once we make it back to the capital and you're speaking with Orpheal."

"While you do that, please don't torment Jimmy… I know you have fun, but he doesn't."

"That fat squirrel needs exercise. I'm helping him," the dragon scoffed. "I'm sure Éabha is feeding him more than usual."

Owen removed the shade overhead. The sun's heat returned harshly, causing them to squint slightly as they got used to the light again. It was always hard to go from dark to light. "If Jimmy dies because you ran him until his heart wore out, she will be very upset with you."

"It's a squirrel."

"I'll be upset that you killed Jimmy. That squirrel is a legend."

"To you and only you. Jimriel is literally entertainment for the rest of us."

He might have been right. Maybe Owen was the only one who thought Jimriel, the fat, massive, albino, Seraphinean squirrel was a legend… But if it weren't for that squirrel, he wouldn't have got Fostri down for a performance a few years ago. Fostri was very squirrel-like and Jimriel was Owen's inspiration.

Jimmy was a legend.

Missiletainn took off again, keeping relatively low as they went towards the sense. The life-filled spring to their left was a contrast to the bog that was on the right, divided by a small wood. There wasn't anything of interest in the wetlands, just a few birds, that was until a clearing seemingly out of place came into view. A large collection of rocks looked like several large boulders were dropped on top of one another from a high height, making a significant hill of rock chunks that sat in the middle. Vines grew through them with a few flowers decorating the surface.

They landed as the magic sense was somewhere in the rock. But standing in front of it, the magic felt off. Missiletainn etched towards it, his black and yellow scales raising on their own to show off their slight purple undertone in discomfort like the hair on the back of Owen's neck.

It wasn't Daemonias magic, that was clear, but it wasn't like anything they were familiar with either. Not Dagdian, not elemental… It felt almost like a life force, something that he was sure that if any of his knights were there, wouldn't have been able to sense it quite like he had as they weren't necromancers. But they would have noticed the rawness to it – reminding him a bit of his nephew's magic. Untrained and just pure energy, but not quite that either. It was old, archaic, and unruly, following its own laws that weren't fathomable to either of them.

Owen got off, the magic from the rock somewhat stained the earth even several metres from the source. The grass sounded different under his boots, similar to the grass in Elwood Garden. It was tall, thick, and unfazed as he moved through it. He reached the rocks and found a hole that laid between them. He looked around the area a bit more before finding that to be the only way in, but it wasn't a big enough space for Missiletainn to continue farther.

Should he continue or should they leave it alone?

"You should head inside; we need to make sure this place isn't of use for Ciar."

Owen gave a slight nod. *"I'll be back shortly."*

His partner laid down as Owen slipped through, barely fitting between the rocks. The air cooled swiftly as the rock path went in one direction before switching in on itself like a maze. The rock wall held no light as he could barely see their edges and faces but was thankful that he could see that thanks to his elemental advantage. Eventually, the back and forth winding, and downward path stopped into a much larger cavern.

He pulled out a flashlight from his belt and turned it on. The magic surrounded him like the strangely carved and shaped walls of the room, obvious and otherworldly. It was light and dark magic on top of the living magic, woven together in perfect harmony that put his and Solomon's intricate form from days past to shame. The carved walls were cut perfectly into a cube, the entrance he had come from was greatly damaged, but clearly had beams etched in, a trapezoid on each end that would have outlined the large doorway long ago, matching the size of Absalom's.

He turned ahead to the large pillars that held the ceiling. They were cracked, but their rounded nature was almost organic as it curved from a thicker base to that of a slightly thinner top before forming out into what he could only describe was a lotus flower. Other carvings decorated the pillars themselves, but whatever they were supposed to be, he couldn't tell as he drew to the closest one.

Perhaps a more trained eye to the details such as Azarias's would have been able to figure out the columns.

He pulled out his CT to call him only to find that there was no service. A small noise escaped his lips in acceptance and continued through the ancient path towards a raised rock at the end. The light reflected off of gemstones that were still embedded into the rock pillars, some of them no longer in their spots but on the smooth, blue stone floor.

"This place is…" Missiletainn started but like him, was speechless.

There was nothing like the architecture or culture anywhere on Orithin. They had been to all corners of the planet, but there was a faint resemblance to the room to that of Ley Line Temple in Dagda. The doorway to the great library and the large, tiled flooring being the only resemblance. Other than that, nothing else matched the room he was in now.

He turned the flashlight to the ceiling and stopped in awe. Carvings and stones decorated it in a beautiful mosaic that he had seen in the holy water pools in Orithina's Temple and the solariums in Ley Line Temple and the castles in Absalom and Asylotum. Though, a small bit of it reminded him of the gateways to Asylotum – only this one wasn't done in dragon stone. The Black Phoenix was etched across the ceiling in a day filled sky, mirroring a similar looking dragon but in white soaring through a night sky. The land encircling the edges of the ceiling was like one was looking up to see the dance between the two of them.

He had never heard of a dragon that was the opposite of the Black Phoenix, even Absalomian Phoenix Dragons weren't as large or coloured like such as they tended to be reds and oranges like the mythical bird they were named after. This one had gold-yellow veins decorating white scales, the opposite to the red veins on black scales of the Black Phoenix. They shared the same colour of purple on their talons.

He managed to lower the light from the ceiling and continued forward, wary of a feeling that had crept into him while he was occupied. This place was old, without question, but something had happened within the walls that surrounded him, and he wasn't sure why he was so certain about it.

The feeling only grew as he walked to the end of the room where a stone block sat away from the wall. Behind it was some sort of altar and what looked like a pool, but whatever was placed in or around it had long disappeared. He looked to the stone and his light showed an object abandoned. A figure carved from stone to look like a person. Speckles of black and red paint were on the body. He wasn't sure how he missed it but picked it up out of curiosity. Suddenly, a familiar pulse of energy went through his body.

The figure in his hand now had its full painted décor on it, showing off long, white hair with parted long bangs and golden eyes. A painted on black and red gown decorated its stone body and was lit up by lights elsewhere in the room. Movement came from in front of him and he moved swiftly and silently out of the way and off to the side, next to a column. A girl with dark hair, braided to tame its messy curls held the same doll he had. She wore clothes that were like priestess robes, but not quite, and prayed next to another girl who looked similar to her. A second doll was held in her hands that was much more familiar to the depiction of Orithina, also with long, white hair but with short bangs and a white, gold, and purple dress.

Neither of them seemed to notice his presence as he looked around the room. There was a tense air to it that wasn't there before. Magic orbs sat in sconces on the pillars that were beautifully painted in stories of other gods he vaguely knew of and others not at all. Ancient Dragon was scratched above and below the pictures in words he couldn't read.

He turned back to the stone that the girls were knelt in front of and noticed the altar in front of them. It held flowers, gifts, and a fountain with water tranquilly moving through it. A unified painting of Orithina and Valrdis holding hands like a sibling picture sat in the blank space of the wall. They looked both fondly and seriously in every direction of the room, their eyes following him as he shifted uncomfortably and silently hid more.

A desperate call in Ancient Dragon came from the entrance in an accent he was not familiar with. Not that he had heard many people speak the language, but it was unique to be sure. He turned to it as the two girls had. The entrance way, tall and wide, was large enough that even the largest of dragons could fit through if they didn't mind the cramped interior that was similar to the vaults under Siofra Castle. "Ahura! Ta'Ur! Tiid eínunt esos dýuo práxite edic?! Emebis échet naque fýnquo!"

"Emebis eínssexi prosantes sen elpes ótut Valrdis kat Orithina thaitexi-" the first girl started to protest, leaving the doll on the altar as a woman with the same dark curls as the girls came through the door, exasperated. Her clothes were dirty, and blood dyed her skirt like someone had bled onto her lap.

"Ta'Ur! Esos anóiltum korítella!" The woman interrupted, swiftly coming to the end of the room. She wiped her eyes and now that she was closer, Owen could see the heavy makeup that lined her eyes was partially washed away from tears that stained her cheeks. She grabbed the girls by the wrists, urgently. "Élani epíper!"

"Perínere-!" Ta'Ur squeaked out as she went to reach for her doll, but it was just out of reach.

The room shook, knocking the three of them off their feet as Owen braced against his pillar. Growls came from the entrance. He went to draw Eclipse to defend the family but was frozen in place by a wave of despair nothing like he had felt before. The mother's face went hard as she tried to push through it, shoving the girls towards the nearest pillar. A purple shield of some sort was created in front of her as a massive stream of energy ripped through the walls that he knew far too well as the Seraph End ability. He wanted to scream at them to hide, but knew that if they heard him, they would only freeze. The energy was swift and blinding as he hid behind the pillar, not aware of how many walls it had traveled through to get to the interior.

A small whimper came to his ears as the light died, letting him know that he was still alive and unharmed. He looked around the pillar, searching the room, but only found one of the girls, Ahura, hiding behind another column. Or at least, most of her. Her legs were sliced and gone from the energy, not hidden by the pillar's shadow.

Ash started to snow down as she looked around, still not noticing him as he went over to her. A terrified expression was on her face as she tightly held onto her doll. "Ta'Ur... Mitérater... Ópubi-?"

"It's-" he started, kneeling in front of her only to see movement in the corner of his eye.

They snapped to it as a monster came through the entrance, stopping her mutters. He analyzed its signature to figure out the best course of action. It was an Outland Monster of an extremely long-legged bear, five and half metres in height at the shoulder as it sauntered in. It was nothing like he was used to.

He dashed ahead, leaving the girl and his flashlight behind, sword drawn and ready. Tendrils came from his field that formed underfoot, but like a shade, the monster went through him and his defences like they didn't exist. He spun around as the monster pinpointed the girl in moments and charged. It's fangs similar to a tyraulia within its massive jaws bit into the girl's lower half. An agonizing scream pierced his ears as he watched both the girl and the monster go through him and out the entrance way. It left him shook to the core.

The room changed back to the uncoloured, flashlight lit room. No blood was on the floor, no ash falling. Just the cracks, the damaged doorway, and him. He did everything he could to keep standing, breathless.

"Owen, what's wrong?" The familiar voice of Missiletainn went through their link and Owen swallowed. *"What happened?"*

"A memory…" He turned to the doll still in his hand, clasping to it tightly. *"Did I bring my grimoire?"*

"Yes… What happened to you? You shut down the link and were gone for the last five minutes."

"I'll let you know when I do…" he said, putting his sword away.

He shouldn't have felt responsible for what happened, but he did. He felt everything, saw everything, yet he could do nothing. He went back to where he had dropped his flashlight, where Ahura been moments… no… thousands of years ago.

Picking it up, he turned to the altar. *"What do you do with something that belonged to someone long dead, but you don't know the customs of treasured objects when they die?"*

"The doll belonged to Ta'Ur…" Missiletainn was sifting through the memories of what Owen witnessed. *"You should call Io, let her team of archaeologists and anthropologists deal with it. These people died a long time ago, they might know more about their practices."*

He agreed, setting the doll back where he found it, but it felt wrong. He wanted to give it a resting place, not to leave it abandoned like it had been before, left to the horror and the inability to share what it had witnessed until now. But he did leave it behind, looking up at the blank altar wall, knowing what was there before with a bit of disgust.

Two little girls, praying to both of them, and neither one protected them from their fate. It was this very reason why he didn't worship like his friends had and still did. The gods helped who they saw fit to help, it didn't matter how devoted one was.

He left the cavern, taking the opportunity of having signal again once outside to call his old friend. It was a quick explanation of what they had found, but he didn't share the details with Io of what he witnessed, ending the call. Missiletainn handed him the book he had asked about and started going through the contents. Owen knew what he was looking for, the ability's name reminding him of exactly that: Echo.

He flipped to the page, finding it to be a short read, but it explained everything from his necromantic powers acting on their own to what he saw. His inherit ability tapped into the object that had a memory, a traumatic one, and was filled with that energy. His powers acting on his curiosity, but not out of line as objects had the habit of wanting to tell their stories without the holder's consent.

He put the book away, mounting up with nothing else to do. He had received the message the doll wanted to share, but there wasn't anything else he could do with it other than live with the knowledge that, at some point, a mother and two daughters had lived and died to… something. Something that could perform Seraph End and a primitive Outland Monster. He didn't even know what race they were.

They had slightly pointed ears, suggesting that they could have been Absalomian, but their pupils weren't slit. They were like Dagdians where the mother had tanned skin, but when she used magic, it was more like life force energy mixed with light and dark, and her eyes didn't glow when using it. The same energy that the old temple was built with.

He let it go, keeping it close, but not on his conscience. He had much more pressing and present problems to deal with. When those matters were dealt with, he could look into it then.

00000

Owen got off Missiletainn at the Directors' Demesne's entrance, letting him go to the Gordin Family Manor for a much-needed rest, and headed in. The place was empty with the exception of the receptionists and a few guards.

"Lord Director Orpheal hasn't left yet, General Owen," the receptionist on the right told him. "He's in his lab."

He gave a curt nod and headed that way in silence. The walk was just as quiet with the only noise being his steps on the floor and the hum of the ley line spires on the walls. He entered Gordin Labs and found Orpheal and Solaria speaking quietly at her desk. They looked to the noise as the doors closed softly, ending their conversation. He gave a small wave of greeting. "Please, don't mind me. I'll leave if it's private."

"Not at all, Owen. Join us," Orpheal replied, waving him over. "What can we do for you?"

"Came to check in on statuses and friends. Aerrow was concerned about governance as well and hopes that it isn't too overwhelming along with everything else."

"Funnily enough, we were just talking about that," Solaria shared, less formal as the office hours seemed to be over. "Orpheal is looking for a date to pick for the vote, but also who to replace the Verdant line."

He frowned as he got closer and saw the papers on the desk of academic achievements. "Is there no heir for the line?"

"No one old enough or with credit to back them," Orpheal explained, looking over the sheets bitterly. "Vígdís had a cousin working with her who had many accomplishments, but going through her logs, we found that Vígdís murdered her when trying to complete her bioweapon to kill my daughter a couple of weeks ago."

"Her son is the only one left?"

"Negligence to create heirs due to safety has been on the rise for many of the directors." Solaria eyed Orpheal. "Including our leader."

A growl barely left as Orpheal's words were said carefully, "You know why I haven't."

"I meant before Iðunn was killed."

"Oh… well…"

Solaria sighed. "At any rate, it has left a hole in the government that wasn't thought to be a problem until now. I suppose we should thank the four of you for finding it before something catastrophic happened."

"I don't want to say you're welcome, but… I suppose our meddling certainly brought to light some rats," Owen commented before moving the conversation along as a flushed Orpheal seemed to be elsewhere, most likely thinking of Éabha as he always did with that doting expression. "Well, it seems to me that you have two options. You can follow the rules of your government and replace the house that can't provide with a new one as you can't have an already established family member of the directorate take their spot. Or give it a second chance to thrive by substituting it until a later date. Perhaps you could have this house be a new pillar if the Verdant line becomes active. An eighth pillar never hurt in the chance that a sub is required again."

"Reforming at a time like this…" A scoff came out of Orpheal as he came back to the conversation. "But I suppose it's times like these that force reformations… I don't want to leave Vígdís's son on his own at the age of ten – whether or not our northern friends strike the city."

"Then I suppose you have your answer on what needs to be done."

"Now it's just a matter of having a vote to fill in the other directors and then another vote to pick a family as this eighth spoke."

"So many votes… The new heads will need time to get into their positions before you can ask them to vote correctly," Solaria told him, and he nodded. "Give them two weeks to figure it out, handle the ropes – from there you should know which families could be candidates."

"That does give me some breathing room, yes. Thank you, as always." He passed her a grateful smile.

"Too early to thank me yet. You still have to pick a date for the first vote."

"Right…"

Owen crossed his arms. "You could work it with the schedule of the Zerach."

Orpheal nodded. "That would probably be best. Have the vote be afterwards… a week from now should be good. This will let us see if Seraphina is still a kingdom by then and not have them focus the rest of their lives on experiments and paperwork should it all just…"

A dreaded tension filled the space as Orpheal couldn't finish and Owen inquired. "What are the defences like?"

"As complete as we're going to be able to get them. Hopefully, we can avoid as many casualties as possible… but well, you've dealt with invading hordes before."

Owen had, many times over. But this wasn't a horde, it was a genocidal mission who has had more time to think about what they would do to a kingdom longer than anyone he knew had been alive, including Helah. "The Zerach will be completed before the kingdom is wasted away. We'll defend this city for as long as necessary to get it working."

Orpheal didn't say anything as he pulled out his CT and started typing out a message faster than Owen could ever dream of creating phrases on the device. There was a little triumphant send noise once he was finished and his shouldered relaxed briefly. "For now, I will continue to focus on beyond the doom in hopes that there is something at the end of the line. The director houses know of the times, it should give them a bit of hope that things will turn out."

"They're going to need it. Schedule and goals tend to work better than misery on the mind."

"Glad you agree, and since that's done, shall we take a stroll to check in on Naftali?"

"If you wouldn't mind."

"Solaria, you should join us on this adventure and end it with a nice meal at my place. I'm sure Éabha would be thrilled to see someone other than staff and her treacherous dad."

"I'll walk with you to see Naftali, but there is a small thing I must do before hand at home. It's been a while since we've had tea together."

"Too long." Orpheal turned to Owen. "I'd offer you to join us as well, but I'm sure you want to head back to your base as soon as you can."

"I do. Aerrow is waiting, patiently as ever." They started walking towards the biology labs, leaving the main foyer to halls more active as Solaria made a pondering noise. He looked to her in confusion. "Something the matter, Solaria?"

"No… just speaking of Aerrow, how's he doing? The last time anyone checked his health was several days ago."

"He could be better but could be a lot worse considering the circumstances."

"He's still weakened by the affects of Asylotum? It's been more than two weeks. That seems unusual, especially if we look at your case."

"Some people are more sensitive." He shrugged, not that he wasn't concerned but knew that up until yesterday, other issues had built up and he doubted greatly that they had helped. That morning, Aerrow had looked significantly better than he had in months. "He's improved and improving, time is irrelevant. But I'll pass along your concerns to him… though you did bring up something I wanted to talk about."

"What is it?"

"I was at the embassy before coming here in hopes that it would be fixed by now. But the repairs are going slower than expected…"

"Only a few people have been able to pass our screening in order to have the most protection of the staff and those visiting," Orpheal explained with a small sigh, apparently knowing what he wanted. "The tyraulia did significant damage to the structure of the building along with the obvious destruction. Without our usual Dagdian constructors on it, I don't think it will be finished before the dragons arrive making it no safer than the safehouse you're in."

"I see…" Owen couldn't hold back the frown that formed.

It would have been nice to move Aerrow not only to a larger space, but a safer one that was made to defend those inside. He withheld a sigh. The kid was doing incredibly well with the weight of everything, that much he had to give him credit for, but it was apparent to their fight yesterday that he was anxious and getting cabin fever. His blows when he was irritated were almost savage, nothing like he had anticipated. He had to do everything just shy of seriously hurting or killing him to defend – not that he was sure if he could if it were a serious match to the death. With his new shield and the years of training they had done together, Aerrow had grown to be more formidable than Solomon by a lot...

It was just too bad that they couldn't have sparred to know for certain. Now if only he used magic too, he could maybe take Azarias and Cyrus. It would certainly knock their ego down a few pegs. Then again, if that happened, it would just confirm that his nephew had lost his mind... A mind that was innocent and shouldn't be forced to decide between killing raging victims to protect innocents. Unfortunately, Aerrow wasn't going to sit idly by once those dragons started their assault. Not for long at least.

"He needs to get out before they come to Domrael..."

"I agree, Little Dragon needs to get out for a short while if Éabha is accurate," Orpheal concurred, changing to a nickname basis as a group of students left one of the rooms.

"Éabha told you, did she?"

"Wouldn't say told and more so retorted as she stormed off to her room yesterday."

Solaria frowned. "You two get into it again?"

"Yes, but I don't want to talk about it now..."

The conversation ended with that as they went down a hall that had a few more doors on its walls with people coming and going and walked into a lab. Computers, spires, counters of equipment, and models of animals and people alike laid about the room in an organized mess. Several people were working at stations, but the only one Owen cared about was the semi-frail looking man at a computer.

Orpheal addressed the room, grabbing the attention of everyone but Naftali. "If I could have the lab vacated for a moment, I need to speak with the department head."

The scientists left the room in a couple of waves as some needed more time to put their projects in a stable position, but eventually, the laboratory was empty save for them and Naftali who hadn't looked away from his computer, flicking through what looked like modules.

The blond Seraph shifted ever so slightly; his voice filled with concentration as he moved the mouse carefully. "I suspect that the conversation about to take place has to do with more than just the data we've finalized tonight."

"Yes, a plan to let Aerrow have a breath of fresh air for a time," Orpheal agreed. "It's just a matter of how to let him investigate and take leisure safely. Being that everyone's trusted here, I figured that our genius could formulate something."

"Safely, inconspicuously, and in-" Naftali's voice caught as he grabbed his head. "I just had to run out of painkillers, curse this body."

"Bad day?" Owen asked, concerned.

The biologist nodded. "The treatments are coming but it's not perfect. I'm waiting on an ingredient that's taking its sweet time."

"I'll grab you something, then after we're done chatting, you should head home and rest," Solaria suggested even though it was more of an order before quickly heading out. "Make sure he doesn't move around."

"Yes, ma'am…" Orpheal muttered before turning to Naftali who gave out a small sigh. "You sounded like you had an idea."

"A small idea that might work. Since he's got a ready to help persona and he'll probably want to talk to the locals for any information we're missing, Aerrow could go out in disguise as say, an officer. He could carry his sword and if anyone came up to him, he'd be able to assist without suspicion. Since lawmen patrol the streets, either for a nice walk or for investigation, it wouldn't be noticeable to anyone if he and one of you three went with him. There are four of you, you could do pairs just in case someone does get wind suddenly and you need a diversion."

"That's a surprisingly good idea…" Owen admitted. How he thought of it in only a few moments astounded him into disbelief. "Suspiciously so…"

Naftali waved his hands in front of him, innocently. "I've been thinking on it yes, but only because I heard about the embassy and figured as the days crept closer, this was going to come up eventually. He's like as his mother called him, even now, yes? Little Dragon… he loves being outside. It was only a matter of time before he got stir-crazy, Outland Dragons or not, he needs to get out for a bit and play."

Owen relaxed slightly, "Yeah... some things don't change in that aspect... I think the idea will work. But his time outside needs to be safe. This city has a lot to offer, but to someone new..."

"That's actually the easier question to answer," Orpheal told him, his mind seemingly whirling as his thoughts quickly came out. "There are two districts in the city that could provide perfect routes of protection from above by the dragons, allowing him to enjoy a few stores and nature, all without needing to be out for long. Both can be done in the quickest time of an hour and have a prescient in the area that could be used as a cover to let you to use a Chaos Portal to head back to the hideout safely. Even if there are a few corrupted officers, they wouldn't dare expose themselves in such a place, even for their god. They'd never have the chance to act."

Owen raised a brow, curiously. "Which districts?"

"The Domrael University District and Central. Central has a lot of people, more places to explore, and places to try out food and Seraphinean culture. The university on the other hand has more nature to it and open – actually if he's being more his age, it wouldn't be as obvious if he went there. Quite a few of the younger officers like to enjoy the little things, like flirting, joining in games, or messing around at the park when they need a break. Not to say he couldn't do that in Central as there are many street performers in that area that he's probably never seen, but he might be more comfortable with people his age if he spends half the time he's out talking with them and the other half actually enjoying himself."

Both held good cases. "I'll check them both out tomorrow before picking a specific location... The problem becomes how we're supposed to get uniforms without zealots caring."

"I'll just order a dozen, say its for research. Since Absalomians aren't uncommon to the law enforcement here, there will definitely be a uniform for each of you without having to turn to the women's uniforms."

"The day Cyrus is caught in a skirt will be the day the world ceases as he would end it," Owen chuckled. "We'll go the day the order comes in if it's early enough to not draw suspicion about missing uniforms and lack of research. I'm sure Aerrow can wait until then for the surprise."

"He'll be surprised alright. Freedom at last," Naftali agreed. "Now that that's settled, I'm sure you didn't come all this way just to figure out an excursion."

"No, I came for an update originally. You mentioned yesterday that today would be a better assessment."

"Ah… about that…" The doors opened behind Owen. They turned to them and found Solaria walking in with a box in hand. "I was actually going to present the finality of it to Orpheal before heading home so he could let you know."

"Finality?" The secretary asked as she handed Naftali his painkillers. "For what?"

"Ciar's samples." He passed Owen two reports before taking a couple of tablets. Owen looked them over briefly, but he didn't need to look farther in to make him feel ill. "We can't continue. There are no connections between him and anyone in our system. Add the missing elements, we don't have the necessary ingredients to figure out what could be used to counter his venom or a weakness to kill or detain him. We need new samples that are less contaminated."

"Great, I'll get right on that…" Owen growled sarcastically at how simple he was making it sound. "Is there really nothing else? I thought you mentioned that there could be a way to get around this whole problem?"

"We tried using the table of elements to fill in the blanks – even tried to make new elements. That went nowhere since nothing matched the biomolecule structures. We turned to the venom itself to try and replicate synthetically – but that also didn't work. Took a magical approach, but the magic frequency is contaminated with Aerrow's. We could make something with it, but it wouldn't deal with Ciar efficiently if at all since we can't separate the signatures. If they didn't have a similar magical presence at the time, it would have been easy but…"

He didn't need to finish for everyone to get the picture. The only way they were going to be successful with an antidote or vaccine would be to find Ciar and take whatever they could from him… which was a whole set of problems they wanted to avoid in the first place. Owen sighed, putting his anger on the back burner. "I appreciate the hard work you and your team have done to get this far… If more samples are obtained then perhaps enough work has been done to complete the rest of this, quickly."

"There would have to be a trial process to make sure it's safe, but yes. Another fresh sample would do wonders to completing this. But until then, this is as far as we can go."

00000

The walk out of the demesne was relatively quiet between Orpheal and himself, leaving Owen to try and create strategies to bring the demon to rear his head long enough to get the samples without risking lives. The planning was not going well and Missiletainn also wasn't contributing much as he tortured Jimmy in the back garden. A sigh escaped.

It didn't matter what they could do to play it safe, they didn't have enough information on Ciar to even get a guess on what would work. They had his fighting style, but that was it. They could throw all sorts of things at him, which if it were three months ago, would have worked, but they believed he had become a lot stronger since so chances couldn't be taken.

A small mumble escaped Orpheal next to him, and he turned to the Lord Director, confused on what he didn't hear. The expression on his face was foreboding. "Orpheal…"

"Hm?" Orpheal turned to him, coming out of thought. "Sorry, I didn't realize my thoughts escaped, yet again."

"If you're not mumbling about something then there is a problem."

"I suppose so…" He sounded broken and Owen read him over again. He wasn't as lively or spastic as he was used to.

"How have you been these last few months, honestly?" he asked assertively, breaking the Seraph's guard.

Orpheal looked towards some trees along the path to his house, a distant expression on his face. "Honestly? Not great. I didn't realize how much I depended on our chats. How simple they were, a couple of mad men at work to create absurd and insane things. How helpful they were for me and for Éabha… Solomon's helped me raise Éabha to the best I could but since he's been gone… I feel like I've only done everything wrong. Lately all we've been doing is butting heads and passively arguing, and not so passive arguing, more than usual."

"Like last night… Teenagers tend to be rebellious by nature. It's their job to make their parents' lives as miserable as possible."

"Perhaps… but these last couple of months have been particularly bad. She's been more distant; I've been distant… She's wanting to fight and help with the border like it's her job, pointing out how the leading houses of Absalom often become knights to protect the realm. But trying to tell her that it's not necessary for her to do so, how we are different from your kingdom, and any other fact I could throw at her to dissuade her has been like asking an Outland Monster to tea."

"She gets her mouth and duty from no strangers."

"No, she doesn't. Iðunn's wit and my tenacity to protect this kingdom, just like our ancestor did were fused together. And like nuclear fusion inside a star, her energy is thrown to the cosmos, making weapons, familiar ones like my bladed gauntlets, or completely unheard-of ones like her rifle. She's trained practically herself just by reading Domrael's journals and clarification of basic training from Solaria which I had to shut down before it got out of hand. She means well, but that's how people are killed; she's too young and foolish to see that."

"Solaria helped with teaching her? I didn't think she could harm anyone outside of necessary medical purposes."

"I think she learned to help Éabha since she was using the forms inside the journal and no other types of fighting, not that I know how long that was going on for. Solaria sides with Éabha on the matter and refuses to tell me." He sighed in disgust, "I know that I'm being controlling, but she is just so headstrong that if she isn't tied down to reality, she would think she's immortal and can do anything! I'd love for her to do anything she put her mind to, but I can't lose her due to naïve recklessness."

"Which makes her more frustrated with you because you're trying to keep her alive."

"Yes, Athnuracha forbid!"

"This might not be what you want to hear but… you might have to give her some space. She's going to be eighteen soon, and if she's been studying Absalomian culture, she knows that she has been considered an adult there for almost a year. She's trying to prove herself to you that she isn't a little kid anymore. To treat her as an adult."

"I know… but I can't lose her too. Her proof tends to be… extreme. Like, she could have used any of her inventions to be a part of the demesne as an inventor – hell she wouldn't have had to do anything if she waited three years. I was planning on inviting her to work with me as her eighteenth birthday gift. But at fifteen she just comes right in the middle of a board meeting after weeks of trying to make me let her join and drops down the ley line spire like it wasn't a two-thousand-year-old problem – forcing my hand so that the other directors wouldn't take advantage of her work ethic."

A small laugh came from Owen. He would have paid a lot of money to see the look Orpheal had on his face when she did that. "That sounds like something you would do."

"It does… which makes me worried that she might hate me now."

He wasn't expecting that switch. "Why would she ever hate you?"

"Because I would if I were in her shoes. The delusion of holding her back, limiting her capabilities. I want to give her the vote of confidence in her abilities, the ones I happily let her dive into instead of being forced into a rigid system, but I can't will myself to let her go any farther. She doesn't have any blessings from Orithina that we know of; the blessings that would be normal for an eight-winged Seraph. No special abilities, no higher levels of magic potential than average for her age and training. She's a genius, but that's it. She only has herself if I'm not around. If Valrdis found out that another one of Orithina's soldiers were born… she would end up like the rest of her kin." Orpheal winced from unpleasant thoughts. "Outland Monsters hunting her down to the ends of the world. It's not just superstitious ramblings of a fearful father. I've seen it happen, multiple times over the last three hundred years. I believe wholeheartedly that because of their rivalry, the divine accord – any advantage that one of the goddesses might have, the other has to remove it to keep that balance. Even if it's no one's fault. If she died just because she was born…"

"Have you told her about the incidents?"

"No… I haven't had the heart to tell her that her dreams to explore the world would most certainly end in death. It would solidify my wishes of protecting her, but at the cost that she wouldn't be Éabha anymore. She'd freak out before completely disappearing into seclusion more than she already has."

Owen wished he could help the situation, but he didn't have anything. "You could try a different approach, offer to talk with her, telling her about things that you might not want her to know to show that you trust her… Have more family time perhaps if you don't want to go to that extreme, especially if things get far worse."

"If she wants to… but as of right now, since I had grounded her, she has refused to speak with me, even when I try to bring up conversation. She will simply ignore me and leave the room, even her own bedroom."

"She's bitter, I'll give you that, but I don't think it has gone so far as hatred."

"If she's anything like me, her pride would say otherwise. And it's all my fault."

"Then you better own up to your mistakes and fix them," Owen growled; the soft-handed approach wasn't working. "It doesn't have to be today, but when she starts talking to you again, perhaps try talking about what she wants without shutting down her ideas or changing the subject that you might not want to talk about. I gave shit to Aerrow for this very thing – treat her like an adult and she'll respond accordingly."

"And if she does hate me for everything?"

"Then you can call me, but you should be worried about that after it comes up, not before."

Their conversation came to an end as they got to the manor door and Orpheal unlocked it before walking in. A large staircase in a foyer was the first thing that greeted them, but no one else.

A sigh came out of the director. "Éabha, did you send Erik out again? He's supposed to be here watching you."

The small tsk from Éabha was faint but clearly came from down the hallway to their left, but nothing else. Owen shook his head, turning to Orpheal. "This is not a great start if you're-"

"General Owen! I didn't know you were here!" The girl quipped loudly, poking her head out of what he knew was her private lab, completely ignoring her father. "I need your help, like right now."

"Maybe I could be-" Orpheal started, attempting to be friendly but she went back into her room with a sharp no and closed the door. "I would like to say this has been going on since yesterday, but that would be a lie... It's been like this since Solomon died and I can't break it."

"I'll try talking to her... maybe you can get something welcoming. She likes tea, right?"

"Pretty sure it's divine law for a Seraphinean to like tea..." he muttered out, not happy at being in the back seat.

"There you go, a nice warm drink and some snacks is a great start. If communication through words doesn't work, Azarias and Cyrus have time and time again proved that bribery works most of the time, especially with kids and teenagers."

"And if it doesn't? What else do they do?"

"You stop following their methods. Look, it will work, and I'll be here to help moderate a bit until Solaria comes."

Orpheal gave a bit of a nod and Owen left him at the door, heading towards her lab. There was barely a second before he could hear the man practically running for the kitchen and Owen sighed.

Good gods was he ever a mess.

He gave a small knock on the door when he got to it and let himself in to a relatively large room that wasn't dissimilar to her set up in the demesne. Counters, projects; one thing that was different was the discarded wires and conduits placed in a messy pile. Éabha was working over Aerrow's coat very carefully, threading conduit through the modified metal that she would have forged in the forgery in the backyard.

"You needed me for something?" He started and she looked up for a moment before turning back to her work.

"You have an idea of how heavy his gear was before, right?"

"About... need me to make sure it's not too much?"

"His smaller gear bits are over there. I forgot to weigh them before getting started... Carried away and whatnot."

He went over to the counter she indicated where the gauntlets, sword guards, pauldron, and boots all sat finished. He picked up the pauldron first. "That's not a surprise considering..."

"I don't want to talk about Dad," the girl growled, apparently seeing right through his approach.

"He's just worried-"

"There's worried and then there's freaking out at everything."

"He has a lot on his mind and has his reasons for being a bit obsessive but believe me when I say there is a good reason behind it."

"Sure, he'll tell you those reasons but me? I had to get some outsider to take a gander and even that doesn't tell me the whole thing."

"Did you try talking to him after this... outsider gave you ideas as to why, besides Outland Dragons on the kingdom doorstep?" He heard her stop working behind him as he set the last piece of gear down and turned around.

She looked conflicted. "No... for the first time in my life, I'm too scared to get an answer."

"Scared of what?"

"That he hates me."

Two peas in a pod... "He doesn't hate you. He told me himself only a dozen times on the way over here."

"Well he has a funny way of showing it. Watch, he's going to come through that door and he's going to see all of this and freak."

"Wait... you didn't tell him you were working on Aerrow's armour yet?"

"No because he'd think I'm being a pain in the ass."

"Éabha-" He didn't get to finish as Orpheal came in with tea and treats in hand before stopping in the doorway.

The father looked around the room before turning to his daughter in disbelief. "Is this... Why on Orithin do you have Aerrow's armour?!"

Éabha looked at Owen with a small hint of 'told you so' before turning back to her father. "Trying to make sure he stays alive."

"How could you be doing that if he has no armour?!"

"He has a spare-"

"A spare that is probably made for training, not actual combat!"

"Well it would have gone a lot faster if I knew you weren't going to be against the idea!"

"Of course I am! There happens to be a group of psychopaths trying to murder him and Outland Dragons at our doorstep!"

"Alright, that's enough," Owen ordered, grabbing both of their attention. They went silent and he continued. "You both have the same endgame, just different ways of doing it. Now yes, it was reckless of Éabha to ask Aerrow directly about upgrading his armour-"

"You're siding with him?!" She exclaimed in disbelief, but he trudged onwards.

"Not entirely, but we've already established that Aerrow's not always about the here and now and often looks at the future outcome like the optimistic kid he is. With this said, it would have gone quicker if you, Orpheal, could be called upon without getting angry with her."

"Oh, so you're actually on her side," Orpheal derided, and Owen took a small breather.

"I'm on neither side. The armour upgrade is wonderful, but the timing was reckless. Perhaps you two need to be strapped to chairs and left in a room for a few hours to figure things out, but since we can't do that, you're both going to assist with the other's problem. Orpheal, you have some tea that needs drinking and Éabha, you have armour to finish threading. Talk something out during this time."

"And what if I don't want to?" Éabha asked boldly and he leaned back against the counter.

"I'm not giving you a choice. I can gladly stay here all night with that door shut until you come to an understanding over literally anything. This infighting needs to stop because teamwork, of any kind, is our only advantage if Ciar does show up again. You cannot fight efficiently if you are sidetracked with personal issues on and off the battlefield."

They looked at each other, one with disdain, the other with disapproval. Orpheal made the first move, bringing the tray over to the free counter near the armour.

Éabha ignored him, going back to the armour for a few moments then sighed. "That's Drenyrae tea... isn't it."

"It is..." Orpheal answered quietly.

"Can I have some... please?"

"You can."

The awkwardness between them was almost unbearable, but Owen stayed where he was, unmoving. They might not get far tonight, but it was a start.

The tea was poured and Éabha took a step back from her work to take the cup from Orpheal. "Thank you."

He looked away, not giving much of a reaction to her attempt as he scanned the armour nearby. "What's left that needs to be done?"

"Threading, activating, calibration, deactivation, reactivation, calibration, testing," she replied quickly and took a sip. "I swear the Goddess of Love herself invented this blend..."

"It is named after her."

"I know I was just... never mind."

Orpheal shuffled over to the armour and picked up where she had stopped. She took a seat in one of the counter chairs and watched, sneakily stealing one of the cookies and shoved it in her mouth before Orpheal could notice. Or at least, probably to her perspective. To Owen, he knew that Orpheal had as a small smile had formed on the corner of his mouth where she couldn't see.

The silence was broken after several peaceful minutes by Orpheal. "You've done a good job so far, but there is still a lot of work ahead. When were you planning on finishing this?"

"Tonight so it can be technically ready by tomorrow if the dragons suddenly showed up, but it'd be better if it was perfected and ready for the day after tomorrow."

"Why wait that long?" Owen asked and she looked at him, happily.

"The Zerach along with Deigh's new spear will be ready then. I know that I'll be helping with it and wanted to show Deigh how her weapon works in case someone doesn't let me leave the house."

"It's not like I'm never going to let you leave," Orpheal told her, breaking away from the armour to look to her. "Just right now. Vígdís could have other experiments out there or a cultist might try and kill you."

"At the hideout? Who the hell is going to find that place in the middle of the city with over a million people in it?"

"It's not about finding it but rather if Ciar made his attack with the dragons. I'm trying to protect you, foolish child!" There was a hint of anger in his tone as he tried to hold back his frustrations with her. "It's like you have a death wish."

"I'm not a child anymore," she spat back, enraged by the very thing Owen had told him not to do. "But maybe I should have a death wish. Maybe then I wouldn't be such a nuisance to you anymore!"

Orpheal was at a loss of words. "I... É-Éabha, that's..."

There were a few, agonizingly long seconds of silence before she gave up on him trying to find his words and scoffed. "Figures..."

"Éabha, wait!" Orpheal tried to call her back as she left the tea behind and went for the door. "There are just some things that-"

"You can tell everyone else, but not me, huh?" She paused for a moment, an emotionless pallet on her face. "Clearly something I shouldn't care about... right?"

"No-"

"I don't care. I'll be alone in my room, exactly where you want me to be so I'm not a bother to anyone or any thing."

"That's not what I want-" She walked out the door, closing it behind her, and ending his attempt to fix his mistake. "Fuck."

"That was a bit unexpected…" Owen admitted, accidentally out loud, and he glared at him.

"You think?! Now she thinks that I hate her!"

"She probably does now, yes. You have to tell her something."

"How could I now? You saw her face; it's the look that is reserved for things she hates the most."

"All I saw was a mask to hide how hurt she was to say those things, not hatred."

"You wouldn't say that if you saw her when someone asks if she likes liver… Gods, if Iðunn was here, she'd be brave enough to tell her."

"Well she's not so if you want to let Éabha know how you feel, you're going to have to tell her directly and indirectly. Passively help her out to show that you don't hate her. Projects, little things in the background. More of her favourite tea. Ask her to come for supper tonight so she's not in her room, alone, crying herself to sleep in fear of not only genocide but her own father wishing she were never born."

Orpheal looked to the armour in disgust.

"Solaria will be there and so it won't be just the two of you. She knows you well enough that I'm sure she can dissolve any arguments that might come up. Don't let it escalate. Literally anything you do will be noticed by her – you don't have to talk to her to show that you care, but you will have to say something once she asks again." There was a moment of pause as Orpheal processed his words before nodding. "I have to get going, but for the love of any god, don't push her to talk unless you are going to tell her everything. She's got just as many concerns as you do about your relationship and she defends that insecurity through quips. You already know this, so don't instigate back."

"I'll do my best…"

"She's your daughter, so as long as you try, she will know."

Chapter Thirty-Six: Escapee

Two days had passed since I had my talk with Owen, two days since I had managed to talk to someone who didn't know about Ciar or Theodora, and two days to get over the relief it was. The crashing halt of it all came the following day with the news that an antidote or vaccine couldn't be completed until new samples were received. It was, admittedly, a bit hard to accept and since… I had been left to stew in the mess of it all. It took my high and brought it down back to reality. Atlamillia was silent as ever and when knowing something was wrong, she flat out refused to acknowledge that there was anything of the sort.

Nothing had been found in the searches, and no updates on Absalom… Then yesterday, the Outland Dragons broke through the barrier. Just like Zegrinath said they would.

I got up from the desk, finishing with learning what the book could teach me on partial changes. It wasn't a question on whether or not I could do it, it was a question if I should. And that debate, sent me spiralling back to problems I could not solve.

I left the room, restless. I didn't know what time it was, but it was early, the sun was rising brightly into the common room window between the buildings. I went over to the window and stared out. It looked no different than it had when I left its existence. It had been forever since I was outside…

I needed to get out. But not yet… Soon.

How long was soon?

Time, days… they had merged together, and I had to mentally divide them up to make sure I was keeping track despite it seemingly not mattering. The dragons were here now, somewhere beyond the city's limits. But I couldn't think about being caught in the crossfire, keeping up a front of optimism that the whelps could be found. And in that optimism, the thereafter, and my obligations towards my own kingdom, had to be addressed.

Thirteen days had gone by since arriving in Seraphina, five days it took to get to the island itself after leaving Asylotum. Eighteen days meaning it was the twenty-first. Organization for the Thinnus Festival would start that day. It would have been nice if the Zerach was completed and brought back so the people could celebrate it in Absalom. Sure, it would've made complications, but I doubted anyone would care about putting in extra work if it meant being home.

I sure as hell wouldn't about going the extra kilometre and would gladly do so if someone else didn't.

Movement came from outside as people started their day, mostly walking, some driving, not many flying. Long shadows were cast off the figures as they went across the crosswalks, the only breaks between the buildings. A few trees were in my view of the steel and glass city, and they blew lightly in a wind I couldn't see or feel.

I knew I shouldn't have been staring out the window, it wasn't making my restlessness better. But I didn't leave, embracing the sun's light. Perhaps the light was warmer outside. That, or maybe it was a cold morning sun and the window just made it warm. I wanted to put my hand on the window, just to see what it was like out, but didn't. Instead, my hands went into my pockets, leaving me to watch the sun rise a little higher. Its light refracted and reflected off the buildings and people. The city was quite beautiful at the hour, a different light to how it looked at night and certainly different from how it looked at midday.

But… my favourite, seeing it now, this time was probably it.

My CT made a noise, receiving a text message and I looked away from the window, pulling it out. Éabha was up. I opened the message to find two capitalized t's and a dash between them, making a crying face followed by actual words. She finished the armour last night, Deigh's weapon was being finalized, and now was bored.

A bit of relief set in as she seemed happier than she was the other day after she got into a rather large argument with her father, despite being bored. I knew she hadn't talked it out with him yet but hearing about her complaining that he completed the threading of my armour told me that their argument might have been a misunderstanding. I sent her a small thank you and told her that Deigh had been practicing with me since she had offered to make the weapon. There was a pause as I thought of a way to deal with her boredom.

It wasn't a long pause and I typed it in, suggesting her to play one of her games and sent it. And if that wasn't what she wanted to do, then maybe she could have a list of new ones for me to try before I had to go. She could get bored of Harvest Valley or sick of me failing at Death Tolls, so who knew what else she had in mind.

I waited a few moments for her to message back. It was prompt and short. A written-out sigh and an agreement before finishing off with a 'talk to you later'.

I wrote a small text to encourage her to try and ask her questions to Orpheal. Another moment passed before another short answer of maybe before saying that she had some serious work to do with picking games I had to try. I didn't push it further and the CT went back into my pocket. She wasn't going to be messaging me for a while, for more than one reason.

I looked back to the window and was surprised by the number of people going about the day that was still slowly growing. How were they enjoying the tedious existence of routine? I wasn't sure... but it was probably better than being stuck inside. A small sigh came out haphazardly as the sounds of socked feet came to my ears. I didn't need to look to recognize the steps as Owen's. He came over to the window, not far from me.

"Morning, Owen," I greeted quietly, letting him know I wasn't that deep in thought, but didn't look away from the outside world I so dearly wanted to join. "Have a good night?"

"Good morning and I did. Finished reading a play. I keep forgetting about this one part. It always makes it rain indoors every time I read it."

"What does that mean exactly?"

"Ah, never mind..." He cleared his throat, changing the subject. "Interesting view?"

"Not really, but the sun feels nice."

There was a bit of an agreement from him. "Did you sleep well?"

"Considering... no, not any worse than usual. Didn't throw up right away either." I shrugged. "But since I didn't have anything in my stomach, it didn't last long. Let me finish the first section of the skill book."

"Thinking about trying it out?"

"Not right now. It's too risky."

"Ciar may not be close enough to notice."

"No, but in the off chance he is, this city doesn't need him on top of dragons... Where were they last reported?"

"Heading south towards Infinite Spring. A second force was heading east towards Domrael, but they are still a couple of days out if they keep their pace," he answered, looking outside. "It's going to be a nice day today; it'll will hinder their approach."

"Will it?" My voice was neutral, my heart split between relief that they couldn't proceed quickly and heartbreak about not being able to enjoy the city while I still could.

It was wrong for me to want joy in such a moment, but I wanted it anyway. But I also couldn't be miserable and ruin it for everyone else.

The general nodded and I forced a smile. "That'll be good for Cyrus and Azarias then. They'll be able to cover more ground, camp if need be where the Legion and Dragons aren't. They're maxing out range for same day return."

"They will be on that tomorrow if the siege allows it," he said, and I turned to him in confusion.

"Is something else happening?"

He gave another nod, looking over with a bit more hope to it than I was expecting. "A plan was made and solidified last night after you retired. You get to explore the university district following a specific route to keep you safe outside for a short while. The route isn't long, but it allows you to talk to people, investigate, and enjoy the things on it without missing too much. Orpheal will be teleporting us just inside a small booth already prepared after he gets here and recharges. Naftali and he will be dropping off parts for the Zerach for Éabha to piece together in a couple of hours. Once on site, Deigh will be here with Orpheal to give him details of where you are in case you're separated for whatever reason. Éabha and him can then rescue you with their Teleport Glyphs."

"So… I get to go out and help and the Zerach will actually be finished before the Outland Dragons get here?"

"Yes, meaning we can protect this city, quite a bit of the surrounding area, and the displaced people until we can find the whelps."

My heart leapt for joy at the thought of being free from the tower and the impending doom leaving, but my demeanour was calm on the outside. There was something… off about the idea, I just wasn't sure why a part of me was saying that I shouldn't go. Not saying, almost a whisper was begging me not to go. I disregarded the idea that I was hearing any disembodied voices as paranoia but kept the caution. "Are you sure that's alright?"

"It'll only be a couple of hours at the most. The other three dragons will be flying around overhead, using the brightness of the sun as a way to deter people from being able to get a good look above. Cyrus will be your main guard as you take a small patrol around a couple of blocks, checking out stores and messing around in a park if you want. The city patrol goes every so often to relax and mingle with the students there, so you won't be suspicious with a weapon, asking questions, or having fun while in uniform. Azarias and I will be around the grounds as well, watching for anything strange and can act as decoys should it be necessary. The journey will end in a precinct where I'll portal us back here."

"This seems like an unnecessary amount of planning. I don't need…" I trailed off as he raised a brow. I turned back to the sun outside. "I love this idea, but I don't want to risk lives in case someone does recognize me."

"No one will be able to organize an attack in such a short period of time, over a large area, and pull it off effectively with the arsenal that you and Cyrus have. I scouted out the area to make sure that you can't be attacked from afar without being noticed and they would have to confront you to do so as long as you stay on the route."

"So, the only way they can attack is on the ground, where one of us would notice."

"That is the idea and with Guðmundr, it'll be quite the challenge to try and get through if I couldn't. And just in case, you're going to have a bit of assistance in not being recognized with a Dagdian illusion spell."

I was still a bit uneasy about everything, but I couldn't stay in here any longer. I needed outside. "Alright… I appreciate everything you've done to make this happen."

"It's nothing. You've been cooped up in here for over a week, working constantly. If anything, it's a way to force you to have a small break and you get to stay sane doing it."

A couple of hours went by where a skip should have made its way into my step, but it never did. The ambiguous whisper still remained, like a breath on the back of my neck and it set me on edge. I put on the black, under armour t-shirt of the uniform, its tightness I thought would be a problem but realized quickly that it was a stretchy, breathable material with hints of magic woven within for a bit of protection. The white jacket was left on the chair along with its belt that I had already put Winterthorn on. It wasn't a bad uniform, very monotoned but not bad. A knock came to the door just as I finished tucking the shirt in to the black pants.

"Come in," I called to it as I threaded the uniform belt through the loops.

The knocker came in showing Éabha in a lab coat who looked me over with a surprised look. "Holy shit, wasn't expecting you to actually look the part."

"I'm not sure if that's a good thing or a bad thing."

"It's good." She took a few strides, swiping the cap off the table and stuck it on my head. "I don't even have to cast a Dagdian spell, you don't look like yourself at all."

"Er... thanks, I think." I looked at the mirror near by and found that she was more correct than I would have liked. The tighter clothing was not something I generally wore nor was the hat. I turned back to her. "Can you still do it anyway? I really don't want to chance it."

"Of course, but it will only be a small illusion, any big changes would be noticeable to people more susceptible to Dagdian magic."

"That's fair. What are you going to change?"

"You'll see when I tell you to check." That told me nothing and made me a bit nervous, but I kept it to myself. She looked at me with a bit of an intense stare that lasted a few, uncomfortable moments before tapping me on the nose. "Well, if nothing else, you can probably pick up a date if you find nothing."

"Is this a bad thing or a good thing? What did you do?"

"Nothing really, just chose a genetic trait and brought it out in your hair and eye colour. Whoever it belonged to probably turned heads more so than your outrageous red and orange."

I eyed her a little bit, not feeling any different but looked over at the mirror regardless, guessing that it was caused by my inability use the magic. What I was met with were startling emerald green irises that turned sombre in the light. My hair that was a bit darker and made me looked far more like my mother than I wanted.

"You don't like it?"

"No, no it's fine. I just wasn't expecting you to pick out that gene." I turned back to her with a forced smile.

"Well... Alright."

"So you think I could get a date, eh?"

She blushed slightly, looking away. "Well, I don't know what a preference is in Absalom but, green eyes are pretty big here for attraction and with the red-brown hair... that doesn't help things."

"I see, you made me your type."

"Oh get over yourself, I did as I said I did. Just happened to turn out like that," she spat as she snubbed me off, her blushing long gone. "But... yes, I suppose it turned out that way. You look surprisingly good as a brunet with green eyes; I thought the change would make you look strange, but it fits."

"Probably because your magic skill is advanced, and it made it look normal."

"Nope, it wasn't. Anyway, I'll let you get ready to go here. I need to get back to my work if I have any hope in getting the Zerach up and running."

"Thank you."

"No problem, oh, I should also mention that you don't need to worry about the spell fading or anything. I formed it to stick around for the next six hours just in case something goes wrong."

"Was that difficult to do?"

"It took a bit, but nothing for you to be concerned with. Just going to need a snack once I head back downstairs."

I laughed lightly. "Have fun raiding the cupboards, I'm sure there is something you'll like."

"Thanks!" She skipped out of the room, and I followed not too far behind her with the jacket. The boots on my feet tapped a little lighter than what I was used to on the floor. In the living room, Owen turned, also wearing the Seraphinean uniform and his expression went from one of greeting to shock, a look that Éabha didn't miss as her skipping stopped and she looked back at me for a second. "Uh… I didn't fuck up. What's with the expression?"

He looked away to his jacket, hiding behind the task of putting it on. It wasn't very convincing as even his excuse wasn't one, the atmosphere of the room changing drastically to melancholy. "Nothing, just… nothing."

"I'm missing something."

Owen didn't share or expand as he changed the subject entirely and started for the stairs. "I forgot… right, my CT. I'll be back shortly."

"Owen," I started but it meant nothing as he was already in his room, the door closing behind him. "Sorry…"

"Sorry for… what?" Éabha asked, moving in front of me. "What the hell was that about? He looked like he just watched his love interest die when he saw you."

"Not so much as that but definitely a loved one…" I sighed. "My mother's genes were what you picked out when you did your illusion. Owen was close with her."

"So that's why you… Why the fuck didn't you say anything? I could have changed it?!"

"Because I didn't think that it was worth it, especially after finding out that you used quite a bit of magic the first time."

"Well… yes, but…"

"Owen will be fine," Missiletainn stated behind me and we looked over to him. "He just needs a bit of time; we'll head out when Orpheal is ready without hinderance."

"Are you sure?" I asked and he nodded.

"Don't mind him, just have fun while you're out. That's all he cares about."

00000

The sunlight after exiting the security booth hit hard, blinding me but I didn't mind it one bit as I relished in its warm embrace. The breeze of the space that lightly played in the leaves of a nearby tree was better than hearing I was allowed outside. I turned to the knights and Owen, my glee and excitement to be outside devoured the uncertain paranoia that I had before. "This is amazing!"

"Can you even see properly without your sunglasses?" Azarias asked, crossing his arms and I shook my head.

"It's still bright as hell but I don't care!"

Owen chuckled lightly but the grief he had before was still present. "Well put them on and go have fun for a bit, Azarias and I will watch from a distance, pretending not to notice you messing around."

"I won't mess around…"

"Sure you won't. Try to behave – you may not be a certain someone right now, but you are wearing a reputation of the city patrol, keep within their misdeeds." He turned to Cyrus. "Especially you."

Cyrus said nothing and started walking. "Come on, Officer Bough, we don't have all day."

"Bough?!" I exclaimed, not sure if I was mad or shocked, possibly both. "What kind of name is that?!"

"Yours."

"It's not much different from yours…" Azarias muttered. "Just wished I thought of Bough first."

"Owen, are you seriously letting them pick?" I asked, just shy of a whine but he started laughing. "This isn't fair…"

"It's not forever," Owen said through the laughter he tried to tame but couldn't. "So have fun with it."

I was not going to have fun with such a stupid name, nor was I bothering to talk to Deigh as she was laughing more than she should have. I left them in a huff, chasing after Cyrus. I put my sunglasses on and the annoyance I had a few moments ago vanished as I could finally see how beautiful the campus was. Unlike the city around it, the buildings were stone, spires, and pillars. Some glass ones but it showed off the age of a time before the steel towers. Buildings, while still large, were similar to Elwood University as they were spread out with pathways for people to get to and from places, benches, trees, and gardens. Waterways lined many of them as I moved to the side of the path and looked at the beds seeing sterlets swimming up and down the streams. They were much smaller than their sturgeon cousins that I've caught many times before.

Cyrus waited for me as I crouched and stuck my hand in the water, brushing the fish as they went by. Some of them seemed to like it, coming back for seconds and thirds before swimming off, others avoiding me all together. They were much softer than their cousins too, smooth but also bony. I got up and dried off my hand as we made our way farther into the campus.

"Where do you wish to start?" Cyrus asked and I looked to him.

"We should go around and ask some questions and about rumours. I'm sure everyone knows about the dragons so they might know something about whelps or even some underground cult network."

He gave a curt nod and we walked over to what looked to be a student under an ancient tree. He looked innocent enough, clearly daydreaming up until he noticed us. His eyes went wide and fumbled to a stand but couldn't get farther than that as Cyrus greeted him, a bit different from how I was used to him being.

"Lovely afternoon, isn't it?"

"Y-yes… Officer sir…" He couldn't meet either of our gazes and while clearly anxious, he looked out of it.

I frowned. "Are you okay?"

"Of course sir! Why wouldn't I be?! Just sitting out in the lovely day." He gave a forced laugh and I looked to Cyrus then turned back to him.

"We were wondering if we could ask a few questions, if that's alright?"

"Q-questions? I'm just sitting here under this tree minding my own business. Nothing illegal, I swear!"

For some reason, I seriously doubted that. "Well, it wasn't so much about illegally sitting under a tree and more of if you've heard any talk about Outland Dragons."

"Outland Dragons?! They're here! Oh gods I only meant to spend an hour under the tree not days!" The kid looked ready to have an accident and Cyrus grabbed the situation, just not the way I would have as he clearly knew what was going on.

"It's been a few days, colleagues back at the precinct were wondering how long you'd be here. They were taking bets."

"Bets?!"

"Yep, bets… betted also about what you're taking…"

"I took nothing! I was just here listening to people walk by on… on the grass."

"If you talk to us about what we need to know, we'll pretend we were never here."

"Anything! Wait… I'm not on anything. You have no proof!"

"What colour is the tree?"

"Green, obviously!"

I looked up at the violet flowers of the tree. "Yeah, you're not exactly making your case any better."

"It's green! It's a tree!"

"I didn't realize that Seraphinean Jacaranda were green in Kalokairtas," Cyrus toyed with him as he grabbed at one of the petals that fell in the breeze. "I thought that happened in Cheimoiems…"

The student looked to the petal and caved. "Please don't arrest me. My mother would kill me if she knew!"

"Just answer Officer Bough's questions and we'll be on our way."

"Bough… like a bow and arrow?"

"Yeah…" I sighed, glaring at Cyrus who was enjoying himself too much. "We're trying to find leads about missing whelps and a monster known as Ciar and his followers. You wouldn't have happened to hear anything about it while you were daydreaming?"

"Oh! I thought this was… ah, no. I haven't unfortunately, officers. I know that there was some recruitment earlier in the semester for this god dude but, I didn't join it. I'm happy with my goddess who has blessed me with a stern mother to keep me… mostly out of trouble. As for whelps, I only heard what was on the news."

"Do you happen to remember where initiates would go when recruited."

"I was high- I mean completely sober and on absolutely nothing and threw their pamphlet out. I should have given it to someone but at the time, this Ciar guy wasn't the Kingbreaker, you know?"

"I know," I tried to sound neutral about the name, but the name only gave a reminder, and my hand went for my chest to ease it. "Alright well, if you hear anything, see anything, go to a precinct, and don't tell it to one officer but many, alright?"

"Yes, sir, always sir."

"I also want to tell you that you haven't been out for days…"

"I… wasn't?"

"No," Cyrus told him, a rare grin on his face. "A suggestion if you want to get high on Dagdian Mushies, don't pretend you are sober; you're obvious."

"Yes… Sir…"

"You looked perfectly sober when you were relaxing under this *violet* tree."

"To you it's violet; to me it's a beautiful rainbow…" The kid relaxed quite a bit and Cyrus patted him on the shoulder, leading the way to the next destination.

"Best not to tell anyone else either – Mushies are illegal in public places. If you head to a church with a solarium, they are free there."

"Oh shit! Really?"

"And they are good quality too."

"Uh… how do you know that?"

"When you are needing to solve a case, sometimes you have to drug your partner."

The kid went a shade paler and simply nodded as I shook my head. "Good luck with your adventures…"

"Thanks… Sorry for your partner."

We went to several other students and teachers, asking around about Ciar and the whelps with nothing conclusive. An old pamphlet that the Mushies guy had mentioned was given over and it went into Cyrus's pouch to be dealt with later, but I had my doubts that the meet up was still used. The dates on it were printed before the attack on Absalom. A few of the students came up to us, immediately knowing that we weren't the usual suspects and had tagged along on our small investigation, asking about, and reporting back to us. Some stuck around as my curiosity finally exploded and I started asking more about the campus itself.

Tales of urban legends and ghost stories were told in various ways from excellent to bare minimum depending on who was telling it, but I listened to it all the same. They were unique yet so similar to the tales I had heard about Elwood University in Siofra. Every old school had stories it seemed and while not helpful to the investigation, they helped with my sanity.

A few of the female students were not so subtle with their flirts towards us which was a bit unexpected as I hadn't believed Éabha fully. Sure enough though, she was right when we went into a botanical garden and I took off the sunglasses. Thankfully, the more assertive women and one guy who had been following us around didn't get heartbroken as I wasn't able to decline their offers due to an exam.

They ran off and I took a seat by a massive flower, needing a breather. It was far too much excitement for someone who had been locked in an apartment building for over a week.

Cyrus laughed at my suffering, teasing me about it and I rolled my eyes and teased him back knowing full well he enjoyed it about as much as I did, which wasn't a whole heck of a lot.

I got up and we walked out of the beautifully symmetrical glass building and stuck on my sunglasses once more to marvel at it in the middle of an outdoor garden space. Hedges lined the campus walkways along with flowers in the middle of the green field. Beyond the glass and stone steps lined what seemed to be stores. We ventured over, checking a few of them out and casually asked our questions before leaving. I knew I wanted a few things but didn't buy anything while 'on duty'.

"So you want to come back then later?" Cyrus asked as we left the final store along the strange strip and I gave a bit of a nod. "It's okay to say yes."

"I know, just… you know."

He gave a small sigh but seemed to understand before looking behind me. "You want to take a small break?"

I looked at him in confusion. "Like what?"

"The park over there."

I turned around and saw a playground sitting in the park he mentioned. Seesaws, animals and other modes of transport on large springs, a massive play structure with several slides and ways to get up, rings on pillars that I guessed to be a ring course for small, flying children, a giant net maze, and swings. Beyond the obvious structure, a larger ground for the older students had several sports fields for Seraphs and non-Seraph games. One of them very active as moving hoops on either end glowed while the participates seemingly beat each other with sticks to get to a flying orb. Some of the team members were flying through other hoops and as we moved closer, I could hear it had quite the crowd with a projection showing the score of what seemed to be four teams and highlighted players who were near the orb.

I turned away from it and found several less than clothed Seraphinean woman and a few other races playing volleyball in the sand. It was a game I actually knew how to play but never got around to really playing it with others. I was caught staring at the game and the girls waved. I waved back politely with a sheepish look on my face, and they offered for us to play. A large part of me was in for it but knowing that time was running out and things yet to do, we declined.

They seemed disappointed but understood and mentioned that they play later on in the week, every week, after the dayshift ended and other officers also came from time to time if we ever felt like joining in, picking up on our accents that we weren't locals. One of the girls was planning strategies far beyond what I expected a game of volleyball to bring.

We left them, heading towards the kids' structure, and walking past a splash pad where there were more than enough ways to soak one's friends for flying and non-flying children. Several of the children, who had abandoned the play structure for cold water, had tried to get us with the toys. I had to leap to the side to avoid the rascals where their parents quickly scolded and apologized.

Eventually, we succeeded in getting to the playground where I stopped in front of the large net that was four metres high and wide and tangled in rope that created a three-dimensional climbing space. It looked... well amazing didn't quite justify it. It wasn't made for children that couldn't hide their wings, but it probably satisfied many energetic and competitive children all the same.

"Bet you can't get to the top of that thing," Cyrus egged, and I scoffed at him.

"Please, it's a simple rope obstacle."

"Without getting stuck."

"What's the wager?"

"Your dignity."

Ouch... "And if I don't?"

"Then you don't... but are you really not going to have a try at it?"

"It's for children."

"Suit yourself... but I'm sure this simple obstacle couldn't be helpful in the future..."

Son of a... "Fine... but if I climb to the top and get back down without your help... we're having what I want for supper tonight."

He gave a shrug, apparently quite sure that I wouldn't succeed.

I got onto the rope structure and easily made my way to the top. Once up there, I took a moment and looked at the view around us. It was a massive park, even more to do farther in and- "There's an ice cream forrum!"

Cyrus looked up at me in confusion. "An ice cream forrum?"

"Over there!" I pointed in the direction. "I've never had ice cream from an ice cream forrum!"

He looked over at the vehicle before turning back to me. "You didn't know what an aftrus was… but you know what a forrum is?"

"Well… it is a forrum right? I've only heard about them so… I'm guessing."

"That is a type of forrum yes."

"Okay! Can we get some?"

He gave a doting smirk like he was dealing with a kid. "On our way out, it's in the direction we have to go."

"Great!"

"But first you have to get down."

"Right…" I looked at the pathway I needed to go and found that the shapes on the way up were very different on the way down. I grimaced as I caught Cyrus's smirk grow sadistic and ignored him. I could get down without getting stuck!

I got stuck almost immediately.

One wrong move and my foot slipped off the rope and I fell, landing hard on the little collection below and slipped past only for my boot to catch a different rope leaving me to hang upside down. My arms entangled in one geometric shape while a rope was pressed against my back as I had managed to get between shapes where another was strapped across my chest. The cap fell off thanks to gravity as I shifted, trying to get my boot to let go. A click went off and I looked at the noise seeing Cyrus holding his CT. Another click and I glared.

"You bastard…"

"You wagered your dignity." Another picture taken and then he turned the device to the side, clearly recording a video. The grin on his face was both sadistic and amused. "I wonder how long it will take for you to ask for help."

"Never…" I tugged at a rope I could reach. "I'm not losing two be-ah!"

The rope let my foot go and I dropped, landing on the safety net underneath, and tumbled onto the ground, backwards. I looked up at him from the ground as he had a surprised look on his face.

"Told you I could get down without help."

"I see that."

"We're having O'Merald's."

"That place is so bad for you…"

"I know and dammit if I don't love it all the same."

He took another picture before I could get up and brush the sand off of me. We wandered over to a safer part of the playground, heading for the way out as I stopped in front of the swing set. About a minute went by of staring, my embarrassment of never playing on one became abundantly obvious and he showed me how by sitting on the other one. It was a weird concept of motion that I have never experienced quite like it before despite playing with the kids and my own childhood adventures. It wasn't like swinging from a branch or a rope. It was unique and relaxing which made it immensely enjoyable. Cyrus also seemed to enjoy it too and relaxed for the first time the whole trip. He passed me a rare smile. We got off after spending longer than we should have and headed towards the vehicle with the ice cream in it.

Cyrus looked over at me. "What kind of ice cream would you like?"

"Chocolate…" I reached for my pocket and realized something very quickly. "Ah… I don't have any money… I forgot I left it back with Deigh so I wouldn't be tempted to buy anything unnecessary."

He seemed to ignore me and walked ahead as the kid that was there took off with their popsicle. "Are you the owner of this venue?"

"I am," the ice cream man said with a bit of a cheery tone that was quickly dropped at Cyrus's next words.

"Got word that your products taste a bit suspicious. For testing purposes I'd like the largest cones you have and loaded for best results. One chocolate, the other…" He looked to the menu. "Harlequin… just to make sure that everything is right."

The man raised a brow. "Ahuh…"

"I am sure it's fine, that kid shows it, but I can't go back to my captain without a thorough testing of it."

He rolled his eyes and got to the order. After a few moments he passed the two cones over with three scoops escaping the top of it and my mouth salivated. It looked so good.

"Thank you for your services."

The man in the forrum was not thrilled but let it be as Cyrus came over, handing me the cone. I kept my voice down. "That was stealing."

"I'm doing a public service."

"Owen told us to behave."

"The general told us to have fun." He ate some of the ice cream and turned to the ice cream man. "I don't know who called this in, but they're an idiot for thinking this was bad. I'll let the captain know that you have amazing ice cream."

"Tell him to bring money next time he wants to *test…*" the man muttered barcly within our hearing leaving Cyrus to shrug.

"You're a menace…" I grumbled before trying the treat. "But you're right… this is amazing."

"I never said I wasn't one… and I'm glad that it was worth the effort."

We made our way to the next part of the adventurous time while eating away.

00000

I shifted the bottom of the jacket sleeve, nervously for the fifth time in the last few minutes. The outside time was almost over with the station at the end of the road. I turned my attention to my hat and lowered the visor to keep the sun out. Cyrus passed me a small look and I just smiled back. There was no reason to be nervous, the trip was almost over and there hadn't been any real incidents.

And while it was a wonderful time… the paranoia I felt that morning had returned shortly after I finished the ice cream. It was like someone was watching us since we left the park, like the beginning of a horror story, but I tried to pass it off. Of course people were watching us, they had been the entire time. Besides the few times of being childish and delinquents, we had acted like officers and lawmen should have. Perhaps it wasn't the uniforms but rather the university district ending and turning into a new one where the tall buildings were back and no longer spread out.

I gave out a small sigh, one that Cyrus didn't miss. "Not enjoying yourself?"

"No, I am. I had a lot of fun but coming to the end of this made me remember how dangerous it is to be here." I looked over at him, he was more rigid than a steel beam. "Something wrong?"

"Not that I'm aware of… but you have been fidgeting meaning you are sensing something I cannot."

"I'm just being paranoid." A glimpse of a shadow was cast down for barely a moment but looking upwards couldn't tell me what dragon had gone by with the sun blocking the view. "Don't mind me and relax. You're not going to be able to react quickly if something does come up."

"I am relaxed."

I gave him a sly smirk. "Sure you are."

Suddenly, a small Seraphinean child darted out of a tiny alleyway, barely in front of us. Cyrus stepped in front of me threateningly and caused the boy to scream. I sighed as I moved past the barrier he made.

"So relaxed, just like at the park." The knight said nothing as the kid took a step back and I moved closer before lowering myself, almost to his height. He gave a look to the alleyway before looking back at me, wide-eyed and upset. Something was wrong. "Sorry, my partner is a bit jumpy… Is something wrong?"

The boy nodded slightly as he looked to the dark alley, tearing up. "Mummy. Mummy said to find a patrolman when I needed help. I don't need it, but she does. She fell down in there when we were going to the store! I can't get her up!"

"Show us where; we can get her help."

"You'll help me?!" He asked in surprised before looking up at Cyrus.

I noticed him motioning slightly to me from the corner of my eye and I stood up. His words were hushed, "I don't think we should. Azarias and Owen aren't far, a few minutes."

"She may not have that time," I answered quietly, not needing to explain to him how those minutes counted.

"It's off the route and a maze in there. We won't have backup."

"Just stay close then, Deigh knows where we are now and can tell Orpheal which alleyway he needs to go down and I have Guðmundr if it's a trap." I turned to the kid. "Show us."

The kid nodded and started off into the alley, forcing us to chase. He rounded a corner, one I didn't expect right away, let alone one he could take so quickly on his tiny wings. I sped up from a jog to a run, listening to make sure

Cyrus was not far behind me. I turned the corner, careful not to bash the side of the wall, only to see the kid was far down the next straight away, turning another corner.

There were many other pathways to go down and I ignored them. It was a maze, but it was interesting at how it was built, cutting through blocks as it did. Both ingenious and terrifying as the walls were really close together, reminding me a bit of the Gracidra's maze.

After what seemed to be forever, we finally made it to the corner and rounded it. A dead end was all that we were met with. The light was blighted out from above by a tin roof. I carefully walked into the space, no complaint coming from Cyrus as I heard him give a small sigh behind me. It was possible there was a passageway in the dark that we were missing. I reached the end found it was as it seemed.

Dammit… I thought I got the right turn, but all the paths looked the same. Hopefully, the kid had noticed that we weren't behind him.

I turned around, ready to call out for him only to find that I was alone. My heart jumped in my throat as I quickly went back to the spot where I knew Cyrus had been a moment before. "Cyrus? Cyrus?!"

Silence once again and I formed Guðmundr into a small dome. The feeling of dread coming back from before. I needed to find Cyrus and leave. I brought out the CT to contact him, but it wouldn't turn on. The shield sputtered out and I silently went back into the dead end slightly. There was only one-way in. No way from above. It was the best defensive-

A small pain hit the side of my neck and I dropped the CT in surprise as I grabbed at the bug that bit me. The bug crumbled in my hand not like a bug would have and I looked at what I had squished. A small, metal thing sat in my palm.

What the hell was-

The world started to spin as my legs collapsed under my weight. I tried to catch myself on the wall only to fail, landing on my hands and knees. My cap fell off my head from the jerking motion as I fought to stay conscious, the world trying to darken. "*Deigh, I need help.*"

No answer came despite our connection being still stable enough.

A small tsk came out. There was some sort of Dagdian illusion at play. I went to activate the shield, knowing it would work now that I knew someone was messing with my head but before I could, someone in heels stepped on my back.

They forced me down onto the pavement, ending any concentration to activate it. I focused on keeping the link open as I struggled to get up. It wasn't successful as each time I tried, a heel dug into my spine, stopping my focus on Guðmundr to activate it.

The weight shifted on my back, forcing most of their weight of whoever was on me down into a single point, making it harder to breathe and I couldn't scream for help. They got close, but I couldn't see through the darkening world what their hand looked like as they removed Guðmundr from my wrist and my sunglasses, getting a view of my face. The shield was tossed in front of me, tantalizingly and just out of my reach. I tried to grab for it only to seethe in pain as they dug their heel again.

A female voice I didn't recognize came to my ear close by, but tauntingly kept herself out of my view. "I can't have you activate that… though I'm surprised you're still conscious."

I ignored her, struggling still, and turned to magic, but no fire came. No hints of light magic. No plasma. "How?"

"I sealed your elements," the woman answered with a hint of amusement. "A neutral ability I'm sure you heard of."

My jaw clenched, trying to keep my shock from her. I did know it; it was one of the first things I had learned from my mother when I was starting my magic training. But it also meant that she knew exactly who she was dealing with. "What… do you want?"

"Money, but not from you. That would be bad business to go against my contract, Your Majesty."

She was a mercenary… but for who? "You won't… get far-arg!" She pushed her heel into my spine again.

"Please, I have class. I'm not carrying you." A circle of light started to form below me as I tried to figure out who hired her, what the circle was, and what was taking Orpheal so long.

"Deigh! Where are you?!"

Silence was all that answered my pleas. A second sharp pain stabbed into my exposed neck. "Good night, Little Dragon."

The name caught me off guard for a moment then I gritted my teeth at the taunting use of it. I tried to get up as the fear of being taken overtook the anger. Running came to my ears. Deigh was so close. *"Deigh! Hurry…"*

The link closed as whatever she injected me with a second time kicked in and my body gave up on moving. The world went dark as I tried calling for my partner one last time, her name barely a whisper on my lips.

Chapter Thirty-Seven: Gone

Owen reached the corner of the alleyway, breathless from his run when the incomprehensible mutters of Deigh reached his ears. Azarias continued on, Cyrus was still missing. Owen walked into the dead end to find Orpheal on a knee, investigating the space as Éabha, who he had followed, wandered over to the sapphire amulet that was Guðmundr, one of the only things that were left of his nephew. His CT, sunglasses, and patrol cap were also left on the ground, but he didn't care. His main concern was the dragon in Absalomian form on the ground in front of him in a state of shock. Her tail and wings were out as she wasn't able to keep the transformation perfect, still muttering. She didn't look away from where Orpheal was, so pale she matched her white clothing.

Owen knelt in front of her. "Deigh-"

"He was right there. I couldn't..." Her words stabbed his soul with each syllable, threatening to shatter him.

"Deigh."

"He called for me, pleading for help."

"Deigh, listen-"

"He was terrified... his last breath conscious was begging for me. He couldn't hear me." Tears broke, but she still wasn't seeing him. "He depended on me to help him. I wasn't there in time. He was right there..."

"We're going to find him," he told her with every bit of confidence he could give, pulling her into a hug. Her sobs barely contained as her body shook in his arms. "You did everything you could."

"You didn't hear his calls... he was so scared. I couldn't even reassure him. He could hear us. We were right there! I couldn't help him!" She broke entirely, something he had seen more than a few times in his life from other people, dragon and Absalomian alike when their partner went missing. But it was something he wished he wouldn't have to see in his family.

Expiration shock was in full effect and she wasn't going to be able to eat, sleep, or think right until Aerrow was found. If they took too long, she was going to die and with the things she had been muttering, the guilt, it wasn't a whole lot of time. Twenty-four hours, maybe thirty-six if nothing stressful happened... That would probably be her limit.

He was going to have to figure out how to keep her from slipping too far, using his experience in hopes that something would keep her stable or better yet functional to a degree. Anything to keep her from getting worse – give them more time. If she died, it wouldn't matter if they found Aerrow. He'd be dead within eight hours after her.

Owen tried again. "We will find him and we're going to need your help to do it. He's still depending on you."

"I failed-"

"Not yet, you haven't." No, she didn't fail him... but Owen had. His nephew was wary, more so than usual that morning and he didn't heed his unsaid instincts. His grip tightened around her. "I'm so sorry."

She shook her head but was unable to speak.

Noises came from his right, startling Deigh as she snapped to it and he looked up to see Cyrus skid to a stop in the alley looking like he had been through hell. His clothes were tattered, blood stained his jacket, and a gash was easily seen on his arm. His spear collapsed inside itself as it fell out of his hand. The small cylinder form clattered to the ground. Azarias came in slightly, giving a wave before leaving to search from above for their king. Missiletainn was waiting with Sage at the street.

"I was right there, he was and..." Cyrus's fist went into the wall causing the cement to crack and break under the hit. His body trembled almost as much as Deigh's. "Fucking Dagdian magic made me think I was still following him! I was right, fucking, there and I couldn't do anything!"

"What happened?" Owen asked him. He needed the full story, not the bits of rage the knight was giving.

"A kid came out of the alley claiming his mother had collapsed and wouldn't wake up. Aerrow offered to help and when I said it was dangerous, he insisted. We were together, we had his shield, we were going to be fine. We should have been fine. We chased; time was of the essence so we couldn't wait for you to come by. The kid was fast... When I turned a corner that Aerrow had gone down, it was just a series of alleyways and both him and the kid were gone. I heard him call me in the distance and I tried to get to him but ran into a group of fucking cultists. They were waiting for me..."

"Did you-"

"Yes. What's left of them are down there somewhere." He ran a hand through his disastrous hair. "I should have noticed the illusions, if I had, he would still be…"

"Cyrus-"

"You don't get it! I've been trained to notice this shit before I knew how to fucking read! I should have… It's my fault he was taken!"

"It would have been difficult to notice illusions against someone with this much talent," Orpheal stated, and they all turned to him. "There's barely a trace of a Teleport Glyph being made. Their signature completely masked. Deigh, what accent did the woman have?"

"She…" Deigh trailed off, trembling worse than before and grabbed her head. "She toyed with him…"

"Was it Seraphinean, Dagdian-"

"I was right there…"

"What accent? Did you see anything? Did she say anything unusual?"

"Orpheal!" Owen snapped at him, ceasing the questions. "Keep the pressure to a minimum. Too much stimulus won't help."

"I'm just trying to-"

"Little Dragon… She called him Little Dragon. Seraphinean accent," Deigh answered, releasing her head. "She wore heels, stilettos, I think. We've never heard her voice before. A mercenary… She sealed his magic using a neutral element."

"Could you guess her weight?" Orpheal asked and after a few shaky breaths, Deigh nodded.

"Incredibly light. She placed her heel into his spine to control him, but I don't think it would have worked anywhere else…"

"A Seraphinean mercenary…" Cyrus spat. "One who is good at Dagdian magic…"

"Someone come to mind?" Owen asked and he shook his head.

"No… but it might come to someone else's…"

"Cyrus, don't-"

"I'm going to check a few places."

"Cyrus, you need to rest."

"I'll rest once he's safe!" He seethed in rage. "He was my responsibility! No one else's! And some bitch beat us by using our conscience, abusing his altruistic-"

"I'm ordering you to rest, Cyrus," Owen cut him off as the air around them gathered a charge. "For an hour at least to calm down."

"They took Aerrow, Owen! He's your nephew and my… my king…" He pushed past the hesitance of what he refused to admit out loud what Owen had known but was still taken aback by the lack of a title. Even in the stressful times before, never once had it dropped, until now. "I can't fail again… Please let me do what I was raised for."

"You fought a bunch of zealots already. You're a mess and not thinking stra-"

"Will it help find Aerrow faster?" Deigh asked suddenly.

Cyrus gave a small nod. "A lead, hopefully…"

"As King's Dragon, I order you to do whatever it takes to find him."

"Deigh!" Owen tried to reason but she wasn't listening. She turned back to his chest, barely holding sobs of distress. "He needs to rest and heal."

"Then someone heal him and let him go do whatever he has in mind! Just find Aerrow… Please… I can't take the last thing he said repeating over and over again anymore."

His jaw clenched at the recklessness of what she was ordering. But if it helped her cope… Beggars couldn't be choosers. "Fine… Orpheal, if you could please heal Cyrus…"

The Lord Director got to work immediately.

"Cyrus be careful. We're heading back to the safehouse. Call both Azarias and I if you find something. Do not go after a lead on your own, understood?"

He nodded as Orpheal finished. He left the dead end and Owen turned to Éabha who was uncharacteristically quiet. She looked paler than normal but noticed his gaze immediately with a look he couldn't read. She turned back to the left behind things on her lap with soft words, finally able to speak. "Who has this kind of power for such powerful illusions?"

"Absalomians are susceptible to illusions if they aren't aware of them," Orpheal answered her, carefully. "But if Cyrus has been training as long as he says he has, then someone very, very well versed. A six-winged Seraph, maybe even an eight-winged one."

Éabha flinched under the idea but didn't share her thoughts. "What does Little Dragon mean?"

"It was Aerrow's nickname as a child. Aelia gave it to him," Owen told her before turning to Deigh. "Can you stand?"

The dragon was back into an unresponsive state but tried to stand with him. She lost her balance, falling into him, but didn't collapse like he thought she would. He comforted her with strokes on her head like a cat. He had seen Aerrow do it enough times to guess that she liked it.

"Aelia… she's his mum?" Éabha questioned, still staring at the objects.

He nodded. "Yes."

"When did she die?"

"Thirteen years ago."

"When did the nickname fall out?"

"Around that time. He didn't like being called it because it reminded him too much of her."

"So, it would be someone who knew Aerrow or his family before then, either the mercenary or the person who hired her. She taunted him with it meaning she was ordered to torment him or she's a sadist."

It limited the number of people significantly, but it wasn't a lot of help in the short term. They hired this woman to kidnap him meaning they wanted to experiment on him with who knew what. Everyone who knew in Seraphina: directors, Io, some older friends on the list were all scientists. That was only if this person kidnapped him was a Boffin or an opportunist. For all they knew, it would have been a follow up to what Oliver and Friea started, and the cultists Cyrus met were coincidence. There were too many variables.

"Orpheal, can you get anything from the leftover magic?"

"No." He leaned against the wall, a disgusted look on his face that lessened for a moment. "But maybe I could scry for him. Did he bring anything that he treasures?"

Owen gave another nod and formed a Chaos Portal. There was nothing left for them to find and he needed to get Deigh to a safe place, physically and mentally. The four of them left and much to his surprise, Deigh stayed in her Absalomian form. She had wrapped her arms around his, tightly holding it as her nails dug through his coat, but he didn't dare tell her that she was hurting him. She was thinking, which was more than what he expected from her. He brought her over to the couch and looked over his shoulder to the two Seraphs. "Orpheal, in Aerrow's room there is a distinct, purple bag on Deigh's saddle. Impossible to miss. Inside there should be a little stuffed dragon inside. You'll probably recognize it."

The man left quickly while Éabha set the four objects that she held onto the coffee table.

"Éabha." She perked at her name being called. "I need you to get blankets from the closet downstairs, the fluffier the better."

Her brows furrowed in confusion and nodded, heading downstairs. He turned to Deigh and noticed her eyes were closed in concentration. He put a hand on hers finding it icy. That was far from good.

"Deigh, can you hear me?"

"I'm trying to find…" Her voice caught.

"You're not going to be able to if his side is blocked."

"Maybe I can push through… I can sense he's alive, I should be able to know where."

"You know that won't-"

"It…" She released him only to curl up into a ball, hiding her face in her knees, crying again. "He called and no one came in time. Alone in that dark place. He couldn't even scream."

Owen moved closer and did his best to hold her. She was freezing, but she didn't shiver. "Deigh, I need you to be strong, okay? Aerrow still needs you, but you can't help him if you're comatose."

"He's gone. I'm never going to see him-"

"You'll see him again. We will find him."

Orpheal came out of Aerrow's room, holding the plush but before either of them could say anything, screaming from Éabha came from downstairs. "Naftali! Dad! Dad help!"

Orpheal dropped the toy, taking off towards the voice and Owen instinctually went to chase only to be grabbed by Deigh, her nails cutting into his hand. A small gasp escaped his mouth in pain, but she didn't remove her nails until he was back exactly where he had been. "Please don't…"

"I'm not leaving," he told her, reassuringly as he glanced at the damage she did. Blood dripped down his hand and he wiped it on his coat to keep it off her. He didn't know what her reaction would be if it touched her. Nothing positive that was for certain.

There was no noise as he looked to the stairs, waiting, wondering what was going on. After a few minutes, Orpheal and Éabha came upstairs, carrying blankets, but Naftali wasn't with them.

"What happened?"

"He collapsed…" Orpheal answered calmly, but his wings betrayed his worry. "I teleported him to Solaria to take care of him."

"He should have stayed home," Éabha growled. "I told him he didn't look well, and he just couldn't listen."

"He's just anxious to finish," Orpheal told her, but didn't disagree.

Owen asked Deigh if it was fine to stand, and she let go. He took the blankets from Orpheal and started to swaddle the dragon in them as Éabha stood by, waiting to give hers over.

"Why is she like this?" The girl asked him.

"It's the relationship between an Absalomian and dragon. Devastating events like illness or kidnapping can cause the unharmed one to slip into this state. If it were the other way around, Aerrow wouldn't be much different. We call it expiration shock."

"Oh…" She apparently understood the implications of the name and he took the last blanket from her, lightly putting it over Deigh and completely burying her other than a small place where her face was. "Will she be okay?"

He didn't know, so he didn't answer. He turned to the dragon who looked so far gone. "Deigh, are you warm enough in there?"

"I want him back…" she muttered out and he bent down to make sure she could see him.

He put a hand on her knee that was buried underneath, checking the air flow coming out. It was warm and he relaxed ever so slightly. "We all do. Orpheal is going to scry for him; he's setting it up right now."

"That woman is powerful, right? She could have…"

"Cyrus will get information about who took him. No one that strong is invisible."

"Is scrying limited?"

"To the user's ability. Orpheal is strong in Dagdian magic, he will find him."

There was silence as he looked over at Orpheal who had dropped a map of the kingdom from Aerrow's desk onto the floor beside them. He paused for a moment and then looked around. "Is there a gemstone around? I need a medium."

"Guðmundr… but it's a bit large," Éabha offered, picking up the pendant and handing it over.

"That's fine, we can use other maps for accuracy." He set Guðmundr on the corner of the map, keeping it off the picture. He picked up the stuffed dragon, holding it in one hand while the other was placed on the map. A Dagdian spell came out. "Invesigh quan homuine qubé aestide haeo read."

The gem glowed, flashing like a beacon for a moment before a chime echoed the room. It didn't move. He did it again, but the result was the same.

Deigh's voice pierced the silence. "Did it work?"

Owen looked to her, finding that she was still hiding in her ball. He made a decision that made his gut twist. "It's a bit confused, but it's got a relative area."

She gave a small breath of relief. "Okay."

He turned to Éabha. "Stay with her."

She looked at him in disbelief before hardening her expression with a nod. She sat next to Deigh and wrapped her arms around the bundle the best she could. "It seems so nice in there… Can I come in?"

There was a tiny movement of a head nod and Owen left them to hide inside the fort, turning to Orpheal who's expression was that of dread. They went into Aerrow's room and Owen closed the door, moving to the far end before speaking quietly. He did his best to keep the anger and fear out of his voice, but some of it slipped. "What the hell was that?"

"He's not in the kingdom," Orpheal answered looking away in disgust. "I can only scry by region and I'm more than certain that no one can block out the skill, not at my level at least… So, I'm going to have to leave to scry, one region at a time."

"How many?"

"Seraphina Lake has eight due to it's depth, Lake Jaya to the west has two, north of Seraphina Lake has three but also encompasses the mountains, east has two, south – two, and west: three."

"How long would that take?"

"Two days, mostly waiting for the Teleport Glyph to recharge. Add in the dragons and other places I'd have to fly to since I don't know the area well enough to teleport it becomes three maybe four."

"We don't have that much time."

"No, we don't. That mercenary could have gone anywhere within five hundred kilometres with what I could gather. Then with how fast she formed it…" He sighed. "Just in the time he's been missing, she could have gone fifteen hundred kilometres in any direction, probably reaching a limit of two thousand before she would have to stop."

He knew the average use of the Teleport Glyph, but Orpheal seemed to be more familiar with the skill that this woman presented. "For how long?"

"For the night, teleporting is taxing plus the illusions of not just visual, but audio to two separate people in an area. She's going to be forced to rest for eight hours at least if she has any hope in protecting her bounty from Outland Monsters."

Eight hours was barely enough time to find him even with scrying. "Scry the lake, if nothing comes up, come back. I'll check the Outlands for any convergences come night, find locations for you to teleport to come morning so it doesn't take days, but I can't leave Deigh here alone."

"I'll watch her while you're gone." He looked past him to the door. "In the meantime, you need to stay with her as long as you can. Her shock is more than I've seen in a long while, twenty-four, maybe thirty-six hours is her max."

"That's what I was thinking and to keep it, we can't have another issue come up. I'm not going to be able to lie to her a second time. She's going to notice." He lost composure at the thought of her state. Her words of Aerrow begging. "This wasn't how it was supposed to be. There were signs and I just... I shouldn't have let him leave."

"Owen, this was beyond what anyone could prepare for."

"How did this woman know?"

"Dagdian locator spell is my guess," his friend replied and expanded on when Owen looked at him in confusion, needing a refresher. "It's like a scry but acts more like a surveillance system. It picks up your target if they walk by and notifies the creator. These spells can last up to a week and you can create about twenty of them at a time, spreading them out across a city easily. They don't work well in high concentrations of magic which is why you've rarely come across them in Absalom. But here, officers are tasked with disarming such spells when they're found."

Owen thought it over. "Meaning she has probably been hired for a while..."

"Most likely, but patrols had already gone through that line before hand and would have noticed new ones being set and reported it."

A frown formed. "Are you suggesting there's a traitor?"

"No. Only you, your knights and I knew of the route. Naftali only knew of the possibilities and I haven't exactly been talking to Éabha as of late." He turned solemn. "I have to prepare for the journey so while I'm gone, Owen, can you do me a favour?"

"What is it?"

"If something happens... can you take care of Éabha for me?"

Owen stared at him in shock. "Where is this coming from?"

"Just a feeling... it's hard to explain but over the last few days, something has felt amiss and Éabha had a nightmare last night..."

"A nightmare or a prophetic dream?"

"I don't know, but she checked in with me and left without a word, seemingly fine so it's unlikely a prophetic dream. Still, I can't shake the ill intent of murder."

If it were a dream, she wouldn't have walked it off so easily, so a nightmare... He nodded regardless of the outcome. "I'll take care of her, but I have to ask, why not Solaria? She knows her far better than she knows me."

"Solaria is my friend yes, but if Éabha stays, she will be forced to be a director and I don't want her to be one so soon and so young. And with the directorate as it is, she would be promoted to Lord Director without being asked. The remaining directors don't want that responsibility and will pawn it on her as she's well versed on how things are run without needing much instruction. I can't let her go through what Aerrow is by letting her take her dead father's place. I want her to live and let her decide if she wants to be a director or not later and she can't do it here."

"What about the family legacy? She wouldn't abandon that."

"I know and it'd be a pity for the Gordin line to end, but we were never rulers to begin with. She knows this and will understand and accept my wish. She knows that Domrael only became a leader to fill the void that was left behind, forming the directorate, and moulding it. With the kinks that have been found and fixed, our job is done. I want her to make the decision to continue the line or let someone else take over. If she's with you, I know she can explore and learn for herself what she wants in life to the fullest without being killed along the way. I won't let her be alone the rest of her life. So… will you do this for me?"

There was a heavy silence as Owen agreed again. "I'll take care of her; you have my word."

"Thank you, Owen."

"But this doesn't mean you have the freedom to die," he told him with a glare. "I will take the risk to summon your soul back, disregarding all your faith and spiritual rights if you die scrying just so you can explain to her why you thought it was okay to die so young."

He paled. "I'll keep that in mind…"

"Good. Now get going. It's going to be dusk soon and you'll have Éabha worried."

00000

Hours went by with the only change in Deigh's state being a couple hours ago. She thought she could sense Aerrow for a moment before going hysterical. Her body went rigid as her sharp nails ripped into the couch, then her throat before losing consciousness for a few seconds. When she came to, she was blocked off from whatever she had felt. Éabha instructed her to take calm breaths – mimicking what she had seen her father and aunt did and healed the wounds Deigh was afflicting herself still as Owen did his best to keep her from mutilating herself.

Eventually, she calmed down and stopped trying to rip out whatever she felt burning through her. All Owen could do was hold her as she explained the pain Aerrow was in was nothing like he had been through. The pain so intense she felt like she was there, suffering just as he was. It took everything he had to hold himself together and push past the thought of his nephew going through hell to keep her optimistic and calm. After cleaning up the blood and more time passing, she was back to holding herself as Éabha cuddled her with all eight of her wings.

The soft hushes and words came to an end as Cyrus came through the door a little more than aggravated. His jacket was gone, and he had somehow looked worse than he had in the scuffle with the zealots. He took a moment, judged the room before marching downstairs, taking off his tattered shirt as he went with a small hiss. Cuts, blood, and bruises lined his body.

Owen looked to Éabha. "Watch her, I'll be right back."

She gave a small nod, going back to her calming explanation of quantum physics and he went downstairs to meet with the knight. He reached the bottom, finding Tempest eating in the far corner while Cyrus was cleaning off blood at the sink.

"Was this one tavern brawl or two?" Owen asked, trying to lighten his mood a small bit.

He was successful as a small laugh came out of his pupil and he looked over at him with a painful, tired, and slightly wild glance. "Don't insult me. This was clearly five tavern brawls of work."

"Was it worth it?"

He turned to the sink, rinsing off the blood on the towel. "It took a while, but I managed to get a name. Aevorii… One chatty fellow mentioned that she was around this morning but checked out."

Owen didn't know who that was. "Chatty before or after you beat him?"

"After I beat the shit out of one of his customers on his bar… I want to mention that I didn't start any of these fights."

"You never do…" That wasn't what he was concerned about. What did was how many underground people he had pissed off in the process. "Anything else?"

"None of the places offered previous jobs or information about an offer to kidnap Aerrow… I have a few other places I can go but…"

"You need to heal first, get some water and food," he finished, and Cyrus nodded. "I'll send Éabha down. Don't get in over your head."

"Yes, Sir." Owen went to leave but Cyrus gave out a disgusted sigh. "There is something else I should mention."

"What is it?"

"The reason why Aevorii… She knew my parents, often took jobs from them. She knew me and that's why it went flawlessly for her."

"So, you know what she looks like."

"No, she changes her look constantly and I've never seen her wings. Someone knew that I was there and tipped her off. If Azarias or you had been there, she wouldn't have-"

"I picked you to be his guard because you're familiar with the dirty aspects of Dagdian magic that someone could use. Don't blame yourself because the one person on this damn planet who knew you from years ago was called."

He only gave out a grunt of disbelief. "I'll believe that when you don't blame yourself for everything too, General."

Owen didn't say anything as he left for Cyrus's room to get him his gear and switched spots with Éabha, letting her heal him and pass along the armour and new clothes he could probably use. She wasn't downstairs long. Cyrus followed a few minutes later with a peanut butter sandwich, wearing a new shirt and left before Deigh could ask questions. Orpheal teleported shortly thereafter wearing black and white armour and set down his bag. A simple look said Owen's question to which he shook his head.

"He's gone…" Deigh said suddenly, causing Owen's heart to stop for a moment, turning his attention to her.

"Gone, what do you mean?"

"We're never going to find him…" He gave her a tight hug, relieved to hear that she hadn't meant that her partner was dead. "Why couldn't I do anything?"

"You're doing something right now," he told her. "You're looking for him, right?"

She nodded, more responsive than she had been in hours.

"That's more than what all of us can do right now. Orpheal, can I have the dragon?"

Orpheal gave him a confused glance before taking the plush out of the bag. "Here."

"Thank you." Owen took it and Aerrow's CT off the table, making the tiny dragon hold the device in front of her. She looked at it with a grim expression. "This dragon is you, see how she's holding the CT?"

She looked to him. "I don't understand…"

"She's going to use it to call one of the knights out looking when she senses her partner again. Can you do that, Deigh? Can you call one of us if you sense anything?"

"What if I don't sense anything at all?"

"Then it's okay. But if you do, we can go to that location as fast as we can. In a matter of minutes even."

She took the CT and the plush, holding them close. "I will call."

"Good. Did you want to eat something?" She shook her head. "Are you able to keep this form for much longer?"

"I can't switch out of it…"

He forced a smile and patted her head. "That's okay. You stay right here then, alright? I'm going to go out and look for clusters and Orpheal is going to be right here with you."

She hugged the dragon tighter, and he turned to Orpheal. He didn't need to tell him how bad the situation was by the look on his face.

"Do everything you can to keep her stable," he whispered as he started to walk past and Orpheal nodded.

"I brought some of Solaria's Night if need be."

"She might need it if another incident occurs. Call me if it does."

"I will."

Owen started to go get his armour when Éabha stopped him, looking at him, expectedly. "Can I help too?"

"Éabha, I'm going to the Outlands-"

"You're not in a right state of mind, you could get hurt." She turned to her father for permission. "Please, I'll be careful."

Orpheal looked to her for a moment, then to Owen, then to his bag. "You brought your armour?"

"Yes. I wanted to show Aerrow how his worked…"

"Then…" There was a moment of silence before he gave a nod. "Alright… But you are not to leave Missiletainn's back. No heroics. You're going to heal and defend Owen if he needs it. Understood?"

She beamed in glee before taking off downstairs to gear up.

Owen gave him an approving nod but saw the pain on his face from letting her go. Orpheal looked away from the vacated stairs to him. "Keep her safe or so help me…"

"She's going to be the safest person in the world."

00000

Ori's blue light glowed relatively brightly in its waxing gibbous form compared to the red sliver of the waxing crescent of Val. It showed monsters flying about, allowing Éabha to shoot them down just as well as he and Missiletainn killed anything that got in their way. Owen looked out at the horizon.

There wasn't much to look at east of the kingdom, just grass, trees, mountains, ocean when they were higher up, and a river. The monsters were far and few in between the farther they got away from the kingdom. Wherever this Aevorii person had taken his nephew, it wasn't around there. He took a few photos with his CT as a good spot for Orpheal to teleport to, and they headed towards the next section.

He looked back at Éabha. "What's the closest section your father pointed out from here?"

"North-northeast of the island is the third region," she yawned, looking at a map. "That's… are we really going to be able to cover half of these tonight? We've only done a fourth of the regions around the island."

"We have to cover that much tonight," he explained, a little more urgently than he would have liked. He looked at the time on the CT before putting it away. It was almost midnight; it took them about an hour to get to a new section… He could shorten the time using a Chaos Portal to the northern sections since he had been to them before, but it might not have been enough.

"This has to do more with Deigh than Aerrow, doesn't it?" Éabha asked, carefully. "Not that Aerrow isn't a priority but, it's about how she can't change back, right? I don't understand how she can't change back to her original form."

"Her state of mind, the expiration shock, has locked her from undoing or performing any magic. It happens in the later stages."

"So, she's… how much time?"

"Originally, your father and I thought about twenty-four hours after the incident, now…" His voice caught.

"Now?"

Missiletainn answered where he couldn't, "Twelve to eighteen."

"It's already been seven. How are we supposed to find him if we don't even know who took him?!"

"I don't know, that's why I gave Deigh that task," Owen replied, barely keeping his emotions out of his voice. She wasn't who he was angry at and he didn't need her to know how terrified he was. "It gives her a goal, something she has always liked and responded to well – this should give us more time."

"And what happens if she has another episode like earlier?"

"That doesn't usually happen." He went through the times he'd witness the event and heard from others. "Hallucinations do happen from time to time, sometimes the state becomes anger and fear mixed and the sufferer gets violent, but never to themselves. This was… I've never seen such a reaction before."

"Was it possible that she really did sense him for that moment?"

"If she did, I'm praying to any god listening to help him endure."

"I didn't know you were religious."

"I'm not, but for his sake." There was silence as the tension grew only to be cut by Owen's CT. He looked at it, reading only part of Azarias's name before answering. "Did you-"

"Meet me at the scene," Azarias answered, quickly. "I got a lead but it's going to take all three of us."

"Be there in a few minutes." He ended the call and turned to Éabha. "Azarias found something, we're going back to the city. Stay on Missiletainn."

She gave a small nod as Missiletainn created a Chaos Portal and flew through it. On the other side was the street that he had last seen Aerrow walking down. On the roof of the building next to it, Azarias, Cyrus, and their dragons were geared up and waiting. Missiletainn landed and Owen got off, meeting the two knights. "Where is he? How did you find him?"

Azarias didn't look him in the eye, turning to the alley below. "Theodora."

"She's here? How does she-"

"I don't know. She didn't say. What she did tell me was she saw the aftermath of what Cyrus did and knew where he was being held, but it's full of zealots and heavily armed guards."

"A facility…" That was a problem for several reasons.

"North of the kingdom, the old lab." That made part of the problem less. They could do whatever they wanted in the Outlands. "But there was something else before we siege, she mentioned that he would be crazed."

"She said crazed?" Cyrus asked and Azarias nodded.

"I tried getting her to expand, but she was very stingy on it."

"Where is she now?" Owen questioned.

"I don't know. There was a Chaos Portal and she left before I could ask more questions." He gave a small shrug at a discussion none of them were a part of. "Perhaps she meant that he'd be confused, probably a bit scared I'd imagine… But he should be fine once he sees us."

"Hopefully, but in the off chance he's not, I'm the only one who's going to confront him. Stay back and non-threatening. Follow my lead, whether that means we play cat and mouse or have to use force. Interject only if necessary."

They both nodded and he formed a portal beside them to the forest that was just outside the facility.

"Take the portal and start sieging, I'll join you after I drop off-" He didn't get to finish his sentence as Éabha flew in. "Éabha!"

"Guess she's coming with us," Azarias sighed, and Cyrus went in, not waiting for an invitation.

They followed with the dragons behind them. On the other side was the building beyond the bushes and across a small field surrounded by a protective fence. Warning lights flashed while a siren blared out across the property. A broadcasted, computer generated warning came to their ears: **Containment Breach – Danger Level has been raised from Heroepos Experiment to Danger Level Divinukos Experiment! All unauthorized personnel evacuate!**

"Well, at least that will occupy their forces," Azarias commented, and Cyrus gave him a glare.

"That experiment is in the same building as Aerrow!"

"Right…" They turned to Owen. "What's the plan?"

Owen didn't take long to form one. "The dragons patrol out here; we can't risk damaging the building. From there, the front door."

"Strong approach."

"We should be going through the side or making our own entrance," Éabha growled, not as thrilled as the knights were. "The front door will be armed to the teeth! Not to mention, if these people are following the same lab rules as the demesne, that thing running around in there is really fucking dangerous. Regeneration, fast, powerful, and just as deadly as a Divinukos levelled Outland Monster. We need something other than just this."

"We've taken on Divinukos monsters before and if Aerrow is in any decent condition, he's killed one just by himself. If worse comes to worse, we can easily trap it and move on, but we need to go through the front door."

She gave a look of surprise before growing confused. "What's at the front door that you need?"

"The security control room. It won't be far, and it will tell us exactly where Aerrow is. We can hack it for a map and access codes to the building just in case we need them."

"Those… are some good trade offs…"

"They are, so stay out of harms way and close, understood?"

"Yes, General…" She wasn't happy, but he didn't need her to be. There were going to be a few people that were going to die tonight before they got to Aerrow and if she froze or started freaking out…

And of course since she had been here, shoving her back through his Chaos Portal would have been useless as she would have teleported back.

Why the hell did she come to a battlefield?

He didn't get to ask when his CT rang, surprising them. He took it out to silence it and answered. "Deigh, this really-"

"I just spoke with him!" the dragon practically shrieked in his ear and started speaking quickly. "He's not right and talking strangely. I could sense so much yet so little – he's in so much pain. Please find him!"

"I think we may have so hold out a little longer, okay?"

"He doesn't have a little-"

"Deigh, we're going to be storming the building. We will rescue him."

He could practically see her relax but her voice was still etched in pain. "He's hurt but I don't know how. He didn't recognize me… They did something to him. I couldn't help him."

"We'll cross that bridge when we get there, but I promise he'll be okay. Can you pass the CT to Orpheal?"

"Okay…"

There was a soft noise and after a moment, Orpheal's voice greeted him. "Owen, she's getting worse."

"I know, but we're just outside this place."

"With Éabha?!"

"It's a long story," he lied before continuing what he needed to say. "I need you to take Deigh and get any and all medical equipment you can possibly think that he will need. Bandages, detox, blood – anything and everything and set it up. We'll hopefully be there within the next hour or so. There's a breach with a Divinukos experiment by the warnings and he's still inside with who knows how many of them and it."

"We'll set up for the worst-case scenario…"

"Thank you." Owen didn't wait for him to speak further and ended the call, shoving the CT in his pocket.

Cyrus took the lead, taking the ending of the call as the clear to attack and got on Tempest who started for the gate. They followed them on their dragons with Éabha on Missiletainn, catching up in time for Tempest to overload the gate and barrier with several incredibly powerful lightning strikes. It opened, but with it came another warning that announced their arrival. Armed Seraphs came to the gate who didn't get much farther than its threshold when they attacked. Missiletainn blasted out a chaos sphere and Sage created a fissure in the earth. Some of them fell and weren't able to escape as it slammed closed, ending the short-lived screams. The ones who were hit by the sphere vaporized.

Balls of light from firearms came at them only to be blocked by Tempest with a wall of ice using the moisture in the air. It was shattered by another bolt of lightning, electrocuting a handful of the flying guard while Sage and Missiletainn followed up. Spikes of earth skewered any who were near or on the ground while Missiletainn covered the sky, tendrils of darkness came from an over-shield and wrapped any who tried to escape the earth dragon. They wrapped and dug into armour, crushing it loudly over the screams that were silenced on gurgles of blood. The leftovers were tossed to the dirt, severed into pieces.

Missiletainn flew by the entrance and Owen dropped off the side. He landed and abused the distraction the dragons were creating. The door was blasted open, breaking the frame it was latched in with ease with his own dark sphere. He felt Éabha land softly behind him through his magic field as shards and tendrils came from it and drove into the hall where militants were surprised by the sudden assault. They attacked everything that he deemed a foe, running them through and tearing their limbs from their torsos. His dark field grew across the floor and walls, the lights flickering at the excess magic. A couple dozen fell in front of him by the time stone shards and air slashes had joined in on the assault as Cyrus and Azarias met him on the raised platform. They started walking ahead of him, dividing, and securing the area of its off-shooting hallways and rooms.

Owen led Éabha in, telling her to keep close once more and a surge of light magic came from his right. A wall of chaos went up in front of him before it could hit. The attack went through it a bit, leaving several spikes of light. They shattered as he crushed them, absorbing their power. A snarled formed as the wall dropped and he grabbed the guard that attacked him by the collar. The man's light frame was smashed into the wall, causing him to wince.

"I'm only going to ask you once," Owen growled as the man tried to struggle against his unwavering hold. "Where is King Aerrow locked up?"

"H-he's not here…"

"You're a terrible liar." Tendrils crept around the man's legs, digging deep into his flesh, and causing him to scream. "Try again."

"He'll kill me if I tell you."

"And I'll kill you if you don't. I don't have to be here to leave you to suffer as I rip your atoms apart, slowly, and when your living hell is over, I'll flay your soul. So, what's it going to be?"

"Flay it, keep it as your slave, Necromancer. It's nothing compared to being damned to the Comyah-" He was cut off as a scream escaped when his legs started to be shredded more.

"Wrong answer."

"Watch out!" Éabha shouted and he felt the light magic appear from the man over his rage.

He reacted; a dark magic shank drove into the guard's skull before the magic could be unleashed. He dropped him and turned to Éabha. "Thank you..."

"He would have killed you, perhaps its you who should be more careful," she mocked, and he rolled his eyes.

"Don't get cocky..." He looked over the body and found a key card on it. "We can use this to create a master key."

"You're not going to reap his soul and flay it?" She asked, attempting to sound apathetic but he could hear the fear in her voice. He didn't blame her, the thought was horrifying even for him, horrifying and brutal.

He shook his head and they started walking down the hall, trying doors as they passed. "He's not worth it nor do we have the time."

"So, you would do that to someone if it was worth it?"

"There is someone that I would very much like to treat that experience to and one person alone." The card unlocked a door.

Azarias and Cyrus were on him, drawn to the noise somehow through the shouts that belonged to the guards they had been fighting. It became quiet and he opened it. There was hardly a moment that went by when he was forced to put up a wall of darkness to block the attacks from three men inside. He dropped it and the two knights and Éabha attacked, each one killing a cultist.

He gave her a surprised look that she noticed, and she looked to her rifle, suddenly realizing her actions.

"They took my friend and I... oh gods." She looked like she was going to be sick. "I murdered..."

"Éabha." He tried to snap her out of the existential crisis, but she didn't hear him.

"Even those dragons too, all they wanted was their kids back and I... Murder is a sin-"

"Éabha, they were going to kill us," he snapped, a bit harshly but it caught her attention. "This is a battlefield and if you want to live, you need to focus."

"But-"

"No, it's them or us – they can't be reasoned with. You can teleport back to the safehouse or you can help rescue Aerrow, your choice."

She seemed conflicted, but her expression went from fear to determination. "I'm going to help."

"Then prepare yourself; there will be more lives taken before we find him." Soft noises reached his ears and he turned to Azarias. "Stand guard just in case."

Azarias gave a curt nod and left, leaving the console and security cameras to Cyrus.

"Éabha, help search, I'm going to hack for blueprints and make this our master key."

She gave him a look of surprise if not a bit impressed. "You can hack?"

"Yes, the only technology illiterate one out of the four of us is Aerrow." He softened his tone. "Are you sure you wish to stay? This is probably going to be the only chance you get to leave."

"He'd do the same for me, so I don't care how many people I have to kill."

"Don't let him hear that, he doesn't like it when people die, light or not."

She glared, seated in her new position. "Well that's just too fucking bad for him."

Owen caught a crack of a grin from Cyrus in the corner of his eye as they got to work, and he pulled out his CT. He opened his application and forced his way into the server. He managed to set up the key card faster than he had expected and turned to getting blueprints.

Suddenly, a shocked gasp came from Éabha beside him, "Oh gods…"

Owen looked away from his download and up to the wall of screens. There wasn't anything he noticed out of the ordinary of what he was expecting… and then it became very obvious that she was focused a cam just outside a stairwell. His CT dropped out of his hand as he watched, horrified as she was and unable to breathe.

"What's going on in…" Azarias started, coming in to investigate the silence only to stop next to him, staring at what they were all watching. "Oh… Oh that's not good."

"What is…" Éabha's voice caught and it allowed him to pry his eyes off the screen to her. She looked terrified. "What are we supposed to do against… whatever the fuck that is?!"

"Follow the plan. Only engage if I'm overwhelmed…" He turned back to the screen and his fists clenched. The figure in it almost collapsed, clearly writhing in agony, and sent Owen's entire being into an endless pit of dread. "Hang in there, Aerrow."

Chapter Thirty-Eight: The One

My chest ached as I started to come to, a small hiss escaping. It was incredibly cold, but I was too exhausted to shiver as my heart raced in line with a massive headache.

What happened?

Nothing came to mind as it was loopy in the pain.

My eyes opened with great difficulty. The room was just as unsteady as my head. I tried to get up, but something was across my bare chest, keeping me down. I went to remove it, but my wrists were bound in metal cuffs along with my ankles that were protected by boots and pants as I tried to shift. No power came when I tried to use magic. The room started to spin more than before as I panicked, looking around for some sort of familiarity. An answer.

Nothing came. No solutions as my mind was fuzzy from the information I wanted to process but couldn't understand. The only thing I knew was the anxiety was building and I couldn't calm down. The feeling of instinct gripping tightly, screaming for me to run.

"You're awake, how unfortunate," a male voice said that I thought I recognized to my left, freezing my struggle. "I was hoping to do this whole experiment without you being in unnecessary pain."

I turned my head to the voice, and he came into the dim light. My surprise couldn't be hidden as I realized it was Naftali, only something was very off. He looked way healthier than when I had seen him before my excursion into the city. He wasn't frail by any means, he… A look of pleasure made it into the man's orange eyes, pupils slit like an Absalomian's.

But… he wasn't… His eyes were blue…

He was a Seraph; his wings were right there.

"Why are… eyes…" I couldn't construct my question as my brain and mouth stopped communicating.

It didn't seem to matter as he figured it out. A cold smile made it to his face. "Through a very difficult blood transfusion procedure."

A blood transfusion… with what? "You can't- dragon blood…"

"I'm well aware that dragon blood is toxic. I'm not the head of biology for nothing. That's why I needed you, your father, or your sister and an opportunity to get you away from your entourage. Guess which one drew the short straw."

He had used… My heart raced even more as the words from his mouth started to dawn on me and I tried at my bindings again, trying to use magic. I had to leave. Get back to the others.

Deigh. Deigh could-

I couldn't sense her. Why?!

The man gave a small laugh at my struggles, a little more than out of character to the person who I had come to know. "You won't be able to use magic for a couple of hours yet and calling your dragon is pointless; she won't hear you."

"What did you…?!"

"Nothing to her, calm down."

I glared at him. "I will not-!"

"You're missing almost two litres of blood and will go into a coma if you don't relax," Naftali sighed like he was talking to an infant. "I'm sure you noticed something was wrong."

I continued my glare, trying my best to calm down using my anger at being betrayed to consume the fear of being trapped and his erratic behaviour.

"Good, Little Dragon… now let me explain. Your link is severed because of a lack of blood going to your brain."

"Why am I…?"

"You ask a lot of questions…"

"I'm tied to a…" A growl of frustration came out at the lack of sentence structure. The room got fuzzier once more as I focused on trying to get the link working again. I knew I could do it, I had to. I just needed time. A distraction to keep him from doing anything. He said experiment, I had to keep him talking, get more information. "How… you use my…?"

"With a great deal of planning. I'm aware that your blood is also toxic. It's fifty percent dragon after all," he answered all too happily. "But it's not so toxic when it has a binding agent such as Ciar's own DNA to allow me to become anew."

My eyes widened as the pieces started to come out of the foggy mess. He was the one who was behind-

"Thanks to you and him… I'm not going to die! I get to live! Together we can stop Ciar for-" His excitement stopped as he grabbed his head, a terrified expression on his face. Like waking up from a nightmare, he's body trembled. A gasped escaped as if he were trying to fight off something within. "Oh, gods what am… This isn't…"

"Naftali?"

He snapped to me, apparently forgetting I was there and whatever he was freaking over was gone, the excitement returning. "I've become a greater species, completely immune to whatever ailments the gods can throw at me! What I lack in, I no longer! Even new magic that I could never have imagined!"

I felt the air shift before something gripped onto me like barbed wire that tried to rip me apart. A scream exited my mouth, the room growing dark, and as quick as the pain came, it ended.

My chest hurt more, my breathing shallow. The darkening world took a few moments to lighten again, the excited noises of success came from beside me. None of them sounded like I had remembered Naftali. Something was so very wrong with him.

"Sorry, this power is something to get used to. Dark magic, it's so chaotic and unruly, so easy to go overboard when excited. But trying it now was nothing like how others expressed it. It's like your blood is adapted to it, boosting it exponentially – even with my light element. It's so strange since it should be hindered by your bloodline not being natural to it."

"Bastard…" I huffed with a glare. He was toying with me and that stunt ruined a lot of progress to get the link open again, even a little bit. A small beacon for Deigh to know where I was.

He gave me a deadpanned look like I was ungrateful. "I could have continued. There is so much to try and test."

"Why are… keeping… alive?"

"Why am I keeping you alive? I suppose that is a good question. I could have killed you, shipped you off to Ciar, dead or alive. He wouldn't have cared, and I got what I wanted. But… I have had a lot of time to think. Something beyond just being alive. The consequences of letting me have you, we can kill him! We can forever protect the kingdoms!"

"What the hell-" My anger stopped immediately, my tongue freezing as he grabbed something out of the darkened space behind him and pulled it into the light. A large bag filled with a black substance attached to a pole. It had an essence to it that I couldn't figure out, but my body reacted to it, repulsively. My heart skipped several beats and I looked over to him, terrified. "What is that?! Why are you telling me this?!"

"You're regaining some more cognitive thinking, unsurprising since your blood is basically the stuff of miracles and we can't have that…" He muttered, talking to himself in thought as he grabbed a large needle and opened the valve on the bag, causing the liquid to flow through the tube. Some of it dripped onto the floor with the consistency of blood.

"Wait-" I tried to delay. I could feel Deigh's vitals. I was so close. I tried to move from my binds with no use as he got closer. He stuck the needle in my arm and my veins started to burn as the substance went in. It ended the link's progression. "Stop it!"

He moved closer to my ear, causing me to freeze. "You wanted to know why I'm telling you. It's because I was bored and wanted to see your reactions. There isn't a risk to this, you won't remember. Not that you'd want to tell anyone who matters if you did."

"What are you talking-nrg!" The pain reached my heart, each beat stabbing me as I felt the substance spread, most notably up the side of my neck.

"This is Outland Dragon blood. It's effects… well normally it will kill someone. But for you, my experiments with other Absalomians have led to this. And now with the revelation of your magic adaptability, it only solidifies its success! My theory is that the blood will bind to you. My creation to protect this whole world! You'll be a new creature! Just like me."

"Bind?!" What did he mean by that? What was he…? What did he mean new-? The pain forced my questions to a halt as he continued.

"It'll attach to your brain, stem cells, and-" He was drowned out as another scream came out of me.

My head wanted to explode as the rest of my body burned at the touch of the foreign substance I wanted to rip out. Then it went dark.

Chapter Thirty-Nine: Unnatural

Atlamillia looked over the detailed plans, walking with the council about the castle and listening to each member discuss and elaborate the plans of the Thinnus Festival. It was a bit different this year as they had to supply for the whole kingdom and not just a portion of it. But through the effort and experimentation of the Kalokairtas Festival two months prior, the Thinnus event would hopefully go a hell of a lot more smoothly and with significantly less problems.

There were always going to be problems, that wasn't something they were ever going to avoid, especially when dealing with large groups of people. Facilities for food, water, and waste had to be attended to along with necessities for merchants and performers. Many artists of physical mediums also had their biyearly shows that had to be prepared. Their showcases were always in Anoxiver and Thinnus, so it was going to be touch and go in that section of planning.

Guards were needed and some soldiers were also planned to be on standby to assist. The only problem was, they didn't have Dragon Knights to assist like they had for the Kalokairtas festival. Most of them were deployed around the kingdom as it was, very few of them were spending their time with families and friends, and that would bring stress.

She was going to have to figure out a way to give them a piece of the festival just to show that the crown appreciated their sacrifices – to do that, she was going to have to ask around inconspicuously. Surprises always made things better she found… Well. Good surprises at least.

The conversation switched to the budgeting for the event. She winced as she looked over the numbers. The money really could be used elsewhere, but much to her disapproval, emotion instead of logic had to come first. Emotion for morale being raised in the people to rejuvenate their spirits was necessary. That meant spending a lot of money to make things as normal as possible. She supposed that it was better to spend money than have a revolt, pillaging, and murder. But were people so focused on their little boxes instead of looking outside of it?

Apparently, the answer was yes. So, the crown had to accommodate.

She frowned as she looked over the blueprints for the event. She had no idea how to approve it. Aerrow was always better with spatial relations, finding problems with a single glance… He was also good at festival design – something she never really noticed until their father wasn't around. The frown deepened and became noticeable by the council around her.

"Something the matter, Princess Atlamillia?" Archbishop Ailín asked, and she looked up from the details to him.

"No, just thinking. I'm going to take some more time to go over this and then send it to Aerrow for approval."

"If we're to stick to schedule, the final decision needs to be made before the end of the week," Priestess Hazel told her as she flipped through her little notebook. "People have to be paid and prepare… we did it too late last time and it was almost disastrous."

"I'll make sure it's finalized before then."

"Yay!"

Atlamillia closed the book of details and turned to her council. "Is there anything else that needs to be addressed today?"

Víðarr gave a nod, not looking overly happy. "Some of te 'ouses are lookin' for updates on te device and of our king. Tey're not a fan of bein' kept in te dark."

"They didn't agree to get a daily report when they let our king go on this mission."

"It was implied tat some updates would be 'ad, tough. We're a week away from te 'alfway point of te mission time and we've not mentioned a tin' ta tem oter tan tat 'e arrived safely."

"And what good would come of it if they knew the details of that trip?" She asked him and he gave a small sigh.

"I don't mean tell tem everytin', but perhaps just an update of progress. If tey caught wind of te attempts, which 'ave been circlin' around as rumours, it would only cause more strife."

She guessed it couldn't hurt to tell them the device progress. "How do you propose I tell them? It'd be rather pointless to have a full meeting for that single thing."

"It would be… but ya could also tell tem tat ya 'ave a betroted-"

"Absolutely not."

"Princess Atlamillia, there isn't anything negative about the situation," Zephaniah told her. "My wife was an arranged partnership, but we couldn't be happier."

"It's not about my situation as it's more of what it would become for Aerrow. If he finds out, he'll marry Dani without a second thought and while I care for both of them and am rooting for her – I don't want him to think he has to. I want it to be natural or not at all."

Both men seemed to understand, their expressions softening. Zephaniah gave a respectful nod. "We'll keep this a secret then. Perhaps you could have a few dinner parties to spread the news of how the Zerach is going. This will allow you to mingle and meet other partners should the king marry Lady Dani and you don't wish to marry Lord Endymion."

A thought passed her mind at the idea and she hesitated at first before asking. "What's the council's opinion on me finding a partner that isn't a man?"

A round of confusion went through the five of them, but Ronial was the first to speak after a moment. "Are you interested in a female partner, Princess?"

She shook her head. "I'm not interested in anyone right now, but in a hypothetical case – what is your opinion?"

"Well female salacious mediums are always nice to look at," Hazel commented with a slight smile and the rest of them went degrees of flush.

Ailín was the most flustered as he stammered, "Y-you're a priestess!"

"Exactly and therefore cherish all forms of love to the best of my ability."

"I mean, she's not exactly…" Ronial started before stopping and cleared his throat. "What I mean to say is that the princess should be happy regardless of who she wants."

"Have either of you no shame?!" Ailín exclaimed. "Oh, who am I kidding? One's a knight and the other is a dirty priestess…"

"What the hell is that supposed to mean?"

"Princess Atlamillia, my opinion on the subject may not be to your liking, but with the throne at stake, I must state that a male partner will provide the ability to make children and create stability," Zephaniah stated, pushing past the argument and inappropriate conversation. "Your family has never been one to have concubines, of any gender, and polygamy isn't well received by anyone in the kingdom. So, unless our king has an heir and many spares... I recommend this."

"I'm in agreement with Zeph as well," Ailín told her while Víðarr shook his head.

"Goin' wit te crown needs are important, but I also believe tat sexual orientation can lead ta bot 'appiness and despair... scandals and disloyalty will certainly occur if security is paid wit 'appiness."

Ronial nodded. "Happiness leads to good leadership."

"I see... Priestess Hazel, do I dare ask your opinion?" Atlamillia asked and the woman slipped into thought, clearly not pure ones worthy of her title. "Never mind... I appreciate your thoughts. It really was just a hypothetical question, so pay no attention to implications."

"So, there's no one you're interested in?" The priestess asked, coming back to reality and she shook her head.

"No. This question came to mind since we were just talking about relationships. I'm sure some of you are aware that my great uncle Lomám had a husband, Great Uncle Dáithí, much to the dismay of my grandfather so, I was curious to know."

"It's a good question to bring up, but as you can see that sort of freedom can lead to situations less than optimal," Zephaniah told her matter-of-factly but not harshly. "We want what's best for you, of course, but it is your duty as wells as ours, Princess, to put your needs aside for the kingdom."

"I know and I will commit to it just as I always have," she said with a reassuring smile, though she wasn't sure how real it was. "Alright. I'll let you get on with your other tasks. Thank you for your hard work."

The council split after a small bow and Mazaeh joined her on her walk to her study to put the paperwork away for the moment. She looked up at him. "You three are really dedicated to this shift schedule."

"It's got a few flaws... like schedule times..." He gave a yawn. "We're still trying to situate to best fit each of us and when to actually have the shift change."

"Two in the afternoon is a bit of a strange shift change."

"It is... Our stupid idea instead of listening to Bretheena who actually has experience in shift work..."

She giggled a bit. "You two never learn to listen to the wise from time to time."

"Sometimes to make sure something doesn't work; you have to try it and find out why."

"Asking why also that does too, you know."

"But what if it works? That is the treasure that Elias and I seek."

"I feel like the number of times him and you went out of your way to basically commit treason a few months ago would attest to that being a bad idea."

"Well, I mean sure, we were young and stupid, but that doesn't mean that some of the ideas didn't work."

"How many?"

"Ah… There were three ideas that went against better judgement. One of them was sticking around to protect you in Siofra, so…"

"And the stupidity was encouraged." She unlocked the door to her study and set the files on the desk before leaving and locking it up again. "Well, can't fault you for trying new things. Just don't get someone killed or commit treason doing your next one, eh?"

"Yeah… so… Where are you off to now?"

"Off to encourage more bad behaviour."

00000

They walked into the much drier training grounds where Dani with her twin-headed axes and Aoife with a mace were practicing amongst themselves. It wasn't a serious match, so they weren't wearing heavy armour, simply practicing forms for Aoife to learn. Due to it, they immediately noticed of their arrival.

Aoife gave her a very disapproving face. "You promised you weren't going to train for the next few days. What are you doing here?"

"I'm not training," Atlamillia told her. "But I did come to help."

"That's… the same thing…"

"Not when I'm not the one in combat." She turned to Mazaeh. "You're a trained professional, I'm sure you can mimic forms I tell you to perform."

"I have three months of official training, Atlamillia, I wouldn't-"

She cut him off. "Perfect! Dani, Aoife, you're going to fight Mazaeh. No maiming."

"A real fight! Oooh how exciting!" Aoife cheered, seemingly okay with her being in the grounds now as Dani gave a small look of pity at the knight Atlamillia threw under the dragon.

"So, this is what you meant by encouraging bad behaviour," Mazaeh sighed, taking off a silver cylinder off his belt that formed into a glaive. "Alright... how did you want us to do this?"

"Dani, use fire twister. Aoife, use light daze."

"Um... I haven't learned that move yet," Aoife told her, hesitantly.

She shrugged. "Mazaeh, go nuts."

"That's not an instruction!" He yelped at her, appalled, but didn't get to support his argument as Dani did as she was told, forcing him to move or be burnt. "Hey! She said no maiming!"

"It's not maiming if she's burning you to a crisp," Atlamillia called, sitting on the bench and admittedly enjoyed the torment she was causing. It wasn't the most moral way of relieving her frustrations, but they didn't need to know that.

Time went by as she gave out other orders for them to turn on each other. Aoife eventually learned the light daze skill right before Mazaeh was going to strike her with the nonlethal end of his weapon, dazing him. There was a moment of happiness within the girl only for it to be set aside when Atlamillia had Dani turn on her.

Dani was a bit much for the brunette as she was sent running around the arena being chased by small fire twisters that had greatly improved as they weren't so magically loud when formed. Mazaeh had also improved, getting a better feel for random chaos that, at any point could change with an order.

Suddenly, all her amusement came to a halt as a feeling of dread washed over her. The feelings were like what she had felt when she went to rescue Dani... but several times worse. Something happened to her brother, but she couldn't explain how she knew it. Was this what Jakob meant by spiritual, irrational power all those months ago? Was it something that through the ability to use magic without a conduit had also opened an instinct over thought she never had before?

The feeling of dread remained, neither dissipating nor getting stronger, not that she was sure if she wanted it to. She didn't like this new sense at all.

She went to pull out her CT, the need to contact Aerrow or Uncle Owen growing only to be halted as the screams and laughter of children came to her ears. She looked up as the kids, Shamrock, and Ardyn all ran out into an active training ground and a groan escaped. How many times was it going to be before they got hurt because they ran into a stray attack?

She stood up but didn't get to tell them to get off the battlefield that ceased to be as Lyric ran directly into her legs with a bit more force than she had expected. She almost tipped over. The small child hid behind her as Karros tried to tag her, making Atlamillia an obstacle.

"I'm not-" she started only to sigh. "What are you two doing?"

"Tag," Lyric answered, moving to the side as Karros tried to reach her. "I'm the last one. No one will catch me!"

"Get her my minions!" Claudius declared his order and the rest of the swarm of kids started for her. The black-haired girl took off, running straight into Mazaeh as Shamrock chased.

"Guys, we're trying to- Hey!" Lyric climbed up him faster than any of them had expected her to and sat on his shoulders, crossing her legs around his neck. He gripped her legs with a hand to keep her from crushing his throat. "I'm not a pole!"

"But you're tall and they can't get me now."

"Taller than them maybe but I could just kneel…"

"No! Onward my steed! Onward and away!"

Mazaeh sighed and… onwarded and awayed for a bit before turning to the rest of the adults where Ardyn was getting all the attention in the world from Aoife and Dani. "Please help me…"

"You're doing great, Mazzy," Aoife encouraged as the other kids and golden retriever caught up with him, trying to get the small girl. "A big and strong knight protecting the defenceless princess."

"I already have a princess to defend, I don't need a second one!"

"Pretty sure if it came down to it, she'd be defending you."

Mazaeh went to argue with her but Dani stepped in, splitting her axes, and putting them away. "Perhaps we could break for the evening. We've made a lot of progress today and the children worked hard in their studies. We should have a small reward for both efforts."

"Ice cream?" Holly asked and Dani looked over at Atlamillia.

"I'm sure the lady of the castle could provide such a thing, after supper that is."

Atlamillia crossed her arms, pretending not to care though in truth, she liked the idea. "Depends on if you can behave until food is ready. Last thing I want to do is reward a bunch of twerps who ran into an active training ground, again."

"We didn't know anyone was out here," Juno told her honestly. "We thought everyone was busy with other things. Sorry."

"Aw, you're so cute!" Aoife squeaked, grabbing the girl, and squeezed her, causing the seven-year-old to giggle. "How can anyone ever be mad at you?!"

The other kids started to demand hugs from the hyperactive girl, leaving Atlamillia's slight grin at the sight to turn into a frown as the feeling of dread slipped through the distraction. She looked in the direction where the gate was. Why was she feeling like something horrible happened to Aerrow? It made no sense. He was safe in the safehouse... wasn't he?

Her skirt was tugged on slightly and she looked down and saw Gasper looking up at her with worry. "Is something wrong, Atlamillia?"

"N-no... no..." She took a breather. "I'm okay."

"You don't seem okay..."

"Just feeling a bit off. I'll be alright."

"Then we should do something relaxing until you're better... Oh! Can you tell us a story?!"

"I'm not much of a storyteller... That's more of Aerrow's thing."

"You tell good stories about Aerrow's trip... Do you have any more of those?"

"None at the moment."

"Oh... okay then." He seemed upset and she frowned.

"Is everything alright with you?"

"I… don't know. I feel like something is wrong with him and kinda hoped you had a story to make it go away." He looked over at the kids back to playing loudly, still trying to get to Lyric. Kris had seemingly taken her tactic and managed to get on Dani's back who was only a few centimetres shorter than Mazaeh. "They notice it too… They're just too scared to ask."

They didn't seem any different from their normal play, but the longer she watched, the more she realized their laughs and giggles hid small glances and frowns barely on the surface. She had to distract them regardless of if she knew something was amiss.

"I might have a story," she said loud enough for the others to hear. "But it's not the most kid-friendly one."

"A dark story?!" Holly exclaimed way too cheerfully as she stopped trying to get Lyric along with the others before frowning. "That's what it's called right? Dark?"

Claudius nodded. "You're correct, but… is it gory?"

"Of course not… But it's short enough to tie us over until supper… Did you want to hear it?" Seven heads nodded and Atlamillia turned to her friends. "You're welcome to join us… just in case the story isn't long enough…"

Aoife got the hint and smiled. "Sure, we'll come listen and share. Story time!"

A few cheers went about while Kris got off Dani. Lyric refused to leave her *steed*, forcing Mazaeh to carry her to the kids' playroom. Once there, only then did she get off. All the kids sat on the floor in front of the chair that they had all seen Aerrow use time and time again to tell stories and Atlamillia took a seat. Shamrock sat on the floor, belly completely exposed as Ardyn followed his owner while Aoife, Dani, and Mazaeh grabbed chairs around the room, not exactly right for their size. They all looked at her expectedly.

It made her a bit nervous, but she pushed through it, somewhat. She was never good with public speaking in front of a large crowd. "Alright… um… this story is probably going to be missing details but… it was written in one of Theseus's journals he left behind."

"A story from the Hero-King himself?!" Gasper gasped in excitement. "Aerrow never tells us those ones!"

"Probably because they aren't all sunshine and rainbows… It's a collection of journals throughout his travels." Claudius commented only to get glared at. "What? It's not like any of you asked why he doesn't share them."

"It's not so much as that and more like Aerrow avoided those journals," Mazaeh told him, surprising Atlamillia. "Apparently they brought up bad memories or something."

"Why would they do that?"

"I don't know. He didn't tell me."

The white-haired boy turned to Atlamillia. "You do though."

"It's not something I should talk about without him here," she answered, and his annoyed crimson glare turned into realization.

"He did tell me that… Yeah, I can see why he wouldn't want to read them now."

"What'd he tell you?" Juno asked him curiously, and he shook his head.

"He told me not to tell anyone."

"But we're not anyone. We're his friends."

"Sorry, can't do it."

There was a pout but otherwise it was silent, waiting for Atlamillia to start the story. She ran through it once in her head before starting with the setting. "The day was filled with the howls of Outland Monsters that echoed up the lava covered Rile Volcano. Theseus and his comrades were trapped within the mountain once they arrived in the task of finding the fifth chosen hero that Orithina had told them about. It didn't take long to find out that it was the princess of Fiery, Princess Zyanya Gouyen – the first one to tame a vigorid and the strongest fighter out of all the chosen heroes.

"One would think her hot-blooded temper matched that of the volcano she lived in, that she was also imposing and headstrong, but in reality, what Theseus found was a woman who was strong, yes, but who was incredibly soft on the inside. She could fight all day and night, killing monsters for sport – but when it came to people, animals, or even a god, she couldn't bring harm to them. In a fair competition, without a doubt she would make them black, and blue should they challenge her in the arena, but nothing that could ever be fatal. She cared for her people and father, the king of her nation.

"The Kingdom of Fiery then was a heavy patriarchy meaning that men ruled, and women were lesser – not being able to make decisions without a male figure around to do it for them. But for being a princess, Zyanya was more in a position of power as she was the only heir to the throne. She acted like a son would, respected the king's every decision and fought to defend any of them with every ounce of strength she could to whoever had challenged his authority. The day Theseus and his friends came to the mountain, however, was the day Zyanya had her world opened in a way she was repulsed by. But she had to make a decision regardless: to protect her people by answering the call of her birthright or ignore it. To follow her beloved father's wishes for her to stay within the kingdom where he could protect her just as she always protected him.

"Unsure of what to do, the monsters came relentlessly, attacking their great defences and slaughtering all who tried to stop them. Each day that passed, the worse it became, and after the third day, she had had enough. She begged King Wawatam with Theseus to let her help, for him to release the lava flows and fill the Ponipura Desert to rid the monsters that were attacking their weakened and exposed side. The king denied her wishes, asking only of where the other foreigners were.

"'They are outside, fighting for our kingdom,' she answered him and upon hearing those words, he told them that he would aid if they were so dedicated. But upon reaching the outlook over the desert, all he did was watch the heroes fight, holding the lever, but not pulling it. She realized that he was waiting for them to be pushed back and to lure them in so they could be caught in the flow controlled by the king's power. To kill them. Theseus also noticed the way the man watched his friends and saw the corruption that had flowed through the king's heart by Valrdis's promise that for the kingdom, King Wawatam and Princess Zyanya would be spared. The Hero of Absalom went to act, but the powers of Valrdis gave the king senses that he wouldn't have had before, attacking Theseus before he could draw his blade, covering him with lava."

The kids gasped, all with the exception of Claudius who frowned. "Alright, but it wouldn't exactly hurt him… Lava wouldn't be hot to him. Argona's flames were much, much hotter compared to it."

"You're right," she agreed. "They didn't burn him, but they did keep him still once it encased him, the hardened rock on the outside, the molten rock on the inside. While fireproof, Theseus still needed to breathe."

"Oh… yeah, I guess that's a good way of killing someone immune to heat and all you have is fire magic…"

"Luckily for our hero, Zyanya broke the tomb before Theseus could be killed, but not fast enough for him to be left completely unharmed. Left to choke on the remnants of the lava in his throat and lungs that had quickly cooled due to the cruel king turning them into minerals as the seconds ticked by. Theseus tried to use his own power to fight against the king for he knew he was stronger, but his magic had been sealed. The ground they stood on had been trapped before hand by the King of Fiery, sealing all element magic in the area except for his own. Neither Theseus nor Zyanya could use magic.

"Zyanya wanted to help Theseus, to stop her father, but she was unable to act. She cared too much for him. She couldn't believe his actions were his own, that some sort of magic was at work. In a way, she wasn't wrong. Valrdis had preyed on King Wawatam's weakness of selfish desires, the flaw that he'd sacrifice his kingdom and people all to save himself and his daughter. It was the very flaw she saw in all Creatures of Light and put a spotlight on it, bringing it to the surface where it couldn't hide.

"The monsters grew closer as the chosen ones were below, oblivious to their impending deaths. Argona was rushing from the other side of the kingdom, abandoning the front line to try and assist her dying partner. The lever was pulled, but before the king could manipulate the slow flow, Zyanya's eyes went golden-yellow instead of her usual royal blue. It was the sign of the Chosen Hero that her father had been denying from the very beginning, but it was also a very dark turning point of what it meant to be a Chosen Hero should they struggle against what had to be done. Under Orithina's control, Zyanya attacked and killed her father. The moment was only a few seconds long, but they struck Theseus to the core. Orithina had always been merciful… but at the brink of the possibility of losing her heroes, the loss of a kingdom, she put the rights and thoughts of one of her heroes aside and forced them to do an unthinkable act.

"Zyanya was aware of what had happened, coming to her senses but not losing the power of a hero in her eyes, and while upset – she didn't dwell on it. She acted instead as a true ruler should. She removed the seal with her power and then the lava from Theseus before he could lose consciousness. Her rage came forth next, the rage of not being able to make a choice and leaving it to the Goddess of Light to do it for her, and she turned it on the monsters. Argona had come in time for Zyanya to order her to move the other heroes out of the way. Once removed, she unleashed her true power without hesitation.

"Monsters perished in the blue desert that turned purple under the lava's touch. Anything flying met the wrath of the volcano's bellowing stones of fire… And once it was over, her traitorous father was thrown in the Sea of Ahi like all the traitors that had come before. She declared her kingdom to be turned into a chiefdom – ruled in a matriarchy to defend her position as a female in a kingdom of powerful men and should anyone during or after her reign see fit to challenge the authority of a leader: for weakness, corruption, or incompetence – a duel was to be had. The winner became the next Queen, and the succession laws remained the same.

"The first-born female would rule in the death of the Queen Chief unless challenged. Men could rule for a time, but only until their daughter, once they had come of age, could take the throne. If they did not have a daughter, they could not challenge. The rules of government could not be changed like she had done so, for if someone changed how the kingdom ran – the mountain would no longer be a volcano and all Fieries would go extinct without their beloved home, a vow sealed by Orithina's own blessing. After she had created the decree, she joined the mission to stop Valrdis so that no one else could go through what she did…" There was silence after she had finished and realized the children in front of her didn't think it was over. "The end? I guess?"

"That's it?!" Gasper exclaimed. "That can't be it!"

"It was greatly summarized but… That's all there was for the finding of Zyanya Gouyen, the Chosen Hero of Fiery."

"It just seemed… I don't know, missing something," Karros stated, trying to figure it out. "Not finished?"

"It's just one part of a grand story, so it makes sense if it doesn't seem finished," Mazaeh told him, and Claudius disagreed.

"It had a beginning, a plot, a happy-ish ending, patricide, and regicide all wrapped into one bundle. It was told well, and I couldn't ask for a better tale."

Atlamillia giggled at the compliment. "Thanks."

"But you know what would be better than the telling of a two-thousand-year-old story?"

Lyric looked at him with confusion. "What?"

"Our own story to be made."

"You mean like… with pictures? I can read and draw well but my writing is really bad."

"No, no. Nothing that childish. I mean we go on an adventure to help Aerrow."

"That seems scary…" Juno told him. "I feel like he needs it, but what can a bunch of kids do if we can't fly to him?"

"What do you mean?" Kris asked her. "I don't feel like Uncle Aerrow needs help. Uncle Azzy said he's okay when Mommy talked to him yesterday."

"I don't know… but I feel like he's in trouble. I'm not going crazy, am I?"

Atlamillia caught a worried looked from Dani that her friend probably hadn't meant to show, but she didn't get to ask about it when Claudius chimed in. "Exactly. We... except for Kris who has no sensory yet-"

Kris frowned. "What does sensory mean?"

"It means you're five and your magic sucks." The boy's eyes went wide before tearing up. Claudius backed things up before any of the adults in the room had to get involved. "No, it doesn't suck, you're still new to magic, right?"

Kris nodded.

"Which means it's not... er... honed. Yes, honed. It will get much, much better with our help."

"You'll hone my magic?"

"Yeah. It's going to be the best earth magic the kingdom has ever seen." Kris beamed and Claudius gave out a sigh of relief as Karros mocked him for being mean. The white-haired boy ignored him and started rallying his new apprentice. "So, that's why we should go on the quest to help Aerrow. It'll give you tons of experience."

Atlamillia shut down the recruitment speech. "You're not going to help Aerrow, regardless of if he needs it or not. You are kids, enjoy kid things. Adventuring is for later when you can defend yourselves."

There was a round of groans but eventually, after more coaxing with Aoife, Dani, and Mazaeh's help, a round of agreement came from the seven bundles about staying in the kingdom.

A knock came from the doorframe. Jakob bowed as she turned to him, ending discussions about new stories. "Princess Atlamillia, supper is ready."

The monsters dashed out of the room, Jakob moving smoothly out of the way as Atlamillia gave a sigh of relief to be free of them but caught a glimpse from Dani that stole it all away. Something was wrong.

But if she tried to call now, it would only prove to the children that their instincts were right. She didn't need that kind of leverage to add to a plot that at least one of them had been planning for some time now.

Chapter Forty: Outland Blood

A sharp pain ripped through my head, waking me from a void. A hiss escaped as other parts of my body pounded, keeping me from disappearing back into the horrible abyss. I drew a sharp breath and the scent that came with it turned my stomach, fear knotting it up a million different ways. The smell was… not something I should be near. I needed to leave. How did I get… It was everywhere. Anxiety tightened its grip as I tried to figure whatever came before the darkness, but it was out of my grasp.

I opened an eye to find the light to be too bright, forcing me to close it, squinting to adjust. The intense fear of everything being wrong grew. I didn't even want to breathe, terrified that someone could hear me while I was blinded.

Where was I?

I went to get up, but something held me down. My wrists were bound, and I looked through the harsh light in a panic. In a frenzy, I pulled at the metal, breaking free and then ripped off the leather strap across my chest. The noises of the metal hitting the tile caused me to wince as I broke my legs free from the table I was on.

I had to get out… I had to leave. Before whoever put me here came back.

I got off the table, my boots loudly announcing my weight which my legs couldn't hold up. I dropped to the ground, my hand catching the table before I could kiss the floor entirely. The dizziness of the head-rush caused the world to darken and the door that I wanted to get to blurred. A gasp escaped as I struggled to get up, the metal I held bent easily against my grip. Each moment was a struggle to stay awake.

I couldn't pass out… Not here. They're going to come back.

I got to my feet and looked around. The room wasn't large, a small empty medical space. My form relaxed ever so slightly as I listened to make sure no one had heard me outside. Nothing came from the hall beyond the heavy looking door with a lock on it.

Something familiar in the strange place caught my eye and I immediately went to it; a bit unsteady at first until I got used to the slight spin of the world. The pounding of my heart eased in my ears as the familiar object was real and not a figment of desperation. My sword sat in its sheath on the table and picking it up eased the anxiety. I could protect myself with this.

A strip of excitement slipped into my thoughts as I strapped the blade to my side, and I froze. What was that thought?

My head pounded. I gripped at it, feeling like the control I had on myself slip away. Other thoughts that felt foreign entered, influencing mine from the terror to determination. They focused on the noises beyond the door. The smells that I wanted to run away from. I couldn't confront them.

Or could I…

My blade was drawn in my left hand as a ball of white and purple-black fire formed in my right without realizing it. The idea of burning the whole place to the ground blurred out my focus to just hide and escape quietly.

They couldn't take me again.

My body flinched under the growing pressure and pain. Thoughts going in different directions as I fought against the ones that wanted vengeance. They seemed just as confused as I was, just as scared. But they didn't want to hide. My breath caught in the struggle and then my body moved forward without me giving it the order to. The flame that had grown in the fight against what to do was placed against the wall which burst to flames before it could touch it. The warmth of it further took away the control I wanted, threatening to put me out.

My jaw clenched, the only movement that felt to be mine as I made it to the door, the flames melting the lock and knob. I couldn't go unconscious. Another fight to stop myself from leaving the room yet came to an end as my body pulsed in pain.

What did they do to me…?

The question brought more confusion, the fear of not knowing brushed past that didn't seem like my own. Then a growl came out, shoving it aside. It was a distraction to who or what moved my form onward. The true goal was… more important than my fear. The odours of the burning objects offset my balance and I smashed against the doorframe. My flame going out as I reached for my head.

The flames were doing their job. Move on to the next room. Burn this building of light to nothing. Take them with it…

Bile came to my throat that was swallowed and I left the room behind. This was wrong. All of it… The World of Light was excruciating. My foot caught on the floor and my strength at holding the sword failed, causing the tip to drop the floor loudly. My heart jumped in my throat as I looked at it, the

Absalomian knots and dragon eyes were aglow in black and white with magic I had no control over.

A door opened down the hallway and I snapped to it in a panic.

I couldn't be found-

"What was that?" A man asked as he came out of the room, looking in the wrong direction before turning around, spotting me.

My fear seized my action as an unexpected rage slipped passed my defences. He was faceless which destroyed any way of fighting off the other force that gripped at my limbs. Why was he faceless?!

They're monsters. They caused my suffering. I can't back down now. A satisfying feeling crept in, warping my fear as the monster's grew at seeing me. *This wasn't going to be like the last time.*

"How did you-?!"

The other voice didn't let him finish as I charged at him, the sword leaving a melted path on the floor behind me. There wasn't a second that went by before I reached him. The sword was brought up, cleaving him in half. The two pieces of flesh fell to the ground, throwing red liquid along the walls and ceiling, pooling on the floor. The heat of the blade dissipated before it could touch him.

I wasn't going to run. They were going to bleed for everything!

The high of succeeding ended as the blood dripped off the ceiling and echoed in my head. This was… What was I doing?! It was a monster but… when did they bleed red?

They have always bled red.

They… had?

Noises came from the opened door and my head turned to it in a panic, the fight replaced with flight as I couldn't breathe. More of the disgraceful monsters were inside their bright haven. The noise I heard was someone dropping their device onto the floor as they were stunned by their comrade's demise. A grin formed in glee at seeing them as terrified as I had been, already accepting defeat.

Then it wavered as I grappled for clarity. I wanted to leave. I had just cut down one of their peers. That couldn't have been a… Another pain caused me to scream but to my surprise, no noise actually escaped the body that did not move at my action. I looked beyond it. They were all faceless monsters. Why couldn't I just run?

The uncontrollable grin came back as my concerns and objections were pushed to the side, filling in with more direct ones. *Their deaths would be meaningless if they didn't feel like I felt.* I walked into the room, my voice unused and unfamiliar. "One."

The faceless monsters started to move away as I closed the door and turned off the light.

A scream caused me to wince, dragging me to a small halt for only a moment. It disappeared as the feeling of being okay within the darkness gave confidence. I could see so very well, unlike the figures that bumbled around. A fireball formed. "Burn."

00000

I kicked down the flaming door, sending it off its frame and across the hall. The sword dragging along behind me in disgust, dripping with the blood of the vile beings. None of them would tell me how to leave. So, I let them leave this life.

My head pounded again, forcing my body to stop as I stabbed into the floor to balance myself. My breathing was irregular as my thoughts spun in different directions. I couldn't recall everything that happened in there. Some moments, the blood, the enjoyment, moments of panic… then darkness. Had I really asked them how to leave?

This was wrong. Why couldn't I remember only a few moments a-

They needed to be removed. They are Creatures of Light. Me or them.

Creatures of Light… why was that so familiar? They… didn't that mean that the faceless monsters were people? Why was I enjoying this? I wasn't! I didn't want-

A seethed squeak came out as my body pulsed. *It wasn't wrong. They deserved everything. Seven… It wasn't enough. They killed more than seven…*

Why? Why wasn't it enough?! This building and then what afterwards?!

It didn't matter. I am going to burn this whole world if need be. That's what Father would do.

Father? No, there wasn't… Just stop…

I can't stop. They live there, shunning us. They always hide from the dark, just like how I'm wanting to hide from the light. Not anymore. I'm tired of hiding.

There was too many!

My begging to stop was silenced as the other presence attacked. Its indescribable anger stabbed into my head and chest. I dropped to a knee beside the blade, unable to keep standing. The pressure kept growing, forcing me to give in or go unconscious. I gave in, too scared to know what would happen if I fell. The voice took control of the form that should have been mine.

The darker, scared, and violent thoughts stood up, ripping the sword from the floor as the world became steady enough to continue down the halls. Parts of the confusing journey came in and out of my vision, the noises however remained constant, rattling through my head, becoming more and more accepting with each monster cut down. Each time I tried to rise up against the rage that felt fragmented and confused but focused, I was brutally overruled. It wore against my form as it felt like it was being ripped apart. My opinions shifted, my response to danger always turning to fight instead of run. My view of what I thought was right and wrong crumbled.

Why was half of me so determined to extinguish the light despite being just as terrified? What were these monsters? Were they the enemy really?

The other presence didn't have to say anything for me to come to my own conclusion, the smell and actions of those who saw me dictating it.

They were the enemy. They had brought me here. They were the reason why I couldn't stop. They were going to kill me… no… use me. The table, they tried to keep me from leaving. Why? What was I to them?

My blade went into the back of the last one in the room, avoiding a needle that held some unknown liquid in it. They collapsed as I managed to take control for a moment, breathing heavily. The endless cycle of figuring out what was right and what was wrong was like the endless people who were attacking me in each room. I just wanted to leave…

"Aerrow," a voice called, causing my heart to skip a beat and I looked around in a fear that I had missed someone. There wasn't anyone… Who said it? Was there someone- "Aerrow! Why won't you answer me?!"

"I don't have to answer to you." A sneer formed as the rage settled in again, the growl that came out sounded feral. "Who are you?"

"Don't play around!"

The words hit a nerve; the new voice sounded familiar. I went to pause and ask again but my tongue stopped. My body started moving on its own, a fire growing within the room I was leaving behind. The words that fell out to answer her didn't feel like they were mine. While aggressive, anxiety was fuelling them. I didn't know who or where they were. "You weren't in that room. How are you still talking to me?"

"We talk to each other all the time through the link," the voice continued. It was inside my head. *"Why can I smell so much blood? This bloodlust-"*

I scoffed, cutting her off. The bloodlust was to get back at those who hurt me – none of her business. "Another annoying voice. Be silent."

"Another?"

"You missed the important part. Shut up."

"Stop messing around!" The voice urged in fear that caused me to wince. I... knew who... No. Stop. *"Where are you?!"*

I hissed as another sharp pain ripped through my body that almost dropped me to the floor. I was already trying to figure out what was going on... What I was... I didn't need someone else there to torment me more. "Not close enough for me to kill you for being so loud."

"Kill? Aerrow, you don't like killing things."

I didn't. No, of course not. Why would...

"Aerrow?"

She could sense my confusion. An innate drive to kill everything the light had touched collided with my thoughts of not wanting to. Why was I against my want to kill. I... cared about the light. How I couldn't... I wanted to run away.

No. They had to die. They were going to trap me again! They were monsters!

Were they? The blood... their suffering. Monsters didn't-

Shut up!

"Aerrow-!"

"Fucking shut up!" The other will shouted in anger.

Regret came as I felt a bit of her shock and grief. My stomach twisted in the shame that took hold of the rage and I fell against the wall nearby. Bile came up and out at the pain and the voices went silent. After a few moments, there was nothing left to throw up, the urge to stay down threatened my survival. My breathing was more than heavy as I staggered to a stand with the help of the wall.

"Aerrow, please listen to me. You need to rest. Find somewhere to hide."

The anger came barreling in, throwing me to the back, enraged by the very concept I had wanted to do since waking up. The low rumble of the answer froze my actions to try and fight back. "I'm not hiding. They must die."

"This isn't you…"

"Leave me the fuck alone," I answered but it was strained and hoarse. I didn't want to be left alone. I wanted to escape whatever hell I was in…

But I wanted nothing to do with her all the same.

The thought of never wanting to hear her caused my world to pulse, panic overtaking my previous want. I needed her.

My body started down the hall again and the fear grew. I wanted it to stop. To acknowledge my voice. But the other presence just kept on walking, ignoring me. I felt like I was trapped inside a box. The more I frantically tried to take control of my actions, the more shutdown and attacked I was. Beaten and thrown to the floor, the rage tried to take over, taking pieces at a time with ease. I wanted the female voice to come back, for the other voice to unblock the link. Ignored and placed in a cage, I was forced to watch and act against more of the faceless beings that attacked.

Eventually, there was a pause in the fighting as well as the struggling for competition. An acceptance that she wasn't coming back, that I wasn't able to hide had drove deep into my desires. It felt hopeless but at the same time relieving that for the moment… neither part of me was fighting.

There were no other Creatures of Light on the floor. No exit. Upwards it was. I would eventually get out.

I hesitated from proceeding and looked back to the fires that neither grew nor shrank. The bodies and blood that coloured the white floor. I … had done that.

Twenty-six… I needed more.

My sword bounced off each step as I went up them. I was no longer concerned with the noise it made as it echoed. The stairs stopped after only one floor and agitation clenched my jaw.

Whoever designed this maze… I hope I could meet them. Then they could be buried in their creation. It'd be poetic, wouldn't it?

I didn't answer my question, unsure of what to feel about it. I brought up my sword to reach for the door when the light bounced off it and into my face. A hiss of pain escaped.

Dammit. Why did the creatures here need to be surrounded by light?

My reflection caught my eye and part of me shuddered at it. Black eyes with orange irises stared back where the blood hadn't been smeared across it. The pupils were slitted to barely a line, trying to limit the light intake. There was so much blood… my gaze was unfamiliar to me.

A different thought approached the glance, a frown deepening. *I am too much like them.*

It didn't matter… I had to leave. Away from the monsters. Anything to get this pain to stop.

I can get out faster… I know of a magic.

No! It was too much.

No, it isn't. I'm not like them! The less of them I looked, the more of me I can be.

Less of… more? What? It didn't make sense.

My body continued onwards, opening the door and my confusion came to a painful halt as beams of light hit me, smashing me back through the stairwell door. I hit the railing at an angle that almost flipped me over and dropped to a knee. The holes that were put in me started to heal and for the first time, both parts of me were on the same page of pain and anger. I glared up at them, hearing as they readied their next attack and our combined wrath faded to fear.

There were so many…

My blade slashed at them, sending a strip of plasma down the hall. It missed in my disorientation and panic. They fired back and the railing broke behind me. My heart jumped in my throat as I fell off the landing. The stairs were hard and stabbed into my back. My scream cut short from the lack of air. The pounding in my head sped up with my heart rate. The fear. The pain. The rage.

Enough of this! They can't win! I can't be caged again! I didn't need more than a second to access the ability. My own magic made theirs inconsequential. *There was no mercy for them!*

The monsters appeared over the edge of the floor above as I felt the wings form on my shoulder blades. I put them to use, flying up and through the faceless things. They were knocked back onto the landing and I skidded to a stop on the other side in the hall. A slender and spiked tail formed and swished on its own, its scales a strange mix of purple, white, red, black, and silver. I didn't give them a chance to recover, too scared to give them any advantage, and charged with my blade alight. Strategy instead of aimless flailing dictated the next action, much to my pleasure as I felt finally some what in control. The monsters had to be taken care of…

Some of them fired their weapons at me, but my sword went up, blocking and deflecting the light away. Some of the attacks went into the walls, but not all as they destroyed weapons or went into their peers.

The sword slashed through the head of one that had dropped to the ground from an attack entering their thigh. Movement came from the corner of my eye and I slipped past the halberd of a different attacker. The blade was run through their chest and I ripped it out and moved on, not wanting to stay still for long in the small space. Another stream of plasma was sent at a group bundled together. Their sudden screams caused me to flinch, but more guns were fired, distracting me from thinking hard on the bodies severed in two, dropping onto the landing or the smouldering stairwell below.

Similarly coloured, jagged wings bashed against the closer ones, giving me some needed room. The blade jabbed and slashed whenever I found an opening. My dodges far quicker than their attacks. The hilt and pommel of the blade was perfect for bludgeoning and smashing through bones and weapons I had yet to get to – maximizing the potential efficiency of the space. Two and three of them fell at a time until the only four left were trying to stay out of the way. Their attempts though to help their allies was a failure, an affront, and my glare turned on them.

They had learned from the fallen, keeping their back to the wall so I couldn't get behind them. But now they also couldn't get away.

My tail lashed out as I finished up with the one I was dealing with who tried to shoot me and sent the four of them through the wall. Their bodies broke or were stabbed by the spines and might. The wall collapsed and the cement chunks of rubble fell, seemingly killing any that might have survived the blow. One in particular stood out as I watched a large piece of wall crush their head into a disgusting, delightful puddle. Pieces of its brain were sent flying out of the shattered skull.

The strategy and the rush for survival ceased, pausing me from moving farther. This wasn't necessary. I could have just run away. I don't-

They were going to kill me.

This… wasn't a fight. It was a slaughter. So much blood…

This is what happens in war.

My throat felt like it closed in on itself. I wasn't in a war.

As long as light remains, I'm always at war. The other side of me pressed, swindling its words and making me grow dizzy. *The dark will never rest. Let them bleed for their sins.*

The blade in my hand stabbed into the upper chest of one I hadn't noticed trying to squirm away. Their scream was cut short as it filled with choking and gurgling gasps. I winced at the visual, stopping the twisting, and swiftly ended their torment. Their sins… What of mine? This wasn't right.

They attacked first. This is defence. They must die if I want to live.

No! No, they didn't! That wasn't how things worked! It wasn't do or-

A scream escaped as my body rejected both declarations. The pain spread quickly through my head and chest and I stumbled, doubling over and writhing. The edges of my vision darkened at the anguish. My legs buckled, threatening to drop at any moment and I couldn't breathe. My free hand gripped at my chest, trying to find a release.

Why was this happening? Why couldn't I feel peace?! What was I fighting? I… I wanted to stop. For it all to end. They had to perish…

The pain eased a bit and I coughed, trying to get air in. *They will. I'll make them regret ever being born.*

No… I could do this without-

Shut up!

I went silent as my body started on its way again. The bodies and the blood left behind. The smell was almost intoxicating. Part of me wanted more. The light was insufferable now…

Burn it. Cleanse it.

For what end though?

Fifty.

Answer the question!

"Fuck off!" I shouted at myself as my head pounded.

I lost my footing and fell into a room that had a door slightly ajar. An ambush awaited my unprepared form and stabbed me in the side with a spear. The anger took full control and growled. I grabbed at an exposed wing and reefed on it, sending the monster into a nearby wall. He screamed in pain as he hit it. The spear that was in me was pulled out as my voice unheard by the outside world took the brunt of the pain with a hiss, causing me to get dizzy again, but my body didn't seem to notice. It stared at the black blood dripping off the tip and shaft. Then it turned it on the owner, throwing it with deadly accuracy. The spear entered his skull through their eye, obliterating it, and pinning his slightly twitching body into the wall. It was held up like a trophy. I looked to my wound as the twitching stopped. It was almost healed.

This is the reason. The other thoughts strode in, but exhaustedly. *These people can't be reasoned with.*

A battle cry came from the left and I attacked, smashing my tail into the noise without bothering to look over. The raging thoughts having their point be proven as I was shoved out of control of my form.

Predictable, pathetic, faceless monsters. If you wanted to live so badly, you should have left at the sound of the warning going through the halls.

I watched as I picked up the aggressor by her collar and slammed her into the counter. It cracked under the pressure as her scream was cut off with no air. There was a flinch at not wanting to hear the agony and I took it, stopping the act of ripping her limb from limb. "Which way is out?"

"You're never leaving…" the woman replied with a sadistic grin as her face somewhat appeared through the blur.

I grimaced for a moment as the anger took hold slightly, stabbing the sword into her wing. She screamed. "Try again."

"Lord Ciar will make you his dog!"

His dog… That thing wasn't going to-!

My thoughts merged with the intent to kill as I threw her off the counter. She smashed through a small, metal table. She barely got to sit up before she started attacking with magic, and I retaliated. Grabbing the leg that had broken off from the table and shoved it through her. It dug deep into the concrete wall, nailing her there slightly off the floor.

"I'm not his toy… and if he comes back, maybe this will be a good message for him."

She spat at me, blood dripping down the side of her vile lips. "Like you have a choice. Look at what you've become… just a pet who got out before his master could put on a leash. I'm sure it won't be long now."

"I was going to kill you quickly, but I think I'll leave you here to rot."

She chuckled painfully. "Just like the rest of your kind… Just another monster."

My body acted where I froze under her comment, fetching the sword that was left in the wing on the counter. Was I the monster?

I left the profanity screaming monster as there wasn't an answer that came right away. *No… She is. These people are all monsters. They did something to me. I… I'm not thinking straight. They are making me suffer. Ciar didn't matter.*

My heart panged in grief. Ciar did matter. He killed… killed… My head pounded as I couldn't remember.

I don't know who this Ciar person is.

I did know! He killed someone close to me! He… he was dangerous.

I'd have to kill him then. Even if I can't remember why-

No! He's too much for-

He isn't too much for me. Not anymore. My head pounded and the thoughts shifted, tearing the unknown thing away. "Stop thinking… The light will be here soon."

The light… They were going to kill me… I couldn't let them.

"Fifty-two."

The woman's screams were starting to be choked on by blood and I closed the door to muffle the awful screeching. With it silenced, my ears picked up other noises down the hall. The sounds of armour and the smell of evil light. There were quite a few of them. Fifteen. Not like the last group… Their steps were confident – they were going to take me or kill me. A black sphere on the ceiling caught my eye and I looked away from it.

The fear crept in again, wondering how many more had been watching, ordering beyond the camera.

I dropped the blade's heavy tip on the ground and stretched my wings slightly, moving onwards. My fears not addressed. No doors seemed to have life on the other side of them. The feeling of hopelessness clawing as I tried to fight for control, to hide in those rooms. To get away from the incoming army.

No… No more hiding. I was going to kill them for making me think of such things.

I felt my thoughts fade, merging and being replaced by the need for destruction. The one who wanted to get back to the female who had spoke through the link…

That was just the other voice now…

Chapter Forty-One: Desolated

I turned a corner, sensing the monsters were around it and braced for an expected onslaught of magic like the other group had done before. Instead, I was treated with something far more organized. Fifteen monsters – five monsters across and three back like some sort of battalion blocked the entire hallway. I looked them over before a small grin formed as a rush of excitement barely contained itself. The other feelings I had were almost drowned out... turning for tactic instead of the fear and panic that I had been feeling this whole time. I took a step forward and none of them flinched outwardly, but their hearts betrayed them. They skipped or sped up beats and the closer I got, the easier it was to hear each individual's reaction.

Pour, stupid monsters... "You should have ran..."

"Steady," the middle monster in the front ordered, but I could hear his doubt. He was not prepared. He may have thought so before, but now that he faced me, he wasn't. None of them were. "Steady."

Regret stained the words. The darted looks from his comrades showed that they sensed his fear but followed the words regardless. It was admirable... But how many were going to die before they fell apart? It wouldn't be fun anymore if they soiled themselves before they died. I readied my blade, the lights flickering at it charging with only a bit of magic. I wanted to rush them, but my bloodlust was held back with caution. Their weapons were like the weapons the other group had, pumping out light magic in a condensed form. A lucky shot was going to slow me down... I took another step, and the leader repeated the same, short phrase.

How steady was their form really?

I tested it, slashing my blade downwards and releasing the stored energy. A wave of white and purple-black plasma went down the centre of the hallway, taking out the middle row of lights, causing sparks to fly, and dimming the space. The forces divided themselves from being hit. I charged at them. Light magic was fired from the first row as the other two rows reorganized and I slid under the attacks. My wings got me back to my feet. I slashed out my own wave of magic across the hall, forcing them to duck or burn as their armour reached its limit or failed as I drew near.

It was a bit upsetting that only one strike removed the proclaimed, sophisticated technology.

My tail went through one of the monsters that were hit by the stream, easily slipping through her armour, and severing her spine as it continued out the other side. The broken body was tossed into two others, ending their ability to attack. My assault continued as I dashed to the other side of the hall, smashing a new monster into a wall with a wing and stabbing my blade into another that tried to help.

A blasting sound entered my ears, causing them to ring, and a sharp pain penetrated my thigh, dropping me to a knee. I reeled on them, sending another stream of plasma only to get shot in the arm on the other side. Someone jumped on me from behind, trying to put something around my neck. Pulling on their wing, I rolled them over my shoulder and grabbed the thing they were holding and threw it. It hit another gunman's face while my other hand gripped their throat, crushing it. My tail whipped out at anyone else who tried to get too close, and I went to stand. Another shot hit my side, forcing me down again.

I was being surrounded but they were purposely avoiding my head. I looked to the thing that they had tried to put around my neck. It's black, opened ring sat next to the gunman that was getting up. A snarl formed. It was a detention collar; they were trying to silence my magic. They wanted me alive… I needed a new-

My head pounded and I gripped it as a noise escaped my mouth. The world grew fuzzy as they reorganized, getting closer. Fear overtook the wrath from before.

I couldn't let them subdue me. I wasn't their toy!

I picked up the blade that had fallen from my grasp and stabbed it into the ground, charging and releasing the energy quickly. The plasmic lines crisscrossed across the floor and up the walls as a wave of energy blasted anyone around away. The lights went out in a chain reaction, exploding down the hallway in both directions. The armour that they wore went dark along with my blade as the excess magic was removed. They moved frantically, trying to get a better position in the dark as I stood.

The darkness was my world… This was what I needed.

I felt a different sort of magic available to me that wasn't like fire, but was so very familiar… I struck the first monster, smashing him into the wall as one of the lingering ones nearby jumped in surprise at the sudden scream beside him. I channeled the power and it formed underfoot. Its odd nature grabbed at the bystander and caused them to yell that something held him.

I stabbed the one on the wall through their throat and up into their skull. The blood dripped down the blade and onto the floor as he tried to breathe, not dying until it was ripped out. The second one gave a blood curdling scream of agony when slightly aglow, purple, black, and red vines tore into him. They dug and ripped as they climbed up and through his body. I turned to the next attacker, my tail stabbing through their torso and used it to knock over five others that had grouped together.

Six down, nine to go, and five were on the floor.

My attack commenced on the weakened ones, leaping on and stabbing the middle one's head. A new dark pool grew below. Vines grappled onto their newfound prey like starved snakes, weaving into them, and filling their screams with blood. The four remaining monsters of light stood there in horror as they watched their fellow peers die gruesomely in vain.

I went to attack but only made it a few feet before the dim world grew disoriented. I stumbled, my own grunt of pain giving away my position. Shots fired in my direction from two of the four monsters while the other two charged their weapons, making them glow. A spear was thrusted at me, its light lit up the area and destroyed any cover I had. I slashed at it, sending its tip away as the axe wielder went for my shoulder. I caught their arm, but it was all a distraction, keeping me still for both range fighters to attack. One sphere hit my chest while the other went through my shoulder and wing.

Blood interrupted my scream as I lost my balance. The axe-wielder slipped away. I grabbed the fleeting creature through the haze, pushing past the pain and threw their light body at one of the ranged men. My tail was whirled into the spear-woman as she tried to attack from behind. Her legs broke at the knees, bending at an odd shape and the bone tore through the skin. She screamed only to be silenced by my sword shoved into her torso. It was ripped upwards, cutting her upper half in two.

I coughed, spitting out the blood that stopped pooling in my throat and mouth and wiped the bit that had fallen down the side of my chin as she fell. Breathing became easier once more, but the throbbing pain still remained. My body wanted to rest, but I didn't obey its wishes. The fallen monsters fumbled to get up, their gear entangled as I went over to them. Their last standing man frozen in fear. I stepped on the top one, crushing them both effectively under my boot. There wasn't a moment of hesitation as the blade went into both and the fire within was unleashed. Their screams died quickly as their bodies burned from the inside out. Running came to my ears and I looked over to find the final one taking flight.

Like I was going to let him get help.

I removed my sword and calmly walked after him. The movement of doing just that wasn't comfortable as everything pulsed in pain. I sent out streams of plasma fire after him. Parts of the walls, ceiling, and floor caught fire as he managed to dodge each attack, rounding a corner that had some light down it. I spread my wings and flew a slight bit to catch up and landed at the corner. The monster wasn't far as he turned around to face me, braver in the light. Not that it made a difference. The ending was going to be the same.

I sent out another stream, setting the floor ablaze as the lights flickered at the excess magic in the air. The man fired, failing to aim as it went over my shoulder, and I continued my stride. Another wave forced him to move left, and I threw the blade where he was going to be. The sword cut through the armour, powering it down a second time and flicked upwards, the hilt smashed into his head. The force knocked him over, the sword clattering next to him.

He reached for my weapon, but I denied him the hope. My hand gripped onto his arm, throwing him away and into the wall. It buckled and cracked under him, his arm dislocating but still under the torment of my grasp. Their gauntlet was crushed, blood squirted out of the bent and broken pieces. He yelped once but remained surprisingly silent.

"How do I get out of here?" I asked unexpectedly, picking up the sword beside me. The influence from before came back, trying to clear out the rage.

"I… I-I can't tell you," the man stuttered, and I hesitated from attacking again. *I needed to know… he could tell me.*

"If you tell me, I'll release you," I hissed, the other part of me was trying to regain control and continue the bloodshed. The persona was slipping back to being dominant… I managed to squeeze the gauntlet farther and he caved.

"Alright! Go up to the next floor! There's an elevator! Take it to the ground floor."

"That's it?"

"It's behind a false wall. You'll have to look for it."

I let go of his arm, stepping a few paces back, ready to leave. My head pulsed, ending the mercy that the other voice was trying to give and brought down the sword upon his skull, his pleas unheard and ended. My body writhed in agony, dropping me to my hands and knees, and a disgusted feeling fell over me. I gripped at my chest and tried to keep from collapsing further.

Bastards… all of them. I could heal through their damage. I had. What was this pain? Why did it feel like I was being attacked from the inside every time I wanted vengeance? This… soft being that I was… it needed to stop!

The pain softened slightly hearing my plea, and breathing became a bit easier, allowing me to stand and sense the world around me.

I knew that the place was so very wrong… Its existence made me want to be sick. But it would be better once I left. The world would stop spinning. The artificial lights would be no more. The pain would cease. Once I was out and rested… I was going to remove the stain. That thing proved they would go against their vows at the slightest pressure. They made me suffer just like so many others. I was going to rip their insides out, spill their blood like they had spilt mine.

I don't need-

They will drown as they leave this world in the peace it deserves.

Peace through hatred?

Hate. Love. What's the difference if the ending is the same?

The lump in my throat came back. *I wanted peace. I didn't want to-*

I know I wanted peace… and my people were going to have it. One way, or another. "Sixty-seven."

00000

I flicked the blood off my tail as the body I had skewered fell to the floor. My body burned on the inside… but it felt like it was slowly getting easier to function. The small urges of doing things different and wanting to hide had stopped fighting, hushed for the sake of peace and defending my people. The scents of more light creatures came to my nose suddenly and I analyzed it. They were different from the others in the building, but I wasn't sure how…

How many more could there be between here and my exit? It seemed like they never ended. I didn't care about how many disgusting monsters fell, but I couldn't keep going if there were too many. My magic was fine, well out of reserves, but my body needed rest. I wasn't sure how much longer I could keep going. Everything pounded, screaming at me to stop. The world, if I didn't concentrate, threatened to be taken. Every so often I was forced to find something to keep me on my feet.

If I collapsed… If I fell… It was over. Any freedom that I was trying to achieve would be stolen. I couldn't fall. I couldn't let the world disappear. I couldn't let them win.

The fear of being used, trapped, and toyed with, welled up in my chest.

I couldn't be caged again.

Not again…

The different scents came around the corner and I looked over slightly at the new arrivals, not quite ready to face them yet. Three of the four of them were different creatures than the ones I had been fighting. The fourth one had many more wings than the others – she was the same species as the other monsters from before, yet she too was different from the vile things. It wasn't all that apparent until now, but they weren't evil. Still I hesitated. They were Creatures of Light – the risk was too great to think they were friendly. I couldn't chance it if I wanted to be free. A different smell turned my thoughts more logical than instinctual. They came from outside.

Outside…

I needed outside. From the Building of Light – they had to be removed if they didn't let me go. Their levels of power extravagant to the others I fought. Their pulses steady…

They aren't going to let me go.

A grin formed, devouring the fear for sport and anger. I hoped they put up a fight worth wasting my time.

I don't want to-

I wanted to erase them from existence!

The foreign voice was drowned out in my fury as I turned my full attention to them, taking a couple of steps before stopping as they had thirty metres away, cautious to approach any closer. The strategy brought forth of what to do… a feeling of union with the other part of me came as battle was inevitable.

I had to admit, they seemed smarter than the last group. Their formation reflected that they knew what I was capable of. Good. It would make the nagging voice stay silent while I saved myself. "Who wants to be eighty-nine?"

"Aerrow… It's alright," the creature in black, red, and white armour started. He took a step forward with his hands showing he was unarmed and defenceless. I glared in suspicion. What kind of trick was this? "We came to help you."

"I don't need your help," I growled in annoyance and glared. I didn't want to chat. I wanted to fucking leave.

He looked behind me at the body for a brief moment before turning back to me. "Clearly…"

"Let me through."

"We can't let you leave like this. What do you mean by eighty-nine?"

My excitement grew with anticipation. "Why don't you find out?"

They were different, faceless monsters – but they were the enemy. I wanted to be successful in ripping them apart.

Do I?

Yes.

"Aerrow, you're not thinking straight."

My glee turned to rage as my body pulsed in agony, back to being conflicted. "I'm thinking just fine!"

He was just like the voice. The voice that made everything feel wrong and hurt. He had to be silenced!

I rushed at him as fast as my aching form could go and was down the hall and in front of him in a third of a second. He managed to block my attack from my tail, and I slashed my sword down onto his open side. A wall of chaos blocked it and a black sword came through, stabbing me in the leg. I growled in annoyance but didn't get much further than that as he cut across my chest. A pool of darkness formed underneath, and a spike came out of it, stabbing me in the right side of my chest. It shoved me into the wall, cracking it underneath me at a force that took my breath away. The winged one screamed in surprise. I wiped the black blood that had escaped my lips and grabbed the spike.

Finally, something I was familiar with!

I crushed it after ripping it out and the pool dispersed as the man felt me try to take it from him. My wounds healed swiftly as I charged at him again. I slashed and he barely blocked against the blow, his whole body being used to keep my blade away.

"Aerrow, we're trying to-" He didn't get to finish as I took advantage of his hesitance and shoved my wing into him.

A tendril of chaos blocked my blade from following through, causing the plasma to hit the ceiling above us. My tail hit him and sent him several metres away. He landed with a loud thud on his back. His armour no longer glowing as bits clattered to the floor when he tried to sit up but fell back again with a painful hiss.

"Owen!" The winged female shouted, and I hesitated after freeing my sword, not able to grab the magic that faded.

Owen… Why is that name familiar…?

It didn't mat-

It mattered!

No, it didn't! He may use dark magic, but he's the same as the rest!

I shifted my grip on my blade and charged, trying to reach the strange creature and finish him off before the female one could aid. They were defended as the monster in red and golden armour blocked the path using a spear with more skill than I had expected. He parried in his intercept, abusing my strength, and tripped me while I was off-centre. My body landed hard, and I brought my sword up just in time to defend his third attack. His spear sizzled as he jabbed. My wing brushed it aside, removing him enough with my tail to get to a stand. The brown and green armoured one caught my side with a blade, making me lose my footing. A growl escaped as my tail flicked out to compensate and sent him into the wall. His armour blocking the spines from running him through.

I went to attack but the red one jumped at the opportunity, pinning me against a wall of stone that wasn't there before. Stone barbs stabbed into my wings and tail. I screamed. The red monster grimaced in regret as he pushed his spear against my chest and arms, pinning me further against the wall. I pushed against him; he was stronger than he looked. My disadvantage made it difficult to fight him off, but he was struggling to keep me down. Two spikes came around my sides, stabbing me in the chest slightly, threatening to run me through if I pushed off the wall and out of his grip.

Ice started to form around my legs, shoulders, and arms to lock me down – its touch burned, and a sharp gasp escaped. I struggled, stabbing myself in the process to break free from the ice. Fire tried to melt it, but it kept growing as it turned to water and froze again before it could vaporize, spreading it. My body cried in agony and my energy ran out, unable to keep going. The ice stopped forming, keeping its sharp and cold touch contained. Short, raspy pants escaped instead of heavy breathing which was blocked by the spikes. I choked on blood from my recklessness, and it spattered onto my captor. My teeth gritted as I tried to keep up the pressure against him but didn't use dark magic as I wasn't sure if I could keep it from the black one. Not at the moment at least.

I could still get out… I just needed a small rest.

The brown and green armoured blight got up, more energetic than what I expected from the blow I hit him with. If it hadn't been for his armour, I was sure his ribs would have smashed through his organs. "Theodora said he'd be crazed, but no one said anything about black eyes and blood. What the fuck is going on?"

What did it matter to them? Who was this Theo-

I recognize that name…

The eight-winged one finished healing the damage I had done to the one I had almost killed, getting up. She answered his question. "That's not his… It's Outland blood. Several years ago, I read some encrypted simulations that Dad tested long before I was born to see if it was viable as a medical option, but he decided to toss the project because-"

"You think you can just use our kind when it suits you?!" I spat at her. They all flinched. How disgusting could they be? Not all Creatures of Darkness were mindless and soulless! "Just a resource for your benefit?!"

The dark magic user ended the silence that followed, ignoring my questions. "Did it get far enough to see about neutralizing the blood without killing the subject?"

"They were hacked files, but there was an odd-"

My body pulsed, causing me to scream and cut her off. I had to leave. I couldn't let them pursue me. Creatures of Light… They took everything from us! I couldn't be taken again… Not again! "I'm going to kill you all for everything!"

I used the wall as a bracer and shoved the one that held me down, not caring if I ran myself through. The spikes dissolved before I could hurt myself and the ice shattered from a sudden wave of heat. A wall of plasma came out of my sword, aiming for the red one and forced him to move. He went to attack but I countered with my tail. He was smashed into his brown friend who had started to jump in. Both monsters skidded down the hallway and I formed vines underneath them. Suddenly, an agonizing pain tore through my body as something entered my leg and I screamed. I dropped to the ground, losing my concentration on magic. The torment spread quickly through my veins.

My breathing became haphazard as the world started to spin worse than before. I ripped the object that was shot into my leg.

What the hell was- an Outland bolt…

I glared at the monster in black who had started to notch another one into his crossbow. They had these on them… Like I was letting them do that a second time.

I sent several balls of white and purple-black fire in his direction. He misfired when he dodged, and it went somewhere behind me. The floor quickly caught fire, growing up the walls and separating me from them. I got up with difficulty and took a few, heavy breaths. I knew where he was just by scent, but I also knew he didn't have the same luxury. I raised my sword, charging it to attack when a firearm went off to my left. A sharp pain in my hand was followed by the agony of the blast ringing through my head, my sword went somewhere beyond the fire. I turned to the culprit to find the winged one holding a rifle on my side of the flames.

"Don't make me-" she started as her gun's barrels switched into a shotgun and I grinned at the challenge.

"I don't need a sword to kill you."

"Don't fight him!" The creature named Owen shouted at her. "Leave before he kills you!"

She didn't leave, standing her ground and I rushed her, dodging her blast as I went under it. I came up and grabbed her throat in one hand. She aimed with little care, determined in whatever suicidal plan she created before I could crush her windpipe. I smashed her against the wall, high off the floor, and it cracked under her as she squeaked. She lost her grip on the weapon and turned to trying to keep my hand from tightening more.

A small, sadistic grin came at the thrill of something new. "Why struggle? You're only prolonging the inevitable."

"Do you… not know us?" She asked and I growled.

I wanted her to scream, not ask stupid questions. "I know exactly who you are. You're Creatures of Light. You need to die for us to live."

"You're that too." A yelp escaped as I squeezed. She struggled to breathe as I brought up a fireball turned plasma to finish her only to freeze at her next words. "You're a king-"

I'm a-

No. I am not like them!

My people-

A foggy memory of being in a cage. The scaled body of someone I had known, unmoving as they drained her of blood. I hissed as my head pounded.

The memory was mine… but it wasn't.

They are my people!

I don't know who that-

"Shut up! I will burn this whole world and cleanse it of you! Your kind killed my people for no reason!"

"Aerrow-"

"Stop saying that name!" It was my name… but it wasn't. My body refused to move my left arm that held the ball of plasma. I tried to squeeze with the limb I could but refused to get passed her grip.

Why was I holding back? She was just like the rest of them! A faceless monster of light that killed… I couldn't remember. My memories of them were dying and it was all her fault! "Why can't I kill you?!"

She didn't reply with words as her leg came up and wrapped around my arm that held her up. My form refused to stop her. There was a quick movement, and something cracked. My arm dropped her, no longer functioning. She landed perfectly, kicking me square in the chest as I tried to recover from my hesitance and confusion. Ribs cracked as I hit the wall on the other side of the hall. The air knocked out of me at the impact and my body crumbled to the ground. I started to get to a knee, regaining my bounds and breathing as my instincts to survive took hold.

I had to kill her to lea-

Lips were pressed against mine and my head was held gently. Time stopped. My mind cleared for the first time; the feeling of pure rage and fear disappeared as I reacted on a different instinct. A tongue gracefully slipped by mine, through my lips for a moment then retreated. I looked up to see my shocked reflection of one eye being white and the other black in her large, tear-filled sky-blue eyes.

This was- "Éabha…"

"Aerrow, it's going to be-"

I didn't hear the rest of what she had to say as an agonizing pain tore through my head and body. I screamed, grabbing my head with both hands as the world grew fuzzy. Her face blurred out, switching between being there and faceless as I tried to figure out… anything.

What was this pain? What was happening? Why was the room so bright? What were these smells and sounds?

Fire… Fire and others… Éabha. She smelt… good, but I wanted to remove it.

Why did I want to kill her?!

"Make it stop," I begged as she moved closer still, holding me tight in a way that should have been relieving, but a part of me was disgusted. A plasma ball formed in my hand on the ground next to us. "Éabha, I can't-"

"I know," she whispered in my ear. "I'm sorry."

I didn't get to ask why she was apologizing. I didn't want to. She was a monster.

My body tried to jerk out of her hold, revolted by her existence but she didn't let me go. I went to attack when something entered the left side of my chest. A painful, breathless gasp escaped. My heart stopped beating as the object was impaled farther and its magic seized through my nerves. The pain was unbearable. A noise came out as I tried to breathe, some last attempt at life, then fell onto the one who stabbed me.

Everything ceased to be.

Chapter Forty-Two: Don't Panic

Sweat dripped down Owen's face as he tried to end the fire's hold, doing his best to douse its grip using his magic. But it kept burning. He couldn't see beyond the flames fuelled by some primal rage, the words of Io coming to mind at her small simulations. The healing, the anger at what had happened to him and whoever's blood that was. The anguish. Owen almost let Aerrow go to wherever his mind was set, the only thing holding him fast was the amount of blood that covered him. Owen couldn't let him continue whatever rampage he was on. It was his body, but it wasn't Aerrow that moved it.

A hiss came out as he backed away from the flames that grew stronger. Struggles beyond it came to his ears. He told Éabha to run. Did he catch her? Even somehow through it all if they managed to get Aerrow to realize what he was doing, if he killed her...

He put everything he could into the chaos field, physically handling it as Cyrus tried to summon water, but the flames kept them both at bay, vaporizing the forms before they could get close. Éabha's sharp squeak was followed by a raging growl that his nephew wouldn't have been able to make before. What either of them had said was muted by the crackling, the floor and ceiling pealing and melting farther and farther from the source. Hot smoke filling the corridor and their lungs. The smell of the burning materials assaulted Owen's nose whenever he had a break to breathe through the coughing. The heat pushed them farther and farther away.

Then suddenly, the flames dropped. He wasted no time searching the smoke, dashing forward. An agonizing scream came from Aerrow somewhere in front of him.

A painful plea came ahead to his left, "Make it stop."

A glow broke through the smoke on the floor, directing Owen to where he was. His eyes grew wide as he realized that the light was plasma, with a hidden intent to kill that he had grown to know over the years.

"Éabha!" Owen screamed only for the orb to go out. A different noise entered the ominous silence that caught his breath. He broke out of the smoke as the bolt he had accidentally fired was shoved deeper into his nephew's chest. His run came to a stop as the one he came to rescue fell onto his murderer. His words were quiet as she gripped the body. "What did you do?"

"I'm so sorry," she cried softly, her words were cracking as if it hurt to talk. "I tried... he was back and then he... I'm sorry."

"You killed…" He managed to pry his eyes from the bloodied body to her, enraged with grief. "You killed him!"

"The Outland blood had to be quelled!" She screamed back before bending over, coughing violently. Her hair moved to the side showing off deep, dark bruising around an obvious imprint of where someone had gripped around her neck. Her words were barely breaths as he struggled to hear her. "It was the only way… I'm sorry."

"Only way for what?!" He tried to keep what little control he had left, failing as she subtly shook. "Éabha, why didn't you listen?!"

"Because I was trying to save him…" she muttered, moving the body on her, finally letting him go and placed him on his back. She looked over at Owen, determination behind the grief and fear. "I need you to remove the bolt; it's stuck. I can't heal him properly until its out."

His fury came to a halt as he heard what she said, finally registering the healing magic coming from her. The entire time he was losing it, she was… He went over to them, kneeling on the other side. He gripped the bolt and pulled, the blood that flung from the tip was black and hit his face, still warm. He didn't get to put the bolt down before she started healing more aggressively, the glow on her hand brightened and etched into some of the veins that were seen around the wound, contaminated by the poison.

After several moments, she looked to him, tears still falling as her voice was hoarse. "I got the bolt's poison out and his heart's healed, start resuscitating. He's only been dead for forty-five seconds; there is still time."

He followed her instruction as she moved away from Aerrow's lifeless chest slightly allowing him space. The seconds dragged on as his compressions continued in beat to the pacing he heard from Cyrus as the young knight silently fumed – barely keeping himself together. He closed his eyes, working autonomously, and turned to a skill he rarely used. He couldn't lose him. It was different from Solomon, from Aelia, he could sense Aerrow's soul still lingering inside. There were other senses there too, something other than just the warm glow behind the cooling corpse. One he recognized as the Outland Dragon essence, faint and not worth paying attention to, but the second sense that wasn't natural caught him off-guard and he almost miscounted. It felt off, but after a slight scan, he didn't find it harmful. It anchored his nephew down, tethering him barely as its strands that were weaved inside the light frayed in the middle, losing their grip, one at a time. He had to assist whatever it was.

As if hearing his thoughts, the strands that had broken away shifted towards him. He reached out mentally, and a familiar pulse went through his being. His necromancy activated and he followed instinct, down the pathway the strange connection had made. When he reached the end of the road, all he could sense was raw death. A gripping claw threatening to grab his own life away, tugging and scratching at the sense that was fleeing. Owen put a barrier down with a slight grimace between it and his energy, forcing it and whatever primal intentions that archaic anchor was trying to a stop. It wanted everything he had, terrifying him at how hungry and persuasive it was, but he wouldn't let it. He may have been inexperienced, but he knew well enough of what the life-stealing ability was and how to avoid it.

But what was it doing inside Aerrow?

He didn't get to ask as more strands had broken, leaving only a few remaining. A cold embrace of a shadow crept on the wall across the hall, something Cyrus couldn't see as he continued to pace. The shadow gave a sense of a figure, an emotionless, snow-white face that seemed almost like a mask under its hooded robe, blacker than the chaos he commanded. It stood and watched, unmoving. Waiting. One of Valrdis's reapers.

He went back to compressions, keeping himself from tensing physically as he magically gripped onto the tether, pressing his own will into following the helpful instructions that wouldn't kill him. He wasn't going to let Aerrow go. He couldn't let him go even if he wanted to. He had promised Solomon and Aelia. He promised them!

The threatening side of the anchor whispered silently for him to take its road instead, hearing his anguish. He stayed with the side that was harmless and felt more like the ease his nephew gave despite everything thrown at him. Owen's magic drained quickly, not being used in such a way caused his chest to compress at the strain.

A growl came out as he went back to compressions again from breaths. "Aerrow! Come on, dammit! You're stubborn with everything else! Don't leave us like this!"

"General… I don't-" Azarias started softly then tsked, unable to finish what they all knew. It had been almost a minute and a half.

"I don't feel so…" An exasperated noise came from Éabha suddenly and Owen looked away from the network of souls as she fell over, unconscious.

Azarias was at her side before he looked up. "Éabha!"

Owen turned back to the network again, the strands that he hadn't been watching had gripped onto her, silently drinking at her unprotected form. He held back a look of disgust and they responded, removing themselves swiftly like scared animals. He kicked his magic up a notch. If they wanted to feed so bad, they could have what he provided, not whatever innocent snack was hanging around.

They struck at his barrier without a second thought, starving for more and a painful grunt escaped at the aggression that wasn't like anything he knew. Whatever laid within... it wasn't normal. Not for an Outland Dragon, and certainly not for Aerrow. But as it fed, doing its hardest to break through his defence, etching and crawling through it like worms, all he felt was Aerrow's presence within.

Éabha groaned, Azarias waking her up now that she was freed and slowly sat up with his help. Pale and tired, she still continued to heal. The stands lessened their attacks, feeding off the healing light that Owen could never provide. They seemed to be in awe at her magic and no longer starving for his. Then, they retreated, forming and winding themselves once more to the soul that he was desperately trying to keep from being reaped.

A shallow, sharp breath came to his ears and Owen stopped resuscitating. Tears broke through his physical barrier. Aerrow was breathing. The cold numbness of the reaper receded in the corner of his eye, leaving a shadow behind as Owen took his pulse. He didn't need to do a full minute to know it wasn't going to be any more than thirty beats. His breaths became irregular along with the heartbeat, skipping or stopping and trying to regulate itself, failing.

"His body is rejecting the Outland blood," Éabha clarified, somehow still healing. She looked to them, exhausted but terrified, matching how they looked at her words. "We have to get back to Dad now!"

"Éabha, you're not capable of taking a Chaos Portal in your-" Owen started, but didn't get to finish as she slapped the floor with her free hand, still not stopping. A glyph was forming before he registered what she was doing. "Éabha!"

"Cyrus, fucking get in," the girl growled, ignoring him and Cyrus did as she asked.

There was a bright light and then the smoke, the awful smell of burning, and the flickering lights changed to the familiar lighting of the safehouse living room. Her healing orb stopped as she swayed, and Owen caught her before her head hit the tea table. "Easy there."

She looked up at him with a thankful glance, but whatever she had to say was interrupted by Deigh coming out of Aerrow's room. She stopped next to her partner, pleas barely audible as she gripped his lifeless, blood covered hand. "He's in so much agony… Aerrow… Aerrow, don't die again. Please don't…"

"Éabha!" Orpheal called as he exited the same room and one look at her made the Seraph go pale. "Oh, Orithina, what happened-"

"Help Aerrow," Éabha stated, stopping her father in his tracks from continuing towards her. "I'm alright-"

"No, you're-"

"He's dying!"

Orpheal looked to Aerrow, as if just realizing he was there and turned to the two knights. "Cyrus, Azarias, help me with him."

They acted, doing as he asked swiftly and efficiently, leaving Owen, Éabha and Deigh outside for a few moments. Deigh followed them, keeping her Absalomian form and Owen turned to Éabha. "Thank you for saving him."

"He's not saved yet…" She looked to the door in pain and fear. "He wasn't like this before I stabbed him. Maybe I should have-"

"No, you did the right thing," he told her, finally accepting what she had done. "He would have never forgiven himself if he killed you. He probably won't be able to forgive himself for attacking you. I'm sorry for yelling at you."

"You watched your nephew, your king, get murdered by someone you trusted. Who wouldn't become enraged?" She shook her head as she looked at her black blood covered hands. "He didn't know better, I did… If I listened, we could have… He came back, but I still… I killed Aerrow, my friend, trying to ease his suffering and I shoved that bolt so easily though his chest…"

She broke down, and he did his best to soothe her. "It's okay, Éabha. He's not-"

"It's not okay!" She was shaking in his arms. "I only knew theoretically that it would work, but I still went ahead and killed him! A part of me even felt relieved that monster… he was a monster. He tried to kill me and… What kind of monster am I for thinking he was a monster?!"

"You saved him, Éabha, even when he was like that. You're not a monster."

"I didn't save him alone… I saw and felt you using magic…"

"Nothing that could be done without you. When Aerrow wakes up, he'll tell you exactly that."

"Perhaps… but I'm also scared."

He gave her a confused look. "Scared?"

"That's he'll be… that thing. I'm so sorry…" She looked back at Aerrow's room. "I can't go in there. I can't help him anymore, but you can. He needs you to get the Outland blood out of him that wasn't neutralized by the bolt."

"Éabha-"

"Stop being sentimental and go! I'll be fine… It wasn't him. That terrifying and terrified creature wasn't Aerrow. I know it wasn't him. He knew me for that brief moment. He held back… he couldn't kill me. He was even more terrified and scared about everything than I was. Scared and angry…"

She hugged herself, struggling to rationalize her experience. He couldn't find the words the help her nor did he want to leave her as she was, but Orpheal called for him. He got up quickly, heading to where the others were, stopping for a moment in the doorway. He didn't know what she went through once the fire separated them, what she had done before she stabbed him. He couldn't ask her, not then at least. He passed her an apology. "I'm sorry… we'll talk once he's stable."

She didn't respond, simply crying silently on the floor.

Chapter Forty-Three: Dream Alone

I gasped for air, bolting upright from a nothingness. My head pounded and my breathing was heavy. All around was the white world, its ashes had already started falling, etching out much of the dead flora and corpses, and covering the white jacket and black pants of the uniform like a light layer of snow.

I put a hand through my hair, still not calming down despite being in a calm place. It felt like I had woken from a nightmare… But I didn't know what the nightmare was. I tried searching for something, a clue to how I got there, but nothing came. Nothing except for an existential dread. My heart raced as my anxiety grew.

What was going on? Why did it feel like something horrible happened?

A small, familiar purr calmed me down almost instantly to my left. I turned and the Black Phoenix was there once more, looking down at me from her laying form with contempt for a moment before it faded to melancholy. Her gaze fell to the floor in what seemed to be guilt.

Why was the proud dragon of a goddess ashamed and full of despair?

"What's wrong?" I asked but she didn't answer, still unable to look at me. Her claws flexed in a similar manner to how Deigh's did when she was upset. I stood up and cautiously approached her as it seemed like this single time it was alright to do so. I stopped about a metre away. Tears streamed down the black and red-lined scales on her face. "Why are you crying?"

There was a moment of silence and then, for the first time in the realm, she spoke with the same voice that had tried to coax my will. The young maiden voice was quiet, heavy in grief. "So many were killed…"

"Who was killed? By whom?"

"The puppets of him. They tortured them. Killed them… They stole you too."

"Stole…?" My voice trailed off in my confusion and I grew anxious. "I don't… stole. What do you mean? Am I not… Was I killed?"

"Yes."

"But I'm…" I looked around before turning to her in disbelief. "That can't be. I'm breathing. I can feel my heartbeat. I'm talking to you… right? This world is just a realm in my mind – how can it be if I'm…?"

"This world is not just in your mind. It continues until all ceases to be, until there is nothing left that can die…"

"So, I… I'm…" None of it made sense. How could I come to this world when I was alive… but when I wasn't…? I still came here. "What am I doing here, breathing, speaking if I'm dead?"

"You were killed, but you are not dead."

My face didn't hide my surprise. "I'm… alive?"

"Barely."

"But how did I… What happened? I don't remember anything after the mercenary injected me with something. She wouldn't have killed me. Where did she take me? Who-?" My body pulsed in agony and writhed as a squeak came out through the lack of air. "What happened to me?"

A little ball of chaos formed in front of her, and she pushed it forward. It hit my chest softly, and immediately the pain recoiled. A familiar power spread to my limbs like a warm blanket and allowed my body to relax. I stood up straight as she looked me over then away again. "Your body was rejecting its new existence…"

"Thank you… but what do you mean? What did you do? What was that orb?"

"I simply protected your being while your comrades try to fix what has become of you, granted a little more aggressively than what you can handle without dying a second time."

"What has… I don't remember."

"No… and you probably won't but trust me when I say it's for the best that you don't. You won't remember just as you will never remember your times in here in the waking world. Once you leave, you will come to understand."

"Understand what?"

"I'm sorry. You were supposed to be protected but time and time again, she stops it."

I wanted to know what she meant; she knew but she didn't seem like she was allowed to say anything. Her tears flowed heavier, her eyes closing to try and contain her emotions as a tsk of disgust escaped her mouth. I didn't understand anything… but whatever happened was something that never should have. I stepped closer and did my best to wipe some of the tears away to comfort her. Her eyes promptly opened and looked at me in surprise.

I pulled away before I overstepped further. "I'm sorry…"

"You were trying to comfort…" She gave a small huff.

"Trying but… I'm sorry for the loss of those you cry for. You mentioned that there were others you cared for. They were tortured and killed. I wish there were something that could have been done before that happened."

"You were never going to find them and it's not only them that I show weakness for."

"Who do you…" It was obvious by the look she gave me. I shifted uncomfortably. "You have no reason to be concerned for me. You're Valrdis's dragon and I'm just a king of a Kingdom of Light – a descendant of hers and your enemy."

"Yet you try and ease the pain of your enemy."

"Out there perhaps you could be an enemy… But I don't believe that to be so here. In here, I can't bare to see your torment. I can't stand by and watch you suffer despite you killing my soldiers and knights in the past. It feels wrong to see you as an enemy. All I want to do is try and ease it, even if that just means staying here until you're okay."

"You strange, little king… You have no idea what has become of you and yet you concern yourself with me."

"No, I don't… but I don't care. You're someone I can help right now and that's all that matters presently. Outside, if I can still protect people from Ciar and whoever else is out there, then it doesn't matter what happened."

"Would you say that once you leave and it happened again?"

"Yes. Tortured, maimed, even if I die again – I want to protect them and will do so to the best of my ability." My answer was surprisingly confident, conquering the anguish and concern of what I wasn't aware of. "For the kingdoms, my sister and uncle, even the friends I've made and am yet to make, people I will never know and certainly those whelps that haven't been found; they are worth it."

"If that is your desire… then my life being taken might have had some purpose to it," a young boy said behind me in Ancient Dragon. I turned around in surprise to see an Outland Dragon whelp standing a little less than a metre tall. He didn't seem any older than the kids back home. He looked up to me with no expression. "You spoke to Zegrinath… You promised him."

"I did…" I started, changing from Ori to his language and looked away. If he was there it meant that… but why? "I didn't find you before they killed you. I'm sorry."

"You did what you could, I know that now. Anger was all I had after…" He choked on his words as I looked back to him. "But I understand now, not all Creatures of Light are bad and I regret not living long enough to see that."

"There is nothing to regret. Creatures of Light and Dark can be scary to each other. People a hundred times older than you never realize that someone different might not be bad so there is no shame with learning after death," I told him, moving closer only to stop as his scales prickled at first before settling. He took a few steps towards me, bumping my hand and allowing me to brush the ash off his head. "It'll be okay when you go to the next world. I heard it's beautiful. You won't be alone."

"I know… my parents told me about it. It's beautiful for everyone. No one cares, it's supposed to be peaceful, just like the peace you strive for. It wasn't something I knew I needed, but I cannot go there."

I frowned. "Why can't you go to Athnuracha?"

"I may be dead, but my life isn't over on Orithin yet. There are people to protect from Ciar and whoever else is out there. Tortured, maimed, even if I die again – I want to protect them to the best of my ability. For my new kingdom, my new sister and uncle, the friends I'll make and the friends I left behind that have to be saved; they are worth the pain."

I was tongue-tied at how he almost repeated the very thing I had just said. I turned around to the Black Phoenix, hoping for her to explain, but she was gone. I turned back to the tiny dragon. "What are you-?"

"When you see my parents again, tell them I'm sorry… and not to be mad. To move on without me. Tell them that I keep living, just differently. Promise that you will find my friends and to tell my parents I love them. Okay?"

"I'll find your friends," I agreed. "I'll tell your parents if I remember once I leave this place…"

"You won't remember… but I'll remind you." He looked to the floor in misery. "As an apology for everything I've done to you. I'll make sure that even when you sleep, you won't ever dream alone."

I knelt in front of him, incredibly confused by his words, but I didn't show it. I rubbed his head and behind horns that would have grown to be massive in reassurance instead. He moved his head and set it on my shoulder, silently crying. "You don't owe anything; things will be okay. You've no need to stay and hold onto past mistakes. It's okay."

"I'm so sorry…"

"You're forgiven." I wasn't sure what he was sorry for, but he relaxed greatly at the sound of the words. "Everything will be alright."

The tiny dragon said nothing for a moment before growing rigid again. Scales stood on end as the red undertones powered through the black and purple. He looked up quickly, almost hitting me and his orange eyes grew wide at something behind me. "They're here."

"Who's-" My sentence was cut short as he disappeared into dust with a short yelp. The wind picked up. I stood, turning around. No one was there, nothing but a growing storm of ash. The ash fell in large clumps, burying even the bodies and fallen trees. I looked around as the silence dragged on. "Kid? Kid?! Where'd you go?!"

Nothing answered, even the wind I felt stinging against my skin was unnaturally quiet. The tension of the world sent me into a panic. The fear was subsided by my head that pounded suddenly, and a scream escaped. I grabbed it, trying to do anything to ease the pain but it only grew – nothing like the pain that I had felt earlier. It felt familiar, but something I couldn't place as it burned. My legs buckled, dropping my weight. A barely audible whisper came from the silence like that of an order, but I couldn't make out what it wanted. The pain spread as I didn't complete its wish, agonizingly into my limbs but mostly my chest. I gripped at my jacket, trying to ease it as it compressed my lungs. I could barely breathe.

What was this…?

Shoes stepped in front of me, and I looked up only for whoever that stood overhead to be blurred out by the pain and ash. Two hands gripped around my unprotected throat, knocking me backwards. I tried to get them off, but the strain of not following the order grew worse as they started choking me.

They were strong… So strong…

I couldn't fight against them.

My thrashing came to a slow stop, giving into the person's hold. A distorted voice broke the silence as the ash started to bury me. "Kill them all, Little Dragon."

I wanted to glare at the name, to give a response of telling them no, but nothing escaped my mouth as my body burned from the pain and lack of air. Then, it went dark.

Chapter Forty-Four: What I've Done

Pain was the first thing that I registered in the darkness. A whisper of a groan escaped my lips as I attempted to open my eyes, but they were so heavy. With a great effort, I succeeded and found myself in my room in the hideout. It was much brighter than I remembered, but it was the room.

How'd I get here? I was out with Cyrus... Then a kid... An alleyway? What... happened after that?

My heart sunk at a thought I couldn't reach. Tears tried to break the surface and I held them back. It must have been the remnants of a nightmare I couldn't recall. I went to sit up only to find it impossible to do so. My muscles refused to cooperate with a small throb of pain, warning me of what would happen if I moved. Dizziness hit hard when I tried to push past, and I closed my eyes to force the world still. My thoughts were fuzzy and incoherent as the lack of vision stimulated my other senses. Scents I did and didn't recognize flooded my mind, similar to what would happen when I opened my senses to Deigh's... But I didn't have the link open that wide.

What was this?

Small thuds came to my ears in steady paces, other noises and scents invaded causing my head to hurt. It wasn't just the sounds and scents, something inside me was different. Why was everything... different?

"Deigh... Deigh, what... why was..."

"Aerrow!" Her voice entered my head like a warm blanket, more delighted than what I had expected, but it was the only normalcy I felt. Her voice became vocal. "He's awake!"

The sounds of chairs moving came to my ears and my eyes opened. I tried to sit up again only to get about halfway before falling against the bed frame in regret. My head and body pulsated and made it hard to breath. I was only clothed in a pair of briefs underneath the blanket which was very different from the uniform before. The air was cool, but I didn't grab for the blanket, too sore to do so. Owen, Azarias, Cyrus, and Éabha came over to each side of the bed while Deigh in her Absalomian form practically leapt onto it, laying close and wrapping arms around me. A small gasp of pain came out and she lessened her already soft hug, simply cuddling up to me like a cat. I looked at her in confusion before turning to the rest of their faces finding only concern.

My throat was dry as I swallowed, my voice unused. "W-what's… going on?"

"Well for one-" Azarias started strongly but Owen cut him off.

"How are you feeling?"

Good question. The answer was a bit difficult to pin down. "Awful… like I was turned inside out and then put back together… I don't know…"

"Considering what happened," Éabha muttered, looking over a sheet on a clipboard on the other side. "Anything else?"

"A migra-" I stopped, noticing faint bruising around her neck. "What happened to you? Were you attacked?"

She froze for a moment, hesitating as she looked at me with a lost look. Her voice was her usual neutral, a contradiction. "What do you remember?"

Why was that always the question I hated being asked? "Cyrus and I were only a few blocks from the station. A kid came out of an alley…"

I tried thinking really hard to clear some of the muddiness of my head. A memory flashed past of someone's wing being separated from their body, the wing locked in place on the counter by Winterthorn. The victim stapled to the wall with some metal piece. Blackness formed as the screams of someone begging for their life were taken by the sounds of choking on blood.

"Aerrow," Éabha's voice broke through the nightmare of memories I wasn't sure were real.

"There was someone impaled into a wall, their wing ripped off… then someone begging for their-" A memory cleared slightly as I saw my hand wrapped around Éabha's throat. She was trying to hold me back. Had I…? "Did… D-did I attack you?"

She said nothing as she turned back to the clipboard. I looked to the other knights and all I received was silence and neutral expressions. They were hiding something from me.

I turned back to Éabha, sensing that a lot of healing magic was used on her. "Please, I need to know. Did I do that?"

"You weren't yourself-"

"I tried to kill you? Why would I do that?"

"It wasn't your fault."

"What are you talking about?"

"You were given a blood transfusion with Outland Dragon blood. It changed your cells, and you became an Outland Mons-" She corrected her analytic answer. "Creature. Part Outland Dragon, part Absalomian. Due to the nature of Outland Dragons and the high percentage of dragon already in your DNA, the combination of the magical properties changed what you perceived to be the enemy and how you approached them."

"So, I..." My throat closed in on itself as my heart raced. Deigh tried to comfort me as I went through my head, wanting to know what happened. What I remembered. But nothing else came. Just those three moments... Though, it was more than enough. I was... "I became a monster... I killed- Oh gods!"

"Aerrow, you need to calm-"

"Calm down?! I don't even know what I did as... as whatever *that* was!" I exclaimed and they all flinched except for Deigh. An ill feeling dropped in. "That sort of personality doesn't just come out of thin air! I tried to kill you and you're fine with that?!"

"Of course, I'm not!" She shouted back as her tears slipped out. "You terrified me then and you scare me a bit now."

I froze as my heart skipped a beat. What... What had I done?

She wiped the tears away, clearing her throat and seemed to calm down. "But... I know logically that you aren't scary... You're my friend. What happened wasn't your fault."

"But I still attacked you..."

"You did, but you held back... you struggled to go through with it. You were still in there somewhere and you recognized that we were trying to help you even though you attacked us. We saw some of what you did inside that Outland zealot base; it wasn't even comparable to what you did to them." While her words were meant to reassure me, I couldn't help but feel like she was trying to rationalize it herself. "You knew that they were going to hurt you and acted accordingly. When you met us, you were angry, but I think you were more desperate. You couldn't risk trusting a Creature of Light after everything you had gone through."

"Wait... I attacked you three too?" I asked, turning to the knights and they remained silent on the subject, but it said everything. I looked to Deigh's white and red head where I could sense that she wanted me to pet her, but I couldn't bring myself to touch her, terrified. "What kind of monster attacks his own people?"

"One that wasn't the same species anymore," Owen told me, but it didn't help. "You were fighting for your kind's survival, adamantly so… Just not the kind you are now."

"How noble of me." The sarcasm was a little more than dry. I looked up to the four of them again. "How did you rescue me if I was consumed by Outland blood?"

"That I can't fully answer."

"What do you mean?"

"I was the one who did it," Éabha said, grabbing the conversation. "Several years ago, I think I was twelve, somewhere around there, I got mad at Dad and hacked into his abandoned research vault just to see if I could find something. Show him up by completing it. What I found though was so tightly secured because of how dangerous and immoral they could be if he finished them. There was one where he was researching if Outland Dragon blood was a viable source for medical research."

"He was going to use Outland blood as a resource?"

"The plan was to synthesize it if it was worth it since he didn't want to harm relations with Outland Dragons anymore than what they were. But as you can already guess, he knew that if he published any of his work down the line, people wouldn't care about the options available and just use it as an excuse to hunt innocent lives for the sake of further research and progress."

"I see…" There was a hint of irrational anger that formed inside me to hear that at first, but as she explained, it stopped and faded. "What did you find in the research?"

"He did a few simulations of what side effects could come to fruition when an Absalomian was introduced to it like you were and how to fix it since he was more concerned about what would happen if so and so happened rather than knowing what benefits would be. The side effects were similar to yours: aggression, anger, fear, and confusion. By activating certain memories, these side effects, in theory, would remind someone of who they are and would end or significantly lessen. These memories had to be close ones that were more instinctual than anything else such as a parent or a child."

"Did you have a picture of my parents with you or something?"

"No, even if I did, they would have had to physically be there for it to work and since you have no living parents or any kids, I went for a different approach with the same stimuli. I tried reminding you that you're a king which allowed me to break free but not enough to snap you out of it, so I went for full instinct…"

"What do you mean?"

She hesitated, looking away sheepishly and a bit red. "Well, you're a young male looking to create offspring as most young people do."

Azarias crossed his arms. "I feel like this is going into a territory that is considered-"

"You…" I cut him off as the memory of her lips touching mine came back, her tongue. My face grew very warm. "You used my… you kissed me?!"

"That is not where I thought this was going," he sighed in relief, not that it was incredibly relieving for me to hear.

I wasn't sure if I was more embarrassed or mad about the kiss. I hadn't kissed the only person I fell in love with and Éabha went ahead and stole my first one while I was possessed! "Why was your second thought of possible options to kiss me?!"

"Doesn't get more instinctual than your basic instinct to fuck someone, that's why," she muttered harshly, still as embarrassed as I was. "For the record, it did work for a brief moment, but it wasn't like the simulations had suggested and you started to lose yourself again. So, I, er, stabbed you in the heart with an Outland bolt."

The emotional turmoil left in a whirlwind. The knights and Owen weren't so surprised anymore. "You what?"

"You were going to kill me and knowing the properties I… thought it was the quickest way to subdue you long enough to get you to safety and remove the blood's control. I revived you shortly after killing you with Owen but…" She faltered before bowing. Her grip around the clipboard tightened and her knuckles went white. "I'm sorry for kissing you and I'm so, so sorry for killing you. It took hours to talk it through with everyone but I still… If you don't want to be friends anymore I-"

"Éabha, it's fine…" I told her, relieved to know that she was still herself even after that horrible nightmare. "I tried to kill you and that alone is unforgivable. You were just defending yourself. In fact if you could stab me a few more times for my actions…"

She stood up straight with wide eyes. Then she looked away, tears threatening to break through, trembling lightly. "If I'm forgiven for defence, you're more than forgiven."

It didn't make me feel better about the situation. My head pounded and a small gasp escaped as I grabbed it. "So, what happens... now that the blood is out of me?"

"That's... not exactly what happened after we got you back here," Owen told me carefully. "Orpheal did a full examination and you had almost two litres of blood transfused into your system. With the amount of magic and ratio – it changed your very DNA so it wouldn't be seen as a foreign object to your immune system. At least, that's the theory with the percentage of dragon blood you already had, allowing you to adapt. With how much you got hurt, the blood's natural healing ability along with yours worked constantly, fusing more and more with your original cells, then the Outland bolt's properties..."

"What are you saying?"

"Even after using an antidote, Orpheal tried to cancel the blood out with his light magic and when it didn't work, I tried manipulating it, but all we were doing was killing you..." He trailed off, looking away in disgust. "We couldn't get it all out. I'm sorry."

"So, it's just... there? Does that mean I'm-"

He shook his head. "No. The blood's hold on your mind was neutralized by the bolt's poison, thankfully, but you're not fully Absalomian anymore..." My surprise wasn't hidden well as he let it sink in for a moment and when I didn't object, not that I could really say anything, he continued. "I'm sorry, Aerrow. I shouldn't have suggested leaving – I should have followed your instincts, thought of the possibility of-"

"You were doing your job as both my general and my uncle," I cut him off, trying my best to push past the horrifying crisis of my existence for a later time. "You were trying to keep me sane and when things went awry, you came to rescue me. I can only imagine how stressful that was."

"Nothing in comparison to what you went through."

"I don't remember, so I couldn't tell you."

"No, but Deigh could. She slipped into expiration shock when you were kidnapped. The two times she got through to you were... rough."

I looked to Deigh who hadn't moved from me and willed the courage to pet her. She purred in delight through the link but was silent on the outside. I understood now why she was acting as she was. She was terrified of letting me go. "I'm so sorry, Deigh."

"No, I'm sorry I couldn't save you when you called for me."

I hugged her, pushing past the pain. "I shouldn't have gone into that alleyway."

"You were trying to save a child from losing his mother," Cyrus said, and I looked up to him, hearing the regret in his voice. "The mercenary preyed on your morals to help someone in need, there is nothing to apologize for."

"Cyrus, this isn't your fault either. If they got the best of you that means they did their homework and knew you were a threat."

"Yes, they did but…"

"We can use this experience to be better… right?"

"Maybe."

"Maybe?"

"He's worried about other side effects," Azarias explained when he didn't. "The ones that weren't researched and thrown into a digital vault."

"Like… what? I hurt, but what other side effects could there be?"

Éabha took my question. "Nothing happens without consequence. So far, you're a little more eager, less passive – but that could fade away as your system equalizes out."

Was I being more aggressive? "… I don't…"

"Even if it stays around, it's not necessarily a bad thing if you have a shorter temper – it'll help you against enemies as you're less likely to hesitate, but one thing that had consequence is your dragon form."

"My dragon form?"

"You… right."

"You used the partial dragon transformation while you were attacking the zealots," Owen explained. "You had wings and a tail that were mixed between an Absalomian Dragon and-"

"An Outland Dragon's…" I trailed off, trying to picture that mess.

Azarias gave me a grin. "You looked really cool. Terrifying but cool."

That did not make me feel better. "How... h-how many people did I...?"

"Er, I don't think that's-"

"I can't be ignorant to what happened regardless of who they were!" I growled out. "How many people?!"

His happy-go-lucky spirit left. "You took count..."

"I counted..." My entire being dropped into dread and Deigh tried to ease the anxiety with no success.

"Eighty-eight of them if you were counting correctly."

"Oh... gods..." The words were barely coherent to my ears.

I killed eighty-eight people. Not just killed them. I toyed with many of them. I slaughtered them in... how long? It couldn't have been very long.

What I've done...

"Aerrow," Éabha called my name and I looked to her. "It's okay."

"How is any of this okay?!" She flinched under my raised voice. Realization hit me, even if she said she was okay, she wasn't under it all. She was terrified of me attacking her again. She couldn't tell the different between me and... whatever I became. "I'm sorry... I've never killed anyone of light directly before. I can't imagine myself doing anything like that."

"They were going to use you to kill more than just them," Cyrus stated, looking at Éabha with a bit of concern. "We had to kill just to get to you, I could only imagine how you felt going against so many of them alone for you to turn on people you knew to be alright."

Éabha gave a small nod as she took a breather. "He's right. You seemed scared when we met you, angry, yes, but scared."

"I... don't remember entirely, but I think a small part of me enjoyed it," I told them as my throat went dry. "I know I didn't, but a small part did. I remember arguing in my head. I hated the amount of blood being spilt, the carnage I was causing. But I also wanted more. It was so angry, it despised everything that was light. Whenever I fought against it, it fought back, and it was agonizing... I couldn't do anything."

"Adrenaline and the vicious cycle between your nature and the primal instincts of a scared and angry dragon. Outland or not, that basic instinct to want those who caused you suffering to pay for it, to fix it, is normal." Owen moved closer to me, putting a hand on my shoulder to reassure me. "You were fighting for both of your lives last night and you did nothing wrong, even if you enjoyed it a little. They were going to enjoy making you their pet a lot more."

"That doesn't erase what I've done... none of it feels right to just leave it as is. Nothing feels right at all."

"You can blame whoever did this to you as their sins, not yours, and not that poor creature they took the blood from." My heart dropped again as the thought I had earlier came back, still out of reach. "Do you have any idea who that would be?"

I thought about his question, doing my best to try and ignore the hatred I grew for my existence. The dreaded thought that I had forgotten something more important than my kidnapper kept prying at my conscious. Experiments eventually came to the forefront, but that was it. "I think they knew of your father's research, Éabha. I can only remember the word experiments... I definitely wasn't their first subject, the other people that were kidnapped died sometime before me."

Éabha gave a pondering expression. "Very few people had access to those notes before they were locked away and as far as I'm aware, I'm the only one who had been able to hack into Dad's system. So, that limits the search."

"Sorry for not having anything else to go off of..."

"It's more than what I thought you could give," she said, trying to be cheerful as she hugged the clipboard. "Alright... I'm going to let Dad know that you're awake, pry him away from the Zerach. He'll want to look you over first so we can ask him about possibilities after that, okay? I think Owen mentioned that there was someone else that might have had more information on the fusion."

"Maybe later, I'm fine for now..." My head pounded, trying to deny my words as my mind slipped back into the spiral of self-hatred and guilt. "I... I need to be alone for a bit."

"Are you sure? They're almost done so you're not bothering him."

"Please... I'm fine. I just need some time to think."

Owen took the hint and nodded. "Alright. We'll leave you be for a bit. Call us if you need anything, we'll be right outside."

They left with the exception of Deigh who, even if I threatened her or myself, wouldn't have listened and stayed wrapped around me. I managed to sit up right, going through everything she and I knew as she leaned against me, trying to help with my searching by organizing anything I came across. But there was so little to gather.

Who was I now...? I felt different and not in a good way. The lights in the room were brighter than before. The smells and sounds were more defined. The person I thought I was made no sense in some way. I had the urge to spill the blood of my enemies without question, but I also wanted to have peace and take them down through words. I wanted to kill the person who did this to me and the dragon they bled for their experiment. The thought of mercy was almost comedic.

My stomach twisted.

The door gave a creak that I hadn't heard before and we turned to it. Éabha came in, looking at Deigh for almost permission before turning to me. I frowned. "Did something come up?"

"No... No." She sat on the bed next to me. "I'm sorry..."

"For what? You saved my life. Deigh's even more ecstatic about it than I am and I'm quite happy to know that I wasn't left to roam as that thing any longer."

"Yes... but what I said afterwards was wrong. I didn't mean to say I was scared of you. I'm tired and more emotional than usual." She grabbed my hand with her warm ones, trying to be reassuring but all I could think of was accidentally doing something that could hurt her and remained as still as possible. "I overreacted and you shouldn't feel guilty about anything. I'm not scared of you, okay? You should be mad that I..."

"I can't be mad at what you did. What I was like..." I looked away. Her words weren't true despite what she said. It was plain as day that she was trying to fight it away by forcing her emotions to be more logical. But that wasn't how emotions worked. "It's okay if you're terrified. I tried... I was a savage monster."

"I'm more terrified that I could murder my best friend," she muttered, tightening her grip.

"Don't be. You did what was necessary. If I had killed you..." I couldn't finish the thought. I didn't know what I would have done, but it was far from forgiveness.

"But still, that wasn't you, was it? Would you torture and kill someone before last night?"

"No."

"Would you do it now?"

"No."

"There we go, it wasn't you. You noticed this tiny little mark, knew I was hurt, and were worried. That is who you are. You care about others before yourself. No monster would do that. Even last night, when you killed... you had a goal: protecting your kind and yourself against a lot of awful people. Would you kill to protect your people?"

"I... would... if I had no other choice..."

"You're a king, so of course you would do whatever it took to protect them against a violent and dangerous enemy. You put your heart into everything you do. Your morals and instincts to protect those that can't protect themselves even if that means killing someone. I killed last night for you. It didn't feel good. It felt disgusting actually, but I did it and now you're safe. So, if that's so wrong then what is right?" Her grip eased as she came to terms with her own conflicting thoughts of taking my life, something that eased my heart a bit to know. "Your knights and uncle don't seem to think that it's wrong when I asked them, and now I somewhat understand why you guys aren't mad at what I did. So if they and you aren't, then why would it be any different for you? You killed to defend yourself and acted as a good ruler would, exactly as you would normally. If that moral compass to protect your people sticks with Outland Aerrow, even if it was slightly demented, then how could I be scared of you now?"

Her words were somewhat uplifting, but a void still consumed me. "But I still tortured people. I didn't just murder them."

"That part wasn't you. You get cocky and apparently pull pranks, but I know you don't toy with your enemies like the Outland blood had in order to get revenge. You're not vengeful on that level. The ones who should rightfully be afraid of you are your true enemies – both Creatures of Light and Dark. Seeing you fight when not held back was, yes, terrifying, but it was inspiring in a way as I've had the privilege of sparring with you. How much mercy you truly give is amazing and if there is anyone that threatened you to that level... I'd feel sorry for the hell you're going to put them through, even if its only a few moments long."

I remained silent as my mind turned back to the question of who I was. Noble, sure... but I wasn't a Creature of Light anymore, was I? I wasn't like my people anymore. I wasn't like my friends. I wasn't a Creature of Darkness either, yet I was still a part of them. A part of the same realm that monsters hid in and threatened the ones I cared about. There were no Creatures of Twilight.

Who the hell was I?

She squeezed my hand, drawing my attention to her. "Don't concern yourself over what you think should be or how you were. Just be you because you will always be that no matter what. Sometimes upgrades might come along but that will only benefit you."

"Are you saying the person I was before wasn't good enough?"

"No, but this new aggression might help in more ways than one."

I furrowed my brows. "What's that tone supposed to mean?"

"Nothing! Just… keep going with your instincts since they never seem to be wrong. Instincts and heart, they haven't changed. You'll make the right decisions when they count."

"I'll do my best…"

"Oh, and one other thing I should mention, it's important."

"Uh… what?" She was more casual now and while I was grateful, I was also scared at what was going through her head.

"From a scientific point of view, do not take this the wrong way, but Outland Aerrow is fucking incredible at kissing. If the person you find as your consort doesn't get that kind of love, it will destroy your future lives together as you get more sexual."

"I… uh… what? I don't remember kissing back."

"Ooh, but I do."

"Your tongue was in *my* mouth."

"You're the one who invited."

My face went warm in discomfort. It was embarrassing but I was certain that a small part of me did enjoy it, which made it worse. It was like some sort of stupid Norian Tale. Being rescued by a kiss…

Deigh giggled at my confusion and Éabha got off the bed, letting my hand go. "Alright, I'll leave you be."

"I feel like you only ended on that to tease me…"

"Well, it was quite clear that you're deprived of sexual needs, so it's rather easy."

"Hey! I'm not… I have control over… that. I've just never kissed anyone until you rescued me."

"Really? Last night was your first kiss? I figured someone of your title and age would be more experienced."

"Oh, like you're one to talk."

"I don't know what you're-"

"Your father for one and for two, you were waaaaay too eager to be in my mouth. Mock the pot all you like, but you're the kettle."

She became flustered, apparently not expecting me to turn the teasing back on her and she stumbled over her words. "S-so what?! It's not like that was my first or that you're really… Look! You started it!"

"I know… I'm sorry," I said, throwing the lighthearted discussion out the window. "I hope you can forgive me for everything."

"I already have. Consider the kiss and stabbing you as payment. How many people get to say they killed and kissed a king, right? Just… er, don't tell Dad. Your kingdom will have a new ruler if you do since I don't think I'll be able to revive you after he's done."

"Noted."

"And just because I was eager doesn't mean I like you that way. You're a good friend and not a prick, but I did it to save you."

"I know and I didn't expect you to like me that way. You're also a good friend, willing to give up a first for a friend; the feeling is mutual."

"Alright…" She shifted her weight before giving a smile. "I'm going to help Dad and Naftali finish downstairs. Gods know how that's going since Naftali's been acting weird all morning."

"Weird?"

"He's been agitated all day. I think it's because he collapsed yesterday so he didn't get to finish working on a section. But he was very happy to know that you were rescued."

"If you could give him my thanks, I'd appreciate it, but also not to work too hard. Owen told me his condition has been acting up lately."

"It has, but he did mention that whatever his medicine he was working on finally finished and Solaria helped him take it last night at some point at the lab."

"He's going to be alright?"

"Hopefully, he certainly seems much better, but still agitated…"

"Maybe a side effect…"

"Perhaps, so we're keeping an eye on him." She gave a breather. "Sorry for keeping you with these details… the others are just outside if you need them."

"Thanks. If you need to leave, take one of the knights with you, just in case."

"Thanks. Oh, and one last, last, last thing. Your armour is in your Dagdian bag in the living room. I can show you some neat things about it when you're ready."

I gave her a small smile. "I appreciate it. Good luck."

She left the room, leaving me alone with Deigh and my inner self… whoever that was now.

Chapter Forty-Five: Streets of Gold

The silence that filled the room as soon as the door closed became unbearable immediately even with Deigh there. It wasn't enough to satisfy what happened as being... fine. None of it was fine. Not to me. Even if I had believed Éabha, that whatever I did, didn't engrain itself into her head, it didn't destroy the fact that I had killed people. And not just two or three... eighty-eight people. It didn't matter if they were the worse people on the planet, that none of it was illegal, that they tempted fate... They were still people. They had friends, loved ones, and I snuffed it all out like cattle in a slaughterhouse.

"They were going to make you hurt people that hadn't asked for it or created the outcome in that lab," Deigh told me, and I gripped my head, feeling it pulse with her words. She switched to speaking out loud and the pain dwindled slightly. "Perhaps you need an outside view."

I looked at her, a bit stunned at the preposition. "Who?"

"Atlamillia. She can tell you exactly as she sees it and help you sort through the concerns about being... different."

"Different, that's a way of putting it." It felt like one the greatest understatements of the century.

"You're still the same to me," she reassured and while it was nice to hear, I couldn't agree. There was something else... something that definitely wasn't the same and it wasn't because of the new DNA that ran through my being. "I'll let you dress... Did you want me to come in after?"

"N-no... no." I took a breather. "I'll talk to her alone, ask her opinions on everything."

She got off me and gave a reassuring smile that soared through the link. "I'll be in the other room with the others. Don't disappear on me."

"I won't and... I'm sorry for making you go through everything while I was missing. I can't imagine what it was like."

"Nor will I ever let you know but having you back and relatively well made the struggle worth it."

"Shouldn't have had to struggle at all. I should have been careful."

"You can't always win, sometimes the enemy is better than what we can plan for, especially when we didn't know what to expect. Isn't that what you told Atlamillia?"

"Word for word... but it wasn't for me to-"

"Doesn't matter what you think, the facts are truth, whether you like it or not."

I didn't like it, but I didn't argue as she got off the bed and left on her toes with light steps. She closed the door behind her where I could hear Owen asking her how I was. I ignored the conversation that turned to that of a slight muffle that I wouldn't have ever heard before.

The bed's warm embrace left as I wandered over to the dresser carefully. My body was sore – but it kept surprisingly steady. The task of finding clothes was successful, and I put on my usual long sleeve shirt and black pants. I shifted slightly and caught something different in the bathroom, something black hanging out of the waste basket. I didn't need to get closer to realize that they were the pants from the uniform. I looked to the floor below the bit that hung and saw a pool of red, red-brown, and black that had dripped to the floor, now dried. The white stripe that lined the outside of the leg was stained in dried blood. Obvious holes and rips etched themselves against the cream-coloured cabinet. I turned away from it in disgust.

How much was really there that I couldn't see? What had I looked like when they found me? How much was mine? How much was theirs?

A scent that was barely on my conscious came forward like a slap to the face. Different smells along the smells of metal were mixed with what I could only presume were the people that the blood had belonged to made me grab the dresser in disorientation. I gagged, covering my nose and mouth with a hand and rushed to the bathroom, closing the door and out of breath.

It was so many people... too many to process.

The scent faded ever so slightly as I went back to the bed and sat down, removing my hand. The seconds turned into minutes as I came to terms with it all. The new smells were never going away. The distance mutters were never going to stop unless no one was talking within range. I looked to the lights of the room and found them to be off, but the light from the curtained window was more than bright enough. Even that was going to be different. My hands gripped the soft, cool sheets. The sense of touch was the same. Thankfully, there was something that stayed familiar. The blood came back to the foreground and I froze.

Whose blood had I covered myself with? Scientists, corrupted guards? What about the innocent? Did I kill children that were taken just as I was? Gods… I hope not… I couldn't have…

My chest tightened at the prospect of what that… what *I* was. I searched through my memory as fragmented and broken as it was, praying to whoever would listen to tell me if I had done something so horrible.

Silence responded, but where no noise answered, a small feeling of reassurance embraced the void that I hadn't gone so far to kill children or innocents. Of the eighty-eight of them… they were all the enemy.

But how could I know? Was the feeling just my mind protecting itself? Was it something else or a god as I had asked?

That wasn't shared, but the previous answer remained strong and unwavering. It was the only thing that stood truthful amongst the uncertainty. Bile began to crawl up from my stomach and I swallowed it, holding back the urge to be sick from the actions I committed. The new senses… I couldn't go to the room, not with-

I wasn't given a choice on the matter as my body and instincts decided for me and rushed to the bathroom, barely making it to the toilet to throw up. I avoided the basket next to me that was forgotten about between the heaves and breaks. Eventually, my body settled, and I left, collapsing onto the bed in exhaustion. A small reminder came from Deigh to call my sister and I gritted my teeth. I didn't want to know her opinion. I was terrified of what she would think. Her big brother, the king of our nation, wasn't even…

I wasn't fully Absalomian anymore…

"No, your dragon percentage went up to sixty-seven percent. The Outland has a percentage of around thirteen percent, and Absalomian is-"

"Twenty…" I muttered out loud in slight disbelief. "Twenty percent from fifty… I shouldn't even look the same…"

"It went into your dragon form mostly according to the discussions that happened when you were resting, that and your senses and magic."

"Probably the only miracle that came out of this…"

"It would be rather weird if you grew horns or a tail… your physic did change slightly though; muscle strength and your pants seem to be slightly tighter, so I think maybe your-"

"Thank you Deigh for your concern," I cut her off, realizing where she was going and did not want her comments on the matter. *"I'm going to call her now."*

"Glad to know shame still motivates you."

She left me a little more than flustered, but less in my head as I sat up. The CT sat on the table next to Guðmundr and I stared at the shield bracelet.

Should I wear it? What if I did become that thing again? I wasn't wearing it when I was… but if I had, that battle may have ended completely differently.

I made the decision to leave it there and grabbed the CT, unlocking it, and went to the only contact that could help me. It rang as I put it on speaker and set it on my lap, too tired to hold it to my ear.

It rang for a few seconds more before Atlamillia answered. "Brother! You have the best timing. We were just talking about you."

"We?"

"The kids. They were wondering how you were doing." A series of hellos and yelling came through and my stomach sunk. "They miss their big hero king and have been begging for stories on you. I've run out… three times over."

"I don't think…" I stopped myself. "Atlamillia, I need to speak with you about something."

The excitement on the other end died as I heard some uh-ohs. She told them she'd be right back and that it wasn't important, just concerns about finding a girlfriend. A few giggles and ews came from them before it went silent as I guessed that she took the device off speaker. A few moments passed before a soft click of a door came to my ears. Her tone was riddled with worry upon her return. "What happened? Are you fine? Is Seraphina alright?"

"Domrael Hill is fine," I started, not knowing the rest of the status of the island and my throat closed in on itself, trying to find the next words. "I… I don't think I'm fit to be king anymore."

"Did a politician there get under your skin in the stress? Fuck, here I thought it was-"

"I just killed eighty-eight people."

There was silence for an agonizingly long time only for it to be broken by an uncomfortable laugh from her. "You're kidding right? You've never killed anyone in your life."

"I've killed Outland Dragons-"

"No, I mean, People of Light."

"Until now... I was kidnapped and-"

"You were kidnapped?! How?! When?!"

"Please, let me speak," I growled way more aggressively than what I wanted. It almost sounded feral to my ears.

"Aerrow, you don't sound like yourself... Right, story. Go ahead."

"I was kidnapped and..." I swallowed as the feeling of wanting to hide in a hole gripped my tongue for a moment. "I... don't remember by who or what happened afterwards except for a few times when I..."

There was silence as I couldn't finish, and she gave unexpected reassurance. "Take your time. Maybe start at how everything happened."

I gave a nod, not that she could see, but it gave me a direction. "I was given a blood transfusion with Outland Dragon blood, about two litres of it and... I-It changed me into an Outland Monster. The research lab I was in was ran by Boffin Zealots, somewhere in the Outlands so I don't know what other possible things they did other than that or if they had the chance to do so last night after I woke up as... that. I know I hunted down and most likely tortured any one I found when trying to escape. I almost killed Uncle Owen, Cyrus, Azarias, and Éabha when they came to rescue me. A goal to protecting my- their... kind, no matter what."

"How noble of you, protecting Outland Dragons," she sighed. "You obviously aren't a monster now, so what's the problem?"

"What do you mean 'what's the problem'? I just slaughtered a bunch of people! I don't kill people! I barely tolerate the killing of cattle and only because we need meat to live, and they are bred to be killed! These were people!"

"Yes they were, but they were going to use you to do more than just kill horrible people. Imagine what would have happened if you came home under their control? What you could have done to Seraphina right there? I've seen you fight, Aerrow. If you weren't in control of yourself, using magic to the best of your ability, you would have killed hundreds if not thousands. What if they found a way to keep you alive without Deigh? What if they captured her and forced her to stay alive to keep you? What could they have done to her? They started a war by taking you. They were already your enemy and the nation's, and they solidified their stance on the willingness to do anything. You ended it doing exactly as they had."

"But they were-"

"People who were trying to kill you, figuratively speaking. You defended yourself, Deigh, and your nation before they could destroy it."

"But I enjoyed killing them! I almost killed my friends when they came to rescue me! That's… I don't even know who or what I am now."

"What do you mean?"

"M-my genetics were… altered."

"Put on the video, now."

I didn't disobey the order and grabbed the device, holding it up and turning on the lens. A tiny rectangle of my face appeared in the top right corner, looking tired but not any different from what I remembered. The grey screen switched to Atlamillia who looked studious as ever.

She took a moment to analyze the screen before shaking her head. "You look the same to me."

"That's what Deigh said but according to tests, thirteen percent of it took over the Absalomian part along with adding another seventeen percent dragon. My senses are all… uncomfortably enhanced and it shows in my dragon form. It's certainly affecting my personality right now, but that might simmer down over the next few days once my body equalizes out, I think that's what Éabha said."

"But could you be that creature again?"

"As of right now, no but I'm sure Uncle Owen is watching closely along with Deigh. But no one knows what else could happen since this hasn't happened before."

"No, it hasn't. But if your senses and body have been enhanced as you said, that could be more beneficial than detrimental, especially on the battlefield. You'll react faster, you might even be several times stronger physically. You would be if your dragon percentage is higher, which you said was seventeen percent more? That's sixty-seven percent instead of your original fifty. Add the Outland Dragon in there and who knows what you could do and learn."

"That's great for some things, but what of the views from a citizen? From the houses and court?" I asked carefully, bringing her back down to reality. "Would you want the king of your kingdom to be part monster? You know, the things he's supposed to be protecting you from?"

"Er…"

"And what about completing the other duty as king and finding a woman to marry? Would you want to have someone who isn't entirely a Being of Light anymore? What about kids? What are the consequences of having children? Could they come to term without dying or killing you in the process?"

"I… I don't know."

"Exactly, no one does." I sighed, "How am I supposed to complete my duties if all I'm going to do is get the woman I love, and our children killed? Can I even go into Asylotum where the rest of our people are harboured? There are just so many things that could go wrong and I don't want to be a liability."

"I'll check the gate as soon as I can get away from the kids, but I think I can turn off the Outland Dragon feature and hope that no hordes try to get through."

"Atlamillia, we can't risk-"

"You are the king, no matter what anyone says if they find out. You have risked everything and anyone who judges you on something out of your control can be damned for all I care," she voiced strongly before easing a bit. "I can't see the future of what might happen if you have kids, but I know it will be okay. You're the king, you can call upon any and every physician in the world to come and make sure your wife and kids are strong and healthy, even if it makes Helena jealous."

A small smile formed. "I suppose that's a pretty decent perk."

"As for your confidence from the people… I think there might be someone else who isn't as biased to the situation."

"Who could you ask without telling anyone?"

The lighting changed as she left the room and didn't answer. The video blurred as she moved from one room to another. She eventually stopped, switching the camera lens from the front to the back to reveal seven little troublemakers colouring or reading at tables within their playroom.

My heart skipped a beat as I realized what she was doing. "Atla, please… Don't-"

"Aerrow!" Lyric squealed, drawing the attention of everyone else and they all sat down on the carpet as my sister sat down in a chair. It was probably the chair I had sat in many times before and one I wasn't sure if I was ever going to sit in again. "Did you find a girlfriend?! Is she pretty? Did you kiss her?!"

"I…" My face grew warm. It wasn't that I hated the memory because I didn't, but I did not have feelings for Éabha in that manner. Unfortunately, I didn't get to defend myself before Atlamillia attacked.

"Oh? You didn't tell me about that tiny detail," she started but I noticed almost a hint of sadness in her tone before it disappeared in cruelty. "You'll have to share that story but first, little monsters, I have a question for you. If you don't answer truthfully, I'm going to make sure that you have several random tests and huge amounts of homework for the next week."

Claudius growled and crossed his arms. "You can't do that!"

"You bet I can. I'm reigning regent; my word is law."

"Fine… witch. What is your query?"

"What would you think of your king if he was part Outland Monster?"

My heart skipped another beat as her words registered and a snarl formed. "Atlamillia-!"

"Shush. Thoughts? Opinions?"

Kris was the first one to answer as he shifted his weight back and forth, cross-legged. "Monsters are scary… But I don't know. If they were good, like Uncle Aerrow, then I'd like them."

"I'm not sure if I'm in the same boat," Claudius mutter with a glare at the floor. "Outland Monsters killed my parents. They killed a lot of families and friends and they destroyed my home, forcing us out of our kingdom! Who's to say that he wouldn't be in allegiance with them?"

My heart sunk.

"If it were some random ruler, king or not, I'd riot." He looked up at Atlamillia. "But if it was someone I knew, someone I trusted…. Then, maybe they wouldn't be so awful. I've been taught not to hate someone even if they are different or have some sort of stigma behind them. So it really depends on the person. If they are a prick, then no. If they were Aerrow or you, Atla, then sure. Why not. You'd probably use that part to really protect us."

There were nods of agreement but his words from before stuck and stung. Not everyone citizen knew me like they did.

Atlamillia filled the silence. "There, you got your answer."

"Still…" I trailed off.

"Why is Aerrow asking such weird questions?" Holly asked. "Outland Monsters don't breed. That's what the book said. So how can a king be part monster?"

"Outland Monsters, the ashy ones, can't," Atlamillia clarified. "But other ones like Outland Dragons, can."

"Aerrow, is your new girlfriend an Outland Dragon?" Gasper asked and I tsked, feeling both embarrassed and uncomfortable.

"Of course not! Don't be absurd."

My sister grabbed the floor again. "He was curious because he had a nightmare. But what is really curious is how you reacted to Lyric's question."

"Aerrow kissed someone?!" Juno asked in shock before quickly getting depressed. "But… he's… He's not allowed!"

Karros looked over at her. "Says who exactly? He's a king."

"I do!"

"Gods above. We've told you a bazillion times, Aerrow is an adult and is not into you."

"He's a hero. Why wouldn't he be into a beautiful maiden?"

"You're seven!"

They got into an argument with the others joining in and leaving Kris silent and confused about why they were arguing. The screen changed to show my sister's face with a sheepish expression on it. "Kids… getting crushes on their elders. She'll get over it."

I tuned out the background yelling and glared at her. "I can't believe you asked them that!"

"Kids are also honest, who better to ask?" She had a fair point, even if I didn't like it. "But seriously, who did what?"

I felt my face heat up slightly. "When I was… er… doing the thing in the lab… I was a bit of a handful. So Éabha substituted what she knew and came up with a brilliant idea of using my, er, primal instincts and duty to deal with that, and…"

There was silence from her as the children continued to be oblivious to our conversation. Then, she spoke. "Going to be honest, I wasn't expecting that. Your Seraphinean friend doesn't seem capable of emotional contribution."

"We both agreed that it was just a thing that happened and nothing more. We're not attracted to each other."

"Yeah, sure you're not."

I grew warmer as Deigh didn't help, laughing through the link. Éabha was beautiful, very different from the other Seraphs… from Theodora. Not to mention incredibly smart, easy to- What the hell was I doing? "Atlamillia, we're not-"

My defence was cut off as an explosion went off outside, rocking the building and the windows blasted inwards. The CT fell out of my hand when I grabbed the side table to keep myself from falling out of bed. My tongue was working faster than I could filter it. "What the fuck was that?!"

"Aerrow?! Aerrow, is everything okay?!"

The arguing on the other side ceased as I picked up the CT from the floor. Eight heads cluttered together on the camera.

"What was that?" Atlamillia asked and I shook my head.

"I don't know…" I got of the bed, putting on a pair of boots and wandered over to where the windows had been. Glass broke underfoot just as a loud roar came from above. Zegrinath dropped next to the building, landing in the crater that I could only imagine he had made.

He turned to me, scales raised and shouted in his native tongue, "Aerrow Fionn! I smell my son near you! Where is he?!"

What the hell was he… We hadn't found- He was supposed to be days out! I turned to the CT slightly, their expressions varied from confusion to fear. "I gotta go."

"Aerrow, wait-" Atlamillia started but I didn't wait, ending the call before she could finish.

I turned to the dragon below who was already scaling the side of the building and backed away from the window. He crawled inside, his horns and wings smashing into and through the walls. "Zegrinath…"

"Where is he?!" The dragon raged, claws digging into the floor. "I smell him on you!"

He smelt... My eyes widened in shock. Was the blood I was given Tad'Cooperith's?! If it was... "Oh gods..."

"The gods will not help you-"

"No! That's-" The door opened behind me and we snapped to it as Owen barrelled through with Cyrus closely behind. They started to attack but my order came out faster. "Leave."

"Aerrow-" Owen started but I glared. I couldn't let a confrontation happen.

"This is between us."

Owen and Cyrus looked between the two of us before Owen sneered slightly in dismay. They curtly bowed and left, closing the door behind them. I turned to the dragon that was seething with rage but also confused at my response to help. "What is the meaning of this?"

"Bloodshed isn't needed, Zegrinath... We didn't find your son, he's not in this city... But if you smell him on me now..." My words caught in my throat as some sort of memory of a small dragon flashed before my eyes in a white world and I looked away. "I'm sorry... I'm so very sorry."

"What are you saying?" His claws relaxed slightly, a crawling disbelief growing in his voice. "Why can I smell him on you?"

"Not on... I was kidnapped by the same people who took your whelps and they transfused me with Outland Dragon blood in some sick experiment..." I turned to him, trying to keep myself together. The pit of my stomach sinking into an abyss. I hoped his next answer was something else. "How old is your son?"

"Eight..."

A tsk escaped. The dragon I saw... That was him. I knew I met him... A memory of a dragon in a cell next to mine, lifeless and unmoving... I knew her. But I knew I never met her. The words that came out didn't feel entirely my own. "They used him."

"They used who?"

"They used Tad'Cooperith... they drained him. Just like Yzelia." Tears fell for something I should not have known. For someone I didn't know. "He watched them kill her and he... They killed him."

My head pounded as a small noise escaped from the pain and I grabbed it. The dragon in front of me had no words.

"He fought against them, but they were…" The words stopped flowing out, but the pain didn't disappear. "I'm so sorry."

"He… no… How could you know if you didn't see them?!"

"I don't know. I don't know anything other then they paid for it in a way I wouldn't have done it. The rage of being trapped wasn't mine alone, the fear and confusion-"

"They used him… They put him in you…" Zegrinath took a step back in horror, not expanding on whatever else he was thinking. Whatever it was, it terrified me. Then, his emotion changed to rage as dark magic pooled on the floor from him, tearing into the wall and floor, but surprisingly not into me. "I will destroy this whole island if I have to. I will find him!"

"Wait, the lab wasn't-"

"Get off this island. A victim shouldn't be in the crossfire."

"You're not going to find him here! They drained two litres – that's all he would have had!"

"Then I will find what's left! I will put him to rest with his mother and all these Creatures of Light will die for killing them!"

"Please, don't-"

"You hold what's left alive of my son. I do not want to have to destroy it but if you get in my way; I will kill you and any remnants of his soul left!"

"Zegrinath!" He didn't listen and left, blasting a black beam of destruction in his wake.

Chapter Forty-Six: Red Cold River

I rushed to the hole in the wall, calling him back but it was futile. He wasn't coming back. So many people who knew nothing of his distraught and anger were going to be killed.

Seraphinean soldiers flew overhead after the large, grieving dragon only to be intercepted by another Outland Dragon. Outland Monsters drew my attention away, chasing and attacking people that were trying to escape, flying or running. The screams carried, hurting my ears as the monsters destroyed their way through buildings and fires broke out. Blood and limbs started to paint the city in gore. I backed away from the window, keeping my presence to a minimum in disgust.

This had to stop... before anymore would die needlessly; before Zegrinath and his people were killed.

I went into the common room where Owen, Azarias, and Cyrus were geared up and waiting impatiently. I acknowledged them ever so slightly, heading for my armour where Éabha had placed it. Pulling out the jacket, Owen started to ask his questions. "What was that about?"

"Zegrinath... We have to stop him and help with this mess."

"The Seraphineans can deal with the monsters-"

"It's not just the monsters; Zegrinath is going to destroy this whole island if we don't do something."

"Why did he abandon his original raid plans?"

"The blood I got was his son's," I answered, breathlessly and Azarias started cursing while Cyrus and Owen remained surprised but silent. The realization of needing socks for my boots came to fruition and I started back into my room, closing the chest piece together. It lit up slightly with a white and black light through the treads, but other than that, it didn't feel or look any different. "Where are Éabha and Orpheal."

"Safe downstairs with Naftali. The building has a barrier that hides our presence from monsters, but it seems dragons can bypass it. They're avoiding our building for now so it's giving us more time to work out the last kinks of the Zerach."

"Okay. Azarias, Cyrus, go help them finish it. We need that thing working now."

There was no reply with words as I heard their footsteps quickly make it to the stairs. I came back out, swiping Guðmundr off the side table and my cape from the chair I left it on yesterday. I took a moment to steady the dizzy world by sitting down on the couch then put the socks on. Across from me, the other couch had large tears into the cushion, but I wasn't sure how they got there.

"You aren't well enough for this," Owen stated, noticing my pause.

I shook my head, not bothering to ask about the damage, and grabbed my upgraded boots. "I know."

"Then why are you pushing yourself?"

"Because I should have done more to find the whelps. Should have been more cautious so I wasn't kidnapped. Tad'Cooperith might have lived. They wouldn't have killed Yzelia. Zegrinath is grieving and shouldn't be killed by the Seraphs and they don't deserve to die because of his loss."

"His actions are his own, you have no responsibility-"

"And what of all the innocent people?! He's here killing them! If I wasn't kidnapped, I wouldn't have his son's blood that drew him here in the first place!"

"None of this is your fault!" he snapped, freezing me just as I stood up. He lowered his voice becoming calm once more. "The people who brought this city to where it is, who kidnapped and killed that child, who kidnapped and turned you into a monster for that brief time are to blame. I understand that you may not wish to believe it, but it's the truth."

I looked away in disgust.

"I'll gladly help you try to stop Zegrinath, help him leave and hopefully take the rest of his people with him to save lives. Perhaps he can find out more if we tell him where we found you. But I will not go if you think that every person you see in a state of distress or dead is your fault. Out there is chaos and you need to be focused if we have any chance of finding him."

"But what if-"

"Not what if. If it really was your fault, we wouldn't be having this conversation. Zegrinath would have killed you."

I went to argue then closed my mouth. Zegrinath hadn't killed me, instead he told me to leave. Why would he do that if I were to blame? I tried to get out of the spiral, but it didn't sit right. In fact, it made me feel sick. "I don't know if I can fully accept this…"

"As long as you don't commit to a suicide mission, I'll be content."

"So, you're going to help me?"

He gave a nod and handed me my pauldron. "I said I would help with anything you ask; this is no different."

"Thank you, Uncle Owen…"

"Don't thank me yet and finish getting ready."

I followed his order and did just that, putting on the pauldron and grabbed the gauntlets, easily putting them on as I looked around. *"Deigh, where is-"*

"Owen, if you could?" Deigh's voice came from behind me, and I turned, seeing her coming up from the first floor. Her armour was done up in places she could get to, but not quite all of it. Owen walked past me to help her as I put on my cape. *"Winterthorn is on the desk."*

"Thank you." I sprinted back to my room again, attaching the shield bracelet, the band that was originally white shifted into black every so often. I missed hearing her voice in my head and not having it hurt.

"I miss hearing you too. But you need to hurry."

"I hope Zegrinath will listen…" I found Winterthorn on the desk just as Deigh stated and hesitated to grab it. It sat so innocently on the wooden surface. The things I had done with-

The sounds of people screaming below made me pick it up and draw it from the scabbard. No blood laid on its surface and I sheathed it, putting it on my belt. While the blood was long gone, the taint of what I did with it needed to be rectified, helping one person at a time.

I headed back out to Owen who turned to me. He gave me a small look over before a slight sigh escaped. "Gods, you've looked better… Once we get Zegrinath to leave, we are leaving as well. You're in no condition to get into a fight with even a Marsutsepi classed monster."

I nodded in agreement. I certainly didn't want to fight, but a fragment did. Thankfully, I wasn't in the position to do so with the massive headache and my body feeling a little more than off. Something was still very, very wrong, and I didn't want to find out why in the middle of combat with, at best, an Outland Monster, and at worst, Ciar. Missiletainn came upstairs along with Éabha dressed in armour. Iðunn and a bag were over her shoulder and a strange, barrelled weapon was on her hips.

I looked at her in confusion. "What are you doing?"

"Watching your back," she answered, and I frowned.

"It's dangerous, your father-"

"Is busy. Azarias mentioned you were going on a suicide mission so I'm making sure that doesn't happen."

"By coming?"

"Yep. You can't be stupid if you have the Lord Director's Daughter with you. Right, Owen?"

Owen gave a nod of approval, much to my dismay. Both of them clearly underestimating my level of idiocy – not that I was going on a suicide mission to start with. "Fine... just stay on Deigh unless one of us tells you otherwise."

"I have wings you know," she stated in annoyance, showing off six wings. "It's not like I can't just fly out of the way."

"And there are just as many flying things out there. Stay on Deigh or don't come at all."

She rolled her eyes but didn't argue and got onto Deigh's back. I looked to Owen who had nothing to add, and we mounted. The two dragons left through the living room wall where no glass panes blocked the way. Once outside, the sun blinded me instantly. The screams and sirens that were somehow muffled by the building were no longer and blaring out, hurting my ears. A small grunt of pain escaped as I grabbed my head.

"Are you okay?" Éabha asked and I nodded.

"Y-yeah... just have to get used to... this."

"Is there anything I can do?"

"I have a pair of sunglasses in the pouch behind you."

I heard her moving behind me and she tapped my arm with the object I asked for. I put them on but even then the sunlight was still incredibly bright, and they certainly didn't help with the noise. I was going to have to get a new pair to compensate for my new light sensitivity. My hearing and nose on the other hand were just going to have to adapt. Deigh flew up above the buildings, following Missiletainn in hopes that we could spot the tribe leader. My eyes adjusted slowly. Fires and explosions ran across the gridded buildings, Outland Monsters and Dragons razed the city at every block, but from what I could tell, none of them were Zegrinath.

Where did he go? It's not like he was tiny… He was twenty-three metres of massive death.

Something else caught my eye as a different set of scales glided in the distance and I turned to the purple swirls. My heart skipped a beat, recognizing the nebula-looking dragon. Armour layered his scales, woven in Seraphinean tech not unlike my own. He turned slightly, showing off his rider.

"O-Owen…" I stuttered out, but thankfully, my uncle heard me.

"What is it?"

"Is that…" I couldn't say her name as the armour she wore, even from where I was, was plain to see. Revealing, form fitting, everything she had told me in our little talks that she wanted as armour one day. She was alive and clearly doing well if she could get exactly as she wanted. Then, my image of her turned sour. A Seraphinean on a tyraulia charged at her and Gabriellos blasted the creature out of the sky. His rider threw her beautifully crafted polearm through the Seraph before having it return to her. I swallowed. "W-what is she doing?! Why are they attacking her?!"

"Looks like she has made a new friend," Owen growled out an answer and I searched beyond the woman to the darker clad creature also on the dragon.

My heart jumped into my throat and I couldn't breathe.

Ciar was here… Ciar was… with her…

"Aerrow."

I didn't look away from the two of them. The white-haired monster was on the back of her dragon, a bit different from my last encounter as his tail and wings were missing but still, it was him… partnered up with her. "Why is she with him?"

"Aerrow-" Owen tried to reason, and my disgust came out.

"I know!" I turned away from them, taking a deep breath to calm down my new-found emotion of jealousy. "I know. We need to go."

"We can fight him another day," he agreed, and we flew lower, hoping to hide between the towering buildings.

A screech came from behind us and Éabha grabbed around my waist as she saw the turn coming ahead. "What was that about?"

"It's nothing-"

"You're paler than Solaria and being this close, I can feel that you're shaking. Don't tell me it's nothing. Who's the broad and the dark armoured guy?"

"That… is Theodora-"

"That's Theodora?! Fuck, she's gorgeous!"

"And Ciar."

"Well… an equally hot Seraphinean was not who I was picturing Ciar as, at all. Nor did I think she would turn to him."

"I didn't think she would either," I muttered, pissed off. She was supposed to be providing a reason to let me lift her banishment, to let her return to the kingdom, not turn to my greatest enemy and start leading an attack on a helpless city. The screeching was a lot closer, and I turned to it, seeing the monster doing it was leading a party of other monsters. A sneer formed. "We were spotted."

She turned to look at what I was seeing, and a surprised expression appeared on her face. "Oh! That's a lot of monsters…"

"We're going to have to deal with them before we-"

"I got this!"

"What do you mean by that?" I asked carefully and she let go. She unattached her strange weapon and clipped in what seemed to be a capacitor crystal, but it was in a weird, rectangular shape. "What is that?"

"I need you to go around the building ahead and then stop behind it," she stated, not answering my question as an excited glint twinkled in her sky-blue eyes. "This is going to be great!"

"Why do I have a feeling that this is not going to be great?"

"Trust me!"

"Alright…" I looked ahead and shouted at Owen to follow. Missiletainn slowed, allowing Deigh to take the lead around the building she wanted. We came to a stop on the other side, and I listened for the monsters. They were coming loudly from each side and through the glass and steel. "Éabha, I don't wish to alarm you but… they are coming around and through the building, quickly."

The crazy Seraph just nodded, setting her weapon on her lap and opened the bag she brought. She looked to me for a moment and dropped the bag in my unsuspecting arms. "Can you hold this?"

"I kind of already am... why?"

"When I ask, hand me one of the clips."

"Clips? What are you-"

"Where are the closest enemies coming from?"

I sighed but didn't argue for answers. "Monsters, left side."

She picked up her weapon again and unfolded a segment that became a shoulder bracer of some sort. She unfolded it a second time to show its full length. It was a gun with a bayonet, that much was obvious, but I had no idea what kind or what it did. It wasn't the largest thing in the world, much smaller than her rifle, but slightly smaller than the shotgun and seemingly more durable in its stout nature. I went to ask her what it was, but the first monsters came from around the corner. She looked down the scope slightly, taking off the safety then pulled the trigger. Tiny balls of light blasted out of the barrel at rapid succession, and I covered my ears at the sound barrier breaking in the muzzle that probably wouldn't have bothered me before. The orbs sprayed the entire region of monsters with scary accuracy. The monsters turned to ash within seconds of being hit, wasting away the first swarm completely in a matter of moments.

She unloaded the strange brick. "New one please."

I reached into the bag, hardly a will of my own and handed her a new one, taking the one she set between us. She clipped it in and waited for me to cover my ears again before firing more rounds of the concentrated magic into the monsters.

What kind of weapon of mass destruction had she made? It was... brilliant, yet extremely concerning.

I removed my hands, getting used to the noise, and got out another one of the clips from the bag. It didn't take her long to empty and I handed her the new one. Monster noises grew closer. "Right side."

"Thanks, charging station."

"What?"

"You're charging the capacitor clips. I didn't get to do it beforehand at my lab," she replied cheerfully and switched to the right side. "It's so nice to have a friend who just oozes magic and is practically a radar now."

"You're just…" I had no words as I noticed through the noises of her fun that something had come from behind. Owen saw Deigh and I looked over and turned to it. Several large Outland Monsters that had no business being on the island were narrowing in on our position. Missiletainn attacked them. The zealots were involved now. "I'm going to have to help in a-"

She interrupted me. "Nope."

"What do you mean 'nope'?"

"You're staying out of danger."

"I'm already in danger!" She flinched, misfiring her weapon into a window. I tsked in disgust at myself and she said nothing, continuing to fire at the monsters. I handed her another clip, staying obedient to her request and took the empty one away. "Alright… I'll stay here, out of danger. Sorry."

"I just don't want you to get hurt. You're not in a fighting condition."

"But what about monsters if they come for us?" I asked her, keeping my tone softer as I watched Owen and Missiletainn deal with the large land monsters just fine. "If you don't want me to fight that is."

"I have bladed gauntlets for that."

"Bladed what?"

"Just let me know if we have a new friend, okay?"

"Alright. Building now."

"Thank you."

"After this wave, we should be able to go back to searching."

"As you command."

I didn't feel like I was the one commanding anything but kept watch regardless. Deigh started blasting monsters that came close as Éabha mowed down the ones that came smashing through the glass building. I looked behind us and a monster snaked through Owen's guard. "Éabha-"

I barely turned to her when she shoved her gun into my chest. Its weight caught me off-guard as she leapt to her feet and stepped behind me. I looked just as she punched the monster that blinked in front of us and came down on our heads. Blades both straight down like sleeve daggers and two curved, metre long blades came out of the top of her gauntlet, swinging out to the sides, and shoved themselves into the monster's skull. She ripped the blades out and the monster turned to ash.

Where did… how did the blades… "What the hell?"

"Bladed gauntlets, Dad's creation." She took back the gun with a grin as the blades folded back into the gauntlet. "Every range, I'm covered."

"I… see that…" A familiar roar reached my ears from the southern part of the city, away from the last place we saw Ciar. I grabbed Owen's attention as he finished with his monster. "Zegrinath's that way."

He nodded as Missiletainn finished off his monster and we left towards the noise. It didn't take long while swerving through the buildings for Deigh to pick up Zegrinath's trail of destruction. The end of it becoming increasingly louder where the grieving father would be.

"*Deigh…*"

"*Yes?*"

"*If he doesn't listen, we need to ground him.*"

"*Tell Éabha to pass on the message. I can't grapple him alone.*"

I told Éabha and she left for Owen for a few moments before quickly coming back. "Is Missiletainn on-board?"

"Neither of them like the idea, but they agreed."

"Good enough."

We rounded a large building as a stream of dark energy came out of it, cutting it in half, and almost hit Deigh as it went a foot past her wing. The building crashed and crumbled, revealing a desolated area of rubble, smoke, and pieces of road. Zegrinath was in the middle of it all. I called to him as we got closer, but he ignored me. He blasted away at anything that moved before turning his attack on us when we didn't leave. Deigh dodged it and Missiletainn came from below, colliding with the much larger dragon. Deigh went above and smashed him downwards. The tribe leader landed hard onto a crushed building.

I got off Deigh as she landed, telling Éabha to stay on and went over to him. She didn't listen and landed behind me. Debris and broken glass cracked or shattered into pieces under our boots as the large dragon staggered to a stand, furious.

He hissed in almost unbridled fury, barely raising his voice, and it sent a chill down my spine. "I thought I told you to leave…"

"You're attacking innocent people for someone you won't find here," I told him, and he snarled.

Owen came forward, guessing at what I said in Ancient Dragon and switched the conversation to Ori. "It's true, Zegrinath. The kids are probably in the lab where we found Aerrow, off the island-"

"That means nothing! They could be here!" The dragon growled.

"If you can't smell them now, I highly doubt they are. There could be more information at-"

"And even if they aren't. Give me one good reason why every single one of these creatures shouldn't perish, Dragonbane? They fight amongst themselves using powers they do not understand for a god that is false!"

"Not all of them do," I answered as Owen stayed silent, his jaw clenching from saying anything that could agree with him. I knew how much he detested the zealots and Ciar. Of course he would only agree – who knew how many just in the city were in leagues with Ciar. They had killed countless of his friends and co-workers and their leader killed his two best friends, all seemingly in the name of power. But even if it was fifty percent of the city at fault, the other half was still innocent. "You've seen the ones who aren't following Ciar-"

"Is that who that foul creature is? He reeks of Valrdis's blessing and is using it well, yet he is the leader of the creatures that took my son?"

"Yes… but you knew that already. Why did you-"

"He wants to take control of this kingdom away from them." He hinted at Éabha behind me in anger. "It's only a matter of time before her kind came to my mountain."

"Just because some people are bad doesn't mean they are all bad. Ciar is not your ally no matter what blessings of Valrdis he has."

"Of course he isn't! But I will deal with him once I've no further use for him."

"You'll never get the chance. He'll kill you just like how his people killed Vothedissith and how he killed my parents. He'll take your power and use it as his own against your people!"

"He cannot-"

"He can! He did it to me and attacked my knights. He then turned to my father's dragon and resurrected him as his new joyride! If you continue down this road, your body will be his new, undead pet, and will be forced to attack whoever he pleases."

The dragon remained silent, torn in thought of what he should do.

"These people did nothing wrong and Ciar is using your tribe's anger to do his work, not the other way around. Please sto- gah!" A sharp pain ripped through my head and I grabbed it. Zegrinath growled as he seemed to lose his balance before blasting a beam out at seemingly nothing. Shrieks of monsters came from behind me.

"Éabha, watch him," Owen ordered, passing me a wary gaze. "I won't be long."

I gave a brief nod, and he took off as Zegrinath seemed to regain himself. "What... was that?"

"I don't..." My words trailed off again as the feeling of wanting to be sick overcame me. The sound of a soft mumble of a voice whispered in my head, someone I recognized. I turned to Éabha. "Why can I hear Naftali?"

Her concern turned to confusion. "What do you mean?"

"I can hear-" A small scream came out as my head pounded. Zegrinath roared loudly in pain. A CT beep came after the excruciating noise and she pulled it out of a pouch.

She looked at it for a split second before her eyes became the size of saucers. "Fuck! The Zerach!"

"It's..." The words sunk in as she started tapping on her screen and brought it to her ear.

She looked to the dragon. "You need to go home, Zegrinath!"

"I... can't just abandon-"

"If you don't leave, your people are going to be mindless weapons. Do you want that?"

"You're lying."

"She's not," I defended, trying my best to get the urgency across. "You need to get as far away from here as possible. I'll find your son. Just leave before you start killing your people!"

The dragon didn't argue as another mutter came into my head, one I couldn't understand and caused me to almost lose my footing. A Chaos Portal appeared behind him and he gave a call of retreat. The noise repeated throughout the city of sirens and destruction, but I couldn't tell if they also had portals. The tribe leader fled, the portal closing almost immediately just as Tempest and Sage landed nearby.

Azarias and Cyrus came over to us, one more chipper than the other as Azarias announced what we knew. "Hey, we finished the Zerach... Why'd the dragons flee?"

"Aerrow?" Cyrus questioned when I couldn't answer, wincing instead. "What's wrong?"

"Nothing... hopefully..." I turned to Éabha through gritted teeth who gave a small look of reassurance. "We... told the dragons to leave before they were controlled."

Azarias crossed his arms. "Why? It would have made cleaning out the monsters easier."

"If they were a horde, I wouldn't care about the morality of it right now, but they aren't."

"Assholes only, fair. So, what's next then?"

"We leave once Owen and Missiletainn deal with the monsters nearby, presumably to a new hideout. Out of Outland Monster scent and Ciar's way."

"He's here?"

"He is... and he's with Theodora." A shocked expression went across both their faces and my head pounded worse than before causing me to lose my balance in the dizzy world. Cyrus caught me as I stumbled and helped set me on my feet again. "Thank you."

He gave a nod, letting me stand on my own, but stayed nearby.

Chapter Forty-Seven: None Shall Survive.

The pain didn't subside as Éabha tried calling whoever she was trying to contact a third time. Owen had joined us as Missiletainn and the other dragons kept watch, but all the Outland Monsters seemed to have vacated the area. The Zerach was doing its job… Unfortunately, it wasn't doing me any favours. There was a minor discussion about leaving between the knights, but Owen made the decision to stay low and where we were. Ciar didn't know where we were, and we didn't know where he was. Owen didn't want him spotting and forcing us to defend while down.

Suddenly, a small cheer came from Éabha, scaring me. I turned quickly to the sound and the motion caused the world to spin. My stance fumbled further when trying to compensate and tripped over myself. Owen caught me and I gave barely a thank you before Éabha started talking.

"Naftali! Where's Dad?" There was silence for a split second, and she continued. "Are you with the Zerach? Yes, good. Change the frequency off Outland Dragons. They aren't here anymore so the machine should focus on-"

Another searing pain ripped through my head and a scream escaped. My legs gave out and I slipped through Owen's grasp. Glass cracked underneath me as one hand gripped at the ground, trying to find a way to ease the pain while the other continued to grip at my head. The glass and cement broke within my gauntlet as it took the damage that wanted to go for my blade. I held against the urge as Cyrus dropped next to me but couldn't do anything to help.

"Just turn it off!" Owen shouted and I looked up for a moment to see he had swiped the CT from Éabha before ending the call. He gave it back to her as I turned back to the earth, trying to focus on the suggestion of breathing from Cyrus. He set a very quiet, peaceful rhythm that was easy to follow. "Naftali sometimes really pisses me off with questions that don't matter."

"What did he want?" Azarias asked and I didn't have to see the scowl on Owen's face to know it was there.

"He heard Aerrow and was asking half a million questions."

"Why would he-" I started only for a much louder scream to interrupt me as my whole body pulsed in pain. Naftali's voice was louder than just a mutter in my head and the message was quite clear. A breathless huff escaped, "Bastard…"

Owen knelt on the other side of me. "Talk to us, what's wrong?"

I seethed in pain, trying to fight myself as my body got up on its own. They stood up as my hand went for my blade, but I stopped – holding off somehow. Another sharp pulse ripped through me at the disobedience of the order.

"He didn't stop it?"

"No... Naftali... he's... nrg." I tried to breathe normally, to speak, but my chest felt compressed and locked. "He wants me to kill the directors."

"Why?! How does he... He shouldn't know about what happened! No one told him!" Éabha exclaimed and I shook my head.

"I don't-" Another painful pulse went through me as they stood by, unable to do anything. I grimaced, feeling the blood that wanted to follow his command. It was excruciating and triggered an instinct that I had lost to once before, one I knew I couldn't win as I was right now. Another order entered my head, asking me to kill the directors' families. My will wavered under the surprise and the stress. "Éabha... leave. Now."

She took a step back in disbelief. "He ordered you to kill me? Why would he-"

"Go and hide! Please!" I begged. I couldn't hurt her again! "Before he wins!"

"Aerrow, you need to fight it," Owen ordered, trying to be a steady pillar, a voice to focus on, but the Zerach's grip only became stronger.

"I'm try-" The words stopped coming out as I lost the ability to breathe. I wanted to claw at my throat, to try and release the invisible grasp that tightened around it, but my muscles were seized.

"Hold out, Azarias and Cyrus are going to-"

I didn't hear what else he had to say as the boiling rage came back and hit me like a tail to the head. I dropped like a rock to a knee as my vision blurred before an abyss overtook my senses.

My breathing was released and a few breaths later, the pain eased slightly.

Neutral Beings of Light, one enemy.

"*Her kind killed them...*" a whisper encouraged. "*Strike her down and others like her... They were the ones that killed them. They are the ones that make you suffer. The pain will end if they stop breathing. Make them pay for their crimes."*

If that was all that was needed... a small list was hardly an effort.

I drew my blade as the first creature on my list seemed to say something, her mouth moving as I got up, but nothing came to my ears. I didn't need to hear what she had to say... The dead did not speak.

I went to strike only for someone to jump on me from behind, locking my arms and shouted at her to leave. The girl left, wide-eyed and hurt. A growl escaped my throat.

I wasn't letting her get away!

I summoned a pair of wings and a tail; the wings breaking through a bit of my armour and throwing off her defender. A wave of plasma was thrown from my blade and the fleeing target dodged as someone warned her. I turned to the creatures who had no reason to interfere. "Stay out of the way."

The blond one spoke, but even though his lips moved, not everything he was saying was voiced. "... You're being... You know who... ... Stop before we make you."

I sneered, readied to attack but was knocked down from behind and stepped on. White claws dug into the broken earth, caging me from being able to move. A feral scream came out as the pain increased drastically. My body fought against something...

I had to go. I had to kill them! Whoever was keeping me in the glass, metal, and dirt was my enemy. Fire wouldn't affect her... but other elements did.

I summoned a dark pool below me, the vines crawling over her claws in my view forced her off as the thorns pierced through her scales. A pool shifted as the blond tried to take its control. Spikes attempted to grow, tendrils weakly grabbing at me and I slowly got to a stand. His magic was more skillful than mine, but it wasn't effective against someone who had more strength and was learning from him as the struggle went on.

I stabbed my blade into the earth, spreading the dark chaos and broke the stone slabs that the brunet had tried to trap me with. A dome formed around the four dragons and three neutral enemies and was set ablaze, leaving the floor untouched by the fire. They were enemies... but I couldn't kill them. It was wrong. They weren't going to end the pain.

The ground of neutral chaos formed vines and grappled onto all of them, forcing them still and unable to attack. Their pleas to stop echoed through the cage, but I ignored them. What did they want me to stop? I wasn't going to kill them.

"Stay here... out of the way," I ordered. "You are not who I need."

"Aerrow!" A familiar voice called, freezing me in my tracks. I turned to the white dragon who seemed to be the most distraught. For what...? I didn't know. I wasn't hurting her. "Their deaths won't make it better! He's using you!"

"*Leave,*" the whisper said, coming back. "*Kill your targets and be done. The pain will cease after such an easy task. It's all you need, right?*"

It was everything I needed. Simple instructions. Simple plans. A set goal that was easily obtained. "Then so be it... His word is law."

"Aerrow!"

The name fell on deaf ears as it lost meaning. I left the dome, releasing the vines to allow them to wander about inside. They couldn't leave, try as they might, but it was futile.

A new order came. "*Kill the Lord Director first, Little Dragon. Strike him down and the others will fall with no resistance.*"

No resistance, that was what I wanted. The less painful path to silence their horrendous acts.

I used the wings on my back as the Lord Director's location came to me. It was a beacon almost and it was a long way up, at the very top of the hill inside a white building. Inside the Directors' Demesne.

Good... The light was too bright. It would be easier to fight inside. Anything to make the pain stop.

A small, different kind of pain entered my head, causing me to lose altitude. A different rage dripped into the feelingless existence. A pure form towards them. The winged creature who did this, the voice. He was-

A jolt of pain ripped through me, forcing me to land and grovel. The grip around my throat came back and I couldn't breathe properly. He was using me?

Of course, he was... I was his instrument. He needed me. The pain will stop if I just...

A scream came out as the different source of pain came back, trying to stop me from completing my mission. My sole mission to serve. My clawed gauntlets dug into the dirt as I tried to regain my bounds, to not go against the orders. I didn't want the anger. The hatred. The suffering of being trapped. I wanted to feel nothing.

But what of the whelps?

Nothing! I wanted nothing! To know nothing... I wanted the agony to stop...

The pain eased a bit as the rogue thoughts went away and I coughed harshly, the grip disappearing. The directors had to die. For him. For the rogue thoughts. It was better this way.

I got up and started on my way again.

The Directors' Demesne was silent as I flew over and nothing stirred on the grounds. It's fences, walls, and gates were untouched by the commotion that had overcome the rest of the city. I landed at the entrance way to the building and slipped inside, silently. No one sat at the desk, the glowing spires were the only light in the darkened building. I took off my sunglasses, no longer needing them to blot out the burning sun's rays. It was still bright in the building, even with the lights off, but it was more comfortable without them. I set them inside one of my pouches and looked around. The Lord Director was here... I could smell him.

Movement came from behind a pillar, and I turned to it. The man I was looking for came out of hiding, tall and lean, dressed in black and white armour. I readied my blade subtly, thankful that I didn't have to go looking for him in such a large building.

The voice confirmed my target with a calm greeting. "Hello there."

"Lord Director." He had no idea... good.

"Where are your knights?"

I gave no answer as I walked over to him. I had no knights. Right?

"*Kill him,*" the voice ordered.

"Is everything-"

The target's words went silent as the voice came back. "*Don't waste time with talk.*"

He was right. I didn't need to hear the target. He would only try and bide time for help. His armour was going to be a problem as it was... There was a chance that he would try and beg before I broke through it.

I didn't want him to…

A sharp pain pulsed through my body as I let something try to fight against my mission. Anger and pain. I wanted to feel nothing! To be nothing!

They killed them… but not… The voice.

I held back a growl as I got close enough to rush and strike, doing just that. A gauntlet defended the attack with ease, leaving me a bit surprised at how prepared he was. He brushed me aside. His wings were protected with armour that formed blades, showing off their edge in the spires light. Three of his wings swung at me, clipping my armour. I moved before the other three could hit. His gauntlet shifted, blades coming out from them, but he didn't press the attack. He stood in composure. His lips moved but no voice reached my ears. A part of me wanted to know what he was saying as he looked down at me. The look seemed to be pity.

I wanted to remove it.

I charged at him, swinging a plasma blade. He didn't move until the last second, once again avoiding my attack and purposely not attacking back. He went back to being still in a manner of seemingly unpreparedness. It made me hesitate. It reminded me of someone I had known, a variation of it at least.

Why wasn't he attacking or running away? It didn't matter… He was going to be killed regardless. Naftali wanted it…

Naftali… he was the one who killed Yzelia!

I gripped at my head as it throbbed. Something was wrong. This was wrong. "Stop…"

"*Attack and the pain will cease,*" the voice of Naftali reassured.

"I don't…" I didn't want to attack anyone.

I recognized the form; it was my father's fighting style, just altered with Domrael's. I couldn't fight Orpheal. He was my father's friend, my ally. I didn't want anyone else to-

Another sharp pain ripped through my body. "Please… stop…"

"Aerrow, you're stronger than-" Orpheal's voice came through only to be silenced once again by the voice.

"*You do want to! Attack! Attack and be nothing! As your god commands it!*"

I charged at my target; the hesitance gone. There was no significance to anything other than obeying the will of Naftali. Faceless, meaningless lives. They were nothing. All shall be struck down at my god's command!

I sent out a stream of plasma ahead of me, knowing how the creature would avoid and struck where he dodged. My blade clipped his armour, somehow avoiding his wings. Guðmundr went up as he went to try and disarm me. I pushed back, swiping out my tail. The tail smashed his light frame into one of the spires. The spire stayed intact, more durable than I had suspected. I flew up before diving at him with my blade. Two bladed gauntlets braced against the attack as I pushed down. The bladed wings slashed out, forcing me to retreat and put up the shield again to avoid the damage. The shield disappeared and the target came at me.

I put up a fire dome, catching him in my trap. The floor below us caught fire and melted, forcing him airborne but unable to get far. A look of disgust went across his face… a look I couldn't have cared less about. Plasma waves were sent at him, the first two being dodged while the third hit him square in the chest. He hit the edge of the barrier then dropped like a stone. I twisted the barrier to that of flaming chaos. Vines of darkness gripped at the target that had attempted to escape the burning floor. Armour activated as the vines crept across his body, forcing him on his back, but not ripping him apart like I had hoped. I was going to have to break his armour forcefully.

I walked over to him, charging my blade. Suddenly, a bright light came from him. It blinded me a bit painfully, and I lost my concentration on the vines. I peeked out from the blindness and was punched in the chest with a precise, light charged strike. Something cracked as the hit bypassed the armour's defence and I was sent into the far wall, losing my sword in the process. The air was knocked out of me as I hit it. My body was forced to a knee while it struggled to stand, but my chest refused. It ached with even more pain, each breath agonizingly expanding my lungs.

"I'm sorry, but I cannot allow you to kill me," the target stated, and I growled in anger, looking up at him as he came close. "You would regret it."

How dare he hurt me?! Did he not see that this was the will of our god?!

"I wish that my words could-"

"*Silence him before he taints you from your true purpose!*"

Purpose… The word hung longer than it should have. It felt heavy.

It mattered not.

I stood up, ignoring the pain in my chest and attacked, a fireball of white, purple, and black in hand. He moved out of the attack, the fire sent across the room, damaging the wall, but the flames didn't go far. The blades on the gauntlets came back as I charged at him, blocking my clawed gauntlets from reaching his armour. Guðmundr went up as he slipped under my guard. Each hit bounced off my shield, but he didn't need to get past it as the strikes were strong, forcing me to put my weight against it. Light magic gathered into his gauntlet as the blades disappeared and wings bashed my shield upwards. A second punch came from the opening, colliding with my chest again, and sent me across the room. A short shout came out from the pain of hitting the floor and I slid to a stop.

It hurt to breathe. To move. To scream.

I sat up against my wishes to stop and a reflection of light came from the left, just behind one of the spires. My blade sat there, a few feet away. A light descended from the sky as I went towards my sword. It hit my back, locking my muscles, but not painfully so as I landed on the ground. Other small pillars locked my limbs in place as I struggled. None of it was made to be physically damaging, but it felt weird on and inside me. Its power threatened to hurt me, barely contained. It was more than uncomfortable being on my chest.

A sigh of victory came from above me as I felt the god come back and continued to press me about moving. Each order pierced my body as I couldn't follow them. I couldn't even writhe in pain let alone scream due to the paralyzing ability. Tears threatened to fall. It hurt so much.

"*Move! Attack him!*"

I couldn't! Could he not see-

"*You must kill him! Be my dragon! Use anything! Use everything! Magic, skills, anything is necessary! Fire! Light! Darkness! All of it! Get to your blade!*"

Darkness… Dark magic was strengthened when in the presence of its greatest weakness… I didn't have to move to use it.

Like the flash of light that was used earlier, I commanded the darkness to do the same. The room went in a pitch-black state for him after a moment of charging the attack, but only dimmed for me. The light's grasp ended, and he moved backwards in a panic. I launched myself at my blade. The spires' glow was faint, gradually coming back as the dark flash receded. I grabbed my blade and turned back to the target, moving quickly to strike while I still had the advantage. The pain from before was tolerable. I slashed, aiming for his head only for the armour to block the unsuspecting man, still unsure of where I was.

I struck a second time, across his chest and the armour stopped glowing. It took most of the attack, but not all of it as he grunted, moving away from me quickly and swinging out his wings, hitting nothing. I placed my tail in his way, tripping him. A pool of darkness formed under us and vines grabbed at him as their long thorns pierced his armour. He screamed in agony making me hesitate. My blade stopped its stab to his chest; an action I wasn't aware that I was doing.

Small gasps came from him as he looked up at me, blood dripping from the side of his mouth. "What... finally coming to some sense?"

My body pulsed with the order to kill but I remained stiff. I couldn't see the blade through. It shouldn't have mattered to me if he lived or died. It was what Naftali wanted... But I couldn't do it... He was familiar in some way. A scream I shouldn't have ever heard.

"Naftali really got us, didn't he...?" A small, painful chuckle came out of him. "I wonder if Éabha will forgive me for this... forgive herself."

Éabha... forgive herself for what?

"Not dealing with Naftali before her friend killed her father," the man answered the question I didn't recall asking. "Or maybe she wouldn't care."

She cared so much...

Naftali's voice stopped ordering as a pulse of anguish went through my head. A sharp noise escaped my throat as I took several steps back, and my legs gave out, finally free to do as they pleased. I swallowed down bile, regaining some sense... Deigh came back, but it wasn't like it should have been. She felt faint and far. Realization crawled in.

I just tried killing... I attacked my partner and locked her up in a cage. Her, my uncle, and my knights. What the hell was wrong with me?!

Naftali... how could you make me...

You monster.

I looked up as I heard movement in front of me and saw Orpheal sitting up with a painful, tiny smile on his face directed at me. I went over to him, leaving Winterthorn behind and attempted to help him. "I'm so sorry, I don't-"

He only shook his head. "It's alright... Can you help me to the spire?"

I nodded, doing as he asked and then knelt in front of him. He was bloody, armour crushed in some areas and impaled in others. I almost killed him... "Are you going to be alright?"

"I can heal myself, but it's not going to be quick." Another small smile that was weirdly out of place as he flinched. "You're a more capable fighter than I gave you credit for, even for being a clunky puppet."

"I'm sorry... I tried but I couldn't... I should have tried harder-"

"You got him out of your head before you killed someone, that's what counts," he interrupted, starting to heal himself with a small, yellow orb to his chest. "Once things settle down, I'll have to ask about your experience with the Zerach."

"If it helps make things up with you; I'll gladly answer any of your questions... I happen to remember this time around."

"You might regret agreeing to that."

Perhaps... but it was a small price to pay considering. He was the leader of a nation, my ally, and my friend's father... and I almost-

A pulse went through my body, causing the room to spin, and a grunt came out. I grabbed at my chest, trying to fight off Naftali's influence again.

"*You can help so many,*" he whispered and I tsked.

I wasn't going to help anyone by killing people.

"*Together, we can defend all nations. We can kill Ciar and anyone-*"

Orpheal broke through. "Is he still trying?"

"Yes... he's abusing my instinct to help peo-" A breathless scream came out as my head pounded. A part of me wanted to follow him again, but I refused to let it. Being controlled once was enough. I got out of it with help... Naftali's hold, while incredibly painful, was a little more manageable, but I doubted it would be for long. It was like the Black Phoenix's mind control, but different. The pain settled enough for me to speak. "Why is he doing this? Why would he want you and Éabha dead? I thought you were friends."

"Power... and whatever he used to heal himself," he pondered, adding things together. "If he used your blood, he would've needed a binding agent. Daemonias magic is the only thing that we know to do impossible feats like absorbing power. For the best results for healing quickly, he would have needed blood or marrow meaning he probably used Ciar's blood since I doubt he would have managed to get marrow."

"Why would he use Ciar's blood? He might not be a physician, but even as a biologist he would have known before hand that it wasn't natural."

"He was dying, only had a few months to live unless a miracle happened. I tried to reason with him that we could come up with something between all of us, but everything we tried didn't work. Eventually, he became almost irrational as the days started to count down. Projects left unfinished. Things he wanted to do, not done. Then, he started to get better a few months ago, but it wasn't enough… It was never enough. Like trickles of sand falling in an hourglass, he still couldn't outrun it no matter how much better he seemed to get. It never seemed to last."

"So, when he finally beat whatever was killing him…"

Orpheal nodded. "Owen mentioned he could sense something off when he came to help with the Zerach this morning… but it was before today that he had been acting strangely. Less patient, thinking quicker but almost warped in a way at times before going back to normal. I didn't think anything of it, just the psychology of a dying man. But if it weren't for Éabha, I would have followed his direction of meeting you here and you would have taken the blame for his deeds."

"So he was getting treated with Ciar's blood before we came with his samples…" I looked to the floor to help think through the pain. "The Daemonias was corrupting him even though all he wanted was not to die."

"When you're desperate enough, you try anything despite the consequences."

"And being the head of the biology department in your lab, he knew of your past projects with Outland blood and probably knew of Vígdís's work of her pets and thought he could have one too."

"With the corruption growing, changing him into thinking he was more than the rest of us, without a doubt. Who knows how long he's been planning all of this; using my work and hers to further his delusions?" He gave a raspy breath, breaking from his healing. "I apologize for my subordinate's actions against you."

"It's not your fault-"

"It is. I should have seen the signs. We've known each other for almost a century and were good friends. He never gets pushy or desperate, even when he found out he was going to die… That was until he asked for a few days of retreat and upon his return was the beginning of the Zerach – when I presented the blueprints created with the help of Solomon. Almost immediately he wanted one of your family to help, saying it was the only way to complete the project. Éabha and I were sure than any random Absalomian could provide what was necessary. If one wasn't enough, a collection of volunteers to synthesize the signature for Outland Dragons. Some of them had the dark element needed to help build the frequency for Outland Monsters… but none of them worked.

"Eventually things were getting desperate, but I didn't want to impose. The barrier was placed around Absalom already when I talked to Solomon about problems, how it was failing despite everything. And that's when he agreed to help, to send someone that would be of a higher dragon ratio and hearing that he was going to send you surprised me. Naftali, who was upset that a noble was going to be sent even though it was going to be the eclipse and shouldn't have expected any help at all, became ecstatic that he was getting his way."

"He was dying even with Ciar's blood… He must have seen that not only could royal blood help with the machine that needed the dragon percentage, but it could save him too."

"Something I should have seen, but I was blinded by all the other distractions and noises… Then hearing how Ciar killed Solomon, I didn't see what he was becoming; what he became, and he abused it. Swindled his new god… a god I'm sure he wants to overthrow now that he has everything he needs. What better way of claiming himself as divine than humiliating the false god by using the kid that he failed to kill as a pet."

"It'd certainly assert his dom-ah!" Another scream was barely stifled as my head and body wanted to rip themselves apart. It became harder to breathe as Naftali's whispers, while incomprehensible, came back. He was trying to get my being to move without clouding my thoughts. It was like last time. "I need to find him before he succeeds."

"You're in no shape to fight him even with your new healing ability. Éabha went to find him-"

"Something clearly happened, or she couldn't find him." I winced, almost biting my tongue. "I'm not going to be able to keep him out and I don't want to attack either of you again."

"She can handle it. I know she-"

A sharp, distant scream of the girl we were talking about came from outside and I snapped to it. She wasn't far. "Éabha…"

"You heard…" Orpheal turned his attention to the doors, no longer calm and collected. He went to get up but didn't get very far, smashing back into the spire with a hiss. "No. No, dammit!"

"Orpheal," I started but he only struggled to push himself, ignoring me. "Orpheal!"

"I have to help her!"

"You're in worse condition than I am. You can't-"

"She's my daughter! I can't leave her to Naftali and whoever fucking else!"

"She's my friend so I won't let her." I grabbed his hand and put it to his chest. "Stay here and heal. Éabha would be really upset if you died."

"I can't just-"

"You can't even get off this spire. Please, stay. I'll find Éabha and bring her back here."

"What about Naftali?"

"Hopefully, he's nearby… If not, I'll make sure she comes back on her own. Just come rescue me if he wins." My joke fell a bit flat as my head pounded again and I shook off the influence. "She'll be alright."

He gave a scowl in disgust, his yellow orb forming again in his hand. I picked up Winterthorn and was about to leave only to stop at his chilling words. "If she dies by your hand, even if it was under Naftali… I will not hesitate to do the same in return. Don't take all I have left."

I clenched my jaw with a nod, acknowledging his warning and left his glare to the blindingly bright day.

Chapter Forty-Eight: Corruption

I followed the sounds of fighting around the building. The sun was blinding me from seeing far, but I didn't stop to fumble with my pouch. A fireball of smoke blocked the sun's light for a moment dimming the world and showing a courtyard garden in the back corner of the demesne. A battle was taking place by a few trees, several of them large and ancient beyond bushes that fenced in the area decoratively. Naftali appeared between the leaves, a strange light coming off his features as he used the Zerach, pushing buttons before stepping back and disappeared. Movement came from the bushes as Éabha flew away from him, landing on a branch high up only to be knocked out of it by an Outland Monster. A wall of brambles blocked me from seeing if she was alright. I went tried flying to move faster only for a pulse to tear through my body and head.

A cry of agony escaped my closing throat as I hit the side of the building then crumbled to the ground. My gauntlets dug into the earth, trying to steady the world before it could grow dark. Éabha was right there, being attacked and in need of help. I couldn't let Naftali take control again.

I struggled to get to a stand, huffs of effort came out from the short breaths. The entrance of the garden had to be nearby. I kept on the ground, not wanting to crash a second time or for Naftali to get creative. My steps were slow and shaky before they got a rhythm again. An opening appeared around the corner of bushes. Quick movement came from the other side as my steps fumbled and my blade went up in response. It blocked an equally sharp blade that was aimed for my throat held by a familiar armour set in front of me. My attacked stopped. "Éabha…"

"Aer-" She stopped as she looked up at my face, her eyes growing wide in fear and disengaged, ready to leave when I called her back.

"Wait, I'm not… Where's Naftali?"

She looked back into the garden with a glare before grabbing the collar of my armour and dragged me farther into hiding within the garden's outskirts. She kept a distance as she let go and allowed me to follow and see her entirely. She looked better back in the space Zegrinath had destroyed. Her braided hair was loosened in some areas and while her armour clearly took the damage, staying alight, it had dirt all over it. Dirt and ash.

Finally, once she was content to a degree, looking over her shoulder slightly, she answered me. "He's over there, but he's… different. He's using magic that felt like the Daemonias Portals and has Outland Monsters. We can't fight him."

"I don't have a-" I couldn't finish my sentence as a squeak came out when a much louder noise was smothered. I grabbed my head, my gauntlet slipping a bit on the sweat. "I-I don't have much time. You have to leave, go see your father in the demesne and leave if I can't stop him."

"You can't fight him by yourself! Just run and hide, far from its reach."

"He knows where I am, what I'm thinking, saying…" I looked through the bushes to see if I could see Naftali and came face to face with two eyes of an Outland Monster staring back just on the other side, but it didn't move to attack. It didn't have to as Éabha looked and got the same message.

"You'd never make it…"

I gave a nod as neither of us looked away from the monster. She tensed in my peripherals. I took a small breather to get the words I wanted out in one go. "You have to leave. Your father is waiting for you."

"I'm not abandoning you to a fate of blood and murder… We might never find you again if I leave you to fight him alone."

"But what if I-"

"We'll cross that bridge when we get there… Should I bother to make a plan with you?"

"Not unless you want him to know."

"Alright… follow me."

I did as she asked, managing to tear away from the monster. I wanted to know what she had in mind and where we were going, but I refrained from asking. She went back to the corner I met her at, a beautiful vine covered arch with flowers and on the inside was a wide, open space for gatherings. Shrubs and garden plots along the sides, a few benches and a tiled floor for dancing or tables – all surrounded by garden hedges that formed entryways to decorative mazes. Naftali was looking at a large CT on his lap and sat away from the Zerach on a makeshift throne made of glass conjured by most likely Dagdian magic. It sat on top of a mound of light, dark, and Daemonias magic tendrils weaving in a sick balance.

At the foot of the creation, three Heftvarys classed monsters sat. two of them were surprisingly beautiful, white feathers and fur with a black strip down its spine and mirror markings on its face. The fox-like creatures had elongated necks like that of a long-necked bird. Large, majestic wings sat on their shoulders, folded calmly to their sides at the edge of the dais. Between them though was a monster that was as demonic as they were divine in appearance. The bulky creature looked like a bear, fangs, claws, and all, but instead of fur, it had rough, bumpy, wet skin, and a long tail. I recognized them from the bestiary.

The fox monsters, aleklors, were more dangerous than the saligorsa in both potential power and flexibility. They could fly and were intelligent, but it probably wasn't something we'd have to deal with as they were being controlled. As for the demonic bear, I was just happy that we weren't inside somewhere. The last thing I wanted was to lose track of it and have it suddenly come down on us from the ceiling.

I looked up to Naftali, slightly disturbed even further. He looked the same in a way. Healthy and not frail. But he was also very, very different. His eyes were draconic and orange, nothing like the Seraphinean blue they were before. An earpiece that belonged to the Zerach for remote control was on his ear and the sense Owen mentioned was physical now. A ghostly grey-purple shimmer of a nihilistic aura protruded from him and penetrated the pain my body felt. A harsh chill went through my nerves. It was like the Daemonias Portal energy only somehow more corrupted and mixed with life in a way. I could smell the individual scents from the blood mixture running through him: Naftali's own Seraphinean presence still lingered under my own, and Daemonias.

Éabha readied her rifle and I realized she wasn't seeing what I saw. "Éabha, wait."

"He's going to-"

"I know, but I don't want to fight him like this. Not without trying to reach him."

"That's what Owen said the last time and guess what happened."

"Make the call when you feel is right, but there's something wrong with him."

"No shit…" She lowered her weapon slightly. "But everything in my being says he's just a shell, nothing like how you were."

I didn't agree with her out loud but agreed all the same. He was… something else now. But against my better instincts, I had to try anyway. We drew closer, stopping at the edge of the open patio as his monsters growled, baring their fangs, and he turned to us from his tablet. A smaller bird-like monster took it from him and put it behind the Zerach then flew off elsewhere.

"There you are," Naftali welcomed like he hadn't noticed us which I knew was a lie. His voice was both in my ears and in my head causing me to wince. "Come to my side and protect your creator, Little Dragon."

I took a step, starting to obey but stopped, fighting him off somehow. "Naftali, you need help. You're sick-"

"I'm perfectly healthy and its all thanks to you." A memory of being strapped to a table and injected with Outland blood came back. I took two steps back in fear and the familiar excruciating pain danced at the edge of my conscience. A cruel smile placed itself on his face, knowing the memories that went through my head. "You saved me, Little Dragon. You did what no one else could."

"And this is how you treat your saviour?" Éabha spat out in rage. "By torturing him and those that brought him here?!"

"I had to make sure it would succeed at all costs, Éabha."

"Why didn't you ask for help before resorting to this?!"

"None of you would understand! You're so set in what's wrong and right without thinking of the opportunities. You're all pawns who get in the way and nothing more. I knew that delinquent would be the main guard, so I had to plan a way to remove Cyrus from the equation – even if that meant causing him and the others to suffer. For the better good and my new creation."

"Stop calling me that…" I growled out, trying to ease out the influence. He called me it before… and thinking on it broke my will a little more.

"You are my creation though. My Little Dragon who should be at my side-"

"No, I'm not! I shouldn't be by your-" I could feel him trying to block out my memories of the commitments to my parents, trying to erase them from existence. Their faces and voices. "Stop it! You didn't create me-"

"You have no allegiances but to me. You're nothing without me."

"And you'd be nothing without Ciar's blood!" I snapped back and his influence lessened in surprise. My breathing became a bit easier as I took exasperated breaths. "But it wasn't enough, was it? You had some and it made you better for a time but never for long. It helped with not allowing my blood to kill you, but Naftali, it only works because it wants power. It's using you."

"It made me anew! I'm a god now!"

"You're turning into a demon, nothing more…"

His shocked expression turned to that of a savage grin. "On the contrary, I've compared my existence to the records that Domrael collected on Valrdis and Orithina… I'm so close to them."

"You're sick! You're no closer to being a-" A yelp escaped as I lost my balance and dropped to a knee. His declaration of divinity was loud and clear in my head as he repeated himself. My body wanted to follow through, worship him as such and I gritted my teeth. I didn't worship well-known gods; I wasn't going to start worshipping a biologist that had a few brain cells corrupted by a horrific magic from beyond. "Naftali, we don't want to fight you. Please listen-"

"Once you've accepted your new purpose, you'll never have to worry again. Be nothing as you wanted. I'll protect you."

There was a small piece of me that wanted that, but I didn't fall into its hold again. A sharp pain ripped through my body. "Naftali-"

"The pain will stop, Little Dragon, just as soon as you accept it."

"You want me to kill people for it! I… can't… I won't!"

"You can and you will. I'm your creator. Your-" He didn't finish as a loud bang went off to my right. The shot that was fired out didn't make it closer than three metres from Naftali before it was blocked by a wall of magic. A second bang went off and a massive orb of light went for the Zerach but failed just the same.

I looked to where the attacks had originated, and a disgusted sneer was on Éabha's face. A mutter of seethed rage came out of her, "Fuck off."

"How dare you?!" Naftali yelled in anger and it took all my will not to turn my blade on her. "I've been sparing you-"

"Good gods do shut up, you fucking poser," she interrupted maliciously before toning her tone down ever so slightly. "I was hoping Aerrow could talk sense into you, but you're no longer Naftali. If you're really a god as you say, prove it! Fight us like one! Unless you're too fucking scared to fight a couple of mortal children?"

Naftali didn't wait for a second invitation and the three Outland Monsters stood up from their protective positions.

I struggled to get to a stand, forcing through the order to stand aside. I noticed Éabha looking over and gave her a small glance, trying to ease the worried expression on her face. "We'll stop him... I won't let you do this alone, okay?"

She gave a small nod, her grip on Iðunn tightened. "I don't want to fight him... but I couldn't watch you suffer anymore."

"We don't have to kill him, just knock him out." I looked to the monsters as they closed the gap. "Until then, I'll try to keep him out, but keep watch. I might act out suddenly."

"Go after the bear thing, I'll keep the other two occupied."

"Éabha, wait-"

She didn't wait, flying up as she put Iðunn away and met the monsters with her bladed gauntlets. I wanted to have a better strategy but there wasn't time to argue with her as the saligorsa was swiping out claws. I flew out of the way, feeling the wind of the attack brush by and readied to dive it.

"If you're going to defy me, you'll have to do it the hard way," Naftali growled in my head and immediately his promise was followed.

A sharp pain ripped through my back and wings. My scream was silenced as I hit the hedges, far from the monster. Or, at least, that's what I thought when I dragged myself out of the bushes against everything I wanted. The bear's maw was on top of me within in moments, teeth aimed for my chest and throat. A fireball formed in my hand, not entirely made of my will but Naftali's, and I threw it at the monster. It hit its chest and left a horrible smell of burnt skin and mucus. It made me dizzy.

It backed off, thankfully, just as the sky turned a blinding white. A hiss came out as I was forced to close my eyes, squinting to try and adjust, and looked up. The area was covered by a light magic dome, tendrils and vines of light weaved between themselves, protecting the barrier. Something dropped down beside me. I reacted, a plasma ball forming in my gauntlet as the order to attack ripped through my head.

"Friendly!" The monster screamed in a familiar but somewhat distorted voice.

Naftali came back. *"Don't listen. It's lying."*

"Friendly," Éabha repeated, coming through more clearly though her form was static while struggling to untangle herself from the bushes. It made her seem more like a pnevallidum than a living person.

I tried to listen to her and put out the plasma, but my body pulsated. I had to throw it... But I couldn't use it against... Movement came from just behind her and I attacked. The ball went passed her head, hitting one of the aleklors square in the chest. It yelped as Éabha looked behind her, opening an eye from her brace. I winced under the building pressure in my head. Suddenly, her blades extended out and moved faster than I could, shoving them into something on the right. Her crescent blade was pulled out and the saligorsa backed off, shaking about its bleeding body in a frenzy. A white and black gauntlet presented itself in front of me through the bright blur. I took it and she helped me to a stand.

"New plan, work together," she told me, and I gave a curt nod.

"What happened to the sky fight?"

"The dome. I can't fly any more than a couple of meters off the ground before I'm grabbed and thrown."

I turned to the monsters that had regrouped in front of Naftali again, the Zerach that was off to his right was blocked by the barrier.

"*She's threatening us.*" Naftali's voice came through my head.

I gritted my teeth. "I don't think this is a good idea, Éabha."

"It's the only one we have-" she started before I interrupted.

"I'm going to turn on you if you're close by."

"Stay in front of me. I know if you're going to attack me if you're suddenly not facing the enemy."

"Okay... I'm sorry if I-" Another hiss escaped as I stumbled forward, losing my balance. "Naftali, stop! This isn't you!"

"*You know the conditions, Little Dragon. Attack!*"

"Fine... if you want me to attack so badly." My blade went straight to plasma.

I rushed headfirst towards the monsters, not thrilled about the situation. My heart skipped in panic at the idea of being torn to pieces but didn't stop, praying that Éabha knew what to do in my reckless abandon. We had only worked together against a thinking enemy once before, and it failed miserably. But it was all I had. I couldn't control myself if I paused to think. I couldn't kill her. If I did... Naftali would win both the battle and the war for his *creation*.

The saligorsa roared, about to meet me halfway when I dodged to the side of its attack. The energy in my blade was released at the aleklor that I attacked earlier. Iðunn went off behind me and the bear monster yelped in pain. I turned to it, shoving my sword through its hide. Scales and mucus burned once more as the blade's hot edge sizzled against it. It turned its head on me and my free hand went for its muzzle. The clawed gauntlet dug deep into the flesh of its bottom jaw. I squeezed, taking control of where it went as more shots went by my head into the aleklors. Movement came from the corner of my eye and I swung my tail out, hitting one of the winged foxes that tried to attack.

The saligorsa whined as its bones cracked within my grasp. The grip tightened, the claws digging deeper, then I ripped it off. The sounds of bone, joints, and muscle tearing, breaking, and popping turned my stomach as the lower jaw that was no longer attached became ash. A tendril of light caught my sight, and I tore out the blade, backing away before I could finish off the monster. The tendril stung as it brushed past my ear, causing me to wince as it snaked through the armour's defences.

I glared over at Naftali, but it didn't have much merit as there was more than just one tendril. Several vines of dark magic and tendrils of light came from the throne followed by balls of Daemonias magic. I brought up Guðmundr for a few of the attacks, smacking others away with Winterthorn. The distance I had closed to get to him was lost within only a few seconds of avoiding and blocking, unable to attack back due to the orders. A few more attacks came from Éabha's new gun behind me, striking the aleklor and slowing its attack from above.

I followed up, chasing after its falling form and grabbed its delicate leg. The bone broke almost as soon as my hand closed around it, unable to hold my strength back. My blade powered up by Naftali's command and shoved itself through its spine and into the back of its head. The monster didn't make a noise as it turned to dust. A warning came from Éabha of something coming from behind. I brought up Guðmundr and a tendril and vine of light and dark magic, twisted into a spire, collided with it. It pushed, trying to stab through and forced me to brace. My boots slid a few paces on the smooth stone.

Something caught my eye to the right, and I peeked over. The saligorsa was barreling in, its jaw almost grown back. The shield started to turn into a dome but stopped, listening in on Naftali's orders. The spire split apart, pushing still to try and break through, and small tendrils and vines started to move to the edges.

"I wonder how you will do against both elements, Little Dragon, as you are now."

"I'm not an experiment!" I grunted out and the shield stuttered at the distraction.

"You don't have a choice."

The vines and tendrils gripped onto my gauntlet where Guðmundr was attached to. "Stop it!"

He didn't stop and I tried to pull away, but they held fast. They squeezed, putting pressure against the armour's defences. It pulled at the bracelet as Naftali toyed with my head so I would slip. Another roar came from the saligorsa and a split-second decision was made. A really, stupid decision, but not one that Naftali expected.

I dropped the shield as the bear slammed into me, knocking me off my feet with ease. The vine and tendril spire went through the monster's side where I had been standing a moment before. The bear mauled it, swinging its massive head at attacks it couldn't reach. The spire digging deeper and unable to reach me underneath. The magic lost its grasp on my arm and I shoved it into the bear's chest, gripping at something inside. It turned its fangs on me and I pulled. The dragon stone claws dug deep into something squishy and what came out was turning to ash. Its teeth never reached me as it exploded to nothing.

I took a breather as the weight left and inhaled ash from the cloudburst. Coughing, I tried to get up but couldn't get any further than to a knee when my body pulsed and collapsed. Tendrils gripped me from out of the cloud of ash and threw me into the dome. My shoulder hit it at a bad angle, causing me to scream which was silenced by falling hard onto a tree root in the garden's maze. The world was dizzy as I tried to pick myself up. Exhaustion ripped through and I dropped back to the ground.

I needed rest… but if I did, Naftali could just-

A chaos pool formed underneath. Vines came from within, gripping onto me without much of a fight. Its chaotic nature emphasized the ignored commands despite knowing it wasn't breaking through. I writhed. I tried to mutter out a plea, but it was met with agony.

"Prove that I should stop. Get up and attack."

I tried and the vines held me down. The order considered disobeyed and the grip around my throat closed.

"You're my guardian. I need you to be my sword and shield, Little Dragon."

"Stop using that-" My voice stopped working and I grimaced.

"Get up."

A sharp noise that should have been a scream came out. His hold was breaking what little control I had left. I tried to look through the bushes to where I heard Éabha fighting the last monster. I had to warn her.

"No, you don't. She is nothing to you other than a source of suffering."

She wasn't causing my misery. She was-

"If she was your friend, why didn't she come to your screams?"

The monster-

"The monster... she sees you as that too."

He pried in my head; memories slowly being blocked that I couldn't fight against. Her attempt to talk over her fear, the times we had. "Why are you doing this?!"

"They are lies! She stabbed you straight through the heart. What kind of friend does that without hesitation?"

"She didn't-"

"She did. You remember her doing it. She held you close... and then she stabbed you."

The memory came forward from the fog. The noises, the smells, the confusion, and anguishing torment of fear and pain – mine and the remnants of a scared dragon.

Then, the bolt.

The struggle stopped just as my heart had for a moment.

"No one thinks you're a person now. Only me. Not your uncle nor your knights. Certainly not that girl who pretends to be your friend. No one but me sees that you're not a monster."

I... wasn't a monster though...

"No, you're not," he soothed the wound he dealt. *"You're my creation so I know that you're just a person. But no one will believe you, no matter how much you prove it. Not even those closest to you, and not your kingdom."*

The words stung, hanging as the world I tried to savour in, melted out of the illusion. I was alone... Éabha, who I trusted, thought I was a monster. My people who didn't know, would answer as Claudius had. They would hate me just like her and see a monster as their leader. Atlamillia and Helah were followers of Orithina. How long before they thought I wasn't fit? Would they do what Éabha did? Would they shove an Outland bolt in my heart as they apologize? Who knew if they meant it?

I wasn't a monster… that wasn't me and yet she still thought that I could… The kingdom would be like her, seeing no difference. I wasn't a pure Absalomian anymore…

I was his creation.

"You are, and being an Emissary of Death, it would only pile on top of everything else. The people in the lab, the Outland Dragons, your citizens, even your parents; they would blame you for it all. You can be exactly who you are though, my Little Dragon of Death. I accept you."

An Emissary of Death… the title made me relax ever so slightly, like a familiar embrace but one that I hadn't felt in years and still remembered like it just happened. The world went dark as I couldn't take the stress anymore. The barrier of will ceased.

I couldn't take anymore loss. Anymore failures or hopes dashed. I wanted to be nothing and restart.

The small rest ended as the voice that offered me that chance came through the darkness like a warm blanket. *"She's coming. Kill her before she kills you. You can rest once she's out of the way, continue again another day."*

I opened my eyes, the calls from a female voice registered in my ears but not of what they had said. The language was foreign. My ragged body got to a stand using the tree. It was a shaded spot and made it easier to adapt to the lighting. Easier to see the glow of the dome that caged us and reflected off armour just outside the brambles. I set my blade back, a dark pool creeping just behind the target – ready to counter her backing away.

I charged at her. The monster unexpectedly went to the side instead of blocking my attack. She rebounded off a light step and used her wings to power a knee strike to a weakened spot in my armour. I doubled over, the hit breaking a rib beyond the protection and blood speckled her boot. My glare barely made it to her before a gauntlet powered with magic was brought to the side of my face. The chaos pool dissipated from the loss of consciousness for a moment as I stumbled backwards and fell. I didn't stay down for long, getting up before she could make another move and thrusted my sword. Bladed gauntlets blocked and brushed aside the attacks for a few moments. The rib healed enough to breathe easier, and I started to overpower her.

This wasn't like the last fight. She didn't have the experience as the last target I had failed to kill for my god.

She tried to get higher than me, but I grabbed her ankle and threw her back to the ground. Chaos vines formed and didn't allow her to get away. She squeaked and my blade hesitated from bring brought down. A small blemish of disgust formed on my face at the delay as she blocked. A bright light flashed from her. Its touch was harsh, causing me to hiss as I was blasted several feet away. The chaos field disappeared. Something gripped at my wrists and then my legs, forcing me to the ground as the voice of the creator came back loudly through my skull.

"Why did you hesitate?"

I didn't-

"Fight then."

The vines of light held me down. She gave a warning I couldn't understand but wanted to. A feeling of not wanting to fight – the familiarity etched its way through me. It made me question everything.

Why was I attacking?

It was for him. He accepted... He created-

He killed so many-

She killed me. She wasn't going to be the last.

Only to protect herself. I was a monster and she healed... I had a responsibility to my kingdom.

"My kingdom," the voice reiterated, organizing my thoughts. *"You want it to stop. The pain, the memories, the nightmares, you want all of it to stop, don't you? Don't think."*

"But... they are who I-" My voice was cut as air stopped going through. Those memories, the pain also had good within... didn't they? I had made promises. I couldn't just leave them behind. They slipped out of my grasp as another jolt ripped through my head. The screams from the memories that remained echoed. "Stop... make them stop."

"Aerrow, can you hear me?" A new voice entered, and I did my best to look for it. A faceless distortion knelt in front of me. "I'm sorry."

"She's doing what she did last time," Naftali warned but my body refused to tense at the statement. Refused to fight for the will to live.

I certainly didn't want to die... but if this was all that remained... I didn't want to live either.

A breathless question came out. "Are you going to kill me again?"

"Aerrow-"

The screams of people, people I knew, people I didn't. Absalom. Seraphina. The ones that tried to kill me that I tortured in return. They all howled. I wanted to cover my ears, but my wrists were locked to the ground. "I can't take it anymore... Make it stop."

"Kill her and they will stop! I need you, Little Dragon! Don't offer her anything!"

A sense of rage came from the god and ripped through my head, trying to absorb the guilt and pain that he had brought forth.

"I'm not going to kill you, Aerrow," the girl answered, breaking through once more. "I-"

She didn't get to finish as a sphere of Daemonias magic was thrown, forcing her to dodge away gracefully. More attacks came, light and dark spheres that were tiny and fired in quick succession. Her tether loosened and then broke.

Naftali came back, his voice inside my head and ears. "I've assisted the best I can, Little Dragon, but I'm not a fighter. You wanted the simple path? To rest? She wants to kill us! Kill her now!"

"What?!" Her words were silenced by his rage fuelling mine.

Some unsaid thought brought itself forward and caused my head to ache differently than the commands that I had disobeyed. She killed dragons remorselessly like some sort of game. Her people did the same. They were slaughtered. They killed Vothedissith! She was my-

Yzelia... This whole kingdom needed to be cleansed! Starting with her... the Daughter of the Lord Director.

Her gauntlets' blades came down as I went after her, fire in one hand, blazing sword in the other. I threw the ball ahead and she moved out of the way. It was an attack pattern I barely recognized, yet still one that caused me grief and rage. I followed the movements, countering each one. Vines were broken as she tried to hold me down. A sphere came from her unexpectedly. I knocked it back, hitting her in the chest. Her scream was cut short as she hit a tree. Winterthorn threw a stream of plasma, ripping everything in its path. She dodged it when she tripped. The tree and gardens behind her were split in two, catching fire. I was over her before she could barely get to a stand. Familiar, terrified eyes looked at me as I grabbed her shoulder to run her through.

She screamed, "Wait!"

My muscles seized.

"Please, stop. He's killing you… I can't see you die again."

"You killed-"

"I know I did, and I regretted every second afterwards! I can't do it again… not for anyone. Not for my life… not even for you." Her gauntlet blades folded away as she grabbed my blade. The technology protecting her from the plasma sizzled slightly when she brought the tip up to her heart. "You said you couldn't kill unless you had to. I believed you because I know you're not a monster. But… if you want to be, it's only fair that you stab me where I stabbed you, right?"

"I…"

"*What are you waiting for?*" The god asked and I didn't know how to answer. If I… her armour was at its limit. "*Finish-*"

"I want to protect you for real this time. Like a real friend does… like what you did for me in the street with the zealot. Not what he's doing. No favours are needed. I won't force you to your lowest and strip away everything that made you feel, good and bad. He's killing you by turning you into something you've never wanted to be. Just like how he killed those whelps."

"The whelps…" I muttered but Naftali countered before I could think on her words.

"*She's lying. This is what you wanted! I'm giving it to you like a merciful god.*"

"Slowly, painfully, kidnapped away from their homes, just like what he's done to you," she continued. "Admittedly, it'd be easier to be his puppet. But is that what you want? You've always made decisions, you're a leader and a noble one, sacrificing and risking your life for your people even though it terrifies you."

Her face came in clearer, her grip on my blade tightened as I struggled under the order to see the blade through. To be or not… "I don't… I can't. I never wanted to be king… I never wanted to hurt anyone but it's all I do."

"No, it's not all you do. You've helped a lot of people, me included." She gave a small smile. "You wanted to be an adventurer, right? You would have been really good at it."

"A long time ago... but she died... because of-" My voice cracked as the memory of her was blocked... someone I cherished, her relation, her face... Not even her name remained. "No, stop... Give her back!"

"*I want to protect-*"

"Get out of my head!"

Naftali's voice boomed around the dome and in my head. "She's dead! You killed her!"

"No... No I... Ciar-"

"You are an Emissary of Death! He just answered the invitation."

"He's manipulating your thoughts, taking away people you hold close to isolate you," the enemy stated as she came through the anguish and I turned back to her. I felt like I was being torn apart at every level of existence. "You didn't kill that stolen person, Aerrow. You'll never avenge her if you go down this path."

"This is the only way you'll get vengeance!" He growled back and my head felt like it wanted to explode. "Kill her!"

My arm shifted, pushing slightly as the blade started to break through her armour's defences.

"Aerrow!" The panicked scream stopped my attack. It was just like that night. Not in fear for her sake. She was scared for mine. Just like...

My sword dropped from my hand as it gripped at my head. If what Naftali said was true, Éabha would have stopped a monster from killing her. She wasn't stopping me... She was telling the truth.

The influence broke, the voice and his demented will left quickly and released mine. I started to lean too far, and she caught me, keeping me steady. I grabbed her arms to assist, my head dropping on her shoulder in exhaustion and distress. Tears broke through the small barrier I had left, and she held me a little tighter. The memory of my mother came back, undamaged by his attempt to take her away. A sense of relief filled me, but a dreaded idea followed afterwards. I wasn't going to let what happened to her happen to Éabha. Not because of me. I wasn't going to let her make that choice that so deeply tore her inside. I couldn't let her do that again. "I'm sorry... I'm so sorry..."

"It's not your-" Her sentence stopped as we both felt a malefic presence coming in close.

I turned quickly, placing up Guðmundr through gritted teeth as the Daemonias sphere hit it. It exploded upon contact and ripped through the bushes and trees, putting out the fires. I glared as the smoke dissipated. Naftali's magical presence had shifted again, the underlining power was surfacing and strong, getting stronger by the moment.

"You bitch…" the biologist spat in rage. His voice wasn't the same as it was a few moments before, growly and rough. "Now I have to beat down my pet all over again!"

"He's not your pet!"

"I created him!"

"You're lucky that the Outland blood isn't controlling me as it once did, Naftali," I warned, interrupting their fighting as a dark wrath surfaced. "It wants to tear you to pieces!"

"You're just a rampaging whelp, like you've always been."

I almost fell for the taunt, but I held my position. He was trying to get back in and with each moment that past, the exhaustion of fighting, physically and mentally, was taking its toll. The attacks were quicker and quicker. I couldn't have him isolate me again. He had almost suppressed my most cherished memories – there wasn't a third chance for me.

Something tapped the side of my hand and I looked down to see Winterthorn being held out to me. I turned to Éabha who hinted at it. "Let's finish this in case Ciar is coming."

"Ciar…?" My eyes widened in fear. "Oh gods, I've used…"

"Don't panic… I'm still here, just as I said I would be, Airhead."

The nickname was soothing and made it easier to think. "I'll guard you. Tell me where to go and do whatever is necessary. I'll do my best to follow and knock him out."

She nodded and I rushed ahead, my blade charging up as I held out Guðmundr. More attacks pelted it from Naftali, desperate to break our cohesion. Ciar was coming, there was no sense in not using magic now.

"Go left after this wave," Éabha ordered just above the noise of my steps and I followed.

She fired Iðunn and Naftali turned on her, the magic blocking the attack. I unleashed mine. It connected, hitting him and shattering his throne. A scream of agony came from him, part of me enjoying it, the other part ceasing the burning as the smell of flesh and cloth came to my nose. He dropped from his pedestal and Éabha followed the mark, shooting his exposed body in the leg. I went to get closer only for a pulse of light magic to knock us off our feet.

The familiar sense of death from chaos and Daemonias came from him and I darted for Éabha, barely getting to her as the attack hit part of my badly formed shield and myself, blocking her. A sharp scream came out as my armour shut down on my back and wings. The shield failed as I fell, unable to keep myself upright. Another attack came and I braced, barely conscious. It never arrived, smashing against something. A warm feeling of healing hit my body. Through the darkening blur, Éabha knelt beside me. Guðmundr was on her wrist as the blue dome was encased with vines and tendrils. More spheres attacked the open spaces.

"Thanks," I muttered breathlessly.

She gave a small smile. "No, thank you. That would have killed me. Here." She passed me one of her capacitor clips for her automatic weapon. "This will recharge your armour if you stick it to your chest. It'll help your own magic fuel it."

"Do you have-"

She took out another one, sticking it to her chest. "There's two extra ones after this. It won't be a lot, but it'll let us deal with him and run from Ciar if he attacks."

I sat up with her help, finally able to and reached into the bag, using my free hand to help recharge her armour faster. My head pounded as her healing was forced to come to stop when she started coughing. "What's wrong?"

"I'm maxing out my limit... I used a lot of magic and didn't rest-"

"Can you use capacitor crystals like the spires?"

"Yes-"

"Take my second one."

"No!"

"Éabha, you lose half of your weapons without magic and my armour is already recovering from mine." I put the clip in her hand. "Use it... just in case you need to teleport away."

"I said I wouldn't leave you-"

"If worst comes to worst, leave and find the others… They'll do what we can't."

"What about Ciar?"

"I'm sure Naftali knows when to pull out if he has to…" I grimaced again; the growing pressure started to expand from my head to my throat and chest. "He knows my limits… He won't want to lose his *creation* forever to someone he wants to kill."

"Are you sure?"

"Yes." I made sure the clip was emptied in her palm before gripping Guðmundr, not taking it just yet. "When I take this… watch my back."

"Wait, what are you doing?"

"Unplanned, stupid shit." I gave a small smirk to make her feel better. "I can't plan, remember?"

"This is suicide…"

"It's just change… It's what Dragon Knights and leaders are supposed to deal with and admittedly a really stupid game my sister and I used to play with Uncle Owen and Father. Use me accordingly. I'm trusting you with my life and what needs to be done. If that means abandoning me for both of us to live, then abandon me." She didn't look happy but gave a brief nod and I took the bracelet from her. "Go."

The shield dropped and we booked it through the gap that was made. On the other side, the light dome greeted us along with something that made our mad dash come to a staggering halt.

"Oh… gods…" Éabha managed to mutter out but I wasn't sure if that summarized the horror we were presented.

Where Naftali had been shot, his leg had grown, breaking through his pant leg. It was scaly like that of a dragon's and bending as such before going back to normal where his shoe was still on. His wings where I had hit him with the plasma were grotesque. The arch of three of them had lost their feathers, turning fleshy and veiny like they didn't have skin to block the muscles and tissues inside. Strange eyes grew out of them that were mixed between an orange dragon's and red or blue Seraphinean. His coat was shredded beyond where I had attacked and a new, lanky, purple-red arm thing had grown from it. It split at what would have been an elbow, separating between a long, four fingered hand with claws and dozens of teeth within a mouth on its palm. The other segment was several tentacles like some sort of squid.

I wanted to be sick but didn't have the chance to express anything as the scientist, or what was left of him, wasn't wasting time. Spheres of the three magics he had at his disposal were formed and fired. The attacks were less calculated, more spastic, making it somehow easier to dodge, block or deflect away. Éabha kept behind me, firing when an opening came, but it was easy to tell that her heart wasn't in it. Not that I blamed her. This was someone she grew up with and now was… whatever the Daemonias magic had done to him.

"What's happening to him?" I heard her ask and I shook my head, sending another attack back at Naftali. It was blocked by a tendril.

"I don't know."

"Can… Do we have to…?" She couldn't finish.

"Hopefully, we can still save him. He doesn't deserve any of this just for wanting to live."

"Maybe if I didn't focus so much on weapons… maybe I could-"

"Éabha, what more could you have done? You only just started learning about healing."

"I know." She fired at a sphere I couldn't block. "I know… Doesn't mean I can't wish."

I knew what she meant more than I could tell her as my head pounded again. The orders were gibberish, but it didn't hurt any less.

"We need to ground him. I'll tell you what to do when I think of something."

"Will you be-" I didn't get to finish my question as she left, tendrils and vines chasing after her as I wasn't given much of a choice: knock him out of the sky before she was caught.

It wasn't much of a plan and I hated it but accepted it. It's not like I'd be helping if I tried. The question was now… how the hell was I supposed to get him to our level without a plan?

I dashed at him, keeping him busy with slashes of plasma. Several of them were blocked with tendrils or orbs, but a couple went through, hitting and knocking him around. It didn't do much else as I kept the burning to a minimum. Each attack I gave, the gibberish was becoming clearer, making it difficult to keep up. A grunt came out as an attack strayed from my control. It went wide where Éabha was forced to backpedal whatever strategy she was trying to set up. I apologized and she gave a nod before leaving my view again.

I got close to Naftali and dropped the shield to send several fireballs at him. A strange snarl came from him as they tried to make their way but were blocked. A small growl came out as I tried again, trying to get closer but there wasn't an opening. The tendrils and vines blocked me from getting within three metres of him. The ground had a light field waiting for me to slip past. The dome above prevented flying…

"*You can't win,*" Naftali said, reading the depressing thought that passed my mind. "*Give in and I'll let her go.*"

"*Like hell you would.*"

"*So, you'd rather suffer-*"

"Now!" Éabha yelled through his words and I charged.

I didn't have a clue what she wanted me to do but went with instinct and put away Winterthorn. Tendrils blocked the way for about a second as Naftali focused on me only to be hit in the side of the head with a softened blow from Iðunn. The barrier vanished. He was barely in the air when I leaped at him. He looked at me just as I tackled his light frame out of the sky. The sound of a bone snapping in his chest came to my ears as I landed on him. The minor success was stopped as the mouthed hand tried to grab at my face. I reeled back before grabbing its wrist. The gauntlet's claws dug deep into the soft flesh and he screamed from the pain. I winced but the small part came back to enjoy his suffering.

It made me sick.

His wings tried to offset me while his extra appendages of tentacles wrapped around my arms when I tried to keep him down. They twisted, forcing me to decide to get off or break more bones which would have taken energy to heal. I took a third option, an idea that came from somewhere within. My head pulsed as I lunged forward and bit down on the main arm of the mutation. Blood reached my tongue within milliseconds as my teeth easily pierced through. I didn't think too hard about what created the thing I had in my mouth other than it was similar to being inside the Daemonias and I wasn't swallowing any of it or the saliva and blood that dripped down the side of my chin. The last thing I wanted was to ingest whatever was twisting him into some delusional monster.

The tentacles let me go through the screams. I grabbed the extra limb with my free hand, moving my knee to his chest. The claws dug deeper breaking the fragile bones inside and ripping skin. The idea built on itself, unsatisfied and not done with simply being free. I tightened my bite and tore. Muscle, skin, the broken bones between my teeth and hand severed and separated from each other. Blood spattered the ground and across my face. It powered the need for more. It finally ripped off with one final pull from my teeth. It wiggled still, nerves moving as I spat it out along with the blood, wiping my mouth with the back of my gauntlet. The pain that went through my head from the savage, animalistic action was topped by the physical screams of Naftali going through his earpiece. I reached for it only for him to notice immediately. A horrible jolt shot up my spine, forcing me to recoil.

I fell to the side as my screams went silent, the grip around my throat tightened at the denied orders. My muscles seized as I grovelled at his feet. He got up with the help of magic tendrils and a glare was sent down at me. A shiver of pure fear went through me. I didn't need to hear or feel the rage that came ripping through to know it fuelled the Daemonias sphere growing in his hand. I wanted to move, but my body and the blood that coursed through it obeyed the order to stay and suffer the consequences for my actions. A blur appeared through the growing darkness as something flew by his head. My body relaxed as soon as it hit the earpiece, ending the attack, causing him to scream.

He grabbed his head where his ear used to be, blood dripping down his arm. I started to get up when something grabbed my ankle. My head hit the hard floor – the world disappearing for a moment as I found myself dangling upside down. Reaching up for the light tendril that grabbed me did nothing as I was tossed violently to the side. I braced for a hard impact against the dome. It shattered just before I got to it when Naftali dropped in front of Éabha who was lowering her gun between the trees. I landed and rolled to a stop on some grass far from the garden.

My breathing was ragged as I laid there, wanting to relax… but knew that it wasn't over yet. The Zerach continued its automatic message. It wasn't as bad as direct control… but it was far from comfortable. If I passed out… I wasn't waking up my own person. I rolled over, picking myself up with a groan after several minutes. My head and body pulsed and staggered. My hands went to my knees and I puked. The action was painful all on its own and my vision darted in and out.

Why hadn't Éabha turned off the Zerach yet?

I looked over, trying to figure out what happened to see a dragon dart in, smacking something in a tree, and the familiar scream of Éabha came to my ears.

Chapter Forty-Nine: A Rancorous Reappearance

I was left to watch, not steady enough to move as a nebula dragon dropped back out of the blinding sun. He attacked Éabha as she flew in and out of sight. When did he show up? I wasn't down for that long, was I? Even if I was... Why was Gabriellos attacking her at all? Why was Theodora...

If she was there, where was Ciar?

I looked around, hearing fire crackle and the smell of smoke reached my nose. There was no evidence that he was around. Not that it mattered. Éabha wasn't in the condition to go against Theodora and Gabriellos, let alone trained to do so. I stood up straight and dashed for the opening again. My run came to a tired stopped under the vine arch. It was too dizzy to keep going and my legs threatening to stop working all together. I scanned the open gathering spot, a bit surprised that it wasn't as damaged from the fights as I thought it would have been. Both women were on opposite sides of the dance floor, Éabha getting up from a broken bench, using what was left as a crutch and retrieved Iðunn that had fallen nearby. Theodora on the other hand was flicking her ponytail aside, her hair a bit longer than the last time I had seen her.

The woman I still loved got up from a destroyed garden plot and sent out a loaded magic strike at Éabha who had started to aim her gun. The seraph stopped aiming and threw up her gauntlets to defend, but it wasn't enough as the attack knocked her back into an ancient tree behind her. A sharp scream was cut off and she landed on the roots, unconscious. My heart skipped a beat as Theodora stalked up to my defenceless friend and my body finally let me move again in desperation. She went to stab as Éabha woke, eyes widening in terror and I stepped between them. My blade blocked the blow. Theodora's aggression turned to shock as she moved away in a backwards bound.

I glared at her as my blade lowered and a growl of rage came out. "What are you doing here with Ciar and attacking innocent people?!"

She said nothing, only giving a similar look I had seen on her face as few months prior: shame.

"Are you truly working with him? If you are, do you know what his people have done?! They've kidnapped-" A new, excruciating pain ripped through my head and body causing me to scream and drop to the smooth floor as the Zerach was used again but very differently from before.

"Aerrow, what's wrong?" The concern in Theodora's voice wasn't how I wanted to hear her again after so long and it hurt almost as much as the Zerach did. I glared over at the machine but couldn't see who was using it. The attack grew, searing my vessels, and I writhed. She knelt beside me for a moment and tried to comfort me but the slightest touch of her fingers moving through my hair caused another stifled scream. My chest compressed. The orders were incoherent, but simply breathing seemed to be against them. She asked a different question. "Seraph, what the fuck is happening?"

"The Zerach," Éabha answered and sounded just as terrified. "Where's Naftali?"

"Stop…" I begged, knowing that even if it wasn't very loud, he could hear it. It was him, Naftali… The orders were the same pattern. A squeak came out as my heart rate felt like it was slowing despite the feeling of electricity tearing through my body at rapid propulsions. The attack continued and begging only served to fuel his warped ambition.

Finally, the voice came back, the strain of a new earpiece being added to the throbbing torture that the machine was doing on its own. *"You're not getting away..."*

"Naftali, stop it!" Éabha demanded as Theodora stood up. "You're killing him!"

"I know I am..." he agreed in my head and a dial was turned. I wanted to scream, but it was impossible from the lack of air. *"Join me, Little Dragon, and I'll give you rest. The pain will stop, and you'll be able to help me help the world. Or you can die here."*

Each word pelted my brain as I curled up, coughing. The taste of blood came to my tongue. "N-no…"

"So, that's why you came here…" Theodora's voice was more than cold and sent chills up my spine at the ruthlessness of it. I managed to look up at her for a moment as she stared at the bushes where the Zerach sat. Her glare deepened. "There you are."

A scream came from Naftali as I felt the claws of Gabriellos slice through his back like it was done to my own and my body stopped struggling, unable to get the energy to seize. My breaths were hardly considered shallow. I couldn't keep him out…

"Aerrow-" Éabha started but Theodora interrupted her.

"Don't move."

"He needs a doctor!"

"He'll be fine in a moment, heal from there and nothing else."

A small warmth came from Éabha, but it was weakened by the lack of magic she had left. A dark shadow flew over as I felt Naftali stumble out of the brambles, forced out by Gabriellos. He attacked, the ground turning into a strange hybrid of light and dark magic. Daemonias magic came from more than his hands as he somehow grew the limb I tore off and then some with two other limbs, all ready to attack.

"Lea-" I tried to warn but was stopped as another silent scream came out. His will shattered through the movements I wanted to make.

Theodora's polearm was suddenly thrown out, its edge sliced through his exposed neck, limbs, and wings behind it. The blade lodged itself cleanly into a tree further past the Zerach as the head of the mutated being rolled off to the side, bouncing off the machine, and sprayed blood from the severed ends onto everything around it. The body stood there longer than I thought it should have with its normal and mutated legs before it fell out of sight.

It took a moment for the last bit of brain activity to die out through the earpiece before the anguish ceased back down to levels where it was just the machine. The malice that had been contained to his body and extra limbs stayed with the graphic scene, glimmering almost on the blood. It was fading slowly. I knew it wasn't being fuelled by anything now, but still it fed on what it could for its final moments. I grimaced at the prospect of its true nature.

The healing from Éabha gave out a large burst then stopped as she gave out an exasperated noise. She fell back into the tree and I gave her a thankful glance, feeling a million times better than I had been. A glow coming from Theodora's wrist drew me back to the revealingly dressed woman. A bracelet sat on her fair skin in a design that I didn't recognize but felt like it was uniquely hers. Her blade returned to her awaiting hand and the bracelet stopped shining.

I swallowed in discomfort, trying to find my words at her new creation and managed to get to a stand. "Thank you but… why did you do that? He is one of Ciar's wasn't he?"

"I was planning on killing him for kidnapping and torturing whelps and you once everything was said and done, not realizing what he was doing with his machine." She gave a sneer in disgust. "Or what he had become."

"Wasn't he following-"

"Ciar doesn't give out such barbaric orders, certainly nothing that can turn into this. He tries to avoid confrontations that are unnecessary. He didn't want the Megalona Danguis Tribe involved, Naftali and his parade of followers disobeyed the interest of what their god wanted."

"Their god, but not yours?" It wasn't much of a question but rather a statement, hoping that she wasn't really in league with people who had killed so many.

A cold, blank face was all I received that reminded me of the days when we hated each other, neither confirming nor denying my question. Gabriellos landed next to her, barely giving me an acknowledgment. Her tone lightened, a hint of affection came through, warming and tearing at my heart. "I'll keep your little secret to myself."

"Wait, Theodora-"

"I suggest you put on a pair of sunglasses; easier to see him coming."

"See who-"

She didn't let me finish my question as she mounted her dragon and took off. I dug out my sunglasses, putting them on to try and see where they went only to be met with a black mass diving down. I grabbed Éabha by the wrist and bounded backwards. The tug to get her out of the way was more of a throw as she landed in a small bush on the other side of the space. She squeaked as she bounced off and onto the ground. I placed up a large shield and gave her a quick look over to make sure she was fine.

The mass landed just as I turned back, a powerful wave of energy expelled from it. It bounced off the shield, protecting the two of us from the magic that cracked the stonework underfoot, ripping up the bushes, and causing several large branches to break. The magic dissipated, showing the damage around us was only a fraction compared to where it had come from. The tree where we had been a moment before was uprooted and destroyed and the stone patio was turned to gravel. Ciar stood up from the centre of the small crater, pulling his sword from the earth with ease even though it was half embedded into the rock, stretching his four, massive, black, draconic wings. He turned to me and the shield dropped as I lost concentration. He took one step forward. I took two steps back, my neck and chest scars aching.

I didn't want to fight him. I couldn't-

A blank expression came from under his hooded cloak that he didn't have before, red eyes aglow as his glance moved from my face to the rest of me, stopping briefly at the appendages I couldn't get rid of due to the Zerach. No words came from him nor an expression that he was surprised other than a small flick of his own tail that seemed to have become a little larger since the last time.

He took another step forward and I tried to take a few steps back but was stopped by a bush. Éabha was beside me, but I didn't look away from the monster. I couldn't look away – could barely breathe let alone tell her to flee. He stopped moving towards me, sending out a black sphere of magic instead. I reacted, deflecting it away with Winterthorn. The rebounded attack hit one of the ancient trees, blasting half of its trunk into nothingness.

Éabha's healing did a lot of work, but the movement highlighted my body's exhaustion was back to about where she healed me the last time. If I had to fight… it wasn't going to… It had to be as long as I could hold out.

How long was that truly though?

He charged and I panicked, thankfully not freezing but dodging out of the way. Éabha moved before I could trip over her and went behind him. Another sphere of death came at me and I moved again, not bothering to deflect. He cut me off and brought down his blade. Winterthorn met his, both were pulled back then clashed again. The strikes were definitely stronger than the last time… but somehow, I held them back without much difficulty.

His blade activated and changed the dynamic power difference immediately. I pushed back, surprisingly getting him off of me and moved away. I couldn't let him take any of the energy I had left. The prospect of him killing me because I collapsed gripped harder than expected, stopping my retreat immediately. I swallowed, trying to get over the paralyzing fear.

Ciar looked surprised for the first time at how far I had pushed him away before going back to a neutral expression, adjusting his blade. Movement came from behind him, and I looked to it, seeing Éabha aiming her shotgun. The look betrayed her as he noticed the split-second shift in gaze and swiped out his tail. She was caught with it, the scales creating a loud, cracking noise as they hit her armoured chest, and smashed her against the damaged tree. A splintering snap went through my ears and I saw that the tree she laid under about to fall.

"Éabha! Mov-" My warning was cut short as his tail turned on me.

My body found another large tree and a small squeak escaped from the lack of air that had been knocked out. I bounced off it slightly, landing on the ground as Éabha screamed. I looked up to the tree that had fallen and trapped her, the world spinning and darkening. Ciar moved away and abandoned me, easily seeing I was a mess, unable to get up as my arms gave out, and went for her. My body screamed at me to stop, to hide from the creature that had hurt it so deeply, but I ignored it, using my wings to help pick myself up and charged.

I couldn't let someone else I cared about be killed by him!

My sword loaded itself with magic subtlety. "Your opponent is me!"

He turned, not expecting me to be there so fast and got my plasmic sword through his chest. It burnt and tore his cloak off as I ripped it upwards and through his broken armour. Guðmundr went up and bashed him across the clearing with an adrenaline fused battle cry. He smashed through a larger tree, causing it to fall over, and into the bushes of the garden maze but he didn't get up. I turned to Éabha, breathing heavily as she stared up at me in what seemed like awe.

I went to help her only for her to shake her head. "Leave me."

I stopped. "But you can't stay under there."

"I can," she sighed, propping her head under folded arms. "I built amazing armour… somehow still active after that. But it's just a bit fucking uncomfortable and not going to last so, you know, take care of his ass sooner rather than later?"

"I'll do my best…" I heard movement come from my left.

We looked over as Ciar got up with a growl. Blood was spat out and he charged at me again. I met him halfway, fuelling my blade with magic and keeping him as far from Éabha as I could. Guðmundr formed, catching his blade as it went under his strike. His blade went up and I stabbed in his open flank, releasing the excess energy. He moved away before I could shift the blade to do more damage and sent several balls of energy at me. I retreated strategically, keeping his focus on me so nothing could stray towards Éabha while still keeping in range just in case he tried to do what he did to Father.

A field of dark magic formed on the ground from him that was nothing like the element magic I knew of. I left the ground, using my wings to get away from the daunting horror that awaited below. He countered, knowing what I would do, and flew directly into me before throwing my helpless form onto it. Dark wisps grabbed at my body, thorns somehow forming and piercing through the clothing and armour that was still active. A sharp scream came out as I fought against their hold.

Ciar came down on me with his blade. The memory of him impaling me came back and I activated the shield at the last second. His thrust penetrated the shield but stopped only a few inches from my chest. He tried to push through it but couldn't and had trouble withdrawing his blade. The shield repaired the hole that was made. The wispy thorns dug deeper, trying to crush my armour but couldn't get around the new upgrades which saved me from getting the full attack.

I struggled further. I had to get out before they broke through. I was still a light element being. They were going to rip me apart with ease, painfully if he so chose. They squeezed, making it hard to breathe as another scream came out. Their very touch burned.

"Cease the struggle and give in, Godling," Ciar growled in irritation with almost a rasp to his voice, clearly trying to hide his pain. He clenched the wisps again. Their thorns penetrated the dragon scales as another cry came out, but I didn't drop the dome. He tsked. "This could have been merciful."

"Merciful... you don't know the meaning- ack!" The wisps crushed, the armour keeping strong, but the unarmoured places were starting to lose the barrier the tech provided.

Ciar struck the shield again as I glared, trying anything but all the effort caused the wisps to attack more. My fire was quickly absorbed into it instead of forming into a plasma ball.

Was there anything I could do? If not... how long before he gave up or helped arrived? Would he go after Éabha?

The Zerach called again, and my head pulsed in pain. The shield fizzled out for a moment before forming just as Ciar hit it. The wisps tightened and I heard something in my chest plate crack. Thorns stabbed into new areas relentlessly and another scream came out. A wisp went around my throat, cutting off air flow almost as fast as it had attacked. The thorns tried to prick through my skin but couldn't get past what was left of the armour's shields. But it didn't need to. I couldn't breathe.

I fought against it further, getting somewhere and nowhere, trying to free at least an arm to try and get the thing strangling me. The shield wavered under a strike. Éabha's warning about Guðmundr being useless if I was unconscious repeated in my head.

A different voice spoke inside my head, but the words were muffled and sparse. It wasn't the same voice as the woman before, certainly not Deigh... It tried again, coming through as a young boy that I somewhat recognized, but didn't know how. *"Use his magic like I did with Owen."*

That was easier said than done as I did what he suggested and tried to manipulate it. The magic trying to rip me apart, trying to crush my throat and windpipe, was so very different from Owen's. It felt older. Much, much older. Nothing like the element's evolved form. The wisps gripped tighter, threatening to succeed at any moment.

The voice pressed, "*It's the same chaotic state. Like fire to plasma, plasma to light. Darkness to the eldritch abyss.*"

Eldritch… That sounded pleasant and exactly like something I wanted to play with.

"*Strangle to death then. See if I care.*"

The voice's presence disappeared and left me with two choices and no time to decide. My will to live answered the call and forced itself onto the dark field, letting me analyze it better.

The field was different and as old as it was… it wasn't weaker, but Ciar's grasp of it was significantly less understood by him compared to Owen's control over the element. Perhaps I didn't have to battle for control using pure magic potential. I knew more of its properties and how it worked compared to Ciar after spending most of my life training against it. It wasn't like his spheres or his wall that he hadn't been able to put up this time. They were far stranger and a very different kind of magic, not something of this world. A small tsk escaped.

Yet it wasn't enough for him… He had to find more and get stronger. Somehow coming across whatever this new, or rather ancient, form of magic was.

I gripped at the pool, physically and mentally, and applied my will and understanding to it. The thorns removed themselves as their grip lessened, allowing my poor throat to pass air through it. I started coughing as I rolled over slightly and almost puked in the process. Ciar stopped pelting against my shield as he tried to regain control of the field, but I didn't give it back. I solidified a large wisp, giving him a glare to say what my damaged throat couldn't, and shoved it through his chest. It spread throughout his insides like tiny vines climbing a fence and he gasped in pain. The shield dropped as the Zerach threatened to take over my mind again. I chose to focus on the wisp inside him.

Ciar swung his sword in my open form but was stopped with a quick movement of the archaic shadows. They gripped around his blade, not allowing him to move it at all. I staggered to a stand and shifted the wisp inside him. He grovelled and knelt before me, trapping him from being able to do anything. I readied to bring my sword down on him but stopped.

He had murdered so many of my people. He killed my father in front of me in a cheap tactic. Caused my mother to suffer by injecting her with his venomous virus. He had made my sister cry almost every night in her sleep, taking away a mother before she could remember her and a father she loved like no one else. I wanted to kill him for everything he directly and indirectly had done. But I hesitated and the words I told to Claudius came back in the gory tunnel.

If I killed whoever it is out of vengeance, what makes me so different from them?

It was up to the king… and that king was now me…

Killing the person responsible won't bring them back.

The question he asked after that still had no answer. Ciar had killed the king, but I still didn't know what I would do.

I wanted him to suffer, to be brutally murdered by my hand… But still I didn't want that.

It wouldn't heal the wounds. For a moment it would feel good… but the people who had deserved and received a similar fate only left my conscience horrified.

I couldn't kill him like this…

The few milliseconds that had passed had allowed my taken wisp to rip into him further, blood dripping down the side of his chin. This was enough. He was defeated and captured.

I went to lower my blade only for Daemonias magic to scrape briefly past my senses from him not surrendering. My sword came down on him, the outcome of self-defence and pure fear as my head slipped back to that day. It connected with his unprotected neck and chest plate, slipping past the protection of his pauldron just as he blasted a sphere into my chest with his empty, trapped hand.

The attack knocked the air out of me for the millionth time that day. I hit a tree, breaking branches with my back and fell through them as they were unable to hold my weight, landing on the ground. My armour powered down – succeeding in doing its job of keeping my limbs attached.

A screech from hell came to my ears and I looked up just in time for him to retreat with a glare, bloodied and holding his neck and effectively bringing the fight to a draw. I went to get up, just in case, but the portal shut with another scream. My body gave out and fell over, laying on my back, breathing heavily. The fight went better than expected… even with his new ability and strength… I had managed to keep up. Who knew Naftali's insanity did me a favour after all this?

A different thought crept into my mind. The feeling of something being off. The new power I was capable of it... it didn't make sense.

Something landed on cracked stone and I panicked, gripping at my sword and lifted it slightly off the ground, charged. Had Ciar-

Deigh, Uncle Owen, the knights, and their dragons saw me as I recognized them, and dropped my sword and arm in relief. They came over but I didn't get up. It hurt too much to do so. The adrenaline ending now that helped had arrived. My throat felt like it was healing as I used my voice, a bit painfully so, but put as much feeling as I could into the breath of a whisper. "I am so very, very sorry."

"Oh, we know you are since it wasn't your fault, but how could you leave us to rot in a heat box of awful!" Azarias spat and I flinched. He was a little more than pissed off, but I didn't blame him. "Then you were gone when the cage dropped and Deigh couldn't find you! We thought you were kidnapped again and Deigh almost went into expiration shock a second time! Do you have any idea how long it took to find you?!"

"Azarias, enough," Owen sighed, noticing that my apology I had tried to say again didn't come out. He knelt beside me and inspected my neck. "Don't get him to talk too much with your complaining."

"Look, all I'm saying is that he should leave a postcard or something next time."

"Yeah, because that's something he could have done." Owen turned back to me with a small frown. "That Daemonias Portal, was that Ciar's?"

I gave a nod, not answering with words and he looked to the tree beside me.

"Are you feeling well enough to sit up? I don't want you moving too much, but we're going to have to leave shortly."

"Y-yeah..." I winced and he sighed, muttering a breathless insult at my stupidity of not following the implied instruction to not talk and helped me lean against the tree.

I flinched again. My wings and tail didn't enjoy being pressed against in the slightest. Deigh became my focus as I noticed blood covered her front claw she barely stood on, and I gritted my teeth. I couldn't read her thoughts, but I could feel a bit of her emotion and she was upset if not furious. Everything from me attacking her to her not being able to stop me.

"Is there any…" My voice stopped working but she understood what I was asking and gave a small glare.

"I want you to forgive yourself. I know exactly what you were going against and Naftali knew your condition was perfect for the least amount of resistance." Her glare softened a bit as she read my answer that I was unable to say. "If you can't do it now… then fish me one of the water monsters that lives in Seraphina Lake."

I gave her an agreeing look.

"And I want to go shopping with you before we leave."

I nodded.

"I'm buying something expensive."

"N-not too…"

"Not too expensive so we can pay for the trip back," she agreed.

I relaxed only to tense again as a loud, dramatic sigh came from the outskirts of the clearing. We all turned and saw Éabha looking about as thrilled as a turtle on its back being eaten alive. Her voice held the same amount of joy. "Wow, such a heart-filled moment. Now if only I could have enjoyed it not under a fucking tree."

I got to a stand with the help of my tree. "Oh gods… I forgot."

"I didn't, fucking, notice…"

I started towards her, not thinking it entirely though on how useless I would have been as Owen stopped my approach. Missiletainn carried out the task, removing the tree easily and releasing the poor Seraph. Owen sighed again, sounding a bit disappointed in me. "I wanted to go slowly, but I suppose you're up now."

"Sor-" My apology was cut short with a raspy scream, if it could be called that, as the Zerach attacked again. A sharp pain went through my body and my vision darkened. Winterthorn dropped out of my hand, clattering to the broken stone floor as I gripped my head, trying desperately to stay conscious. "The Zerach… it's still…"

"Where's Naftali?" Owen asked and after what seemed like forever, my voice seemed a little less sore, but I wasn't sure if it was because other parts of my body were higher in pain priority.

"In there, somewhere."

Cyrus went over to the machine. A small noise of disgust came from him and then suddenly, the pain ceased. My legs gave out from the freedom leaving Owen and Azarias to catch me before I fell too far. The partial transformation ability finally came to an end and all the extra weight went with it, but the gone limbs still left behind the pain of being injured. It wasn't something the book mentioned and knowing it, was something I had to be aware of going forward. A breathless thank you came out, but they didn't test to see if I could stand on my own. I certainly didn't think I could. They adjusted me; an arm placed around each of their shoulders.

Owen gave a small, cheeky smile of reassurance. "Easy there… you've had quite the day."

"No kidding…"

"Aw, your coat is soaked in blood!" Azarias growled in distaste but didn't let me go. "What the hell did you do this time?!"

"Thorny wisps mostly… no, it doesn't make sense but it's Ciar's new power."

"He didn't do his venom bullshit, did he?"

I shook my head as Éabha answered for me, joining us. "He didn't get close enough to attack either of us with it." A loud screech from a very large Outland Monster came to our ears. "Right… They're still around."

"We need to go," Owen stated mostly for Éabha to hear rather than the rest of us. He turned to me. "You're riding with me until we can heal Deigh at the next safehouse far from the city."

I gave a small nod then remembered what I had promised earlier. "Éabha, your father is in the lobby of the demesne. He needs medical attention and is extremely worried for you."

"Dad's hurt?!" She squeaked and I nodded but before anyone could say anything, she took off towards the main entrance.

Cyrus and Tempest went after her as Azarias and Owen helped me on Missiletainn. Azarias called Cyrus to tell him to take care of Éabha and Orpheal and to meet us at the safehouse with the Zerach. Once Owen knew I wasn't going to fall off in case I passed out, we left.

Chapter Fifty: Torn in Two

I looked over the machine in front of me. Blood of its co-creator was still smeared on its surface from a few hours ago but the corruption I had seen before had faded. I turned to the plans in my hand for a final check before grabbing the portion I wanted and ripped it out, purposely breaking its slot so nothing else could be placed there. It evaporated in the matter of a second within my hand as I looked to the others in the room. Éabha looked devastated at what I had done while Orpheal seemed impartial. The knights gave little to no care at the decision.

"*Good riddance...*" Deigh muttered, still curled up in her bed upstairs. "*Hopefully, this is the last of this nonsense.*"

"*Hopefully... but you're supposed to be resting.*"

"*I am resting, you want me sleeping.*"

I laughed a bit through the link and let her be, addressing Orpheal who was looking a lot healthier than when I had left him in the demesne. "The machine is still a great use... but I want all records of it being even a possibility to be able to control Outland Dragons from every source erased: hard copies, logs, digital records, everything. Outland Dragons or anything with a soul should not and will not be controlled, doesn't matter how awful they might be."

"Understood, King Aerrow..." Orpheal answered almost hesitantly under my tone. It was a bit harsh, but after dealing with the affects personally, I was a bit bitter. I didn't want anyone to go through what I had. "I'll make sure everything is gone when I head back to the city."

I relaxed, changing the subject. "Is it safe for you to go back there right now?"

"The monsters have been killed. My general just reported that once the dragons left, it was rather easy to clean up the monsters and as a bonus, she and her team have captured several zealots and placed them into custody."

"Io's actually beat me to something for once..." Owen muttered with almost amazement and I looked over at him.

"You know his general?"

"I do, but it's a story for another time."

Must have been a long one. I gave a small nod, going back to the zealots. "Hopefully, they can give more information about Ciar."

"That and if they can't with words, their blood samples should provide some key elements we're missing to figure out Daemonias magic along with Ciar's blood that we grabbed from your blade." He turned somber. "It's too bad that the handful is hardly a victory compared to the cost of lives in their murder-suicide tendencies when in a corner. We lost a lot of people today... but it would have been worse if the dragons had stayed and were under Naftali's control, so thank you for doing that instead of running like you should have."

"The dragons were rightfully upset, but they had to know that they weren't going to find their answers in Domrael Hill, I'm just sorry I couldn't have stopped it sooner."

Orpheal looked ready to apologize for something else when Éabha cut him off. "Just stop... you are both sorry for things you didn't do. We get it. Move on."

"Éabha..." Orpheal sighed, giving up on scolding her further. He turned back to us. "What are your plans now?"

"I think it's been decided that we're going to stick around until things are more settled, help patrol if need be until your barrier is repaired. Azarias informed me that three of your barrier towers were destroyed."

"We have spares that will be fully installed and activated over the next couple of days. You should rest for the time being, all of you... Like taking off your armour for starters."

I looked down at the damaged armour before giving a small, cheeky grin. "It was originally in case monsters followed us... but then I forgot I was wearing it when I woke up..."

Éabha facepalmed while her father simply shook his head. "At any rate, Fyliel has agreed to come tomorrow to assist with your healing and to do a thorough look over to find any adverse affects between the lab incident and the Zerach as a second opinion. She hasn't been informed of the details other than Naftali had experimented on you and any of her findings will not leave this house. If anything else is required, I'll proceed but I pray that there are no other surprises."

"That's not necessary."

"It is. For my conscience and your kingdom's," he answered with a finalizing tone that I last heard from my father. I stopped arguing by instinct and gave a nod. "Good… in the meantime, you should rest and before you leave, maybe you can explore Rath Hill. It's a city like Domrael and I doubt that any zealots would expect you to be there."

"That sounds nice… I'm sure Deigh will be happy to go shopping someplace new."

"I've never gone to Rath Hill," Éabha commented, almost excitedly. "If you want company, maybe we could explore it together."

A smile formed. "I'd like that."

"It'll have to be after the memorial if you're going Éabha," Orpheal said in a way that sounded annoyed for her not asking for permission first. I could feel her wanting to roll her eyes, but she didn't. He looked back. "I'd offer you to come join us for the mourning of those who died, but it'd still be unsafe even with Ciar defeated."

"A lot of people could get hurt at the ceremony. The zealots will be expecting one of us to attend," Owen agreed and Orpheal nodded.

"I'll tell those who attended that you wanted to be there but could not when I chastise those following Ciar. The people of Seraphina will understand your absence."

"I'll make sure to visit the location before leaving. It'd be wrong not to do so even if it's only for a few moments," I told him. Suddenly, something moved behind him, distracting me. I focused on it as an outline of a small dragon appeared, moving about before disappearing again. A shiver went up my spine. "What the…"

"Everything alright, Aerrow?" Owen asked and I turned to him, cautious to look away from the last place I had seen the small shadow.

"I don't know… I think so but, I could have sworn I saw a ghost."

He furrowed his brows, turning to where I was looking. "There doesn't seemed to be anything now nor am I aware of this place being haunted in anyway… perhaps you need that rest now."

"I've rested-"

"It wasn't a suggestion. Napping on the way here and for an hour while we waited is not resting. You need to actually sleep."

"But the whelps…" I was not happy about being sidelined.

"Most likely in the facility that we found you and likely heavily guarded. It'd be suicide to go with the number of monsters around right now."

"I see… It's been a while since something was suicide for you."

"Some of us know our limits," he jabbed before growing a little more serious but endearing. "We'll get to them, but we can't help them if we die in the process."

I gave a tiny agreement, thinking back on the building I was in, not that I remembered much. "How did you guys find me anyway?"

"Azarias had a surprise visitor when we were split up and searching for you."

I turned to Azarias, noticing the dragon outline appeared again, almost prancing around the knight then disappeared. I kept the weird hallucination to myself. "Who visited you?"

The usually chipper knight put his hands in his pockets, turning to the picture on the wall on the other side of the room, sombrely. "Your ex."

"What?"

"Theodora, she was hiding in a dark corner of the alleyway you were taken when I was triple checking the area since the best place to hide is right under someone's nose. She told me that you weren't going to be right in the head, crazed was the word she used. I asked her how she knew, but she didn't give an answer as she disappeared through a Chaos Portal, not of her making. I think her dragon made it, he's a fire-dark element dragon, right?"

"As far as I'm aware."

He gave a small nod. "She was really pissed. Not at me, but at whoever took you, which I guess we know was Naftali… She still has feelings for you."

"Explains why she refused to attack when I got there and killed Naftali without hesitation…" Regret and satisfaction collided for a space in my head making me a bit numb on how to feel about the outcome. "Sorry that Naftali couldn't be saved."

"She might have done us a favour," Éabha said after a few moments of silence. Her voice was a bit shaky. "We tried everything we could, and he still wouldn't stop trying to have you – if it wasn't for her, he would have won and killed me at the very least."

"Still…" The regret won against the victory of revenge as Orpheal stayed silent. "But you're probably right… and if it wasn't for her vaguely telling us that Ciar was coming, he would have killed the both of us just at his grand entrance."

"He would have…" She shook her head. "I want to be mad at how it turned out but… It could have been so much worse."

I gave a small nod as a wall of exhaustion appeared from out of nowhere. "Okay… If no one minds, I'm going to retire for the rest of the day I think… you guys should get some rest too. Orpheal, please let one of us know where and when if you need help with anything."

He nodded and I started walking towards the stairs of the large, wooden lodge. I got about halfway up the stairs when I heard rushing air coming from behind me.

Éabha's voice called, "Aerrow, wait."

I turned as she landed on the step below and gave her a confused look. "Something wrong?"

"No… well, yes. I appreciate you saving me, again."

"Always happy to do that." I smiled a bit at her sheepishness. "I'm just happy Theodora didn't kill you. She's a dangerous opponent."

"Yes… strong, talented; she's terrifying. I wouldn't be surprised if Ciar was the one who recruited her and not the other way around."

"You think so?"

"No, I know so. Her weapon designs are part of the standard Dragon Knight gear and even her armour is beautiful crafted. That's a custom build created by a genius… speaking of custom builds, I have an offer I wish to propose."

"Like what?"

"I want to rebuild your armour, fix it to accommodate your wings in case you decided to use them again. I'll even attach wing armour like Dad's. It should keep you from getting dark thorns of death piercing through you. If you fight Ciar again, that's going to be a problem, especially if he gets stronger. You're still part light and that makes you very vulnerable to them."

"He's certainly developed a new trick in only three months…"

"Yes, along with his power rating. It's already a thousand, the same as yours."

"I'm sorry, what? Last we checked; it couldn't reach nine-hundred."

She tossed her meter at me and I looked at it to see the number for me was nine-hundred-eighty-five, more than a hundred points from the last time she brought it out. "The Outland blood spiked your magic potential. When you were fighting Ciar, I had nothing else better to do other than do something productive or get myself killed by trying to help. So, I did both of your readings out of curiosity. Both of you went up to a thousand with ease, playing around the thousand-ten mark at times. Your natural elements are fire and light, right?"

"Last I checked…"

"Make a plasma ball as pure to light as possible."

I eyed her with uncertainty as I handed her back the device but did as she asked. Keeping it small and the heat contained, I did my best to focus on the light aspect over the fire. It was black and white at first, quickly thickening into an incredibly bright, white orb that forced me to look away from it slightly. "Good enough?"

"Yeah, it confirms my theory," she stated, and I closed my gauntleted hand, removing the orb. "I think with this new add-in, the blood broke your little rule about Absalomians never being able to use an opposing element. This plasma ball was almost pure light and in that last battle, you used dark magic. I don't know what the consequences of that would be since it's never happened before without the Daemonias, but I do know a great deal of magic is coming from you. My new theory on why the new DNA didn't register as a foreign object but a necessary one once it was low enough is because the magic created a similar symbiotic relationship with your cells. As to why none of the other experiments that came before you had a similar outcome well, that is still in the air. Might have to do with the percentage of dragon in your blood, the same reason why you, and theoretically your sister, are able to survive Ciar's venom under the right circumstances."

"Maybe…" I didn't have much to say as my thoughts couldn't focus on words.

I hadn't registered that I had used dark magic. I knew I used it, but… it hadn't entirely clicked until now. It should have been impossible. The consequence of developing an opposing element was death. That's it. End of discussion. I should have been dead. The evidence of it had been seen time and time again within my kingdom where parents of opposing elements tried to have children and the child, unfortunately claimed both. They never made it to term, a miscarriage. It was heartbreaking. It didn't happen extremely often with a ten percent chance, but it was a risk the lovers would have known about.

And yet... I was still breathing.

"So!" Éabha started again, breaking me out of the horrible path I was about to go down. "Hand over your armour and I'll get started on it right away!"

"Uh... right now?"

"No... I was thinking after Ciar attacks you again."

"But it's-"

"Does it look like I give a shit if it's covered in blood, Airhead? No, they can be cleaned with a Dagdian spell so take it all off and hand it over. I have to upgrade them."

"I..." I sighed and took off my gauntlets, putting Guðmundr on my wrist and handed them to her. She stood there, waiting, and I rolled my eyes. "You want all of it this very moment?"

"Certainly more than just your gauntlets. These things weren't damaged in our fights."

I shook my head, taking off my pauldron, my belt, removing Winterthorn that had been cleaned when the samples were taken, and then my coat, dropping them loudly on top of the gauntlets. Blood stained my white shirt as she grimaced ever so slightly before turning to my boots. I gave them to her with a sigh. "Have fun... I guess..."

"I will! Good night!"

My annoyance at stripping an entire layer faded at her enthusiasm and a small smile formed. "Yeah, good night if I don't see you later."

She grinned cheekily before bounding down the stairs and I turned around, seeing the outline of the dragon at the top of the stairs. It stared down at me before disappearing. I looked back at Éabha as she went around the corner and my shoulders dropped in defeat. She would have said something if there was something truly there.

I climbed the rest of the way, asking Deigh to check my head for trauma. I was either going insane or an injury I caused that my healing ability or the healing I had received had yet to take care of. I knew the external healing magic had reached saturation from everything else that had happened over the last twenty-four hours, so hopefully, the weird hallucination would go away sooner rather than later.

I crossed through the kitchen, swiping a bag of unprotected jerky instead of the salted fish-shaped crackers and left, shoving a piece in my mouth. I was starving again, despite eating food when the others-

This jerky was amazing.

I popped another piece in my mouth as the first one was devoured and went to my room, closing the door behind me.

00000

A loud ringing noise woke Deigh and I to the darkness of night. It stopped after a few moments as my exhaustion registered it as nothing more than noises from the city. I rolled over. The ringing came back, reminding me that I wasn't in the city at all. I groaned in irritation.

What was that noise?

The vibrating of a table came from beside my head and on it was a small light of the CT glaring onto the bedside table, barely seeping out of its slight ridges. I grabbed it and hit the answer button, bringing it to my ear. "H-hello…?"

"He's going after the gate!" Atlamillia practically screamed in my ear, waking me up. Her voice cracked in a way that made my heart skip a beat. "He's going to open it!"

"Hey, it's okay, slow down," I started, sitting up and trying to calm her down. I adjusted my pj top and stifled a yawn. "Who is doing what with gates?"

"Ciar! He's going after the gate!"

"Absalom's Gate?" I left my bed, allowing Deigh to go back to sleep as I tried to figure out what she was trying to say.

I was confused, a bit annoyed at being awakened, but she sounded like she was holding back tears. I closed the door behind me quietly. The rest of the house was dark and silent. A figure moved slightly on the couch, catching me a bit off guard. I relaxed, recognizing it was just Éabha sleeping, her blanket on the floor.

Atlamillia kept rambling out a bunch of nonsense, nothing I could register as words, and panicked over something. She was talking at a million kilometres an hour. I went over to Éabha, picking up her blanket and set the CT between my ear and shoulder, freeing up my hands. The blanket was set nicely back on the small Seraph. I left, wandering over to the kitchen and closed the door behind me as I could guess her rambles were going to end soon and I didn't want to wake Éabha by talking.

After a few more moments of fast talking, her words came to an end, allowing me to ask the important question that she never got around to answering. "What gate is Ciar trying to open?"

"The one under Dagda."

"Atla... There's no gate of anything under Dagda... Maybe district gates-"

"There is a gate under Dagda! It's the same feeling as Ciar's spheres. The Daemonias came out of it when he opened it!"

"Alright, alright... So, there's a gate that possibly has to do with the Daemonias?"

"No. It is the Daemonias Realm. That's where the tear happened."

"That's where... How can you be so confident that that is exactly where Orithina and Valrdis ripped space? This planet is huge."

"Because I just do! And Ciar is going there soon if he hasn't left already! You have to go stop him!"

"Have you talked with Owen yet?"

"Yes. He mentioned your fight with Ciar but that means nothing! That gate-"

"I know, it's important. But I can't just go to Dagda, tell Thaloth that there is some gate under his kingdom, and some monster is trying to open it," I explained to her and wandered over to the fridge. There was some leftover rare steak from supper. Before yesterday, I had never tried steak that was barely cooked before but was happy that Orpheal brought them over. I took a slab from the container and stuck it on a plate. "I need evidence and to be invited. For all we know, there isn't a gate."

She gave out a growl as I slightly heated up the meat with magic before bringing it over to the island counter. "It's there and I'm sure as hell that he's aware of it! You have to go or the seals that remain will mean nothing!"

I didn't like the sound of that, especially since she had yet to look up the information on them as far as I was aware, and I knew nothing more about them. I went to the drawer and pulled out a fork and knife, bringing them back to the table and sat. "Alright... I'll call Dagda, see if Thaloth is free and can hear the request. How exactly am I supposed to bring to this up without making a fool of myself?"

"Just ask how his kingdom is doing and then bring up the text you found on the wall of Seraphina's seal. It mentioned a gate, did it not?"

I swallowed the bite I had. "Yes… I completely forgot."

"Well, I did wake you at three in the morning, so that's no surprise. Are you eating?"

"Yes. I'm hungry."

"You shouldn't eat at night…"

"I'll eat when I please. I take it you don't want me to mention your nightmare?"

"No, I do not." Her answer was very clear on the subject. "Keep this within your party if you must tell someone. If Thaloth allows you in, please get there as soon as you can. You still have about a month or so for the Zerach excursion, the other houses shouldn't complain about this if you use your time wisely and still make your way back at the deadline."

That certainly didn't leave us much time, but it's not like Ciar was going to need much time to recover. I didn't like thinking that the world could end within the month. "We're going to need some extra money to pay for this new excursion. We didn't plan for this."

"I'll send a messenger to the demesne to drop off some. How much did you think you need? How long to prepare?"

"I don't know. Don't know the best route to take to get to Dagda from here either… I'll have to ask Uncle Owen."

"I'll just send you an excessive amount then."

"Thanks."

"Be careful. You were there too."

"Do I get killed?"

"Yes… crushed to death by rocks."

"And you want me to go to a mysterious gate, underground?"

"I'm sorry, but it's all over if he opens it."

I gave out a sigh, shaking my head and tried my best to play it off. In reality, I was terrified. I just got out of a life and death situation; I didn't want to go back into another one. I didn't want to die. "It's not your fault. If I get crushed to death, so be it, but I'll make sure that it happens after Ciar or that gate is dealt with."

"Theodora was with him."

"Because of course she was…" I trailed off as the outline of the dragon appeared again, hopping off the counter and disappeared. It was, admittedly, a good distraction from the prospect of how painful being crushed by rocks would be and the thought of seeing Theodora again. "Hey, do you know if Outland Dragons can haunt places?"

"Um… weird question. Where did this come from?"

"I think I keep seeing a ghost, but not a detailed one. More like a shadow. It's been like this since I got here, but no one else seems to have noticed or it's hiding from Owen whenever he's actively trying to see it."

"I-I don't think an Outland Dragon would be haunting a hideout."

"Why the stutter? Is there a special thing with ghosts that I'm not aware of?"

"No, no. You know that ghosts, if powerful enough, can show up to people who aren't necromancers. Father used to tell me about a few that he had seen over the years, including an Outland Dragon."

"Could a baby one become that powerful?"

"A baby?"

"Well, a whelp… probably the same age as the kids, maybe a bit older." I pushed the bloody plate away as I finished eating. "Ah, never mind. It's probably nothing. In a few days we'll be leaving so I can tolerate it until then. Maybe Owen will catch it."

"There you go, optimistic thoughts."

"Was that everything that you wanted to talk about? Anything more about your nightmare?"

"No. No… that's everything. I'll let you get back to bed, you had a very long day yesterday."

"Alright, sweet dreams, Atla," I told her, and she made a sound of agreement, but not a confident one.

"You too. Talk to you later."

She ended the call without another word. I set the CT down on the table, looking at the time. Three-twenty-one in the morning. I would normally be getting up in an hour or so… but the thought of going back to bed was stronger. It was still a bit too early to call Thaloth even with the five-hour time difference. His meditation started at noon and I had managed to figure out that they lasted for two to three hours. He said that was when he was the freest and therefore in the best mood. That was when I could ask for such a ludicrous request. So… that was in six and a half hours from now. That would be more than enough time for some extra rest.

I got up and washed the dishes I used, dried, and put them back into their homes before returning back to my bed with the CT. I wasn't sure if she would get another nightmare or if she wanted to talk more later.

I laid down and as soon as I closed my eyes, I was met with a face full of Ciar. I bolted up, my heart in my throat and was blindsided by the sun. A small growl of irritation came out as I flopped back down onto the pillow where the sun hadn't crept, breathless.

Was it morning already?

I looked to the time on the CT, reading a quarter to ten in the morning. I rolled over and threw the blankets over my head. I didn't want it to be so late… I didn't get any rest at all!

Deigh gave a small chuckle through the link. *"You can sleep more if you want."*

"No, I can't. I have to call Thaloth. He'll be finished his meditation soon…" I whined out loud. "It's too early for this…"

"I haven't heard you say ten in the morning being too early in a long time."

"Well here we are… Dammit!" I threw the blankets off and started to get ready for the day. I had showered last night to make sure I got all the blood off of me before heading to bed. "Being awake is exhausting."

"You had a rough day yesterday; I'm not surprised that you're tired."

"Who else is up and about?"

"Everyone. Fyliel is here and ready to exam you."

"Great…"

"You also got a message from Atla that I looked at briefly for you. She wants you to finalize the Thinnus Festival layout. I recommend looking it over while you eat and before you make that call, even if it's something small. You're hungry and a grumpy wumpy isn't going to get Thaloth to invite us to search for some mythical gate."

"I'll come out and eat, look over the plans, but could you warn everyone that I'm not going to have a lot of time to chat? I'll give out a new plan of action for us depending on how well this goes."

"What if it doesn't go well? Atlamillia seemed to be on the verge of tears last night."

I honestly thought she had cried before calling. Whatever she saw terrified her. *"Then we'll have to think of something else. If Ciar is heading for the tear in space, and it's there, we can't let him reopen it."*

"Not if those warnings on the walls have anything to say at least."

I left the room, grabbing a quick bowl of cereal with some simple good mornings to Azarias and Cyrus. I could hear Éabha speaking with her father and Owen downstairs as I devoured the food, but not what they were discussing, and I marked down my suggestions of change for the Thinnus Festival. I went back to my room after sending the plans back to Atlamillia and closed the door, heading to the bathroom to quickly brush my teeth. It'd be embarrassing not to mention make my request less professional if there was something on them.

I tapped on Dagda's contact information and it started to ring as I set the CT on the table to simulate a conference call. Hopefully, someone would pick up on the other end. It wasn't at the top of my priorities to tell the other leaders about the CT, which might have been a mistake, but not something that couldn't be fixed. A simple message to Atlamillia would do it once I was finished with Thaloth.

On the other end, no one answered. It made sense, so I tried again using persistence and patience as my weapons. Eventually someone would answer to tell me to stop calling. I tried a second time… and then a third. Had something happened to the continent nation?

The call was answered, ending my worries and an exarch looked ready to give hell to whoever was pestering their communications room. He stopped part way, recognizing me.

"King Ae'row! This's a pleasant and unexpecded su'prise."

"Sorry for the different number, I picked up a CT when I arrived in Seraphina. Is Archon Thaloth available? It's an urgent matter."

"I was just thinkin' of you on your fi'st excu'sion, King Ae'row," a moderately deep voice said in the background as rich in the Dagdian accent as the exarch's. The exarch bowed, looking off camera and left the beautiful room of floating, soft-purple flames. It reminded me of one of the rooms in Orithina's Temple.

The young-looking leader came into view and a door closed somewhere within the room. The man looked like he was carved out by a god and it always left me speechless at how perfect his features were between the chiseled jawline, piercing blue eyes, and never out of place blond, medium length hair. His frame was like my own – lean, but that was all I could compare to. He was much more accustomed to magic and while he looked about the same age as Theodora, I knew he had to be much older.

He had been the leader even before my birth and there hadn't been any mention of a leader that came before him in my lessons. No possible leader or apprentice to take his place. He was just… there… Like a statue crafted for his position and no one else could stand on his pedestal.

I greeted him. "Good afternoon, Archon. I hope I caught you at a good time."

"Good mo'nin', Si'e. And yes, your timin' is, as always, pe'fecdly timed." A sly smile formed on his face, one I had come to learn to mean he was in a good mood and not planning something horrible or about to get snarky, the exact same way Óðinn's did. "What can I do for you teday?"

Getting right to the point, as expected. Made the ease into the conversation a bit more difficult but not impossible. "Domrael Hill had some monsters attack in plenty yesterday along with Ciar. I was hoping to know if the monsters have laid off there at all."

"Unfo'dunadly, no. They're acdive as ever, but it's 'efreshin' te know that our common enemy's far from Dagda; not that I wish tu'moil in Se'aphina."

"It seemed like Ciar was only targeting the capital for political seize which is fortunate as he failed. He'll be healing in hiding someplace, but because of his actions, something was brought to my attention." I stepped up my lying skills that had been refined over years of dealing with Father's council. "During the fighting, an altar under the capital was found along with several of his cultists. After translating the ancient text on the walls, they mentioned a gate of great importance under Dagda. Talking it over with my knights, we believe he will be heading in that way."

"Te find a gade of some ancient language? I don't know of any gades that lay under my kingdom, especially ones that we'e wridden in a language he might not unde'stand."

"That is true, we're not sure if he can read it himself, but we know he has conversed with Outland Dragons who would."

"A'e they also on his side?"

"Not anymore. It was a mutual relationship until the leader realized that he was being used." That wasn't entirely a lie. Ciar could have betrayed them, he may not have, but I didn't put it past him. Naftali though certainly used their presence thanks to him.

"He lost a lot yesde'day then, meanin' he'll be wandin' te compensade." Thaloth made a small hum like he was contemplating, but the decision he came to was quickly delivered without much thought at all. "So, of cou'se you're mo'e than welcome te come and see if you can sea'ch for this myste'ious place that your aldar mentions. Dagda has many ancient places under her su'faces, a lot of magic and connections te the sacred 'ealms of O'ithin. Who am I te say I know eve'ydin'?"

"Will it be alright if my team and I go through some of your records and kingdom's underground?"

"Anydin' if it stops that he'etic from doin' mo'e ha'm te this sacred wo'ld that belongs te Lady Orithina. But I should wa'n you, we're havin' some civil strife on top of the monsde's. Nodin' te be conce'ned with, just some a'eas won't be safe as I'd like them te be. The embassy's locaded far from it, the same grounds whe'e I sleep peacefully at night. I'll have inquisido's with you if you need te vendu'e off inte the oder disdricts of Dagda that a'e cu'rendly, shall we say, messy at the moment."

"I appreciate it, Archon. I don't know what lies beyond it, but the text mentions Od Symalum and of the Daemonias."

"Od Symalum, that means The Calamidy in Ancient Dragon, the Language of the Gods, co'rect?"

"Yes." I was a little more than surprised at the fact that he knew that.

"If our grace, Lady Orithina, has placed the wa'nin', then it's my dudy te make su'e that this gade doesn't fall inte the wrong hands."

"It wasn't just Orithina that made it. Valrdis's will was placed into the warnings as well."

"Valrdis and Lady Orithina wo'kin' tegeder...? Dear me, it must've been quite the expe'ience for them te've wo'ked tegeder at that aldar. I'll make su'e that a team's 'eady for your a'rival at your beck and call te find it."

"Thank you, Archon. We won't be leaving Seraphina for a couple of days as we have to prepare for the trip across Akirayuu."

"Take as much time as you need. The ocean's a dange'ous place and it'd be a shame for you te die befo'e you could find this gade and see my beloved nation. In the meandime, I'll have schola's lookin' for wo'ks and sifdin' through them te lessen the load when you a'rive. If anydin' comes up, I'll call this number." The man fixed his white, golden-yellow, and purple robes, the colours of Orithina, and pushed a few buttons on a console I couldn't see but certainly could hear. "The'e, your numbe's now 'eco'ded so it won't be igno'ed in the fudu'e. Was that eve'ydin'?"

I gave a small nod. "Yes. It was good speaking with you, Archon."

"Undil next time, King Ae'row. Safe travels and may Lady Orithina be with you."

I gave a similar reply through habit and ended the call, hitting the red button. I sat back with a small, exasperated sigh. He was intimidating at times... I could never read what he was thinking, and his presence made it almost impossible to relax, even though it was through a screen. He just oozed with power and ambition. I wouldn't be surprised if one day he decided to start colonizing the other continents, but I doubted it would be without great preparation.

Ruairí set a fine example of what happens when you don't, and that was within the same land mass. There wasn't much one could do if something happened to the colony across a massive ocean, far from the motherland. A small laugh came out as I thought of Thaloth.

I wondered if he was as intimidating in person or if I was just socially awkward. It was probably a bit of both. Though, it was always a million times easier to deal with in person than over communications.

Movement caught the corner of my eye and I turned to see the shadow dragon bouncing on the unmoving bed. Suddenly, the dragon jumped at me.

I panicked with a small yelp. The chair tipped at my recoil and I fell backwards, kicking the table and crashed to the floor. I looked to the air and then the bed next to me, but the dragon was gone, leaving me feeling ashamed.

A muffled voice came from the other side of the door, sounding similar to asking if I was alright.

I muttered that I was fine but didn't bother to move. My shin hurt as the table was solid, but other than that, I was incredibly comfortable. The voice came in, the door loudly announcing it was being opened and the light steps of Éabha walked for a few strides before stopping. I didn't look over as I stared at the unimpressive, wooden ceiling. I could just close my eyes and rest. Who was to stop me?

Éabha hindered it almost immediately with a very appropriate question. "What are you doing on the floor?"

"I fell, couldn't you tell?"

"I figured with your massive mass hitting the floor. You scared the shit out of us downstairs."

"Sorry." She came up pretty quickly to be at my door almost immediately. Must have been quite the bang.

"That doesn't answer why you're there."

"A spider dropped in front of me while I was spaced out, scared me," I lied, sitting up a bit regrettably. "How's it going down there?"

"It's going well. It's going to take all day tomorrow, at the very least, to make sure that calibrations are done correctly. That is if we finish the work that needs to be done today. Adding wing armour to form and come out when your wings do is a bit of a challenge, Dad's area of expertise so I know he'll figure it out. He also wanted to add tail armour too, all of which will match Deigh's armour – stole it so I could upgrade it if you were wondering where it went off to."

"So, that's going to take a couple of days, eh?"

"A couple, yes… Is that okay?"

I nodded. "We aren't fighting Outland Dragons, so she doesn't need the extra armour right now."

"Okay! Great!"

"Also, I was wondering if you could show me how to fix both armour pieces if something happened. We're not going to be able to ask for repairs any time soon."

"Huh? Why?"

"I'll explain once I get everyone in the same room. There's been a change of plans."

Chapter Fifty-One: Instinct

I gathered up the people in the house, much to the prodding of Éabha wanting to know what I was talking about and to Fyliel's irritation who just wanted to make sure I was healthy. It wasn't a long explanation of the new plan to head to the Makonogah continent with the quest to find The Calamity's Gate. I kept the details about where the idea had come from until after I knew I wasn't going to be overheard by anyone. Atlamillia wanted to keep her nightmares a secret for some reason; I was going to keep it that way.

Thankfully, I didn't have to say anything to explain myself to the people who already knew what the seal actually had on its walls as Owen seemed to pick up where the idea came from and agreed to the change. Azarias and Cyrus followed with a bit of confusion.

Orpheal cleared his throat from his seat and continued building new armour. "So, how do you plan on getting there? There are no islands or Outposts once you leave Yasuquinn and the journey is a little over four times as long as the one you took to get here."

"Boat… though I'm not entirely sure how long that would take," I admitted, not thinking everything through. "I would say fly but twenty-thousand kilometres in one trip is impossible for a dragon."

"You could go by airship, even in bad weather you'd get there in about five days."

"That's a bit much for our budget. We only planned on the trip here and back. I don't think even with Atla sending money would be enough to hire a crew and an airship since we can't risk going by public transport."

"But would you take an airship if it was available?"

While I've never been on an airship, it was the quickest way to get to Dagda. "Without question."

"Then consider yourself the captain of an airship," he stated, not bothering to look up from his work like he was casually greeting someone.

"I'm sorry?"

"Once I'm done with this section here, I'll find you a ship and crew that can take you to Dagda and then fly you home once you're done. Though they won't be able to stay there, you can call me when you're finished. It'll give you some time to enjoy the strange little kingdom. It'll be like looking back through time."

The tone he used on that last phrase made it seem like he detested Dagda for their aversion to technology. Thankfully, the Absalom embassy was very up to date. "I don't know what to say... It's absurdly generous."

"You rescued Éabha, it's the least I can do."

"I appreciate it, Orpheal. Thank you."

"Um..." Éabha started, drawing attention as she shifted back and forth like that of a small child. She looked heartbroken. "So, does this mean you're not staying until the Zerach is ready for you?"

"I would like to, but-"

"Then I'm going with you."

"Éabha!" Orpheal scolded swiftly and sharply. "You cannot just invite yourself to join someone on their tasks! Especially not something so dangerous-"

"They need someone to repair their armour if it gets damaged," she retorted, standing up to her father strongly. "I can also heal. It's not perfect like yours but it's better than most as it can heal fatal wounds if acted on. I can teleport and I'm well versed in combat. I can help-"

"I don't care. You're not going."

Devastated was an understatement for the look on her face. Then, it turned to that of fury. "I'm not a child anymore! I have the capabilities to help, and I should be helping! Not hiding away!"

"Éabha-" I tried to intervene only for her to cut me off, not looking away from her father.

"You stay out of this! I can't stay here forever, unable to spread my wings! You're just afraid that I'm going to die just like Mum did! I'm not Mum! These people have risked their lives for me, they won't leave me for dead like our so-called colleagues left her!" She choked on her words. "Another kingdom actually needs help and its our duty to provide all the help we can give! Domrael did it for Theseus-"

"You are not Domrael!" Orpheal snapped, no longer working on his project. "You have no godly protections like he did! So yes, I am scared of you dying because you're just a normal girl against a whole world of monsters that will happily kill you! Is that so wrong that I don't want you to die?!"

"I'm not going to-"

He interrupted her, trying to calm his voice, but it was clearly forced. "We are helping by doing what we can here-"

"It's not good enough!" She took a shaky breath. "You didn't see him, I did. He looked just like us but he's more monstrous than anything I've come across, fiction or not, and he's growing stronger by the moment. If they go without some sort of backup, no one to repair their gear, to update and upgrade it, they will not keep up. If they go without the skills and talents I possess; even if they are ordinary, they are going to die on that island! One, powerfully protected, undead guardian is all it's going to take since none of them have pure light abilities. They can't learn Dagdian magic. What happens when a Dagdian zealot decides to mess with their heads like that Aevorii chic did?

"We already know what happens if someone can't disarm the skill since it almost cost Aerrow's and Deigh's lives! What happens when Ciar learns those skills? They'd be more than fucked if he managed to beat over Aevorii's skill and exploits them. What happens if he hires her? He's around a thousand on the MFM, they'd be fucked without me who can grow without limits just like he can because of my birthright. I can compete against that! I have to go!"

There was an unsettling silence that fell upon the basement level. My tongue refused to move, both not wanting her to come since it was safer, but also wanting her to. She was a good friend and a fighter that we needed… but I couldn't ask. Orpheal needed to make the decision without the added pressure. If he said no, then that was that. Somehow, we'd have to make do or fail trying.

The seemingly unending silence ended as Orpheal stood up from his station and came around, stopping in front of his daughter. The girl looked like that of a large doll compared to him as he placed both hands on her shoulders. She looked up at him with determination, tears briefly held back. It was easy to see she wanted her father's approval but was terrified of leaving him alone. She, like any normal person, was scared of dying just as he thought would happen if she did leave.

Why did he think she would die without failure if she left the island? I looked over at Owen in hopes of an explanation but only saw a troubled expression as he watched Orpheal. He knew whatever it was. Some unsaid fact that they had yet to tell either of us for Orpheal's deep-rooted feelings other than just the death of Iðunn.

Orpheal gave a stern look as he asked his question. "Do you believe that wholeheartedly? Do you believe that they will fail?"

"If Ciar continues to grow, if he has followers in Dagda he can learn from, naturally or not, they will die," she answered, her volume back down to normal. "That gate needs to be protected and if they fail, it won't matter if I stayed home, safe with you. We'd be dead if whatever is on the other side is scary for Orithina."

He searched her face then drew her into a tight hug. "Then… you should go. But you have to come back home, understand?"

She gave a nod somewhere buried beneath his arms.

He turned to me, ashen. "Keep her safe, just like your ancestor did for ours. If you don't…"

"I'll keep her safe," I told him stronger than I thought my voice could muster to try and reassure him. "Even at the cost of my life, I will make sure she comes home alive and safe. I won't let her die for this or any mission."

He just nodded, turning back to her and squeezed. "Come back home, Éabha."

"I will…" she replied with a bit of a muffled response and another nod. She broke free from his hug, but not leaving too far from him as she wiped away tears. "Now we just need a plan. What to bring… I've never left the island before the other night and it wasn't very far. Only seen a bit of the ocean from the edge."

"Well, the ocean air is wet for starters," he laughed slightly in amusement, but he looked ready to cry. "But first, I think we need to work on everyone's armour and get them upgraded, only then can we start to worry about what else to pack for you."

"Okay." She turned to me with a smile on her face that should have eased my worries but only made my heart sink at the thought of her dying. "I hope you don't mind having another party member."

I shook my head, refusing to let her know of my concerns. She was so happy about finally being able to leave. I couldn't take that away.

"Good. And since this conversation is done, Fyliel has a patient to see."

"Er… right."

"Once I'm done with the armour, we should have another practice before we go to Rath Hill and be ready for anything."

"Sounds like a plan." I turned to the doctor. "I guess I'm all yours?"

She shifted her weight. Her voice was a bit monotoned, "Upstairs, Sire, unless you want to be examined down here?"

Azarias answered before I could, "Oh yes."

"Oh no." I rolled my eyes with a sigh. "Definitely not."

"Strip tease?"

"No! I thought you liked women!"

"I do but watching you squirm is hilarious."

I had a few choice words, but my jaw locked before I could say something really mean and walked away.

00000

I found myself trying to find a snack after dealing with Fyliel for what seemed like forever. According to Deigh, it had only been three hours, but she wasn't the one that was being asked half a million questions and had cold instruments placed on her. I looked in the cupboard, seeing the great, glorious, grandiose, salted fish-shaped crackers waiting to be eaten... and looked elsewhere for food. I wasn't looking for them, not that I knew what I wanted at all.

But it wasn't them.

I looked further only to find that the only thing around was cereal and crackers. A depressed sigh came out and I grabbed the crackers as I heard someone reach the top of the stairs.

I turned to the noise and saw Owen with a look of concern on his face. "Someone sounds upset.

"Just a bit hungry..." I looked back to the cupboard in disappointment. "But nothing looks appealing."

"Not even the crackers?"

"No. I don't know what I want, but its not these." I shook the box slightly before sitting down and he joined me. "Is someone going to be shopping soon?"

"Cyrus has started a list of things that we need for now and the trip. Though I don't believe we have to worry about food for it as Orpheal will have it covered... Is there something you wanted in particular?"

I shrugged, indecisive. "The jerky I found yesterday was good… and the steak was too, maybe something like that?"

"Really?" He looked at me strangely. Why? I didn't know. "Alright. I'll find Cyrus and let him know you want red-"

"Like, a lot of it though. The packet of jerky didn't last long."

He shook his head with a small smirk, changing the subject from food. "How did your examination go?"

"Long… but she said there wasn't anything unhealthy about me. All the serious injuries I got yesterday are basically gone thanks to the healing efforts both internal and external. She told me to relax and not do anything too strenuous as the healing factor isn't exactly as it was before and has a limit. The bruising from my ribs breaking allowed her to determine that while great, it focuses on deadly and first dealt then shifts to something else that needs attention after a point and uses a lot of energy."

"So it works best when you're asleep. How did you break your ribs yesterday?"

"My fight with Orpheal. He somehow bypassed my armour… probably because he helped designed the technology, and then Éabha kneed me right here."

He winced even though I was being lighthearted. "Well, besides it's quirks, that's a handy little trait you've gained from Naftali, eh?"

"I suppose…" The dragon outline came back behind him on the counter and my brows furrowed as it started chasing its tail before sitting.

"Is something wrong?" It disappeared before he could turn around to see it. He gave a small sigh, looking back. "Are you still seeing the-"

"Maybe… I don't know what it is," I sighed. "It's probably nothing."

"Are you sure?"

"No… There is just… something wrong, but I don't know how to explain it. The primal instincts I had, like the bloodlust, have mostly faded thank the gods. But it still feels like something is off."

"How so?"

"I don't know. It just feels like there is this suspense just everywhere, like anxiety, but not. Almost like walking into a horror house and you know something is going to jump out at you except it's a fifty-fifty chance that something is actually going to kill you."

"That sounds like anxiety."

"But it's different. Something else happened and no scientific instruments are finding it." Another sigh came out. "I've had Deigh look me over, pay attention to anything that is psychological such as an anxiety attack, but everything seems normal to her."

"If it's not anxiety, could it be your subconscious pestering you about the whelps?"

"Maybe? But while it feels like anxiety, I also feel... I guess the best way to explain it is simply weird."

"Weird how?"

"Like you have a spider on you-"

"Please you another example..."

"An ant on your skin." I changed the bug type and he shivered causing me to stifle a small chuckle. "But it's not quite the same temperature as your skin as you can kinda feel it. It sends a small chill up your spine every so often as you remember that its there, but you can't brush it off for whatever reason."

Owen thought it over but was perplexed. "I don't know why you would be feeling that, but I'll keep watching for anything strange and ask the others to do the same. Between all of us, perhaps we can figure it out."

"I appreciate it. We still don't know everything about the situation, and I don't want to hurt anyone else, just in case."

He gave a soft look. "I don't think we have to worry about that, but you're right, caution is important, especially over the next few days."

"If nothing changes really over the next couple of weeks, I'll be content about the situation, but not before," I agreed and shoved a couple of crackers in my mouth. As soon as they hit my tongue, it reminded me how much I loved them. "Why the hell I didn't think I wanted this right now is a mystery all on its own. These are delicious!"

"You've had a rough couple of days and probably forgot when the Outland Dragon instincts took over for a brief time," he laughed then grew serious. "Can we take this conversation outside?"

I nodded, adding more crackers to my mouth and followed him to the back door, crackers in hand. We stopped our epic journey at the railing of the back deck that was several metres off the ground and the sun was beaming down from above, blinding me. Owen patiently waited for me to get my bearings. Once I adjusted, the view was quite stunning. There was a bit of a field, perfect for training, which turned into a great forest. There wasn't a single building in sight and no other people. Just trees and wind. It was a view I rarely got back home or since I arrived, and certainly not one I had been able to enjoy in the Outlands.

I turned to my uncle as I doubted he wanted to bring me outside for just the view. "What did you want to talk about?"

He went to say something but stopped as he searched my face for an answer for an unknown question. I felt a slight magical presence come from him. It faded just as quickly but not before I realized it was necromancy.

Why was he using necromancy magic? "Uncle Owen?"

"Sorry. Missiletainn made a terrible joke about a ghost following you and I fell for it." He shook his head and I held back a frown, hiding it within a small laugh at this apparent prank. He was lying and was exceptionally bad this time around, but whatever he had on his mind, he wasn't ready to speak of it and it made me a bit paranoid. What was he looking for and why was he so bothered by it that he couldn't be straight forward? He switched to a different subject of concern. "The reason we're heading to Dagda, your sister had another nightmare, didn't she?"

"Yeah. She called me this morning in a panic. It took a while for her to calm down and tell me what she saw. I honestly don't think I handled it as well as I should have." A sigh came out as I set the crackers aside and leaned against the banister. "I never realized how traumatizing her prophetic nightmares were until now. I've never heard her so scared or upset in my life... not even talking with her after Father was killed... I only wish that I was there and not trying to comfort her through a CT."

He leaned perpendicular against the railing, not looking overly happy in my peripherals. "If she managed to calm down, you did well. Prophetic dreams are like night terrors only worse."

"She was in a bit of a better mood once everything was said and done, helped me figure out how to get Thaloth to have us come, but it still doesn't feel right. I should have been there."

"One of us should have."

"Maybe if we were, she would have told us everything."

"Everything?"

"I feel like she was hiding something."

"She might just need more time to analyze it. She knows how you can be when given information that could mean something."

I laughed a bit, looking to him. "Yeah, I guess I tend to weigh things more than what they should be at times. But that's why we're going. She said Ciar was heading there to open this gate that no one has heard of, somewhere under Dagda. But not even Thaloth knows of an ancient gate."

"Or he's lying."

"Why would he lie about something like this?"

"He's a secretive man and I'll be the first one to tell you I don't trust him. But… perhaps in this case he may not be." Owen crossed his arms, contemplating. "He cares about his position and his kingdom; he doesn't want someone coming and ruining that for him."

"He was pretty on-board with letting us come. He already has scholars preparing works and places of interest for when we arrive."

"That is rather generous of him. You must have caught him in one of the best moods I've ever seen him in."

"He did say I had good timing," I joked before frowning. "I just hope we find this gate first. Atlamillia is convinced that the gate is the same one mentioned on the cavern walls – the tear that the goddesses had made and then closed."

"You think otherwise."

"There are no records of where the goddesses' fight took place. That final clash that ended the First God War and brought the Daemonias to us. Zegrinath had no information on the gate other then the seals and the one seal we could investigate only mentions it… somewhere. Yet somehow, she knows it's under Dagda? How do you know and not know of where something is? The kingdom isn't overly large compared to the others but it's not small either. There are thousands of kilometres to search through if not hundreds of thousands. It's a continent with ancient buildings full of ancient magics, who knows what was buried where or what traps could be left behind?"

"From the few times I've gone, traps could be anything from pop-out paper cut-outs to an undead guardian."

"Like that… or worse."

There was silence for a few moments as I thought about her other warning. My hands clasped together tightly as I looked back out to the wilderness. An overwhelming sense of dread rolled in and while I thought I was hiding it; Owen caught the slight shift. "Did she see you die?"

I gave a small nod. "Crushed to death by rocks…"

"And yet she wants you to go find an underground gate?"

"That's basically what I asked, but she insisted that if I didn't, Ciar was going to succeed. Oh, also Theodora was there. So that's great."

"So much for never seeing her again. Then again with her being around, you might find it easier to get over her and move on."

A laugh of disbelief came out of me. "Yeah, right. If anything, this is making things worse. She's with my worst enemy and helping him. The way she spoke about him, it wasn't as an underling. She was her own person, doing what she wanted… She was his equal."

He had a surprised look on his face. "You're jealous."

"Well, yeah! He's a Seraphinean and, as Éabha pointed out to me that I hadn't noticed before, is an attractive one that can will away any of his monstrosities he forms including his wings. He could go anywhere, and they could be doing who knows what. I shouldn't care but I do and seeing her again is way worse than thinking I had sent her to die."

"I understand your feelings, but as I said before, it will get easier, and this new development may be more of a blessing than a curse."

"Well I don't want to see her hurt either. It's a dangerous game she's playing. She killed one of his scientists, one that I'm sure wasn't low in ranking. She's helped me twice now and we know nothing of Ciar. What if… What if he kills her for those actions?"

"I doubt she would be with him and take those risks without knowing the consequences. She's a smart girl and knows how to play her cards."

"If she was so smart, she would have never joined him at all," I grumbled as the outline of the dragon came back, dancing about the field and chasing a butterfly. It looked at me, gave a wave, then dashed into the forest and disappeared as Owen turned to lean heavily against the banister with a sigh, probably unsure of what to say. A strong urge dropped on my shoulders to leave and find the whelps. The whiplash turned my stomach a bit. "Owen... I know this is going to be a bit random, but I need to ask for a favour."

"What is it?"

"I need to go find the whelps. It's incredibly stupid but I cannot have you come with me."

"Aerrow, this is not the best time to go. Fyliel literally just told you to rest."

"I know but I have a really bad feeling..." I looked to him, getting off the railing. "I have to go tonight or whoever is left is not going to make it."

He turned to me slightly, but didn't shift too much, his brows furrowing. "I have a bad feeling of you going on your own. But if you're ordering it, I'll have no choice but to obey."

"Not ordering, I just know that if there is anyone other than Deigh and I, the Outland Dragons will attack."

"I still don't like it, especially with the monsters..." He sighed. "So I'll escort you part way to the lab, give you a portal once we're close enough for me to summon one."

I relaxed a bit. "I think Deigh would appreciate the assistance of skipping whatever lays at the border and inside. Hopefully one of the Outland Dragons can escort us on the way back."

Owen nodded, looking at his CT for the time. "Then we'll head out after supper. Speaking of... I think Cyrus has already left for the supplies."

I pulled out my CT and started messaging about the food I wanted. "I feel like Deigh right now, completely derailed by food."

"But it does mean you're eating, so I think it's worth the price. I'll tell Éabha to finish what she's doing with your armour while you're messaging. You don't think this will result in a fight with Outland Dragons, do you?"

"No... No Outland Dragons will be fought tonight, even if they show up at the facility before we're able to leave."

"Good."

He left me to finish my list to Cyrus and I put away the CT once it was sent. I looked into the forest that reminded me a bit of Baiwyn's, grabbing my crackers again, but didn't snack on them. A small chill went through me as a sudden cold breeze blew by.

"*Get in here,*" Deigh scolded, "*before you catch a cold.*"

"*Alright… We have to get ready anyway.*"

"*Like a small bit of practice?*"

"*Sure.*"

Chapter Fifty-Two: Lonely

Atlamillia ended the call, staring at the black screen. It was fine... it was going to be fine. Optimism... Optimism now that he knew... it wouldn't happen. He had a plan. He could plan. He had Uncle Owen and the others. They knew what they were doing and what battles to pick. It wasn't...

It was going to happen.

It didn't matter. She couldn't tell him about the one who caused it, who probably knew when she did. And she sent him, knowing that...

Just like her father.

The CT fell out of her hands as she lost her grip and it hit the bed, bouncing off and onto the ground. The prophetic dream came back immediately despite the brief moment she had calmed down, it wasn't enough.

It was never enough.

Lucilla came over, doing her best to comfort her. She swept her off the bed and into a protective embrace as she started silently crying again in terror. The nightmarish dream was horrifying.

Her living nightmare.

They were never going to stop.

Lucilla never saw what she saw. She never saw the memories of it even afterwards. She could only understand what her partner had seen and heard when Atlamillia had calmed down enough to explain it.

But until then, Atlamillia had to suffer through them alone even though her partner was right there. She thought she was getting better. She had had so many, so close together... But each one proved her wrong over and over again, wrecking her soul like a whip with hooked spikes, one flogging at a time. Her cries became a little louder as the memory of the last one came back.

Her father had been there for her, just as he always had. He would comfort her, shower her in warmth and confidence... but Lucilla just couldn't offer the same answers. The same reassurance. She felt the terror, the horror of the experience yet knew nothing of it. Feeling every ache and frozen heart-stopper. And it made the comforting actions she tried to give all the more flawed. Her dragon was more passive than her father ever was – she was reserved, much like Atlamillia, and wasn't very good at being the one to give the lies she needed to hear.

Lucilla was a terrible liar.

The dragon tried to squeeze and warm her cold, cold body but the more she did, the more it made Atlamillia feel how distant and alone she really was from everyone else. The only person who made her feel like she wasn't, who kept her grounded, was the former king. He knew… He knew how to handle her cursed existence…

Her door opened suddenly, and Lucilla turned her head with a hiss, ready to annihilate whoever dared to walk in on her lowest moment. She settled as the door closed. Atlamillia looked through the blurry tears that she couldn't stop, hearing the quick steps and a familiar blonde was invited into her dragon's attempt to console her. The hug, which was more of a cradle, was warm and confident against her shaking body. An exterior expression that almost mimicked her father's, clearly taught by the man.

She gripped at Bretheena's night shirt, crying into her chest. The pain and the grief growing under the soft hushes she gave.

He taught Bretheena. He prepared just in case… He always prepared for the just in case. But now he was gone. No plans to be had. No hopeful wishes. No blissful alterations. Nothing at all.

Because he was never coming back.

He would have known what to do… He wouldn't have done what she had just… But who else could do that task? Who was already prepared for such a battle? Who else knew Ciar better to stop him from opening that strange gate? That large, rectangular, stone gate deep underground… That thing that stared back as it opened. It saw her and whoever witnessed the dream.

It saw Orithina… It wanted everything her world had.

The room grew colder as she could feel it encompass it. Everything inside her.

It wanted her. "It's coming…"

"What's coming?" Bretheena asked, sounding like she was soothing a child, but Atlamillia knew she was more like a toddler. Bumbling around without the faintest idea of the battlefield she entered.

"The thing… it's going to come." She wanted to rip the senses she had of it from her head. "It's waiting. It knows. It knows everything. It wants to consume all it can. I can't fight that!"

"Princess Atla-"

"It saw me… It knows where I am… It can get in."

"It's not going to-"

"It can! It will! I can't stop something like that! No one can once Ciar opens that gate!"

"Ciar will not open any gates and let anything in."

"He's going to… I sent him on a suicide mission… He's not going to stop it! He's not going to let him. It's suicide… I… Oh gods, what is wrong with me?!"

"Atlamillia," Bretheena said stern enough to stop her rambling and brought her hand to Atlamillia's chin and lifted it, forcing her to look into her blue eyes. "Nothing is wrong with you."

"You don't have any idea what I've done!"

"You sent your brother on a mission-"

"He's going to die! I should have just called him home! He'd never have to meet that-"

"You wouldn't have given it to him if you knew deep down he couldn't succeed," Bretheena said firmly, brushing Atlamillia's messy hair behind her ear before resting her hand on the side of her face. "You were acting on instinct and that is everything when it comes to prophetic dreams. King Solomon told me that. If you act on instinct, no matter how horrible the idea when thought out, has a purpose and it will work in your favour."

"At the cost of my brother?!"

"If it turns out that way… but I don't think it will. Did your dream feature his death?"

Atlamillia nodded. The sharp, heavy rocks digging into her body came back and she winced.

"What else was in it? A gate that Ciar was opening, something on the other side – that is your concern."

"Yes but… I just sent-"

"The person and his team that you know who could stop it." She pulled her into a hug. "I don't want Aerrow to die, and I can't imagine how scary it was to send him, or how scary it was in your dream. Of what you saw that makes you so cold… but it will be alright. We can plan right now, do something to clarify it all."

"Like what? What else is there? Aerrow is going to die in Dagda and that thing is going to come out of that gate and eat him! Him… and everyone else as it spreads. It wants me. I heard it call me by name! I can't… I can't fight that…"

Bretheena gave some more hushes as she started crying, unable to finish her thoughts and shaking in fear. They sat, surrounded by Lucilla trying to give Atlamillia a sense of security that she needed for several minutes.

She started to calm down as her retainer stroked her hair, starting to softly speak out a plan. "First… we're going for a walk. That's what you did before right?"

Atlamillia nodded.

"A walk then and some fresh air to sort out the dream. From there, we'll do whatever you need to do, be it research, have dessert for breakfast… Chocolate cream pie is what your father told me that you usually turn to for comfort food when you're drained. If you want that, I know exactly where to get one at this hour."

"I… I don't think I should…" She looked away, her tears coming back, and she smothered her face into Bretheena's chest. The woman hugged back firmly. It was as her father did for her. "I'm sorry…"

"Shh, it's okay… You're safe and sound. It will turn out for the best. It's not coming."

Lies. All of it.

And she drank them in like it was life itself.

00000

Atlamillia had expected that she and Bretheena would have had to traverse the city to get the treat she wanted from a mythical place, but to her surprise, that wasn't the case. After Bretheena had left to allow her to change, she opened the door to find her in a homely pink sweater and pants. Bretheena brought her the long way to the courtyard garden where Elias, Tatian, and Scarlett were waiting. The knight, while a bit bed ragged from probably being

724

woken up, held a box that he delivered to Atlamillia's hands. Inside was the pie that Bretheena had mentioned.

It took every once of strength she had to not break down again as she accepted the gift. Bretheena led them into the garden where Atlamillia set the pie down on a table to share with them. Elias seemed a bit unsure before joining the two of them at the table, scraping the metal chair on the patio stone tiredly and sat. "I don't think you should be eating chocolate pie at five in the morning, Atla."

"Do you want some or not?" Atlamillia asked with a glare and he sighed.

"Well, yes, obviously, but… Bretheena, you clearly know about eating healthy and all that; why are we encouraging this?"

"Because it doesn't hurt once in a while," Bretheena started so innocently before growing a bit cold. "So shut up."

"I… I'm missing something…"

"Yes, so why are you still talking?"

"Needlessly mean… I didn't have to get up to get you-mrph!" He didn't get to finish his complaint as the blonde shoved a spoonful of pie in his mouth. "Fis is acfully really guf."

Atlamillia gave a small giggle then ate a more reasonably sized piece of the dessert. It was really, really good, and it filled her with much needed comfort.

He swallowed, not keeping quiet. "Mazaeh would probably want some of this…"

"Probably," Atlamillia agreed. "But he can get some later…"

"Oh, so he gets to sleep, I see how it is." He ate more of the pie. "Bastard's missing out, it's been a while since we all hung out together."

She gave a small nod. "It's been rather quiet when you two aren't bouncing off of one another."

"I know! I miss hanging out with him!"

"We shouldn't drop the shifts just yet," Bretheena said, ending his next proposition. "Not until the king has returned at least."

He pouted. "Fine, that makes sense…"

"If you don't like it so much, you shouldn't have suggested it," Atlamillia mocked, and he grinned.

"It's nice to know you missed us too."

She was surprised by the answer before giving a small smile. The sun's glow on the horizon starting to turn the dark, starry sky a deep blue. She looked up, finishing her piece and just stared at the stars. The sky was mimicking how it should have looked, making her think it was more of a projection than calculated equations of star positions. Magically speaking, god or not, just having the sky mirror the real world would have been easier and made more sense for what mortals needed. The sun, the moons, the stars – there was no space outside the flat realm of Asylotum. There was a sense of simplicity to it.

Simplicity... perhaps that was what Atlamillia needed.

"*Are you sure you should try?*" Lucilla asked her, reasonably wary of her idea. "*I don't want you to go through being ignored when you're like this.*"

"*I should also try... maybe she'll provide guidance.*"

"*And what if she doesn't? Atlamillia, you can't keep taking shit and not have any wins to separate them. I'm seriously worried.*"

"*If she doesn't answer, she doesn't answer... But the world is in danger if my so-called instincts are wrong.*"

"*Atla... fine... but if anything else goes wrong, I'm taking matters into my own claws.*"

"*What do you-*"

"*It'll be for your own good.*"

Atlamillia frowned at the bluntness of the answer as she looked over to her partner. Lucilla gazed back with a serious glare before taking off, back to their room. She gave a silent sigh. Lucilla really didn't want her to go pray in the solarium. But her decision was made. She looked to the rest of the table as Bretheena watched her carefully while Elias was cautiously stuffing his face with a second piece. The relaxing, meaningless conversation was long gone.

"Thank you for the pie, Elias, Bretheena."

"Anytime," Bretheena told her, and Elias nodded.

"Why is everyone up at such an hour anyway?"

"It's... nothing important," Atlamillia answered, not wanting to talk about it.

He didn't need to know, and she didn't have the energy to explain things, nor did she want to slip back into the state of mind she had been in an hour ago. It wasn't dignified or proper for her position and she didn't want to be seen in that state by him or Mazaeh. There was a level of pride and image she had and... she wasn't ready to break their vision yet despite knowing that Aerrow had told them to be wary of the secret power she had.

Power... No... It was a curse.

She'd rather be oblivious to everyone's demise than know and fail to stop it.

She got up from the table and left, needing to clear her mind before she spiralled. Bretheena quickly followed her, ordering Elias to take the pie inside – keeping the knight as far from the problem as possible much to Atlamillia's gratitude.

They walked about the garden, going through the decorative mazes as the fireflies started to end their lights along the dragon stone lit paths. Their light reflected off of the other dragon stones and created a kaleidoscope effect on the bushes and flowers. The lights gave her warmth to the cool night and the cold, cruel dream. Eventually, she stopped in front of an Absalomian rose bush with its white, red, and black roses decorating it, beautifully alight in the magical light. Bretheena stood close by, ready for the storm that was barely held back.

A few tears fell from the reminder of the night she spent with her father by similar flowers. The same lighting as the day she had last seen Eadric alive.

Her voice cracked a bit. "Why is everything so hard and complicated?"

"I don't know, Princess."

"Was it simple when you were in Baiwyn?"

"In some ways, the people there are simple and easy to predict. Visitors were similar, sometimes they were more complicated than they seemed. But my life was simple because I wanted it that way."

"So, why did you take this job?"

"Because simple is boring. Gives you tips though..."

Atlamillia giggled. "Simple also keeps you alive longer."

"Yes… but what's the point of being alive if you don't enjoy it? The simple life was fine, safe until the Gracidras and Gracidra showed up, but it wasn't what I would call enjoyable."

"And following me around as a shadow is?"

"It is. Not to mention the men hitting on me are usually sober and smell a whole lot better even when they just came off a battlefield."

"Looking to settle down, are you?"

"A bit, yes… Still trying to figure out with who now that my options are so much wider, less drunk assholes and more rich ones," she chuckled. "I enjoy being your shadow, following you around and protecting you from people who might try to hurt you and learning about things out of your range. It's fun and it's productive."

"You would have made for a good mercenary."

"My parents were actually."

Atlamillia turned to her. "Really?"

"Really. Can't learn all the things I have come to know in that simple little fishing town."

"Explains why you moulded so easily into this job…"

"The skills aren't too dissimilar from what my parents did, but also growing up after leaving Baiwyn for a bit, I knew I didn't want to live off of each paycheque and not have a place to call home. I wanted a home and a place to put my stuff. Not on a boat or an airship, or on Scarlett like Citlali stores his trinkets on Noelani. I live off of protecting my home, so I returned back to the town I was born in. At one time it was my home, working as a bartender at the barracks and now it's here in a castle where I protect a cold, bold, little princess from herself and anyone else she asks me to."

Atlamillia eyed her as she turned back to the roses. "I'm not little…"

"Well you're smaller than me so that makes you little." A small pout formed on Atlamillia's lips as Bretheena wiped away the tears that had fallen. "Life is complicated for you and unlike me, it doesn't seem like you have a choice to openly oppose it or not… But I know that it will get easier because it eventually has to. It might not be today, tomorrow, or a year from now… but it will get easier."

"It doesn't have to…"

"That whole balancing thing found in Orithina's Law."

"I guess... but what if I'm dead before it becomes simple?" Bretheena looked at her in surprise but she didn't have an answer. "There is... a lot I've been thinking about both my life as... this... and as my life as I want it to be. I haven't really thought about doing normal shit until recently. It's always been thought of as a distraction, a waste of time... A burden. Those might be my simple moments and a part of me doesn't want them because I don't want to lose them."

"Sometimes even if you lose it in the end, it was worth having the moment in the first place."

"Like playing?"

"Playing, shopping, fucking. Friends, lovers... they are worth it even if they do hurt. It makes you mortal and makes living complicated lives, in my opinion, worth the complications."

"So... even if I'm not sure if I'm going to live out my path... you think I should think about it and fantasize anyway?"

"Fantasize, partake in it. Either way, it will become a new road for you when your mission is done. Saves a bit of time too if you do plan or enjoy a bit of it before you get there," she agreed.

There was silence as Atlamillia thought on it. What did she want if she did live? It hurt to think about losing it all even if she didn't know what she was losing. She was tired of losing.

"You don't have to think of anything right now. Life plans and fantasies take time and are often shared and discussed with multiple people such as friends."

"Perhaps that's not a bad idea. Just sitting down and discussing this shit at ungodly hours with some people."

"The best time to discuss such things. You can get really deep in those hours and that might just help you better understand both yourself and those around you."

She gave a nod and moved closer to the bush, picking a few roses from it. "I'll try it sometime... but there is something I need to do first."

"With roses? Oh, that does remind me. Did you send the king the plans for the Thinnus Festival?"

"Ah, no… shit. Okay, two things first."

There was a small laugh between them, and they started back out of the garden to head to her study where she could complete her crown duty before attending a personal one.

Chapter Fifty-Three: That Place

I started putting on the armour as Éabha watched with great concern, handing me a new piece every time I finished gearing up with the one I had. I gave her a glance. "You realize I know how to put armour on, right?"

"Yes, I know. But I haven't got to test it as much as I wanted to. The slots made for your wings are basic at best. Dad hasn't finished the wing armour yet and-"

"You don't want it malfunctioning, I get it. I think you forget that I'm not as fragile as a Seraph. I'm used to armour not being infused with magic or technological enhancements and am typically careful in fights."

"Doesn't mean it can't hurt you," she growled.

"I know, which is why I abused the fact that Ciar isn't coming right now to enchant my wardrobe so I can't break your hard work in case I use the ability again."

"Learned that did you?"

"I did a while ago... just didn't get around to using it."

She shook her head and got closer. Her steps somehow still light in her heavy, slightly over-the-knee, work boots as I placed on my gauntlet. She closed the jacket up, the pieces snapping together, and a small, white, black and purple light came from between the plates and reflected slightly off her sleeveless, black crop top. She tapped on my chest and I looked down just as she flicked my nose. "Pay attention to what you're doing. You didn't buckle up your main source of protection."

"You can't just flick me in the nose! I'm a king!"

"I just did, Airhead." She moved behind me, throwing my cape over my head and blinded me from the outside world. "Do me a favour and summon some wings; I want to make sure this is going to work before you leave."

I hesitated for a moment out of instinct then summoned them without much effort. The armour plates moved out of the way as the wings formed. She played with the moving parts, but I couldn't tell what she was doing from underneath the cape other than she was purposely avoiding my awareness. She gave a small sigh of relief. I went to dismiss the extra limbs only for her to stop me with an unexpected question.

"Can… c-can I touch them?"

"The wings?" I looked back slightly but the cape blocked all of view of her. "I guess?"

I didn't need to see her to know she was hesitating before she ended her curiosity. "They're… so smooth. They look rough but…"

I hadn't got around to stroking my own scales, but I took her word for it as she etched and brushed across them with her fingers. I never realized how sensitive they were until her soft touch went over their scales. A touch I didn't associate with that of a weapon's smith or that of a fighter. Fingers smooth and kept away from harm. My stomach dropped. I didn't want her to come. She was going to end up hurt. "Maybe you should stay here."

"No. I'm not staying. Dad gave me the permission I've always wanted and I'm going to make him proud."

"But it's more than just-"

"I'm going. Even if I have to sneak on-board that ship. For your stupid kingdom's sake and my own." She moved her fingers to the base of the wing where it stretched from the main bone and I flinched. "Oh, ticklish are we?"

"Maybe…" She did it again and I dismissed them, throwing the cape back into place, and looked down at her, not amused. "You're cruel, you know that?"

"Sometimes I am." She moved to my side and lifted the cape again to peek underneath before looking back up at me. "But I'm happy to report that the basics of it are working. It should be alright to rescue those whelps even if you do something stupid."

"I won't do anything stupid."

"Well, Deigh's not going to be able to fit down those corridors in her dragon form. You're going to have to be her shield and therefore, do some really stupid thinking."

I remained silent on the matter and grabbed Guðmundr from the side table next to the couch, placing it over my gauntlet.

"I could go with you, or maybe one of the knights."

"They know Owen as Dragonbane meaning they will attack on sight just as they would if they saw you. Cyrus and Azarias are unknown to them, and any patrol seeing more than just Deigh, and I will attack without question. We know this from experience. Since we've already been to the tribe's home, they will assume that we're bringing their children home, so we'll be fine."

"Okay… but how are you supposed to get the whelps from the facility, if they are there, all the way to the tribe's mountain?"

"We'll figure it out when we get there. We always do."

"That is something I have noticed." She gave a small giggle before sighing. "Be careful… You're my only friend and only ticket off this fucking rock."

A small smile formed. "We will."

"One other thing…"

"What is it?"

"What were you and Dad talking about before supper? You were in your room for a while."

"Oh, that was… Well ideas and future endeavours for governance, all very optimistic. I don't want to say anything until it's a little more realistic."

"Politics… I suppose I shouldn't have expected anything less," she sighed, clearly a bit annoyed over how boring the answer was. She looked me over one last time then took a step back and place her hands behind her grease-stained denim short shorts that had a belt holding many heavy tools, tools that were the only thing clean on her besides her hands and forearms that were gloved when she worked. Much of her had some form of grease as she only seemed to care to cover up when it came to working in dangerous environments, like welding. "Alright… you should get going. Owen's probably waiting."

I nodded.

"If there are any leftover dickheads, wankers, or cunts, give them hell."

"Uh…" It took a second for me to register what she had said. "Where did those words come from?!"

"These, and others, are the things I say to people I don't like."

The memory of our first little adventure came back to mind. "Wow… alright then."

"I'm the Lord Director's Daughter, so I didn't learn them from any stranger."

"Remind me not to get on your father's bad side…"

She smiled proudly before her expression changed. "Oh! Does Deigh have everything? She left to warmup before I could ask."

"She has the weapon you made for her and a cloak."

"Okay, good. Take advantage of that and don't go in there alone. It might mess with your head if you remember anything."

"She wouldn't let me go alone even if I asked."

"Good. Good… okay. Are you sure-"

"Éabha, we'll be fine. You have things here that only you can do, and we have ours."

"I know…"

"Make sure you go to bed at a decent hour, alright?"

"You can't tell me what to do," she grumbled, crossing her arms as Deigh landed in the yard behind me. "Good luck."

"Thanks." I gave a curt wave before leaving out the back door and got on Deigh. She took off as Missiletainn opened a portal to shorten the trip to the border.

00000

It was dusk as we exited Owen's portal near the building, not getting too close so we could look around without being spotted. Nothing moved, no guards and none of the vehicles in the side yard. There were lights from some of the windows, some flickering, and others had something blotting out parts of the glass. We did another sweep before agreeing that if there was anyone still around, they would be inside.

My stomach gave a small hint of a growl and I tsked in annoyance. I shouldn't have been hungry.

"*You did remind me of something,*" Deigh commented as she took us towards the forest. "*I bet those whelps haven't been fed right.*"

"*No, probably not. What do you think they would want?*"

"*Meat… something large enough to hold them off until we can get them home.*" She dove towards a river as I saw a large group of hefty bears that were catching fish on the rapids. "*Never had a bear in the south before…*"

"You just ate."

"As did you and we're both hungry."

"One bear for the whelps. That's it."

"Fine, party-crasher. You could have tried it too."

I gave out a sigh, keeping back the thought that I was vaguely curious to know what a Seraphinean black bear tasted like. She snatched one of the unsuspected bears that stood as tall as I was on all fours with her claws. It barely gave a noise as she snapped its neck, killing it instantly. She flew it back towards the building and dropped it by the vehicles. When we found the whelps, if there were many of them, we were going to have to use one of the forrums in the yard in order to get them home… How to use it though was going to be an interesting time.

It couldn't be that hard.

She flew back to the wooded area nearby where the only entrance we managed to see was directly through destroyed gates. I got off and looked out from the bushes. Nothing continued to move, and I relaxed slightly. If there was anyone there, they would have noticed the bear dropped in their yard.

Deigh came up beside me in her Absalomian form. Her white cloak covered her head and casted a dark shadow over her face. A white and silver spear was in her hand. The air around the tip was heated. I put a hand on her shoulder to try and help her nerves. This would have been her first real battle in this form and unlike me, she didn't have any armour besides her high resistance. Hopefully, she didn't have to use her spear at all.

The tip cooled and the spear folded into itself. She stared at it a little longer then put it away within the holster attached to the belt on her skirt. *"I'm ready…"*

"Let me know when you aren't, alright?"

She nodded.

"Stay close."

We moved to the door, swiftly and silently. The fence and the gates had been destroyed long before we got there, but whatever remained of the fighters was gone. Melted metal and clearly rearranged earth that wasn't natural compared to the rest of the smoothened ground; they were the only things that showed that the knights, Éabha, and Uncle Owen had been there. We got to the door and I went to try the handle to find that it was slightly ajar with the frame bent and broken. Slipping inside, the smell hit both of our noses first. A stifled gag came out as I tried to stay silent and hold down what was left of supper, covering my nose and mouth with my hand. Corpses covered the entrance lobby and parting halls. They were rotten and slightly eaten by small animals that scurried away at our arrival.

Only a couple of flies buzzed, and some movement came from the bodies. I got a little closer, wondering what it was, and regretted it immediately as tiny maggots were squirming about. I walked away quickly from them and continued down the hall. A small, hushed laugh of amusement came from Deigh as she gracefully moved around them. I rolled my eyes.

We were exposed to the same amount of death and right from day one she was fine with it… It wasn't something I quite understood.

We went to move forwards, deeper into the facility but I stopped as the outline of the Outland Dragon appeared again, wagging a beckoning tail before rushing into a closed room. I narrowed my gaze and followed it as Deigh questioned where I was going. I looked back at her. "*Just a feeling…*"

She followed as I walked up to the room the dragon had brought me to. The door, unlike the front entrance, was closed. I tried the handle, but it was locked. A panel sat next to it on the side of the wall and showed a red light. It needed a key card. It didn't do its job well at keeping us out as the handle melted under my gauntlet. A small spark of the security system overloading from magic came from the panel. The metal dripped down the door and eventually, nothing sat in the socket, releasing the door from the lock. Deigh passed me a strange look. I didn't ask about it and focused on our surroundings instead.

I pushed the door open slightly and peeked around the corner. More corpses laid on the floor of the slightly lit room. I opened the way fully. Screens were alight on one side and underneath, a console for them sat on the table. Each screen had a different view of a hallway or a room, many of them covered in bodies, blood, and scorch marks. Some of them flickered from damage. My stomach turned as I scanned over them, avoiding the less disgusting corpse behind me. The screens had tiny names of where their video feed was in current time and with a map of the building that had a little highlighted square to detail its exact location. The building, if the map was accurate, was huge. Huge and at least one of the massacres on the screens that were left abandoned was my doing.

I looked down to the console and saw a collection of buttons that mimicked the video buttons on the CT to fast forward or reverse feed along with a stick. I moved the stick and all the cameras moved in the same direction. There was probably a way to do each camera individually, but I wasn't testing what button did what. I pushed the reverse button and sat down as all the feeds moved back. We could find something important, but it was going to take a while to get to that point.

Deigh joined me as we watched the animals that had come into the building, scurrying backwards between the feeds at a much faster rate than what they would have been going forward. Eventually, the animals were gone and the view of the knights, Éabha and Uncle Owen appeared in the light of a Teleport Glyph with my body between them. The part where she healed me as Owen started resuscitating my dead form. The bolt entered and removed from my chest. The attack on Éabha before switching to Owen beyond the flames, Cyrus and Azarias.

My jaw clenched as I watched and hated every second of who I was. I followed the person I should have recognized from one screen to the next, killing everyone in sight with the wings and tail of an Outland Dragon. They were jagged and cruel looking mixed with something similar to Deigh's scale structure, colours, and patterns.

Deigh put a hand on my arm in comfort and I placed my own on it, squeezing it. "Are you okay?"

I looked to her and gave a brief nod. "I'm alright…"

She gave a reassuring smile and looked up at the screens again. "There, you came out of that room."

I turned back to the screen and found Naftali going back into the room for an extended period of time. "Maybe he went and got the blood… if he did, we could follow his actions to figure out where he came from."

She didn't say anything, just agreeing with a nod as we waited for him to come back out. Which… would have him going in…

Reversing time was stupid.

We waited for what seemed like forever until he finally came out, holding several bags of black blood. He moved from screen to screen, down two floors until eventually he came to a door. A loud zap came from the console and we both backed up quickly from it in surprise. My chair hit the floor, falling over a corpse behind me. The screens went weird with a bunch of strange, coloured blocks. A loud shrieking noise suddenly came from it. We left the room at a breakneck speed and I slammed the door shut to the best of my ability when no door handle existed, lessening the horrible noise.

It eventually died out and I gave a sigh, "At least it worked for a little while…"

"I'm surprised it didn't break sooner…" Deigh admitted, turning back towards the hall. "Too bad this place is a bloody maze; it'll be difficult to navigate down to that floor."

"We could just go through the floor… like in Fort Hammond."

"I'm going to tell you what you told me: we don't know where the supports are. That isn't mentioning that you lit some of these floors on fire. How safe would it be for the whelps if they are below?"

"R-right…" I cleared the idea aside and looked at the wall behind her where a map of the floor sat. I went to it and punched its case, easily causing it to break with my gauntlet and pulled out the map. "It's convenient that they have floor maps of this place. All we have to do is get to the next floor and find a new one as we go."

"There's the thinking king I've missed."

"What's that supposed to mean?"

"Nothing. Come on, we don't know if anyone else is hiding about."

She walked ahead and I quickly caught up. We went silently through the halls, listening for anything that could try and ambush us. Just like outside, nothing stirred other than some moving maggots and the occasional small animal that had come to the smells of corpses. Each floor had a map as I predicted by the entrance making the search for the next set of stairs not much of a search at all.

Eventually, we came to the floor I had first started my crusade and it was crispy to say the least. The charred floor made it impossible to step without a sound as we walked through it, carefully trying to figure out which room was which so we could follow Naftali's steps. We turned a corner to find a charred door slightly embedded into the far wall and a corpse laying on the floor, burnt almost entirely but clearly in two pieces. Blood spatter still painted the ceiling and walls.

A sick feeling came over me as I partially remembered the deed. The man in front of us was the first one I killed. It was a swift death, but a brutal one. I looked into the doorway where the lights were off. One of the bodies hung upside down against the counter, but in a way where his insides were strung across the lab bench. It was the only way the top half had manage to stay as it-

I froze, unable to breathe or move from the doorway. I did…

The memory of it was only that of screams. Living people bumping into things in the dark, unable to escape. Blood hitting surfaces. The tearing of flesh-

My head pulsed in pain and I grabbed it, losing my balance. Deigh caught me before I fell, and I landed hard against the doorframe.

"It's okay," she hushed as the feeling of wanting to throw up came over my senses, but I still couldn't tear my eyes from the gruesome scene I had created. *"It's okay. You didn't do this. A very angry and scared primal force did after they tempted fate."*

"I'm not so sure about that... Naftali was the one who did this to me... Who knows if anyone knew what he was doing..."

"They knew. They were right down the hall. I very much doubt that they weren't aware of what his work consisted of if not his intentions. Aevorii had to drop you off to someone while he was back at the hideout pretending to be innocent of your kidnapping. He didn't do this alone, and those whelps weren't for this single purpose." She grabbed my hand and dragged me from the door, sensing my body was steady enough from the headache. *"None of this is your fault and you are righting their wrongs by finding the whelps."*

"If they are still alive... even if they weren't killed – they may have been moved or abandoned... It's been two days-"

"We don't know what we will find on the other side of that door." She squeezed my hand. *"If they aren't there, there might be a clue as to where they might have gone."*

"Which will just lead to more fighting..."

"It will end quickly if nothing else."

That was true. Neither of us were going to be messing around. *"How many people do you think?"*

"Who knows... but if I have to, I will kill hundreds just to start getting even with what they did to you."

"Deigh, revenge isn't-"

"I don't fucking care. I'm a dragon, not a knight. I didn't take an oath and I sure as hell am not allowing any of them to get away without punishment."

"I agree, but depending on how many, I don't want you to get hurt for it. Plus, it's not just us. We promised to bring them to Zegrinath. He has every right to lay punishment for their actions just as you do."

"Then I hope they are too difficult for us to capture." She stopped in front of me and gave me a tight hug, burying her head into my chest. *"I will never forgive them for twisting and turning you into that."*

I was a bit surprised before wrapping my arms around her with love and appreciation for everything that she was. She felt every torment and fear I had. *"I'm sorry."*

"Please don't leave me ever again... Don't become that monster again... I can't see you suffer anymore."

"I'll have you to make sure I don't, both as a knight and as king..."

She nodded and eventually let go. I took the lead again, passing the room where that thing we were both terrified of was born. I avoided looking within and continued onwards as the outline of the dragon ran out of it and ahead, disappearing around the corner. I looked at the map to see the stairs were around the bend. We went down two more floors and grabbed the new map. Naftali had come from the direction just ahead. I saw the dragon was back and ran where we needed to go, vanishing again. A few twists and turns within the maze later, a new hallway laid before us and the door we were looking for had the dragon waiting outside. The feeling like it was judging me was evident, like I was going to get lost, and it was not a welcomed feeling.

Did it not realize I was carrying a map? It's not like Naftali took six dozen turns... The floor was built asininely so, but it wasn't hard to follow. But of course, it didn't notice... It was clearly a figment of my imagination since no one else could see the damn thing.

We stopped in front of the door where we had last seen the biologist. I placed up my shield as Deigh moved behind me and I grabbed the handle. It turned and opened with a soft click and I peered inside. It was dark, but not dark enough to hide the lab benches, the strung about papers, computers turned off, and equipment. Nothing moved and I put down the shield, moving forward. The shadow dragon jumped onto the counter and raced to the other end of the room where it went through a second door that wasn't very noticeable. I left Deigh to look about as I followed the urge the shadow brought.

Opening the door, on the other side were empty cages and a subtle scent of blood that belonged to someone I recognized but couldn't place. The shadow stopped, no longer chipper in the middle of the room, looking back at me before disappearing. Sudden anger and depression tried to grip my rational focus to find clues and left me a bit disoriented on what I was supposed to do next. Deigh brushed my arm, and the alien feelings went away in an instant, bringing me to reality. I looked down to see her looking at me strangely.

"Are you alright?" she asked, and I looked around the room, trying to figure out where the sudden feelings came from but not knowing how to answer her.

"I think so?"

"Are you sure? You were spaced out when I came in."

A frown formed. It didn't seem like I was… "Let's just look around and see if-"

Steps came to our ears from outside growing closer. She turned off the light I didn't realize she turned on in the back room and we hid behind the wall. The steps stopped in front of the entrance followed by the soft click of the door to the main room. The person walked in. A bag being opened, and the sound of a computer being turned on followed. I looked to Deigh before peeking out. A Seraphinean was looking away from us and to a monitor. He stuck in a stick to the tower. A gun was strapped to his side with a bag on the counter next to him. Nothing else gave indication that the man had friends or if he was more armed.

"He must be getting information left behind," she said, and I gave a small nod. *"I could take him now."*

"Let's hold off for just a moment and let him get the information. We can take it from him and hand it over to Orpheal."

"But what if he portals out of here?"

"He's not going to without us. We should sneak up and prepare to ambush him – he will know where the whelps are."

"He has a gun."

"Which is why I'll be the one he meets. Take him down while he's distracted." I handed her Guðmundr, and she gave a worried glance back. *"Just in case, my armour will take the hit even if it hurts. You don't have anything to protect you."*

"Don't get shot…"

We snuck into the other room, quietly making our way around the lab counters and waited. Deigh's heart raced nervously as I kept a calm demeanour, a switch in what our roles tended to be, but one that was necessary. A few minutes went by of watching the Seraph moved data from one folder to another and eventually, pulled out the stick. I struck swiftly and attacked from behind, controlling his arms from going anywhere near his gun. Deigh came out of hiding, her spear ceasing his struggles as it touched his throat. She removed the gun and consumed it in a ball of white fire and dropped it at the man's feet. The tension in his body lessened in defeat.

"I'm going to put us both in a more comfortable position and then you're going to take us to the whelps," I told him quietly and heard his heartbeat pick up, skipping in fear and his lie.

"Whelps? I don't know where any-" He was cut off as Deigh added heat to the tip of her spear and he screamed causing me to wince. The attack wasn't more than a moment, too quick for me to tell her to stop, but it was enough for him to give in. "Alright! Alright! I can take you to them!"

He wasn't lying as his heart, while quick, was a lot more steady with his claim. I let Deigh hold the man at spear point as I unlocked my hold and grabbed one of the lose cables nearby, tying his hands and arms behind his back. I took his information stick and stuck it in one of my pouches.

"I thought you said this was supposed to be more comfortable?"

I walked in front of him, and he paled a bit, recognizing me. "Is it not more comfortable than the grapple that could have broken your arms?"

"You're supposed to be… where's Doctor Belenos?!"

"Dead, now I suggested you stop talking and take us there before my friend here loses what restraint she has left."

He looked to Deigh with a swallow and gave a nod. A Teleport Glyph started to form on the ground at his feet and we stepped in with caution. The odds of him taking us to the whelps and not into a trap was less than zero, but that didn't mean the whelps weren't going to be nearby.

Chapter Fifty-Four: The Return Home

The bright light of the Teleport Glyph ended and immediately commotion came to my ears that we were not alone. Deigh acted first, long before my eyes could adjust and when they had, she was standing in front of a console with Guðmundr blocking any way for the other person in the room to get to it. The man we caught gave warning that there were two of us but the Seraphinean guard didn't turn around fast enough before I attacked. Dark vines came from the pool that formed seemingly a bit out of instinct wrapped her up and silenced both seraphs. Glares with both anger and fear were passed to me as I placed them against the wall, off the floor. The pool was removed as it wasn't necessary to keep them out of the way. Deigh dropped the shield and passed it to me.

I looked them over and kept my voice quiet. "I suggest you don't try anything else; the vines have thorns that will activate upon the smallest change in magic. You're sensitive to it and my control is very limited at keeping its power contained. This is your one and only warning."

The man looked shocked while the female guard glared, noises of most likely insults were almost fully muffled. We ignored them and looked at the more important thing that could help us: the map on the console and the video feeds. Each feed was labelled with a number that matched to that on the map and doing a quick over, the lab that we were in now was a bugout lab. It was large, but it didn't have as many features and probably even less people, which was best for us. A morgue had a camera placed inside, empty and clean with the lights out. On the map however, it sat near a room wonderfully named Species Lock-Up which was just down the hall to the security check room we were in. How well designed…

"*How should we do this?*" Deigh asked and I passed her a small glance before turning back to the table.

"*Keep this as covert as possible. Get around that corner there, hopefully subdue anyone that might be in that room, check the morgue, and leave with whoever we've managed to snag.*" I peeked over at our prisoners. "*It's late and the halls and rooms of this place seem to be barren, but that doesn't mean there won't be a security switch soon and I don't want to be in the crossfire with the whelps.*"

She gave a small nod but was clearly unhappy about the pacifist route.

"And maybe don't turn to torture… I know you're frustrated, but we can't stoop to their level."

"It's efficient… fine… but only because I don't like how you reacted to it."

I didn't like where that lack of care could take her, but it was a discussion to bring up another time if it was needed. Her word was more than enough to know that she wouldn't stride for it. For now at least. Later down the road if things continued to get worse… I left the pessimistic thoughts behind for optimism that things in the grand scheme would lighten up from here on. It couldn't get any darker.

I looked over the camera to make sure no one was standing right outside the door and headed out, Deigh following just behind. In the hallway, it had a nightshift feel with not all the lights being on and it being dead quiet. We kept our steps as quiet as possible as we made it to the end of the hall that was much larger than what it seemed on the map. Steps reached our ears followed by a door closing beyond a corner. We placed ourselves against the wall, waiting to see if the noise would come closer. They were fading and I took the chance to peek around the corner.

There was a Seraph scientist walking towards Species Lock-Up. He entered the room and called to someone inside. There was some whimpering of whelps, but I couldn't hear the exact words other than it being hopeful recognition and it stabbed our hearts. Deigh tensed, barely keeping behind me as she fed off my reaction. My jaw clenched to try and calm the sudden rage. The man yelled at them to be quiet as the door shut behind him and silenced anything that might have come afterwards.

"They smell Tad'Cooperith," she commented which didn't make me feel any better about the circumstances. They probably thought he was alive. *"They might blow our cover if we wait too long."*

An unexplained, irrational thought obliterated the idea for covert operations. *"We found them now, let's be quick before anyone else is around."*

"I could kill them…"

"Subdue before we have to kill. Remember, they are Zegrinath's before anyone else's."

"We have every right to them just as he does after what they did to you."

"I don't think you'll have any issues with his way of doing things since they killed his son and subsequently his mate." I looked back to her for a moment then around the corner. *"Looks to be clear. Ready?"*

She gave a nod, and we went to the door in silence. *"Are you able to keep up the vines from here?"*

"Yes... and it's providing good practice to not tear things apart," I answered, and clenched my gauntlet as a physical medium to keep the vines that held the Seraphineans from expelling their magic. *"That part of the magic is really, really difficult to do. Keeping it within the vines and not hurting them... This magic was not made for restraint like light magic is."*

"I guess it makes sense why you sense it trying to escape even when Owen is using it on you."

"Yeah..." We reached the door and I listened, but nothing came to my ears. *"So, what do you think we should do? We don't know what is on the other side, where the whelps are, or what other element if they have a secondary – we can't hurt them anymore than they have."*

"Probably something that will surprise the Seraphs. It'll give us more freedom to decide what to do if there are more than just two people and the whelps." She looked up at me. *"The room wasn't large compared to the rest of the scaling on the map, there won't be a comfortable fight with four people and at least one cage, let alone anyone else added to the mix."*

"We can bust down the door... the hall doesn't echo so we'll use that to our advantage. But it's not like it would be very disorienting for anyone other than us and the whelps." I scanned the hall to see if there was anything we could use only to be blindsided by the light on the ceiling. Then, the idea hit. *"These guys need the light."*

"I'll use your sight..." She gripped her spear tighter, uncomfortable about literally going in blind. *"When you're ready..."*

I gave a hint of a nod as the dark flash charged and she moved ahead. She gave the door a firm kick, breaking the metal frame as the door bent in on itself and went flying inside, loudly hitting the floor. Three different screams that weren't the whelps came from the room as I moved in front of her and released the dark energy. The room was encased in darkness. A quick look around the room gave Deigh a target to go after off to the right while I charged into two male Seraphs with the shield smashing them against the research benches, keeping in mind of the row of cages off to the left. Five dragons cowered at the backs of them.

The dark flash started to fade faster than I had anticipated as they started to fight back with cattle prodders. I blocked one with Guðmundr while the second one was parried with Winterthorn, offsetting the man. The action allowed me to focus on the first one, the one that had yelled at the whelps earlier, and put a boss to his chest. He was sent into the corner of the counter and he dropped. A swinging sound came to my ears and I turned back to the other one, barely moving out of an electrical strike. Wings came at me and I ducked, forming a small pool of darkness under us. Vines gripped at him, forcing him to drop his weapon and cave under the pressure. He gave off a small yelp at the chaos's touch not being contained well.

Deigh almost tripped over us as she was forced back. Her spear's shaft hit the side of the woman's head. The Seraph fell unconscious and Deigh turned to me, looking for approval at her work only to barely give out a warning. I turned, Guðmundr already formed but the man I thought was down, was up and knocking it out of the way with his wings. I lost my balance from the strength behind it and an Outland bolt activated in his hand, driving it towards my head. A spear suddenly went by, skewering him through his chest, pinning him to the far wall. Blood dripped from a drooped head onto the shaft that was driven into his heart and the bolt dropped to the floor, reminding me to breathe.

I turned to Deigh. "*Thank you.*"

She only gave a nod, and I walked a few steps to the entrance way and picked up the bolt and snapped it in two. The power that ran through it stopped. The energy was still in my senses as I pulled out her spear and turned to the counter where the man was shoved earlier, and the upper cabinet was opened slightly.

"I'll destroy them," she said, knowing what I was going to ask as she took her weapon, and the whelps squeaked behind me. She turned to them with an apologetic look. "The bolts, not you five. You're going home."

"We're going home?" The closest one to me asked in Ancient Dragon, translating what Deigh had said correctly.

I nodded and walked over to them to look over their prison cells. My language changed to hers. "Once I figure out this cage, Mygeeria."

"How do you know my name?"

"I…" I froze. I didn't know how I did or why it came out so easily without hesitation. It was like I had known her most of my life. But that was impossible. This was my first time seeing an Outland Dragon whelp this close.

The realization of where it had come from spilled out on sombre words. "Tad'Cooperith…"

"You know him?! Is he safe?! I can smell him on…" she trailed off as I shook my head and lowered myself down to her level.

The other four dragons: Dreomivog, Koderrym, Qin'Darrea, and Cazzrir all backed up, but fearless Mygeeria stood her ground. All of them had detention collars around their necks. They would be useful on the people we were taking with us as it stopped them from using magic just as well as it stopped the whelps.

The little dragon with a blue stripe down her spines brought me out of my head. "He's… He's like Yzelia, isn't he? Not… moving… He attacked them when she stopped breathing and they took him away."

"I know…"

"How do you-"

"I don't know, but what I do know is that you five are going home to see your families again."

She glared at me in suspicion. "We've never seen you before… Are you lying to us?"

"No." I scanned the cage again, trying to figure out how to open it with no success. "We're going to get you home along with your fallen friends. No one gets left behind."

"Tad'Cooperith always said that we'd go home together…"

"And you will. Do you know how this cage works?"

"They had some sort of thing. They hit it a few times and then the door would open."

"A controller and lock probably," Deigh commented as she came over, looking at the cages. She turned her attention to the whelps. "Stand at the back of the cages."

The whelps did as they were told without argument and she summoned a white fireball. She put it to the cage and melted the metal without hindrance, drawing doors for each one. A foul odour came from them as the material was turned to liquid but thankfully, nothing else happened. After a short bit, the cut-out parts fell off one at a time and clanked to the floor. The dragons wandered out warily only after Deigh stepped back and with tails between their legs. They eventually started to move a little more as Qin'Darrea wandered over to the trapped and knocked out Seraphs.

She sniffed the awake one as he looked at her with a terrified expression then turned to me. "Can I kill them?"

I was left a bit shocked at how casually she asked that question. "N-no."

"Why not? We were taught to defend ourselves against them." Her scales flexed in anger showing a green undertone. "They took our friends and us away from home. They should pay."

"It's not defence if they aren't in the position to attack you," I tried to reason. "I know that you're angry, but the decision of what happens to them isn't yours to make but Zegrinath's. If you act out of anger, you're going to hurt someone, even if you think or they do deserve it."

She turned to her friends. "I don't like that a Creature of Light sounds like Father… It's weird."

"Are you sure he's like them?" Dreomivog asked and sniffed at my boot. "She smells like them, but he… I don't know…"

"Let's just remove these things from around your neck and then we can find the rest of your friends," I started, changing the subject. I took off my gauntlets and set them on the floor. "Who wants their collar off first?"

"Do you know how to take them off?"

"Believe it or not, I know a trick that doesn't requite a key," I said as Mygeeria came forward and I felt around for the little indent. "When I was younger than you, my mother taught it to me just in case someone took me."

"You have a mother?" Mygeeria asked and I nodded, pinching the piece I wanted. It came undone with ease, freeing the whelp as it retracted inside itself, clearly an upgraded model to fit the dragons.

"Everyone has a mother."

"Outland Monsters don't…"

"Not directly, but Valrdis did create them according to stories, so I'd like to think that she's their mother."

"Where's your mother?"

"She…" I swallowed the distaste in my mouth as Dreomivog came forward. "She died a long time ago. She's buried in a sacred tomb in my homeland."

"What about your father? What did he teach you?" Koderrym asked shyly but just as curious when he came forward after I released Dreomivog.

"Lots of stuff. To be silly, some fighting, kingdom duties."

"Is he around?"

"No… He's gone too."

"Oh, sorry." The collar came off and he walked away.

Dreomivog looked at me, his head tilted in curiosity. "Does everyone have a father too?"

"I don't know. Many things were created by the goddesses in the stories so, maybe not."

"Weird… I'll have to ask my parents when I get home."

"They would know a lot more than me," I admitted and then looked over to Qin'Darrea and Cazzrir. "Who's next?"

Cazzrir went first followed by his friend and I stood up, tossing a collar at Deigh. She went over to the knocked-out cultist as I put the collar around the trapped Seraph's neck. We left them where they were with a small exception of the woman as I put vines around her in case she woke up while we were looking for bodies. The two zealots that I had left in the room were brought out with a simple thought and placed on the wall next to us. They were collared easily. I turned to the next destination. There was one more collar left and where the other collars had gone – we weren't bothering to waste time looking around if we didn't need to.

I searched through the fragmented memories that weren't mine, seeing the dragon that Tad'Cooperith had cherished in hopes that there was something he would have known about. There was more, but nothing pleasant. At one time, there were nine of them. These people had taken nine of them in the last napping but now, only five remained. I held back my anger and drew Winterthorn instead. We went to the door down the hall. There was no sign that dictated it was the morgue, but for some reason I didn't need a map to know that bodies were behind it. It sent a small shiver down my spine as I looked at the whelps that had followed close by me and avoided Deigh to the best of their ability in the hall.

It was all a bit unnerving.

"You five need to stay out here and against the far wall, okay? Tell us if you see or hear anyone coming."

"What's on the other side of the door?" Cazzrir asked patiently as he followed my instruction and sat down.

"I don't know for sure, but hopefully your…" I couldn't finish, not thinking, and he eyed me.

"Hopefully what?"

"Your friends."

"Alive?" I shook my head and his wings that had been lifted in glee, lowered their magenta and black grandeur. "Oh, that's why you… Okay. I want to go home now."

"Soon."

I turned back to the door and raised the shield as Deigh readied her spear. We barraged the room like before and found it empty. The dark flash receded, and we looked around. A few bare medical tables sat in the middle of the room with a wall of metal cupboard doors at the back. The outline of the dragon appeared again on the table, leaping towards a door on the second of four rows. I wandered over to it; a dreaded feeling entered my stomach. It opened with a small click as I pulled on the handle and tugged it outwards. On the stretcher sat a corpse of the dragon inside a clear bag that I recognized but shouldn't have. The shadow I had been seeing matched the outline of the dragon. Deigh opened the one next to me and inside was Yzelia.

"I'm guessing that they were kept for Ciar," she said quietly, hinting at the fact that neither corpse had been cut into for examination. She closed the door and I followed, the freezing air from inside lingered on and through me. We opened the other ones finding more and more tiny corpses, frozen for preservation and not tampered with other than their initial reasons for dying. Nineteen bodies in total were inside the mortuary wall. "This is disgusting."

All I could do was nod as I felt frozen to the core and without words. I knew every one of them. Their names, ages. What they liked and disliked… Even their birthdates and their parents. And they were all just laying there. Deigh brushed my cheek, wiping away more than a few tears that had fallen. I cleared my throat, trying to regain some sort of composure. I took a step back and wiped my face. "Sorry, I don't… you know."

She gave a small smile that knew of the grief I was fighting against. "I know and we're gong to get them to their mountain for a proper rest. The question now is how we're going to do that. There are a lot more bodies here than what we thought there would be… not to mention we don't exactly know where we are."

"If we're near the other base we can use the transport vehicles. We'd just need one with a cooler since it's a warm night out tonight. We can put the cultists in there with them." I looked over my shoulder and called out to the zealots in the hall, pissed off. "I hope you like it a little chilly."

A muffled response that came back was a noise, surprisingly loud under the vines, but it was quite clear that the guard had told me to go fuck myself.

"I'll take that as a yes." I turned back to the wall. "We can use the examination tables here to move the bodies, but it will be a bit difficult to get them to the entrance without being seen if there are others around. Then if we take too long outside Outland Monsters are bound to show up."

Deigh looked around before landing her gaze to the wall where the doorframe laid and walked over to it. I watched her in confusion, and she turned back to me with a hopeful feeling going through the link as she tapped a framed piece of paper. "There's a tunnel on this map that isn't on the one in the security room. It leads to an elevator and a shipping yard."

"That's a lot better than going through this place, good eye."

"We should be able to place a couple on a cart at a time."

I agreed since it was a million times better than any other option and we got to work, bringing four of the rolling tables over. We were careful about putting the frozen bodies on them and I tested the weight of it before letting Deigh try. She pushed easier than I did, and we silently agreed that moving twelve bodies instead of eight would be the best solution. Then, once in the yard, she could watch the dragons while I went back to get our prisoners on the third trip.

The trip wasn't a long one after I had the whelps follow us down the hall, taking turns going up the elevator as we all didn't fit in at once. Three of the whelps went up with Deigh first while the other two went with me. The anxiety of being inside the death box was clear as soon as the door closed and quickly noticed by the whelps. Thankfully, the ride wasn't a long one as they teased me about my obvious fear of being in it. Their laughter and jokes spread to the others and a sigh escaped as we walked over to the transport forrums.

I was just so glad that tormenting people over *silly*, rational fears was universal.

I looked around and noticed that the lab that we had left was a bunker and well hidden inside a rock face that if we hadn't come out of, it would have been hard to tell it was there at all. The yard we stood in was the very same one where we dropped the bear about a hundred metres away with the large lab building standing not very far. I looked back at the way we came out of. It was so stupid at how close it was for a bugout lab… but so very clever.

We stopped at a larger forrum and opened it to see that it had a cooler inside as the whelps saw the bear and charged for it. A small chuckle came out at their enthusiasm of chowing down the meal and Deigh went inside the trailer, noting there wasn't an easy way to adjust the capacitor's resistance.

"Guess we better hurry up so we can go as far as we can with it. If the trailer isn't attacked, it should keep it cold in here," I sighed and started passing her the bodies to set them at the back. Once we were done, she hopped out and went over to the large section where the driver sat. "I wonder what this part of the forrum is called."

She looked at me with amusement. "It's called a cab, or at least that's what the magazine said in the mall."

"Why were you looking at a magazine of vehicles on your trip?"

"I was wondering what was inside and there are a lot of different types of aftruses and forrums all by different companies… but I don't know what any of the types are."

I laughed a bit as I joined her and looked inside the cab. "This should be able to fit the whelps and me. It even has a mattress."

"What's a mattress?" Mygeeria asked suddenly beside us and I jumped in surprise. "You're jumpy…"

"A bit…" I cleared my throat. "A mattress is part of a bed for a lot of Light Creatures. They are often soft and sometimes can be bouncy. Perfect for sleeping for the road trip we have to take."

"That seems weird… but if you say so."

I turned to the other whelps who were cleaning up the kill like the poor, starving creatures that they were. "Hey guys, we have to get going soon."

They stopped eating, apparently not wanting bone and the bits of bear left and licked their chops as they quickly came over. Without instruction, they climbed into the cab. One of their tails hit the cupholder and sent a small clinging noise to my ears. The key to the vehicle sat happily inside. I grabbed it and spun the ring around my armoured finger then dropped it in Deigh's unexpected hand.

She looked up at me with concern and I explained. "If I happen to… you know, die, get the kids home. You have several hours after I-"

She glared, shutting me up. "Don't die and drive them yourself. Who is going to cover from above if it's just me?"

"Well, it's not that much safer since I've never driven anything… but I guess it's better than having an Outland Monster crashing it."

"Like you think I'm more qualified. I'm a dragon, remember? We don't drive."

"Well, maybe, but-"

"I forbid you from dying. Ever. Now stop and go."

I did as she requested and left, taking two carts with me. The second trip went without a hitch as I came back with the fallen, helping her load them in the back before heading back to get the final body and the four prisoners. I got them first, doing my best to keep the magic contained to the vines that allowed them to use their legs to walk ahead while I got the last body. It was easy to catch up with their slow saunter, but I didn't force the issue. I wasn't cruel and let them have their last hurrah of dragging it out, much to Deigh's annoyance.

We finally made it outside, and I watched them carefully as Deigh took the last dragon from me. She hopped out once the body had been placed down and I ordered the four zealots to get in. They obeyed after forcing my hand a bit to use thorns in persuasion. Once in, the vines dug into the side of the trailer, easing the necessary concentration needed to keep them where I wanted. We closed the doors, locking them in the same format we had unlocked it, and a small sigh escaped.

Dark magic was hard to control when one got frustrated… but a part of me knew I should have been having a harder time with it. It wasn't like the magic training I had, yet it was almost purely instinctual to use. Like breathing in a way. How I learned from Owen when he tried to hold me down, it was like an old memory that my body knew but couldn't remember. But unlike the fragmented memories of what remained of Tad'Cooperith, this one was mine and mine alone. Which made it all the stranger. How could I be so adapted to it if I had never used the magic until a couple of days ago?

Deigh transformed back to her usual self and I looked up at her as she dropped the key from her claw. I caught it and she gave me an endearing gaze of reassurance. *"You're overthinking things. You're more skilled than you give yourself credit for. Even your sister can't form plasma and she's been training for years."*

"Perhaps..." This wasn't the time to worry about coincidence. *"You ready to go?"*

"You know how to start the vehicle?"

"I've seen how it's done a couple of times now."

"Good. Just worry about the go and stop peddles, or whatever they're called, and obstacles, like this fence. Pay attention to your speed and put on-"

"Deigh, I got it. It's just a vehicle, how hard could it be?" I asked, leaving her to head for the cab and got in.

I put in the key and turned it forward like I had seen it done before. The engine came to life and the vehicle lifted off the ground slightly. Its energy gauge needle neared the F which I was pretty sure meant full. I looked over the console to find the cooler button along with the other trailer buttons and pushed it. The trailer vibrated to life behind me, and I adjusted the temperature dial to the farthest it would go on the cold, blue side before seeing the snowflake button and pushed it.

It had to mean cold, right? Snowflakes were cold...

It meant cold.

I took a small breather as I turned to the next objective: my seat. It needed to be brought forward quite a bit as the last person who drove it was at least a foot taller than I was and the pedals were far from my reach. I was tall for an Absalomian, but in the world of Seraphineans, it did not matter. All of them were so fuc-

"Where's your friend?" Mygeeria asked from the seat next to me. The other dragons looked at me with the same question on their faces from the mattress, none of them seemingly wanting to sit on the seat like she had.

I turned back to Mygeeria. "She's going to be keeping watch from above."

"How? She doesn't have wings."

"Heh, she's got wings."

"I didn't see any."

I hinted behind her as Deigh moved next to the forrum window and I put on the seatbelt. "She's right there."

The little dragon turned away with scepticism and her tail gave out a thunk as it hit the seat, no longer wagging. "Oh my... She's the dragon from the stories..."

"She is the same species, but not the same dragon," I said as I took note of the gearshift that I had seen the chauffeurs use to take the vehicle out of park and into drive.

"Really? Then she's not Argona the dragon of Orithina's Hero Theseus?"

"No, her name is Deigh."

"Deigh... What is your name then? You never gave it to us?"

"Aerrow."

"I see... Aerrow and Deigh..." She looked out at the window again. "We were taught that she was scary and that you were scary... but if it wasn't for you, we wouldn't be going home right now."

"You still should be wary of other Light Creatures, not all of them are nice and some of them are even scared of you."

"Hehe, yeah they are. Did you see that mean man's face in there when Qin'Darrea was beside him?! We're super scary!"

"You are pretty scary," I agreed and tried to move the shift. It wouldn't budge. I stepped on the break and tried again, and it moved, shifting up and down as I overestimated how much strength was needed. The gear went up one notch and I took a moment.

I had this...

I stepped on the accelerator pedal, sending it to the floor and the forrum lurched backwards only to come to a violent stop as it hit the building behind me. My foot left the pedal, my stomach returning as I stared at the wheel in front of me in disbelief. Calls came from the trailer behind me and a fit of giggles from the cab. The shame of it all dragged me out of my shocking mistake.

A sigh escaped. "Yeah, yeah. Quiet. This is my first time."

I moved the shift down two steps and the D lit up on the board in front of me, off the R and P. The realization of figuring out what the letters meant made it even more embarrassing as anyone, if they were paying attention, could have avoided the mistake.

Turned out I was an idiot.

I stepped on the accelerator again, much lighter this time and we crawled forward, much slower and calmer than before. My foot pushed the pedal a little more and it picked up speed, but not a lot at first.

Deigh came in to add insult to the injury I had received. *"There you go. You only had to smash the entire bumper and jammed the locks to the point of never being removed from the inside of the door again. But you got it."*

"So what? It's not like you can't open it and this thing was going to be used again."

"That's a valid point, but it would have been nice to brag about how you didn't destroy the vehicle on your first try."

"Shush... It's not destroyed yet. Don't give the universe any ideas."

She laughed lightly, leaving it as that and destroyed the fence as I neared it. I carefully maneuvered the vehicle over, not sure of the clearance but found that its hover shifted as the terrain did. A large boulder stood as the next obstacle that I moved around with a surprising amount of grace despite the forrum's wide turn. It picked up speed as I pushed the pedal more, but after testing waters, I kept it between eighty and a hundred kilometres. Going any faster than that on the rough terrain made me feel like it might miscalculate and scrape the bottom and it was easier to avoid things and follow a path through a massive forest without having to slow down too much. The last thing I wanted to do was lose control in the middle of the Outlands.

Hours went by and I carefully shifted in my seat, getting a bit uncomfortable from driving for so long. There was probably an easier way of keeping a constant speed without shifting the pressure on the pedal, but I wasn't going to go out of my way and break the vehicle to find it. Instead, I kept it relatively the same pace until we hit a wide open plain where I gained about twenty kilometres. A couple of hours ago and about halfway to the mountain, the cooler had broken down and scared the whelps. It was only a matter of time before the forrum followed.

They had been quiet for most of the trip, even when they weren't sleeping like they were now. I expected them to be more like the kids at home with an inexperienced driver driving through a valley, to try and hide the anxiety by chatting away... but they didn't. Instead they watched out the windows at the dark world and the few fights with Outland Monsters that Deigh had to take care of, before curling up and falling asleep. It was depressing. I took a glimpse at them and sighed silently with a bit of contempt. They looked and sounded happy from the soft purrs of dreams. At least they had that going for them and it was more than I could hope for after dealing with what they had for weeks.

"*I see movement ahead. Something big,*" Deigh said, and I gave my full attention to the pathway ahead.

My foot eased a bit on the pedal, gradually starting to slow the vehicle down to not disturb the whelps. "*I hope it's not a Heroepos monster… I don't think we can take it and defend the forrum.*"

"*Not well at least… but I think it's an Outland Dragon.*" I looked through her gaze and gave a nod, recognizing the flight movement. There wasn't just one dragon either.

I nudged Mygeeria softly and she looked up at me with an annoyed expression. "We're here, can you wake the others?"

Her eyes went wide in surprise and glee and bounded in behind, her high-pitched voice quickly woke the others. Zegrinath landed in the distance, the headlights lighting him up in a terrifying way, and I crawled the vehicle to a stop a few metres away. The whelps, recognizing their leader, started bouncing up and down in excitement, the sleepiness long gone. Deigh opened their door with a claw and they practically fell out, tripping over one another as I turned off the forrum. I got out on my side like a normal person and met Zegrinath halfway as he drew closer. He did a small count as the little bundles of scales danced around his legs. Movement came from behind him, the night's lack of light didn't hinder me as I watched Cindreiss and her party land not far, but out of Deigh's view.

The whelps moved to the newcomers and Zegrinath came over, a sad tone in his voice as he spoke Ori for my benefit. "Was… that all of them?"

"All that weren't killed," I answered, and he winced. "But we made sure to bring all the children who were taken. They deserve a proper send off."

"Who else is in the back of that… thing?"

"Prisoners. They were all who we found in the complex and could bring back. One was killed in a skirmish during the rescue… Sorry for not keeping the full promise."

"This is more than I expected, thank you for bringing them to me despite their obvious sentence."

The massive dragon moved to the back and ripped the doors off with a single swipe of his claws. The zealots screamed in surprised, and I removed them from the trailer wall, forcing them out, and released them of their binds except for their collars. It wasn't necessary to use magic on them now. Trying to run or fly away would have been futile.

I stood by in silence, waiting to see what he would do besides glare at them as my stomach dropped. I already knew what would happen, but I hoped that it wouldn't come to that. Unfortunately, I had no say in the matter as I had surrendered them to the leader of the tribe that they had ransacked of children.

"You and your zealot companions kidnapped, tortured, experimented on, and finally killed my tribe's youth. You kidnapped, tortured, killed, and manipulated my son's soul, the next leader of my tribe, all in the name of your sick science. To further your filth, you kidnapped, tormented, and used the king of your allied nation against his will, put your entire kingdom in jeopardy, and broke the truce between the two goddesses all so you could continue your work and collect more of my kin..." The large dragon paused as his glare turned somehow deadlier. The rage barely held within made me wish I hadn't witnessed it and it wasn't even directed at me. "What you all deserve is eternal damnation in the Comyah, but that is not something I can provide with this sentence of death. I pray that Valrdis may judge your disgusting souls as I see them and give what you truly deserve to the best of her ability: stripped of them and turned into her eternal savages where you will be killed over, and over, and over again by the very creatures you've betrayed, your own kind."

There was a minor plea from one of them only to be silenced as a black wave went through all of them and they were ash. The wind picked up, blowing the ashes away to nothingness.

I looked to the smashed bumper with a bit of disgust. Somehow, even after what they did, I still pitied them.

I noticed Zegrinath turn slightly, and I looked up to him as he asked his question. "What of the building they were from?"

"There are two and a lot of it is underground. It would be difficult for you to destroy it without help."

"Unfortunate..."

"If you would, Orpheal had asked me to tell you that he's willing to send his most trusted to thoroughly search and destroy anything within or the very structure itself to your heart's content. He feels responsible that some of his people had turned from Orithina to Ciar and betrayed the trust you had with the kingdom and wishes to compensate anyway he can."

"Do you trust him to keep this promise?"

"Yes, without question. He believes in the truce between the two goddesses as much as you do and has already started to lay down plans to have better communications between the kingdom and your tribe in hopes of reconciling and the mutual interest of diplomatic affairs. With it, you two will be able to communicate conflicts and problems that arise so nothing like this can happen again."

"So, if I wanted a message to be sent to your kingdom, you believe it will be delivered without hindrance or hesitation?"

I nodded. "During our conversation, I offered the idea of a continental communications with your tribe and hopefully other tribes in hopes we could all work better together, both for monstrous beings like Ciar and basic needs or even friendships. He openly agreed that it was a good idea." I looked to the dirt, shame entering my tone. "I know it'd be hard to establish considering what my kingdom and ancestors alone have done to the Outland Dragons, in self-defence or not, but I don't want that cycle of death, fear, and hatred to continue."

He gave me a look with a hint of disbelief as I turned back to him. "You want to create a treaty?"

"Yes. This has been going on far too long and after speaking with my uncle, Dragonbane you call him, he agrees. He thinks a proper and protected truce would benefit everyone. And should hordes, which I know affect the tribes, try and disrupt your want for peace, Seraphina and Absalom would defend alongside you should you ask for aid and in return ask the same. Food, travel, all of it for mutual benefit whether or not we know if we're going to need the same aid in the future. There isn't a name for it yet, but this was the general idea of it that we can hopefully iron out together in the coming months if you wish to participate."

"This clearly is less beneficial to your kingdoms than our tribes. Why would either of your kingdoms agree to this?"

"Because it's right and that's it. Lives were taken without it; I can only imagine how many we can save from future events and harm." I sighed out a bit of frustration that wasn't because of him but at life and its complexities. "It's optimistic, I know, but I don't care. I don't want anyone else to suffer like you and your people have and I want to repay what your son did for me. His influence is what got me out of that laboratory and is the only reason why I'm alive right now."

"There isn't a debt to be paid even if what you say about my son is true. You are not to blame over what happened. As a ruler, you need to know that putting everything that is in and out of your control on your shoulders will kill you."

"So I keep hearing… but I don't think I'll ever be able to learn that advice," I chuckled slightly as the shadow of the little dragon came back and sat next to the great dragon that could not see him. The urge to tell him a message started to fall out of my mouth before I knew I was talking. It gave me an unexpected headache that I did my best to keep out of my voice. "I have a message from a dream I vaguely remember having from Tad'Cooperith… He told me to tell you that he's sorry and not to be mad. He's living, just differently and that he loves you and Vothedissith… but I guess I wasn't able to tell her that since she…"

"She knows," Zegrinath said confidently as he fondly looked at me. "And you have a great journey ahead of you. Be careful, my son."

My head tilted slightly in confusion. "Pardon?"

The dragon took a step back and looked upwards at the cloud covered sky. "Just a prayer."

I turned to Deigh who gave no indication that the whole interaction was weird, and I set it aside. It was probably just cultural differences, something that if the treaty much later down the road came to pass, I could learn more about. I looked back to Zegrinath with a nod. "I'm sure he's alright."

"He's where he's supposed to be," he replied and ripped the top part of the trailer off. The two sides fell off and hit the thick grass with a soft thud. He scanned the bodies, his gaze drifting far, and unshed tears formed. "Thank you for bringing back our dead, we can take them from here. You should head back before your people worry about you further and tell the leader of Seraphina that I am interested in working with him. He can send an emissary or two along with himself, should he choose, to come to my mountain and they will be brought to my council without harm."

"I'll tell him."

"Cindreiss, escort them back to Seraphina. There's too many monsters for their trip."

I mounted Deigh as Cindreiss walked over to us and we left the rest to their dead.

00000

The late Kalokairtas sun started to rise as we got back to the wooden lodge in the woods, exhausted from the journey and staying up all night. We slipped through the backdoor that was unlocked for us and instead of going to bed as I planned, I went for the snacks that Cyrus had brought back. I made it to the kitchen and immediately started eating.

Starving didn't even cut it, but I knew I shouldn't eat too much before heading to rest, despite what I had told Atlamillia the night before. I looked back to see if Deigh followed as I knew she was also hungry to find that I was surprisingly alone. It didn't feel like I was but knew it to be true when our bedroom door closed behind her. I prodded at our link that she had closed since we left Zegrinath, and she let me in only to speak but not to know what she was thinking.

"*You need something?*" she asked, not harshly exactly, but distracted and I frowned.

"*You expelled a lot of energy today; I think you should eat something.*"

"*I'm not hungry.*"

"*Is... something wrong? You only don't want food when you're sick or really stressed out.*"

"*It's nothing; just tired.*"

"*There's been something bothering you all night, maybe talking about it will-*"

"*It's nothing, Aerrow. Good night.*"

The link was closed completely before I could get even a good night in or a prompt to argue, throwing me completely off.

What was with the sudden silent treatment?

I sighed silently as I guessed that whatever it was, she needed some alone time to figure it out. If she wanted me to comfort her, she wasn't shy about it and would have asked... It reminded me of the repeated times we had shut each other out during our early teens and it only bothered me more. I was going to have to wait and see if she wanted to talk about it or ask someone to help figure it out. I was sure I hadn't done anything to hurt her, but I didn't want to get the receiving end of her unbridled rage after bothering her one too many times.

It wasn't a mistake even the dumbest made twice.

An exhausted groan came out as I finished off the package of jerky way too quickly. I had meant to save it. After tossing out the paper packaging, I headed downstairs to put the armour back on the crafting tables they were on before. There wasn't need to make Éabha's and Orpheal's jobs more difficult by keeping it in my room. I got to the final step and saw Éabha had found a sleeping spot on Deigh's armour with a small light on what she was working on. A small, quiet laugh came out at the sight. She was like a child, falling asleep in the middle of tasks. No wonder her father worried about her.

I dropped the armour off at the stations, left a note for Owen to get the information stick to hand over to Orpheal, and wandered over to her. As comfy as she looked, it didn't look like it was going to feel good if she stayed like that. I removed the tool she was using from her hand and set it on the table and then picked up her extremely light form. It was a quick walk up the stairs as she didn't move or make a noise from the basement and through the kitchen, nor did she when I placed her on her *divine claim* to the resting spot that was the couch. Why she didn't want a bed that was offered was beyond my understanding. I grabbed the blanket nearby and placed it on her. She curled up, practically cocooning herself within it and I shook my head. She could claim that I was the kid, but frankly her actions made her just as much of one as I was.

I left her to sleep and went to my room, closing the door quietly behind me where Deigh was curled up but not sleeping. I went to shower and found nothing to what her troubles were within, and then headed to bed.

Chapter Fifty-Five: The Unexpected

The holy pool Atlamillia knelt in the centre of was warm against her skin just as it had been when she got in hours before. The soft lights of the dragon stone ceiling reflected off the water's surface behind her eyelids as she clenched to the rosary wrapped around her hand. The small, white and gold, dragon stone beads coursed with power, but nothing different from how they usually were. She didn't need to see to know that the stone and amethyst had probably embedded themselves into her skin, but not enough to bleed as she prayed silently. Her words were in Ancient Dragon – something she knew was the preferred language. Then, she brought the rosary from her chest, splashing the water in frustration as her arms came down with a sigh in defeat.

Orithina was silent, as always, and she had gone the extra mile save for getting high to see if she could commune with her. She even removed her clothes in humility to meditate in the holy pool of the solarium within the castle. And yet, the goddess didn't come to even whisper some sort of comfort.

She stood up and got off the meditation platform. Her hair covered her breasts well enough as she waded over to the edge and got out. A towel waited for her by her priestess robes where she dried off. She hated the water. It never helped her think and yet the best way to connect with the divine was in a pool with a light trickle of water echoing throughout the open room. She gave the lighting of the room a point for being nice, but the water was the worst. How Aerrow abused the element to sort things out was beyond her comprehension. He didn't even meditate!

She looked to the simple rosary in her hand, Orithina's Crest sat at the end of it. It was the only thing that was simple about Orithina's Light and it was testing her patience.

She had spent hours praying and meditating in the pool for nothing. The solarium had an altar for sacrifice, which she had brought incense and the roses from the courtyard that had long burnt out and still nothing. The practice of blood sacrifices was not something she was going to start practicing and she was religiously against being under the influence of anything while she was temporarily regent and that included alcohol, so she definitely wasn't going to get high just to talk to Orithina even if she had the means or want to do so.

She tsked in frustration as she went over every possible means to try and connect with the matron goddess. She was doing better than how she was before, but it didn't make her any less angry about her prophetic dreams. Just significantly less terrified.

How many times did she have to see her brother murdered before she could have some sort of audience with the matriarch goddess? Did she have to hear about it from someone else that he had truly died before Orithina would talk to her without offering to be divine? She just wanted to know why her prophetic dreams were as they were.

She understood Ciar, he was trying to end the world as she knew it, but why was her brother always a part of the misery? She wanted to know why, but also if she had made the right choice of what she asked of him. If her impulsive decision was based on instinct or the whims of delusion that her big brother could do anything. It was selfish, but she didn't care. She was alone despite Bretheena's best efforts with no one to comfort her from what she saw under Dagda. There was no one that could understand.

She just wanted someone who knew… But there wasn't anyone alive that fit what she wanted.

Tears dropped onto the crest that she wanted to throw into the pool behind her and she closed her eyes, trying to push them away without much success. She wanted to scream and wail like a banshee all over again, but she stifled the noise. She was tired of it.

Tired of everything.

One victory on her journey only for it to possibly not matter. She wanted Uncle Owen home. She wanted Aerrow home. She wanted them far away from danger and to coddle her in a false sense of security for eternity. She just wanted to know that no matter what happened to her, they'd be okay.

Aoife's words about heroes dying came back, how there wasn't a victory if everyone didn't come home to celebrate. She was right in the context Atlamillia was concerned with. What victory would there be if Ciar was defeated but at the cost of Aerrow? What if his death was in vain? Her uncle there after… She doubted that even with his strong stature he'd be able to take another blow. It only took one, it didn't matter who, and one of them would lose him too.

Her CT went off in her robe's pocket and she looked to it in surprise. She thought she had silenced the thing after the message about the festival, but perhaps in her tired state, she hadn't. Atlamillia took out the device and opened the message. It was from Aerrow and it wasn't the first one.

She was concentrating so she guessed it wasn't that much of a surprise that she hadn't heard the first message.

The notes for the layout revised and… Thaloth agreed to let him in, pleasantly even. He would have told her earlier, but he had to be checked over by

Orpheal's physician for the last three hours. But that wasn't what concerned her. Thaloth letting him in without a fuss...

But of course he would... Had he...?

She should have felt content, happy even that her ridiculous request was successful, but all she felt was distrust. She met Thaloth in person once during a world meeting held by her father, but she was only eleven at the time. Still, they both seemed to be aware of the other's power. He was terrifying then, and in her eyes, still was in a way as he felt off, but she wasn't sure if it was due to his magic potential being so far from hers at the time or if it was because he was a Dagdian. Though, even knowing that he was strong, she knew that he knew her own capabilities.

She had heard him talking to Uncle Owen and Father about her untapped potential. He had wanted to take her as a ward to study further to make sure she had the proper training she needed. And while she should have been honoured if not pleased for a foreign leader to see her skill just by talking to her for a few moments, it didn't compare to seeing the smugness of his proposition being wiped away when Father said that the matriarch of Orithina's Light, the religion he was the voice of in his kingdom, was personally teaching her. Even the Archon didn't have that privilege.

The memory helped calm her down again. She finished reading the rest of the message, the plans for moving forward, the lie that had been orchestrated, and replied back through the blur, telling him that she'll tell the council and the other houses on her rounds. She wiped the tears from her face and got dressed. She couldn't spend the rest of the day wallowing away in the solarium when she had to inform people of the development.

Atlamillia left and just outside, Helah was talking quietly with Mazaeh. They both heard the door to the room open and turned to her with wary expressions on their faces. She looked at them in confusion. "Is something wrong?"

Helah stepped a few paces forward, looking her over for a moment before shaking her head. "We were just worried. How are you?"

"I'm fine, just lost track of time," Atlamillia lied. "Sorry for meditating through our lesson."

"It's alright, I heard from Bretheena that you came down here early this morning and have been in there since... We were starting to think you had an accident inside."

"Please, I'm not Aerrow," she growled and rolled her eyes. "I was just meditating, trying to get some answers."

"Did you have another nightmare?"

She didn't want to answer with the truth, looking to the time on her CT. She had been in there for almost nine hours, not in the water the whole time, obviously that was bad for the skin, but it made sense why they'd think that. "No, just worried after Ciar's attack."

"Atlamillia, you know you can talk to us, especially me. I've been teaching you for years, I know how scary-"

"Was there anything that was brought up about any of my relatives not in the tomb and buried elsewhere?"

"Maybe one of us could-"

"Helah don't take this the wrong way, but you have other things to be worrying about. Even if I did have one, you wouldn't understand."

She looked a bit hurt, probably seeing and hearing something very similar from someone in the past over a similar issue but answered her question. "Nothing has been found within the temple's research. Your uncle, Prince Lucius, was killed at Fort Noruin when he was holding off an Outland Dragon horde. Many bodies were found and buried there, but none of them were of him and the area became Noruin Village. I've already sent a few priests and soldiers to re-evaluate the area and the mountains beyond it, but as far as the story goes, he was eaten whole, and his dragon went after the fiend that had killed him. Neither were seen again. Prince Lomám was killed in a similar manner at Absalom's Gate. He wasn't recoverable and his dragon's corpse was turned to ash. We have Princess Scarlet and King Ruairí."

"What of Theseus's parents and their parents?"

"Theseus's mother wasn't recoverable during the attack on Siofra during the Second God War, her parents are in there. His father is also there and since he married into the family, his parents had their own crypt. It is being watched."

She wasn't too concerned about family members before Theseus but knowing that at least two of her dead relatives could have been resurrected and put back together with some sick necromancy disturbed her. They had to either find who Citlali saw if it was a Fionn or the remains of either her great uncle and uncle, or both. Anything to put ease of mind that even if an impostor strolled up, it would not become an issue for the crown if they were to challenge, not that they had claims. It wasn't something she would have ever thought could be a problem, other monarchies had those problems, but she wasn't going to risk it. Not after knowing what had become of Aerrow…

She had yet to tell anyone, and she wasn't planning on it. He brought up good reasons why people, including the court that supported him, could turn against him, and the last thing he needed was an impostor abusing that fact. It was going to be hard enough to fight off the houses if the time came and she rejected their wishes to take his place. He wasn't different in terms of being able to use magic, therefore he could still use the barrier – his rightful claim to the throne and that's all they should be happy with. She even checked by attempting to create the barrier with the altar just to make sure he was still the recognized ruler. The orbs went white with slight patterns of black and purple – displaying the shift of his magic, the tether that bound him as ruler, and then dimmed once more.

But even if she showed that off, people weren't that simple to accept it, were they?

"Let me know if you need more assistance. The knights are spread out, but this is more important than retaking the borders right now and there are soldiers available," she offered, not showing the turmoil going through her head. "The odds of finding any remains of Lucius are unlikely as it's been at least five hundred years, but the scars and dragon bones should still be there."

"I'll let you know immediately," Helah agreed before bowing her head slightly, more formal than she was expecting. "I'll head to the temple for the time being. Take care, Atlamillia. Don't push yourself anymore than you have."

She gave a small nod, not promising anything, and a Teleport Glyph formed under the Matron's feet briefly. Helah gave a small farewell to Mazaeh and disappeared to most likely Asylotum's Arch.

It must have been nice to be able to teleport… She had yet to get to that lesson. That came with the territory of learning how to use magic without a conduit. She turned to Mazaeh. "Anything else that came up while I was meditating?"

"Just concerns over your wellbeing. You've been on edge, even after the surprise attack on Domrael Hill… Has something else come up?"

She hesitated and then shook her head, deciding not to tell him about her dream. It was enough for Bretheena to know, she didn't want anyone else to try and *help* her when in reality all they were going to do was make her feel worse about it.

"Are you sure?" She stood her ground and he sighed, "Okay… but just so you know, we worry about both of you, even through the secret stuff. All we want to do is help, including with your prophetic dreams and whatever else comes along. You… did have one of those, didn't you?"

She glared. "Who told you that?"

"Elias when we switched earlier. He guessed at the way you and Bretheena were acting… So, he was right, you did have another one?"

"Maybe."

"It's a yes or no question."

"Yes… I did."

"Why didn't you say something earlier to us, we could've-"

She shook her head. "It's not that simple as talking and helping… a lot of the time it just makes things worse. Perhaps in time, but it's also not easy to talk about. I'm sure you have some secrets or personal issues that you don't share to anyone."

"I guess… but the rest of us aren't running a nation. I know how those secrets and hidden worries can build up and control our decisions. I know I've made a few irrational ones when stressed."

"Well if I need to let off steam, I'll ask you. Unlike my brother, I actually like pulverizing to release tension."

"And him?"

"He's got lots of people to talk to. If you're worried, call him yourself later."

"Don't want to listen to that conversation, eh?"

"It'll probably be a quick one."

"Ow…"

"But regardless of him ending the call on you or not, we have somewhere else to be."

He looked at her in confusion. "Where do we have to go?"

"Rounding up the council. I have to explain the new plan."

"Uh, new plan?"

She nodded. "Aerrow is going to Dagda."

00000

"What in the world do you mean His Majesty is going to Dagda?!" Zephaniah exclaimed, surprisingly uncharacteristically and she crossed her arms, unamused. He calmed down, pinching the bridge of his nose. "My apologies, Princess Atlamillia, but he just got out of a mess in Domrael Hill with the Outland Dragons and Monsters, not to mention the cultists and Ciar… Why in Orithina's name is he going somewhere else besides home? His mission's complete, the prototype of the Zerach is finished."

"Something came up, specifically dealing with Ciar."

He lowered his hand as his angry surprise turned to astonishment. "Ciar is going to Dagda?"

"He is. There was mention of a gate within a cavern where a seal was found. This seal is dedicated to keeping the Daemonias out of Orithin and her fellow realms."

"I'm sorry, but could ya give a small refresher on seals and folklore?" Víðarr asked, rightfully confused as she realized that while she and Aerrow talked about things of that nature. The new council didn't exist when it was first brought up when explaining the Gracidras's and Gracidra's appearance in Baiwyn.

"The Daemonias is the realm of demonic beings who infiltrate our world any chance they get," Priestess Hazel answered almost lightheartedly. "Sometimes they possess people so Ailín and I have seen our fair share of the likes over the years."

"How do tese seals come inta play? I've never 'eard of seals anywhere pertainin' ta tis realm of demons."

"That… I couldn't tell you…" She turned to Atlamillia. "What did the king find in Seraphina that led to this?"

"It wasn't in Seraphina where it was first brought to our attention. Four months ago, when the attack on Baiwyn happened, he was sent to investigate the lack of shipments and communication by King Solomon."

"Talkin' about te demon 'unter attack, are ya?" A medium deep, Absalomian accented voice came into the conversation and caused Atlamillia to jump. They turned to the newcomer. Governor Óðinn was leaning against the far left of the two entrance ways that led out to the sunny balcony they were chatting on. "My fater skipped out on tellin' me te details, so I'm curious ta know 'ow tat massacre occurred."

"Governor Óðinn, what brings you to the castle?" Ailín asked and he shrugged, seemingly without purpose.

"Was bored, wanted ta come see what's been 'appenin' around 'ere." He had a mischievous look in his sea green eyes. "So, te king's gonna be 'eadin' ta all te nations eventually? Must really suck ta be 'im, eh?"

"Not all the kingdoms, just Dagda," Hazel corrected, and he gave another shrug.

"Two kingdoms, one trip. I know 'im well enough tat 'e'd rater not."

Atlamillia nodded. "You're right. Aerrow just wants to come home, but that's not possible right now unfortunately."

"I get it. Don't know why 'e's out but I can 'elp spread te news and calm the 'ouses and teir noises... Gods is it only ever just noise."

"Really?"

"I'm a governor; it's kinda my job ta be content if it's for the betterment of te people and do what te crown needs ta stabilize te kingdom. Besides, even if I did 'ave a problem, 'e's still within te time limit of 'is mission. So as far as I'm concerned, 'e can do whatever 'e pleases if tat machine is done. A 'oliday never 'urt anyone. If 'e needs a few extra days ta deal wit Ciar, ten 'e needs a few days. It's not like te kingdom could be attacked in 'ere." He came out of the casted shadow and parked himself on the banister, inviting himself to their meeting. "So, what's it got ta do wit te demon 'unters?"

"You know, you're bolder than I thought," Ronial commented. "Considering you've never gone on to be a Dragon Knight like your father."

"Less bold and more stupid, I'd say," Óðinn stated though Atlamillia didn't believe that for a second. He didn't act arrogantly, nor did he seem clueless. He knew exactly what he was doing and why. "Could 'ave used the trainin'. But I'll admit, I'm not stupid enough ta tink I'd be a good Dragon Knight. If I 'ad, my 'ouse wouldn't exist anymore tanks ta everyone's favourite monster."

A frown formed on her face at the grin plastered on his. He wasn't one to berate himself, nor did she think that he wouldn't have made a good Dragon Knight. He wasn't scrawny. That blue pullover sweater didn't hide anything and while he didn't have a weapon on him, she could easily sense his elemental potential. It had only been a few weeks, but the dark magic in him was a hell of a lot stronger and honed than it had been when Aerrow had the house gathering where she had seen him briefly on his way home.

Óðinn had been training on his own and she didn't know him well enough to know why. He was smart, that was a fact, and Aerrow enjoyed his company the few times they had been together, but it still unsettled her as to why he was taking those steps now. She didn't ask though and answered the questions already set out. If there was time later, perhaps she could converse with him more. Allies never hurt.

"The Gracidras and Gracidra were originally thought to have come to Baiwyn in hopes of feeding and gathering strength to fight against a demon called The Effigy and monsters called pnevallidums that found a home in Elwood Garden. But there were aspects that hadn't added up such as the kill count or why they had shown up practically across the country. There wasn't anything else to go off to answer those questions at the time, so it was left as an anomaly. After Ciar's attack, we used magic scanners to look for his signature using his presence within Siofra Castle shortly after the evacuation. He not only had a presence that matched the Daemonias Portals, which we already knew of, but his showed up in Baiwyn. It was faded, but he had definitely been there just before the demon hunters spawned."

"The demon hunters came because they were hunting Ciar?" Hazel asked, her eyes growing wide. "Yikes! They killed a third of a town! I knew he was strong but... two demon hunters, seriously?"

"It's because he's not only part demon but also part Seraph. Whoever his mother is comes from a powerful line."

Víðarr crossed his arms. "So, 'ow's tis relate ta te seals?"

"Aerrow was directed to a man who had been helping the local Dragon Knights by identifying and sharing what he knew on that mythic level that the knights were missing. While doing so, he created a very poor cosmology chart of the realms and how each one was connected: Orithin in the middle; Athnuracha, the Kingdom of Orith, and the Kingdom of Valr on top; and on the bottom, the Comyah sat between Orithin and the Daemonias. This realm, as Hazel said, is where demons come from. Orithin never had a demon problem until after the First God War when the goddesses broke space and were forced to seal it to keep something on the other side from closing in. This story, while seemingly outrageous, was confirmed by an Outland Dragon Aerrow met recently."

"So, te goddesses broke our realm fightin' and sealed it up... but not perfectly since demons still try and get in," Óðinn summarized and she nodded.

"Alright, but what do tey 'ave ta do wit Ciar? But also, back up a moment, te king 'ad a conversation wit an Outland Dragon? When te 'ell were ya gonna tell te rest of us?!"

"It… honestly didn't seem that important to bring up."

"Tat right tere is gold. Anyone doubtin' 'is leadership would be 'umbled by tat shite…"

"Watch your tongue, Governor," Zephaniah warned, and the black-haired young adult waved him off slightly.

"She's probably said worse."

"That's not the point, respect is."

Atlamillia took the sigh that had come from the councilman as a good time to answer the question presented. "After knowing he was in Baiwyn, we figured out that he was after the man Aerrow had met but had decided that it was more than what he could chew at the time and left."

"The man in that little town was more than even the full might of the Dragon Knights and King Solomon?" Ailín questioned and she nodded. "Who or what could be possibly more powerful than the former king?"

"A god."

There were blank and surprised faces from the council, the provincial leader, and even Mazaeh who had been pretending that he wasn't listening to the conversation from afar in the other doorway. The glance he gave for a moment was one of almost fear.

Ronial was the first one to find his tongue. "The man was a god? Why was he in Baiwyn of all places?"

"Apparently trying to gain inspiration to write."

"Write?"

"He's a storyteller, one that we're all aware of. Aerrow, his knights, and General Owen met Valoth Nor."

A scowl formed on Óðinn's face. "Tat's neat and all but why'd te god, I don't know, not smite te demon 'unters while 'e was tere?"

"He explained that he wasn't much of a fighter, which makes sense when you think of other gods, minor or not, that aren't powerful in combat and that's not mentioning the fact that they were preparing for Ciar. According to Aerrow,

Valoth seemed like he could do a one on one with his crescent blade and the power he could sense off him, but he didn't think he could do anything more than that. All Valoth claimed to be was a simple wizard."

"I suppose I would ta if I weren't confident of holdin' my own… So te goddesses sealin' te damage was tat seal you mentioned earlier?"

"There was a seal located behind a destroyed wall just before the Dragon Knight Trials that Aerrow, Mazaeh, and Elias could probably paint a picture of what was found inside," she confirmed as Mazaeh grimaced in her peripherals but didn't disagree and she continued. "I'll spare the details but there was a ritual sacrifice. On the walls however was Ancient Dragon script but nothing that could be studied as the cavern collapsed shortly after they found it. It, unfortunately, wasn't a single incident as a second one was found in Seraphina. That one was broken similarly over thirty years prior. Needing answers, our king went to Zegrinath, the Outland Dragon leader I mentioned earlier, and asked about what was pissing them off and hoped that he knew something about the matching caverns."

"I'm sure he's aware of how dangerous that would be, yet Ciar's going after them?" Ailín asked. "It's dangerous and mortal souls are easily corrupted by its presence and end up in the Comyah. What is his end goal?"

"We don't know. All we know is Ciar is going after some gate that was mentioned on the seal's walls and it's in Dagda. That's why Aerrow is going, to find this legend and stop Ciar."

Zephaniah frowned. "Shouldn't we be sending an army for this? I don't wish to imply that His Highness can't succeed, but Ciar almost killed him, twice now. It's reckless to send him."

"No, this way is better," Ronial disagreed. "There would be no way that Archon Thaloth would allow us to send an army to locate a gate in his kingdom. A king and his party, sure, but not an army or even a squad of specially trained units like Dragon Knights."

She added to it. "That along with time and resources. They'd have to make it across the ocean just to get there and that would take too long to gather a task force and move them there before he arrives. Aerrow can make it there in at the latest eight days – about the same amount of time that Ciar would need to arrive due to his strenuous injuries from his last fight."

"And what if he faces Ciar again?" Zephaniah questioned.

"He's not going there to fight but if he does… hopefully it doesn't break out into a fight. Luckily, Ciar wouldn't have much time to grow with his absorption skill and with the Dagdian Inquisitors and Bishops, he'll have a lot of backup." She turned to the city below as a sigh came out. The memory of Aerrow's death was still fresh in her mind... just as all the other attempts were. "He's the only one who's been able to find the seals that we know of, so he's the best chance we have in finding the gate and protecting it before Ciar opens it."

"They're right," Ailín agreed with an equally depressed sigh, a hint of regret staining his tone. "Ciar could know where the gate is long before an army could get there if they could even be allowed into the nation. If by some miracle that the Dragon Knights could get there and find it before he does, he will know of our weakened state and counter without ever having to be on Yasuquinn. He could fail there and still make us pay for it."

"'e's probably goin' ta do it anyway," Óðinn shared, tactically. "'e wouldn't want ta risk failure if 'e's just failed in Seraphina. If I were 'im, I would make everyone else quite busy wit shiny distractions while I went ahead and ended te world as I knew it. Makes te search for te gate if I didn't know where it was much nicer since no one was gonna boter me."

"Good Orithina... It's possible that the monsters' actions lately are just a reflection... I'll bring up patrols and have more soldiers take to scouting," Ronial told Atlamillia, asking for permission ever so slightly. "I'll make sure everyone knows it's a covert operation, but this tactic is highly likely from the information you told us yesterday on how he almost took Domrael Hill. If he didn't have a tactician before, he has one now."

"See to it... Make sure anything new that arises is reported back to you and myself. We need to know of any changes to pass along to the king and General Owen; they might see something that we aren't. They may be heading across the ocean, but the stance of being able to make it back here in an emergency is still at the forefront and they can do it using portals. Luckily for us, Akirayuu doesn't have the issue of finding oneself inside a building or a tree making it easier to travel just by using a map. Are there any questions about the new mission?"

There weren't any and she withheld a sigh of relief. "Then that's it... Meeting adjourned."

The council broke apart, Ronial heading out quicker than the others to do his mission and a bit to her surprise, Óðinn didn't leave. Instead, he got off the banister and looked to her, a bit sheepishly. "So... it's been busy aroun' 'ere..."

"It has been." Oh, he had no idea. Another thought came to mind. "I've been meaning to tell the other houses about the details of Seraphina, if you have the time, we can speak about it now. Ramsey should be just about ready to serve food if you're interested."

"'aven't 'ad a meal in te castle since te coronation, so ya 'ave my interest, Princess."

She was glad to know that food was a motivator for the young governor. They walked down the halls towards the private dining hall as he observed the place almost secretively. The kids would have been in the larger one and while she had gotten used to their tendencies, she wasn't going to have the governor eat with them unless he asked to. She eyed him a bit before starting a conversation. "How has governing a province been?"

"Particularly easy when te province isn't 'ome," he answered cheekily. "All my problems come ta my doorstep instead of dozens of letters or messengers like it was for my fater and frankly, tere 'asnt been many of tem."

"It'll be a change then when the kingdom is able to go back."

"Yes, but not an unwelcome one. Seeing te people under my protection is nice, but gods do ya not 'ave any privacy."

"I'm presuming this also means that the ones coming to your door are other houses and provincial leaders."

"Yeah, some of tem don't tink I can do te job, but I suppose tat comes wit te territory of being young." He looked down at her with a smirk. "But ye'd know all about tat, Princess Atlamillia."

"More so Aerrow than myself. I've thankfully managed to avoid much of it."

"Right, ye're te one tat te 'ouses 'ad more contact wit before te shitshow." A chuckle came from him as they got to the private hall. "Well tat'll go away once ya tell tem about all 'e's done in Seraphina. Tough, I wish meetin' a god could be on tat achievement list…"

A lighthearted giggle came out at his obvious disappointment. "Even if I could, I doubt they'd believe either of us. Not on top of all the other unbelievable things that have happened."

She opened the door, and the smell of food welcomed her blissfully as Óðinn walked in. A small whistle came from his lips. "I 'eard tat some kids were livin' in te castle so ta 'ave tis place set witout bein' ordered is sometin' special. Not ta mention tis room. Tis castle is amazin'."

"It's flashy but it's not the warmest or the most technologically updated place," she admitted as she remembered her first time seeing the layout. It was in fact one of the most beautiful pieces of architecture she had seen. It was sculpted out literally by a god, but due to that, it had its problems, mortal problems. "As for where we're eating, Jakob takes great pride at knowing what is needed around the castle."

"I'll admit, I'm a bit jealous of 'is work etic."

They sat at the small table and after digging into the delicious meal for several minutes as Atlamillia was starving, she finally talked about everything he was missing. The progress of the Zerach to some of the other misadventures. She kept parts out, like the kidnapping, the personal things that only Aerrow would tell her, but she did tell him about the activity of the zealots and how there were at least two types. It wasn't for the sake of causing worry, or in Óðinn's view showing off, but for spreading awareness in hopes that the knowledge could bring out thoughts and ideas that may have crossed his mind or whoever he talked to about other possibilities within the cult. She stuck her fork into the mashed potatoes, readying to grab another bite. "And you already know of what's happening now that the Zerach's complete."

"Finalizin', miniaturizin', and replication," he guessed, his dish was eaten as much as hers was, which was most of it. "'e's been through quite the experience, 'asn't 'e?"

"That's one way of putting it."

He gave a small chuckle at a discussion she wasn't a part of. "Ah, but I wish I could've assisted in te matter. Admittedly, I didn't come 'ere simply because I was bored. I was curious about 'ow te two of ya were doin'."

She passed him a confused look. "You mean how the crown is-"

"No, personally 'ow te two of ya were 'andlin' everytin'." He had a distant look for a few moments. "We bot lost our faters, it's 'ard ta fill tere spots. Well, maybe not and I'm assumin', but for me it's been difficult. Aerrow and I 'ad only a small discussion on te matter, but I could tell it 'urt. I tought at first tat 'e was gonna be a snobby rich prince, ya know te type, but when 'e wasn't, it was nice ta 'ave someone ta relate wit. Unfortunately, tere 'asn't been a lot of time ta connect before 'e left so I never got te chance ta tell 'im 'ow much I appreciated 'im ignorin' my mannerisms and mistakes."

"He spoke to me a little bit about you," Atlamillia told him, and he gave the briefest expression of surprise. "You helped him along as well since you were one of the first house leaders he met with. You gave him tips on how to deal with certain houses that he was very grateful to have."

"It's nice ta know tey 'elped. I consider 'im a developing friendship, but when we discussed matters, it was quite obvious of te wall 'e put around 'imself… So hopefully once 'e's back, I'll maybe come over more often ta see if I can knock it down."

"Luckily for you, those walls you mentioned were softened since he's been in Seraphina."

"What stubborn bugger managed to do tat?"

"An equally stubborn Seraph, but I'll keep the details, so it gives you two something to talk about. Make that friendship a little easier to develop."

"Aw, not gonna put in a word for me?"

She was about to give a sassy reply to his equally cheeky response only for the dining hall doors to open loudly. They turned their attention to the one who barged in unexpectedly to find Jakob bowing lowly. "I'm sorry, Princess Atlamillia, Governor Óðinn, for interrupting your dinner."

"What is it?" she asked, and he raised his head.

"Brigadier-Commander Delram Tadhg is in the throne room. He requested your audience, it's urgent."

"I'll be right there."

"Never quiet 'ere, is it?" Óðinn question and she gave the smallest of sighs.

"It can be, excuse me. This shouldn't take long."

"Take yer time."

She left with Jakob and walked briskly to the throne room. She had been avoiding the place but should have guessed that eventually she was going to have to hold meetings in there like the proper regent she was supposed to be.

"*You'll be okay,*" Lucilla reassured. "*And if you aren't, you can always ask them to walk with you. But I believe this is a good opportunity to know if you can stay there.*"

"*Glad one of us believes that…*"

They reached the side door into the throne room and on the other side was like she had remembered it when Aerrow had his last audience. She felt a small sense of accomplishment for being able to avoid the room for weeks on end. The red and white draconic throne on a dais was lit up evenly like the rest of the large, circular room from sconces on pillars and chandeliers. The massive walls and balcony were built and carved from the mountain itself and mosaics on the domed ceiling sparkled. The architecture, while not her most knowledgeable subject, was very different from the architecture of her home. It was older, designed like Ley Line Temple as she had seen in textbooks, but it seemed like it was older still.

It had been a question on her mind for a while, whether the designs were the gods' preference or if it was some long-gone people that the gods had incorporated. It seemed like a mixture, but she wasn't sure. Azarias had went out drinking with her one time with her friends and went off on a long tangent on the mythical history left behind. He was drunk, but it was a fascinating series of stories.

Delram and several other knights stood near the throne, geared to the teeth. She didn't need to see their expressions or hear their words to know the tension and concern that smothered the massive room. Hearing her steps, they turned to her and she greeted them with a hint of caution, stopping a few feet away from the dais. "Brigadier-Commander, what is it? Shouldn't you be in the Province of Maritemps?"

"We were. The mission to take back the west coast was going well, too well." Delram shifted his gauntlet uncomfortably. "The tunnels there are still being attacked, but the coast is completely barren of monsters."

"Barren? Citlali was just there; there were monsters everywhere."

"This is true. The farther you get from the coast, the more monsters. But even the monsters that remain are smaller. They ran away in our presence, seemingly terrified, and anything that we were prepared for, something substantial from the reports, was simply gone from the area."

She frowned. The monsters wouldn't have wandered off. They'd stay, knowing that a Creature of Light would come along. Then, there were the smaller monsters… Monsters didn't run in fear unless something else much, much scarier within its ranks was there. "Where could they have gone?"

"Systematically cleaned out, Princess Atlamillia," Commander Kail answered. "We found several remains of large camps in the area, but they weren't ours. No remnants of who they could be were left behind other than disturbed land and charcoal. We looked to the radars in the area to see who was using those campsites or killing the monsters, but their signature wasn't strong enough to be registered or they were hiding it."

"Tat's an oddly specific detail for tem ta take considerin' tey're fightin' overpowered monsters," Óðinn stated from behind her and caused her to turn around in surprise. The knights behind her drew their weapons. He came out of the shadow of a pillar, brushing his black bangs slightly. "Apologies, I didn't mean ta startle."

"Governor Óðinn, we didn't see you come in," Delram greeted as the weapons were sheathed.

Óðinn brushed the topic aside. "You were sayin' te ones clearin' out te land 'ave left no trace oter tan shifted land?"

"That's correct, my lord."

"Well I assure you tey aren't my soldiers or any of te soldiers of te 'ouses in my province." He pondered a moment longer. "We know te other kingdoms wouldn't boter trying ta 'elp wit tis as tey 'ave teir own issues ta address, correct Princess Atlamillia?"

"They would have sent word if they were going to aid," she agreed.

"A rogue party ten… Brigadier-Commander Delram, was it?"

Delram nodded. "Yes, Lord Óðinn."

"Where 'ad tey set up?"

"Forests mostly, once at a mountain, but their camps have been limited and never used twice."

"No where near civilization?"

"No, my lord."

"Odd… if tey were opportunists, tey should've swarmed what remains of towns and cities, but tey are clearly avoidin' tem."

Atlamillia narrowed her gaze at the prospect he was bringing up. "They have further information about the land and were prepared. But from where? Who are they?"

"Princess Atlamillia, if you'd have us explore the area more," Delram started, bringing their attention back to him. "These people might be trying to take kingdom land for their own goals. Zealots, mercenaries, they are resourceful and if we don't get the upper hand, they could force us to take it back with resources best spent elsewhere."

"Which direction were they heading?"

"Towards the capital, Your Highness, at least that was the pattern."

"If they are making it to the capital, it would be easier to track their movements and who they could be working for, if anyone, as they'd most likely go for the castle."

"We'll attempt to stop them moving that far. Fighting for a taken city, especially the capital with its defences let alone adding a castle would be incredibly more taxing to take back without the intent to destroy."

"Do your best, but don't overstrain. They could be clearing out monsters for the sake of trying to prove a point such as sullying the crown and distract us from their real goals."

"So you wish for us to go after the phantoms, or shall we continue our original mission?"

She wanted both, but with their resources already stressed, she knew she couldn't have both. "Strategically continue your mission and spread the message to the other generals and brigadier-commanders that there are intruders in our realm. Have them keep vigilant. Report camps as you find them, use scouting soldiers. If they make it out of the province, inform other parties of their location. We need to keep to our original goals but also find out who they are… though that doesn't mean we can't take advantage of their hard work."

"I'll send a messenger should any other camps be found, Princess Atlamillia."

Delram saluted and his company followed suit before quickly leaving the room with her, Óðinn, and the throne. Surprisingly, there was no tug to go towards it like there was before. She gave her full focus to the young governor, keeping her relief to herself. "Looks like your province might be available sooner than expected if we hunt down these strangers."

"Perhaps…" He didn't seem as thrilled about the idea. "I 'ave a bad feelin' tat tis's sometin' more… I'm gonna look inta tis furter. I'll get back ta ya if I find anytin'. Tank you for te dinner, Princess."

She gave a nod and he strolled out the way the knights had went through the large doorway. She turned to the throne and a small pang struck her chest.

She hoped that she did the right thing. To focus on the mission over finding whoever was in the kingdom.

A sigh came out as her brother came to mind.

Hopefully, nothing else could go wrong.

Chapter Fifty-Six: Phantom

I brought up my sword, blocking a sneaky attack from a pistol that Éabha had fired from her hip while her magic attacks had forced me to back off a moment prior. I went in, the soft grass under my boots gave me grip that the sandy training room didn't and allowed me to avoid her light vines. The blades on her gauntlets blocked Winterthorn and pushed upwards, throwing my arm off to the side. She took the opening, flying overtop and hit my back with a second strike. I turned as Guðmundr formed and blocked a third. A light field formed under us and I countered with a dark field, neutralizing both. She raised an eyebrow before shrugging and formed several light orbs in a grid in front of her, mimicking what Naftali had done a few days ago.

She let them go and I reacted with several of my own fireballs still white with hints of purple and black in their forms. They connected with some of the orbs and caused them to blow up at the interception. Winterthorn was used to send a few back while Guðmundr took the rest, and I closed the gap in her distraction. She turned from her recovery, her eyes growing wide at my sudden appearance before it changed to a smirk. My triumphant feeling of making it went with the breeze as a flash of light came from her. A grunt came out as the pressure from the attack sent me several paces back. If it hadn't been for the armour, her light flash would have seriously hurt.

My sword was twisted out of my hand in my blindness, and it created a soft thud of the blade stabbing into the grass far off to my right. I tried to regain my bounds, swiping out my clawed gauntlets at movement to my left. The sound of something hitting Winterthorn's blade came shortly after I struck out a second time, finding her as the heated claws scraped against her armour. A surprised squeak came out of her. My eyes finally adjusted as the light had completely faded and felt her land on the field behind me. Magic came to my senses and I backflipped over her. A large blast of light went through the space I was in a moment before. With the landing, I brought around a kick, noticing that she also took Guðmundr from me while I was blinded.

It connected with her attempt to block her chest with her gauntlets, but it wasn't enough to stop the dragon magic that it was loaded with. The magic was released, and she was sent quite a ways from the house and closer to the forest. I went after her only to be hit by a stray vine within her field as mine lost focus and pelted me right in the middle of my chest. It took my run and momentum and planted me face first in the dirt. The air was knocked out of me as it was both hard and unexpected. I got up slightly disoriented. A glint of armour reflected in the sun came from my right and I activated the semi transformation in a panic of not wanting to have a gauntlet to the face. The wings came out, taking the attack and throwing it and Éabha off-centre. My tail came from the side, knocking her over with a loud thump as the armour on it hit hers.

My wing armour finally finished unfolding itself, protecting them with carbon steel. Sharp, jagged blades matched the jagged form of the wing and I stretched them out, feeling a bit more normalcy than I had without them as Éabha glared up at me. I gave a cheeky grin only to realize that she was holding a vine of light in her hand, keeping it from forming out of the field. I didn't get a chance to react as she whipped it out and my leg was pulled out from underneath me. I hit the ground before being dangled upside down for a moment, then finally was flicked away and off to the side.

The landing on my side and wing was uncomfortable and caused me to hiss. I rolled onto my back to get up as the sun was blotted out. Éabha dropped on top of me, pinning my arm above my head to get an opening. I went for the weapon on her hip with the free hand that she forgot to pin with her leg. Her gauntlet's forward blades were placed against my neck, easily ready to enter and skewer my brain.

Neither of us moved from our spots, breathing heavily though from her shadowed face, her gaze seemed wild in expression. I huffed out a grin as I realized that she hadn't noticed what position she was in. "Good tie, Éabha."

Her look laid off the aggression and turned to a furrowed brow of confusion. "Tie?"

I moved my free hand slightly, rubbing the muzzle of her pistol I had grabbed in the struggle against her stomach. She looked down and her eyes went wide in realization that it was loaded with enough magic to destroy her armour and then some.

"Oh. I see you figured out how my gun design works…"

"It's heavier than I thought it would be," I admitted, and she turned back to me, a bit perplexed. "What is it?"

"I'm just surprised that you used magic for this skirmish. I thought you hated it."

I looked at her in confusion before going over the fight and I panicked. I set the gun off to the side and dismissed my wings and tail immediately, dropping us a couple inches into the grass. "Oh gods, I…"

"Aerrow?"

"What if… no he wouldn't be…" My head throbbed and I brought my free hand to my head. She removed her gauntlet from my throat. "Why would I use magic?"

"You alright?"

"No… yes… maybe…" I gave out a sigh. "I don't know… I got lost in practice and… but I never use magic and yet… You're getting better-"

"Don't change the subject. What is it?"

"It's nothing, really. I guess I'm more air-headed than usual today." I sighed again as the pain went away and I looked up at her with a smile, trying to ease her concern. "Your attacks made me forget about why I don't use magic. You should be proud."

"If you're sure it's nothing…"

"I'm sure… but I have to ask, how long are you going to keep me pinned like this?"

She looked confused once more then realized that she was still on me, growing a bit red and immediately stood up next to me. "Ah, fuck… Hope no one was watching us."

"Uh… why?"

"What do you think my father would think if he saw that?" She asked, offering a hand and I took it, getting up.

It took me a few more moments to understand what she was talking about and my muscles froze. "Oh gods, please tell me he's not there…"

She peeked around my arm then relaxed. "Nope… no one there."

"Thank the gods… your air-headed move almost got me killed!"

"Yeah… it probably could have. Sorry." She went sombre, a look I had seen a few times over the last couple of days between bouts of helping her with the armour and meals. It was practically every time she wasn't distracted with something else.

"Thinking about Naftali again?"

She nodded and I sat back down in the grass, taking off my gauntlets to feel the coolness of the ground. She took out her bun and sat next to me. The ghostly dragon illusion came back, sniffing at her and then wandered out of view.

I ignored it and there was silence between us as she also took off her gauntlets and set them next to mine.

A few more moments went by before she broke the silence. "Is it wrong that I miss him?"

I shook my head. "Of course not."

"But he tried to kill me… he tried to get Dad killed, all of the directorate… The things he did to you. They were so monstrous, and I can't help but miss him."

"It wasn't Naftali doing it though, was it?" I asked her and she hugged her knees, resting her chin on them.

"I don't know… It could have been. The things he said to me before you came to help, they were things he knew would hurt. It wasn't like how you were… You didn't know me, and I've gotten over what happened thanks to him… but because of him, I knew that he was still in there."

"Maybe it was a small part of him that was still around, but if he never did it before, then it wasn't him. It's not who he was. That thing controlling him, bringing out the worst of him was the monster, not the person you cared about. Unless someone forgot to tell me that he could grow tentacles and hands with mouths before that fight."

She giggled at my joke and shook her head. "No. No, that was new."

"He was sick, and he had no one else to turn to. Not even Orithina helped him and if he was religious… I could only imagine how much of a blow that would be to someone's faith in life."

"And then he turned to the thing that killed your father… Why would he do that?"

"The same reason why anyone would: he didn't want to die. He probably heard rumours that Ciar could help him by passing alleys or in the demesne, didn't know he would become the Kingbreaker, who knows. But I doubted he would have taken the offer if he knew what Ciar was or what would become of him, right?"

"No… he was so caring. He listened to my rants, to Dad's, offered solutions whenever he could. He took care of everyone in his division. Everyone except for Mum that is…"

"What happened that day?"

"It was a routine mission, Mum said she was going that morning. She gave me a kiss before I had to go to school… and then a few hours later I got called to the headmaster's office. The other kids thought I was getting in trouble because another teacher was escorting me, but when I got down there, Erik was waiting. He told me that there was an accident and Dad was at the demesne waiting. By the time we arrived, I had already figured out what happened. There wasn't even a body to recover from the ambush. Naftali and Dad were both in silence as I walked in, asking where Mum was. Dad couldn't say a word. Naftali attempted to apologize but it didn't come out."

She paused and I moved a little closer to give her some comfort. "It's okay if you don't want to continue."

She shook her head. "Naftali… he was the leader of the mission, so he oversaw look out and equipment, but his sickness was acting up that day and was forced to return to the island. Not long afterwards, the one he put in charge slacked off, focusing defences into collection because Mum was apparently taking too long despite following procedure and schedule. Mum and her team had no idea that they had been compromised. She died, protecting them when they were retreating… I never found out the details of how it happened but the blood I saw on one of the expedition members who tried to apologize… it was a lot. Dad became so furious at him; I have to this day never seen him so mad. Everyone on the mission that was part of defence was fired and charged with negligence, manslaughter, and disobedience…"

"Gods, did your father have to participate in the trials?"

"He did… he was the Lord Director then and the head of Gordin Labs which the expedition team was under. I was at Solaria's during the whole mess because no one wanted me to be alone and see him as he was." She looked to the trees that blew in the light breeze. "He never blamed Naftali though. Not once – it wasn't his fault that his illness had started to turn. But Naftali did. He refused to be the field mission leader again after that, taking coordinator instead. He made sure that everyone that wanted the leader position would know what to do so that shit wouldn't happen again. But the event took a toll on his health and it went for the worse. Each year it got exponentially more difficult for him. More hospital trips, more incidents. A section of the lab was renovated into a small hospital with its own standby doctors that could be called on if Solaria or Dad were unavailable. Then, a few months ago, he got his expiration date… you know what happened after that."

"It must have been hard to watch, I'm sorry."

"It was and it wasn't. I got to help create things with him, spend time there instead of in that house. He even got me into learning biology which turned into wanting to learn medicine, something that I could bond with Dad easier over – it even saved your life..." She buried her head, trying to hide her tears but her body shook, and her voice cracked. "I was so happy that he was getting better, not realizing that he wasn't. He was slipping and I never thought to bring it up. I wanted to believe that it'd be fine. Then, Solomon died. Dad disappeared for a while because of that. His temper and my headstrong nature collided more and more, and Naftali abused it. If I had said something, you would have been home for your kingdom. For your dad. You'd be home now. You wouldn't have been kidnapped or tortured, controlled like a doll."

"Éabha, it's okay."

"No, it's not!"

"It is. If I didn't go, maybe I would have died in Siofra, never would have left my kingdom, never would have met you. There's a lot that could have changed and none of it would have been your fault."

There was silence as she cried a bit and I stroked her braided hair, hoping it would help ease her mind. Several minutes later, she sniffled. "You must hate him for what he did to you."

"I..." I looked to the trees. The shadow of the dragon was still around as it stopped playing in the bushes as if hearing her question and sat to glare at the earth. I sighed. "Yeah... a part of me does, very much so. The things he did... Read my darkest thoughts and threw my insecurities and greatest mistakes to the forefront to break me, to make me wish I never existed. I hate him for turning me into someone I'm not... But I know that it wasn't him. It was just a demonic force using his body, so I'm doing my best to see it as the Daemonias who did it, not even Ciar this time. I don't know what Ciar's intentions were behind helping him, but it gave Naftali hope and allowed me to meet him for who he was before it took over. I'll try to keep him in memory as that and not what he turned into."

"He'd be grateful if he could hear that. I hope he knows that you won't remember him as that thing..." She peeked out from her knees. "Was it easy?"

"Was what easy?"

"Ripping that arm off with your teeth like an animal..."

"I... I-I'll be honest... I kind of did it without thinking."

"You just... decided to rip it off?"

"It's hard to explain… but believe me when I say that I never intended for it to end like that."

"He grabbed you, right?"

"Yeah, and it was all I had to stop him… So, I just… you know."

"Well, it was gross, scary-"

"Sorry-"

"And kind of awesome? I don't know. I have mixed feelings about how disturbing it was to watch my best friend tear off a mutated arm off of a family friend with his teeth."

"When you put it that way it sounds wholesome."

She shoved a shoulder into my side. "Not what I meant, Airhead."

I laughed a bit. "Sorry."

"Did it taste like anything?"

"I didn't taste anything, no. I refused to think about what it was made of and I did not swallow anything that made it inside my mouth."

"At least you were thinking that much… it reminded me a bit of a dragon when you did it… Never noticed how prominent Absalomian canines are."

"Didn't realize you were so fixated on my mouth."

"I mean, you did tear off an arm… it's rather hard not to look at."

"Fair enough."

Both of our CTs went off in our pockets and we pulled them out. I looked at mine and found Orpheal had messaged me. The messenger from Atlamillia had arrived and the airship was at the sky port and being loaded for the trip. I was free to start sending our things that way any time. I wrote back, telling him thank you and asked for an estimate time of departure. There was a moment before his answer came through for tonight around seven.

I sighed; I didn't want to wait that long.

"What was your message about?" Éabha asked and I looked to her.

"Orpheal was letting me know that things are moving smoothly, that our things could be sent over now, and the time we're leaving. What was yours about?"

"Owen wants us to come inside, pack up and what not. Deigh also wants to talk to me."

"Deigh? She wants to talk to you but not to me?"

"Yeah, I tried to get Owen to see if she'd elaborate but not a word other than she mentioned you were hungry."

"That's it?"

"That's it."

I frowned. "Mind asking her why the silent treatment when you're talking with her? I have barely spoke with her since we got back from rescuing the whelps."

"I'll ask because it's weird not having you more spaced out."

"I don't space out when I'm talking to her."

"Oh, but you do… Are you sure you don't know what's bother her? Maybe something you did? She's been avoiding you a lot."

"Not that I'm aware of. We were fine up until the other night… Maybe she's mad that I let Zegrinath deal punishment instead of her? But… she's usually forward about that sort of thing."

"Is she always forward with her feelings?"

"I mean… when we were young and hormonal teenagers no, but that was three years ago when we had our episodes. Ever since, we've been straight forward if either of us has pissed the other off."

"Maybe there's something she's concerned with for you."

"You mean something she's hiding from me? Why would she do that?"

"I don't know… but maybe it's that. I'll let you know if she tells me."

"Well… since she won't let me even speak to her mentally, can you let her know that I miss her asking for snacks and head pats?"

"Yeah, I'll tell her along with letting her know that you're getting really worried about her."

"Thank you."

She stood up and I followed her back inside to wash up and head to our missions.

00000

I looked over the things piled in the corner of the house after doing a final walk of the place, snacking on some sandwich meat. Everything seemed to be there that was on the list. I shoved another piece in my mouth. It wasn't what I wanted, but it worked. I did another walk around the house for paranoia's sake, checking rooms to make sure nothing was left behind and then came back to the empty living room again.

It seemed like everything was in order, just needed to load it on the dragons and bring them to Domrael Hill… Well, not all the dragons. There was still the shopping trip to do, one I promised Deigh I'd take her on and then there was fishing after that. It should have brought us to about the time the ship would be leaving. I just hoped that her weird mood wouldn't affect the outing, even if we weren't talking. I knew she was looking forward to all of it.

The back door opened and the one I was thinking of walked inside in her Absalomian form and all dressed up in a white, strapless Kalokairtas dress and little boots. A smile was on her face and I gave her one back, super happy to finally feel anything but her vitals. "Hey, look at you. Already to go?"

She gave a nod, her smile unfading which warmed me. "Come on! Owen and Éabha are waiting!"

I laughed at her anxious impatience and set the list down for Cyrus and Azarias, raising my voice for them to hear me in the basement to tell them that we were leaving.

"Okay kids, have fun!" Azarias called up and I shook my head, walking out the door with Deigh on my arm and my gear in a bag in the other.

We went around to the front to find an aftrus where Uncle Owen and Éabha were talking at the open trunk. We went over to it to place in my stuff and inside was the expected gear but one extra bag. I looked to them. "What's in the bag?"

"Nothing for you to be concerned with," Éabha answered as I grew curious and reached for it. She stopped me by closing the door and I pulled back my hand before it was caught with a small yelp. "Nice try, Airhead."

I pouted and turn to my uncle. "I order you to tell me what's in the bag, Uncle Owen."

"I'm sworn to secrecy," he replied, and I glared slightly.

"I'm your king."

"And I'm a Dragon Knight; we keep our vows."

"You're fired as King's General."

"No, I'm not, now get in. You'll find out what it is later."

I sighed and gave up, letting them have their secrets and got in the front passenger seat. I didn't want to try driving in traffic much to Deigh's displeasure.

The road trip was a long one, but I enjoyed looking out the window, watching the water of Infinite Spring through the trees that were similar and different from Absalom's. A train moved along its tracks beside the highway. I looked over at Uncle Owen's side and saw Domrael Hill in the distance. There wasn't smoke and the buildings I could see reflected the sun's light like nothing had happened. Past it, the fixed barrier shimmered slightly in the sky and I turned back to my side. My eyes closed for a moment and a sudden drop startled me awake causing Éabha and Deigh started laughing. I rolled my eyes and let them poke their fun at my short nap. Thankfully, it was just long enough to rest a bit but short enough to not dream.

Uncle Owen came through the laughter and pointed out the city we were drawing closer to. A large ruin that looked like a castle sat at the top, away from the rest of the much newer buildings and a small feeling of sadness came from it. I held back my feelings and a frown from Deigh as I eyed it a little longer before looking to the buildings and scenery of Rath Hill. It was weird thing to notice, but it didn't seem like anyone else had so I left it be. It was probably the sun's rays shining off of it and my Outland DNA was causing the strange reaction to it along with enjoying darker places. Some weird shimmer on some buildings, like the ruins, could just be one of the many new things I was going to be stuck with.

I turned back to it and saw it through the now growing buildings, not letting it go as I wanted. It felt like a lot of death happened there… some tragedy and I wanted to know why. I didn't go after the want and let Uncle Owen turn away from the ruins at the top of the hill.

At the shopping centre, it was about as I expected. Many, many stores within an air-conditioned building with some people coming and going happily and others not. I got bored after finding some new sunglasses that could keep the sunlight out better than the pairs I had but kept up a façade as Deigh seemed thrilled. I talked with Uncle Owen as I watched her go from one shelf or rack to the next in glee, ready to assist when she asked. It was fun to talk about nothing important and playing a stupid game of guessing how expensive things were in stores.

Turned out I was terrible at it and guessed way too low. He gave me a consolation prize of reminding me that I often didn't shop so it was already unfair. We played other games which eventually stopped at an art store. There was some push from the others to try and get me to head in, but I didn't dare follow the impulse. I had no idea what kind of new things that could have been in there and there was no way in hell I was going to leave with a reasonable amount of money spent if I went in. Deigh read my distraught and came on my side suggesting a late lunch instead.

Lunch turned into more shopping as she and Éabha went from one store to the next, trying new things and picking out clothes. A mini fashion show in each place and the smiles and overwhelming joy that came from Deigh wasn't something I had seen or felt in months. I encouraged it and she dragged me around one of the stores to try on clothing she wanted me to try on. Some of it was alright, others not so much. I got a couple of outfits to give colour to my wardrobe other than white and black much to everyone's approval. Somewhere in the distraction of dress-up, Uncle Owen followed through with his offer from what seemed like ages ago and got me a dark blue scarf that was soft and something I was definitely going to be using as the seasons shifted to Cheimoiems.

Eventually, the trip came to an end and the girls were in a formal gown store. I wasn't allowed to see the gowns that they tried but was left to painfully pay for Deigh's. It was all in the idea to being prepared for Dagda and Thaloth throwing one of his famous parties that even I was aware of. Still, I hoped to any god that he didn't throw one when we were there. Parties and dances weren't my thing and being of any importance, it meant I had to stay for a long, long time. There were things to be done and a party was the last thing on my list of procrastination options. Once the whole gate mess was over with then, and only then, could I be content with going to a party and enjoying it to a degree.

We left the shopping centre in the aftrus once more and Owen drove us quite a bit out of the city, heading back towards Domrael Hill before turning off to a road that led to the edge of the island between the two hills in the middle of nowhere. We got out and Deigh transformed back, stretching her wings.

I closed the door and leaned against it. "Did you have fun?"

She gave a small nod. "Yes, but I wish we had more time to explore other places like downtown… We could have gone to a tavern or a club."

"Why would you want to go to those places? We have those back home."

"Yes, but everyone knows you there. Here on this hill, you can enjoy yourself and I could have fun drinking people under the table."

"You… you want to drink?"

"It's a thing I want to try. I won't get drunk without breaking more than just our wallet, but I think it would be an interesting experience."

"I suppose…" I didn't entirely understand it, but I wasn't going to turn down her curiosity. "Maybe we can try something like that when we have more time."

"And you could teach me to dance."

"If you want to learn, I'll do my best."

"You can dance?" Éabha asked behind me and I turned around. Her head barely poked over the vehicle.

"Yeah, it's part of my studies along with many other skills."

"Are you any good at it though?"

"Yes…" I wasn't sure where she was going with this. "I'm sure your social class also has that requirement."

"Well obviously. It's just interesting to know that fairy tale ideas of royalty actually transpire outside of fantasy."

"It's not like the idea came from nowhere…" I trailed off as she adjusted a large collar. "I don't remember you getting anything with a collar."

"That's because I didn't."

I went around the vehicle as she looked down at herself. A soft click came to my ears and what I expected was not what I was greeted with. The high, folded over collar was connected to an armoured, royal blue trench coat not too dissimilar from my own. The armour was black with white accents mimicking her original set. Pauldrons of the same colour and design sat on and were built and weaved into the long sleeves of the coat. The sleeves extended to large cuffs that went from her wrist to the middle of her hand. Like her gauntlets, the underlining cuff was triangular and went to the middle of her fingers.

The coat wasn't long in the front, showing off her armoured skirt but was layered on the side to its full length just above her ankles, split at the back. White and black Seraphinean meander mixed with Absalomian knots lined the edges of the coat and collar. The two designs, one geometric and the other not somehow worked really, really well within the piece.

But the question still formed on my tongue. "Why the mixing of designs?"

"I should have expected you to focus on that first," Éabha sighed, rolling her eyes. "Simply, I liked the Absalomian infinity knots. Your sword is really, really pretty when it's got magic running through it. Then there's the crown's design. I went and mixed it with the Seraphinean meander and gave it a framed form... It turned out well, I think. The other reason why I did it was because the idea for this armour came from your kingdom, so I wanted to pay homage to it."

"Well it's beautiful. You greatly outdid yourself this time."

She blushed slightly as she sat down to change her footwear for more armour. "I appreciate the compliment... but I do suggest you also stick on some armour, Airhead. Unless you want to go below with just the clothes on your back."

"Ah, nope. I'll pass on that, thanks."

I left her to put on my armour and once we were done, Uncle Owen left with the items we brought and headed back to Domrael Hill through a portal that swallowed the vehicle whole. Éabha and I climbed onto Deigh's back and left the island, heading for the enormous lake below. There was a giant lake monster somewhere within and it was my quest to get it.

Deigh flew around a bit, finding a cliff side with deep water in the middle of the lake. Its creation was probably from when the island rose from the earth millennia ago. Éabha and I got off and I started unfolding my fishing rod while Deigh went to catch bait large enough to draw in the attention of our quest item. She came back in no time and it was hooked on the line. The line was cast out and the three of us sat at the edge.

It was relaxing. No Outland Monsters bothered us as they were focused up at the island above. The sun was setting in the distance like a storybook ending and I was finally able to enjoy one of my favourite hobbies in real life and not in a game. It had been too long since I last fished. Deigh fell asleep sunbathing and I looked over at Éabha who didn't look bored.

She caught my glance. "You seem to know what you're doing."

"I've fished similar things throughout the years." I shrugged.

"I doubt that. The monster you're looking for is a prehistoric animal that hasn't changed in millions of years."

"I've caught sharks before."

"It's a little bigger than a shark..."

"I don't know, the sharks up north are pretty big."

"You'll see what I mean if it decides to bite your line…" she sighed and looked about. "So, this is fishing…?"

I gave her a surprised look. "Have you never fished before?"

"No, this is actually the first time I've seen a fishing rod in real life." She scanned it over before looking to the water. "Yours is a bit different from a video game."

"The rod in Harvest Valley is made for smaller fish so this doesn't shock me. Did you want to fish?"

"Maybe… but not this time. I wouldn't know what to do if a fínralua grabbed it."

"So the monster has a name. What other things are around here that unique to this place?"

"There's a lot of flora and fauna around here that don't live up north, but I wouldn't really know where to start or where to go to show you some of the safer things."

"It'd probably be better if you had a textbook," I agreed thinking about if she asked me a similar thing. The line jerked ever so slightly, and I stood up. It pulled again and it wasn't something small.

She got up beside me and looked at the rod then to me. "You think you got it?"

I stayed silent, judging the thing on the other end. It was much bigger than the northern sharks. I pulled slightly, tempting it and it pulled back hard. Deigh put her tail under the pole to help me reel in the creature I misjudged. I reeled it in carefully to not snap the line and Éabha flew upwards. The creature rose out of the water in a massive wave leaving me in a bit of shock. A long-neck beast that was covered in spines and a long mouth full of needle thin fangs was much, much larger than a northern shark. It screeched loudly, not happy about being fished, and we prepared for a fight. A shot echoed across the water and it fell anticlimactically dead in the water before I could draw my blade. Éabha gave a cheeky wave from behind it and I relaxed with a small smile at the save.

Deigh ecstatically dove for the water and dragged the creature up on land. "Aerrow! Take a picture of it with me with it!"

"Uh…" I looked past her at the catch. The thing was three and a half times longer than she was and easily twice as tall if it was standing on its four flipper-like claws. "I guess I could do that… sure."

"Thank you. I want everyone back home to see this thing… It's huge!"

"Yes, it is," I laughed and took out the CT readying the shot. Éabha snuck in from the top corner of the camera with a silly face as I took the picture. Without waiting a single moment later, Deigh took a huge bite from the fínralua and gave it the seal of approval for excellent food not with words but a purr of delight.

I shook my head as I walked over to her. "There aren't many water-based creatures that you don't like, Deigh."

"They are the best kind of food… Can we bring it?"

"I don't think that-" I didn't get to finish as Éabha suddenly came from behind and pushed me forward before dragging me closer to the large animal. "Hey!"

"Up we go!" Éabha declared and before I could protest further, the Teleport Glyph was formed, and the bright light took the scenery of the lake. The light died and I opened my eyes to find that we were in the sky port where crew, random citizens, and my knights had stopped to gawk at the sudden appearance of the carcass stretched across the docks.

"Azarias, where did-" Orpheal started, coming from behind a pile of crates and stopped at the sight of us. His face was a little more than surprised that eventually made its way to us. Éabha gave a wave with a cheeky grin like that of a cat who had brought its owner a kill and wanted praise. An aggressive sigh came from the leader as he pinched the bridge of his nose. "Good Orithina… What am I going to do with you…?"

"Free food?" his daughter suggested, and his shoulders dropped in defeat.

"Yeah, sure… good job at teleporting… that… along with a dragon."

"Thank you!"

00000

The sun was gone behind the buildings and hill, leaving behind the closing in Thinnus chill that my dark green coat protected against. The only light was a large, beautiful, purple-pink and blue, ley line spire glowing softly in the centre of the city where a building would have stood before the assault. It sat in the middle of a small park that was designed like Orithina's Crest. Eight pathways led to the spire and a ring walkway edged the space. Garden plots lined the pathway with green space between. I walked up the steps and brought my scarf closer to my face as a surprisingly cold breeze blew between the buildings.

Familiar steps walked up just behind and stopped next to me. I glanced over at Uncle Owen before looking to the flowers, toys, and photographs that were placed around the base of the structure and then to the plaque that sat in front of us. It was simple and metal with its purpose pressed within it:

In memory of those we loved and lost during the Seraphina Assault
Octius 20 – Octius 23, 2018 TE.

My chest tightened. Like the time visiting the tomb, I wasn't sure what to do. So many people died… for a man not wanting to die, parents wanting their children, and a monster wanting a kingdom…Was that all there was to do? Just reflect? Memorize the memories left behind? Know that the people that were recognized through objects weren't everyone that had suffered?

I withheld a sigh of frustration for not knowing the right answer. I went to ask Deigh for advice but found that she had blocked me out again. I knew she had been silent but didn't know she went that far again while she was busy with something. Maybe it was for the best though. My head gave a small pang, it felt cluttered, like she was still there with a million thoughts.

Owen caught my flinch. "Are you alright?"

I gave a slight nod. "Yeah, just a bit of a headache. Too much excitement I think for today."

"It was an eventful day," he agreed before teasingly ruffling my hair. "But you had fun."

"I did," I laughed a tiny bit. "It's been a while since I've had that much fun."

"It's good to have fun once in a while." He turned back to the memorial as I had. "This is nice…"

"It is, but it would have been nicer if it didn't have to be made at all. That way people are alive, and we aren't standing in front of it awkwardly."

"Aelia wasn't very good at memorials either. Never knew quite what to do or how to feel."

"Is there something that you're supposed to feel?"

"Whatever you're feeling is the correct answer."

"So a horrible tension of sadness with a bit of guilt."

"Aerrow-"

"I'm not blaming myself for this. There wasn't much I could do to prevent it and I did everything I could to try." I gestured at the memorial, taking my hand out of my pocket. "The last couple of days has taught me a lot... Yes, there will always be that small bit of self pity but moving forward is far more productive and better for my conscience."

"That's good that you've learned this. I didn't want to give a lecture on why this isn't your fault."

"But you're just so good at them," I said, and he rolled his eyes as I looked back to him. The tiny shadow dragon hopped onto a bench behind him, but I ignored it. "Thank you for coming with me, Uncle Owen."

"It's not like it was-"

"No, I meant through everything and still sticking by."

He gave a sad smile. "Happy to be there, nephew of mine."

There were a few moments of silence as we turned back to the memorial and he gave a small, sad sigh.

"We should head to the ship before someone recognizes us."

"Pfft, impossible. I'm not wearing my cape or my usual colours."

"Yes, well I'm sure they are keeping a look out for a cute redhead and a dashing blond all the same."

"Just cute?! How dare you. Out of the two of us, I'm the dashing one."

"You wish, my scar is cooler than yours."

"I think that might be subjective, but you're right. Yours is the cooler eye scar."

He chuckled and we went on our way back to the sky port.

00000

I gave one final look from afar at the gorgeous airship after changing out of my coat and scarf and back to my wonderful cape. I had seen them before but never this close. It was a battleship with many decks, windows, cannons, turrets, and guns. Huge sails covered its masts and had two large propellers aimed at the ground, not turned on as its lower deck was still opened for boarding.

The ship was majestic, though saying it with its hull and sails painted in Seraphinean black and white colours, made the description fall flat and understated. I kind of wanted an Absalomian flag on it... but I knew it was a stupid idea. We didn't want to be spotted and sticking a bloody flag of the country was not subtle. So, I stood there and pictured it instead of boarding like I could have ten minutes ago. The ship was powered like that of the train and had to be calibrated before I could get on, but that was long done and all I was doing was wasting time. I looked around the sky port and island once more before sighing.

I didn't want to venture off and out of safety again.

I wanted to go home...

But that wasn't something I could do for a while yet. Atlamillia depended on us to find that gate... or perhaps the world did if it was as bad as she said it was. A heavy weight dropped on my shoulders and my feet dragged me along towards the ship. I walked up the ramp, following the large dragon walkway up to the top deck. Uncle Owen was at the top and I asked a quiet question to know if everyone was on board.

He nodded. "I'll tell the helmsman that the captain is onboard and ready to set sail."

"Thanks." I moved onward and let him do his tasks as the ship's shields came online, creating a small distortion to the sky.

I walked ahead as the final whistle blew and got to the railing near the figurehead of a silk clad Seraphinean woman. The ship moved forward in a strange grace that made me think I would get airsick. Eventually though, the queasiness left as I got used to it. The shields blocked the majority of the wind that would have happened, reducing it to that of a soft breeze as the ship picked up speed. The feeling of being on the deck and watching the world around was refreshing and made me feel a little better about not going home right away.

Two hours went by as the ocean was very much in sight as the sun had finished its set far behind us. Ori was slowly rising above the water's horizon, its blue reflection appeared on the water's soft waves. The sound of familiar claws hit the deck behind me.

I turned to her and my stomach dropped when her scales bristled slightly. It took a moment for the words to get to my tongue. "Deigh... is... is everything alright?"

"I..." She sighed, transforming to her shoeless, Absalomian form and drew me into a desperate hug like I was going to disappear. "I don't know..."

I hugged back tightly and tried to reassure whatever doubts and fears she had, but it felt worthless against the ocean that was brushing at the link. "Maybe I can-"

"It's you, Aerrow. You're… different," she started, not looking up at me as her face was buried into my chest. Her nails gripped at the back of my shirt. "At first… I thought maybe it was nothing. Something that would pass like your urge to rip out throats… but I talked to the others and they… they've all noticed."

"Noticed what?"

"And you haven't. You've been eating things you wouldn't normally eat. You opt out of things you would. You have been staying up later, sleeping more in the day. Then when you're being your air-headed self, you don't even realize you're using magic. When you do notice you stop and panic like you're coming back to reality. It's like you're not consciously here all the time… It scares me." She somehow squeezed tighter. "Owen thinks that it's great that you're eating more regularly but I know better. You don't snack, especially on meats. You like those stupid crackers and when you keep forgetting that you like them, it's suddenly a surprise that you actually like them. You don't use magic. Not in fights and never to solve casually small problems. You figure them out… But lately when there are other things on your mind, when you're not here… you start using it without a care – like it's breathing. That's not… I… I-I don't know what's happening, but it feels like you're disappearing. I can't lose you again!"

The feeling of what was off finally snapped into place as the pieces fell together. I felt someone looking at me from the railing behind me, but I didn't dare turn around. More pieces fell, building a picture that made my heart race, skipping beats as it went. The conversation within a white world with Tad'Cooperith came back slightly and not just the message he wanted to give to his father. The words that Zegrinath had said… It all made sense.

He knew… he knew since the day he sensed his son. Why he acted as he had…

I shut the link down between us as I felt the wave come crashing in. The fear and shock, the devastation and crisis of existence overcame my other senses and caused me to get dizzy, unable to process… But it did process. It had to…

My blockade did nothing to relax my precious partner. She felt it come, heard the anxiety grow, and saw the tsunami before it hit. Her tone was forced to a calming state, but it shook. "What is it?"

"I… I'm no longer…" My tongue froze as I tried to figure out my thoughts. The thoughts that couldn't organize themselves into words amidst the

chaos of my head. Separating the thoughts that were truly mine from…
"Tad'Cooperith… he's in me."

"His blood was-"

"No… Not- That's not what I mean at all!" My throat closed in on itself as the reality of everything came down. "His soul is physically bonded, it's in me. I can feel him. He can't… He's there. He's always been here since… It's who I've been sensing this whole time, who I've been seeing. Zegrinath knew; it's why he called me his son. Whatever Naftali did, he… he's bonded like the blood did… Oh gods!"

"Aerrow, it's…" She couldn't lie to me.

None of it was okay. What could one say to even try to make it sound fine? We both knew it to be the truth.

How she couldn't see the dragon while I could. The nagging feeling of never being alone… Constantly being watched. Thinking but not actually thinking. Acting without acting… Why I wasn't always there… The headaches caused from him switching places with my conscience.

My mind raced as it tried to figure it out, to calm down. But it couldn't keep up.

What were the implications of it? What happens?

When a soul was corrupted by the Daemonias, it went to the Comyah… but what happened to two fused souls in some experiment? Where did they… What would happen to them?

What happened after this life for either of us?

I had never cared about the details, the end of it other than death was assured once everything was said and done… That the people who left the world went somewhere else, Athnuracha or not. I never could care until now and not just the thereafter… What were the consequences of being here? Being alive? The snacking, the absent-mindedness, sleeping schedule, the use of older names like calling Owen Uncle like I had when I was a child – constantly without regard to setting.

Now that I was aware, I knew that some of it would separate from my actions like the bloodlust had. But what about the things I wasn't aware of? What else was bound to change? Would those things stick forever, or would they fade as I separated myself from the entity's will? Would we merge into some other person that was neither him nor myself? "What… What am I?"

"You… You're you with a bit of an upgrade…" she said as some of the thoughts had slipped through the barrier I had made. She tried to be optimistic, a forced outlook of everything turning inside out as I tried desperately to hold the fragments of my existence together. An outcome I hopelessly wanted to be real that it was just going to be two minds separated forever and not the latter. "The changes are manageable. Different, but something that is still within the realms of normal."

"But… what happens afterwards? What happens if…"

"I don't know…"

"I… I have to tell the others. Just in case if… if I…"

She gave a nod, knowing what I couldn't get into words and unwillingly let me go. She left to gather everyone in a secure location where I couldn't be overheard.

The feeling of never being alone… to never dream alone… it was foreboding. A death sentence that I felt like was hanging over my head, but never knowing the day it would come, only that it would.

The feeling of someone watching me continued as I saw Deigh's figure disappear below deck. I turned to the feeling, knowing who it was. The railing was innocent enough but on top of it was the dragon I had been seeing. It wasn't an outline or a shadow anymore but more solid and kind of ghostly within Ori's blue light as Val's red light started to rise.

The voice from the time fighting Ciar came from him as his tail flicked out in a greeting. "Hello, Aerrow."

"Tad'Cooperith…"

Epilogue

She waited outside the door to his quarters on the ship. He had requested her, and she wasn't ignorant to the reasons. But they were her choices, what she wanted to do, just like they agreed on. And even if it wasn't, she had gained a reputation that had helped him bring in many of his outlier zealots. They respected many of her decisions which were enforced and encouraged by Ciar.

There was also the other matter that she doubted he knew about and never would as she and Gabriellos had managed to get around his habit of reading people's minds. They had used the same talents he sought them for to do it. The magical technology was strung through their armour and other accessories allowing them to never be without the protection that Ciar had offered to help with. He wanted to respect their agreement of being equals and that meant not listening in on everything even when he hadn't meant to. It was a skill that had grown over the months and he was constantly honing to better grasp it's range. But there were times when he did get distracted and it just happened, like breathing, and having to keep his people in check, he tended to listen in on everyone's reaction in the area. So, they developed a way to get around it and it allowed them even more freedom to their thoughts and actions.

She did as he asked, and she did as she wanted without him ever knowing. She had done nothing to get in his way, but she certainly didn't let him have him so easily. Not when he was like that.

She flinched at the memory of seeing Aerrow on the ground, tortured by that tentacled, mutated thing… It wasn't the first time she had seen such mutations since joining Ciar, but it was the first time she had seen Aerrow in such a state: pale, bleeding, writhing in agony all because of that machine Naftali's followers had been bragging about. It was mostly superficial anguish, but it didn't matter to her. Those few moments were even worse than how he broke things off with her. The pain in his eyes that were black instead of white as the Outland Dragon inside was manipulated by the Zerach. It was more than what she could bare.

Naftali was already on her kill list after she had found out what he was doing but letting him get up after she came to defend him under a favour was a mistake and not one she was going to make again with someone else. People who got drunk off power, even if it was influenced by something out of their control, was something she had seen too many times. To her and Gabriellos's surprise however was not something they had seen Ciar fall into yet.

He was always composed, keeping himself in check despite the impulses that even she would have done under certain conditions and chose not to straight up slaughter everyone that pissed him off. He could get angry, it wasn't something that one could easily spot visually, magically even less so, but he had kept it together. He would ask for her counsel when he needed help or even just for conversation about whatever was on his mind. It was something only she and Gabriellos could provide. The rest of his company was devoted, insane maniacs at times, while others were scientists and inventors that were too zealous about their projects. None of them were basic, normal people or were people that he could console with. In this case though, it was a bit different.

Theodora hadn't seen him in three days, not since the battle he lost to take the city and as far as she was aware, he hadn't talked to anyone about it. She wasn't even sure if he had let a doctor tend to the wounds that would have killed a normal person in moments and if he had, it wasn't to anyone else's knowledge on the airship that they were using as a base. Whispers had come to their ears though, that the ship wasn't leaving because Ciar was waiting for someone. Other whispers thought that their *Lord* had died and were concerned for his wellbeing but didn't dare tread near his quarters.

The door opened and she got off the ship wall, standing up a bit straighter. The proclaimed god came out of the dark room, looking a hell of a lot better than when he first went in. He wasn't in armour and wore a black, long sleeve, collarless shirt and similarly coloured pants and shoes. It was still proper in a way that he could address his people, but it was very casual from her understanding. She had never seen him in anything less than slacks or a respectable long sleeve shirt. She wasn't even sure if he owned a t-shirt or a sweater of any sort. As for what he went to bed in, she hadn't got around to asking much to Gabriellos's disappointment. His curiosity would have got them both killed if she didn't put a stop to half of the things he wanted to know. And it wasn't just Ciar that he asked the strangest things about.

She looked Ciar over and found that he was healed and without his grandeur tail that he only brought out for extra power. Instead, he was, like his clothing, in a more comfortable state with eight draconic wings that none of his other followers or enemies knew of. He only brought them out in front of her and Gabriellos or when he was alone. Or in this case probably too tired to bother to try and hide them in their secluded spot. A secret he wanted to keep due to Seraphinean legends.

Many of his followers would leave by principal of him being born to be a soldier of Orithina, not a god as his power suggested. She didn't see where they were coming from. She was never one to dwell in superstition and as far as she was concerned, some godly gifts simply given because one was born with eight wings was outrageous and stupid if people believed such a thing. She understood inherent skills, just simply being naturally gifted… but for these religious scientists to be so engrained in the idea and not having these gifts being sacrilege was… something special.

He looked down at her not with anger like she had predicted, but with confusion for a brief moment then went back to a neutral state on his pale face. He asked his first and most likely only question. "Why did you execute Naftali Belenos when you were sent to protect him? You knew he was working on something useful for us."

"Not for you, for himself," she answered. Her response was ready from the moment she had made the decision that that prick had to die. "He was using you after your blood started to corrupt his thoughts."

"There have only been a few times when I have allowed my blood to be given to the sick, but never has it devolved a man to turning on me."

"Have you ever given over as much as you had to someone before him? He was considered a genius, that added power would only influence the insecurities that he probably had because of his degenerative nerve disease. He was going to try and overthrow you with those experiments."

It wasn't often that her tone went harsh with him, but in this case she had warned him after finding out that Naftali was the one who wanted a Fionn to start with. There was something fucking suspicious about the whole thing and Ciar hadn't thought that it would be an issue.

"He created his own cult and became the sole reason why the Megalona Danguis Tribe didn't join us. He had kidnapped their children for experimentation – and because of him, Aerrow got to them first. The only reason why they joined us on our attack on the city when I went as your ambassador the second time was because they wanted to find their kids that the Seraphineans had taken."

"I see…" Ciar slipped into thought as she watched him work out all the signs that she had stated before and what happened when he hadn't heeded those concerns. It didn't matter to her if he took her advice or not, but it bothered her particularly this time because it got someone she did care about almost turned into some pet. "I apologize for not taking your advice when I should have. You have yet to lead me astray and I ignored the writing on the wall… Perhaps if I had not, you would not be angered, and those children would have been protected."

"I'm aware you don't like innocents to get in the crossfire, which is why this plan to take the city was made so you wouldn't have to violently conquer all of Seraphina to have the kingdom. But yeah, this could have been avoided and this loss wouldn't have happened if you weren't so confident in a changing man who promised to get Aerrow out of Asylotum for you."

"That is a name you have not brought up in a while with such a tone… What else did that pathetic anomaly do?"

"Naftali was going to try and make him his pet to kill you. It would have been a fantastic plan to overthrow you and get all your followers in one swoop had it worked."

"Do tell how he was planning on doing that."

"Aerrow was injured before hand; I don't know what Naftali was going to do in order to get him under his control. I only knew of what his endgame was and the vague planning I had tried to warn you about, nothing else." It was a lie of course. She knew exactly what Naftali had done but Ciar nodded, believing her.

"That is unfortunate. Too bad I have yet to perfect necromancy for summoning souls… The things he could say…"

"If there was much of his soul left. His body was already half consumed by the Daemonias mutations."

"Well, at any rate, I will be asking for your assistance for finding any other anomalies within my followers. Allies are important for the final motion to lessen the lives taken and I will not let this happen a third time."

"I'll gladly help-" She was cut off as another woman interrupted her with a sharp, scolding tone.

"Maybe they would follow your orders better if you aren't bested by a simple child not only injured but sick due to his hidden kingdom."

Ciar tensed as Theodora turned around and prepared to call Gabriellos to remove this random bitch but stopped. She was completely taken aback by the woman with pale, pale skin and white hair. Her eyes were just as white, only a pale grey defining the Seraphinean pupil within. Ciar didn't remove his four extra wings as Theodora had expected but rather stood up straighter and with a slightly ashamed look on his face.

The woman walked over to them and stopped not far, standing about the same height as Aerrow. She looked down at Theodora with disgust then turned to

Ciar, apparently not done ripping him a new one. "I'm not angry that you didn't manage to kill him, but I am disappointed in you. On top of everything else he was weakened by Orpheal, kidnapped the night before, and then fought against Naftali and his Outland pets before he got around to you. Yet somehow after all that, you couldn't come close to overcoming him and left it in a tie. You boosted his morale!"

"I apologize, Mother," Ciar said, the only shame Theodora had ever heard from him. She looked over at the incredibly endowed woman in black. The resemblance was uncanny now that they were standing in front of each other. "I underestimated how strong he could have become in such a short time."

"Next time, don't. I thought when I came to heal you that you had to fight a horde of them only to find out today that wasn't the case at all. That boy king is resourceful and adaptable if nothing else and has a growing number of allies while you have lost an entire facility to him, a tribe, snakes within the directorate, a kingdom, and any sense of pride. And yet you want to make us proud..." the woman scoffed remorselessly. "That child is leaving, to where, I don't know. But they are loading a ship and leaving tonight. I suggest you get moving so you aren't noticed. You're not in the position to fight them all."

"We will leave shortly."

"Do you know what you're doing once you find the gate?"

"Opening it with the ritual you gave me. I have memorized it already should something happen to it."

"If you succeed, you'll be able to meet your father... But I fear you may have to grow more, so much more before you can open it. But once you do, he'll be pleased to meet you. He's been waiting for thirty-one years."

"I will succeed. Dagda has a ring full of elites and rebels just waiting to join my cause. Some of which would be worth absorbing."

"That's my boy." The woman turned to Theodora with disdain. "And who is this... woman that you've shared your secret with?"

"This is Theodora Rinn. She has overseen our operations, weapons growth, and is my diplomat."

"She's doing a fantastic job..."

Theodora glared at the sarcasm, but carefully constructed her sentence to not seem rude, not in front of Ciar at least. It was his mother after all, and he was apparently fond of the cunt that only reminded her of her pathetic excuse of a

childhood. "Operations and growth within the missions have gone five times faster and exponentially since I was asked by Ciar to join him. We have also kept many active and potential threats at bay due to my tactics that I learned from King's General Owen in Absalom which have allowed us to predict many of not only Absalom's movements but of the other kingdoms, demon hunters, and Outland Dragon Hordes."

"Lord Ciar you mean," the woman scowled, and Theodora felt a sinister smirk slightly play on her lips. It always amused her when someone thought they had the upper hand when they didn't.

"No, Ciar to me." She moved closer to the son of the foul woman, possessively. The woman tensed. "He asked me to be his equal and we have become a little closer since we've met."

"But nothing more than friends… why?"

"She is dealing with her own emotional distraught," Ciar answered bluntly, bolder than he had been since his mother arrived. "I am a god, not a lustful monster that would deny her time to heal."

The mother looked from him to Theodora. Her rage wasn't held behind her gaze well but stayed out of her tone. "You decided that this… woman, will be your partner even though she hasn't gotten over someone else?"

"In time you will see that she is the most talented woman this planet can produce."

"More talented than the one who gave birth to you?"

"I am sorry, Mother, but yes."

She was left without words and simply nodded. A few moments went by before she finally found her tongue. "I must head back to the demesne now before Orpheal needs my assistance… I wish you well on your mission, my son. Don't forget to do me proud."

"I never forget."

The woman left in a hurry and Theodora took a few steps away from Ciar, looking up at him. "Who the hell was that?"

"My mother, Solaria."

"She doesn't like me very much."

"She is a possessive woman, so no. I did not think she would have or ever will."

Theodora looked back at the woman's four, white wings spread out at the stairs on the top deck, a contradiction to her black outfit. She took off from the airship. "I guess I should tell the helmsman to get this ship in the air."

"Yes... I think that would be wise. I cannot have another battle with him yet. His new power is... unexpected."

"What do you mean?"

"He is supposed to be a Godling, Orithina's Golding. One of several and yet he used dark element magic."

"He did?" That was something she didn't know... but now it made sense why Naftali was going to use light magic on him and not just dark. Gods... no wonder Aerrow looked like he'd gone through hell. As far as she was aware, his tolerance to dark magic was good and well but being attacked by light magic as a dark elemental being was a whole other story. She knew the difference personally.

Thankfully, Ciar started talking before those memories surfaced. "He did and being a light and fire elemental; dark magic should not be available to him... unless I am mistaken. He may not be a Godling and just that of a bastard son between his mother and general. According to my mother, Owen Castrum had an infatuation for the former queen and never got over her even after she was married to Solomon. They could have had an affair."

"If she was the royal line, perhaps the theory could hold, but the genes that hold Aerrow's right to the throne were carried by Solomon, not Aelia."

"I am aware... It does not make sense. I absorbed some of his magic the night I killed his father, the power was there. But something has changed between then and now. Dammit... maybe he was not the Godling I sensed in Siofra and the real Godling is either dead or in hiding with nothing to force their hand."

"I'm going to presume dead... Most of Siofra's population was slaughtered."

"And going through what was left, I did not find anyone that had the blessing meaning they might have not been awakened entirely or were hidden by their parent due to my attack thirteen years ago. They would not be any older than Aerrow is now. Does anyone come to mind for who that could be?"

Theodora shook her head after a moment of thought. "No. The mourning of Aelia was heard across the kingdom, even in my shitty little hellhole in Noruin. If any parent were smart, they would have seen the attack as a warning."

"And Orithina would have responded as she is possessive of her Godlings to the point of harming those closest to them…" Ciar gave a brief sigh of annoyance.

"Are you going to stop trying to kill him now that you know he isn't a Godling?"

"Not after what he has done to me. He might not be one of Orithina's Godlings, but I know he is something else… He is incredibly powerful, a being that can use light, fire, and dark magic and from what you said he has hardly any education in magic but is wielding it like he has. I need that strange creature in order to grow. In the meantime though I will stop hunting him. He is most likely going home with his mission complete, and we are heading across the sea. Another Godling awaits me there and from the last report from our rebels, someone even more interesting that could be our ally or my growth."

"You're talking about that kid… I don't know how factual that information is considering the source didn't know how to spell his own name. For all we know that lack of education has him confusing basic knowledge with grandeur myths."

"Once we arrive, we will know more about this fable." Four of his wings disappeared. "I will be up momentarily to speak with those travelling with us. I leave the rest in your capable hands."

She gave a small nod, taking her leave to the helmsman, not saying anything else to his decision. It wouldn't have been heard anyway if she did speak her mind. He was prideful despite her wishing he weren't, and he wouldn't heed any warning about chasing after someone who had wounded that pride quite a few times now. That same pride was just going to lead to more irrationally caused failures until he learned or died.

That decision was on him.

End of Book Two

Seraphina

Glossary

Achia (Ah-Key-Ah)

Áed (Aid)

Aera (Air-Ah)

Aesear (Eh-Jher)

Aestide (Eh-St-Eyed)

Afitus (Af-Eh-Tus)

Aftrus (Aft-Rus)

Aftruses (Aft-Rus-Es)

Ai (Eye)

Ailín (Ail-Lean)

Akirayuu (Ah-Keer-Ah-Yu)

Aleklor (Ale-K-Lore)

Annadh (An-Na-Th)

Anoxiver (Ah-Nox-Eh-Ver)

Aoife (Ee-Fah)

Apex (App-X)

Áskétill (As-Keh-Till)

Asylotum (As-Lo-Tum)

Áxigna (Ah-Zig-NA)

Cazzrir (Kaz-Rir)

Cessarfidh (Cease-Ar-Fith)

Cetaykos (See-Tah-Kos)

Cheimoiems (Chee-Mo-EE-Ems)

Ciar (Keer)

Cindreiss (Sin-Dre-Ehss)

Citlali (Seat-La-Lee)

Conchobhair (Con-Koh-Var)

Corraidhín (Kor-Aith-In)

Cruylia (Kruu-Lee-Ah)

Daemonias (Day-Mon-I-Us)

Danguis (Dan-Goo-Ehss)

Deigh (Day)

Denon (Den-On)

Deòrsa (Door-Sah)

Divinukos (Div-Eh-New-Kos)

Doge (Doj)

Drakco (Drak-Coh)

Drakcooletis (Drak-Coh-Leh-Tis)

Drakcovíssus (Drak-Coh-Vis-Us)

Dreomivog (Dree-Umi-Vog)

Drixula (Drix-Oola)

Éabha (Eh-Va)

Eadric (Ee-Drik)

Edic (Ee-Dik)

Eggo (Egg-Oh)

Eínunt (Eh-New-Unt)

Eísammeo (Eh-Sam-Mee-Oh)

Elaftrus (El-Aft-Rus)

Élani (Eh-Lan-Ee)

Endymion (En-Dim-Ee-Uhn)

Esos (Eh-Sos)

Eudoxia (Oo-Dox-Ee-Ah)

Évus (Eh-Vus)

Fionn (Fin)

Fontis (Fon-Tis)

Foux (Foh)

Freegdred (Freeg-Dred)

Fyliel (Fi-Lee-El)

Girra (Gi-Rah)

Gloinne (Glin-Nin)

Gracidra (Gra-See-Dra)

Gracidras (Gra-See-Dras)

Graemerae (Greh-Mee-Rah)

Guðmundr (Good-Mun-Der)

Haeo (Hay-Oh)

Heftvarys (Heft-Varies)

Heirobha (Hair-Oh-Va)

Helah (Hell-Ah)

Hepseptus (Hep-Sep-Tus)

Heroepos (Hero-Ep-Os)

Hexsexus (Hex-Sex-Us)

Hildebrand (Hild-Brand)

Homuine (Ho-Mu-EEn)

Hudvíkin (Hud-Vehk-In)

Hugberaht (Hewg-Ber-Awt)

Iason (EE-Son)

Iðunn (Eh-Dune)

Igteine (Ig-Teen)

Invesigh (In-Ves-Eye)

Jósteinn (Joss-Teen)

Kalokairtas (Kah-Lo-Kar-Tas)

Kánite (Kahn-Ite)

Koderrym (Koh-Der-Rim)

Lachesis (Lak-Eh-Sis)

Laïono (La-Ee-oh-no)

Makonogah (Mak-O-Nog-Ah)

Makrýongus (Mah-Kree-On-Gus)

Marcaigh (Mar-Kay)

Marsutsepi (Mar-Su-Sep-EE)

Monónum (Mon-Oh-Num)

Mygeeria (Meh-Gear-Ee-Ah)

Nekarios (Neh-Kar-Ee-Ohs)

Nerqua (Ner-Q-Ah)

Noelani (No-eh-la-nee)

Óðinn (Oh-din)

Orba (Or-bah)

Ori (the language) (Or-Ee)

Ori (the moon) (Or-I)

Orithina (Or-I-Thee-Na)

Orpheal (Or-Feel)

Pefror (Peh-Froh-Er)

Penquinus (Pen-Quin-Us)

Pértra (Per-Trah)

Pnevallidum (Ne-Val-Lid-Um)

Prosecro (Pro-Sek-Ro)

Prosocave (Pro-Sok-Ehve)

Pýta (Pee-Tah)

Qin'Darrea (Quin-Dar-Ree-Ah)

Quan (Q-Awn)

Qubé (Q-Beh)

Raghnall (Rag-Nall)

Rórdán (Row-Dan)

Ruairí (Roy-Ree

Salicia (Sali-See-Ah)

Saligorsa (Sall-Ee-Gore-Sah)

Seraphina (Sera-Fee-Na)

Sfragillum (Sif-Ra-Jil-Lum)

Sigeweard (Sig-Ward)

Siofra (Shehf-Ra)

Spímum (Spee-Mum)

Suerius (Sue-Eh-Ee-Us)

Symalum (Seh-Mal-Um)

Symalumtoi (Seh-Mal-Um-Too-Ah)

Tad'Cooperith (Tad-Coop-Er-Ith)

Tadhg (Tayg)

Tatian (Tat-Ian)

Thaloth (Thay-Loth)

Thanatem (Than-Ah-Tem)

Thinnus (Thigh-Nuhs)

Tode (Toh-Duh)

Tois (Toh-Ehs)

Tria (Tree-Ah)

Typoregula (Typc-Oh-Re-Goo-La)

Tyraulia (Teh-Raw-Lee-A)

Valoth (Vay-Loth)

Valr (Valer)

Valrdis (Valer-Dis)

Vasígnum (Vah-Seeg-Num)

Víðarr (Vee-Dar)

Vígdís (Veeg-Dees)

Vlirrith (Vleer-Rith)

Vothedissith (Voth-Dis-Sith)

Vragi (Vrah-Gee)

Wyrtha (Weer-Thah)

Yasuquinn (Yah-Sue-Quin)

Yzelia (Yeh-Zeh-Lee-Ah)

Zegrinath (Zeh-Greh-Nath)

Zerach (Zair-Ahk)

Zotae (Zow-Tai)

Manufactured by Amazon.ca
Bolton, ON

35029969R00446